Praise for *Byron Easy*

'Cook has sufficient gifts to ensure his protagonist is good company for the ride ... the descriptions of Easy's fellow passengers have a malevolent brio that calls to mind Martin Amis ... with many passages of real beauty and humour.'

Times Literary Supplement

'Cook's tone moves from a bleakly glamorous existence in the capital into a darker account of a rapidly destroyed life... There's an addictive charm ... that gives a potency to this ambitious tale.'

Financial Times

'An exuberant, stealthily shocking debut ... razor sharp.'

Daily Mail

'[A] darkly comic novel. The hero sits on a train, half drunk and with his worldly goods in a bin bag, contemplating the mess of his life and wreck of a marriage. As the train heads up the country, he travels through his painful memories, to hilarious effect. Daring, moving, imaginative and, above all, funny, this is a great debut from a promising novelist.'

Sunday Mirror

'*Byron Easy*, the eponymous antihero of this beautifully written debut from Jude Cook, is, like his namesake, a poet. However, unlike his namesake, his love life is characterised by failure. Sitting on a train at King's Cross station, destitute and broke, recently separated and with suicidal impulses, Byron cuts a sad figure ... As we share this long journey, we traverse through Byron's innermost thoughts ...Themes of masculinity, the self – he is a poet after all – causality, divorce and deep emotional pain howl through Byron's mind in this most intimate novel.'

Irish Examiner

'Comedic moments . . . come as a perfect contrast to the equally well wrapped poignancy. . . . Entertaining and rewarding.'

'Ravishing in its evocations of beauty, sexual candor, suspense, and unusual insights into the soul-battering consequences of abuse and violence. Cook's debut gathers force as a rolling and rocking ballad of survival and love.'

Byron Easy

JUDE COOK

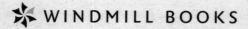

WINDMILL BOOKS

Published by Windmill Books 2014

2 4 6 8 10 9 7 5 3 1

First published in Great Britain in 2013 by William Heinemann

Windmill Books
The Random House Group Limited
20 Vauxhall Bridge Road, London SW1V 2SA

Addresses for companies within The Random House Group Limited can be found at:
www.randomhouse.co.uk/offices.htm

The Random House Group Limited Reg. No. 954009

www.randomhouse.co.uk

A CIP catalogue record for this book
is available from the British Library

ISBN 9780099558699

The Random House Group Limited supports the Forest Stewardship Council® (FSC®), the
leading international forest-certification organisation. Our books carrying the FSC label
are printed on FSC®-certified paper. FSC is the only forest-certification scheme supported
by the leading environmental organisations, including Greenpeace. Our paper
procurement policy can be found at: www.randomhouse.co.uk/environment

Typeset in Bembo by Palimpsest Book Production Limited, Falkirk, Stirlingshire
Printed and bound by CPI Group (UK) Ltd, Croydon, CR0 4YY

To my mother and father

. . . I am not asleep.
I weep; and walk through endless ways of thought.

Oedipus the King
Sophocles

1

Negative Capability

M y name is Byron Easy and I am sitting — or rather, sardined — in a tight table-constricted booth on a train at King's Cross, and, until a few moments ago, I was alone with my thoughts. I am pointing north, waiting to depart, and already dying for a cigarette. The fuzzy reds of Santa hats out on the bracing concourse remind me dismally that it's Christmas Eve. Oh, and not just any Christmas Eve, but, on a more dramatic level, the last one of the twentieth century; hence the atmosphere of millennial panic inside the carriage, the general feeling that the human race is reaching escape velocity. That it is dealing with last things. I must confess now that I am returning to my mother in Leeds — pathetic really, at this age, this altitude. And I'm trying to remember a lot of facts in order to forget them. Believe me, it's the only way. If you want to close the door on the past, *remember* it all first; otherwise it keeps returning, like the Christmas puppy discarded two streets away, or the breeze-blocked corpse that refuses to sink in the Lea Valley reservoir. Yes, I'm trying to remember it all, while waiting to depart.

You probably won't get much in the way of the train's interior or the wintry English countryside as it flashes unstoppably past, because they constitute the irrelevant details. The unrecallable facts. The minutiae of a journey. The surface gloss. But I do have a story to tell. And I think it's for the best that I'm out of town over the festive break as I've begun to cut a sad figure in the taverns of north London, what with all the trouble a couple of months back. Not the usual writer's trouble – money-trouble, soul-trouble – but *special* trouble, of a type you may have problems identifying with at first. Anyhow, you can most likely imagine what a non-smoking carriage of a British Rail train resembles on Christmas Eve: the abbreviated space packed with shrieking saliva-mouthed infants; the solitary sons and their gold-brocaded luggage (their inevitable spectacles parked on waxy nose-bridges); the long-married grandparents deep in the tartan seats, sipping lidded styrofoam teas that dangle cotton tags. The tang of whisky. The parps of blown noses. The palpable and depressing sense of anticipation. You've all been here before – in the needling heat, the mince-pie air. Yeah, the faceless cast is all prepared for departure. Present and correct and Christmas hungry, Christmas randy; all with the common purpose of Yuletide repatriation, of being with their loved ones on the twenty-fifth of December.

However, today remains stubbornly the twenty-fourth of December, and there is still the journey to shoulder through; those memories to recall.

My name is Byron Easy. I am a writer sitting on a train; and I think about this shit way too much.

Of course, the following shit you just couldn't make up. Who would want to? This kind of shit is always present in people's lives, waiting to be recorded, dissected, embarked upon. Like a journey, I guess. Like the journey I am about to begin, half drunk and headachy at three-thirty on a winter's afternoon.

If I look onto the concourse, I can see a quick wind making ripples in what could be a puddle of urine. Also, a haggard pigeon spitting a cigarette butt. Further still, an apoplectic traveller locked into a dispute with a ticket inspector. In other words, the usual troubled waters of the earth, which I fully intend to forsake.

I am trying to bear all this in mind when a human voice wakes me.

"Scuse me? Is anyone sitting there?"

A timid young couple, slightly blurred around the edges from all the wine I had to sink to board this train, enters my field of vision. The man, whose reedy Estuary vowels formed the question, is dressed in the dichromatic uniform of the trainee accountant. Maybe he is an accountant. Maybe they both are, and spend their Friday nights in Pizza Hut discussing the small progresses made on their investment portfolios. His avidly defiant eyes gaze down at me: an estate-leer, once learnt never eradicated, like the rude glottal stops. His forehead, a bubbling Icelandic spa of acne, gleams under a hairline itself largely a strip of exposed scalp due to an over-application of wet gel. He stands in prickling anxiety of my reply. I must look drunk, or slightly dangerous. If he were a poet he would adduce that I had not loved the world, nor had the world loved me. But it is unlikely he is a poet, not with hair like that. Maybe it's my two days of stubble and florid colour that cause him to hover there uncertainly. Maybe it's my clenched fists, which lie taut-skinned and raw from the cold on the bare Formica. I should mention again that this churl is flanked by his partner, a bony, bloodless woman who wears a crinkled A-line skirt and a complexion as pale as a sheet of writing paper. The man's face twitches slightly. There is a lengthy silence; his question still poised and resonating. I have faced him down. I note that his expression has modulated into the counterfeit smile reserved for the job interview. My blood-drunk eyes survey his dripping scalp, then meet his stare. I growl, 'Is it still raining out?'

The couple exchange rapid, nervous glances. He doesn't get it. He thinks I'm mad. With a strangled timbre, he repeats his question.

'I mean, are they taken, mate? The seats?'

A theatrical pause before I relent.

'Nah, you go ahead.'

There is a tangible gust of relief; a relaxation. They make to sit down opposite me. Rapidly contorting my face into an expressionless mask, defiant of every conversational opener known to man, I allow myself a long sigh through the nostrils.

Oh well, I always was a pushover.

My name is Byron Easy, and I must never get my hands on a gun.

Why? Because I would blow my own head off, that's why. Not somebody else's head, but my own horny, just-turned-thirty, drinker's head, with its retreating hairline that seems to be constantly saying to Time: 'Okay, brother . . . you win.'

To be frank, just lately this is an action I visualise performing once, twice, three times a day. Oh, and once more before I fall asleep at night, like some kind of morbid nightcap. The unwanted, *unwarranted* vision upon closing the eyes: the clip slammed chunkily into the stock, the hammer coaxed back, the short journey made by the barrel to the back of the mouth, then . . . then blackness, like a suddenly extinguished television screen. Not even a sound to accompany the shot, because there wouldn't be a sound. You would go before you heard the sound. Like the soldier says, you never hear the bullet that kills you. No, there would be no bang and nothing more to see for ever and ever, amen. Although that, I suppose, depends on what you believe.

Is this unusual, or do you harbour the same reckless, annihilating impulses? They say all great men have been heroes, conquerors and cuckolds in their time, but I can only be certain I belong to one of those categories. That's not to say I believe I'm great – if I am, it will be of the variety that is unwillingly thrust upon one. Maybe I am more gravely ill than I at first suspected. But I am not making things up, unlike some I could mention.

My name is . . . A note about the light: the carriage has, predictably, eye-tiring fluorescent strips blinking invisibly at two-hundred frames per second. This will ensure at least a third of the passengers will be nodded-out over sports pages and last-minute Christmas cards by the time we trundle into Doncaster. By then, of course, it will be dark; the white neon tubes will paradoxically appear to originate from the station platform in the rain-dotted, reflective windows. All very misleading. I know it will be dark because it is dusk now. A London dusk of measly rain; hostile and blade-cold, with red stricken clouds clinging low to a black horizon. I know they will be asleep because I will be awake; deep in my own abyss of thought.

Why plumb such an abyss, you may ask? What could precipitate such an urge? Well, the events of last night, for a start. Though it might be some time before I feel ready to share them with you. The plain facts don't do them justice. I spent the majority of the evening drinking champagne at the house of an old friend – my oldest friend, in fact. Sounds great, does it not? I can still picture the jewel-bright bubbles, their inevitable effervescent journey to the meniscus; still hear the soft burr of Rudi's familiar voice above the discordant clanking of metal or tin from outside . . .

Then something occurred that changed everything; that accounts for my current state of disturbed, amped-up intensity; of dangerous melancholy; of near-clairvoyance. This state had its genesis in the small hours, and was still going strong this morning, which for me fell between eleven forty-five and midday. Waking unshaven under my coat, on the sofa of my shared flat, magnesium light penetrating the blinds, I decided to skip breakfast. Grim laughter, a kind of debauched chagrin, chased me around the room as I gathered my meagre possessions. The gloomy egoist is always at his best in the morning, so I was relishing my strange mood of vindication, achievement, fear. After my second or third glass of lunchtime Rioja (straight from the bottle, so I'm guessing here) I began to pack. Not that I am wealthy in worldly goods, but I managed to strip it down to the bare essentials. All my leather shoulder bag contains – all I have under the sun – is a notebook, a Leeds street-finder, the now empty bottle of red, a toothbrush, a wad of crumpled fivers in a Jiffy bag (both courtesy of Rudi), and a change of socks (why socks and not underwear isn't coherently explicable at the moment).

Oh, and a single pamphlet of poetry. Its author? Me, actually.

Well, I did declare that I was a writer. And one has to cite proof for one's assertions. The story of my *succès d'estime* is too circuitous to discuss here, suffice to say that I have a single copy of it left, the one I carry with me now – like a talisman of dormant talent. Taking it from my bag, I hold it to my nostrils. It smells faintly of cat litter. The very sight of it troubles my heart. They say train journeys often precipitate poetry, and, before one knows it, the past. Both require time to do them justice. Well, for once I have time on my hands: the nasal announcement that disturbed my thoughts a moment ago informed us that, due to a person under a train at Stevenage, we were subject to 'a substantial delay'. So for the foreseeable future I'm going nowhere. And I plan to do a fair amount of writing, along with the obsessive acts of recollection – the industrial amount of thinking I intend to do before my inevitable end; my long-anticipated *felo de se* . . .

Don't believe me? Just watch me now, as Bowie muttered at the end of 'Star'.

The celebrity psychologists state that pain only lasts a second – that it's up to us to decide whether we want to perpetuate it by morbid reflection. But the pain of the last two months, caused by the *special* trouble I mentioned, has begun to feel chronic. I have decided, at last, to put an end to it. I just haven't settled – in the manner of famous cowards – on the best method yet.

———————

Think I'll take a quick look around.

Hey, I was wrong. My company isn't faceless in the least. I am surrounded by more arresting physiognomy than you would encounter on a tier of a football ground. A Hogarthian mob in catalogue clothes. And all so purposeful, so alert . . . There's always a moment during a good afternoon drunk when you become vividly aware that, all around you, people are operating *life* soberly. They're conducting phone conversations without speaking into the wrong end of their mobiles, or gangwaying to the Gents without tripping over, or turning the pages of a newspaper without blacking adjacent eyes. It's a great moment, like putting your contact lenses back in.

A door hisses open to the rear of me, allowing in a blast of fridge-cold air, dust and the smell of fried onions. The hair in my nostrils prickles, my eyes weep from their corners . . . then the warmth is mercifully restored. If I were a philosopher I would ruminate upon the idea that the cold is now the past moment, the dead moment; whereas this is the present moment, the living one. That 'now' seems to hold me transfixed in the glare of its para- doxical headlights – how can anything past be happening 'now'? But there is too much stimulation for such inquiries. A passenger shuffles by, his toilet-cleaner cologne smarting like a smack in the face. Well, that's certainly woken me up.

Newly and thrillingly aware of the teeming variety inside the carriage, I take out my black notebook, one of many that I never leave the house without. It falls open to reveal the skeleton of a poem, in spidery longhand, on the facing page. The Accountant Couple glance away as if I've just produced pornography. Verse? Scandalous! What did they expect, a ledger? I uncork my favourite fountain pen only to witness their ears virtually humming with embarrassment. Fuck 'em – I've always written in these things, especially on trains. And one day I will throw them all on the bonfire, like all good writers should. I commence with a short, if adjectivally challenged, description of my fellow inmates.

Fat, thin, tall, short . . .

Ah, it's no good. There's too much to take in – an over- whelming tidal wave of diversity in search of a seat; an anthro- pologist's gang-bang. Pascal said only stupid people thought everybody was fundamentally alike; referring of course to the interior, not the deceptive carapace we spend our lives lugging around. Giving up, I let the pen drop and simply stare. The man who just bustled past, letting in the cold air, turns out to be a priest; the egregious white band like a pure strip of snow between his black cassock and triple chin. Beyond him there are frowning fathers and slickly hipped girls (all undoubtedly younger than me); patrolling lads in knee-length Saturday night pulling-shirts; giggling sari'd Bengalis; a pair of Upper-Street Sapphic sisters; a septuagenarian dressed entirely in blue denim; a supermarket-shoed fashion-catastrophe bending under the logged and straining luggage racks (O, the varieties of luggage!). Then there are the cuff-linked ex-aviators; the desperate frauds and baldies; trophy wives next to unspeakably smeared infants; faded neckerchiefed blondes, their crisp-packet faces trowelled with slap; Suit-and-Ties reeking from work; growling misfits; teenagers with heads square as televisions; girls with intelligent continental mouths who will incongruously disembark at Grantham; cheeky mites with gurning fissogs; wind-blasted aunts; solemn-jawed Christians smelling of new laundry; hippy mums in earth-brown rollnecks; acne-beasts; sunlamp survivors; once-successful Lotharios chinking under bazaars of catalogue-bought gold . . .

I pick up my pen.

Waistcoated wankers, passage-staggerers, nippers and grippers, seal-bark coughers, self-pitying snifflers, hawkers, tutters, scratchers, groaners, verbal diarrhoeics, carol-hummers, dribblers, tongue-lollers (the proximity of all this hot blood!), balls-rearrangers, piles sufferers, dye-jobs, stroke victims, syrup-apologists, recently suntanned showoffs, cold sores, frowners and debt-drowners, blackheads and smackheads, sad Jacks and six-packs, Johnny-no-mates and fashion plates, cancelled beefcake, vacuum-eyed jailbait, bitter-guts, sweating gluttons, pee-desperate ten-year-olds, furtive scribblers, diddlers, con-men, strongmen and me.

Bosh! The cornice of a suitcase on its way to the angled luggage racks scores a direct hit on my right temple. A gross lardball in a rippling, seething tracksuit is leaning monstrously into my personal space; sharing his body odour – like an olfactory festive gift – with seats thirty-seven to forty-two. He looks oddly familiar. He looks gross. And he certainly hasn't noticed that he's injured a fellow human. Pain, like thumb-pressure to the actual brain itself, enters the right side of my face and vibrates along the lines of my jaw and skull. In clinical close-up I watch the man's T-shirt reveal a vast, pubicly forested space-hopper belly as he berths his case. Then, with a burp, he rejoins his two incredibly bolshy and stupid-looking children further down the aisle, pausing only to clip one of them over the crown.

I huff and I puff and feel a prickling in my nuts. Oh, you shithouse! Oh you clumsy— If it wasn't Christmas (and he wasn't bigger, badder, exponentially *more* than me) I would've definitely called him a . . .

'Kant!'

The man turns in full movie slow-mo to face me. Again that familiar snarl. Oh dear. I've done it now. The word, as a word so often will when you're drunk, just slipped out.

'What did you call me?'

I see at once that his face – lopsided with venom and ovoid under a lawn of bristle – has murder written across it. As he advances, I become aware of the Accountant Couple, now crimson with shame and stress, physically diminishing in their seats; probably wishing they'd cabbed it or chartered a helicopter to Leeds instead. With a burger-waft of bad armpits, the big man is once again back in my personal force field, closer (if that were humanly possible without him actually *penetrating* me) than before. His deceptive height really is something of a phenomenon: taller at a distance, up close he is Danny DeVito as Napoleon. I see that his eyes are deranged with afternoon alcohol. I note the mottled blue of a swift tattooed on his grilled neck. Then my voice appears from nowhere.

'I didn't call you anything. I said *don't*.'

The man's children watch this terrible, thrilling scene like two orphans on a sinking ship. It is surely something they have witnessed before. Just daddy doing his stuff.

'That's not what you said . . .' The big man's voice is graphically deep, an Essex gravel pit of menace and harm. Our stares are now locked like antlers.

'I meant don't hit him. The kid. I was hit when I was a child . . .' (I think the pale woman opposite coughs at this sentence, shifting her weight to the other bony buttock) '. . . and look how I turned out.' He remains impassive. For some reason he doesn't seem impressed by this. I try another tack. 'Okay, I'm lying. I've got Tourette's, which makes me shout out the names of dead German philosophers.'

Hopeless, I know.

An electric pause. Then he leans forward, the tracksuit scrunching in the bends of his limbs. Poking an oil-stained finger at my third eye (almost touching it) he says this to me:

'You – fuck nuts – *you*, I never want to see again. *Capiche*?'

I nod vigorously, hypnotised by how long these moments always seem to take. Then he's off, down the carriage to corral his children; a thousand eyes feasting on my face. Glancing up at the Accountant Couple, I give them my best, my largest smile. They look down instantly at the scratched Formica, as if it held information of great importance.

Ah, well. At least it's taken my mind off the past for a moment and forced me to focus on the journey. And that can only be a good thing. As with any journey, one begins at Point A, things occur (and the really significant things are always thoughts, memories, insights, terrors – not the quotidian narrative of events), and eventually one arrives, some time later, at Point B; usually with fizzing limbs and hospitalising indigestion. The mental journey is always richer, for it contains recollection, fascination; though not much tranquillity in which to contemplate them. Despite the much-vaunted psychopathic state known as 'living in the present', one doesn't want to lose the precious stones of the past. One doesn't want to forget them, to see them drop away through the mind's vast sieve of worthy and unworthy keepsakes. There they go: the good and the bad; the treasured and the negligible; the love and the hate. One becomes a loving curator of a self-important myth. A hero in one's own epic drama. An uncommon desire, maybe, but then these are uncommon times. Above all, one wants to remember before one forgets, before one jumps to faulty conclusions. To remember in order to comprehensively understand all one has undergone, or endured. Quick now! Remember, record, embark. Quick now, before they go; before it's too late.

It always takes something like this — present pain, present smell, present occurrence — to fix one firmly in the horrific Now. Of course, Now is not where I'd want to be if I had the choice. If I could be anywhere in time I'd be anywhere but Now, with its tiresome demands and shrieking infants and blade-cold dusks and suitcase-strikes — that stuff that masquerades as real life but isn't really; that great battalion of distraction ranged against one with its weapons drawn at any given moment of the day. Real life always seems to occur in the past, qualified by perspective. Existence is a mosaic of moments. And one wants to pin down those moments, those memories, like fat-torsoed moths under milky glass, as if one were the soul's lepidopterist. The present, meanwhile, is still too hot to the touch, too raw, too *evolving* for us to call it real. Can you honestly say, gentle reader, that what's going on around you now is real? Or is it the projection of some giant celestial panopticon; God's dream. Perhaps, come New Year's Eve, we will all find out. Overrated, to say the least, is the Now. Living in the present? For people with too much time on their hands, if you ask me. But, for a split-second, being whacked in the face took my mind off her (thank you, Tracksuit Man, and Happy Christmas).

Oh yeah, *her*. In case I forget to mention it later, this half-drunk writer has recently separated from his wife. From his half-Spanish wife of three years. That was the special trouble I was telling you about earlier. The exploding of lawful, awful wedlock. Not unusual for a modern marriage, I suppose. We met when the present century was in its staggering, senile nineties (and it still is, of course, for a couple of high-anxiety days). Yes, we met, fell in love, got hitched, and somewhere along the line became separated. Some vital component was lost. The wife should really understand this better than me, what with her career of bereavement following her mother's death, but something tells me she doesn't understand any of it; not one little bit. Christ, three years of marriage! Three years of microscopic London flats, of shouting and ducking airborne crockery, of sitting opposite each other during a million sweltering meals. All those carrots, those carbohydrates, those trawler-nets of spaghetti, paddy fields of rice, lakes of gravy, Thameses of tea . . . Where did those evenings disappear to? What did we talk about during them? And then there are the friends and family, people who I will never see again, people she is probably scornfully indoctrinating with lies as I sit here, gassy and humiliated on this bristling train seat. People such as her father, vertiginous and patrician Ian Haste with his air of past financial indiscretion, who never thought much of me anyway and had me fingered as a penniless loser from the start. Or her dizzy old bat of a grandmother – Montserrat, monstrous Montserrat – with her beaked Castilian nose; her melanotic skin the texture of beige silk, a result of going to bed every night with her face slicked in olive oil. I can still hear her haranguing voice in our many kitchens: '*Ay, ay, ay! Qué pasa? Qué pasa?*' The outrageous pronouncements that needed delicate translation: '*No hay coño que no está en venta.*' Her! Still going strong at eighty-four; still amoral, manipulative and selectively deaf at that indecent age! And then there's Leocadia, the long-suffering aunt who had to look after the old war-horse. Leocadia, Leo for short; withdrawn, subjugated, meek; the veins on her hands distended and liquorice-coloured from years of domestic service. Leo with her spick-and-span stone-floored apartment by the aromatic Mediterranean where we spent our honeymoon. Yes, they're all hating me now, in that uniquely proud Spanish way. Hating me for that zenith of sin, that ultimate deviation of being a husband who couldn't provide financially, who didn't sire grandchildren . . . As for the others, the others were my friends too, but I suppose they'll cross the street or jump behind parked cars to avoid me now. Antonia and Nick, for instance, the swinging scenesters who were our closest friends; a pair of sixties throwbacks with the finery of their buckled clothes; their amnesiac, sybaritic lifestyle. Nick with his gracious limbs and foppish cuffs, who tried so hard to interest me in the names of footballers over pints of his beloved Guinness. Or Antonia, who grew up on a farm; a heavy-chested *naif* with her intensely nurturing nature; her rustic hands and lactic, silk-screen complexion . . . And then there's the wife herself: tall and physically intimidating, with her charcoal brows and centrifugal radiance (and who, according to her osteopath, could have grown to over six feet if a curvature of the spine hadn't lowered her shoulders into a witch-like arch before the age of ten). Yeah, the wife — another ghost I will never see again, unless it's within the dusty cell of the divorce court. I can picture her now if I close my tired eyes: the wife with her white plastic-rimmed shades, her showy snakeskin knee-boots, her cobalt ring. Her unforgettable pupils, like droplets of ink on a chestnut. The wife with her many coats, her many cats. The wife and her many ailments that mysteriously came and went when it suited her. The wife at full throttle with her Pearl Harbors of vitriol, her dictionaries of prejudice. The wife. *Her.*

'Welcome to Great North Eastern Railways. The restaurant car will be serving hot tea and coffee, fresh soup, gourmet sandwiches and a range of crisps and snack products.'

The nasal, infiltrating whine snaps me out of my lamentable meditation. All around people are hoisting travel bags; marshalling wallets of Christmas cash. Then a nauseating list: *'Hot baguettes with fillings of roast beef, roast chicken, roast turkey and stuffing; toasted bacon and tomato sandwiches plus a wide range of home-made cakes, biscuits, pastries, hot drinks as well as a fully licensed bar. The buffet trolley will also be passing through Standard Accommodation. Thank you — we look forward to seeing you and hope you have a pleasant journey.'*

Standard Accommodation. That must be me.

I close my notebook, re-cap my pen and turn to the rain-sullied window. We are still stationary. Outside, under the cathedral-dome of an umbrella, a woman is kissing her lover goodbye. I notice immediately that she is crying; her generously lashed lids blinking every time the wind sends a gust of drizzle her way; the long runnels forming kohl-black roads in her foundation. She looks small, forlorn, sinister even, among the equidistant lamp posts and agoraphobia-inducing concrete walkways of the platform. A dark, gale-blasted survivor of some terrible saga of love; one purse-like hand pursuing the folds of her lover's overcoat. Why do women cry so much? The world must hurt women more than it hurts men for them to cry so much. Her face turns upwards now to receive the last kiss, the important kiss, the one that needs to hold the correct note of gravity, of poised farewell, of future intent. Then her man turns rapidly and walks towards the glowing interior of the train. In close-up, his face is creased and orange; reflecting the sad ambers of the dusk lights, the bullying wind. He's hunched, swarthy, slick-haired and dry-eyed – just the type, I note abysmally, that the wife used to go for.

Enough! Enough about *her*. I had better tell you about me first while there's still time, while it's still light. We'll get to *her* later. To understand me you'd better know something about my mum and dad. Yes, that David Copperfield crap. Because these are confessions, right? You might have already identified the slightly hysterical tone, rich with grievances. St Augustine, Rousseau, Philip Roth – those whinging bastards all had a record to set straight. It will come as no surprise, then, to learn that I am an only child, the only child of Sinead and Desmond Easy (Des for short). I have a half-sister, born when I was eleven, but she can wait. My father, who also suffered the trauma of early baldness always – to my mind at least – had a strange way of looking at me. He would stare under the heavy, shrouded lids of his eyes, as if squinting, or trying to figure out a particularly tricky equation. Apparently, I just didn't add up. Or balance out. In fact, he had a brilliant mathematical, or rather scientific, mind. Unfortunately, he instilled in me a hatred of the sciences by his very proselytising of them as academic subjects. 'God is dead,' he would proclaim while burning lamb chops under the grill in the white house where I grew up. 'And science will prove it – probably in your lifetime. So stop wasting your eyesight on poetry.' Precociously, I would answer that, for God to be dead, he must once have been alive. My father's squint would then become even warier. His path in life, his golden route to the threadbare carpet of *his* early thirties and beyond, was as unsystematic, as unscientific, as could be. Evacuated from the blighted terraces and V2 craters of Barnet during the war, he grew up on the Isle of Wight. I've often wondered whether those years on an island, surrounded by incurious sheep and paedophiles, weren't the crucible for his strangely insular and reactionary views later in life. I can still hear his pedagogic voice holding forth to a schoolfriend who had just discovered Marxism: 'There are either winners or losers in this life, and giving your money away is the sure route to becoming the latter!' I remember asking him whether he considered Gandhi a loser, only for him to reply that Gandhi didn't count on the Isle of Wight after the war: the only things that did were the price of butter and the availability of primitive condoms. He certainly made me never want to visit the place, the Isle of off-White – a chunk of Great Britain that, once detached, should have just sunk quietly into the Channel, volunteering, as it were, its own superfluousness. At seventeen, and very pleased with himself (with an ingenuous self-confidence that never left him his whole life), he won a scholarship to Cambridge to study chemistry. The old grammar-school boy-at-sea-in-an-ocean-of-toffs scenario. From this pinnacle, it was downhill all the way – on graduating he found a post as a rank-and-file research chemist for a French laxative and cosmetics company based in Bedfordshire called Diatrix, where he remained until . . . You may have noticed I'm talking about my father in the past tense, as if he had already joined the Dead, those watchers and hand-wringers on their plinths of stone. But he's not dead. I just haven't spoken to him for ten years. Or rather, we haven't spoken to *each other* for ten years. The feeling, and it makes me short of breath and bewildered to admit it here, is woundingly mutual. I know where to find him. He knows where to find me. But neither of us *have* found the other, for over a decade.

A psychiatrist could probably make much of this, along with the head-blowing-off daydream (which isn't my only persistent hallucination, I should stress. I have another – of solvency and spiritual calm – involving a spacious timber-floored flat, its bookshelves rich in reference works, its walls punctuated by framed charcoal sketches; a piano, upright or grand, I don't have a preference; and the faint smell of lavender pot-pourri in the immaculate, startling can). Although psychoanalysis, it has to be said, so often misses the point – the subtext to many of its questions about parents seems to go something like: *What were you doing hanging around with a father like that in the first place?* As if anyone ever had a choice.

But my father was, is, an intelligent man. After his emigration to Sydney, Australia, with a new wife, I began to miss the stimulation of his bookshelves (not him, you note, but his bookshelves – why, why, why? What am I that I can be so frigidly monstrous when it comes to the central relationship of my life?). My formative memory is of an entire ranged wall in our living room bearing texts on at least twenty runnered shelves. An odyssey, a magical orange-grove for a child; a gift. As I grew older I could see that some of the erudite works looked suspiciously unread, their spines pristine and uncreased; also that his taste, in his fifties, had come to rest on dry historical accounts, political philosophy, along with biographies of prominent chemists and right-wing politicians. The roman candles of literature (the Lawrence, the Joyce, the Kerouac, the Yeats) had been consigned to the dustbin marked 'deluded youth'. (Though you had to search for this dustbin. The exciting books were often hidden *behind* the volumes of European history, in piles or stacks – concealed like pornography.) But he *did* have books. Books that are probably the cause of all my present heartache and pain; though one doesn't choose the inviolable facts of one's upbringing, good or bad.

Yes, an intelligent man, and sure proof that you can read all the great works of literature and still be as confused about your moral and spiritual life as the dustman who devours the *Sun* every day as if it were *The Book of Common Prayer*. And maybe this is at the core, the rotten root, of why we haven't communicated since I ceased to be a teenager. You see, at that age, Desmond Easy personified the perils, the folly, of the man who has made firm metaphysical conclusions one way or the other (there being no persuasive evidence in either direction, as any fule kno). A lot depends on what you believe, of course; where you stand vis-à-vis the afterlife. In his case, two thousand years of philosophical debate could be distilled into a simple sentence: there was no God. A committed atheist probably from before birth, I would feel corroded, soul-contaminated, every time I endured another spleen-filled rant about how our only destination was the avid soil and its gleeful worms; or about getting and spending and the greasy world of commerce; or the importance of chemistry as an A-level subject. That's not where my head was at, not in the least. I was all for keeping my options open. When the bullet enters my brain (as it most certainly will), I'd like to believe in the slimmest possibility that the Big Man Upstairs will be there, shaking his fist, cursing that I'd arrived too early. And when I engaged my father in argument, I would witness his divorce-injured spirit cowering as I expounded (ludicrously, at that age!) the doctrines of Platonic transmigration, of Lawrence's soaring and solipsistic life-belief and the lyric (largely stolen from the French Symbolists, I was later disappointed to discover) to The Doors' 'Break on Through to the Other Side'. So we agreed to leave it. We agreed to differ. For ten years thus far. The bond cracked twixt son and father.

My mother, however, was a different kettle of ballgames – a free spirit, but most tangibly different in her physical characteristics. While my altitudinally challenged father was always fighting a tendency to flab in the upper arms and was bald as an acorn by the time he reached thirty-five, Sinead Mary Maguire (to use her stunningly beautiful and evocative maiden name) was an elegant raven-haired head above the crowd. Literally. By seventeen she was a giraffe-like five foot eleven. The daughter of an Irish miner displaced to Leeds in the 1930s scramble for work; early photographs demonstrate just why half of male North Yorkshire spent much of its spare time in garages repairing cars they'd crashed while straining to catch a glimpse of her on the street. In one, taken when she was just eighteen, her mathematically perfect legs curl from under a pleated schoolgirl skirt and end in those juvenilely-buckled court shoes that young women wore in the fifties. Atop this, her tiny waist is overfolded by thin but capable hands, which for some time now have tragically borne the distorting tree-branch knobbles of arthritis. Then her face: an oval of health and intuition divided by a long fluted nose; bearing a mouth so heavily lipsticked that it appears black in the creased monochrome of the picture. The only disappointment, in the photo, are her grey eyes – smudged and indistinct, in real life they were the colour of rain. Finally, her hair: a straight burnished cascade of witch-like ebony, mirroring the hue of her permanently raised, questioning eyebrows. A dark beauty, then: someone in whom life's vital appetites vibrated strongly – one of those rare Southern Irish women who seemed to have bypassed the gene pool of freckles and carroty hair and been awarded the full set of night-black attributes reserved for Gothic heroines.

So why did she end up with Des Easy? Well, that's simple. My mother was, for a long while, a terrible judge of men. After the dismal, rationed privations of her teenage years (bananas something seen only in films until the age of sixteen), and a tragic accident in which a faulty gas main killed her mother and much-younger brother at a Butlin's holiday camp, she found herself teaching nursery-school children the alphabet using colourful wooden representations of letters. A brief affair later with the married headmaster, which scandalised the entire Leeds suburb where the school was undistinguishedly situated, and she found herself with the same primary-hued wooden letters at a school in Lewisham, with slightly older, but infinitely more vicious, more worldly, more feral children. She stayed for ten years.

It was in this demolition-scarred no-man's-land of south London that, one night, she attended a party thrown by graduate teachers in a Habitat-infested flat. That providential evening she arrived late, finding the hashish-demented revelry in full swing. Twenty minutes in, and her gaze fell on a shortish, balding man wearing square clothes, grappling with a 45 rpm single held by the host, himself resplendent in beatnik black. The two were face to face, eyes bulging.

'I don't care if they're the latest thing,' the shortish, balding man protested, 'it's those unbearable voices and that thud, thud, thud – the tyranny of the beat!'

A foreign female voice (of the erotic type always present at parties) offered, 'It ish only rocks schmoosic. Don't ve so anal!'

'Yes, Des,' said the host, now slightly calmer, 'this ain't your party – and we'll have the bastard Beatles if I say so.'

A cheer went up from the few interested souls who had over-heard this deeply embarrassing exchange between two men in their late twenties.

'Here. Vivaldi. *The Four Seasons*!' said Des, desperately. 'I'm sure if we did a quick poll of the room, if we put it to the vote, then Vivaldi would come out on top.' A sweat – for it was a broiling summer night in the mid 1960s, with all the sash windows thrown open to the static, dust-flavoured air – had appeared on the unap-petising dome of Desmond Easy's head. 'Think of your neighbours! You've come close to being slung out already . . .'

At this point, the single over which the two men were still tussling snapped crisply down the middle and a disapproving groan could be heard around the room. This seemed to decide the matter. And so the old Venetian had his way. Soon the cramped quarters swelled with the rarefied pizzicatos and tiptoeing melodies of 'Summer'. The cackles and chatter resumed, escaping out to the bewildered street below.

It also decided something in the vertiginous Goyaesque beauty holding a lonely glass of Cinzano that was Sinead Mary Maguire. Here was a man, she mused, with whom she could fall in love; a man of sensibility, intellect ('slung out' – she loved that! And, over the years, it would become a phrase she would grow to hate more than any other on earth). Here was a man not afraid to give his opinion, to fight for it (again, a quality that would eventually drive her to paroxysms of Irish distraction). Above all, he sported leather patches on the elbows of his diseasedly brown corduroy jacket.

This, for her, denoted adulthood. She had finally arrived. Sure, he was almost shoulder-height to her and she had seen newborn babies possessed of more hair, but in that split-second . . . (that manful struggle over the record, representing the battle between two extremes; of high culture with low, of black rollnecks with professorial corduroy, of Ringo Starr with Vivaldi – plus the sexy 'snap!' made by the vinyl in the stultifying night) . . . in that split-second something had been decided: here was the man who would father her child.

And that child was me.

They married within the year and moved first to the blighted satellite town of Luton, then to neighbouring Hamford on realising that a concrete post-nuclear wasteland of piss-filled underpasses (and where, indeed, most of the buildings resembled public urinals) was no place to bring up a child. Hamford, with its broad avenues of deciduous trees, placid, murky river and Norman church, its outlying estates that promised (and delivered) unimaginable violence, would soon become a mythical place for me; but for newly-wed regular hardworking Desmond and his attractive wife it was just a place to send a kid to nursery school that wasn't Lewisham. Things were good in Hamford for a couple of years. After I appeared, Sinead took eighteen-months' leave from the local junior school where she was again making fast progress with the magic wooden letters. And Des, tired from a day analysing a new commando-strength laxative, would appear every evening with his tie askance, hungry for the phenomenal Irish stews that had played such a vital role in Sinead's wooing of him. Every night at six p.m. she would hear his key in the lock and there he'd be – every night (if that were possible) slightly balder and ready to rest his head where it most naturally fell due to their height difference: on her sternum.

Yes, things were good for a couple of years in Hamford, if not a little . . . well, boring. In retrospect, this could have been the end-of-life-as-she-knew-it for Sinead Easy (the atrophying of those vital energies) if it wasn't for what happened when she returned to the school. She met a man. She met a man who would eventually (and literally) sweep her off her feet – that most destructive of female aspirations. To quote my namesake, maidens, like moths, are ever caught by glare. His name was Delph. Delph Tongue. Scandinavian in origin, so I'm told. And he was (very Lady Chatterley's this) the assistant caretaker, the man who painted the glutinous, supernaturally straight pure white lines on the football field every summer. And also a man who had watched her – married, unavailable Sinead Easy – walk through the low gates every day like a galleon-tall, devil-black vision of erotic invitation.

I've often wondered why my mother – so nurturing, so at home in the bewildering polytheistic universe of the under-five – only ever wanted one child. It has taken a number of years to realise that, for her, dealing with children every day brought her close to tearful and justified mass murder. It looks like an easy gig, teaching: those endless holidays that stretch long into scorched August; the early finish to the day leaving the evening free to run a red biro facetiously over a couple of exercise books. But you would be wrong. I read somewhere that only airline pilots and those in the nursing profession suffer the same stress-levels as teachers. Cases of burn-out, if not outright crack-ups and suicides, are high. A teacher's mornings and evenings are often filled with interminable meetings, sandwiching the daily descent into the braying aviary of the classroom. And then they have to take it all home with them, in the form of essays to mark, lessons to plan, administrative assessments to wade through. It must be like having homework for ever.

So it was this life that Sinead Easy (aged thirty-three) found herself leading; and it was into this life that strutting, cocksure northerner Delph Tongue walked. The truth was, after a couple of years in Hamford, Sinead's veneer was beginning to chip off. Every night she'd flop crimson-eyed into bed after a day of un-intelligible mayhem and five hours of epic marking. Every night a little less beautiful. Every night a little less certain why life had to be lived, or what it was even *for*. Desmond would be in his armchair, listening detestably to Radio Four, some half-brick-heavy tome open on his lap. Often he'd be picking his nose. She felt like the classic neglected woman. Then along came Delph.

It helped that he was a northerner too. They had that instant rapport born only of geographical serendipity. Though of Dutch or Danish parentage, this Viking had grown up in the grim wool-town of Wakefield and had spent his early twenties drifting from job to job, itinerant and predatory. A narcissist with shaky self-esteem, he was an aggressive, dominant man. Also, it would tran-spire, a very strange human being. He was even taller than Sinead, an attribute she had learnt to value ever since her teenage days of towering over sweating suitors in the cinema queue. When he was finally introduced to me as 'Uncle Delph', I remember thinking he had the ugliest name I had had the displeasure to hear up to that point in my short life. *Tongue. Delph Tongue.* How the forename seemed to me phonetic of inadmissible sloppiness. Like the sound of a flannel or towel roughed between coalsack-hairy buttocks. The squidgy 'ph' mimetic of drying underpants. Ignorant of its Nordic roots, it sounded to me like one of those mid-fifties American boy-names like Ralph or Wayne or Duane or Dean, made all the more ludicrous for its displacement to grey rain-racked Wakefield. An awful used-johnny of a name. A stupid, juvenile, jaunty name for a man. A name never forgotten once injected into the fire-bright bloodstream of a young life.

And then the surname: Tongue. So biologically explicit, redolent of meaty flesh and puking; strangely congruent when appended to Delph, perhaps the most perfect onomatopoeic for chucking up you will ever find.

The two of them embarked on a torrid secret affair which lasted eighteen months, containing all the usual pulse-quickening rendez-vous (store cupboard, groundsman's hut, staffroom sofa after-hours), plus lies and evasions of such labyrinthine complexity that even Richard Nixon would have had trouble keeping up (the Watergate scandal running roughly concurrent with their great *amour*). After almost two years of adultery, they were at the stage where – like in all the most terrible TV movies – the phrase 'we can't keep doing this' would conclude their every liaison. Then fate threw them a hand. Diatrix decided to transfer temporarily some of its less vital employees to France. So Desmond Easy found himself leaving his groaning shelves of beloved books for a one-room coldwater flat in smoke-belching Lille for a fortnight at a time. This was the green light the affair needed. In Desmond's absence, athletic (but mentally tortoise-slow) Delph would take up residence, leaving only when the joyously unwitting cuckold returned to see his five-year-old boy – me.

Previously, Sinead had been neurotically fastidious about secrecy. She had learnt her lesson from the married headmaster up in Leeds. I once asked her why she kept referring to Delph as my uncle, when my father had reliably informed me that I didn't have any, only aunties. I remember my mother suddenly averting her eyes and straightening the mauve headscarf which she always wore in those days.

'Well, your father's not always right.'

'But either he's right or you're right or someone is fibbing.'

'Jesus wept!' moaned my mother, her eyebrows raised at this interrogation. 'Will you give it a rest. He's your bloody uncle. You've been asking the same question all week. Now go and play.'

'But I don't like to play,' I pleaded. 'The big boys say they will steal my bike.'

'You tell me which boys next time, and we'll see how big they are.'

I remember Delph entering the room at this point. Unreliable Uncle Delph – long before he became my stepfather. He always appeared from nowhere, like a gargoyle-faced ghost. He was tall, physically taut and overbearing. I hated him.

'Are you my real uncle, Delph?'

He didn't answer. He merely gave his equivocal smile which often looked like a sneer to me. My mother flashed him a glance of desperate appeal.

'Will you hark at him!' she cried. 'He's like a stuck record. As if I didn't have enough books to mark.'

Delph turned to me, and spoke in a voice much louder than I had expected. This always scared me.

'Don't cheek your mother!' he boomed in his porridgy Yorkshire accent. Then, with real nastiness, when mother was out of earshot: 'One day your bloody mouth will get you hung.'

For eighteen months nobody in the school knew about their 'shenanigans' (as Sinead herself described them). Their affair had been conducted as *espionage*; with coded meeting times left in pigeon-holes or playground bins. Now she didn't care. Let the world know she had been neglected; that she was deliriously in love with an assistant school caretaker! Let the net curtains twitch until they fell to pieces in the hands of those with nothing better to do!

Somehow I made it through to my thirteenth birthday alive.

I am standing in the mica-bright khazi of the train, sweating. I'm also shaking, hyperventilating and invoking Allah. I can't be sure if my teeth aren't chattering too. My forehead, that dome of shameful retreat, that Dunkirk of the follicles, is resting on the mercifully cool plane of the steel mirror. Once I've squeezed the tears from my eyes I find I'm staring at a thundering stream of my own urine as it hoses away the fascinating stains already present in the aluminium thimble of the toilet bowl. Impressive. That's a lot of puke for four in the afternoon. The part of my mind that is still rational informs me that it would take a Scottish football team a number of hours to produce that much vomit. I've seen troughs on cross-Channel ferries or in the Gents of a rugby club at six in the morning on New Year's Day that held approximately the same amount of sick. But never in the cramped can of a British Rail train at four in the afternoon. We haven't even moved yet. The bar isn't open for another twenty minutes!

As I watch the expressive rope of piss (still going strong one minute in) churn through the regurgitated prawns of a thousand hors-d'oeuvres, the carrots of a main course, then finally the laval swirls of a colourful dessert, I start to laugh. The kind of laugh that sounds like sobs to anyone who doesn't know you well, or isn't in the immediate vicinity, like the queue that's surely beginning to form outside the bolted door. I start to bang my forehead rhythmically against the sheen of the metal, producing a pleasing concussive effect every time I pull away. Oh dear, oh dear. The pain of providing all that — it must've been close to childbirth. Whoever came up with that much spew must be walking around with half their original body weight. The confined booth of the bog has taken on a different atmospheric pressure due to the stink of it. I let out a last hoot of derision as I zip my fly. Then I stop. Hold on — that puke. That's mine. That's *my puke*. That's what I did first before I finally unloaded the seismic pressure on my bladder . . . So what happened? And why am I still shaking?

This is what happened.

Five minutes ago I was sweating on the tartan seat of the train, in a kind of suspended state; a levitation or trance from the stress of remembering. The stress of encountering so much past in the present. This, after all, was half my mission, but I didn't feel equal to it. Hamford isn't a place I visit very often when trawling the archives. For a start, I haven't been back for ten years. There doesn't seem any point. Nor have I spoken to my father. After my mother's second marriage (to Delph, who else?) ended in a trauma of broken furniture and immense vindication for everyone who said it would never last, she moved up north. Back to her people. Or what few of them there were, with her mother dead and her old man a toothless miner who, like Delph's, sat wrapped in a travel rug by the coal scuttle all day, conjuring myths and roses from the flames. She was happy there, she said, with her *own*.

So my mother was gone. I was barely nineteen. And then, around the same time, my father decided to emigrate. Always a man to take life's blows lying down, always too *easy*; always conforming to nomenclatural accident, he found himself involved with one of the research operatives Diatrix employed in Lille. Research operative was a euphemism for human guinea pig, those drifters and loners who willingly allow fearsome strains of newly patented drugs (in this case laxatives) to pass through their systems in exchange for francs. Usually people who'd tried everything in life *twice* already, and still hadn't found their place in the world. Wasters, economic migrants, *clochards* – haggard survivors of bottom-dollar hotel work, stints of fry-cheffing, college terms of life modelling, prostitution, begging, smudging and skanking. This particular woman, Des's chosen *chérie*, was a sparrow-thin ex-grape-picker named Emmanuelle Deborache. A woman who habitually found herself in Lille when the vine harvest ended, knocking on doors for cleaning jobs. The chance to take her life in her own hands (or at least, the future of her colon) by ingesting the sulphurous and virulent shit-inducers concocted by Des and his colleagues must've seemed like a gift from heaven. The money was fantastic; the hours great, although they often tested full-strength on a Friday to give the operative the weekend to recover. This played merry havoc with my father's courtship of the Piaf-like Frenchwoman when cinema seats had to be hastily vacated on a Saturday night, or when entire restaurants were cleared by a single fart as new 'X-Shift' found its tenure in Emmanuelle's digestive system.

They married in a leaf-strewn registry office on a rainy morning in November 1990, six months after meeting each other. The best man was Des's French boss, Didier. The witness was Emmanuelle's scowling sister, Marie (as strikingly fat as Emmanuelle was strikingly thin). There were no other guests. A year later they emigrated on a whim to Sydney. I have often thought my father's island upbringing, somewhere in the lost patterning of his subconscious, informed this move. And I am sure I have many emaciated and bald little half-brothers and sisters who are impressively bilingual. But I'll never find out. Unless one of us picks up that telephone.

So Hamford – that sweet Ithaca – isn't a place I visit very much, physically or mentally. The long, elm-shrouded avenues must still dance with tree-thrown shadows under the blissful agitation of a

June breeze. The mythologised sandpits and treehouses where I played (and once found a sodden, discarded flat cap seething with earwigs) must cringe to the sound of other children's laughter. The fag-strewn, rotten-vegetable palisades of the market where I ingested my first tab of acid, the one bearing the cartoon squiggle of a Pink Panther, must now be suffering vandalism by other biker-jacketed lads, their collars up against the tidal teenage night. The place is still there, in the memory, but I'm absent . . . So, back there in my cramped seat, I found myself in a kind of altered state, a translucent stasis. After ten minutes of intense meditation – the soul visiting, enraptured; dazed by vividness – I discovered that I was bursting for a piss. And not a little sick. I caught a flash of myself in the darkened train window and saw a half-bald, salmon-faced tippler who hadn't spoken to his father for ten years. And I knew I had to go. My mission: the khazi.

It wasn't easy.

For a start I upset the game of dominoes the Accountant Couple had been playing ever since I put my notebook away. Such a simple movement – onto my feet, palms pressed against the bare surface, a twist of the hips and then out – but so much carnage. Ten apologies later and I was snaking down the aisle, absorbing the punishment of innumerable glances. Yes, I'm drunk! It's Christmas Eve, for God's sake! A quick pratfall over a suitcase someone had helpfully left in my path (and which seemed to intensify the steel blade in my bladder) found me in front of the flimsy door to the loo. A strip on the ridge of the handle showed red. Engaged. I started hammering.

'You in there long?'

There was no answer. I started to feel the first bilious twinge; a pigeon-like undulation of the Adam's apple. 'I'm bursting . . .'

I knocked again. Silence. 'Look, whatever you're doing, I'm, I'm . . . in great need here.' No response. They could at least answer, it being the season of goodwill and all that. I changed tack and kicked the door instead. A sort of shuffling sound came from inside. Then the unmistakable scrunching of harsh toilet paper being broken into strips. Oh, Christ. A number two-er . . . I must, I must piss! 'Oh, come on, take your time. When are you coming out? Some time within the next decade would be—'

The toilet flushed: a muffled evacuation followed by a serene hiss. Under the cover of this sound I started to shout at full throttle: 'How long does it take to pull your trousers up? I mean – for God's sake!'

Then the door exploded open. It was, I'm not happy to relate, Tracksuit Man.

At this point my memory gets a little hazy, but I remember feeling something like the sudden disintegration of all my limbs at once, as if they were filled with hot washing-up water. Simultaneous to this was the sensation of a sweat instantly covering my entire head, like an icy tea cosy. The huge man searched my face until our eyes met with a dismal familiarity. His intensely blue, mine intensely afraid. I was about to say, 'Haven't we met somewhere be—,' when he pushed past me, knocking me into the obstructive suitcase for the second time.

Then I was throwing up.

I'm back in my booth now. The game of dominoes continues at a cracking pace. Tracksuit Man is fifteen seats away down the carriage. He still looks familiar somehow, like the Ghost of Beatings Past. His brutally shorn head is now wearing a Santa hat – at the insistence of his delightful children, no doubt. I'm hoping we can co-exist for the duration of the journey without me actually dying. For the moment we seem to have a fragile symbiosis – like Chamberlain's with Hitler, like Antony's with Octavius. Ah, the respect that comes from facing down the oppressor. I bet mine was the *last* face he expected or wanted to see as he pulled open that toilet door! My first playful thought was: we must stop meeting like this. Admittedly this was before I fell backwards over the suit-case (sustaining injuries to both arms – the pain of which has now joined the throbbing in my head). But, all in all, I'm feeling relatively spruce after throwing up. There's nothing better for lifting the spirits than a good yodel.

I should tell you that there was another catalyst for puking, aside from my encounter with Tracksuit Man and the considerable quantity of red wine I've put away since breakfast. There was a poster in a sealed frame, advertising life insurance, on the way to the loo. It featured a psychotically healthy Nordic-looking woman and her gurning companion; a man with one of the most punchable faces in late twentieth-century advertising. They were both sporting the kind of grins usually achievable only after dropping three tablets of ecstasy. The simple tag-line read: 'Getting Hitched?'

As you might expect, this brought me quite low. And made me not a little nauseous. Yes, it was the poster that really did it. *That* finally uncorked the bottle.

Well, my thirteenth birthday came and went. It was around this time that I realised I was a writer. I hadn't actually *written* anything at this point, but, to my mind, this was merely a technicality. I'll fill you in on what happened after that epiphany a little later; suffice to say that I had the usual single-child, commuter-town adolescence – shitty comprehensive; innumerable and astonishingly barbaric beatings outside Burger King on the midnight High Street; Saturday jobs; a parental divorce followed by ten years starving in London. Just the usual. The usual transition from provincial to urban. The predictable fate of the connectionless, gormless hick who comes to the big city to seek his fame and fortune with seventy-five pence in his pocket, and no firm understanding that talent is only two per cent of the equation, if that. I'd like to lie to you and declare I'm a teacher of foreign languages, or an oil-rig worker or a postman and this is my story covering three dynasties of stoic Royal Mail Operatives (as the dole-office computer sinisterly likes to term them now). But I hate those phoney heroes. No, I'm a writer. Why else would I be noticing the long-married grandparents or going on about what's inside my head? Other people, normal people, *postmen*, are safe from the impingements of these things; of the subtleties, of the increments; the nuance and tone of daily life. Unmanageable thoughts, in other words. They don't need to write it down. That's how they can be postmen without donning a baldric of bullet belts and spraying down the occupants of 28a every morning. You just wouldn't believe me if I said I was anything else. Other people, normal people, would get over this trauma – this vicious separation – with a combination of mates, spirits and that great counterfeit healer, Time. Above all, they would display an innate negative capability – capable, as Keats had it, of 'being in uncertainties, mysteries, doubts, without any irritable reaching after fact and reason'. But, with writers, things hang around. The chronology is lost. Writers don't want to forget, to be healed by time. Writers want to write it down. Writers want to remember before it goes.

I also work in a shop, but that can wait for the moment.

So, something went wrong with my family at a crucial age, and I didn't manage to get an education. Though not for want of trying. My one attempt at scaling the towers of ivory, which I may share with you later, was soiling in the extreme. Instead, I suffered the trials of the autodidact. For years I bluffed it on wit alone, mispronouncing a sizeable lexicon of words, including heterogeneous and Goethe. I was twenty-eight before I understood a fifth of the evening news. What saved me was the English public-library system. After ten years of sharing hushed tables with reeking job-shirkers and Italian language students I was able to get by. And anyway, my birthright demanded that I take up the pen. When my mother was heaving me about in antenatal classes she was instructed to find a mantra suitable for getting through the ordeal of labour. She chose the line 'I wandered lonely as a cloud', which she mistakenly thought was written by Byron. Thus I became Byron Easy: retailer and poet.

A writer, then. Of largely unpublished poems, as it happens, as you already know. If you, dear friend, are a scribbler and happen to have a bundle of poems you want out there you could do worse than publish a pamphlet. My magnum opus was entitled *Hours of Endlessness*. It was my first (and only) foray into print. And it was well received, though a pamphlet hardly turns one into a lion of society. You will, on the morning of publication, awake, as I did, to find yourself dramatically un-famous. But, as Virginia Woolf said, for a writer, it's not what you've done or read that counts, but what you've thought and felt. That's the most important thing. Also to write it all down. Not everybody does that.

If, say, another writer were called upon to describe me he might draw attention to my banister-thin legs, the weakly sensual lopsided lips inherited from my father or the unassertive nose. Oh, God – my nose. That great drawback of my adult life. As time has elapsed I've made comparisons between myself and those proud possessors of Roman, equine, or boxers' noses and been almost fanatically certain you could take my sexual history and *double it* to reach their number of partners purely on account of their strong, male probosces. It's a ski-jump nose, really. Boyish, tweaked at the end like the victim of a Beverly Hills scalpel-job. It photographs satisfactorily only from the dead-centre front, any other angle giving the impression of a third earlobe rising like a pale pimple from my upper lip. It's not a nose that demands to be punched, but it has trouble getting served in pubs or throwing a shadow, or creating a profile that would be worth casting in bronze. It would certainly be no good in a fight.

My hair (what little of it there is left) is black, and – since growing it long gives the impression of wearing a kind of permed, pubic hedge – currently very short. This other writer would be quick to point out that it's a dye-job, tapering to thin, daringly spare sideburns that terminate an inch above my now-aching jaw. Sideburns, not mutton chops, he would hasten to add, as Dino my Italian barber has laboured years with clipper, razor and cuticle scissors to create the ultimate masterpiece sideburn while quite ignoring the fact that he's got the neckline wrong or taken too little from the back. I reassure myself that this is merely the Sicilian way.

Then the eyes. He would say they were always too girlishly wide and long-lashed, too under-evaluating, too *easy* on others to be the eyes of a man who had just turned thirty. Those emotional peepers of mine: too demonstrative, too candid . . . Distressingly, I have always looked younger than my years. Maybe there's an oil painting of me somewhere that's horribly agèd. This writer would note that the strong brows occasionally push the lids down, producing a somnambulant, half-awake look, as if a photographer had forgotten to ask for a stare or a 'cheese' or a 'shit'. And my domey forehead would also be singled out, its convex bulge evidence of too much brain in too small a skull or of the fact that I'm a distant relative of John Merrick.

I suppose my only redeeming feature, if he were called upon to provide one, would be my strong jawline: arrow-straight and non-parallel with the singed sideburns, its powerful line regrettably undermined by my button-nose and lunar forehead.

For the rest of it, I'm not a hunchback or a one-thumbed survivor of a factory accident, or a eunuch, but I am thin. As thin as a Giacometti. And short with it – the booby-prize combination for any man. The wife always told me that I was too short and thin to wear a suit; that I looked like a schoolboy on his first day outside the intimidating gates. Oh, that castrating bitch! In addition to this, my spine, like my father's, failed to grow straight and strong and is now resigned to its agonising curvature under my shoulders. I used to spend hours coveting the supple, pooltable-flat backs of men on beaches, wondering just where their vertebrae had got to. How easy, I thought, must it be for them to sit erect on buses and bar-stools. How their girlfriends must love to pull tarty nails over that expanse of non-deformed flesh. How pleasurable for them to bend over from the waist and not feel that dangerous whip of pain from coccyx to cerebellum. But at my age – at this altitude; this great distance from childhood, from the maelstrom of adolescence – one puts up with such deformities. At my age you get the body you deserve. Or the body you paid for (the latter never being an option).

Which would bring our writer onto teeth. My lower-deck is dangerously overcrowded, like a teetering rush-hour bus crammed to capacity. This state of affairs is more than vaguely connected with my childhood dentist's vast talent for incompetence. I can still remember the doomsday visits there as a teenager with my half-sister, Sarah — across Hamford's green and undulating Payne's Park (how apt a name). Even then, at six years old, she had that defiant look in her champagne eyes that made her a fabulous squabbling partner. After the hour-long fight over who would go first, we would arrive at the scrotum-tightening suburban address. Together we would tremble up the shovelly, crunchy gravel to a door bearing a plaque the bastard had screwed there to ensure he inflicted agony on only the very highest class of toothache sufferer: DR DEMJANJUK — DENTAL SURGEON. NO WORKMEN'S BOOTS OR SOILED SHOES PLEASE. Well, that disqualified two-thirds of the town's population straight away. And you're just talking about the women: the puffa-jacketed, gum-chomping, scarily confident *spreads* who did men's jobs on the labyrinthine industrial estates. How he ever got any work I'll never know. He had the same unassailable conviction in his own purpose as does a serial killer. And then there was his suspiciously Eastern European name: Dr Demjanjuk. Was he the distant cousin of one of Ceauşescu's blood-drunk henchmen? Or the son of an exiled Nazi? One almost expected to see the arrows of an SS ensign peeking from under his fumey white gown as he greeted us at the gates of his torture den; lime-green mask dangling beneath his smile. From a tender age, his jaunty manner didn't fool me for a moment. He was always a little *too* pleased to see me shaking there, engulfed by the springy sofa in the converted downstairs parlour of his house. Years later I discovered that other tooth-surgeons had *practices* with computers, clinic-style waiting rooms and fragrant nurses in fantasy costumes. But, with Dr Demjanjuk, one was never sure anyone else knew he was involved in this, this dental lark — as if he'd cobbled together all the necessary drills and equipment, nailed his stupid sign in front of his gravel path, stuffed some initials after his name and settled down to a day-job of fulfilling sadism after night-shifts in an abattoir. For years afterwards I would check the latest tabloid exposure of some House of Dismemberment or other to see if it wasn't *his* impenetrably netted sash windows in the innocuous photograph.

Anyway, he systematically failed in his task of draining my lower field. Once, after eight extractions in a single morning, I messily spat a mouthful of alarmingly black blood into his bidet or sink or whatever makeshift apparatus he'd stolen for such a purpose, only for Commandant Demjanjuk to grin: 'Would you normally do that at home?' To which my strangled, pipe-voiced reply was: 'I never have teeth taken out at home.' Now that – that *really* put a smile on his face.

So it came to pass that I have two rogue incisors in the basement: one pointing out to catch my lower lip and one leaning in at a ridiculous angle that has snagged on my tongue for ten misery-filled years. Nothing they can do about it, so I'm told. It's giving me a speech impediment. It's *given* me a speech impediment. Only thousands of pounds of costly Harley Street orthodontia will enable me to speak Spanish now. The best the tooth-quacks could offer was to grind down the inwards-facing offender, but that brought unsettling visions of medieval torture.

I'm stuck with them. No Californian beach-grins for me. That's what the extractions were for: so I wouldn't have fucked-up teeth. So I wouldn't have to spend my teenage years in an anguish of enforced celibacy, a railway-track brace deterring every fourth-form carpark-wench from hoisting her navy hockey skirt up her moley thighs. In retrospect this was clearly a double disaster. I didn't get to see any moley thighs and I've still got terrible teeth.

As time passed I became convinced that the continual erosion of my tongue's cells by my shark's fang was giving me too much saliva. By twenty I habitually found myself with a mouthful of spit, a gobful of gob. For no good clinical reason. Talking became an obstacle course of headachy swallowing and avoidance of any sibilant word or experiments with languages that required rolling Rs.

I was arrested three times for spitting in the street. The noise of my hawking in the early hours precipitated a petition from my neighbours. I lost out on three absolutely cast-iron nights of debauchery by half-blinding newly acquainted girls with drool. Any friends with glasses had to invest in windscreen wipers.

And still it got worse. Only recently, just before the separation, I checked myself into the Eastman Dental Hospital in an attempt to clear up the matter once and for all. It was a blindingly bright, rare July day of sunshine. An embarrassment of amber glories and vibrating symphonies of light. It just so happened to coincide with a sudden deepening of my lifelong melancholy. That's right: lifelong. I'm a writer, what did you expect? I suffer from mild depression, like all writers, comics, crazies, depressives. It is their *modus operandi*. Except many writers oscillate in their misery, have manic phases of credit-card spreeing and street-shouting – dizzy epiphanies followed by curtained afternoon bed-residencies where their manservants have to hide the shotgun cartridges. And they're the lucky ones, those bipolar popularities. No, for me it set in for life at around thirteen, that magic age. I don't go on about it for reasons I might elaborate later. Suffice to say that no Lithium or Prozac or self-help doorstopper will snap me out of it, will lift the malaise or provide the heaven-sweet analgesic. It's there, like rolling, chasing thunder clouds in a spasmodically disturbed sky; a constant like tinnitus, a background hum. It deepens, it expands, it multiplies like cancerous cells, but it never *lifts*. And it's especially heavy on blindingly bright, rare July days of sunshine with their obligation, their hot imperative, to fun and shorts and ice-creams and loose times in loose clothing.

That morning, the sudden deepening had manifested itself as a weight, almost a physical sensation, like somebody standing on my chest in concrete waders. The weight of accumulated stress, accumulated knocks to one's self-esteem, accumulated failures. Ten years of London-damage, money-damage, all distilled into each dreadful sigh that unsettled my fellow tube passengers. Plus the weight of *her*, of what was happening with the wife, even though I was trying to deny it, bypass it. The sour tang of our daily argument had been fresh on my tongue as I journeyed towards the hospital, thinking about the twin subjects of metempsychosis and divorce. Earlier that morning, as she rocketed through her bathroom ritual, I had walked into the narrow galley of the kitchen to discover it under a fog of smoke from a grillpan of burning sausages. I must have forgotten about them as I sat in the living room, engrossed in Raymond Williams' *Culture and Society*. On extinguishing the blue jets of gas I could hear her calling from the bathroom, her voice carrying the assertive edge that forecasted fireworks: 'Byron – what the hell is that smell?'

'It's under control,' I shouted back, throwing a dripping cloth over the blazing grillpan, somehow sustaining a third-degree burn to my thumb in the process. 'Fuck!' Instinctively, I dropped the whole apparatus. Oil, molten bangers and shards of charcoal flew to the four corners of the kitchen lino. I yelled, 'Would you like the window open a little?' Then she was in the room.

'I don't believe it. Can't you smell? Can't you smell burning?' Unsurprisingly, she wasn't concerned that I had my thumb under the blast of the cold tap, a lip of crimson skin hanging from the knuckle. 'As if I'm not late enough for that crappy place as it is.'

She barged past me, hurling windows open. Then she began shovelling the sausages from the floor and depositing them in the bin. I watched her carefully as she did this, trying to gauge her true Richter-scale reading. She sometimes moved with a fantastic hauteur, that terrible conceited scorn for the *watcher* you occasionally see in the outraged faces of paparazzi-snapped celebrities. It was both frightening and magnetic at the same time. An awful cynosure. I observed her silently, my thumb now without feeling under the deep-cold water being drawn from the tap. I began cooking up excuses for myself, any excuse other than the sin of reading. But instead I opted for attack – always the best method of defence with her.

'You're not throwing those away are you? They've only been on the floor. We can't afford to chuck 'em away.'

She span round, her eyes full of cat-like venom, a sneer on her wonderfully thin, crisply outlined lips.

'*You* can't afford to. I'm paying all the fucking bills.'

'And I'm paying the fucking rent.' I slammed the tap off and wrapped my hand in a tea towel, tourniquet-tight. 'All you do is spend, spend, spend.'

In the last fortnight alone she'd taken delivery of four new pairs of trousers, a climbing frame and mischief-centre for her beloved Siamese cats, and an in-car CD-system for her vintage VW, a car she couldn't afford in the first place. She stood before me, a shaking wall of perdition, her impressively ironed and coordinated work clothes almost trembling with righteousness.

'It's my money!' she cried, and sent a coffee cup skidding across the surface until it exploded against the toaster.

'It's never just *your* money when you're married!'

I started to search for a dustpan and brush for the shards of the cup; always my first instinct when objects were smashed, regardless of the perpetrator.

'And what were you doing to set the house on fire? You're an idiot! *Cabrón*!'

'I was cooking your breakfast.'

'No you weren't – you were reading.' She disappeared into the living room, returning a moment later brandishing the copy of *Culture and Society*. 'Why don't you make some real money instead of filling your head with this shit?' She was screaming now, at full-philistine-throttle; hurling the book into the bin to join the still-fuming sausages. 'If you're not *reading* . . .' (she pronounced the word like some sort of religious curse) '. . . then you're getting pissed with that idiot Rudi.'

'Oh, so now we're going to hear all this Rudi crap again, are we? He's my childhood friend. My best friend. I'm entitled to have at least one, or is that against the bloody law now?'

Rudi Buckle – hirsute, stocky, early-thirties swordsman and all-round good guy – had been at school with me in Hamford. My oldest pal, as I think I mentioned earlier. Although six months my senior, and a pragmatic Scot of Italian extraction, I would always consider him my closest friend. His folks had moved down from Glasgow to nearby Stevenage when his old man had been transferred to the huge British Aerospace plant that provided most of the work in the area. Rudi was effortlessly charismatic, with a kind of swashbuckling confidence, and initially my wife had warmed to him. But gradually he'd become a *bête noire*, probably through every fault of his own. He'd turned up in London five years ago to start a car valeting business after a similar operation had failed in backwards, provincial Hamford. A year down the line and it had become a thriving monster – he was always meeting crooks and casino owners with their needy Bentleys and voluminous Mercs. He never left the house with less than five hundred quid in his wallet, just in case he met some near-autistic dolly bird still impressed by flash Scotsmen with pockets full of dough. But Rudi's pragmatism covered a strong streak of flakiness. He always had money, but he owed a fortune too. And I was always borrowing from him. And, just recently, drinking a bottle of whisky well into the night at his place to avoid the barren Sahara that was now my marriage bed. He called it 'hard drinking', and it certainly was hard to imbibe that much every night without dying. I love that adjective: *hard*. No one describes gluttony as hard-eating. It's that macho qualification – hard rock, hard porn. Hard drinking.

'He's a pisshead – strutting around like he owns everything. Someone should cut his balls off.'

A familiar deranged look appeared in the black points of her eyes. She was one of the few women I'd known mad enough to carry out such a threat. I shouted back,

'Well, that's something you know all about!'

'And you're just a loser. I'm too good for you, and you know it. My mother – God rest her soul – made the same mistake with Dad. She could've married ten millionaires! They were offering her yachts, jewellery, just to have an affair with them. And she ended up with him.'

'Oh, Christ – not this now!'

Her mother Ramona, a beautiful Spanish immigrant who'd arrived at Victoria station in the early sixties with no more than a suitcase and her stunning looks, had worked her way up the ranks in the hotel business until she was manager of one of the largest Bayswater international stopovers. She, like Rudi, was always encountering the dangerously glamorous, rich or unscrupulous in the course of her work – except in this case they were valeting *her*, usually on stolen weekday afternoons in one of the deluxe, white-carpeted suites. Ramona had died in a car crash when my wife was only sixteen, and, to deal with the grief of this defining disaster, she'd devoted her life to *becoming* her mother; mimicking her profligate habits, her clothes, ambitions, qualities. A modest inheritance, wrested from her father, helped her in this costly endeavour. As I watched my wife – that concentration of fluent vitriol – seethe in front of me, I opened my mouth and said the only thing I knew would end the argument swiftly: 'You're not your mother.'

'Drop dead.'

And, with that *bon mot*, she snatched her embossed VW keys and stormed out, slamming the front door with such ferocity that the living-room lampshade plummeted to the ground in a hail of plaster, like a hanged man through a trapdoor.

At that moment I became aware of the smell of burning. Then I looked at the bin. It was on fire – the pages of *Culture and Society* curling among greedy orange flames.

So, that morning, by the time I reached the sun-carved, chalk-white edifice of the Eastman, I was almost drunk on the lethal Black Dog. Like mustard gas, I felt it was jaundicing my face, adding a sickly lime-pallor to my ears and throat. I wasn't even sure I could make it through the richly timbered, impressively slow revolving door without the unendurable weight of Time and Self pushing me out into the street again, like a gravitational force.

I stopped in the vaporising heat, in blinking disbelief that I could sink so low. Poleaxed by the ponderous millstone, the axle-load, the great sum of Self.

'Mr Easy? If you'd like to follow me.'

Well, she's pretty, I thought, the weight decreasing appreciably by a couple of kilograms.

I followed my glamorous, flat-shoed Burmese nurse into a spare, fluorescent-lit cubicle, pausing to reflect that heels, though impractical on the disinfectant-slippery tiles of the Eastman hospital, might have lifted my depression for ever.

'I'm Dr Amir. We're just going to conduct a couple of experiments and then look at the possible analyses.'

Doctor! And I thought she was only . . . Christ, they're getting younger by the hour, just like coppers. Dr Amir could only have been twenty-six and was possessed of the kind of heartbreaking, leather-dark, make-up-free complexion that Gauguin drank himself to death over. Her mouth, as richly lipsticked as a London bus, shimmered and concentrated the bright glosses of the overhead striplights. I glanced around: no winey blood-furrowed parlour carpet like Dr Demjanjuk's converted Chamber of Horrors, just the immaculate chessboard tiles. White, black, white, black.

She handed me a specimen bottle. I had to spit into it for fifteen minutes.

When she returned, clutching a clipboard to her bust, I had only managed a pitiful amount of bone-dry froth. But that's life, isn't it? When put to the test, very few of us can rise to the grand occasion, can do what we promised, let alone surpass ourselves. On any other morning that month I could have filled three bathtubs to the brim with spittle, doused house fires with phlegm, flooded high streets with saliva. On any other morning . . .

As I apologised, hoping she wouldn't read my parlous performance as a sign of any sexual inadequacy, Dr Amir suggested that my problem was maybe only subjective, a perceived problem. After all, how much is too much? Too much saliva? Too little hair? Too much depression? Aren't all complaints, apart from the obvious tangible ones like severed limbs and terminal illnesses, subjective? It was all about putting up with it, adaptation, I was briskly and sexily told. There *was* an operation, she revealed, but this was expensive, risky and usually only performed on slavering schizo-phrenics or multiple sclerosis sufferers. I was just about to ask whether it was not simply possible to buy a whole new mouth from recep-tion when she said this to me:

'Mr Easy, sometimes dental problems such as yours are psycho-somatic; are brought on by stress or depression. If you like we can refer you to the Eastman's dental psychiatrist. Would you like that?'

Apparently, such a thing as a dental psychiatrist existed. I wondered briefly if, the night before, she hadn't been a participant in one of those epic benders that junior doctors legendarily enjoy after their sixteen-hour shifts, and whether this might be clouding her professional judgement somewhat. I also pondered the possibility that, after the conveyer belt of vodkas and pricey bottled beers, some strapping-armed hospital porter hadn't lifted her coffee-creamy thighs around his waist and banged her remorselessly against the bedroom door, her jet, incensey hair and pillar-box lips wet with the reflected light from her studious standard lamp.

'I'm not sure,' I replied, my mouth suddenly full of spit.

'Well, if you do decide, you'll have to fill out one of these.'

She unhooked a form from her clipboard, moving thrillingly close as she did so.

'There's space to list any psychiatric problems or stressful events you may have experienced over the last eight years. I'm afraid the amount of saliva you produced is pretty standard for a man of your age.'

Age. *My* age. Oh God, to be young enough for her, to not be this frazzled car-wreck of doomy neuroses and nightly death-dreams. To be a strapping-armed hospital porter. To have money. To not be shackled to the black ball and chain of writing. To not feel the weight of Self, like someone in concrete waders standing on my chest. To not be married.

'Have you any history of depression, Mr Easy?' asked Dr Amir as I dithered with my ballpoint. A sententious expression appeared on her face. She looked candidly through me, right back to the cot I bawled in, aged one, when I was still unaware that, as bad as this being-a-hungry-baby caper is, there's worse, much worse, much *more* to bawl about coming later.

'I've been as depressed as the next man, I suppose,' I lied, with refreshing simplicity.

And as the sentence left my desert-dry lips I felt two awful and conflicting things at once. The first was a galactic sense of enfolding warmth, like a heroin-surge; a blanket of childhood safety engulfing the nerves and bloodstream. Merely the interest from another human being, a stranger, an unconditional hand of heated care reaching out from the squalid sea of indifferent inscrutable faces one encounters on any given day in London, was enough to lift my spirits. How long had it been? How long since anyone had shown any curiosity over my suffering, into what had fucked up this Grand Old Man of Misery? How many aeons had it been since anyone had taken a look at my black-box recorder to see what had gone wrong, what had malfunctioned? Nobody had. At least not for a long time. Not my mother, nor Rudi, nor Antonia and Nick, nor the rest of my sleazily ambitious acquaintances. Not my increasingly malicious wife. No, certainly not *her*.

The second and simultaneous reaction went something like this: where to begin? Oh, where, where in the universe to begin? I know a lot of life-sentence depressives and, not to diminish their anguish – cold posterity will decide whether what they endured was worth the effort, was worth sticking it out to the bitter end for – nearly all of them have been through some form of counselling, of therapy. I never have. For the simple reason that I know what the root, the core, the cause of the malaise to be. The problem, unfortunately folks, is *me*. No traumas of hypnotism-induced total recall, no mornings spent baseball-batting chunky pillows in anger-catharsis classes, no costly hours dangling my feet from leather sofas and pouring out histories of incests and primal-woundings will ever resolve it, will ever clear the mess up, relieve the weight, the pure tonnage. Because *I* am the problem. The problem is me. In essence, my essence is to blame. That thing that crystallises hard into all you've got after the world ceases to be a horizon-wide playground of possibilities – one's very *quiddity* – is the culprit. In the end, *I* have done all the damage.

And this is not unusual. It's just that most depressives haven't reconciled themselves to the fact. They're still looking outside themselves for a cause, as if the contingent world really had an effect on the Self. Human beings are pervious to things, to the great shit-storm of occurrence that awaits them after the soft bay of childhood, in different ways. For instance, one individual's mother could die and leave him or her with nothing much more than a sweet absence, a sentimental vulnerability to any talk of mothers and their passing away. But nothing that would prevent them from leading a productive, coherent life. On the other hand, for another individual, it could spell a life sentence of bereavement; of perpetual howling after the loved-one; of feeling the raw hole of loss in just about everything they ever attempt, as they hurl themselves through one destructive personal relationship after another, like those iron wrecking balls they use to bring down tower blocks. This was the case with *her*, as it happened. With her, the woman I married.

I filled in the form inaccurately and left. Dr Amir's sapling-brown eyes would never understand. But the process of confession, of being probed in the very interior by such a simple sentence, had left me high; vulnerable as a peeled egg.

I gained the street and stood in the cornea-slicing sunlight. And then they came, the hot tears, like a sneeze, like a sudden, churning faultline split in the soul. I moved off among the indifferent faces; the rib-cracking weight on my chest doubled, if not almost trebled.

———

In case you're wondering whether the train has moved or not, it hasn't. Tracksuit Man is still sitting in his Santa hat, bellicose with booze. A third game of dominoes has just commenced before me.

The tensed carriage is still putrid with the stink of pasties, whisky-breaths, wet cattle, hot leather, sweaty fabrics, migrainey perfumes and burps.

Think I'll take a look outside.

Stationary, abandoned luggage-buggies crouch forlornly on the concourse. A smattering of leather-smocked desperadoes and tubercular grans are sucking whey-faced at last-minute cigarettes (how I long to join them!). A porter with his porter-hands clasped trimly behind his back like a beat-copper perambulates unsteadily, close to the crouched carriages, disguising his six lunchtime shots with a practised ease. Further off, where no people go, a ragged T-shirt caught in a bulging wire-mesh fence flaps madly on the whippet-quick wind. No blessing in that ungentle breeze.

Getting dark out there.

The blood-crimson ribbons of cloud seem to have been cowed, demoted somehow to the bottom of the sky's three-tier colour hierarchy. Red, hospital-white, then boiling storm-blue; like a judgement hand unclosing over sewery, dogshitty London. A quick look around. Everyone seems glad to be getting out. Brightly relieved to be heading off, departing, travelling from station to station. Released from the cage of work or school, or penurious debasement, they all appear lighter than perhaps they would if one encountered them in the street or job uniform; as if they'd all been given an extra lung or a transfusion of new blood. See them smiling: exalted and helium-light. Getting out of the smoke. The dirty old town. Leaving Old Father Thames to receive its Christmas suicides, unobserved by the writhing directional hordes that batter its bridges by day.

Rattle-tattle-spattle.

The rain has picked up from nowhere, announcing itself like a spew of gravel against my smeary window. An hysterical rivulet of water in the corner of the frame, like a mad artery, pulsates and quivers – endlessly replenished. It must be time to go. I need to go. Every stasis-yellowed nerve in my body yearns for movement, extradition. I've never wanted anything more in my life.

To convert the present quickly and painlessly into the past. To slide away amnesic, the chromium rails diminishing to nothing behind.

Go, go, go. Please – let's get out of here.

I suppose I should tell you more about her. No. She can wait. She made *me* wait enough, over the three tarnished, nightmare-vivid years of our marriage. I must have clocked up a thousand man-hours in attendance for her. Not just the usual bum-numbing sojourn outside the women's changing rooms in the alarmingly populous department store. Not just the nervy, tenterhooks evening by the phone wondering whether to ring around the hospitals and enquire about recent traffic accidents. Not just the pregnant millennium it always took her to decide on tea as opposed to coffee in the greasy spoon before quickly reversing her decision. But the season, the lifetime, the *fourth dimension* spent waiting for her to change. To reach her emotional first birthday. To grow out of her scarily psychotic temper tantrums. To stop taking everyone she encountered up and down in her emotional elevator. To cease being a habitual liar and truth-strangler. To take her first faltering, nappy-free steps on the road to having any insight into anything at all, anywhere. To stop being what psychologists amusingly call an 'adult baby'. To learn how to *behave*.

There. I've already started telling you about her. She's burst through what I originally intended to report and established herself centre stage, grossly unavoidable – forcing everyone, through sheer might of personality, to be somehow contingent upon her. She's here now – not physically with me, of course, on this train of pain, but with me nonetheless. And even that's in character: affrontingly omnipresent, she always got her own way. And she never did change.

Which all makes it sound like I hate her. That I despise and reject every wretched facet of her five-note emotional range. And

I do. If I heard on whatever grimly whispered grapevine that my estranged wife had been murdered I would turn myself in at the nearest police station, convinced I was guilty on grounds of mere thought-transference. That she'd perished telekinetically, as it were. But all this doesn't explain why, on a daily basis, for the past three months, as regular as the milkman, I have been poleaxed, soul-hindered, by the most innocuous of phenomena. A vintage VW outside the post office near my Kentish Town flat can cause untold internal disturbance. A tall jar of pimento olives in the supermarket as I make my grisly bachelor rounds is a morning-sabotaging obstacle. A cause of shrill physical pain and panic, like the moment of child-hood drama when you realise you've let slip your mother's hand in a crowd. The wife introduced me to olives. By the end of our three-year tenure I was an olive gourmet; an expert on shape, size, contour and colour in the multifarious universe of the olive. I was an honorary Spaniard, or, at the very least, an honorary Greek, since it was at the orange-tumbling all-night Cypriot grocers that we embarked on our odyssey of olives. I'm certain that their bitter, briny, delectable tang will eternally conjure the potent myths of her cooking; her mother-learnt spice-knowledge, pulse-knowledge, olive-knowledge. I am convinced that, at eighty, the insatiable saltiness of an olive (mostly green, sometimes black) will rein me back to our three varnished, vanished dream-vivid years of marriage; with all chronology lost – every day at once in photographic detail.

And that, I suppose, is a terrible thing. If a jar of olives in a shop can do this to me now, what damage is it going to exact in the future, when the raw edge of memory is submerged? When the soul waits for an object, a perfume, a snapshot to stir a scene from the past, like a focus-puller zooming a blurred frame into crisp, clarified profile.

I am powerless in the face of these impingements. And it's not just olives, those madeleines with a stone at their centre.

Only the other morning, for instance, I was on the lower deck of the unfamiliar bus to the shop, i.e. to work (you thought I made money from writing? Are you mad?); un-breakfasted, separation-crippled, bloodstream ninety per cent cheap red wine from the previous night's saturnalia, when I whooshed past the park where we used to walk the dogs. And I got it all, right between the eyes, all at once. A Nagasaki of recall, and of helpless insight into that recall.

O mister bus driver, if I knew you were going to do this to me, I surely would have walked . . .

We used to have two little dogs. Well, we fostered over the years what seemed like a vast zoo of animals great and small, but these two – two chihuahuas – were, how can I put it, lovers. Like humans, their love was initially courtly, then fantastically, detailedly carnal. And it's these two satanic rodents I remember most potently. Their names were Concepcion and Fidellino, or Fidel for short. I had no choice in their naming, as I had no input into holiday destination, TV channel, emulsion colour, gas versus electric, white versus red as a choice for alcoholic imbibition, side-of-bed-to-sleep-on, variety of supermarket, or what to wear in any given weather. They had to be *her* names. They had to be Spanish names, too. Unsuitable, unpronounceable, unmemorable to even the most fastidiously tuned canine ear. No Rover or Growler for *her*.

Of course, they never came when you called them. She claimed it was in the nature of the breed to be disobedient, a fallacy she had gleaned from the cornucopia of dog books borrowed from the library during our preamble to buying a mutt (the furthest she read in the time I knew her). I, meanwhile, was convinced it was because they couldn't understand what the hell you were yelling at them, their names lacking the single smart consonant necessary to catch a playing dog's attention.

We acquired Concepcion first. I can still picture the sun-settled May afternoon we zipped through Shepherd's Bush to collect her from a gay Chinese dentist who was, apparently, an eminent and respectable breeder of smooth-coat chihuahuas. A spring snowstorm of blossom was everywhere: on the streets and in the breeze, every shade of Japanese pink and cherry. We whisked illegally through the junctions' plenteous ambers in whatever Sierra or banger she had at the time before she developed a profligate taste for sports cars and the slavering, stubbled mechanics who would later sell them to her. My hand-wringing disapprobation of the very idea of getting a dog, let alone ruining ourselves with a costly pedigree, had of course fallen on deaf, impatient little ears. It was all arranged, so I was told. I was merely along to restrain the vomiting, shitting, whinnying bastard on the return journey in the absence of a suitable travel-box.

I sat in the passenger seat in the choicely conifered Close, wearily watching privileged brats act out some urban drive-by fantasy on spankingly minted BMX bikes, while she vanished with great purpose through the dentist's front door.

A last, dog-free fifteen minutes elapsed, during which I gloomily tried to convince myself that dogs only smell if they're not *your own* dog. Then the car door opened.

And then I fell in love.

Into my unready hands was placed squirming, smooth-coated, hot-pawed Concepcion. The dinkiest, most beautiful rat-faced little yapper you ever saw in your life. The engine growled into throbbing anticipation of take-off and the car − me, the wife, and Concepcion cradled like a hot pie in the crook of my arm − yanked backwards in reverse.

If you can still love someone after they've puked and defecated on you (twice) then I reckon you can call it true love. Poor Concepcion. Her maiden voyage in a motorised vehicle certainly didn't agree with her. After five, dumb-struck, trembling minutes cowering under my fatherly palm she looked at me, her pupils zigzagging wildly, with a kind of pleading abattoir-fear. Then she started to foam greenly at the mouth, the shakes coming at regular intervals, like the spasms of an exposure-victim. After this she remained still, as if contemplating (like a seasick drunk) whether she could make it to the toilet in time. Then it was all over. Pigeon-like retching was followed by massive fumbling for the kitchen towel we had presciently taken along.

As her most recent meal dried sadly and wetly on my newly

laundered lap (just not slick enough on the draw with the old kitchen towel), a rank, excretal honk, an ordural cloud, began to fill the car, requiring swift window-windings on both sides. By this time even the driver had begun to have serious reservations about dog-ownership. A few nippy corners, and another whimpering voidance later, and we were home; me staggering with guano-spattered flanks passenger-side, the wife aborting the driver's seat, all five senses fairly blotted out by the pungent flavour of cacation.

Once inside, diminutive Concepcion – surely convinced that she had experienced the most traumatising twenty minutes available to any mammal – was gently set down to await the attentions of our three shark-like tomcats.

It took a while, as it always does for a new animal, to get the run of the place. To stop vibrating under the bedclothes hoping the hellish, unfamiliar world they've been plunged into will vanish and be replaced by the comfort of their old stinky pen and the company of their mother, father, brothers and sisters. To stop pissing like a Tiny Tears doll the moment they're picked up. To stop barking at you or their own berserk reflection in the bedroom mirror. To make friends with three grimly established and territor-ial tomcats (or jungle lions, as they must appear to a chihuahua) . . . But Concepcion managed it somehow. She pulled it off by pretending that she – the smallest dog in the world – was in fact the biggest dog in the world. Her impersonation, standing all of six inches in her stockinged paws, of a drooling, terror-toothed Dobermann or pit bull was really something to be witnessed. She would bark herself to a croak at approaching postmen, friends, vets, in-laws or televised dogs, her rancour becoming progressively more intense (and striped with a certain concussed bewilderment) as she discovered the reaction she invariably received was not fear, but laughter. Oh, what amusement she caused in the street! On the rare occasions that she consented to walking on a lead in that scampy, pizzicato way that all lapdogs have (as opposed to her usual method of transportation – that of being dragged unwillingly across pavements on her belly like a kind of canine sleigh), the looks she and we used to elicit were treasureable. Small children would point in frenzied amazement: 'Mummy, mummy, look at the puppy!' And that was when, at eighteen months, doomed Concepcion was already a fully expanded, six-nippled bitch. Grown men, scaffolders, labourers and tattoo-wristed car thieves would weep openly as the little doll did her heartbreaking, scurrilous wiggle down the sweating High Street. Owners of mangy pooches and lactating Labradors would turn up their commoners' noses with envy when they saw our formidable miniature approaching.

It was then, genetically fascinated, and also not a little sorry for the poor circus-attraction wretch, that we decided it was a good time to find her a mate. Enter Fidellino, or rather, enter a fantastically libidinous hairy Swiss roll called Rusty Gold, sold to us by a devious builder in Totteridge for a hundred and fifty quid. Obviously, he couldn't stay Rusty Gold. After all the Ricios and Juans and Xaviers and Joaquins had been worked through, I timidly suggested Fidel, as his straggled pubic hairpiece of a coat reminded me of Castro's beard. With a slight alteration, Mandy loved it, and Fidellino he became. It was Spanish-sounding after all. We both hoped he would gallantly go on to sire many children.

Didn't I mention my wife's name was Mandy? Always hated it. Wouldn't you, O hip and cultured reader? Wouldn't you despise its silly vowels? Wouldn't you wince slightly at the altar or tatty registry office desk as your sober marrier spaketh the sentence: 'Do you, Mandy, take this . . .?' Or maybe you're married to a Mandy already and the name has become a kind of phonetic blank, something not heard any more. I *always* heard it; always had a problem with it. Always cringed at having to introduce her, at seeing it on an envelope, or calling her name in a public place, or saying the sentence: 'Mandy, I love you.' It was that perky, tooth-decaying last syllable that was to blame. Dee. Like Suki or Debi or Plebi – those abysmal, made-up Page Three monikers. (And before you ask, plain Amanda was never an option. Not even her mother had called her Amanda; her daughter having been conceived to the castrato strains of 10cc's 'I'm Mandy, Fly Me' in the deluxe wedding suite of a Bayswater hotel.)

I used to exhaust myself with tumours of research into an appropriate nickname for her. I even considered cooking up an *acronym*, but there aren't any, not sufficiently romantic anyway, for any girl's name anywhere – unless her initials spell L.U.V. All I came up with was 'Man'. ('Hi, here's my woman: Man. And my name's Tarzan.') Or Dee. Or worse, Dee Dee. But the name refused to conform to any meddling, so there it stayed: irreducibly, eternally, miserably, Mandy.

Let me stop now, lest this effort of hate deform me for ever.

Fidel and Concepcion never did produce that baying litter of fluffy pedigrees (Mandy with one rapacious eye as always on how much she could flog them for). The ratted, roasted beige carpets of our flat never ticked with the patter of tiny, costly paws for the simple reason that the bitch was too small. Concepcion, that is. Mr Morris, our morose and farmyard-odoured vet, gravely broke the news to us one rainy, work-dodging morning after Mandy had failed to obtain the exact date and hour of when she could expect a female chihuahua to reach her first season. For this information we went to Antonia.

Antonia, Mandy's best friend, was also dog-mad. Mandy had called her at *Acquisition*, the fiendishly elitist antiques quarterly she worked for. Antonia, a diplomat's daughter who had grown up on a farm surrounded by pedigree dogs, had just returned from New York, a city she claimed to have first visited while still in the womb. In general, I was distrustful of people who had been to New York early in life – it spoke of more vivid, more worldly upbringings than my own. After all, NY was the great aspirational visit. The one you talked and worried about until you had the money or the luck, or both, to go there – and Antonia had been to the Big Apple lots, and (if she were to be believed, the truth always being negotiable with her) when she was very young.

'Hon', I'm up to my eyeballs in Pembroke tables,' Antonia had purred, when Mandy finally got her on the line. She had one of those upper-middle-class voices that somehow purify and pollute the air at the same time. 'How can I be expected to give advice on your babies? Try talking to Mr Morris – I'll give you his number.'

So Mr Morris it was. A day later he was standing before us on the opposite side of a slab-like, green-vinyl examination table, where he imparted some sobering information.

'I'm afraid you can't breed her.'

'What – you mean she'll never have kids? That's the only reason we got her,' said Mandy, Spanishly alarmed.

I cradled Concepcion on the comfortless butcher's board of plastic, shielding her ears slightly from these harsh words.

'I'm sorry, but it's too great a risk to breed her,' growled Mr Morris in a significant basso profundo as he snapped off his condom gloves. 'There's a ninety per cent chance she'll die giving birth or that her litter would be dead. She's simply too small. Where did you get her again?'

'From a gay dentist,' I offered helpfully.

'Ah, Mr Tonka. I know him well. He should have told you. Although, I have to admit, he's become slightly more unscrupulous about whom he sells to over the years.'

'What do you mean by that?' persisted Mandy. 'We're the best parents she'll ever have. She's our little baby.'

And with that, she yanked Concepcion from my tender grasp and held her upside down in a pietà-like cradle. I couldn't help but notice the stunted bunny's eyes glance anxiously towards her father, as if to say: *Don't put me down. I promise to walk properly. I promise to grow bigger, if I can.*

'I'm sure she is Miss, er, Haste, but that's all there is to it. You'll have to keep her from any male stud when she's in season. I recommend a locked pen.'

'And an armed sentry,' said I. Mr Morris lowered his forehead towards me, as if the only way of training his eyes on something was to physically move his rotund head.

'I'm serious. I've seen male dogs jump through plate-glass windows to reach a bitch in heat.'

'I know how they feel,' I muttered, trying to remember the distant era of the past, the period during late antiquity, when Mandy and I last had anything to do with each other sexually. I unhooked the clasp of my wallet in readiness to pay his scandalous consultation fee. 'Anyway, breeding isn't the *only* reason we got her.'

'Oh, I wish I was dead,' hissed Mandy, and left the room; dumping the terrified dog in my clammy hands on her way out. Yes, Mandy certainly had a negative capability, though not in the sense Keats intended. I turned to the vet, marvelling at how she always left me (literally) holding the baby.

'Sorry about that. She's joking. We got her because we . . . because we loved her.'

'Always the best reason,' nodded Mr Morris, holding the door for me and my trembling cargo. 'That'll be forty-three fifty plus VAT. You can pay at reception.'

'Cheers.'

All this came as grave news indeed to little Fidellino, a dog, if ever there was one, who was born to reproduce. If, in a sick parallel universe (Hamburg maybe), dogs were ever enlisted as porn stars, then Fidel would have been Big John Rocco Fidel; or Fidel The Fuck Machine; or simply, The Satisfier. In the previous few months our dimpled Castro's beard had grown into a tautly haunched priapic love-engine, a young thing never too busy, tired, or Chum-hungry to turn down the briefest of copulations. The fact that most of these acts of love were with virginal sofa armrests, cuddly toys or strangers' legs didn't seem to deter or confuse him in the slightest. For me, there was an admirable simplicity in his basic urges: when a guy had to do it, he had to do it – Hell, yeah! And he wasn't going to stick around to hug or reassure his inanimate partner before trotting off refreshed for a nourishing meal, either. Way to go, big man! I didn't know of any bloke not in prison with such shameless fidelity to his own impulses. But Big Fidel the Fornicator hadn't, as yet, got the chance to practise on another living, breathing animal.

And this was why what we had to do hit him so hard.

At first he thought we were being bloody-mindedly contrary, feeding him and his adorable Concepcion at different times of the day and in different parts of the house. Dogs always keenly notice any incremental change in their owners' routine, but this to him was a grim disaster. Initially, our concupiscent crawler tried to pretend he wasn't crouching satyr-like under the kitchen table at bedtime when it became necessary to separate them overnight. As the potential rapist was carted off upstairs his eyes would plangently, pleadingly meet those of his smooth-coated Juliet (by now wiggling her arse in a randied, readied frenzy at every opportunity) as if we were cruelly extinguishing an epic love. Then he would look to me, the Man, as if to say: 'But you'd do the same, wouldn't you? Given the chance? You understand how I can't help myself?' And I would have to avert my eyes lest the clearly transmitted meaning of his doggie-stare received the thumbs up from me.

Night after night we were woken by pussy-crazed scrabblings as Fidel attempted to gain gallant access to his beloved's bedchamber, the kitchen. By day four of his helpless lust the lino had to be replaced and the door re-glossed where he had clawed the paintwork to splinters. By day five he'd begun speaking Swedish. And it wasn't just him in a lather. On the other side of the divide, fair Concepcion would be whimpering in rampant expectation; an unwitting conduit for Nature's Way, as Fidel tried – finally, one night – to shoulder-barge his way through a locked oak door. Oh, the carnal reveries we denied him! Oh, how he hated us, as no end of spankings and admonishments failed to souse his thundering desire! Behind the impenetrable cell door there yapped gagging-for-it Concepcion, dressed (in Fidel's mind) in stockings and suspenders, a filthy brothel-glint in her eyes; while we, his cruel deprivers, slumbered on upstairs.

The sound of two dogs shagging, when the bitch is clearly in discomfort, is not a sound you forget in a hurry. It resembles, frankly, that of a small baby being murdered with a kebab scimitar, or, at the very least, someone sawing a cooker in half with a hacksaw. It was this catastrophically distressing sound that had me leaping bare-bollocked downstairs in the early hours of the last day of Concepcion's season. One of our tenants, it seems, had disobeyed the clear felt-pen notice on the kitchen door and had left it ajar after a nocturnal sally for a glass of water. And there, as the overhead light exploded on like a police flashbulb, was famished Fidel crouched over his squealing prey in the guilty act of debauchery. On seeing me, he ran like a missile shot from a silo through my legs, leaving his half-raped concubine palpitating in fear.

'Fidellino!' I screamed at his cowed, retreating haunches. But he didn't stop. And then I remembered: he never did stop when called. The name Mandy had given him was about as recognisable to the dog as Morse code, or hieroglyphics spoken out loud.

After that close call, and after Fidel had been taken away to stay at Antonia's in order to undergo a course of cold showers, we decided, to my tearful regret, to sell Concepcion to a babbling old bat with a big house up in Hampstead. If our darling ever did fall pregnant by the unquenchable Fidellino then we never found out.

All I can say is that, as first-time newly-wed parents, we tried our level best.

I find it hard to illuminate, O hip and cynical reader, just how bleakly painful these recollections are to recount. A thwarting emptiness, a cardiac heaviness is expanding inside my chest as I re-run these flickering Super-8 scenes for your delectation. If this were a real film-show, the tickering projector throwing prismatic light through a smoke of dust, then you would find me creased with tears on my plastic chair when the living-room spots went up. And why? Because these were vignettes from a bigger, better, richer life. Despite all the arguments for filing for divorce after the first week (which I'm working up the nerve to get to later), these and other faltering flashbacks constituted the *good life*, the days of laughter and involvement, not the days I torpidly wake up to now: the gruesome impoverishments of a drooling, penny-hoarding bachelor.

They all seem so long ago, the days. Was it really then? It's like looking into the wrong end of a telescope, the detail condensed and miniaturised. All painted from memory, of course. I didn't take any photographs with me. I didn't have the time, what with the haste in which I had to leave.

So the bus took me past the park where we used to walk the dogs. I think it even did a stop there, by the shielding trees that confuse the perspective of what's behind. The park was still extant under the low mirage-mist of a November morning, its concave curves of dogshit lawn extending to blurred boundaries. Yes, the park was still there, but something was missing – us. We, the wife and I, and our tearaway chihuahuas. We were absent. A skeleton park, with all the flesh and warmth and life removed. The view from the bus – the present moment – had struggled manfully to contain the past. And it choked me up, I can tell you. It made me shudder. It throttled the ventricles to get that old conker right between the eyes again; the useless insight that a space takes on meaning only if we, human beings (and in my sorry case, chihuahuas), invest it with something. Without that investment it's just space: concrete, grass, litter bins, climbing frame, goalposts, *air*. Oh, to know the raw edge of that blinder once more! To see Concepcion bulleting after strangers' footballs like a dog-track whippet in the smelting August sun. To witness Fidel, fiddling pornographically with himself on a rich knoll of sunburnt grass. To see Mandy, the glosses of her hair unbearably raven around her delicate collar bones.

How could she wantonly split that closeness, that symbiosis, that cell of love? How could she detonate a whole marriage? Sheer recklessness – like burning a diary. Like cutting apart Siamese twins. Like halving Aristophanes' original homo sapiens. Is that what she really wanted? Because that's what she really got.

Why is it we remember the bad times as if they were better? When you look back rationally, that glowing childhood holiday was in reality an opera of recrimination and cockroach-ridden campsite toilets. That first date was really an agony of suppressed colonic torture, being, as you were, too embarrassed to visit the Gents for longer than it took to piss. Those knockabout schooldays really a Stalag 18 of solitary confinement and beatings. I seem to remember there's a photograph of me from one of those blissful August days with the dogs. Byron Easy asprawl the sun-warmed park bench: grotty pillar-box-red T-shirt; a scowl on his face. I was, I seem to recall – after the bitter day-long argument over money and the dire possibility of moving to Spain for work – in a foul mood.

Hold it . . . we're moving! At last! Or at least I think we are. After a long stationary wait it's sometimes hard to tell if it isn't just the scenery, the *world*, gracefully evolving into motion rather than sore-arsed you – as when the cross-Channel ferry begins to ease out of port and the quayside starts shifting. Like two wide ribbons being unwound, as Frédéric observed at the start of his sentimental education. Maybe life bears an echo of this: we assume we are in motion, forging ahead through time and space, from station to station, when in reality we are static, *stationary,* and it's time that is active, operational around us; fraying us, distorting us. With all the millennial panic in the air, it's hard to tell.

This living in the past – this lepidoptery – it can play terrible tricks with the light.

The rivulet of rainwater, still vivid through the breath-steamed palette of glass, has gone into nervous hyperdrive – shivering centrifugally and threatening to break like a stretched chromium worm. We're definitely off. A whistle blows long and shrill. The train is sighing away from its mark, its carbon-black buffers; leaving the squalling neon burger-counters of King's Cross to their cast of Christmas drifters, their men with nowhere and no one to go to. It makes you feel good and warm inside; hot, like after a bellyful of coffee, to know your mother has left some money for a ticket home at Christmas. Makes you thankful not to be one of those

Yuletide Nowhere Men spitting and swearing their way through the shopping hordes, crackling with bitterness. Those losers. Those swimmers of Acheron. It makes *me* feel good because I have been one of their number, in my time.

I watch the tapering platform pick up speed as I swirl a kitchen-sink of saliva around the basin of my mouth. Goodbye ragged, mad T-shirt caught in wire-mesh fence. Goodbye porters. Goodbye platform-wavers in Santa hats. Goodbye seedy corrupted London. Goodbye Mandy.

The ribbons of horizon cloud now seem lit from within: diaphanous streaks in the dusk over a population of chimneys. There's a sudden, raw noise. A groaning shudder of machinery-squeak announces the train's effort to find its centre of gravity. The carriages lurch: a sausage-string of heavy metal on a tightrope. Then we're released into a ranged arena of points and sidings; a confluence of tracks and overhead cables petering out to low, graffitied brick walls. Open space. Unreadable aerosol-artist tags on an approaching iron-riveted bridge; the rain bulleting down with a sadistic vengeance. Then darkness. A tunnel.

I take a brief gander around. The exterior blackness seems to have concentrated the feverish glare of the striplights. Everyone appears to be absorbed in a paper, a card game, a sandwich, a private life. The septuagenarian in the denim jacket is playing Space Invaders; the white plastic console bleeping and cooing in his frail hands. The Islington lesbian couple, wearing weightless peacock-hued silk scarves, are bickering good-naturedly. Tracksuit Man (whose suitcase smack is still causing me pain) is joyously spanking his defiant daughter across the back of her bare legs. The colourless, office-tanned Accountant Couple opposite me are now engrossed in terrible fiction . . . But I'm thinking about *her*, and what she's doing now – now, in this exact moment, whether it be her insisted-upon twenty stirs of sugar in her beloved tea or her groans of submission with some Italian on the futon we shared for three years.

And I'm thinking about the still unfamiliar sights and sounds I awoke to yesterday morning in my comically empty room; the room in a shared flat that Rudi found for me after the split. The folding chair. The blighted, peeling crust of wallpaper. The daydream of my exploding cranium spattering the carpet with crimson. The commotion of the two haggard croupiers letting themselves in downstairs after an arduous night. The sound of distant, muffled chamber music from the jobbing classical musician behind pitifully slender walls. The low, sinuous sustains of a viola as the rain chucked its buckets against the flimsy panes: bare baroque études – a melancholy concoction at nine in the morning.

And I'm thinking about the view from my high window: a strange, barren, blowy panorama. The stripped chestnut in the garden two doors down, now fully naked almost three months on from its October glory of copper and rust, the day I first flung my three cardboard boxes across my square of carpet.

And I'm thinking about thirty and how the hell I arrived at this famous summit with so little achieved: how royally I've failed in my chosen endeavours of art and love. And I'm thinking about my mother and my estranged father in Sydney, Australia, playing with the step-siblings I've never met while Emmanuelle looks feebly and Frenchly on. And I'm thinking about all those I'll never see again, like Antonia and Nick or Fidel and Concepcion. And I'm thinking how each disappearing year seems like a station left behind, becoming smaller as the tracks thin to a pencil point; how these years come to resemble alien countries or continents, each with their capitals of pain, counties of sorrow, small hamlets of joy.

And I'm thinking about *her*: Mandy. I'm trying to remember in order to forget. Before her image slides unrecallably away into that lost land of the past, like decaying Finsbury Park is now beyond my rain-refracted window. I'm thinking about her face with its almond symmetries and glossy brows; her strongly bridged nose as flat as a ruler; the Mediterranean heat of her leather-brown eyes; the squiggly white childhood scar on her forehead that her fringe used to hide before she settled for a straight parting like her dead mother's. And I'm thinking about her appurtenances of richly raven hair that tendrilled to her swift, exciting waist. Her fashion-model legs. Her quick, uncontrollable smile. Her look that once held love for me.

But mostly I'm thinking about that other *her* – Mandy, the adult baby, the evil little emotional-mongrel who never learnt to share, who almost did for me with two kitchen knives on the day we split for ever (and on other numerously dark occasions). I'm thinking about her, her, her. I don't recall telling you how we met, how our two souls became entangled, fatally enmeshed.

Let me fill you in.

2

Never Met A Girl Like You Before

It was at work. My work. The shop. A music shop on two crumbling, dust-decorated floors in Royal College Street, where I had slaved for five years before Mandy blew glamorously into my life; trembling the strings on the wall-hung instruments. A chance meeting on a snowy morning. Ah, if only the plumber hadn't cancelled his appointment to fix my ruptured heating pipes that day. I would only have had to endure a morning of mild racism. Instead, I got the Spanish Inquisition.

At the time the place called itself Rock On, although it had evolved through many incarnations (*Strings 'n' Things, Stacks 'n' Racks*) due mainly to the fascist and unforgiving attentions of the taxman. It was, and still is, the brainchild of an old rocker named Martin Drift – a low-shouldered, astute-eyed survivor who wore his hair in a tight grey ponytail raked back from an embattled forehead. A lovely, gentle man, with delicate fine-knuckled hands, Martin was from the Old School – the *lycée* that sent its pupils out into the slipstream of the Home Counties Guitar Gods, through the coffee bars and sweat-toilets of early sixties Soho. Martin had endured this breathtakingly exciting time of overnight fame and fortune, white

Jags and scandalous skirts (a time when Making It seemed so much *easier*) to find himself living with an obese Hare Krishna and an acid-addled poet in a Chalk Farm squat. It was the dog-end of the decade and he was, like so many others from the Old School, bewilderingly unfamous and exactingly unfortunate. Out of desperation he formed one last band. And they – a soft-rock combo he christened Drifter, who sported the requisite Old Testament beards and albescent denim – *almost* made it. Why are tales of almost-success more heartbreaking than abject, gruel-subsisting failure? Why is number fifty-nine in the charts always more pitiful than number-nothing in the charts? Why is a support tour that *almost* happened with world-famous rock outfit (insert name here) more calamitous than a self-funded tour of East Anglian mental homes? Is it that parlous proximity to the Holy Grail? Or just proof of the unpalatable parental wisdom that it all comes down to luck in the end?

Anyway, it was Drifter's turn to rocket to number fifty-nine during the hot August of '75 with their immortal summer stomper, 'Bell-Bottomed Belle'. It was then, at the height of his fame, that Martin went and had an accident, the legacy of which is still visible on his face today. He electrocuted himself onstage in front of ten thousand baying Dutch rock fans at a festival in Rotterdam. And, on this occasion, nobody in the audience thought it was just 'part of the act'. The way Mart tells it, he was thrown back into the drum riser with such force that it appeared someone had yanked him from the wings with an industrial pulley. 'It was like being hit by a six from Viv Richards, man. Total impact!' What remained of the right side of his charred face was painstakingly reconstructed by Dutch surgeons over the following year. The modified plateaus of artificially wax-textured skin under his grey stubble testify to this feat of dermatological engineering. Whenever a customer commented on his scars, the saga would be trotted out – lavishly embellished, of course (helicopter air-ambulance from the stadium, Mick Jagger weeping at his hospital bedside), after which Martin would conclude: 'Hey, could be worse – I could still be living in Bromley.' Ah, Mart and Bromley. Bromley and Mart. The place *he* escaped from.

The place that made him the man he is today, with his two floors of bargain Stratocasters and budget recording and rehearsal facilities in the converted toilets. Nothing, according to Martin, could be worse than originating from Bromley. The way he told it, nowhere was geographically further from the epicentre of rock 'n' roll in the sixties than Bromley. No conurbation could be more banal, no town centre more unlike downtown New Orleans than Bromley's in 1965. I once put it to him that Hamford was worse. He said,

'Nah, man. I think you'll find that Bromley had the edge. Even the lettering on the street signs was depressing.'

'Street signs are depressing everywhere. Think of Russia,' I said, thinking instead of Hamford.

'Yeah, but their alphabet looks so exotic.'

'Not when you've queued six hours for a single egg.'

'True,' conceded Martin thoughtfully, lighting his fifteenth Marlboro of the morning.

'And I bet you had a cinema.'

'Yeah, but it got all the films a year late. And no bands. I mean, apart from us and the Thin White Duke, who came out of Bromley?'

'*Us?*' I replied, as if I didn't know who he was referring to. I used to love baiting him in this fashion – he was too equanimous to ever get really angry.

'Us . . . you know . . .' Martin was now looking pleadingly into my eyes, a veil of smoke soft-focusing his features; waiting for me to complete his sentence with—

'Ah, you mean Snifter.'

'Drifter, you bastard – now, there was a band . . .' And he would be off, usually concluding on a sordid tale of rampaging Copenhagen call girls as our sole lunchtime customer made his purchase-free rounds.

So rock 'n' roll almost killed Martin Drift, just as it successfully killed a host of others. After reconstructive surgery he opened a record shop on Camden High Street with his first wife. But drinking soon put paid to that venture, as it did his first marriage. His last chance was an eighties initiative called the Enterprise Allowance

Scheme, a Thatcher brainwave that lent you just enough money to start a small business, but – deviously enough – not enough to make it worth drinking away in style. With this cash, Martin opened Rock On, and kept his second wife safely at home with the children. It was his last chance, and he knew it, which explained his obsessive fiscal caution over the years I worked for him. To Martin, expansion equalled danger: 'Tick along and you can't go wrong,' he used to instruct me in his tobacco-torn husk of a voice.

Which didn't mean he couldn't be philosophical about the glacier-slow trade done by Rock On over the years. Nobody conversant with the almost movie-like reversals and plummeting fortunes of the music business could be otherwise. If somebody had walked in one day and carried out the entire safe containing the unbanked profits for the whole month, I'm sure he would have muttered: 'Ah, well, could be worse – I could still be busking in Bromley.'

It was at Rock On, then, that I met – to use the nauseating phrase – my future wife. Where else do people meet if not in a place of work? Setting aside the bus-stop marauders, the laundrette bottom-pinchers, the palsied personal-column advertisers and the characters in black-and-white films containing steam engines, most *affaires de coeur* initiate themselves in a place of work. John met Yoko at her place of work – a fastidiously white art gallery that said 'yes'. Not much similarity there, you may think – although Mandy at the time was a bass guitarist and I a shop assistant who spent the small hours fiddling with poems, the geographical, serendipitous similarities were present. She just walked in one day when I was least expecting it. Just like John Lennon at Yoko's exhibition.

And she always was an artist, of a kind. Right from day one.

It was, if I recall correctly, March the second. The snow from stamped boots was melting in the grate by the front door; the one-bar electric fire was petulantly refusing to heat the second floor where I was finishing my shift. March the second. The crucible of the year, when the heart thaws, unclenching itself from the emotional permafrost. When the three pairs of socks one is forced to wear brand thick crimson bangles into one's shins. When one is distracted more easily than one should be by the coercion of a pretty stranger's smile.

I was walking down the stairs, she was coming up them.

'Can you fix this?' demanded a voice.

A vision in tartan flares, white brothel-creepers, bare Spanish midriff and ebony-everything-else was pointing to a knackered guitar amp, gripped almost manfully by a bony hand. And that face. Impossible not to be transfixed by that face. Thin, brown, mobile; full of immediate light and energy from her big eyes and triumphant nose. In first meetings, the face decides everything. It shouldn't be like that, but it is.

'I can't, but Martin probably can,' I said, drinking her in.

'It's only one of the knobs. It's fallen inside.'

There was a brief pause that the soul registered as an hour, not the split-second it actually was. In that pause our eyes transmitted the vital, instantaneous information that indicates *you will become involved*. It is written in the fixed stars. Unavoidable. An *a priori* union. A fact waiting to become fact.

Finally, I found the power of speech.

'You'd better sling it in the rehearsal room, then.'

It took five minutes of bluff and quackery to even get the back off, but, with her waiting patiently amid the stale fragrances of male sweat and spent testosterone, I managed to nurse her ageing amplifier into some semblance of signal-carrying utility.

'You're very brown,' I ventured, after I'd finished; coiling leads like hangman's ropes over my left arm. 'Just been on holiday?' The white and scarlet ruff of her knickers was showing over her waistband, and I tried helplessly not to focus on it as I spoke to her.

'It's my natural colour,' she said, and turned the full force of her Medusa smile towards my pale, diminishing face. 'I'm Spanish.'

There was something in her aura, her gait, that held great forcefulness – an assertive brightness that attracted and repelled at the same time. I would later learn that this mysterious anima held

the key to why she never kept any friends. The strength of attraction inevitably led to an equal and opposite repulsion. As she
stood there, waiting for the bill, or God knows what, I looked
her up and down admiringly; and she, incredibly, did the same
to me, a playful grin fixed on her thin, propulsive lips. Under
the peacockery of her fresh-smelling clothes she was somehow
unevenly proportioned – long-femured, but with fine angular
bones in her upper torso; her buttercup breasts fixed high and
happily on her ribcage. Very early twenties, I supposed. Spanish,
she claims. Why didn't I believe her? Very definitely Mediterranean;
her eyes shoeshine brown. Yet there was something about her
attitude to the whole package – her body, her projectile personality – that said she wasn't in total possession of it, or found it a
burden. An uneasy vibration.

She surveyed the tatty room, and I knew she was going to ask
a question that gave her an excuse to make a return visit.

'How much does this place go out for? The rehearsal?'

I was just about to answer when Martin craned his head around
the door. Instead of uttering my name he looked at Mandy and said:

'Mandy!'

'Martin!' yelled the girl, her nutritious voice at full throttle.
'How's it going? Byron's been fiddling with his screwdriver for
me.'

They embraced, and I saw then how tall she was at full stretch,
Martin being about as dwarfish as I am. Of course, they knew each
other. Martin knew every musician in north London. Most of them
owed him money. I watched them there, the old rocker advanced
enough in years to be her father, and thought how much Mandy
comported herself like *his* elder, his mother, even. I also felt another
immediate emotion: jealousy – so unexpected, so debilitating, like
an infusion of icy mercury into the emotional bloodstream, that I
almost lost my balance. I examined myself briefly for its cause. It
was her fully engaged, hyperactive interaction with Martin, moments
after extending the same treatment to me, that rankled. Some people
just make you yearn to be their favourite. I later discovered that

she dished this treatment out to everyone whom she didn't consider a *threat*. She radiated a certain freedom, or at least equally conferred charm; right down to flirtations she didn't intend.

Mandy and Martin noisily descended the uneven steps to the ground floor. I listened to the sound of the pinging till and their boisterous goodbyes.

And that was that.

That was the extent of it for a couple of weeks, until she returned to use the rehearsal room with Fellatrix, the all-girl Stooges-soundalike band with which she was captain, organiser and all-round glamorous mascot. In those two weeks I pumped Martin for every conceivable detail about her band, her life, her inevitable boyfriend. I lost count of the times I asked him to wipe the lascivious smirk off his face. He didn't tell me much, as he knew I was altogether preoccupied with a girl I had been seeing since Christmas – fragrant, diffident, middle-class Bea, Mandy's diametrical opposite. To Martin, his long-time customer was just mad, driven, Spanish Mandy with all the drooling suitors in the world. But to me she was suddenly an obsession; some kind of terrible erotic epicentre. I was in love, or lust, confusingly with someone I had exchanged ten sentences with.

Strange how the little details linger in the mind ... Her flexed, femininely capable rod-thin upper arms. Her fresh-smelling clothes. Her caramel midriff. Her sheeny hair, reflective as a London black cab after rain. Her equivocal exuberance; actressy and assertive. The ring on her third finger: a plastic rhomboid of tacky sapphire, so different to the austere wedding band which would replace it. Or her teeth. Mandy's immaculate teeth, lionised and loved – as I would soon find out – by half of north London simultaneously.

The train is leaving the subterranean rush of the tunnel. The last of the red lights are flecking past as I observe my eyeless face in the black square of the window. The century is ending.

The millennium is ending. Everywhere there is an atmosphere of temporality, of provisionality, of Nostradaman doom and silly super-stitions over last things. My hangover and damaged forehead seem to have joyfully joined forces, having made some kind of pact to double my torment. My need for a cigarette suddenly appears to be life-threatening. I advance a finger around the frame – an aluminium rail, like a new bicycle wheel, set in a richly black tube of sealant. Mandy and Martin: friends for donkey's years, or so it turned out.

First meetings, then. Always potent with the stock psychological truths: *eighty per cent of communication is done by the body, only twenty by conversation,* or: *never underestimate the sense of smell on a first encounter,* or: *attraction is largely pheromonal.* All true, all true. But way off the mark when it comes to adumbrating the complete experi-ence, the sensory cosmos available to us when meeting someone significant for the first time. Mandy had been *too much* that March morning – a telephone exchange of conflicting signals, enticements, vibrations. But there always is too much to take in on these occa-sions, too much for the time we're usually allotted. One really is assimilating a whole being: eyes, body, soul, capacities – not just their cosmetic radiance. In fiction, these initial encounters are usually cack-handedly omen-heavy. The spilt glass of red wine will indicate that blood is to be shed; the clutch of lilies the heroine is arranging in the florist's window points the way to her terminal illness; the squalling children in the playpark beyond that incipient bus stop tells us the couple's family will be large and loquacious. But real life is never so tidily signposted. One rakes the past for signals, only to find confusion, arbitrariness. In fiction, everything is revealed in retrospect as latent; but in life there is no clear map of predestin-ation. There are too many wild cards. You yourself are a factor in the equation too; its crucial determiner. You change the course of the other person's life just as irrevocably as they change yours. Together you create a deadly dynamic. You are both the wild card. Character is destiny only up to a certain point. In truth, it is two people's evolving lives that force the alchemy.

There is another crucial message that can be adduced from first meetings. It goes something like: enjoy this now, this spring-fresh fascination. This is as good as it will ever get. Because human beings have a tendency to go downhill from this point onwards.

It makes me feel no easier, no more placated, to digest all this information as the train hurtles towards maximum speed. The void of the tunnel is becoming a soot-blackened wall, racing at a kamikaze pace beyond my window. The knowledge that I will never see Mandy in the way I did on that day in March seems as strong as the knowledge of my own death — and just as terrifying, just as tiring.

I blow my nose into a serviette left by the last occupant of seat number forty-two. Hopefully the Accountant Couple haven't noticed I'm crying. They both appear rapt by the pink Hiroshima of the sunset; airport blockbusters lowered in their grey hands.

We're out onto higher ground now. The vomit-encrusted portals of Finsbury Park have been replaced by the vista of Tottenham's vast gas works. Beyond this I can see the riding luxuriant barge of Alexandra Palace, its planes of Aegean glass kaleidoscopic in the failing light. There's an old danger in the air, the danger of descending blackness and cold, of having to find shelter and food and primal warmth. The human animal hurrying to its cave, its burrow. Man, could I use some of that primal warmth now. From this vantage, the petering sprawl of north London can be assimilated in all its squalor. There are industrial plants and peopleless water-works. Articulated lorry crates stacked like surreally huge bricks. Glimpsed streets of kebab houses and blackened boozers. Then the sudden strangeness of greenery: verdant geometric patches inter-spersed with estates of shivering semis, all framed by the sighing umbilical powerlines, with their tireless lifting and sagging. One-porter stations are flashing past in a blur of concertinaed posters, their chained bicycles packed like biscuits. The ear-plugging gust of another tunnel cancels any view for a couple of seconds, until I am looking in at the lit windows of a train passing the other way:

a parallel world in reverse time. Then we're out again into the sorry sprawl of the dwindling conurbations – sudden perspectives allowed then blocked; a white house uniquely isolated: glimpsed then gone, replaced by a zoetrope of willows or a flashing row of stripped poplars.

I take out my notebook. This has to be captured, caught – set down (and one day I will fashion it into a poem in the smithy of my bedsit): *A deserted golf course. Half-built houses surrounded by stacked timber. The low sun in its dizzying death throes. Flatlands of arable earth, paths, spinneys, quarries, copses. Sinister hags of trees. Greenhouses. Flying clubs. Leisure parks. Lakes. A trackside stretch of gravel, arcade-game-fast, bisected by the even strokes of telegraph poles. Hacked waste ground. The glittering coin of a reservoir. A distant graveyard; headstones dense as dandruff. Squat cottages with conspiratorial outhouses. The reaching arms of alders under immense cloud formations – fingers and quays and spits, evolving and separating. A horse bending to graze, unicorn-white. Distant, argumentative weathers over parish spires. Darkness descending. Cul-de-sac streetlamps like gannets with their opposing amber beaks. Geese on a path, cherry-winged in the sunset. Rolling-stock on browning rails. Scrapyards of flex-coiled wooden barrels. Rising ropes of hedgerows split by the thread of a canal. A ditched Sierra growing grasses from exploded seats. Broken birches. Gulls over clogged fields of refuse sacks. A private pond bearing a puffed swan; a royal dinghy in the threatening twilight. A barren field, the blasphemous rooks peppering the ploughlines . . .*

Hold it – running out of space. By chance I notice the date at the top of the page. December the twenty-second. Two days ago. But, more significantly, more potently, our wedding anniversary. I let the pen settle on the paper, aslant my almost illegible scribble. I sigh gravidly: a bellows exhausting its chamber of air. December the twenty-second – three days before Christmas; chosen so we would 'never forget it'. Three years ago to the (almost) day. A date that also coincides with the year's nadir: the shortest, darkest day. The winter solstice; the year's true midnight – although I didn't know that fact at the time. Maybe it would have helped to have known that.

Then I see that the bony-buttocked Accountant woman opposite is holding something out towards me. An offering. I catch her eyes: they are ameliorative, weakly brave. I feel sudden surprise at this gesture, this *détente*. After all, I've insulted her husband, almost started a fight (twice), and demolished a game of dominoes beyond repair. I am unsure of what the object is at first. I examine it closer. It's white, folded, very clean – an envelope perhaps? Surely not a Christmas card! My heart swells with unexpected love for all humanity. Then I realise. It's a Kleenex.

They say we're strongly attracted to those most likely to destroy us. Maybe we fatally desire punishment, self-negation, nullity. I had met women like Mandy before. I had her down as a self-loather, an attention-seeker, an hysteric, a sympathy-junkie and expert manipulator right from the start. Just as the most gregarious, bubbly people are often deeply sad individuals on the interior, life-and-soul Mandy proved no exception to this rule in the final analysis. But what can you do when you're treated to the illegal, strawberries-and-cream frillage of someone's knickers riding helplessly from the band of their hotpants on a fortnightly basis? What can you do when your interior damage seems to correspond? What can you do when you get on like an oil rig on fire?

It is both comforting and frightening to remember somebody in this nascent fashion, when you're still bringing out the best in each other. Like imagining the wasp-humming, orange-squash sunshine of the English countryside in September 1939, tranquilly ignorant of all that's to come.

Of course it was good in the beginning. It always *is* good in the beginning. Since that first encounter in the dust-trap of the rehearsal room, intrepid Mandy returned on a weekly basis with Fellatrix – a tattoo parlour of nose rings and dungaree-housed bosoms, who, to a woman, couldn't tune their instruments. For this task I was frequently summoned mid-song, only to be admired and cooed at satirically — and, in the case of Mandy, maybe not so satirically, as she soon extracted my phone number and was calling me at all hours from her dull switchboard job, extrapolating in unnecessary detail her insane escapades in the clubs of Camden. Along with these three a.m. adventures, I also learnt who was suing whom; which lead singer was tooling a female journalist just to get a live review, which executive was scamming a band's tour budget to fund his heroin habit, et cetera, et cetera. Though I feigned a weary disinterest in these stories, I would become unbearably excited when she phoned, and could usually time her call to the nearest minute. It was her energy that overwhelmed me initially — plus her sure conviction that Fellatrix were destined for Wembley Stadium, even if it meant posing naked on vintage motorcycles for the *News of the World*. But we were friends first — light and easy friends, too, albeit with her investing all the energy. And this, it seems, is always fatal, as the transition into a love affair can so often feel like a *capitulation* on the part of the passive exponent.

I remember one call in particular. A rainy Friday night in reading Yeats, trying to write, when the phone rang. Now, how could I tell it was her just by the ring?

'Hello sweetheart!'

'Shouldn't you be out clubbing or something?'

'Can't do that when it's raining. That would mean a cabbage.'

'A what?'

'A cab! Anyway. I've got two friends round — we're all pissed on voddy and feeling a little fruity.'

Giggles and shufflings in the background. I let old William Butler slip onto the desk of my bed, knowing I would be in for the long haul. I suddenly felt like a pipe-smoking father castigating his errant daughter. But also glad of the company; flattered by her attention.

'Fruity? Isn't that that how they describe opera singing?'

A peal of laughter and a sound not dissimilar to a cat being sat upon.

'Listen, the real reason we can't go out is because of Johnny Radish.'

'Who's Johnny Radish? And why does his surname sound like a root vegetable?

'That's his band, you nutter! Don't you read the music press? He's been after me for months. Last week he just pushed me up against the wall at Club Dynamite and snogged me. Oh, Byron, you have to rescue me.'

The sound of hysterical laughter in the background. This is why 'Kubla Khan' is only fifty-four lines long, I mused.

'I'm not the rescuing type. I don't do rescuing. Specially if the men involved are bigger than me.'

'Oh, he's huge!'

This time the laughter almost burst my eardrum. And so it went on. She was a life-force: demanding, infuriating, instigating, inspiring. She told me her band was going to be enormous the following year; that she'd put so much into it any other outcome was unthinkable. I'd never met anyone with such an unshakeable determination and energy. Such fire-proof self-belief. And she always looked stunning, turning up at the battered door of Rock On, shades balanced on her middle-parting, immaculate white mini-dress and a black-blue feather boa trailing behind, like a magpie in flight. At the end of each conversation she would call me her 'special friend', tell me to 'wrap up warm' and blow a kiss down the phone. Without getting too Oedipal, that kind of maternal affection has its appeal.

March gave way to April, which buckled to the seething uncertainties of blossom-blown May, which in turn opened out into a blistering June. Summer. And not just any summer. It never is when two people find themselves uncontrollably, unfathomably in love; in dangerous, lethal balance.

It was after an unconquerable day in early June (the shadows cast by trees in Finsbury Park seemingly as solid as the objects themselves) that she invited me back to hers for a little wine. 'Hers' was two uneven floors above a bakery in Archway, patrolled by the wary watchfulness of her tomcats, all three of which had red, white and blue Fellatrix badges dangling unsettlingly from their collars. I was sweating like a wrestler by the time the expedition of her stairs had been completed. A door on the top landing was knocked open for me by the Trojan horse of her guitar case and I found myself standing in a spacious room reeking of fresh paint.

'Deluxe, ain't it?' said Mandy, kicking off her creepers.

'Blimey. Is this . . . is this all yours?'

'It is now. I used to share the cupboard next door with my boyfriend until my breakdown.'

I let this sudden, significant revelation of her mental precariousness (so casually introduced) pass while attempting to digest the agoraphobic dimensions of her room.

It's not often in London one sees rented accommodation, or a single room, that has any sense of *perspective*, but this candle-softened pad (no other word for it) almost had a vanishing point. To my right was a limo-length sofa counterpaned in ebony fleece fur. Then there were the spanned orange walls, teeming with posters, framed rock stars, flyers and a Polaroid-thicketed noticeboard. To my left were racks of clothes, books and rare vinyl. As my eyes acclimatised to the scarce light, I suddenly noticed the crouched figure of a man by one of the three open sash windows, the black apertures of which were letting in the exquisite June night air. He was holding a paintbrush.

Christ, I thought. She's brought me back for an orgy.

'Byron, this is Steve,' said Mandy, turning on me with a corkscrew.

Steve cocked his head towards me, and my gaze met his booze-destroyed eyes.

'Easy, mate,' said the man, in a bass voice.

'All right.'

Steve assessed me for a moment, sitting erect, like a bull mastiff in a painting smock. Then he spoke.

'Byron. What kind of name is that for a bloke?'

For this, I didn't have an answer. I never did. I had always thought the predictable and dreaded enquiry over my ludicrous name had no defendable riposte.

'Shut up, Steve. I think it's a fab name. Anyway, I thought I told you to have this done by the time I'd finished rehearsal.'

'Sorry,' growled Steve, plopping his brush into a jar of turps. 'You're the boss.' He raised himself to his full height of five foot six and shouldered past me, his transit having that unmistakable masculine tang of staked territory, proffered violence. 'Gloss takes a fucking aeon. You know that.'

Once Steve had disappeared through the doorway, candle flames trembling in his wake, the whole room seemed to relax tangibly.

'Sorry about Steve. He's one of my tenants.'

'You've got tenants?' I asked, overstressing my surprise, as I attempted to reclaim some lost masculinity by virtually smashing the cork out of a bottle of red wine.

'Oh, yeah. I'm the landlady here. That's how I got the biggest room. He's a total nutter, Steve. I'll have to go down in half an hour to put out his fag and turn off the telly. He always falls asleep pissed out of his mind. He's a brickie; got loads of cash – see that?' She pointed to a dinnerplate-sized gash in the plasterwork of the far wall. 'He did that with a baseball bat when he thought Matt was getting out of hand with me. He's very protective. Heart's in the right place . . .'

'Who's Matt?'

'Another tenant. The other bloke who lives here. A total hippy – wouldn't harm a fly, but try telling Steve that.'

'They weren't fighting over you, were they?'

'No, not over me. Over the microwave. Matt was using it when I wanted to. And to Steve that deserved a smack.'

'Very protective, then?'

'Yeah, and very drunk, though he's great at disguising it.'

'So, er, who else lives here?'

'Harriet. Thinks she's a photographer. Almost twenty-one and still a virgin. She told me blokes have got it in, but not up, if you see what I mean. Says she gets tense . . .' At this point I realised there was something profoundly *wrong* about Mandy. Something that didn't add up. Full of innuendos, but very definitely not a sexual woman. Bursting with banalities, but very certainly possessed of a resourceful cunning. I would have to watch my step. She continued on the subject of Harriet, all the while monitoring my reaction. '. . . I thought she was stuck-up at first 'cause her dad's this journalist on the *Independent*, but she's sound. In fact . . .' Mandy suddenly patted a space on the limo-sofa, indicating that I should sit next to her; I grimly complied, bearing the heavy bottle and two glasses, '. . . he's gonna help the band out. Write our first piece of journalage.'

'You mean journalism.'

'No,' and she fixed me with the twin infernos of her stunning eyes. 'I mean *journalage*.'

Easy does it, I found myself thinking. This is someone who always, even when they conclusively know they're not, *has* to be right. Every time. Over the next three hours, as the empty bottles of gut-rot red queued up on her chaotic coffee table, I learnt about the terrible privations of her Windsor boarding school (tabbed by her flash dad), her phenomenally spoilt single-child upbringing in some leafy cul-de-sac (conducted by Granny Monsterrat and Aunt Leocadia), her aloof father's maniacal passion for DIY over parental duty, and her drift towards ever more villainous and violent boyfriends culminating in a schizophrenic drug-dealer now doing time for ABH (the stolen credit card sprees down the King's Road in a hotwired four-wheel-drive; the orgies of house-breaking). This was followed by the tale of her three-year relationship with a self-pitying madman, climaxing in her eventual breakdown and emergence as the Future of Rock 'n' Roll.

Meanwhile, she (when I could get an epithet in edgeways) learnt about my estranged father; Delph and my mother; my 'stalled' literary career; my current diffident yet perplexing girlfriend, Bea; the years of heating my room by taping Bacofoil to the wall behind the electric ring of the cooker (still ongoing) and my current emergence into someone who was very eager to sleep with her indeed. That very night, if at all possible.

It was then that I noticed something, two things, on the sturdy Victorian mantelpiece that dominated the nearest wall: a pair of gilt-framed black-and-white prints on either side of an arch-shaped mirror. A sombre diptych. Not sepia photographs, but 1950s glossies. Hard to make out much detail, the light in Mandy's room being a relentless, subterranean amber that made you feel as if you were in a cave, straining to make out Palaeolithic daubings. In each frame smiled a Mediterranean-looking woman, with grey flourishes streaking a Steinway-black cascade of hanks and tresses. Both head-shots had strongly memorable features – so reminiscent that I thought they must be of someone famous: Eva Peron or Maria Callas perhaps, though they appeared to be family portraits. I was studying them so hard that I forgot the hot proximity of the girl at my side, talking away to the deaf ear of my averted profile. Then I realised who the subject of the photos was. It was Mandy.

'That's you, isn't it?' I interrupted suddenly, pointing to the mantelpiece. Mandy followed my nicotine-jaded forefinger.

'No! That's my mother, Ramona. I wish it was me,' said Mandy, beaming. I made eye contact with a younger, infinitely altered, yet morbidly similar version of Ramona. 'She died when I was sixteen . . . in a car crash. Everybody loved her.'

'You look more like – like sisters.'

'Ah, she would've loved you.'

At that instant the door swung open and there stood Steve: ruffled, grossly panting; a gaseous nimbus of seventy-per-cent-proof air in front of his puckered mouth.

'Ron. I need your help, mate. Gotta shift something.' Mandy went to stand up. Steve held out a trembling, admonitory hand. 'Nah, it's a man's job. Needs a strong pair of mitts.'

'Steve, it's three in the fucking morning. And it's *By*ron, not Ron.'

You had to hand it to her: she had authority, as well as glamour, energy and great legs. Although I could have done without the emasculation of her correcting Steve on my behalf for the second time that evening.

'Whatever,' mumbled Steve.

I met Mandy's eyes with a kind of mute desperation.

'Go on, then,' she sighed, exhaling a rich plume of cigarette smoke into the summer night. I followed the sweating rhinoceros of Steve's back through the open doorway. Then her voice: 'But don't tire him out. He'll need all the strength he's got.'

With this shocking statement jangling in my ears like a fire alarm, I accompanied Steve to the lair-like opening of his pauperised room. Suddenly he turned. I saw at once how evolution had beautifully developed the short man to give him the optimum height and range for delivering a headbutt.

'Don't get me wrong,' said Steve, as I ingested, with the torrent of his breath, what amounted to a virtual *short*, a whisky chaser. 'I like you, Ron. I'm a good judge of a geezer's character. But I've become very – how shall we say – protective of Mandy over the last few months. She's a sweet girl. Sweet girl.'

'You're not wrong there, Steve,' I said, as neutrally as my temple-throbbing fear would allow.

'A lot of people like her a lot. A great many chase after her. Fuck—' And he nudged me with the freckled haunch of pork that was his right arm. 'Sometimes it seems like half of north London is trying to get into her knickers. Know what I mean?'

He was smiling now, his very blue, very drunk eyes flecked with light. But still he seemed to be occupying the entire corridor, his bulked obduracy like an invitation to do or say the wrong thing; his leer full of pre-emptory menace.

'Last week she got alcohol poisoning. Spent the whole day in bed, me bringing her little soups and things – her chocolates of choice. That's what friends are for, ain't it, Ron?'

'She speaks very highly of you, Steve,' I said, with an increasingly strangulated cadence as I reached his name. He clapped me on the shoulders, abruptly and without warning. I jumped, and realised that I had been expecting his forehead to be the first part of his anatomy to make contact with mine.

'You do right by her, mate, and you do right by me, 'kay?'

'Okay.'

'Take good care of her. She's a fucking diamond.' I turned to go but a blood-curdling shout stopped me dead: 'Oi!'

This is where it gets nasty, I thought. This is where I start a long and unhappy intimacy with X-rays and hospital radio. When I turned around, Steve wasn't even looking at me. He was fixated on the floor with full sadness, as if he had been trepanned by some terrible insight into life's futility, or merely alcoholically winded. There was a long edgy silence. He left such a lengthy pause after his barked imperative that I assumed the sad piss-artist had forgotten what he wanted to say. Then his aqua eyes found mine.

'I haven't finished speaking yet.'

'Sorry, I thought—'

'Shut it,' said Steve; though now in a ridiculously high and gentle voice.

'Was there something you wanted me to lift?'

'Nah, nah, nah.' Then he paused. 'Ron?'

'Yes, Steve?'

'Do you want to listen to my new CD? I bought it today. It's fucking amazing.'

So, there was nothing for it but to listen to Steve's Fucking Amazing heavy-metal CD at window-splintering volume, while Mandy, alone upstairs, was probably wondering if I'd gone home – or maybe even died. Eventually I escaped, my jaw aching after having to feign an appreciative smile for so many stomach-convulsing minutes. I re-entered her room, like a haggard veteran of Korea, Vietnam and at least two Pacific campaigns.

But her room was in darkness. Groping my way for the light switch, I softly eased her door to; trying to conceal, with gulps of alcohol-free air, my bilious rage. A vivifying smell of fresh paint started to make my head spin. I found the switch. Then I saw that the big room was empty. About to leave and search for her down-stairs, I heard a voice.

'I'm here.'

I squinted into the distant corner that contained the low, flat play-pen of her futon. There was a person-shaped bulge under a colourful Latina bedspread, at the end of which were Mandy's pyjama-shrouded shoulders and serene face; her eyes intently closed. Without opening them, she said, 'You can get in if you want. It's cold with the windows up.'

I needed – in the phrase so beloved of cheap (usually British) pornography – no further encouragement.

'Tickets please!'

Ugh. The whoosh of the smoked-glass door announces the stout inspector. He cranes over the huddled passengers in his brisk, speechless interrogation. The cord of the past is broken. I must engage with the present. Oh, Mandy! How sweet a proposition you seemed before you disgraced the ring you wore.

Still pissed, I fumble for the documents as the inspector approaches. The man seems to have been born in his nasty navy British Rail suit. I sometimes wonder about the wearers of uniforms, or rather, about the identities beneath the uniforms. How do these individuals appear so happy to be housed in the pressed serge, the crisp white collars? How do they contentedly button themselves up virtually every day of their lives? These actors, these dissemblers! I would feel as if I were wearing a giant conspicuous clown outfit. The man bends over the adjacent seat, though manages to keep me in the corner of his eye for the duration of his brisk ritual. How do officials of all types manage this feat? And why do I always feel a surge of guilt and sickness in the moments before my ticket is scanned? A memory of childhood transgression, of authority evasion? No, I only ever skanked the fare twice when I was sixteen, and on both occasions I felt calmer than I do now. It must be the deep sense that I am not entitled to share the carriage with my fellow passengers, my fellow homo sapiens. That they have more right to this warm seat than I. Or maybe it's consciousness-guilt; a fear that every straight-talking, straight-backed citizen can read my corroded thoughts, and is scandalised by their perversity, their lack of engagement with the present. A panic descends on me, an intimation that everyone in the vicinity has been sharing that breeze-fragrant June night I spent with Mandy.

The inspector takes my ticket from its wallet, a wary look on his fringed face. He scrutinises it for a long moment. I feel all the tension of the double agent at the border crossing. Then he hands it back with an intimate waft of some hideous scent. What is it about Christmas and bad scent? Surely there's enough opportunity to wear it after the twenty-fifth. Aniseed? Bad lemons? I hold my breath for a full ten seconds, then let out a grateful sigh.

Outside, I can see the dripping hedgerows of deep midwinter under vapour-heavy air. A ploughed field, brown as a chocolate cake, tears past. In it stand pylons, like cowboys on the draw, huge and distinct in the rolling dusk. Above them the sky seems drained of light, of the very property itself; dismal, defeated. Heavy with last days, last things. In the near distance the soil is a weltering sponge, at capacity. Soaked, bogged, downpour-logged, exuding steamy emanations at the very deadest hour of the year.

The very antithesis of that night in June, in fact. The following morning I awoke to sunshine exploding in fierce pellucid patterns on her orange walls. That big room: even more surprising in daylight. The surly weight of three tomcats, curled upon the radiator of my chest, heaved up and down with my breathing. I was aware that the slightest movement might tip me from the hard mattress into the narrow gap between the bedframe and the skirting board, as Mandy was occupying ninety-five per cent of the space, arms splayed like a starfish. Cramped and confined as I was, I enjoyed the slow, man-of-the-world, you-old-devil crinkly smile that always appears on one's face after ratcheting up another conquest.

Except that I hadn't ratcheted up anything.

We had spent the whole night talking, interrupted only by hysterical police sirens on the Holloway Road below. When the blackness framed in the big sash windows had begun to alter imperceptibly into the rich holy-blue of dawn, she had produced tarot cards. The Death card had made repeated appearances in my readings, but she assured me it only signified change. Smart girl. Lately I had been doing much thinking on what constituted intelligence. Mandy, with her direct soft brown eyes certainly seemed to sparkle, but she didn't have what you could call any formal learning. She was quick, adaptable, resourceful, practical. She knew how to get by in certain company. But the autodidact is always aware of knowledge as a commodity. How much have you got? How much did it cost to obtain? Put Mandy in a discussion on, say, existentialism, or ask her who Clement Attlee was and she would be at sea. She may try to bluff it with her substantial charm, but that's no substitute for knowing what people are talking about. In many ways her candour provided her legitimacy. In a similar fashion, Martin got through life with only the knowledge of electronics and the family trees of rock bands. But did this make him unintelligent? It was, at that time, a hard quality for me to gauge. It had nothing to do with Mensa or heavy-reading. It had more to do with how knowledge impacted on the psyche. My conclusion was, the more you knew, the more complicated it was to act. When thinking about the future, the questioning mind hits the wall of determinism versus free will before anything else. To the unquestioning mind, everything is *que sera*. For Mandy, everything about her future was graspable, readable. Everything about her past mental instability regrettable but unavoidable. As she shuffled the deck and then merged the two bricks of cards with an expert thrum, I could see lines of strain on her thorax; visible stress from the effort of independence, from being motherless. I could see she wanted us to merge somehow, but not on a deeper level. She was sizing me up. Her brashness concealed a core of people-fear. She certainly didn't have any notions of taking her clothes off. Although at one point I suggested we formulate a game of strip tarot, an idea that was deliciously refused as I gazed into the liquidity of her Catalan eyes.

I later learnt that most of Mandy's friends, male and female, had received the talking-and-tarot-card treatment. With the men, it was her way of neutralising them, of allowing intimacy only up to an invisible, heavily armed perimeter fence. This accounted for her considerable reputation as a cock-tease among the aviator-shaded predators of London's club scene; and as sexually strange among the women.

The smell of yeasty cooking from the bakery below and the summer pollen breezing through the big windows gave me the impetus to make a quick exit. I left as rapidly as I could; unshaven, wine-tongued, with outpatient hair, onto the hot tarmac of the Holloway Road. As I made a list of objects I'd accidentally left behind in my haste to leave (and my even greater haste not to encounter Steve on his way to whatever chimp-house of a building site he worked on), guilt, confusion, and shabby regret vied for prominence in the polluted traffic of my emotional bloodstream. What was I doing in this woman's bed all night when I had Bea to soothe my mortal brow? I counted four things missing: wrist-watch, diary, jacket and cigarette lighter.

Later, I would add sanity.

I should say something here about girls whom everyone wants, girls who are an index of male desire, of the metropolitan erection. Not the sheer-silk sirens of Berkeley Square (too costly) or the bosomy, broad-bummed secretaries that buckle whole offices while bending over the photocopier (too easily identifiable in the porn-hoard of most men's sock drawers) but the unknown quantities, the stream-lined brunettes in Avengers' boots one sees queueing for clubs, usually with *two* male companions. The shadowy epicentres of temptation one catches lighting up murky parties with a flashbulb of heartbreakingly sexy teeth. The glowing Amazons one suicidally notes on the tube-seat opposite, off to liaisons with men far richer, funnier and taller than you'll ever be. *Those* girls. West End girls. Girls fully occupied with their own fantastic desirability under the big, randy Saturday night of their early twenties.

Mandy was one of those girls: brisk, knowing, and just scratching the surface, just beginning to digest *how* much power her looks could exert over the helpless male world. The democratising effect of her looks was a great leveller. It precipitated wood in every male from seventeen to seventy. She had a face that held many hours of love and admiration from total strangers. Sometimes, one observes a man's face (the scowling rough-sleeper, for example) and concludes the only person who ever loved him was, in all reality, his mother. And that love was proffered in the distant past, before his three consecutive prison terms and a prostration before hard spirits. In the same way one looks at the faces of plain girls and is forced to surmise that nobody has ever fantasised over them; one notices the tremendous absence of sexual investment. But not Mandy. She was, at that time, literally *everyone's*. The male gaze, for Mandy, acted like an expensive moisturiser: nourishing, empowering. Ah, the difference between women . . . And doesn't the beauty know it; know exactly what she's got. And doesn't the size-sixteen on her exercise bike with her square, ruddy knees know exactly what she lacks.

I remember during our last holiday together, a week in Cephalonia punctuated by terrible arguments in the hot cell of the hotel room, noting something about Mandy that had always been innate. She shared, with supermodels and the big cats, a certain physical nobility; a grace or astuteness of movement. To the hotel owner's swarthy teenage son this merely resulted in his glueing his eyes to her arse for a week, or practising showy dives whenever we were in the vicinity. But I, fool that I was, had to locate the centre of her erotic fascination mentally. I was compelled to intellectualise her lines, almost from afar, as if she were an exhibit. Paradoxically, I noticed this phenomenon most acutely when she was covered up. When she wrapped the startling orange sarong around her hips, with an intent concentration on the knot. When she swayed along the holiday street in an ankle-length denim coat, the greedy eyes from the gift-shops guzzling her down. Or when her devilish black hair swung like dual pendulums over her high and happy breasts. It wasn't just the cliché that concealment is more exciting than expo-sure. It was more to do with ownership. As her husband, I was supposed to own, or have exclusive access to, all this. This is what got me going: the impossibility of possessing something one should already possess. On our final evening, by the pool with the teenager doing furious lengths of front crawl, with the parsley smell of shish kebabs in the air, I remember telling her she was, 'at the height of her beauty'. And for once it wasn't a phrase I'd acquisitioned from film or literature. She really was a glowing Venus to my time-serving Vulcan. It might have been the last sincere sentiment I expressed to her, there on that barbecued veranda, as every filament of her ebony hair absorbed the ambers of the tragic, setting, ocean-bound sun.

On that June morning (the morning after the night before with Mandy), I returned home to my scarred, shrouded bedsit in time to see the gleeful postman deposit another polar-white, windowed sheath from the bank onto my doormat. I ripped it open with ochre fingers – fingers that smelt of Mandy's scent, Mandy's hair, Mandy's bedsheets. My rent cheque had bounced yet again (what do they put in chequebooks these days? Rubber balls? Old lilos? Bouncy castles?). This unforgivable act, I understood, would set me back twenty-five pounds plus five pounds for 'letter advice'. In more understandable language, I was paying for their gluttonous pleasure in telling me the obvious. 'Oh, you tossers!' I allowed the words to echo in the junk-mail graveyard of the sooty vestibule, then let myself in.

Now, this room – this Camden crash-pad I was barely hanging on to when I met Mental Mandy – well, I wish you could've seen it. For many long and sexually arduous winters I convinced myself that it was pretty good, all told. Convinced myself that I was lucky to have a roof, even a leaky one, over my head. I mean, compared with where I am now (Rudi's bare matchbox; the two croupiers; the classical musician I never see), it was a sumptuous pied-à-terre, a tyrant's winter palace, a *ranch* at the very least. Forgetting for a moment the bread-mould rash of rising damp that greeted you on first inspection, the relationship-ending chairbacks of tattered drying underpants, the mounds of termite-sawdust under the ransacked furniture, the smell of sewerage and the rat problem, I always thought the joint was pretty ritzy myself. Others, especially women, as time went by, seemed to differ in this opinion. To the extent that, when I met Mandy, I was only bringing back girls who were, if not actually blind, then at least partially sighted, very fat or very desperate. 'I've had worse in the past,' I always lied to them. Or, 'Beats a cardboard box and a can of Kestrel.' For some reason this never proved very persuasive, as they myopically gathered their belongings the following morning in front of the guttering gas fire, muttering phrases like, 'Place should be condemned', 'Fucking hypothermia' or 'Writer'.

I had first rented the flat five years ago from a compact little queen called Keenan Peach. 'Keeney' was a fleshy-faced man in his mid-thirties with a permanent suntan. He used to wear the kind of waistcoats that even a vaudevillian would reject as a little *outré*. With his magpie eyes that alighted on the most personal possessions during his infrequent visits, Keeney would still be 'there' an hour after departure, his cologne being of a grandiose, almost radioactive virulence. I would come to dread his whiny, workaday, cat's arse of a voice on the phone uttering opening shots such as: 'Byron – rent,' or 'Ah, you're in!' I waited in vain for the inevitable, backwardly-put cruise of 'If you can't pay me, Mr Easy, there are always other ways of . . .' But it never came. Jesus, was I that ugly? That short? That bald? He must have had some kind of lover, some form of granite-abdomened Sex Führer, or lust-bandit boyfriend to resist penniless, button-arsed me almost winking and panting at him when he came over to collect his wad (which I never had). I would have done it for poetry, for England . . . I like to think he just preferred the money.

The place was in pretty good shape when Keenan first dropped the perfumed keys into my liar's fist. Neglect and seasons spent penning ineptly metred sonnets on semeny bedspreads had left the corners full of forgotten things. It was I who had invited the rats and the termites over, if the truth be told. It turned out he was subletting the place, anyhow, which obstructed all forms of maintenance even further. When the immersion heater gave its yearly last-throttled-gasp it was Keenan, sitting behind the till of his Bond Street boutique, whom I had to phone, not a landlord who might possess something useful like a new boiler. Nothing ever got done. The curtain rail dropped terminally from the wall (the puckered plaster too far gone for drilling), forcing me to black-out the windows with newspaper. Tiles avalanched from around the bath, revealing soily brick-dust, giving you the impression that you were taking a soak in a trench or some kind of dugout. The toilet seat came away in your hand. Rotted carpet sprang from the skirting boards like an unrolled poster that wants to regain its initial centrifuge. Stains widened like North Sea oil disasters until a flood two years in replaced the distressed beige with black carpet tiles. It was a mess. A dump. The glaucomatous women were right: I had let it go to seed.

So, that morning – which would lead to love, marriage, separation and eventually you reading about it – found me in the kitchen. I snapped on the electric kettle and tossed a tea bag into a tomb-brown mug. I pondered, as I often did and do, the existence of the man who lives to create art instead of answering life's relentless imperative to earn cold hard cash on a daily basis. Art versus commerce, that old saw. The more time you spent on one, the more it seemed to dilute the time required for the other. My inability to earn proper money – to support myself – had made me feel emasculated, ridiculous, useless. Or maybe it was the world, with its money mania, that had made me feel ridiculous, useless; an idiot. It felt as if I had spent seven years in London making little headway in either endeavour: a minimum-wage job in a music shop ('seasonal', as Martin's ad had emphasised) and, apart from the solitary pamphlet, not so much as a couplet published in a greetings card. Why couldn't I make poetry pay? Well, all further attempts at getting into print had failed. After the initial giddy rush provided by my good reviews, I found the usual-suspect magazines strangely obdurate in taking on any more of my work. Even a rinky-dink Mickey Mouse operation called Verb*ose*, specialising in the syllabic verse of Ipswich *écrivailleurs*, refused to run so much as a squib, let alone a sestina. Listening to the kettle boil, I recalled the evening when – frustrated with the grand *peut-être* that is the immortality of the soul, feeling masochistic – I collated together all the straining sonnets and verbless terza rimas I had slaved over for what seemed like a decade and folded them lovingly (with full footnotes, preface and critical apparatus) into a Jiffy bag; kissing its gummy hinge for luck, which hurt my lips. This I deposited in the main post office on Camden High Street, after spending my last pennies on stamps. I then sat back and awaited my bays by return of post . . . But even Verb*ose* sent me their standard rejection letter. Not only did poetry not pay, it seemed, but it cost you an arm and a leg (and a soul) to write it. And yes, they really did italicise those last three letters.

I glanced around me. In my kitchen I had suffered extreme cold, and the kind of sexual, emotional, intellectual and spiritual privations that Solzhenitsyn could have romanticised if he were writing about Camden and not the Gulag. I surveyed the square of Formica where I had prepared meals whose hideous collision of tastes made me clean my teeth immediately afterwards. Potatoes smeared with an onion. Rice mixed with a single stale fishcake. Porridge and soy sauce. I took a peek inside the impoverished fridge which held, hilariously, a single egg. I reconnoitred the murderous corners of the flat for anything I could sell in order to afford breakfast. Did anyone else live like this? I thought. Did anyone else remember whole years as *the one they once ate at McDonald's*? Okay, I could've been born in Ethiopia, or on a dollar a day in a rancid Indonesian sweatshop, holding my urine for seventeen hours at a stretch, but this was Camden, the 1990s, for God's sake! Not much at that time made me laugh out loud, but the translated title of a Japanese film, glimpsed in a listings magazine, had been the most recent cause of this phenomenon: *Life Is Cheap but Toilet Roll Is Expensive*. Says it all, really. Says all you need to know about the degraded, pauperised, eked-out, tuppence-hoarding *nuclear winter* of the terminally skint. The grisly hand–to–hand combat of it. The title encompassed the boredom of it too. I mean, you don't really want to hear about this, O cool and media-literate reader, do you? Surely you'd rather immerse yourself in the priapic gallivantings of some public schoolboy methadone-fixer on his first trip to New York? Or the labyrinthine tale of erudite Hampstead wife-swappers? Or a snappy hit of sex and smoking credit cards? Or even the sober saga of eight generations of frugal, hardworking Black Country folk? Anything, really (I know I would). But the story of a man who moans about the price of toilet roll? How diseasedly banal.

Ah, how wretched and all-too-believable is the tiring rhetoric of the bottom-line broke merchant. How void are the days of the grindingly boracic, as enervating to observe as the film that would be produced by pointing a camera at a brick wall for a month. Nothing goes on, really. Life's opportunities, its love affairs, its fast-forward button, are always cruelly out of reach. On a Friday night I would watch the sleek movers and groovers on the corner of Delancey Street and feel as if I were living in some kind of penniless parallel universe. Where did they get their dough? Did they inherit it, steal it, earn it? Or a bit of all three? Their bronzed confidence, their sense of entitlement, was at once revolting and spellbinding. Every fortnight, like Lazarus at the house of Dives, I would pass the mansion of a well-known media magnate which was unhappily situated on the route to the dole office. Often I would spend so long searching his bins that I'd miss signing on. Scarcity was the keyword. It's a condition one notices only in the absence of its opposite: plenty or enough. Most of my contemporaries from Hamford were either making sackloads of cash as builders or plumbers, or installed in the spacious accommodation of the successful graduate, their lives stimulated and rich. Even Rudi, that tax-free tool, had his business.

And then there was the inertia to deal with. The days of leaving the house only to score ten Benson and nick a bottle of milk from a doorstep. And then the moral dilemma: the self-imposed cage of the starving man who lives within the law; the straightjacket of the man who doesn't feel *entitled* to don the balaclava and do a few sub-post offices when the money runs out. The curse of the man who doesn't dare explode a whole dole cheque on a weekend's bender, thus losing his gaff and ending his days gargling and trembling under the Waterloo Bull Ring. This would describe me, who dutifully husbanded his meagre resources for years, always deferring the present to some imagined future of God knows what. I knew then that money really was 'the purchaser of life'. I should've busted out. Grabbed the rope and swung away. I'd been too good, too steadfast, too *easy*, all along. A pushover for the poverty gods. Only the privately moneyed or the very villainous, I reflected, could be chance-takers, could live in any way recklessly. Ah, flat treason 'gainst the kingly state of youth!

I threw the tea bag back in the jar. There was, after all, no fucking milk. And no money with which to buy any. I went for a little lie down. Even though it was barely midday, I found myself anticipating another friendless, foodless, fagless Saturday night in . . . Then I thought about Bea, and felt a bilious twinge of guilt. Through the haze of my queasy grief I thought about how good she had been to me. Not in a financial sense, oh no. Not even in a giving, loving, emotionally opulent sense either. No, the way in which Bea had been good to me, had been heedlessly altruistic, was by being *sane*. And by being female at the same time. Over the years I hadn't been able to pull that combination off, or find the two phenomena co-extant, if you see what I mean. And something told me – experience, intuition, radar, call it what you will – that Mandy was seriously *un*sane, imbalanced, needy; critically brittle.

I had bumped into Bea at Rudi's birthday party six months back and had spent the entire evening gripped by the possibility that the black electrical sheen of her thighs belonged to stockings, not tights. I say bumped into, because I had known Bea before, in another life, in Hamford; though from a great distance. Rudi had kept in contact with her, but then he always did with friends, especially if they were female. In fact, it would be true to say that Bea had been the great unrequited love of my life, if people still talk about unrequited love. What they refer to, I suppose, is a love felt so intensely that the suffering becomes heroic; with the grim side effect that the sufferer becomes sickly fascinating to himself.

O Beatrice! Provider of agony! Burgundy rose of my fevered youth! I was fourteen when I first glimpsed her plum-coloured eyes flickering abstractedly under glossy lashes; her holiday-brown fore-arms disappearing into mysteriously deep pockets. Had I been Petrarch, I could have panegyrised her as my Laura. Every day I would be treated to the same banquet. She would be swaying home from school, leather satchel trailing among the surreal purples of the violets. I would be sweating with Lucozade-sticky hands, acci-dentally present at every street corner she might happen to pass – you know, the usual. It was one of those summers where the July skies turn all the road surfaces white in the mid-afternoon – an eternal summer in the memory, and she was all love, all beauty. She must have been thirteen: awkward, pole-shouldered, chestnut-haired and with that air of vague abstractedness that drives the male of the species crazy. Girlish dimples would appear on her clear face when she was amused; lips twitching outwardly in nervous antici-pation of wryness or teenage irony. Often her attention would be everywhere at once – a devastating smile shared ecumenically among her schoolfriends – yet focused inwardly somehow; involved in her own mysterious interior. Impenetrable, self-contained, yet vulnerable. It is a quality that invites a man to take care of a woman; to assume the role of patriarch, provider, protector, life-giver. By the time I roused the courage to approach her she was leaving Hamford for university (Yes, five years later! Five years of suffering felt so intensely it becomes heroic! Five years of a form of meta-procrastination; five years of addictive stasis). Of course, it wasn't to be. I remember the fateful phone call. Forget the sorrows of Young Werther, this was more like the suicide of a young wanker. I stood in the secluded, pissy phone box for half an hour, praying to the courage gods. Then with a berserk alacrity I snatched up the receiver and dialled. Her mother answered in a sweetly tinctured, cultivated voice, telling me her daughter had already taken the coach for her first term, and who was I exactly? Then a male voice.

Her father (whom I knew to be an irascible chartered surveyor, as I had followed him to work one morning on my bike) was suddenly on the line. He told me the police knew where I lived. Then the receiver went dead. It was too late. I no longer felt sickly fascinating to myself, merely physically sick.

So when Rudi tapped me on the shoulder at his party (Hawaiian shirt rent to the navel, cocktail-stick cheroot proceeding from his grin) and motioned his head towards the quiet chestnut-haired girl in the corner, I knew life had offered me one of its rare second chances. Despite a momentary twinge about my male-pattern baldness (reversed by recalling that I was receding at *fifteen*), I strode purposefully over to Bea and her group of friends.

'Hi, you probably don't remember . . .'

She turned. All love, all beauty.

'Of course. You phoned me after I'd left.'

The same calm interiority. The same plum-coloured eyes, though womanly now, sexually aware. Her adolescent hips had broadened to produce an arousing female enclosure; her moley bust, heavy and compressed, caused me untold upheaval. Her accent betrayed impeccable middle-class manners – a childhood of ponies, holidays in the Auvergne, Weetabix and *Jackanory*. Then it struck me that this was the first time she had addressed me directly. She smiled that collusive smile I had seen her use so many times with her schoolfriends. 'I'm sorry about my father. He thought I needed protecting.' Oh, but you do! It was also apparent that adulthood had exacted a toll on her insouciance, had instilled in her a need to explain. I noticed she had the expected raft of feminine insecurities and anxieties about her attractiveness. She also seemed nervous, intent to make a good impression. This was unexpectedly flattering. As she swished her hair from her eyes I thought I could detect a faint odour of rose water: unostentatious, subtle, grown-up, sane. She said, 'So how are you?'

'Oh, you know – well you probably don't – going bald. Trying to write. One thing seems to go with the other.'

'A writer!' said Bea, her sudden animation holding both surprise and delight. 'I always thought you'd end up doing something like that. I used to see you riding around on your bike, looking mysterious.'

'That's because I was always lost.'

'Oh, *no!*'

It's hard to convey how the way her voice abruptly rose to a pinched, concerned squeak on the word 'no' almost caused my legs to buckle, once and for all, underneath me. I tried for a moment to concentrate my gaze on her kneecaps (stockinged? Please, no!). I was undermined, unstable. An instinct told me I should admit to having been suddenly taken ill and leave the conversation at once. She didn't really believe I had been lost any more than I did, but she had a strong impulse to express concern. This is a rare quality in anyone. She had an altruism that was proffered naturally, almost with greedy interest. And towards me, her virtual stalker for five years. She swished her hair again, her one vain affectation, and touched my arm with two fingertips. I felt a static charge. A textbook couldn't improve on this, I thought. Make her laugh, for God's sake, and you may not have to die alone in an old people's home after all.

I said, 'No, actually I was following you.'

She laughed. Now, that wouldn't embarrass me in a restaurant. Feel free to use that laugh any time you want.

'Yeah, my friends all thought the same thing. So, where did you study?'

I felt a cold constriction at the back of my neck.

'Oh, that didn't plan out as panned. I mean . . .'

'The University of Life, then.' We both winced at this expression. Except I alone felt the jeer of class as a wounding caveat. 'You know, Rudi dragged me here and I don't know anyone. Maybe you can show me around London some time.' Her eyes found mine; slowly, shyly. She needed help.

In the surroundings of Rudi's party, with glammed-up groovers and unsmiling Turkish hardmen fondling their untouched drinks, Bea looked positively ordinary, homely even. She seemed relieved to talk to me. It turned out the characters I thought were her friends were Rudi's cleaning lady and husband. She was on her own, newly single, still awkward and abstracted after all these years, and strangely brave to be there somehow. Standing next to her was, for me, like standing next to deep water. Cool, unfathomable, frightening, delicious. I scribbled her phone number down on my hand (the hand that, so many times, had lovingly – no, you don't want to know) and agreed to meet her the following week. As the front door banged in the small hours, spewing revellers onto the frosty street, Rudi approached me with a smirk and put a hot hairy arm around my shoulder. 'You okay, spunker?'

I stared at the Bea-shaped space she had just vacated, then said slowly, pseudo-profoundly, 'Now is my bliss made manifest.'

Rudi raised an eyebrow, a practised tic. He'd given up asking who I was quoting.

'Looks different now, eh? And she was the lassie you spent your teenage years greetin' over! She's no all that. What you'd call a handsome woman.'

I couldn't reply for a moment. I was still drowning in the deep water.

'Rudi, do I look bald to you?'

'Aye. As a tatty.'

But this cannot have significantly deterred her. One carefully orchestrated week later and she was in the lair of my freezing bedsit, begging me to allow her to sleep with her pop-socks on due to a very real danger of frostbite. And then . . . and then the next morning, snow delicately tornadoing outside, the Busy Old Fool a pale aperture in the sky, the novelty of a new body warming mine and none of the poised, gently demanding enquiries: So, are we an item, then? What shall we name our three children and Gloucestershire cottage? All she asked, in a quiet, level voice, was: 'I'm not too moley, am I?' 'No, your moles are Godlike,' I replied. 'If God had moles, they would resemble yours.' She didn't seem to care that I had no money, no clothes, no perceivable friends or future. She was merely interested (lunatic that she was) in *me*. She was at the opposite end of the Richter scale to the castrating harridans, the triple-breakdown survivors, the hurricanes of female scorn I had thus far attracted my entire life.

Within another week I was crazy about her. More so, if that's possible, than when I was fourteen. But, true to the Bea I had once swooned over from a distance, she kept something in reserve. She was *laissez-faire* to the point of polite detachment. It was her nature. But also, I think, she had been hurt before (how I longed to repair that hurt!). Nevertheless, there was something obdurate, interior about her. Deep water moves slowly, it takes its time. Calm down. But that's always the dynamic, isn't it? The more neutral and reserved one party is, the more fervent and obsessed (despite themselves) the other becomes. It's an impregnable law, a facet of Nature's spirit-level. My notebooks became crammed with imaginary conversations with her, rhetoric on who her favourite poet was, absolute conviction that they *were* stockings and not tights. I commenced an ambitious sonnet sequence: *Astrobyron and Bea*. To die in her arms under the Camden moon would have been heaven indeed. I attempted to play it cool in her company, but privately her pedestal stretched eight miles high – a dangerous altitude, I know.

The strong, sweet poison of her diamondy complexion and classically auburn hair would be at work in my belly for days after each meeting. Her plum-coloured eyes a banquet that lasted a week. The sense-memory of her indolent creamy thighs, wonderfully broad enclosing hips and geometrically beautiful chin would be imprinted in the fingertips. But, above all, she became associated in my mind with London. The London (I'm ashamed to say) that reads like a *Time Out* lonely-hearts ad: cinema, walks, theatre, restaurants, galleries . . . The London from which I'd been ostracised during seven years of living there. The London where the cultured and the moneyed cherry-pick their leisure options from a seemingly never-ending vista of riches. Not that we experienced all of these things in our time together, you understand. I had just survived another Christmas on ten quid and a tin of baked beans. But the crucial thing is that we *tried*, we did things, like lovers are supposed to do. Meeting on a work-exodus Friday night or scintillatingly frosty Saturday, I would actually *take her out*. We saw many subtitled films. The day we visited the Whispering Gallery of St Paul's was, I knew, the closest I'd ever get to heaven. So I may have had to pay for a few meals with a smashed piggy-bank of tuppences and chose only the exhibitions that admitted us free, but the objective was always the same: to step out, to get the most from London and our brief planetary time.

Often, before I ran into Bea, when reading those celebrity questionnaires in the sodden evening papers (listing a star's cherished bistros, choice markets to rummage in, favourite shopping-spree routes, et cetera), I would be struck with the sure knowledge that, not only was I not living London to the max, but if I were called upon to answer those same questions I would surely be officially pronounced dead. I had to be. Only a dead man did less with his weekends. My column would wretchedly read something like: Favourite London Restaurant – my bedsit kitchen (or, when really pushing the boat out, Kebab Magic, Turnpike Lane). Favourite London Department Store – Meg's Fags and Mags, Tottenham Lane. Favourite London View – my navel . . . But not after Bea. No, with her I really made the effort, even if it meant selling my record collection every time we hit the town.

Level-headed, sane Beatrice moved into a flat with three perpetually out-of-work male friends from university. I was pretty sure she wasn't fucking any of them, but then that was the arrogant naivety of the twentysomething relationship-novice. In retrospect, she was probably fucking *all* of them, every night, comparing my performance unfavourably with theirs between little, sexy, submissive gasps of air. Their timber-floored Hampstead flat-share fairly reeked of art, of a greedy immersion in high culture. There were bookshelves of erudite criticism, Expressionist prints on the walls, scripts cracked open on stolen university armchairs, racks of fine wine, the *Telegraph* crossword done as a flat on a Saturday morning, and (the really impressive thing) real Sumatran filter coffee. All so refreshingly novel, so perturbingly *other* in comparison to the knicker-littered mantraps, cosmetics-obsessed bathrooms and citadels of cretinous women's mags I was used to visiting. Bea would spend three days at a time in her thrillingly austere bedroom ignoring the phone, just *thinking*. In other words, my kind of girl. She'd had her summers of nannying, teaching English in the south of France, sailing with (I imagined) ruddy, big-cocked ex-public school boys and was now doing a master's in something fiendishly obscure (genetic theory? differential particle physics? oh, the pain of being half-stupid!) about which I ruined my eyesight trying to mug up on.

But hush . . . these are the surface details. They don't accurately relay or pinpoint the value of what we had in those months. Those few months we spent together before Mandy shoulder-barged into my life. Those languorous Sunday mornings in the wide, hard arena of her double bed; like children sleeping, her inky hair honouring the pillowcases. Or the deliquescent dawns that woke us with the usual epiphanies: the old insight that this warmth was as antithetical to the cold of the grave as you could get; or the certainty that lovers had lain like this since Donne's time and long, long before, in search of affection from each other in the possible absence of a God's unconditional love. And with those epiphanies, the usual confidences: the revelation of unbelievable sexual histories (aren't all our love-histories beyond belief if we're honest, if we speak them aloud?) – my quota of partners doubled, hers undoubtedly halved; though this still left her with enough casual liaisons to inspire a rabid, operational jealousy. They included encounters in France, the Himalayas, at university in Edinburgh and the tale of the Lothario she met in a laundrette with whom she 'flirted like mad' before taking him home to endure the most richly comic carnal experience of her life (the shared sherry; his jeans reluctantly dropped at the last moment; the microscopic penis).

It was those Sunday mornings that I remember and cherish the most. Although we had a lot of sex, I was never sure I was her sexual 'type'. The spectre of the Alpha male seemed forever present in the boudoir (manly, but not moustachioed). There was always the male anxiety that I wasn't tall, rich, dominant, confident, secure, *male* enough for her. Also, I was always too impatient for emotional demonstration. I didn't have the diligence to swim to the bottom of that deep water.

These love snapshots are the only ones I choose to take with me to the desert island of the present. I cannot picture Mandy's face without tears, resentment, nausea. (And we do choose. Even at the moment a caressing hand leaves us we are looking back on it from afar, thinking: I will remember this for ever.) At the time, these pockets of calm, these lacunae, brought with them the unshakeable conviction that, for Bea and me, floating on the lake of post-orgasmic satiety, time had stopped, and all around us the mad, acquisitive world was hurtling headlong in its revolutions – until we reluctantly stepped back on. These are the moments that will remain in the black-box recorder marked 'Bea'.

So why was I jeopardising all this by spending the night with a known runaround, a glitzy, gold-digging self-promoter like Mandy? Simple: she had better legs. (Oh, and it turned out, sanely enough, that they were tights, not stockings.) If you were to distil down, to boil off all the concrete-sounding, persuasive nonsense men spout to explain away an infidelity ('Our inner paths have diverged,' 'Our spiritual space is conflicting,' 'She never puts the special bay leaf in the boeuf bourguignon any more . . .'), you would arrive at the same answer. The new woman has better legs. Or better tits. Or a better arse. No, scratch that: Mandy didn't have better legs than Bea, merely the newest legs, the *latest* legs; they were not actually empirically better. It's a novelty thing, you see.

Bea and I had been rendezvousing every weekend for six months, and it was all getting a little predictable, a little inert. A sense of déjà vu hung over our late-night kitchen confessionals (post flickery US indie movie, or ascetically backdropped fringe production), surrounded by the verbal jousting of the three out-of-work gallants. It was all a little stale, a little out of puff. At least it felt that way then. With the hindsight of three years and one failed marriage I can put my hands to my faultlined face and howl into the November night about not-knowing-what-I-had, about throwing it all away, like the Base Indian, like Bob Dylan on *Nashville Skyline*. Also like a fool. I underestimated the quiet value of our time together. And then I squandered it for a psychotic bitch. I threw away all love, all beauty. That awful expression about being careful of dreams because they may well come true became the defining maxim of my life . . . But back then our relationship was beginning to feel like a stalled car: there are only so many times you can turn the ignition before you magnanimously admit defeat, hop out and go to the dealership for a new one. And yes, I would live to regret this glib analogy.

The problem was that with sanity comes stability, and with stability comes normality. Bea was no virago, termagant, lunatic. But at the time some self-destructive gene threw me in the path of such women. Of course, as with everything else that's malfunctioned in my life, I blamed myself. It was my fault, I thought, for being so crazy about her, for allowing the current to flow in only one direction, for enforcing this obdurate emotional template, this dynamic on the relationship from day one. Obviously she would play it cool, exercise some reticence. For six months, apart from the occasional demonstrative display of emotion, Bea had remained resolutely neutral and restrained in the treacherous arena of commitment. After all, we hadn't promised each other monogamy. We hadn't even promised to exchange birthday cards. It was all implicit in the intense, precious, high-value feel of our nights together. In fact, we hadn't even promised to phone each other after our last meeting. Surely if I, if Mandy and I, wanted to . . . Ah, the self-deluding crap that men feed themselves when thinking about fucking another woman.

I bolted up from the bed, tripping on the bolas of my trousers which were now around my febrile ankles (all those thoughts about Bea, her hard double bed, her indolent alabaster thighs, you understand). I crawled across the pungently minging black carpet-tiles and picked up the phone. I dialled Mandy's number.

'Mandy, it's me. Byron.'

A pause, long enough for her to take Steve's or Jake's or John's or whoever's hand out of her knickers. Oh, the leprous jealousies of the newly ensnared!

Then her bright Spanish voice.

'Hello, lover!'

At least she remembered me without consulting her bible-sized Filofax.

'I left my watch at yours.'

'Yeah, and the rest. Why don't you come round tonight to collect it?

'Okay.'

———

Now, you may have been wondering why, if I met Mandy at my place of work (and work being the kind of activity that's usually rewarded with hard cash, usually of the folding variety and usually monthly), why I never had any money. Well, you'd be right to be curious. Let me tell you the circumstances of a desolate state. I've been lying to you. Or rather, I've been less than generous with the truth. I did work, I did put in the hours, but only when Martin could afford to employ me. When I first phoned his shop, the kippered husk of Martin's voice had repeated the ominous word seen in his job ad. The word was 'seasonal'. When I asked him to expand, he told me that my employment would be 'on and off'. I found out, over the years, that it would be mainly 'off'. And some-times, just to keep my foot in the door when Rock On was undergoing one of its periodic stretches of 'asset sharing' (Martin putting all his old guitars in the window out of desperation), I would work for free. That's right, I did it for free. A mug's game, you'd rightfully announce. Well, maybe. It's no accident that one of my distant ancestors was given the name Easy. It must be in the genes, the gene-memory. He must have been one pushover, one crumbling tower block, if the end result was me. Because, allowing for the female side of the family's dalliance with short, bald, spinally defective window cleaners, I am his DNA descendant, his cellular culmination.

The fact was, for a lot of the time, Martin paid me in fresh air. Well, I did get unlimited free studio time in the cramped eight-track facility in the converted toilets, but I was no musician, and messing around with reel-to-reels and old mixing desks begins to lose its attraction on a hollow stomach. For months at a time there was no cash transaction. I suffered – to use Disraeli's splendid phrase – from extreme pecuniary embarrassment. My only other income was the Rock 'n' Roll, or rather, its totally un rock 'n' roll phoneme, the dole. Forty quid a week and half the scandalous rent paid. Forty fucking quid. Doesn't go far. In fact it goes nowhere. The stripey-shirted graduate ghouls who fix these figures must have conducted their research during late 1950s Great Britain – when tea bags cost one and six and bread was a shilling a loaf. The Great Britain where the mail was delivered by whistling posties and no one stole your bike from outside the dole office using fence-cutters and a blow torch. How could they be so far-off-the-mark, so deliriously out of touch with the actual price of things nowadays? Like, not thirty years ago, guys, but nowadays. Not last April, but now, after the latest hefty inflationary hike on fags, spirits, pornography, volumes of poetry – all the things that made life tolerable at the time. And what was the net result of struggling through life on forty quid a week? Predictably, a life not worth living.

What actually happens is that you do without the things that render life liveable and make do with only those that are vital to its *continuance*. The latter being little things like food, heating, shelter from London's merciless Januarys. And that's no life at all. It's subsistence. That's right, all carbohydrate and no cream – life loses its taste, its pop. It becomes as blank and as bland as plain potatoes boiled in their skins (a current favourite chez Easy), as tepid as tap water, as inanely void as a lunar landscape. I had come to London to write, but instead found myself fading to grey year after year in a bedsit. A burden on the public purse to boot. Some people were just born to make money, I concluded. The world was groaning with money, and they attracted it magnetically, or else it just fell out of the ether into their hands. Others, of course, were born into it, like Antonia with her trust fund browning nicely like a fat Norfolk turkey in an oven. Others still, like me, were born to feel money's keen edge, its scarcity, its alarming absence their whole lives.

I'd been working at Rock On for five years, barely turning a penny. Most of the time I felt as if I were living in an Eastern Bloc city during the mid-seventies. And then . . . enter Mandy, my fatal, my future wife; though I didn't know it at the time. Well, if you were up the Rhine-sized shit-creek I was and someone was foolish enough to throw you the paddle of marriage, you'd go for it, wouldn't you?

I actively hated where I had ended up. Of course, the pavements are teeming with people who are doing one thing but would rather be doing another: postmen who'd rather be waiters, waiters who'd rather be actors, actors who'd rather be directors. There's a community chest of dissatisfaction out there. So I wasn't alone in this. I was toiling every day in the shop and every night over a hot fountain pen wishing I was elsewhere. And then there was the inertia of the 'off' periods. My average day going something like: surface midday, make five cups of tea, smoke twenty-five cigarettes, get depressed, return to bed, get up again, try to write, fail, cycle to the shop for seven, work till midnight in the little recording room and return a thwarted, smoking wreck of despair in the small hours. Occasionally I would work through the night, setting my own syllabic verse to torrents of feedback guitar (this, after all, being my pay cheque) and then send the results off to the indifferent money-men and scalpers of the publishing business. I was twenty-seven. I was sacrificing living for creating art that nobody gave a fuck about. I could have built a paper armada, a Nelson's Column, a life-size papier mâché model of the White House from my rejection letters. I too yearned to be somewhere else, *someone* else, released from the intolerable and tiring bind of hope. I was fucked. I was suicidal. I was having that vision again: every night on the point of surrender to sleep I would mentally picture the snub barrel of a handgun crisply blowing my head off. I was penniless, smoke-less, hopeless. And I was contemplating cheating on my girlfriend.

For the two weeks after I returned to Mandy's orange opera-house of a room to collect my watch I'd seen her every night. Not almost every night, or five times a week, but *every night*. Our evenings followed a thrilling routine: the gauntlet of her six rotting staircases (a meeting with Steve being an ever-present danger), four bottles of wine, talking till three a.m., tarot cards and a cistern of strong tea in the morning, followed by the hollow-bellied scuttle home along the effulgent Holloway Road. Happy, happy days of love! I had been roped in to write the lyrics to all of Fellatrix's songs. Well, every big writer had a money-gig, I thought – even Shakespeare. They were long, alcoholic, unforgettable nights. O how these words, these . . . facts don't do them justice. How can they when what's under discussion is the *novelty* of another human being? When shared bills and chihuahua ownership are a lifetime away. When two are embarking on a monstrous odyssey of love, of hate, of torment.

With July came greater lassitude, greater frustration. It wasn't uncommon to finish a languorous afternoon of songwriting at Mandy's and follow it with an evening of headachy culture and gravy-thick red wine at Bea's. I would step into the late sun, aban-doning the bakery smells and her three cats for the fully leaved trees of Hampstead, the wind inflating their flapping, verdant forms like hot-air balloons. When I wasn't actually at Mandy's she would ring me in the shop. Sacked from the switchboard job, she would often be sunbathing on her roof. One afternoon in late July her voice came on the line with a terrible groan. Martin had just ejected one of our regular drunks who posed as virtuoso guitarists in order to enjoy human contact and the chance to play abominable riffs on out-of-tune guitars. Shocked, I said, 'Mandy, what's the matter? Where are you?'

'In hospital.'

The unbearable heat – the hottest summer for a hundred years, according to reports – suddenly increased by a couple of centigrade. I said, 'Don't mess around, Mandy.'

'I'm not. I'm in the Whittington Casualty. Remember that pain in my leg? Well it's totally paralysed.'

Terrible thoughts ranged through my mind. A fracture she doesn't remember? Or something worse? Deep Vein Thrombosis? The onset of MS or a rare blood disorder? I was surprised at how anxious I had immediately become. But then it's hard not to care for someone who calls you every day. She told me she had been there for four hours just waiting to be seen. By this time Martin had returned to his vigil behind the counter and was giving me an enquiring look.

To Mandy, I said, 'Just hang on there. I'm finished in half an hour.'

'Can't you come now?'

'Well, Martin needs me to lock up.'

There was a pause and what sounded like strangled sobbing. I knew I had said the wrong thing. With Mandy, it was instant gratification or nothing.

'That's all right. I'll get Johnny Radish to drive over.'

'No, no, don't do that.'

Then the waters of her great sorrow broke. A cataract of weeping, very pitiful, hot and close into the receiver.

'Oh, why haven't I got a mother?' she moaned.

Not knowing what to say, I said idiotically: 'You've still got your father.' This only seemed to increase her anguish. Then she told me that she wasn't going to speak to him for twenty years after the previous night's conversation in which he had ridiculed her plans for the band.

'I'll come over right away. Just stay there.'

She suddenly brightened. 'Well, I'm not going very far in a wheelchair am I? You know – I just want you to be my friend.'

'I am your friend,' I said, with as much appeal as I could force into my voice. Then I heard someone whispering in the background: modulated female tones and something being opened, like the cassette drawer on a Walkman. 'Hold on, is someone there with you?'

'Yeh. Antonia. How do you think I got here? Air ambulance? You're still coming, aren't you?' Then, in a little girl's voice: 'I miss you.'

How could I refuse? When I reached the vomit-stinking concourse of Accident and Emergency, Mandy and Antonia seemed to be having the time of their lives; pushing each other around in the wheelchair with Fellatrix demos detonating out of a compact little blaster. I never did find the cause of Mandy's mysterious paralysis. I knew then that she was attracted to something strong and weak in me. She needed the strength (the understanding, the support, the rescue), but wanted to control and dominate the weak part. Once Antonia had gone she told me many things under the awful fluorescent lights of the casualty department. How she had had a comprehensive nervous breakdown after her previous boyfriend and had spent the last three years in therapy. How her therapist had asked her to write a letter to her dead mother. How all of her relationships had been violent (I could see why. It always happens to girls like Mandy – men feel threatened by them, by their immense need to be the boss). She showed me the talismanic photo of her mother she always carried in her wallet – an older version of Mandy on a sun-scorched Mediterranean seafront; the tautness of the skin in her brown forearms intensely alive. I remember thinking, where does that flesh go? It seems so impor- tant, so impossible to eradicate, so eternal. Finally, she put her head on my shoulder, like a little child wanting its father, and related the one and only dream she'd had of her mother after the funeral. In this, Ramona had appeared by her bedside, mute but smiling, only to disappear after tucking her up. Then Mandy said: 'For a long time after that, I used to think my mother was watching over me. But, you know . . . she's not.' With her muffled, tearful face buried in my neck and shoulder, I pondered the spirit world. Was her dead mother watching us there? In the terrible dramatic arena of a casualty room? Was there a spirit-life, or was there just the blue-blank void of eternity? Where nothing contemplates nothingness. For ever.

Two weeks later, we were back in the casualty department of the Whittington hospital, but this time for a genuine injury. That morning I had awoken after incessant, exhausting dreams of ringing telephones, only to find that the phone had indeed been ringing all night. Mandy had staggered home at three in the morning to discover the front door of the bakery caved-in, her two grand-and-a-half Gibsons stolen. In her fury she put her hand through one of the big sash windows and had spent the night having the wound incompetently dressed by a drunken Steve and a terrified Matt. I went round at once. And there she was, in the broken doorway, wearing a pink-print mini-dress, her intoxicating Spanish smile, and a black gouge on her hand that would need fifteen stitches. The scar, white and jagged, would never leave her in all the time we were married.

Once again, we sat on the orange bucket seats, her head on my shoulder. She told me how she hated hospitals because they reminded her of having to visit the morgue after her mother's crash. How Ramona had said only a month before, 'If something happens to me, you will bring me flowers, won't you darling?', and the terrible guilt she felt for not visiting the grave in two years. After the suspicious, recalcitrant nurses had ejected us from the surgery cubicle, I said to her, 'You need a lot of love. More love than three cats and one man can give you.' To this she just smiled. She knew I was hooked, like a twitching fish on a line.

Certain songs have a Proustian effect on me, and, for that summer, it has to be Edwyn Collins' 'A Girl like You'. Apposite, I know. All I have to do is hear the dark voodoo of that subterranean minor chord and I get the works, like poor Swann, in an involuntary rush. One afternoon in particular – one deep July interlude of coruscating heat and rare indium – will always be conjured up by that tune, and probably will be for ever until its tape is erased by whatever gunshot, multiple pile-up or agonising illness brings me the end I so richly deserve. We were lounging on Mandy's spacious futon, an exquisitely gentle breeze fingertipping our foreheads; the champagne breakfast over with (she treated me so well!); the conversation stalled for the moment; her mother's photos watching us sadly from the mantelpiece. And I remember thinking: this is as good as it gets. Yes, this really is as good as it (this life, this plane of being) ever gets – hold on to it, carry it with you down every street you wind, like a precious desiccated flower, like Bergman's precariously brimming bowl of milk. And I remember hoisting myself up at the teeming open window by the bed to contemplate the stripes of sun on the chaotic Holloway Road. The cars zipping home or away from home; the glory of light in the fully borne, fully complected trees. And I knew that the moment would be fixed, branded, tattooed on the retinas by the glare along the windowsills and in the branches – a second or two of high balance: the leaves so sympathetic to the sun, the sun so sympathetic to the leaves.

Given the amount of time I was spending at Mandy's it's a wonder I didn't feel worse, or more guilty, than I did. It wasn't that I was mumbling to Bea about where the apple-red smudge of a lovebite on the throat originated from, or why my trousers were on back-to-front for the third weekend in a row. In fact, no explanations seemed required of me. We had been seeing less and less of each other. I suppose the answer was simple: I was falling in love. I was becoming enmeshed in that fatal balance, that feted curiosity that two can feel for each other; that doomed parity that has to be seen through.

I remember the exact moment I *did* fall in love with her. It was late on another sybaritic afternoon in August when Mandy leapt from the sofa with a sexy, unselfconscious scream to answer the phone. She rejoined me on the limo-settee and proceeded to speak crackling Catalan down the receiver to her aunt Leo in Tarragona. That's *it*, I thought. I'm smitten, I'm under. I watched her there: me blissfully ignorant of every syllable; her all red dust and ochre thighs, liquorice eyebrows and taxi-black hair, midday matadors and snapping castanets.

Once she put the phone down she became melancholy, as was often the case after talking to her relatives in Spain. I gathered that she had asked for a loan and had been turned down.

'If only my mum hadn't gone and *died* on me,' said Mandy, yanking her hair into a tight knot at the crown and searching for an elastic band.

'She didn't mean to,' I offered pathetically.

I watched her ransack her dressing table with a kind of helpless admiration. A white summer butterfly flitted in briefly through the open window, then left.

'She'd help me out, I know it. Leocadia and Gran – they're okay, they're over there, in the sun. They're just *bitches*.'

And then she started to cry. You got that sometimes with Mandy: a sense of dangerous scorn, of almost psychotic venom. As far as I could make out, she'd had all the help money could buy: a bereavement counsellor, a full-time therapist, doting boyfriends whom she gleefully gave the push one after another, a flash father with dodgy loot coming out of his ears, friends who'd do anything for her, a loyal auntie and grandmother in Tarragona. Yes, you sometimes caught the breath of that, her viridian life-force coming back the other way, alchemised into hate, her natural and pragmatic energy now a black gust of negativity; an ill wind that would blow nobody any good.

'You're like me,' I said, getting up to help her locate the box of Kleenex I knew she was searching for. 'You get low in the afternoons.' I felt newly uxorious, attentive.

'The time of day has hardly got anything to do with it,' she said bitterly. Then she smiled, accepting my tentative arm around her still-shaking shoulders. 'Anyway, you don't seem like the type to get depressed.'

'See, that's where you'd be wrong. I'm not a bright guy.'

At this she laughed; a high, gazelle-quick cackle that seemed to come at me along the doorway-wide strokes of sunlight pouring through the open sashes. We looked at each other and without any warning started kissing. The first one. The one you will always remember. The one that will, at some point in the future, return with Francesca's terrible words: 'The bitterest woe of woes is to remember in our wretchedness the happiest times.' Then we embraced, so close I could feel the crackle of roots as I ran my fingers from her crown down the divide of her middle parting and onto the alien surfaces of her forehead scar.

'What's so funny?' I asked, wanting only a kiss for an answer.

But she didn't kiss me. Instead she made a kind of proposition, or bribe, one that I would always recall in the black nights of the future, when I would measure what I'd *got* with what had originally been *promised*.

'Why don't you leave that Bea? Out of both of us, I'd love you better. Come on – stay with me and you'll have . . . lots of fun, lots of sex.'

And as she fixed me with her fully engrossed, fully dilated Latin stare I knew I was done for.

———————

'It's great to see a man able to cry,' announces the Accountant Woman to her husband. 'You know – openly.'

I am sitting on the hurtling, fevered train, staring at the pale faces opposite me. Until a moment ago I had been lost in that first kiss, that epidemic summer. And, obviously, weeping. Oh, I forgot to tell you. I made friends with them. The Accountant Couple, that is. Well, they say it's often the people closest to you that you fail to notice. They're not accountants after all. She is a counsellor, and he is a mortgage advisor. They had to be, didn't they? Or something similar, something crushingly plausible. Where have all the artists gone? The chisellers and ink-dippers? The mad-haired prodigies of poetry? Michelle and Robin: happily married since last July, apparently. First baby planned for next year. After she offered me that Kleenex we got chatting. Now she's looking back and forth between me and the sceptical face of her husband. I feel he needs to speak; to save my embarrassment, my smashed dignity. He rakes a hand through the brilliantined sweep of his hair.

'Well, you can't get much more open than that,' says Robin, restoring some masculine straightforwardness to the slightly Californian atmosphere that has gathered over the intimate space of our table.

Michelle squeezes his hand, and he returns the gesture. I wince at this touching display. Her emaciated face turns towards me. 'Well, I think it's sweet. And very brave.'

'I'm all right now,' I manage to moan with a smile; childish snot on my T-shirt.

'At least she didn't do the dirty on you,' grins Robin, warming to his subject. 'Now, my uncle—'

'Don't tell him about all that!'

'No, go ahead. I need cheering up.'

Robin continues, a certain relish now present in his voice. '—my uncle, he got hitched at the ripe old age of fifty-five to this younger bird. Asking for trouble. Anyway, he was a joiner, so he was at his workshop all the hours God sent. What does his missus start doing? Having all these blokes round, fellas she's been to college with . . .'

I begin to tune his voice out. It's necessary. Some things are necessary to one's survival. I start to wipe the mucus from my chest, then give up and glance at the dark window. Outside I can see the ring of the horizon and its veil of rain; cold showers on steep streets and roofs; the hum of raw weather. Inside, this terrible pain in my heart. Mandy or Bea – what a choice I had to make. I watch the mysterious distances slowly revealing themselves with a stately motion: telegraphed, pyloned, oaked and copsed, with silver birches flashing close to the mad chatter of the rails. How does the song go? *Crashing headlong into the heartland . . . in a night that's full of soul!* All of England seen at once, as if viewed from the air, or in section; or in every epoch, its secrets quiet within the rings of ancient trees, incontinent hedgerows. '. . . Anyway, while he's holed up at his workshop waiting for this hurricane or storm that never happens, she's having it away with this *student* . . .' Late gulls on thermals escort us effortlessly, suddenly peeling off and dive-bombing a lake – streaking Stukas in the winter dusk. There's the movement of wind in skeletal trees; as old a movement as you could hope to observe. Then the sudden disruption of a sewage works. At this speed, the landscape has the power to change within seconds; from broadly plotted squares of farmland to concave valleys hiding steeples amid the tops of rotting elms. '. . . and then when this other fella tries it on, he gets a right kick up the arse. My poor old uncle didn't even get a look-in . . .' The towns tumbling past show the last of England; what was once Saxon woodland tamed into arable sweeps dominated by the six-armed kings of the pylons. '. . . Terrible, ain't it . . . ?'

Mandy or Bea? That decision, as I remember, couldn't be deferred for a moment longer.

'Yeah,' I mumble distractedly. 'It's the old story.'

September. A gloomy morning of showers. The second of September, six months after meeting Mandy, and I was rendez- vousing with Bea to tell her goodbye. It had to be done. We sat together on a bench in Regent's Park as the sun came out briefly over the branches and the rain-puddled walkways. It was the saddest morning of my life.

'We didn't promise each other anything, did we?' I asked, looking at her pale profile. Her brow wrinkled slightly at this; her plum- coloured eyes deep-set, full of what I thought was thwarted feeling. But it was always hard to tell with Bea.

'No, we didn't. I suppose that was partly my fault, most of the time. So you're in love with this – what's her name again?'

'Mandy,' I mumbled, and felt the full error of what I was doing in the utterance of those two awful syllables.

I had told her all about Mandy, about my infatuation, how I thought the weekend-thing between myself and her was going nowhere. Or rather, I had rehearsed the plain transmission of these facts beforehand, but had garbled them out backwards in the last half hour between bursts of rain. Now I merely felt abysmal, like a murderer; the abortionist of our nascent love. The sun had just come out, turning all the walkways white with early autumn glitter.

'So I'll have no one then,' she said, with a steady voice.

I had no answer to this. I saw all her loneliness then, in her upturned chin, her delicate Adam's apple under its precious film of skin. I immediately felt, in my sternum, in my faithless loins, how close we had become, mentally and physically. Putting an end to our relationship felt like killing something inside us both. A brutal act. Sometimes it is only when you cross an invisible line that you precipitate the disclosure of another's feelings, not to mention your own. Now her look was imploring, vulnerable, impossibly alive. I thought I would have to split up with her every day in order to arouse these emotions. Only years later did I recall sentences of hers that took on greater significance. One evening, as we lay naked on my crocheted bed-spread, my feather fingers lightly stroking her pussy, she said, 'I think I'm going to start purring.' Then, in a quiet voice, 'I do like you, you know . . . more than you know.' She said no such sentence in Regent's Park, but it was immediately manifest in her eyes.

'You'll be okay. There's your master's, all those new friends up in Hampstead. You know, despite all this, I think we'll always be friends.'

I looked far into the middle distance at these words. The classic words. I badly wanted this outcome, but I didn't see how it would be possible with brash, aggressive Mandy around. The sun disappeared suddenly behind a rearing, bruised cloud. The indifferent squirrels with their spasmodic watchfulness, gnawing on their acorns, were only witnessing another couple split up in their park, unaware of the flames that consume human hearts.

'Yes,' she said, and I felt true assent, true hope and feeling in her voice. 'We will always be friends. Maybe what we had was just sex.' And her eyes reverted to their abstract, unreadable depths.

The rain started again. Pelting drops hit the bench, the size of amulets. Bea put her brolly up, and I walked her back to the road; finally unable to give her the protection I had vainly offered. Within the church-like sanctum of the umbrella, sheltering us both from the drumming downpour, I said, 'You will always mean everything to me. All love, all beauty.'

Unsurprisingly, this rankled more than anything.

'That's just someone else's poetry, Byron. I'm only a girl you met at a party who's doing a post-graduate course. That's part of the problem. You had me on a pedestal.' But she was wrong (as well as one hundred per cent correct). I looked at her then and she seemed to show a God-like bearing — the raindrops dripping from the brim of the brolly instead of tears; her level, candid gaze: a stillness at the centre of a world turning in futile revolutions.

At the road junction we stopped and she kissed me on the lips. Please, no more, I thought. She gave my hand a warm squeeze and asked,

'So you want a clean break then?'

'A clean break. Yes.'

'That's really horrible,' she said quietly. I apprehended at once a crucial difference between people. Not everyone needed to pick up the megaphone when undergoing intense pain. I had attributed to her a lack of feeling in the absence of my own glib, hysterical displays, but I had got her all wrong. I felt chastened that someone could have a subtler sensibility than me. Fundamentally, I had misunderstood her mechanism. Some people express titanic emotions, grave loss, in unostentatious, unobtrusive language. In no way does it diminish their depth of feeling. But then her behaviour was always understated, always impeccable. Here was a woman, I thought, who would never strike me, never say a sour word without mitigating it with love, who only wanted a steady man to provide her with protection, warmth, children, romance. And here I was throwing it away. As I returned her hand-squeeze, the words of the Soft Cell song swarmed into my head: 'Take a look at my face, for the last time. I never knew you, you never knew me. Say hello, wave . . .'

'Goodbye, Byron.'

My older, present-day self watches this, tears of remorse on my stupid chin, like crabbed Albert Finney in *Scrooge*, crying, 'You fool!' at the young Ebenezer. Indeed, if this were a movie, the crowd would be screaming in their seats: 'Don't leave her, you madman!'

'Goodbye, Bea.'

I thought of all the things she had given me. In February, I had sent her a large Valentine's card with a bad poem inscribed inside. She, meanwhile, had delivered a plain card with a quick message. But I now realise that it demonstrated a simple link of love. It was one of those optical illusion cards; just a pixelated blur until you catch it at the right angle, then all is revealed. In Bea's card, the revelation was the male and female symbols, discreetly linked together. Subtle, but worth the effort of investigation. Later, in August, she had given me a copy of Camus' short monograph, *Summer*. I thought then, in the wanton oven-like heat, with Mandy calling me every day, that the summer didn't belong to her, but in retrospect I was wrong. It would always belong to my chestnut-haired darling.

Bea let go of my hand. We both turned simultaneously and disappeared into the fuming crowds. At a corner, I craned my head around to take a last look at Carthage and its tragic flames, but she was gone. I never saw her again.

Lots of fun, lots of sex.

Well, for a while, Mandy was right. Newly separated from Bea, September turned into an Indian summer of rare magnificence. The rain had lifted. Strange that combination: unimpeachable blue skies and a heart as heavy as a ship's anchor. But somehow I managed the struggle of sharing Mandy's bed. Within a fortnight I had virtually moved in. A visit to Brighton with her dissolute tenants had long been mooted providing the weather held up. I kept putting it off, the anchor too weighty to dredge on board, but eventually a date was set. A fine Saturday saw Mandy's chrome Peugeot rattling towards the coast under incoming Jumbos and a scalding sun; the back seat bulging with Steve, Matt and Harriet; Mandy up front with me, looking like the cat that had just got the cream.

It was one of those unforgettable days. The sieve of memory is unpredictable: what it chooses to retain or lose. Nothing momentous happened . . . until it was time to go home. I can still feel the hotplate of canvas car-seat under my jeans; still see the plastic of the boxless cassettes fed one after another into the whirring slot of the stereo; still anticipate Mandy's hand reaching for mine to place a burnished kiss on my knuckles – one of her few gestures that I always loved.

Steve had been told that I worked in Martin's music shop and spent the entire journey screaming 'Rock on, Ron!' into my right ear. He had started early: the plastic bag of freezing cans diminishing by the mile. Brought up in care, then borstal, then onto a career of petty thieving, Steve had worked as a cabbie until he had blown it by becoming a professional alcoholic. Fifteen of his thirty-five years had been spent behind bars. Another ten pissed. Now a brickie, he was, for a while, one of the most dangerous men in north London. I didn't know this at the time, and neither did Mandy, otherwise we might not have let him loose onto the scorching back seat. Still, he was handy – in every sense – to have around. He was going to be Mandy's bodyguard when fame arrived in its golden chariot.

Harriet and Matt sat huddled together, obviously alarmed to be within Steve's vomiting-range, as The Who's '5.15' rang out along the Surrey Downs. Harriet at that time had an uncontrollable helmet of corkscrew ginger hair which blew free through the open rear window. She was afflicted by hirsute moles, some of them facial, though she had the newly coined beauty of anyone pushing twenty-one. She was so excited, she said, to be going to the seaside. Matt, meanwhile, never said much anyway. Goateed and pony-tailed, a gentle six-foot-two pipe-cleaner, he sat silently with an expression of half-formed mirth on his chops for the entire journey.

Once parked, we all hurtled along the broad perspectives of the seafront — singing, piggy-backing, taking photos. Ahead of us was the dazzling sea, the twin piers; one vibrant with a funfair, the other crumbling fabulously (like a seedy old soak at kicking-out time) into the waves. After fish and chips in vinegar-sodden newspaper, Mandy and I escaped from the others, leaving them to skinny-dip in the foaming shallows.

There we were, two semi-educated idiots, whose inner damage just happened to correspond, with the world all before us. We kissed in the holiday heat, lips already tanging with salt, in the sultry dregs of an exceptional English summer. Then we made our way to the slatted running boards of the Palace Pier with its dodgems, coin-clanking arcades and candy-floss parlours, all wallowing in the day's dizzying centigrades.

Mandy took my hand again and pressed it to her lips. This courtly gesture in reverse always fascinated me. She said,

'Why don't we get married?'

I laughed and looked into the sun, into the light, then pulled away half-blinded.

'Why? I know why. It's because getting married isn't the sort of thing people like us *do*. Straights and suits do it to please their parents.'

And this was the truth: I didn't know anyone my age who had tied the Gordian knot. For many people, marriage and children was just the next thing, requiring the full approbation of their folks, their bank accounts. But not for the likes of us. My mother was merely a voice on the phone, my father on the other side of the world. As for bank accounts, Mandy was a near-penniless musician, I a scribbler of non-remunerative doggerel. My attempts at self-improvement, at further education, at forging a career, had been hilarious. All the same, I felt a warm uncoiling in my stomach, a sense of rightness, of being at the centre of something for once in my life. It was such a ludicrous suggestion. Is this how grown-ups got married? On a daytrip to the coast? It was obviously unworkable. We hardly knew each other, although love deludes you otherwise. And me with no dough, no tenure, no hair. Mandy with her brazen ambition, her recklessness, her changeability. Yes, a ludicrous suggestion. Because it was such a bad idea it started, in the Brighton sun, to look like a good one.

'Did you say, I do?' grinned Mandy.

She wasn't without humour sometimes. And not without conventional notions, either, within all the brittle waywardness, the capricious flutter that was her life. Under all that glitter she was just a regular gal. I decided to take the plunge.

'I think it's the best idea you've ever had.'

'Oh, deluxe! I've told my dad you can meet him next week. If that's all right.'

'Hey, that doesn't mean yes! I just said it was your best idea. Anyway, I thought you two had fallen out.'

'That happens every week. Gran and Auntie are coming from Spain, too.'

This evidence of prior planning unsettled me slightly. But she seemed overjoyed. At the back of her mind, I could perceive the shade of her mother, absent from any wedding day she would ever have, smiling an Andalusian smile. And at the back of mine there was a pair of welcoming angel's wings, bringing salvation. My tacit acceptance had something to do with death and time, too; with the train of my years screaming through its stations. I was knocking on. Most of the time I felt like milk on the turn. I was also romantically convinced that I would die young, like Keats, like Shelley, like Raphael. If I didn't marry now, then when? There is a sense that people without a family get married because they are trying to become each other's family. And this is a dangerous, regressive notion; a dependent merger that can only bring misery. But I needed a family. As Madonna sang, one is such a lonely number. She still had her hand on mine. Abruptly she yanked me forward and raced me to the end of the pier, her black hair blazing with surface reflections from the toiling ocean.

There is a photo of us from that day, that season of unforced laughter. It was taken by Harriet, who had sneaked up behind us with her heavy Nikon, her red locks wild in the sea wind. The pale grey-and-white reproduction of Mandy and me, arm in arm, wearing summer pumps and shades on the Brighton Palace Pier hung in all the flats we subsequently shared and she subsequently destroyed. The two lovers, soon to be married, walking off into the sunset.

Lots of fun, then.

And lots of sex, too. At least when we returned to the generous ceilings of her top-floor flat. We sat on her futon, as I remember it, the sash windows flung high; pebble-filled pumps scattered about. And she hugged me. A deep, double-enclosed embrace. The first time I had been properly *held*, it seemed, since childhood. It appeared unthinkable then that we would ever do each other harm. Eventually I opened my eyes and, with my chin on the warm shelf of her shoulder, I could see a gravid slowness in the movement of the horse chestnut trees outside. Late summer butterflies, white as Arctic snow, flitted about weightlessly. A brittle opacity in the lemon light of evening held swarms of hysterical midges, distinct as stars or satellites. And, as she undid my belt, I noticed that every sill in the perspective of windows out back was brushstroked with a stripe of delicious yellow. If there had been woods beyond Tufnell Park, they would surely have echoed to our ring.

———————

The meeting with a girlfriend's father is always a decisively male moment. If all goes well, the acceptance of a cigarette from the peacock-fanned pack counts as an unspoken bonding between Y chromosomes. Talk should then move onto the re-laying of lawns, the grouting of tiles, the size of a car's engine specific to litres and numbers of pistons. Despite one's best efforts, one becomes acutely aware of how one is walking – too much mince and he'll think you're a woofter, too much aggression he will give you that 'lay one finger on her' look. And all the while, there it is in blazing neon, on sandwich boards along his street, on tannoyed address systems: 'This man is fucking your daughter'. Yes, a male moment, and one corrosive to the nervous system. Anyway, I hadn't actually said yes to marriage yet – and hey, I thought it was my job to ask – this was merely an exploratory visit, a relaxing rendezvous. By the end of the week it seemed all was decided. Mandy did indeed drive us to meet her old man, her wizened granny and her aunt from Tarragona, the following Sunday.

Her little Peugeot dipped between the banks of the circuitous country lanes surrounding Windsor. A day in very late September – the fulcrum of the year. One of those days when, after a good summer, the soil, the sky, the leaves on a blazing row of maples, seem fully permeated with the sun's benevolence. Total satiation: nature at full capacity, with the insidious whispers of a cool October kept at bay, like attendant devils in the wings. A late September afternoon: the hot sky an ocean of breathing azure. The hedgerows persisting in their plenty a little while longer.

The tree-canopies dispersed light in a continual dervish flicker across our faces; a zoetrope of gold, like blinking very fast. Although I had spoken briefly to Mandy's aunt Leo on the phone, I had only seen a smudged black-and-white photo of her father. Significantly, this was taken on his wedding day. There was Ramona in all the flamenco finery of her dress, and there was Ian Haste – tall as a telegraph pole and, as I would later find out, only slightly more talkative. Yes, I had been keenly dreading the meeting for seven days. Why do we tremble over such introductions? There is nothing one can do to prepare oneself except jump straight in, naked. A baptism by etiquettes and rules not yet known. Best behaviour won't get you through, only a kind of instinct; the intuition of the Davy-lamped miner feeling his way along the dripping seam. One is there, whether one likes it or not, to be evaluated. And you better have had a substantial breakfast, or risen early enough, to get you through, to emerge intact. To emerge like a man.

Unfortunately, this wasn't to be the case that September afternoon. I had taken the precaution of drinking three bottles of Spanish sack the night before (and most of a bottle of Famous Grouse as a nightcap) just to get in the mood. To be frank, I was hungover. In fact, I felt titanically wasted. There was a slim possibility that I might have to do some talking later on. This was doubly unfortunate, as ninety per cent of my vocabulary was fiercely marinating in an evil broth of red wine. All verbal agility was lost. Not only that, but the afternoon was shaping up to be a scorcher. By two o'clock, the viscid booze had begun to osmose through every pore of my body, basting my forehead with a sheen of toxic, seventy-per-cent-proof sweat. I could see it was going to be a long day.

Once we emerged from the country lanes (a wisp of straw, blown in from the late summer fields, lodged in Mandy's hair), we took the turn for Slough instead of Windsor. Mandy sheepishly admitted that she'd been economical with the truth about the town of her origin. Soon we were on the outskirts of Betjeman's dystopia. We span fast through the demoralising concrete boulevards, the office blocks that appeared to be made from tarmac, the scarred pubs and fried-chicken outlets. Fast was the operative word. I'd say we averaged seventy for the entire journey. But then she performed everything rapidly, did Mandy, my meretricious marvel. The only thing Ian Haste and I would eventually agree upon was that she drove like a *man*. Finally, we reached an outlying suburb, with gated residences that surely held sentimental Monet and Renoir reproductions in appalling frames. Sure enough, the house of Mandy's father was one of these.

As soon as the car had been parked – and I had scooped my sick and shaking frame from the vehicle – I became aware of foreign voices, screaming. Through a window I could see two hunched shadows inflicting insults upon each other.

'What the hell's that noise?'

'Oh, that's only Gran telling Leo off for letting her down. It's happened every day for the last thirty years. First she blames her for not looking after her. Then for squandering her savings. Then for not being as good-looking as my mother. You'll get used to it.'

I wasn't sure I wanted to. Smoothing the tears of sweat from my brow, I turned towards Mandy, who already had her finger on the doorbell.

'How do I look?'

Mandy had taken me out to buy a pair of flares, a suede jacket and some passable shades during the week. She was wearing exactly the same outfit. We looked like slightly decadent, recherché twins.

'Apart from the clothes – awful. But I don't care if he likes you or not. As long I get some cash out of him for the band, I'll be happy. How's your Spanish?'

'Non-existent.'

'Doesn't matter. Gran pretends not to understand English, just like she pretends to be deaf.'

At that instant the door opened and the screaming abated. A warm gush of Mediterranean cooking hit me in the face, making me slightly nauseous. And there stood Ian Haste, Mandy's father; ghoulishly tall, with liver-spotted hands the size of ping-pong bats, his straight hair coerced back from his forehead with oil and comb into something resembling a quiff. His huge right hand extended.

'You must be Byron.'

His eyes scanned me for signs of previous marriages, sexually transmitted diseases, prison terms. If he had been in any way articulate he would have described me as a classic waster, or a narcissistic poseur of the highest stripe. Instead, his dislike merely registered in minute movements of his thin grey brows.

'The one and only,' I replied, my mouth filling with spittle.

'Well, come in. You must be tired after Mandy's driving.'

We went into the long-corridored house. The deep-pile carpets were scrupulously clean. On the living-room wall hung Renoir's *La danse à la campagne* in an abysmal frame. I followed Mr Haste and Mandy into the cramped kitchen, and witnessed the detailed,

extravagant hugs and kissings between my future wife and my
future Spanish in-laws. Once they had disengaged, the talk turned
to the huge paella simmering under a dustbin-lid, like an offering
to Olympus. I sat with an inane grin sellotaped to my face and
observed the company. Old Montserrat had a dignified, even regal
gait, that I later found concealed great feminine deviousness. She
seemed stooped and miniaturised by age, her eyes sometimes
twinkling with that feral shrewdness old women are possessed of.
She was dressed in a tan summer trouser suit, the type necessary
to keep cool under the scalding Andalusian sun; a long string of
pearls double-looped under her turkey neck. Her hands moved
expressively in time with every crisp syllable. Leocadia, Mandy's
aunt, was pale and withdrawn in contrast, her hair cut into a
greying wedge. She looked frail and malnourished, with a sense
of self-neglect in her clothes and complexion. There was an aura
of self-restraint and repression about her, of properness. I inspected
her meek frame for any resemblance to the fiery Ramona, but
could find none. As the three generations of women began to talk
very rapidly in Spanish, I mopped my brow. The heat of the
kitchen had caused the virulent sweat to virtually urinate from my
face. Mr Haste lowered his gaze to me.

'You're sweating.'

'So I am,' I laughed, and pulled my cuff across my forehead,
feeling unable to stand the Hades of the house for a moment longer.
I must have looked like a human waterfall. 'It's not just the *proverbial* kitchen I should get out of!' Mandy's father examined me with
a dead-eyed stare, not even the glimmer of a smile on his sallow
face. Oh, Christ, I thought: uphill all the way.

'Anyway. So what do you do?'

Of course, I was ready for this one. A week of preparation had
gone into my answer. The almost fifties elegance of his clothes
seemed to twitch slightly as he waited for my reply. His bathtub-
defying legs stiffened impatiently.

'Didn't Mandy tell you? I work in a music shop.' Best not to
mention writing, I thought. Until you were lionised by the world

at large, writing was an occupation that didn't count as something you did. It was something that did things to you. It made you poor. It was an expensive hobby, a silly indulgence; something that prevented you from making a living, from *do*-ing. It wasn't legitimate. It was a guilty, dirty secret, a form of self-abuse. I felt observed and vulnerable standing there with my world-competitive hangover, my height problem; like a moth under glass. Like Pip before Miss Havisham.

'We tried to teach Mandy the piano. But she had no application. This thing she's up to at the moment – I hope you don't encourage her – hardly counts as music.'

'Actually, I think she's got what it takes.'

I felt a sudden surge of rebellion well up inside my aching guts. What the hell, I thought: he loathed me on sight. Ian Haste spoke softly, in measured tones that masked any clear accent. But behind the reticence was an overpowering arrogance. The arrogance of the tall man. He had a stubborn, over-manning presence. His physical carriage reminded me of my stepfather: stringy and dangerous. He pulled a pack of Dunhill from his jacket pocket and offered the filter ends towards me.

'Cigarette?'

Ah, we're making progress. He likes a bit of resistance, of opposition. But – I could sense – not too much. He was beginning to loathe me less, despite himself. I later found out that Ian Haste was also an only child and had become a successful businessman the hard way, with all the unbending conceit that confers on a man. He had been born into poverty in Bow, and had managed to disguise his accent with elocution lessons, fudging and the shining example of Terence Stamp. His parents had run an East End pub, but he saw the real money was with the breweries. In his early twenties he had become a buyer for one of the major companies, snapping up half the boozers in Bethnal Green within a year. He had met Ramona while staying in a Bayswater hotel on business. At that point she was just a maid, whereas he had swaggered in all spivved-out in his skinny black Krays' tie

and Carnaby spats; a high-roller full of vulgar, vertiginous charm. I accepted a cigarette, and he led me outside to show
me the new lawn he'd put down in the spring. He stood there
like a king before his realm, as the merciful air soothed my frying
face.

'Once the topsoil's full of stones you're done for. Trust me, it
needs constant attention. Compost, weedkiller, hosing. I don't
suppose you have a garden in, where is it?'

'Archway.'

'Oh, yes, that grotty little dump. I went there once. Won't be
going back. By the way, they're not as scary as they look.'

For a moment I thought he was referring to the red-hot pokers
bordering his immaculate lawn. He was standing next to me, stud-
iedly smoking, rarely making eye contact, in the pose of the loner.
The man apart: circumspect, masculine. Then I realised he was
talking about Montse and Leo.

'Oh, they seem very . . . vibrant.'

His eyebrows shifted disagreeably. Not a word in his vocabulary,
I imagined. Anyone who used words such as vibrant were highly
suspect. And probably communist. I was dying to get a look at his
bookshelves. You could tell a lot about someone from their books.
In fact, I was of the opinion you could tell everything worth
knowing.

'The old girl's a bit of a handful, but you won't get much trouble
from Leo. Nothing like Mandy's mother.'

'I heard she was quite a personality. And very beautiful.'

'Too beautiful for me,' stated Mr Haste, ruefully. Then he
drew himself up, remembering his reserve. But it didn't last long.
He let loose a bizarre chuckle: 'Her mother spoilt Mandy something rotten. Now she needs someone steady. You seem fairly
steady, Byron.'

I couldn't believe I had heard him correctly. In my advanced
state of dilapidation, the last thing I felt was steady. But then, I was
beginning to suffer auditory hallucinations. My forehead-constricting
headache was starting to buckle my temples, upset my sense of

balance. He continued, 'By the way, I can tell you were a bit worse for wear last night. Don't worry, I used to be in the pub game before I retired. You're a dead giveaway. But I can see you've got your head screwed on straight.'

'Thanks,' I muttered, the effort of doing so almost causing my head to fall from my shoulders. Did this count as his assent, his blessing? Man to so-called man?

'You've no money, mind. But neither had I, really, when I met Mandy's mother. It was all front. You can't do it with just front these days, more's the pity. Come on, let's go inside before they ruin dinner with their rabbiting.'

Soon we were all seated around a circular pine table, the broiling paella sitting heavily at its centre. Montse took command of the serving, and, despite a personal attack of delirium tremens (precipitated by the sight of a glass of red wine), and the equatorial heat, the meal went as well as could be expected. Marriage was only mentioned once, and then it was in the context of a *fait accompli*, as if we'd tied the knot a month ago. I managed a couple of sentences with the verbs and subjects in the right order (in English, of course – what did you expect, Castilian?), and tried not to appear as dangerously ill as I felt. An hour later the old lady addressed me in Spanish with a tigerish smile.

'*Mariscos, bien?*'

Mandy leaned over and whispered in my ear. Under the table she clasped my perspiring palm. 'That's seafood.'

'Oh, non. Merci,' I managed to stammer. Another mouthful, I feared, would bring me face to face with all the others.

Montse looked back and forth between me and Mandy, the feline grin still beaming.

'Ah, they look such elegant young ones! A dynamic couple!'

I was startled by this burst of English. Up until that point she had bewildered me with the machine-gun rattle of her Spanish. There was the old girl arrested before us, ladle in hand, bearing a clump of bilious *gambas* and steaming rice, speaking fluently a language of which I had assumed she was completely ignorant.

I returned her smile. Then there was no stopping her. 'I remember when I met my Pepe. Everyone said he was the village idiot, ai, ai, ai! And you know what they said? Eh? They said that I should no marry. *Nunca*. Not never. And look at us, God bless him in heaven, sixty years of bliss. Let us hope you two make the same marriage. We were like two shoes on the foots of the same person!'

'Oh come on, Gran,' cajoled Mandy, 'you couldn't stand each other.'

Leo interrupted with her matter-of-fact voice: 'They were very happy together, Amanda. I should know, I have had to listen to her all these years.'

Mandy turned to her aunt.

'You were the lucky one. You had Spain, and the sunshine on tap all year round. I had to go to school in this dump.'

'You mean England?' I said, slightly offended.

'That was your father's decision,' said Leo crisply.

'Ah, Pepe!' sighed Montserrat, not listening to us. 'He looked so good in his uniform. Said he would die for the Republicans. And for me, of course!'

'And now I feel like I am married to her,' muttered Leo. There was scorn rather than resignation under her timidity.

A new tension entered the room. The old girl shot her daughter a venomous look and a sad passivity returned to Leo's face. Mandy's father sat back with a manly calm. He had heard all this before, many times. I saw his hand move towards the packet of Dunhill. Montserrat pointed the paella ladle towards Leo like a broadsword.

'And what would you know about marriage? You could still find yourself a man – look at you. God made you beautiful once and you let it go to waste.' Her twinkly eyes were now full of mad poison. Leo, I knew, had been briefly and traumatically married in her early twenties and was now a confirmed spinster. And also a slave to Montserrat. The situation was escalating. I felt suddenly asphyxiated. 'If only Ramona were still with us, she give you a kick up the backside!'

Leo had a strange way of being unassertive and patronising at the same time. She spoke to everyone as if they were naughty children. Her sanguine face addressed Montserrat without meeting her eye.

'Now stop it, mother. What will Byron think? You've only just met him, and you still cannot behave. You've had a very tiring day, insisting on cooking at your age. You should be resting. And this heat – it feels like Madrid in August.'

I could concur with her there. The raised passions were propelling more whisky-flavoured sweat onto my hairless scalp. Every time I dabbed my pate with the heavy napkin, Louis Armstrong-style, the foaming spa would be replenished seconds later. I must have looked like a glacé cherry, sitting there; pooped, full of trapped pain and heat, and longing to go home. I glanced towards Mandy. She seemed to find the whole scene amusing. But the old woman's blood was up.

'Don't give me orders! Do I take orders from my youngest daughter? *Imbécil! Muñón! La más puta de todas las putas del mundo mundial!*' She hurled the ladle into the sink. 'How dare you be alive and Ramona dead?! And you . . .' She pointed a curved forefinger at Mandy's father, who was patiently smoking and rolling his eyes. 'You devil. She could have found better than you. You are no man! Pepe – he was a man!'

Leo got up and walked towards Montserrat, in an endeavour of placation. Mandy had told me that Leo worked with the mentally ill back in Tarragona, so she was perfectly qualified to deal with the old battleaxe. Leo held out her arms as if to comfort a sobbing, petulant child. The stooped woman spun around and stood trembling by the sink, refusing all succour. I watched this scene through engorged eyelids. A waterfall of liquid turned my vision crimson. I felt faint. A crisis was coming. The couple in the Renoir on the wall seemed to be line-dancing rather than waltzing, their expressions of abandonment suddenly melancholy and confused. I was dimly conscious of Mandy next to me taking the opportunity to seize her father's arm. Then her voice.

'Now, Dad. Can you lend us a grand?'

But I didn't hear his answer. I blacked out, face down in my still-molten plate of paella, like Agamemnon with the sword in his back.

———————

Mandy didn't get her thousand pounds. In fact, her father rarely gave her anything, whether it was attention, money, support. And he didn't have any books on his shelf. Only the *Times* World Atlas, Yellow Pages and a tax guide. This in itself was not surprising. But his unfatherly parsimony ambushed me for a moment until I realised he was trying to teach Mandy a lesson. He had done it the hard way, so why shouldn't she? I could never be so cruel to any offspring of mine. He was an odd, chilly fish. It is said that after men who own yachts, women most desire men who resemble their fathers. This cannot have followed with Mandy, as Ian Haste and I were about as different as could be imagined while still belonging to the same species.

After the abortive dinner (which Mandy found grimly comical), there followed a few brief months of frenetic bliss in London. There was a wedding to be organised, for instance. I had previously thought that people just turned up at a church to get married, like in the movies. I didn't know you had to apply for such things as a *licence*. For three weekends in a row we met with the slight, heavily bespectacled woman who would be marrying us at an Islington registry office. There we would go over the words that were to be uttered at the ceremony. Our brief but significant meetings took place with hailstones beating the windows, the weather having deteriorated into a turbulent autumn of dark, dank evenings. Mad, Carel Weight wind blew in the trees outside as we spoke the sacred sentences. I was also unaware that you could say virtually anything in your marriage vows as long as it didn't allude to international terrorism or leave out the bit about 'any lawful impediment'. Our registrar seemed to spend half her time underlining the seriousness of the union, the other half attempting, so I thought, to dissuade us from the whole idea. You had to believe in every word, she said. At that point, we did.

The date was set for December the twenty-second, allowing us to escape to Mandy's beloved Barcelona ('my city!') for the honeymoon. I hadn't been as far as Great Yarmouth in the previous seven years, so the pleasure and the privilege was mine. Every morning, as I leapt out of Mandy's shower, I would feel a liberating sense of increasing life; its boundaries, its possibilities, its aqueous intoxication. Her favourite band at the time was The Who, and 'Love, Reign O'er Me' would greet my ears as I dressed for a day's toil in the shop. Often, when I was stuck behind the counter alone, she would turn up with a full roast dinner under a lid of tinfoil, a gesture I found immensely touching. When not at Rock On, our days were filled with intense activity, most of it centred around Fellatrix. Many a pink-and-gold October morning did I spend with scissors, adhesive and Letraset, collaging together flyers for her gigs, or helping scour directories of A&R men for suitable mailshot targets. The phone in her flat rang incessantly. Friends, prospective managers, promoters; strange liggers she had met in whatever fetid den of leather she'd spent the previous night networking. A hecatomb of panting suitors. Then there was the elusive drummer problem. As Fellatrix was an all-girl band, Mandy had deliberately recruited chicks *less* good-looking than herself. When her regular drummer left upon realising that a rhythm section didn't receive a penny in songwriting royalties, Mandy began an exhaustive season of auditions. I would stand at the back, ushering in the hopefuls for their strictly timed fifteen minutes, only for Mandy to shake her head, 'Nah, much too pretty . . . Way too blonde . . . Tits too big.'

When not in the malodorous rehearsal and recording studios of north London, we would market for vegetables and fish on the Seven Sisters Road. She was a spectacular cook; all learnt from Ramona, so I was told. On our forays, we often encountered the same toothless lecher flogging lighters from a ripped cardboard tray. He would hiss and purr every time my lovely shimmied past.

I sometimes think about this lunatic and why I didn't paste him to within an inch of his life. The reason, apart from me being no good at fighting, was that Mandy gave the impression of being able to take care of herself. In a physical way. She just looked dangerous, rangy, unpredictable. Five-ten of slinky hips, lips, tits and power. After scoring *merluza* and tiger prawns for her Mediterranean concoctions, we would drive into Camden and scour the markets for clothes: skinny-rib T-shirts, velvet flares, vintage party dresses. My favourite top of hers read 'Psychobitch', rendered in the Harley Davidson logo on crenellated pink and silver. She had a genuinely impulsive nature. Anything she saw and loved she had to have. I would feel energised, emancipated, just from being in her company. I often asked her why she liked me, let alone loved me. She would answer simply, her rich brown eyes full of engagement: 'Because you're different. Because you make me laugh.' This made my chest fill with a strange, hot, expanded feeling. It was almost frightening; an unpleasant upheaval. I had been so used to unhappiness that the idea of happiness made me miserable. Rummaging through those clothes shops, those troughs of decaying paperbacks, those furriers with nineteenth-century stained glass over the lintel, I felt as if *I* was the object that had been located in life's junkshop. After seven years of getting lost in London, I had been found.

There were also some tremendous parties in the big top-floor room. One raucous bacchanal seemed to have every popstar, music-biz ligger and journo in London present: all dangling from the banisters, flying on Es and wizz. Mandy had dressed Steve, Harriet and Matt in surreal cabin-crew fancy-dress, and persuaded them to replenish everyone's palate with champagne or charlie borne on silver trays. The three cats, with their Fellatrix badges swinging from their collars, watched the guests come and go with a Rhadamanthine scrutiny, as Mandy's demos splintered eardrums.

By the end of squalling November I had moved into her capacious flat above the bakery. Mandy had picked up my laugh-ably meagre possessions in a single visit with her Peugeot. I really wish I could tell you that it required a second or third relay, but it's strange how little one has that's worth keeping. We clashed over throwing away the tottering stacks of jaundiced newspapers and magazines I had been hoarding for years, but this was quickly resolved by the cunning method of backing down. I had learnt to tread easy with Mandy, very easy. An incident the previous week had given me pause for much thought and doubt. We had stepped out to Club Dynamite with Antonia and Nick, Mandy deciding to bring along her Danish cleaning girl, a fluffy blonde tomboy of twenty named Rikke. From the moment we arrived at the heavily policed doors, there was trouble. Our names couldn't be found on the list; Mandy said she was ill – a migraine coupled with stomach cramps and a cold. Once inside, Mandy and her friends cruelly ignored the poor Scandinavian waif. At midnight, I turned around to find they had all disappeared, except Rikke. Feeling deserted and not a little sorry for her, we trawled the club. It was hard work: her with little English, me less Danish. Half an hour later we were back where we started, the anti-aircraft strobes whiting out recognisable features. Then I was hit in the face. A glass tumbler of vodka, bitter-lemon and ice had smacked me snappily under the left eyebrow, leaving me feeling, after a couple of seconds, as if somebody were trying to force out my eyeball with a spoon. I was stunned. Before me stood Mandy, shaking with rage. She obviously thought I had been trying it on with her cleaning lady, who was now staring at her trainers, mortally embarrassed.

Mandy stormed out, leaving Antonia and Nick to nurse my wound with an ice-pack from the bar. It wasn't the fact of her jealousy that surprised me, it was more that the punishment in no way fitted the crime. The force with which she threw that glass was deeply disturbing – all anger loosed; uncaring of the consequences. The old pint of beer over the head would have been far preferable: a comedy comeuppance for a crime never committed. A panto or a Noël Coward ending. But this? It crossed that unwritten line of respect present in all relationships. I began to wonder at her capacities. I felt humiliated, uncertain of everything.

For the next couple of days I had serious doubts about marriage. These were immediately followed by a list of plausible excuses I made for her. It was only the Spanish temperament, I told myself. I should be flattered that she could be so jealous. Her with half of Holloway drooling on her doorstep. Me so bald and prospectless. Also, she had been ill, stressed out. But then reason prevailed. *She* was the one who had vanished. I had gone looking for *her*. It was, I mused with what now seems a quaint naivety, completely unreasonable. And I had said goodbye to sweet, sane Bea for this? Mandy turned up at my rickety Camden crash-pad the following morning in tears – the first time I'd seen her really upset. But I immediately wondered whether they were equivocal, crocodile crawlers. I'd known girls over the years who could turn on the sobs, a trick they'd learnt in order to manipulate men from daddy downwards. I looked deep into her bereft eyes, into her soul, trying to divine whether they were genuine or not. It was important for me to know; much depended upon it. I began asking questions, fundamental questions that I'd never asked before. Who was Mandy? What did she do with experience, how did she assimilate it? Was she in control of it, or did she let it rule her? Did she ever want children? Did she believe in a God? Was she capable of loving anyone or thing apart from her cats and her band? I eventually asked her these crucial questions over the years, but her answers were evasive, indistinct; non-answers. I also had a catechism prepared for myself. Did I really love her, or just the way she looked in silver tights and black underwear? Did I really think we had a future? And how much exactly did a divorce cost these days?

But a date had been set. And two people newly in love can blind themselves to virtually anything, so immense are their delusions about one another. There was also the very real notion that I didn't deserve anything better than being whacked in the face with a full glass of vodka in a packed nightclub, but let the shrinks get rich on that one.

The night before I was to be married I took a brief walk around the block. The sky was a turbulent sea of black and blue. Deep December, with a nip of ice in the zippy wind. The cars on the Holloway Road were still relentlessly pouring past, just as they had in those high summer days. Some heading home, some away from home. I pondered my last hours of freedom, thinking: this time tomorrow I will be a married man. Well, well, well. What a turn up for the books, Byron, you old devil! Who would have thought it? Yes, I agree. Some deeper meditation at this juncture might have brought me greater happiness in the future.

A white Roller, hired by Mandy's father, picked us up at nine in the morning. The boot was full of champagne. We had decided it was going to be a glam wedding, like Mick and Bianca's, like David and Angie's. Her in peach and me in black. Actually, I had borrowed Rudi's ill-fitting pinstripe suit complete with outrageous chalky stains on the inside leg, whereas Mandy had eschewed traditional white for a shocking pink turtle-neck and six-inch glitter heels. Rudi, the best man in every sense, met us outside the murky entrance to the registry office. I felt strangely calm. The future didn't exist. Just Mandy and me and the crisp December morning.

Inside, on collapsible wooden chairs, were Harriet, our official photographer, Ian Haste, Montse and Leo. We had resolved to keep it a quiet affair: no band members, no clubbers, dealers, skankers or schmoozers. Finally, at the end of the row, sat my mother, Sinead, on a rare trip down from Yorkshire. I had only told her the week before that I was getting hitched. She seemed initially bewildered that I wasn't marrying a nice Catholic Irish dairymaid, but then she had long given up offering me advice. I kissed her on the cheek, and she asked me how I was. I whispered in her ear: 'I'm happy, Mum, for the first time in my life.' Her long oval face flowered into a smile at this, the pain of two divorces present in her etched brow. As I spoke the vows I thought I could perceive the ghosts of my father and stepfather on opposite sides of the room. Des and Delph hovering palely in facing corners, as transparent and weightless to me as they had been in real life. Also supernaturally present was Ramona, her taut brown skin looped with silver bangles, an impetuous smile on her face. As I said, 'I do', Mandy turned and kissed the bare knuckles of my hand. I believed every word.

After the book had been signed, Rudi approached and gave me a generous Scottish bearhug. He shot Mandy an admiring glance as he spoke into my ear: 'You made the right choice, spunker.' And it was only then that I remembered Bea and her imploring plum-coloured eyes. He linked one arm, and Mandy linked the other, and together we strolled through the gates of ivory.

We walked straight out into a snowstorm of confetti. It was everywhere, in the eyes, the hair, the ears. Blinding, freezing. Only when we climbed onto the rear seat of the Roller did I realise that it was mixed with real snow; the London skies emptying their desultory icy shards on our newly married heads. But I couldn't have cared less: in my heart it was May in January. We roared off along Upper Street to a Spanish restaurant where Antonia, Nick and Martin Drift were waiting, already insensible on cocktails. I was twenty-seven. Mandy only twenty-three.

We're decelerating. Reverse thrust. Descent, but a kind of horizontal descent, as emotionally deflating as the clogged, unresolved end of a bad film. I can see the waxy ghouls of passengers at Potters Bar station. They look like rain-embittered penguins on an outcrop of Arctic rock. And then more: fevered movement in the tired light of the station entrance.

There seems to be ice in the rain, just like on that day in December, illuminated in detail by the spectral platform arc-lights.

What is it with railway stations? Is it the draining sense of purpose everyone seems to exhibit? The conflicting speeds of the concourse-walkers, each with his brolly, tabloid, laden golf-cart. Big stations are nerve-centres of nothing-at-all. Conduits for incognito humanity: dirty and grave. Just apexes, faceless connections, with everyone thrown outwards, centrifugally, once the centre has been achieved. Outwards to the dormitory towns, suburbs of lock-knife pubs and mirrorball clubs with names like *Reflections* or *Manhattans*. Or further out, to the Shires, the shaded cottages, farms, maypole villages, enclaves of serene Middle England. But the stations themselves? Just toilets. Once grand and Victorian, with wrought awnings and spanned arches designed to enshroud the noble slip-streams of coal-burning steam engines, now they seemed merely magnets for every pimp, hustler, pickpocket, scrubber, clipper and scrounger on the planet. The averted eyes of the trussed traveller betray unsavoury contemplations and outright fear as he traverses the piss-river of the main entrance and the flickering letter boxes of the departures board. From station to station. Once trapped within their prison-like perimeters, you just want to escape.

The train is slowing to a standstill. The thrilling sense of departure, present since we left King's Cross, is at an end. As I survey the half-empty platform, I think about Mandy and me, tearing off into the proverbial sunset that December day in the white Rolls Royce. By the end of the evening, Martin and my mother were waltzing on the tables. It was a great night. Mandy in pink; me covered in Rudi's old jizz, happy at last. With everything to live for. Even Montse and Leo buried the hatchet for the evening . . . The thought that it has come to this, that this is its inevitable destination, is nigh on unbearable.

The doors hiss asunder, letting in chilly, forbidding air.

Potters fucking Bar.

Looking back, I feel as if my battle wasn't with Mandy, but with Time itself. Choose the biggest weapon you like, and time will always win. Will always reduce people to their worst possible components. Will always distil a human soul down to a set of appetites, paranoias, grievances. Yeah, that's how those two glammed-up neophytes on the back seat of the white Silver Cloud ended up: a mere list of faults and dysfunctions. Powerless in the pull of the big river – barely human in their chains.

3

This Is Only Temporary

Allow me to tell you something about an experience, a recent experience, that should have taken my mind off all this: I fell in love. For a week. Difficult to believe, I know. It's hard to gauge whether I'm still in love or not, but the ancient Greek dramaturgical laws governing human emotional confluence, the fixed mysteries of astrology, the films of Woody Allen tell me that I probably never was in love: I was mental. That seems to be the state one emerges into after demolishing three years of marriage in one abysmal afternoon. One finds oneself – in all clinical reality – insane.

What happened was this. After the final flat-destroying screaming marathon with *her*, I found myself on the street struggling with an Elastoplast to stem the rich flow of blood from the fingertip she had all but sliced off with a kitchen knife. A meagre palliative, I agree, but that's all I possessed, except twenty cigarettes and my hastily snatched notebooks. My first port of call was Rudi's. His only words of wisdom were: 'Life's a bitch and then you marry one,' although said with such Scottish certainty that I'll only ever be able to hear that aperçu (and I hear it a lot, usually just before

I go to sleep at night) in his accent. Over oily tea on the gentle gradient of his back garden he told me there just happened to be a room going in a croupier's flat in Kentish Town, a share with three others. By the end of the evening, as bruised and bloodied as I was, I had moved in.

That makes it all sound so easy. The *difficulty*, the tragedy, will have to wait. What's important, startling even, is that within a week of separating from my wife I was in a state of unwanted emotional turbulence from a different source. The love-atoms, for the first occasion since I fell for *her*, had been disturbed. It did me good, it did me bad.

Her name was Haidee. Sporty, breeze-fresh Haidee; with her French-speaking Swiss father, her insouciant giggle and her drinking problem. She was tall, with rosy cheeks – a real lifesaver; ripe and real. And it was into her old room that I hurled my life's accumulation of three cardboard boxes. She had already moved out to some stucco edifice in Notting Hill with her boyfriend, but was around the flat a fair amount as a valedictory gesture. She wasn't beautiful, so I know it wasn't lust. At least not conventionally beautiful . . . What is it about attraction? One minute you're platonically negotiating a shared spaghetti, the next their very force-field, their twenty-paces proximity, is transporting you to a state of tremulous arrest. I fell, and I fell hard. Like a rock off a mountain. But then, I was mental.

Let me think about her for a moment: hooded, disappearing, expensively grey eyes under schoolgirl glasses. An exquisitely fine, thin upper lip baring symmetrically sexy teeth. A pinched, intelligent nose that descended almost vertically from her forehead, and (best of all) a swarm of natural auburn ringlets, an unruly explosion framing all of this. If I were to hear her bronchial cough again, or her clear, modulated tones grappling with her wonderful vocabulary ('carnage', 'defiant', 'besotted' – as in, 'Byron, you're fucking besotted with me!') I think my heart would snap like an ice-sculpture under a black-belt's karate chop.

Jesus, this heart – multiply broken.

She was only around for a week, thank God. If I were to draw a chart or graph of that week's emotional traffic it would look something like a straight vertical line: a one-way street. After we'd slept together for the first and only time she spoke to me in French: '*À demain,*' she bronchially whispered, and she wasn't to know I'd waited my whole life for a woman to speak to me in French after sex. Of course, the next morning she fitfully regretted it all. What about reality? The stucco mansion in Notting Hill? The doting boyfriend? The father, due to return any moment, expecting her to be married to a broker? What good was I, the half-crazed virtual *clochard* so recently separated?

I tried flattery, I tried humour, I tried putting my arm around her repeatedly, all to no avail. And I realised then how much we project into the future with new people, how we absent-mindedly imagine buggying their kids around the October-sunned park or opening the vast door to the shared Bayswater townhouse. Or at least people as desperate as me do.

Predictably, our natures conflicted wildly: she was a loose cannon, a hedonist of orgiastic proportions, maybe even an anarchist; I essentially a melancholic with a side-order of suicidal tendencies. But there she was: Haidee – five years my junior and a veteran of boarding, boating, backpacking, nannying in Cairo and the coconut-oiled Caribbean. Someone who met the morning face to face every day without trepidation or neurosis. A butterfly, a free spirit. To love her would be like attempting to bottle the breeze! And me the helpless onanist, the love-blind suitor, the hapless cuckold, the furrowed divorcee, incapable of joining the dance.

When she left it merely served to reinforce life's cruelty. A repetitive pain, like hammer blows to a blacksmith's anvil: again and again and again. As if I hadn't brought enough pain with me in those three cardboard boxes – enough frigid pain to re-snow the French Alps.

O for a heart that pumps Evian water like all the rest, not this thick, soul-sour blood.

★

The flat, then. The shared flat whose walls I now wake up to every morning. Only intended as a temporary measure, like much else. But I've been here for almost three months. Does that count as temporary? When does something cease to be a stop-gap and become officially permanent? And anyway, who's counting days, except me?

Once I moved in it struck me that I had never lived with anyone apart from Mandy. No college dorms or years of co-habiting had prepared me. This state of affairs, I find, requires many complicated and unwanted adjustments. There are three other human beings here, three 'equivalent centres of self', as George Eliot said. All demand a different approach to any interaction; all have their hopes, griefs, passions, love-affairs and job-worries to attend to in their little rooms. I try not to burden them with my woes. Meeting in the communal areas is, it's understood, a highly artificial activity. The human animal naturally needs its space, mental as well as physical. More often than not, I leave them to it.

As for the place itself, it's a four-storey monument to solid Victorian brickwork, now crumbling with a great deal of dignity into the Leighton Road. Could be worse, could be the YMCA (and it nearly was). Actually, there are three floors with a basement flat inhabited by a fetid loner who sometimes shares his whisky with me. But that's another story. My room is on the top floor; Haidee's old room, fifteen feet by fifteen, painted stark peeling-white with an oppressive ceiling and a view into the gardens out back. There is no furniture except a camping table and a folding chair. The bed I had to borrow. It is obvious that all four walls once bore posters. There are rectangles of lighter paint delineated like trunk-marks on a suntan; the pale spaces fringed by yellowing strips where sellotape probably held the grinning behind of that tennis player with her skirt hoicked up. Most of time I try not to look at those empty spaces. Most of the time. Instead, I stare out of the window. It's fair to say that the view has kept me alive for three months. I have spent many hours at the rattling sash window in contemplation. Directly below is an overgrown plot belonging to the loner, wild with tall grass and convolvulus. In mid-October, this ubiquitous vine still had some of its delicate lotus flowers attached: unimpeachable whites with mysterious interiors. At night, the stars can be seen in an unnaturally rich, blue sky. Just recently, the musty smell of bonfires has reached my room as I've lain on the mattress; window flung high, masochistically welcoming the raw autumn air. Mornings have arrived with a ravishing freshness; a pure, dank, peaty odour has risen to my high floor from a bed of mists below. Mellow fruitfulness indeed. But the centrepiece has to be the huge horse chestnut tree two gardens down. Almost as high as the house, I have watched it shed its leaves, bend defiantly in storms, shiver in the ransacking rain. It feels like an old friend. By the end of November I was sad to see the last leaves torn from its noble branches. The area below was a russet carpet; pure gold in the early sun, squirrels jumping in the yellow mulch. Strange how dying can look so beautiful.

On the first landing there's a shared bathroom; a sunless, mouldy little cubicle with a startling lime-green blind that's always kept drawn. Very different from the immaculate bathroom I shared with Mandy. The shelves are full of unfamiliar beauty products, forgotten cosmetics. I'm never sure as to which of the others they belong. There is a pile of blue disposable razors next to bottles of French shampoo, colourful unguents and bath salts. Who could need so many razors? Did a previous tenant leave them as a gift? Am I living with a werewolf? Certainly, the two croupiers keep unsociable hours, and I've only bumped into the classical musician once, when we fumbled good mornings on the stairs, but she didn't look the type to howl at the moon. She seemed shocked that I was still alive. But that's not so surprising. Since throwing my boxes across the maimed carpet of my upstairs room I've only used the kitchen twice. Ah, the kitchen – the best room in the house. The big light-filled kitchen with its three yawning sash windows, where I hear the others coming and going with rustling bags of shopping. Where certain nights I have heard the rumble of dancing, scraping chairs, spontaneous laughter, the odd shriek or familiar song; or have smelt the aroma of fried sausages or home-made popcorn. But I have been in no fit state to join them. No fit state at all.

Take last Wednesday, for example. Three in the afternoon found me crucified on the floor as the day diminished outside. A dripping yellow haze filled the screen of the window. I was trying to get several things straight in my mind, but to no avail. Overall, I felt close to how Nietzsche must have when he threw his arms around the neck of the horse. My main preoccupation, apart from how to deal with the terrible physical and spiritual lethargy that had descended on me in the past two months, was how richly I deserved my fate. No, really. Anyone who thought that people were generally trustworthy and good, were basically sane, deserved to be punished. Such naivety had to have its comeuppance. And here it was, in the shape of an abysmal room with nowhere to sit. A trusting, puerile nature such as mine (who ignored Pascal's maxim and thought that everyone was fundamentally identical underneath) was heading for a severe hiding, a rigorous lesson, an education at some point in his life. The fact was, Mandy had stitched me up. She had come out of the maelstrom emotionally and financially intact. She had the flat, the car, the furniture and probably a clear conscience. That must have taken some planning – a process I was too innocent to observe at the time. Lying there in the sickly twilight I felt numb, stupefied, rejected, nauseous, abused. I also felt dangerously close to hysterical laughter or tears, or both. Really, one had to laugh at the audacity of it all. At my own risible gullibility, aged thirty and four months.

Downstairs, in the spacious kitchen, I could hear the whirr of the washing machine. This put me in mind of a task I had been deferring since nine o'clock that morning. Previously, after a break-up with a girlfriend, I have found myself strangely galvanised and purposeful: some life-instinct or survival mechanism always kicks in, forcing me to make lists of people to phone, tasks to undertake. I often thought this was symptomatic of having no immediate family to discuss my latest emotional catastrophe with. The Self magically takes control, knowing what's best for the organism. But this time things are different. I find I no longer possess that open and artless soul necessary to move on. As Kurt sang, something's in the way. Something to do with hitting thirty and discovering my marriage and nebulous career down the toilet simultaneously. These immovable facts have seized up all impetus towards practical activity. In three months I haven't unpacked those cardboard boxes. And anyway, this place is only temporary, right? Until I find somewhere better. Sitting in the centre of the spattered carpet is a busted suitcase that once held all my books. Only these objects have I hauled out and stacked in dusty piles around the room in the absence of any shelf. Recently, reading has seemed too complex and demanding an act. When I have attempted a page of Descartes or Hardy's poems the words have appeared to be in the wrong order. The more I persevered, the more they seemed to be written in Cyrillic – literally meaningless, the signified detached from the signifier. The same went for writing. I knew I should be fiercely hammering or weeping out a *Blood on the Tracks* or an *Ariel*, but the truth was, I couldn't be fucked. The moment I stopped laughing at my own idiocy, I told myself, I would commence fixing this mess in words. But that moment never came. For once in my life, I let myself drift: blown with Neptune's tides. A freefall without any self-preserving intervention from the Superego. For once, this felt like the right course of action. Besides, I was too depressed and tired to do anything else. Too suicidal to commit suicide.

The bare spaces on the walls where posters once hung remain empty. Honestly, you get so beaten down by failure and humiliation that you can't even assert your own character on your own surroundings. You don't feel entitled to. Besides, it takes energy to put posters up, and that I reserved for thought. Circuitous, exhausting thought; pinning the fat-torsoed moths of memory in their appropriate glass cases.

So, lying there in the diminishing light, tangled up in blue, I felt like a communications centre of intersecting thoughts, intense impulses. Yet paradoxically impotent, unable to act. A rain started up in the gardens out back, spattering the blackened undergrowth.

This reminded me again of my task. My great shame. To wash my borrowed bedsheets, preferably unobserved by anyone in the flat. This, I knew, would necessitate a visit to the laundrette. Because in the early hours of that morning, as astonishing as it may seem, and for the first time since childhood, I had wet the bed.

Yes, go on and have a good laugh, ungentle reader.

Maybe it was the rain in the middle of the night that did it. That set me off. That set *it* off. First a soft purring against the sash window, like hoarse ghosts trying to gain access to the room; then a furious vertical hammering into the barren gardens. That old sound-association must have triggered a hot hosing into my mattress and mould-dappled duvet at three in the morning. I had tried in my half-sleeping, half-conscious state to find a part of the bed that wasn't intimately damp, that wasn't a swimming pool of now-cooling piss, but to my fuddled dismay the whole area seemed to be immersed. I was wet, wet, wet, right up to the armpits of Mandy's dressing gown, an item of clothing which I had taken to sleeping in, as I had snatched hers by mistake in my hasty exit from the flat. But this was too much. I must have staggered out of bed and thrown off the robe only to return and find the mattress much, much damper; the rain still cat-o'-nine-tailing the panes. What was once steamy, almost luxurious, was now cold, grimly alien. Yes, it must have been the rain that caused me to piss the bed, aged thirty, in the middle of the night.

Of course, it wasn't the rain. It was the booze. I had made my way home from Rudi's place in the small hours like a blind forest animal, feeling my way from lamp post to lamp post. We'd had a few to say the least. Just the sheer cc volume would have burst Henry the Eighth's bladder. I remember Martin, that old road-hound, telling me a cast-iron way of deceiving hotel staff if such an accident occurred while on tour. The clever, seasoned boozer would heat a kettle of water in the morning and then upend it on the bed, leaving the whole apparatus lying there innocently for the maids to find when they did their rounds. The band would be long out of town before they discovered the sheets were saturated with a more bodily fluid, thus avoiding a hefty cleaning bill charged to the room. However, this ruse was not of much use to me. The only observer of the sad sight of my drenched bed was me. How did this happen? Was this the summit of my degradation, or was there more to come? I remembered reading an article by a child psychologist citing emotional upset as the chief cause for infantile incontinence, but surely this cannot have contributed to my nocturnal disaster. Was I so fucked up to be experiencing a second childhood? But regardless of the aetiology, something told me I had to act fast, otherwise I would be sleeping under my coat on the floor later that evening. The classical musician, who occupied the room next door to mine, had just returned, sighing audibly as she gained the top of the staircase. Minutes later I heard the muted sound of a viola through the walls: stark and beautiful – rich down the bottom end, full of serpiginous melancholy. It was now or never. I jumped to my feet and stuffed the duvet into a bin-liner. Then I hauled the mattress into the centre of the room, to give it a better airing. The rain had begun to step up, so I closed the window. The downpour started to thunder against the panes; the last light glowing gold in the murky distance. Making sure my sleeves were rolled down (a necessary ritual, as I had been trying to keep the scars inflicted by Mandy a secret from my flatmates) I bolted downstairs and out onto the street.

Luckily, the laundrette was nearby. I opened the smeared door of my machine under the accusing eyes of a gaggle of mums with pushchairs, then bundled the reeking bedclothes inside. The cocktail of those intent watchers and the furtive sense of my own humiliation told me I couldn't stay. Standing there in the dead light, I suddenly realised I was ravenous; that I hadn't eaten for twenty-four hours. I checked my pockets for coins, then fled for the caff over the road, my sad sheets revolving in their drum.

Predictably, the place was almost full. Didn't people have jobs to go to? All these busted losers with days to kill; or workmen reading whole tabloids from breasts to betting tips. How did they get away with it? Having said that, I wasn't in a position to judge.

I seemed to have plenty of time on my scarred hands just lately, Martin having downsized me to one day a week. Even this made me count my blessings, because, until I split with Mandy, I hadn't been working for him at all. A sense of pity must have encouraged him to offer me some paid employment. In fact, only Martin had called regularly to see how I was bearing up over the last couple of months. Unlike Rudi, unlike Antonia and Nick, he knew what the end of a marriage felt like.

I took my seat at the window. The artery-clogging air was dense with the pungent aromas of frying. After ten minutes a Macedonian waiter sullenly took my order for egg and chips – without the toast, as I couldn't stretch to that. I stared at the harried bums and jakeys of Kentish Town, shivering in their sleeping bags outside the tube station. This compelling sight always acted as a reminder of the next rung on the ladder: the bottom rung. My chest felt heavy with the weight of this knowledge; with the intolerable weight of my loathsome self. In fact, I felt as if I had slipped down the biggest ladder on the snakes-and-ladders board. One moment I was snoring under our laundered duvet, the next pissing into a mouldy, semen-streaked sheet purloined from my neighbour's cellar. How had it come to this? I also felt vulnerable, self-conscious, sitting there; as if something terrible were about to happen. Eating solo in the caff had been an unsettling experience to begin with. One felt like a virtual advertisement for the bachelor life, a living, breathing poster of what's in store for the hopeless divorcee. There was also the acute shame I felt at the scars on my forearms, the hunted, desperate look I must always be wearing; and also the fact I only ever ordered the cheapest things on the board. But, after a while, I realised there were other men (nearly always men, apart from the obese bag-lady who sat for hours over a cooling cup of tea) doing exactly the same. I had joined the club. The losers' club. Any age welcome. The newly separated or the mentally ill specially catered for. At first, the hum and noise of the place had been disturbing. The croupier's flat, despite its ramshackle ambience, had served as a sanctuary for me. There was a merciful quiet there most days; a lack of turbulence, raised voices, slammed doors, smashed objects. In contrast, the caff was a zoo of belching brickies, yapping cruel misogynist horseshit in coarse voices. Just lately, I had been unable to overhear anyone talking in an aggressive manner. It made me sick to my very soul. A curious phenomenon. I had to have silence, otherwise my centre was upset for days. Like Keats in his tubercular dilapidation, I could only contemplate beauty. Anything else, I felt, might finish me off for good.

The egg and chips arrived: two yolks of orange pus bathing in an Exxon Valdez of oil. Grimly, I forced myself to eat, though I felt too hungover to get much down. There was also the noise pollution of the radio to deal with. Constantly tuned to an MOR station, last week it had played, consecutively, 'She's Gone' by Hall and Oates, 'One More Night' by Phil Collins and 'Nothing Compares 2 U' by Sinead O'Connor. Yeah, they must've have seen me coming. The sad-sack with his drooping antlers. How I moaned inwardly at the monstrous irony. Some gleeful playlister must have compiled that little selection specifically for the likes of me, buckled over my plate of cholesterol in a greasy spoon some-where. And I was especially not in the mood that morning. As I had crossed the road to the caff, a vintage red VW had nearly run me over at the lights, tearing off into the traffic with a guttural roar. It was Mandy's car. It had to be. There was only a handful of the same model in the country. Hadn't she seen me there, about to cross? Or maybe she had, and that was the point. She was merely attempting what she had always threatened to do: wipe me from the face of the earth. Confirmation that it had been her came ten minutes later: there was the same Volkswagen, with Mandy at the wheel – terse-looking, patrician – driving back in the opposite direction. This, as you can imagine, didn't serve as an *aide-digestif*.

I returned in the tooling rain to the laundrette and rescued my sheets. Inside, the mothers and pushchairs had been replaced by a group of teenage girls; tracksuited, gum-chewing, supremely arrogant. They didn't give me a second look as I wrestled with the ripped bin-liner. This added another cut to my heart. But why should they have checked me out? They had their cool to take care of, their conceited splendour to attend to. Who was I to yearn for attention from teenage girls? Me, balding, just turned thirty, egg on my unshaven chin. I was back on the shelf, and I had better get used to it. Slightly shop-soiled, with a 'reduced' price tag stamped on my forehead. Going cheap in the sales.

Later that evening, I carried out another task that I had been putting off for much longer than washing my bedclothes: returning my set of keys to the flat Mandy and I had once shared. A registered psychotherapist (or Randy Newman) could probably give you a better explanation as to why I had held on to them for so long. I set off on this dreaded mission after draping my duvet from the single coat hook on the back of my door. I took one last look at my garret, as if I wasn't expecting to see it again for some time. Like Mr Bleaney's room, it was laughably austere. Is *this* all I had accumulated? The sodden mattress in the centre; the scoured ashtray; the sad socks. It suddenly struck me that the room was very familiar. Its layout was identical to my first room in Hamford, the one I moved into aged eighteen when shuttling between the houses of two indifferent parents had become too much to bear. The bed was in the same position next to the window. There was the same lack of a cupboard, the same veneered camping table with its pile of coins next to a comb. So I had come full circle, then. How we live measuring our own nature.

The walk took some time. I had spent my last pennies in the caff and was without the bus fare to get to the Haringey Ladder, where Mandy and I spent our last miserable months. I literally didn't know where my next meal was coming from. After the noxious ghouls at the bank had closed me down, asking me to return my cashpoint card 'cut into four pieces', Mandy and I had opened a shared account, but my access to this had ceased the afternoon we split. Ah, the mesmerising ongoing humiliation of not having a bank account, aged thirty. I had no credit anywhere. Anyone who hasn't been in this position might romantically conjecture that such a fix would free the soul to concentrate on its higher aspirations. A very middle-class notion. They might see it as a glorious, poetic unfettering. Hell, when you got nothing, you got nothing to lose! Just think of Van Gogh or Soutine. Or of Jackson Pollock, ploughing his Ford into the fatal tree with only a hundred and fifty bucks to his name. But they would be wrong. Walking around with no money in your pocket – no money to your name, anywhere on earth – and with no idea of how to go about getting any – is terrifying. It's like driving a car with the needle constantly on empty, on red. There is the same pervasive sense of insecurity and imminent disaster. And after a while it can affect your personality. Everything becomes provisional. If you were a political system, an analyst would say you were afflicted with short-termism. You can't plan further than the middle of tomorrow afternoon. Once a stoical person, you become a fearful person. Eventually, the post starts to scare you to death. Another bill or a bailiff's notice? Either way, they're having a fucking laugh. You become a trembling suppliant, racking your brains for anyone to borrow from whose patience you haven't already exhausted; grateful for any titbit that happens to fall from life's table. It also alters your physical posture. I looked at the human flotsam and jetsam on the sluiced, neon-lit Tufnell Park Road (all reduced to this for want of a few quid! This indignity! Each a human life!) and shivered inwardly. People who never had any money looked deformed, bent out of shape. They never grew straight and strong. Somewhere along the line they'd been fatally negligent – or unlucky – concerning this vital resource, money. Forget the rich being different to us, it was the poor who belonged to another species. The more savvy I became about the world (and believe me, sagacious reader, it took a number of years), the more I came to realise that nearly *everyone* had a bit tucked away somewhere: shares, peps, ISAs, second accounts, nice little earners, small inheritances, pension-schemes, batty rich aunts twice removed, family heirlooms – stuff they could draw on when the going became choppy. Whereas I had the contents (or non-contents) of my wallet. Fucking scary. These people had obviously done some hard thinking about money and the consequences of not having any. What was I up to when they were doing all that serious, remunerative thinking? Writing poems, that's what.

I reached the Archway roundabout, that magnet for hedge-haired nutters and whippet-thin tarts who always seemed to be bleeding slightly from the nose. I felt unable to go any further, my stomach full of a churning, gnawing heat; a fatal heaviness in my limbs. The worst depression I had ever experienced: a Sisyphean effort to get through each minute. I sensed I was expiring somehow from a bottomless, untreatable despair. The harsh wind Ferraried around the gyratory system, dragging with it, in the gutter, the discarded financial pages from the *Evening Standard*, a halved bottle of Becks, a slew of chicken parts. To the north was the mysterious tunnel of the Archway Road, spanned by its Suicide Bridge, leading to Highgate and Hampstead with their secure implacable wealth. To the south the massed lights of the City, a lurid glare hanging over the hidden chasms of Bishopsgate, of Threadneedle Street, a crimson inferno seen from a miry summit. Once the human components have left a city – have ceased their ant-like industry, their ferment of activity – all that's left is the garbage; a life-vacuum. I felt disgusted with my fellow humans, all fleeing homeward from the light-ringed maw of the tube, ignoring the imploring arms of beggars. I shouted into the crowd, ashamed at my bitterness, my mad unshaven face: 'Go on! You can afford it, you bastards!' The sound of my own voice surprised me. The only other sentence I had spoken that day was when ordering the glutinous egg and chips. The usual, seething thoughts assailed me. How base, stale, unprofitable, et cetera. Then I remembered my mission. My talismanic act of emancipation. I grasped the keys in my pocket, jangling in their plain envelope. I felt I had to divest myself of these symbolic objects. The first step in letting go.

When I finally reached the crest of Seaham Road I realised something was wrong with the street. In fact, something was wrong with the whole area, it just hadn't struck me until I rounded an all-too-familiar bend in the road. There were no lights anywhere. Not a streetlamp or a glow from behind a curtain. There had obviously been a powercut, a regular occurrence in that crumbling nook of north London. The houses stood in eerie silence. What was everyone doing? Crouching by candlelight indoors? Engaged in seances or exorcisms? I looked to the skies, but cloud cover allowed no light. As I approached our old place, a feeling of panic began to rise at the back of my throat. I felt engulfed, threatened. I quickened my step until I reached the front door last seen during my bloodied exit three months ago. As quiet as the grave. I looked up at our old bedroom window. Nothing stirring. I glanced around for Mandy's car. Not present. She must be elsewhere – probably out, spending money, laughing; accepting the lecherous hands of strangers on her superlative behind. No, there was nobody home at our old address. Just blackness, the void. How strange to return and find this funereal emptiness. I had thought the flat was for ever, just as I had thought marriage was for ever. But these were just other examples of my childishness. Naive notions that I must yield to experience, must accept my punishment for. I shoved the keys through, and ran as fast as I could towards the light.

———

Three Decembers ago it was all very different. The day after our wedding found Mandy and me thirty-thousand feet over the grey English Channel. The plane touched down at Barcelona's great airport with something like a long seraphic sigh. On the flight, they had played 'Silent Night' the whole way. The terminal was on the city's outskirts, close to the Olympic Village. I felt intolerably euphoric to be out of London. Once on the tarmac, the air itself carried good vibrations: warm, sweet; slightly scented with intimations of the sea. Mandy kissed the still trembling knuckles of my hand (my first flight in seven years) as she welcomed Spain. So this was what a honeymoon felt like, a holiday from the tired commercial extravaganza that was Christmas in England. A glutted suburb of shanty towns and ghostly buses was the first thing that met our eyes as we cabbed it to the hotel Mandy's father had stumped up for. The journey took half an hour, the streets becoming gradually more salubrious. A black Mercedes here, a Gaudí building there. Eventually we arrived at the gold-thronged entrance. The Royal on the Plaça Catalunya, high as the smudged offices of *La Vanguardia* opposite; with a mini Christmas tree in its own little tub on every balcony. We threw our cases onto the plump double bed, deliriously in love. Later, I went out onto the cramped terrace, fifteen storeys above the street, and breathed deep of life, the future; marriage. I could see couples out late strolling arm in arm; the illuminated ants of cars tearing around the square. My wedding ring felt strange on my finger. It caught gleams from the hooded nineteenth-century streetlamps. Down below, Las Ramblas was festooned with green neon Christmas lights, proclaiming *Bon Nadal, Sí, Sí, Sí, Las Ramblas, Sí!* I thought briefly about Matt Arnold and his desultory honeymoon at Dover, all twisted up over blind armies clashing by night, mourning the sound Sophocles once heard on the Aegean. That old misery guts! He obviously didn't have Mandy with him, slipping into a pink baby-doll nightdress on the big bed behind, cooing his name. Now, that might have cheered him up.

We stayed for five days, high on each other's company, on the mere change of scenery. I felt as if my blood had been cleaned and re-transfused into my body. On Christmas Day itself, we found a number of shops and restaurants open. I remember walking past a jeweller's and having a sudden impulse to buy a crucifix, to have the icon next to my mortal skin. I asked Mandy to purchase it for me, as she said she wanted me to choose my present. I explained, as we walked around the ancient sanctity of the Gothic Quarter, that even tortured agnostics had urges for religious symbolism, had intimations that they should *make a start* on the big questions before it was too late. We spent the rest of the day in the Parc Güell, with Gaudí's kaleidoscopic mosaics blue in the wintry sun, the sound of a flute from the catacombs below. Orpheus playing for the recently united couple.

Every night we ate at the same restaurant on the Passeig de

Gràcia, as it had been so exquisite the first time. Every night we had the same dish: *merluza a la plancha* with the best chips this side of Brussels, Mandy talking flirtatious Catalan to the gimlet-eyed waiters. On the last day, before we caught our train for Tarragona, and the flat of that dynamic duo Montserrat and Leo, I persuaded Mandy to wear *my* Christmas present to her. Stridently secular in contrast to her gift, my offering was a top-dollar black-and-scarlet basque, a suspender belt, sheer silk stockings and a pair of virtual knickers that probably weighed less than a Kleenex. Why are men smitten by such vulgar visual stimuli? I had spent many hours pondering this question, often reaching a conclusion that was more physical than intellectual, and had made the deduction that men are conditioned by pornography from an early age. A vast repertoire of sexual images has been assimilated by the time a boy reaches fifteen. All a woman has to do is provide some of these images in the correct context and bingo, he's yours for eternity. It really is that simple, girls, that Pavlovian.

All day we dodged mopeds and overdressed Barças as Mandy fought to pull the hem of her skirt over the stocking tops; or stopped vexedly on road islands to re-clip the garter belt or yank the thong from between her outraged buttocks. Yes, it takes a lot of getting used to this clobber, a lot of maintenance, but in the end the results are worth the effort (for me at least). Later, on the plump double bed, joined sweetly at the pelvis, Mandy undulating beneath me in a brothel's worth of black, I made a mental note to thank the ghost of Franco for allowing Montserrat's family to live when Barcelona fell in 1939. As our rhythm increased, Mandy holding me by the stem as I slid effortlessly into her, she gently tugged on my lower lip with her teeth. I noticed her eyes were fixed in concentration behind their lids, as if willing some primeval alchemy within. A series of trapped, high-pitched noises made an effort to be vocalised, her shoulders jumping with every thrust. Then she came with a heavenly expulsion of air from the throat, the sensual woman at last central in her sometimes sexually awkward persona. Yes, no matter what else you can say about our marriage, she always came in the end, did Mandy.

Tarragona was different. I had been fearing a repeat of the fire-works witnessed at Slough. In the end, no such nonsense occurred. We arrived at Leo's sea-facing apartment in the early hours, having taken the late train. There we were welcomed by both the dutiful aunt and Montse, the old woman gesticulating and congratulating us in a mixture of Catalan, English and Castilian. She looked as if she were conducting Rachmaninov. They had touched down from their visit to London only the night before, so we had to endure endless dramatic replays of their six unfortunate hours spent with a mob of England fans in the Heathrow departure lounge. 'Pigs, all of them! I always said British men were pigs,' spat Montserrat. 'Except you, *guapo*,' she smiled at me. Mandy always found these demonstrations amusing, like voices from another era. The puce stone floors of the flat echoed to our every footstep. At night, bats could be seen swooping through the Moorish arches of the patio, the ocean distant and salt-flavoured. One evening, towards the end of our stay, Leo put her excitable mother to bed early, after preparing for her the regular meal of nuts and *Caballa del norte*, part of a special diet insisted upon by her doctor. Leo, Mandy and me sat around the simple kitchen table drinking Calvados, the stiff greying aunt appreciably relaxed for a moment. Although thin-shouldered, she was stout in the hips. Pear-shaped and slightly ungainly. If one were unkind, one would describe the flesh moving like blobs in a lava lamp. Her hirsute upper lip – common in Spanish women, and over which they expend so much self-conscious anguish – was also striking, although I never minded this sight, reminding me, as it did, of Frida Kahlo's self-portraits. In her mumsy voice, Leo said, 'Well, I suppose the next thing will be children.'

Mandy and I looked at each other, wondering who should answer this. Of course, Mandy got there first.

'Come on. You know I've got my three babies, and anyway the

band comes first. I have to do this while there's still time. Look at Mum, running around for everyone else until it killed her.'

By her three babies, she meant her three sullen tomcats. Leo understood this before Mandy had completed her sentence, and allowed a sigh to whisper from her prim nose.

'Cats don't count,' said Leo, studying Mandy's face.

'Yeah, and your mum still managed the time to have you,' I volunteered.

Mandy flashed her irresistible smile. 'Don't tell me you want kids! Anyway, I'm too young. Help me out here, Byron!'

Leo was thinking how to reply. The mention of Ramona didn't help either. I could see a certain extra-sensitivity in her brown eyes. Some people wear their souls on the exterior; any incremental change or undermining is immediately made manifest in a physical tremor or tic. They are emotional weathervanes, tilting in response to deeply felt suffering.

'But every woman wants children,' said Leo, faintly smiling, emphasising the word 'every'.

I thought about this assertion for a while. Yes, in theory, every woman had her biological destiny to fulfil, a desire that should come naturally. But with Mandy I wasn't so sure. Something told me that, like Lady Macbeth, she had the capacity to suppress her womanly impulses, had unsexed herself somehow. One only notices the milk of human kindness in its absence. More than once she had brashly proclaimed that she hated screaming tots. Not a good start, I thought. And her stock answer about the cats was, I knew, a cop-out. They weren't so much her children as her toys, her underlings, something to control.

'Not every woman wants kids under their feet,' persisted Mandy. 'Some take care of their careers first. And you know the problems I've had. I get too ill. The doctors said I had an eighty per cent chance of being infertile.'

It was true that Mandy had been treated for endometriosis in her teens, hospitalising her for weeks. It was quite possible that she was barren. But this fact, I suspected, was a source of relief for her;

a good reason to avoid the issue of whether she *wanted* a child. Also, somewhere among Mandy's rebuttals, I knew she was alluding to Leo's childless state. It only occurred to me later that Leo's question might have cost her some anguish to ask. After all, her marriage ended mysteriously in the sixties, and she never had any children. One didn't like to ask why. At the time of this conversation, I thought of Leo as an almost comically timid presence. Transparent and vulnerable. But now I see her as very brave – another example of my people-blindness.

I addressed both of them, in an effort to allay the waves of Spanish passion that were beginning to stir in the night air. 'Kids are expensive. I don't think either of us could afford all that at the moment. Plus it's a difficult question when your family background has been so . . . disrupted. You think twice about bringing another life into the world. It's not a given that you automatically want to continue the species. Perhaps you don't want them to go through the same trials, the same rubbish.'

'Exactly,' said Mandy in triumph. 'Look at my old man and what he did. This—' she pointed to the erratic white scar on her forehead, '—will last a lifetime.'

Mandy often griped about her father hitting her and, once, pushing her through a glass door, causing the scar she was so self-conscious about. For some reason, I never quite bought this. I waited to see if Leo's response confirmed the accusation.

'Well, that was an accident. Your father did what he had to do to bring you up. You were spoilt from an early age – a spoilt only child. That's why you're so pushy. You think the world owes you something. Well, it does not. I can tell you all about that. As you get older, it's what you owe other people that matters. Duty is the most important thing, especially in families. Look at your grandmother: if she didn't have me to cook, clean, tidy up after her, she'd be in a home. You remember that one we saw in Valencia. It was like a Nazi camp. Now, would you like to see your granny there?'

Leo was the only person who could genuinely subjugate Mandy.

Perhaps some of that motherly authority hit the spot. Montserrat, on the other hand, didn't receive such latitude from my pushy darling. This was because, for a large period of Mandy's childhood, the old señora has been in charge of her upbringing. She had moved to England during the seventies to allow Ramona to get on with *her* career. They had installed her in a semi in Slough with a little Mini, a necessary move, as she had clashed with Mandy's father over virtually everything from the start. 'That evil man!' she would moan. And the car was a mistake. Shortsighted and short-fused, she was possibly one of the most dangerous drivers this side of a blind paraplegic.

'Of course we couldn't dump her there,' said Mandy. 'But she runs rings around you. This special diet thing. I'm sure she only does it to give you more work, to make herself feel important. Like a popstar. Did you ever check with the doctor that she needs any of that stuff? *Caballa del norte en aceite vegetal!* Almonds from Africa! It's so expensive.'

'That's as may be,' said Leo firmly. 'But when I'm dead and gone, you'll have the pleasure of looking after her. She's bound to outlive us all.'

Mandy poured the Calvados and lit another cigarette, expelling the first puff like a whale spouting water. The candles trembled as a breeze made its way through the apartment. She had no answer for Leo at the moment. Plus she had to exercise caution – Leo and Montse had bequeathed a substantial cash wedding gift, after all. But I saw something of the virulence of Mandy's female rivalry, how personally she took other women's attitudes towards her, their mere presence. In her mind they were all jealous: of her looks, her youth, her band; or were trying to coerce her into dull, dutiful lives like their own. She really liked to throw her weight around, especially with other women. More than once, I noticed that other females were slightly scared of her, this stormy spitfire, this untameable firebrand. Also, behind all the talk of biological destinies, and my own exhortations about unstable families and money, there was the intuition that I could never trust Mandy with one of our children.

I, too, was secretly relieved that a Harley Street doctor had pronounced Mandy almost certainly infertile. She was far too capricious, aggressive, irresponsible. Her attention span was too short for the lifetime's task of bringing up a child with diligence and love. I could imagine her coming back from the supermarket saying that she knew she'd forgotten something, but she couldn't quite remember what. Olive oil . . . pasta . . . oh, yes, the kid! Or stabbing the poor child in the head with a fork because it chewed its food too loudly, a pet hate that caused her almost psychotic exasperation.

Leo concluded the discussion in her slightly patronising, sing-song voice, 'Maybe it's too early to think about little ones at the moment.' She patted Mandy's exposed shoulder. 'You hold on to your figure, dear.' This elicited a sharp look from Mandy. She would get her own back one day.

'Anyway, it's late. Tomorrow's New Year's Eve,' I said, brightly.

Mandy frowned. I was getting to learn that she really was a great sufferer; a theatrical, Olympian sufferer. 'Yeah, and I've got a migraine coming on.'

New Year's Eve was our last full day in Spain. The flight was booked for the following afternoon. The migraine that Mandy had threatened us all with did indeed appear in the morning. Well, it was always hard to tell with Mandy whether she was swinging the lead for England. Would she take medication for an ailment she didn't have? It wasn't beyond her. One thing was for certain, when she did become ill – usually when she found herself slipping from centre-stage – she got the attention right back again. Lunchtime saw me affixing a cold compress to her fermenting forehead in the darkened room, then running from chemist to chemist to score the horse-pill preventatives that she claimed were the only remedy. She was sick several times; both Leo and Montse fussing around the locked toilet door, wondering if they should call the doctor out. By five o'clock, with the prospect of a good party, her condition magically began to alleviate. The plan had been to see in the New Year with Leo and Montse – including the ritual of the twelve grapes, one on each stroke of the clock – then make a rapid exit and find some young people after so many days of being cooped up with the fogeys.

As the bewitching hour approached, announced by a dapper Spanish newsreader, we all stood and toasted the future, cava foaming in tall champagne flutes, the sad silver Christmas tree throwing artificial reflections around the room. For no good reason I suddenly wondered what Bea was doing – in that exact moment. They had an hour still to go in England, but maybe she wasn't in England. Who was she with? Was she happy? Just before the wedding I had returned to my Camden flat to pick up the mail. In among the wadge of demands for money and technicolour junk mail was, to my heart-racing surprise, a card from Bea. She said she was back in Hamford: she wondered how I was, how my writing was going. Very sweet, very considerate. Reading between the lines wasn't difficult. One could fall between those lines. Drown in that deep water. After much thought, I sent her a card back, telling her I had married Mandy. I knew that may hurt her. The unnatural haste, the fact that I had a wife named Mandy. But I would rather she heard it from me. I felt a sudden twinge, a heart-surge of love, guilt, self-hatred; standing there with my glass raised like a fool, the twelve grapes ready in my sweaty palm.

After the chimes, we took a rattling cab down to the seafront, where we proceeded to get enthusiastically drunk. The youth of Tarragona screamed past on their mopeds; primary colours flashing in an unrestrained fiesta, horns tooting. In the small hours we walked onto the beach. The night was still pitch, the tide out, with breakers foaming in the very dim distance. A layer of fog hung in a ghostly wreath out at sea, with faint harbour sounds emanating from the gloom. A horn groaned low and long. There had been a tension between me and Mandy all day. We immediately found ourselves in an escalating argument; over what, I can't remember. All I do remember was that it was vicious, both of us too drunk to care what we were saying, hurling abuse at each other as the waves moaned their eternal sound a quarter of a mile down the level beach. Then I turned around and she was gone. She had deserted me, in the middle of a strange Spanish town, me with no lingo and no pesetas to get back. The argument had been over something very petty. In Barcelona, I recalled us having coffee and *turrones* together, talking and laughing, when I accidentally dropped a sugar cube into my cup, splashing her cashmere scarf. Her eyes had flashed venom. 'You clumsy idiot,' she had spat. I was astonished at how quickly she could switch. From zero to one hundred within seconds. Apologies had been useless. I was sorely wounded by this, for deep childhood reasons – I couldn't stand discordant scenes over food, it made me heartsick, shaky, inconsolable. I felt the same hurt, desertion, woundedness, walking along the sea-wall, not knowing where I was heading, and on my honeymoon too. After an hour a cab sidled up and stopped, its amber light revolving like a squad car. Mandy's voice called from the window, her face in deep shadow. She said, 'Are you coming or what?'

During the silent drive back to the flat, on the first day of the new year, I could still feel the powerful wind of the beach on my face; still smell the raw, female emanations of the sea. In my ears was the sound of the black breakers crashing onto the pebbled shore, mixed with the terrible things we had said. The sound of the waves put me sharply in mind of Arnold again and his metaphysical miseries. What a change – from Barcelona to this in a matter of days. How brief is the joy, I thought. The poet spoke truly when he said you have to catch it as it flies.

And now we are flying. Or at least it appears that way. Over a viaduct that has suddenly split the Hertfordshire fields. The exhilaration of height! I can see car headlamps down below, finding their way through distant fields; dipping, disappearing. The pattern made by the streets explicit at last. Can't make out much, as there is a horizontal drizzle on the train's window – brushed on with a witch's broomstick. This view always looks magnificent in full daylight, an unexpected lift as your express tears through the commuter towns. Now the diminished light allows only a fragmentary glimpse. My eyes strain to focus in the miasma-gloom. One hundred feet down is a mini-roundabout, a dot at the centre of a village, its sparse streetlamps Victorian and comforting, the tiny cars gently braking in opposing directions, their Christmas beams bright in the dusk. We must be somewhere near Welwyn Garden City – still javelining our way northwards. In the distance, beyond the glut of jammed car parks and office-space-to-let, there is a cluster of newly built homes advertising their promise of soul-death. This is where your life's journey ends, they seem to proclaim: under the brown-tiled roof, next to the too-new fences, the unspoilt mica-macadam driveways, the fitted bathrooms and kitchens that must annihilate the spirit just to enter them.

The ground is rising to meet us, just as the runway does when the plane releases its undercarriage. Soon we will be back on the level track, sunk in its valley of rising banks and impenetrable trees . . . Catch these moments while you can – that seemed to be the dispensation of my honeymoon. And here I am on the rumbling, streaking train, suffering like a fool for not doing so; for expecting longevity. But that's what you get for surrounding yourself with unscrupulous, coercive, flagrant, equivocal, *no-good* people. Actors who take advantage of the sincere, the meek. Was I always so meek? So Easy? In comparison to Mandy, yes. The proverbial town just wasn't big enough for her and anyone else. She was a glossy, brash, rambunctious character, and I was her whipping boy. Strange how we both went along with the pretence that I was her husband. Most of the time I felt I was the target of her vengeance, of past scores that hadn't been settled. How could I have missed this in her? Just one good look at her would have told me that she was an individual bent on revenge. Revenge on her father; on boyfriends who didn't let her have her own way; on men in general. The awful memory of the night-beach in Tarragona has forced a prickly sweat to my forehead. After that debacle, as I remember, things only got worse. From time to time I was put in mind of St Jerome's *Adversus Jovinianum*: 'For three things the earth trembles: if a servant becomes a king; if a fool is filled with bread; if a hateful woman has a good husband.'

Along the corridor of the carriage I can see that people have settled in for the journey. There is a conflation of smells: rich camembert from feet that have slipped the protective harbour of their shoes; the laundered odour of Michelle and Robin opposite, now once again deep in their chick-lit, their lad-lit. Then the musty brush of an old lady as she waddles past towards the smoked-glass partitions, requiring a held breath. There is also the milky waft of a child a couple of seats down. Earlier, the peace had been shattered by his high-pitched shrieks: 'Aiieeowh!' followed by 'Aaargghgoogle!' culminating in a stark request, 'Mummy, I need a poo!' Now I can see that he is sleeping, the mother and son slumped in a touching pietà, her hand gently stroking his hair. How I could use that touch! Did I ever receive such a touch from my mother? Is that tenderness deep within me now: redemptive, stored; like a nest-egg of transmitted love?

I take out my notebook. *Where did all that childhood love evaporate to? Where is the slanting expanse of May? The canopied trees, the joyous light and snowstorming blossom?*. . . No, poetry won't help me now. Keep it rational . . . *I have come to the conclusion that the more one looks objectively at people, the more unattractive they become. Everyone is implicated in time, everyone corrupted. Their faults pile up; even outright dangerous characteristics not noticed before. We should check people more thoroughly beforehand. Like stones dropped in a clear stream, we must watch the ripples widen then gradually disappear, until that deceptive clarity returns. This is how we should sound out others around us. But people rarely give us this opportunity. The real information is concealed. More often than not, the current flows in one direction between two lovers. It's always one soul seeking, the other retreating. One reality* imposing, the other hiding. Only rarely does another's soul appear to fly and be separate from its cage of flesh – like a butterfly. A white summer butterfly. This is what we look for. What we wait for . . . I am over-excited and exhausted at the same time. Pulverised by the past; always on the verge of some mental collapse. Why would I think my mother, or indeed anybody, would want to see me in this state? I should get off at the next station and hitchhike back to London. I am not good company. My spirit is heavy and drags everyone around me down – like a rock in a stream. Full of strong existential pain, mental upheaval; wiped-out; soul-sick; suicidal; brimming with high-pressure anxiety and childish torments; metaphysically troubled; unable to read, write, sit, think or make a phone call. No, I'm no use to anyone . . . And at the same time we are all wrestling with futures, trying to bend others to our will; trying to free ourselves from others simultaneously. And why this ever-present tang of degradation? A shitty odour of belittlement, introduced by the actors one gets tangled up with: people who think they've got your measure, got you all worked out, down to a T. This is what degrades human dignity, because, to them, you are static and not kinetic. And this is wrong. A human being always has an unstable definition, is always amorphous, protean. A butterfly.

Why am I soiling my mind with this ugliness? I must think of the lives of the artists, the poets, the scribblers . . . Chaucer in his room on the London Wall, writing his masterpieces after a hard day's graft at the customs office; Herbert and his evenings of music in Salisbury; Shakespeare and Jonson swilling Southwark nights away; Dickens chained to his desk, dreaming novels in his head on his daily walk; Marvell overhearing the dialogue between his soul and body; Wordsworth contemplating Newton's statue at Cambridge, his own mind moving through strange seas of thought alone; Dante standing in the fuming street and reading for hours; Eliot scribbling after a long day at Lloyds; Larkin tossing off a piece of genius after his evening wank; Thackeray with his beady eye on the patrons of his cigar-smoky club; Sidney taking out his notebook while on a hunt; Hart Crane under the glittering Brooklyn Bridge; Yeats in his tower by moonlight, his mind moving like a long-legged fly on the stream . . . No, this will not do either. I let the pen settle on the page. I must return mentally to Mandy, to the life we tried to have together. The home we tried to build.

———————

The return flight from Tarragona revealed a London shivering under a full blanket of January fog. The change in temperature was the first thing that hit us. From the genial fragrant breezes of the Mediterranean to the rigorous, nipping cold of England. Swirls of icy hail were tornadoing across the tarmac as we made our way to the luggage belts. And I never did get used to flying. For Mandy there was nothing more straightforward. She had chastised me as I trembled in the cramped airline seat: 'You and your death-obsession. You should have someone close to you die, then you'd know what it was all about.' She wasn't far wrong on both counts. It was an obsession, and it was nearly all theoretical. Air travel, I decided, puts you uncomfortably face to face with your own mortality, usually at a time when you least need it. On your honeymoon, for example. The cringing fatalist always imagines that something very bad will succeed something very good, as if the world ever ran on such easily demarcated lines. And for people as morbid as me, death was an ever-present thought on a plane, startlingly juxtaposed with the streamlined comforts of the cabin, the crisp hostesses and in-flight tray (even that, for me, resonated with the convict's last meal).

I suppose it was the totality of the carnage that terrified me. Each body would be subjected to what surgeons gravely term 'massive trauma'. In a car, there was always the chance that you could walk away from the smoking upturned wreck, but with a plane, if anything went wrong, that was it. A comprehensive snuffing out of every soul on board was what one could look forward to. But, strikingly, most air passengers didn't seem concerned about this possibility. Had they all made terms with death before they boarded the plane? Had they all commended their souls to the everlasting? Had they all revised their wills and prepared their visas for a possible afterlife between check-in and duty-free? I often thought about what those last moments would be like, as all aboard knew they were certainly done for. There would be a crude re-appearance of certain atavistic traits, an animal panic that would be horrible to behold in the final seconds before impact. Maybe people would claw the window frames or jump from the exits, like cattle entering an abattoir; a futile, blazing-eyed survival instinct taking over. People would foul themselves. Would say inadmissible, heart-breaking things to the strangers next to them. Would pray out loud. Would perform Hail Marys up to the last split-second. No, I wouldn't want that tableau to be the last thing I witnessed on this earth.

When I returned to Rock On, in the first icy week of the year, I asked Martin whether he was scared of flying. After all, if he were to be believed, he spent most of the seventies in the air. The shop was empty, except for a shifty Goth pinning something to the Musicians Wanted board.

Martin said, 'Nah, what happens is you get used to the fear. You also get a bit cocky. The worst never happens. Tells you that nothing's inevitable.'

'But aren't you unable to think of anything else, every second of the way? Doesn't it make the bread roll and reheated lasagne stick in your throat?'

'When your number's up, it's up, old chum. Anyway, I was always pissed. The best thing is to get totally wankered in the departure lounge, then load up on miniatures once you're aboard. That way you never notice the grim reaper.'

I observed that his face was inflamed under its barnacles of bristle. An angry red, sore to the touch. The old scars playing up as they formed their endlessly fascinating landscape. Must be the cold, I thought. Or maybe it was all this talk of death, of transition, that was eliciting an unconscious reaction. Although Mart liked to bluster it out on the big subjects, I knew he was unusually sensitive to such discussion. He hated abrupt change of any kind. 'Tick along and you can't go wrong,' was his mantra.

'Yeah, but what about the next world, if there is one? Fancy having to deal with that after the in-flight film.'

Martin smiled, tapping a Marlboro onto the back of the red and white pack in readiness to light it. 'Well, if there is a heaven, I get to meet Hendrix, Jim Morrison and Marc Bolan.'

'I don't think they'd let you join their band, Martin.'

The Goth vacated the shop, leaving the tinging sound of the bell and a vapour trail of patchouli oil. I felt as if I were trying to explore fundamental metaphysical questions with a brick wall. Apart from a general fear of snuffing it (after all, he had come closer than most), Martin never had any such existential difficulties. On a day to day basis, he didn't concern himself with the fact of dying; the dread of the grave. Even less the torment or boredom that the soul may or may not suffer afterwards. So I had to let the subject go. Of course he had asked about Barcelona, about Tarragona. And of course, I told him the tellable bits. My first instance of making excuses for Mandy and her behaviour, something I would become an expert in later. But I had learnt not to talk to Martin about negative incidents. He often said I was exaggerating, that I was a wussy scribbler of gay verse. 'Oh, you're not having another "poetic experience"!' he would explode, making the inverted commas sign in the air. 'Leave it out, you ponce! We've got customers to deal with. Do you think some kid ready to start his rock 'n' roll career wants to come in here and see you looking like a wet weekend? When all he wants is a shiny red Stratocaster? Instead, he gets bloody Wordsmith, up his own arse again.'

'It's Wordsworth, Martin.'

'Okay. Morrissey, whoever. Thank God they banned him from making records.'

I allowed him these outbursts at the time. Besides, he had his own marital difficulties to deal with. His missus had offered him an ultimatum: either they found somewhere else to live, or she took the children to Margate to live with her mother. This was due to an unsettling incident the previous week on the piss-slippery corridors of his high-rise. One of Martin's daughters had been attacked by a pit bull in the council block. His child, still in hospital, had been lucky to escape with scars to her legs. The dog had been put down. The Drifts had been told that it belonged to a couple on the next floor. But it didn't. It was a dealer's dog. In the past year the flats had become a centre, a veritable bazaar, for skag and crack. Martin's wife had pressurised him for months to find a better place in which to bring up two children. This was the final straw. And for Martin, who had lived there since Thatcher came to power, who hated change of any kind, it signified an unthinkable upheaval.

The old rocker ran his graceful hands through his greying locks. He said decisively, 'But if there's a music shop up there, that lot will be in every five minutes for equipment they smashed up on stage.'

At that moment the door to the shop opened, and the first real customer of the day made his entrance. It wasn't the ghost of Hendrix, it wasn't even that bloke from the Yardbirds who'd electrocuted himself while plugging in his guitar at his home studio. It was a loping, Irish character known to us both. His name was Pat Coffer, a space-cadet extraordinaire from Martin's seventies rock odyssey. He never spent any money. More often than not he wanted to borrow some. And if it wasn't forthcoming, he'd always nick something. After five years, we still couldn't work out how he did it.

Martin groaned and put on his brave, business face. Pat approached the counter with that curious walk of his that seemed to be the result of a prosthetic limb, but was probably drugs-related. An ex-junkie, he was now a committed alcoholic. It was obvious that he'd been at the sauce early.

'Hello fellas,' he said in his seductively gravel-timbred voice. 'I've got a business proposition for you both.'

'Why do those words make my heart sink, Pat?' said Martin, hiding his packet of Marlboros.

'No, this one's sound. It's a definite pissability.'

'Pitch it in a single sentence, Pat. We might get some real trade in here at any moment.'

'Eurovision, next year. I met this fantastic bird down the Electric Ballroom. Sings like an angel. And if she ain't up to it, I can pretend to be her. If I can still get up there. All I need is the perfect song. You still writing, Martin?'

It was true that old Pat could sing like anyone you could think of. He could do a convincing Diana Ross followed by an authentic Rod Stewart in the twinkle of a diaphragm. The only problem was that the woman from the Electric Ballroom was almost certainly an alcoholic, beyond forty and only shagging him until the Eurovision dream went up in reefer smoke.

Martin said, 'I haven't written more than a shopping list in twenty years. Try Byron, he's got it going on.'

With that, Martin rather ungraciously disappeared into the back room. He never could stand Pat's bullshit. Pat called out, 'Make us a cuppa, Mart!'

Ah, yes, tea. Pat would always extort a cup of tea, before the expert cadge of a twenty, or anything we could afford. He owed his landlord. He owed his mother in Cork. He owed Simon Napier-Bell for those demos in 1978. I remember Martin telling me the whole Patrick Coffer saga once. Pat really did have every opportunity going for him in the seventies. A golden larynx, half-good rugged looks, mates with Nilsson and that whole LA lunatic asylum. Only he blew it by becoming a smackhead. Some of the tales after his fall from grace were almost impossible to hear. Following a platinum album, from which his manager swindled him of every cent, he could be found down Berners Street, hanging on the wall with Marianne Faithfull; strung out, crap in his pants, vomit on his breath. He was offered myriad deals over the years, but when it came to the crunch, he'd disappear to Paris for a month to do a load of gear with the drummer out of the Tubes; or end up punching a producer in the face for a perceived slight about micks. Martin always said Pat was his 'own worst enemy'. That really was the most vitriolic insult Martin could conjure up. In all my years of working for him, I only saw him lose his temper once, when someone repeatedly took his parking place outside the shop. The mild-mannered father-of-two ran out and bellowed: 'There are other fucking people who work in this street, you know!' This must have been loud, as I could hear him from behind the counter with the door closed, the windows vibrating. He confided that Pat was always breaking expensive guitars on stage, telling record company guys to piss off when out of his mind. It seemed such a squandering of opportunity. Opportunity that, as Martin bitterly knew, only ever knocked once. Old Pat, then: his own worst enemy. This made me think about myself for some time afterwards. Was I my own worst enemy? And if so, in what way? What a terrible thing to be, a personification of what Conrad called 'the will to fail'. But now I had to deal with Pat, face to face. He had a slightly intimidating anima. A very persuasive, vain, tormented man; his cheeks purple, his hair grizzled and white. He growled, 'I didn't know you were a songsmith. On the sly.'

'Well, I'm writing lyrics for someone at the moment. My wife, actually.'

'Bollix me! You're too young to be married, Byron. Although I can talk. Three divorces down the line. Hey, they're all bitches, you know. They only show you their evil side once they've swindled you into tying the knot. Then it's too late.'

He let out a Herculean laugh. I didn't want to think about this apophthegm, this pearl of Socratic wisdom, at that exact moment. I just wanted him out of the shop. I knew Martin had left me to eject him, and was sitting in the office, contentedly watching Sky football.

'I don't think I could contemplate Eurovision, though, Pat. Plus it's scraping the barrel for you a bit. After all you've achieved.'

'It's a piece of piss. Just scribble something on the back of an envelope. All the best songs were written on the back of an envelope. You couldn't lend us a twenty could you?'

Pat already owed me a twenty. I could see recognition of this knowledge in his intensely grey eyes. Like pumice stone, but shot through with a sad light. They were cowed but still contained remnants of their old vivacious, confrontational sparkle. He put on his best West Ireland brogue: 'Don't answer me now, my friend.

Think on.' And he tapped his pitted, exploded nose. 'I gotta use your *pissoir*, if I may.'

Pat went into the back of the shop, inevitably to look for Martin. Just then, the bell jangled and a group of Japanese kids with all the latest, most expensive suede schmutter from Camden market entered the shop. They always looked the coolest, these guys with their studied choice of shades, their airline shoulder-bags chosen for maximal retro impact. I knew it would displease Martin to find Pat still around, like pure radioactive waste, with these new customers. Japanese kids spent big, and this lot looked as if they were forming the first non-occidental indie supergroup of the decade. Or maybe they were just cashing in on the spending spree the music business seemed to be on at the time. Yes, if you were young, and owned a Les Paul and a Manc twang, it was very heaven to be alive in that moment.

One of the kids sidled up to the counter and asked me to plug in a guitar for him. I pulled down the most expensive model I could find. Just as his cacophonous, oriental-tinged fretwork began to fill the air, Pat ploughed back into the shop. He was buzzing and wiping his nose on the back of his sleeve. Oh, no.

'Fuck me! Just as well George Martin's not in here looking for new talent!'

The diffident Japanese boy looked terrified. He exchanged glances with his friends. Pat made a lunge for the guitar. He caught it and balanced it on his knee. 'That's not the way to play rock 'n' roll, you bunch of pansies. The first chord you learn on guitar is an E.' He crunched out an eardrum–throbbing E major. 'There! Listen to that. Goes straight to the nuts!'

The Japanese boys began to head for the exit, making apologetic smiles in my direction. Pat shouted out after them. 'All you need is another two chords, and you could end up like me! Heh, heh.'

A shuffle of feet behind me told me Martin had returned. Even though he had just potentially lost a great deal of money, he didn't seem angry. Instead, he said gently, 'Come on Pat, sling your hook.'

'Okay, I know when I'm not flavour of the month. But have a think about Eurovision.'

Pat limped across the tiles to the door, leaving a cloud of whisky breath among the dust motes sparkling in the wintry sunshine. This was the most dangerous moment, the moment when he promised to leave, but didn't. For hours. Then came the handshakes. Some of these went on for so long that they couldn't be termed hand-shakes any longer. In all reality, Pat was *holding your hand*. He reached the door, and we both breathed out long lungfuls of relief. He turned to wave. 'I'll just love ya 'n leave yer.'

Martin called out: 'Oh, Pat.'

'What's up?'

'Stick the guitar back before you go.'

Fact. People not afraid to make enemies always seem to have a lot of friends. I've never been able to work out that little conundrum. What shrinks would call a counter-intuitive phenomenon. Mandy was certainly not afraid to piss people off, to scorch the earth with her opprobrium, to put some flames around the room. Like Hedda Gabler insulting the hat belonging to her husband's aunt, she was deliberately provocative. Maybe this proclivity resulted from a form of boredom as much as malice; from restlessness and ennui. And Mandy was always bored as only truly shallow people can be. She also hated being alone. People with no genuine inner life with which to entertain themselves always hate being alone. Instead, they prefer cosmetic hubbub and activity. A life full of business and pleasure. It takes away from the real pain, the Everest of effort involved in confronting the Self. Just as people who prefer pets to children evade the difficult task of dealing with real human beings.

And Mandy certainly seemed to have a lot of friends when I met her. Her phone never stopped ringing. But were they real friends or invidious characters determined to hang on to the coat-tails of someone – anyone – who seemed to be going all the way? Parasites deeply concerned with catching some of that reflected glory, with acquiring keys to social doors they badly needed to unlock. Individuals obsessed with obtaining what sociologists rate above money in their demographic analyses of the class war: social capital. It's all down to who you know, as tedious media pundits keep telling us; as if this aperçu was up there with Montaigne's. If many of Mandy's friends turned out be passengers or acquaintances along for the ride, I could well understand this. Half the time that's how I felt. But on a deeper level, I also felt a certain amount of guilt about my motives for getting married. Sure, we were sickeningly in love. But I identified another, less noble or altruistic strand: I thought if Mandy made it, she could help my career. Just like those rapacious Jane Austen heroines, I had my eye on the loot. Or rather, the social loot, the kudos; the gateway to getting more of my work published, a goal I had been stunningly unsuccessful in achieving over the years. So, apart from the naive notions of human homogeneity that I was accepting my forty lashes for, there was also the low motive of personal advancement. I didn't think about this on a daily basis, you understand, but it was a component. I wasn't entirely blameless. And I seemed to be receiving my comeuppance almost immediately post exchange of vows. After marriage, I thought I would ascend to the broad sunlit uplands. Instead, I got war. Or three years of bastinado, at the very least.

At the time it was hard to tell whether Antonia and Nick were good friends of Mandy or merely hangers-on. Each party seemed disposable in the eyes of the other. A tacit agreement always accepted with a smile. Everyone knew the deal. In that world, everyone was in it for themselves: there was a kind of Teutonic efficiency about the whole project of self-advancement. The hierarchies were clearly delineated. Only someone higher ranking in media or pop-music terms could afford to insult another or disregard their phone calls. The suppliant of lower rank accepted this with a stoic submissiveness. And this was only natural. One day he or she would be in a position to do the same, perhaps to the person of original high rank who had slipped down the greasy pole during the intervening time. Mandy very clearly saw Antonia and Nick as belonging to a lower rank than her, and treated them accordingly. She stood them up at the doors of clubs, borrowed money without giving it back ('they can afford it!' she would bawl), left their pet cat to starve when it came to stay. And yet she still kept them as friends and allies. Marvellous. All I can say is there's just not enough masochists to go round.

I gained a true insight into how Mandy handled Antonia and Nick one February night after we married. There was a launch for some high-roller from a major record company who wanted to be cool and start an independent label. The usual fortysomething frequenter of prostitutes with the complete works of Simply Red in his CD collection. In a twist of what he probably considered Warholian irony, he had arranged to hold the party at Stringfellows, a notorious London shithole full of potbellied media whores that likes to think of itself as 'classy'. We agreed to meet Antonia and Nick there merely because we were told there was to be free champagne. And not just the odd complimentary glass. But a whole bar full of bottles in a constant state of replenishment. As soon as we arrived I realised how much I liked them both. They had that effortless cool only attainable by having a bit of dosh behind you, by possessing moneyed parents. An hour later, after we had paired off into the corners of voluminous black-leather sofas, Nick became tired of talking about football and transfer fees. I was glad about this, as I thought my disinterest in his conversation might mark me out as a practising homosexual. We'd both sunk at least a bottle and a half of bubbly each.

'Well, you've got your work cut out for you,' said Nick, apropos of nothing, in his reassuring, engaged voice. 'Dear, oh dear!'

'What do you mean?'

'You obviously don't know what went down with Mandy's ex,' he continued, meaningfully.

He focused his limpid brown eyes into the middle distance and shook his head slightly from side to side. Nick was tall, foppish, long-limbed. He was also a man of mysteriously independent means. Initially he had wanted to be a footballer, then tried his hand at acting with little success. He was currently running a glam clothes stall on Camden market, but that in no way provided an income that enabled a man to go out five nights a week and drive a bottle-green MG. He was also full of juicy tales about the movie and music-biz people he effortlessly drifted among. I realised I was about to hear a juicy tale about my own wife. I said, 'The ex? He was a self-pitying loser who caused Mandy a breakdown.'

'Maybe,' replied Nick, with relish. 'But when they split Mand tried to run him over in the street. I have this on the highest authority.'

'She didn't tell me that.'

'Well, she wouldn't.'

We both glanced over to the other end of the settee to check Antonia and Mandy were still deep in conversation.

'What's worse . . .' and here Nick's voice dropped to a whisper that was hard to hear over classic UB40 and Simple Minds. '. . . she tried to torch his flat.'

'Christ!'

'She still had the key. He came back one night to find an entire wardrobe of his clothes in flames. He refused to press charges.'

I looked again at Mandy and saw her, as they say, in a new light. Why hadn't I been told this before? Admittedly, one's first question to a girlfriend is rarely, 'Have you ever at any time attempted to murder a boyfriend with a motorised vehicle, and then tried to immolate all his worldly belongings?' Maybe that one should grace the questionnaires of dating agencies. I felt distinctly queasy. This was followed by anger at Nick for not sharing this with me before. To avoid appearing a complete fool, the man who married the booby-prize, I wiped the look of surprise off my face and said: 'Well, that's mental Mandy for you! Full of Spanish passion. Anyway, this berk probably exaggerated the whole thing.'

'Yeah, but if he didn't,' smiled Nick, tossing his fringe back, 'you're in for a bumpy ride.'

There was movement next to us: the glow of a female presence, pre-empted by a gust of expensive scent. It was Antonia. She had left Mandy talking to a well-known record plugger named Victor

Moore, a man in his early forties and the very spit of Bill Sykes in Cruikshank's cartoons.

'How are you, sweethearts?' she purred in that innocent way of hers. She put an arm around Nick's lanky shoulders and squeezed his knee. I felt a twinge of jealousy at this. Since our return from Spain, Mandy had rarely kissed the back of my hand. It hadn't been on the menu, for some reason. Instead, much affection had been jettisoned as we were forced to face up to harsh financial realities. We were teetering on financial collapse. I had even considered plunging back into further education, but after recalling my one failed attempt at storming the groves of academe aged twenty-three – and Mandy's sneer at its very mention – I ditched the idea. She said Fellatrix had to be signed by April, otherwise we would lose the flat. After all, since the switchboard job, she had been out of work for months. Then she had had a brainwave. Throw out all her old tenants and raise the rent. We had argued much about this. 'You can't just throw out Harriet, Matt and Steve with a week's notice!' I had exclaimed, open-mouthed. 'Aren't they friends as well?' She had trained her eyes on me with full firepower, her lips thinning to nothing: '*I* can do what I like. I'm the landlady.' And so it went on . . . I looked at Antonia's voluptuous body and made a comparison with Mandy. I had been formulating a theory that thin women had a higher capacity for spite than those built on more generous lines. And Antonia certainly was a big beauty. You could probably sleep a small baby in each of her bra-cups. It was more the idea that an abundance of flesh equalled nurturance; the folds of the Earth Mother, the bountiful Eve, et cetera. All this seemed to stand in opposition to the tomboyish qualities of the slender shrew. On the acres of her father's estate, Antonia owned many pedigree dogs, chickens and sheep. She loved them, and conversed with them daily when she was there. Yes, she was very maternal, sensual, fertile. She also had a sexy, marshmallowy voice perfect for fielding calls from the wealthy clients of *Acquisition*; a 'hobby job' she was always too discreet to talk about. 'Look at Mandy chatting up Victor!' she said in her erotic croak. 'Look at her go.

What a professional. At this rate they'll get signed *tout de suite*. Anyway, what have the boys been so busy with to make them look so guilty?'

But we didn't get the chance to answer. Mandy was on her feet, wielding a champagne bottle in one hand and the arm of the bestubbled Victor Moore in the other. They were heading our way.

'Guys!' said Mandy expansively. 'Help me out. Tell this man he's wrong about everything. He's the most cynical person I've ever met.'

I located Nick's eyes briefly. Had she pissed this plugger off already? No, she was merely proving my point that the recklessly impudent always make new friends. Victor and Mandy sat down heavily next to us. Nick nodded hello to Victor. To be hip held the ultimate social cachet for him; to be at ease in all company. He said, 'All right, Vic. How's the bitterness coming along?'

'It ain't bitterness or cynicism. It's realism,' said Victor with his mugger's smile.

'What's realistic about telling me to keep my day-job?' gushed Mandy. 'I don't even have a fucking day-job. The band is my day-job.'

'Okay, you got a lot going for you. Fellatrix, yeah? Cool name. That'll get 'em hot under the collars, those that get it. An all-bird band. The press are interested. You're seen at all the right knees-ups, and that, but . . .' Here I knew Victor was going to allow Mandy into a secret. He was about to let her know that the music business was a far bigger, nastier, more nepotistic beast than she had made provision for. He locked stares with her. '. . . You have to bear in mind that all the journos writing about your band in a fanzine now will be reviewing fiction for the *Guardian* in ten years' time. It's doubtful you'll be still making records. They will come on full of high-principle, oh yes! Be prepared for that. If you suggest that you want to make any money or have any longevity they will call it "selling out", while they've got their big media careers all planned out. Today the *Cardiff Chronicle*, tomorrow the *Independent* and a TV presenter's contract. Same with the record companies. Today's scout is tomorrow's CEO. Always remember the artist is at the bottom of the pyramid – just sausage mixture for the big machine; fodder for other people's glittering careers.'

Mandy stared down her nostrils at this debunker of dreams, this heretic, and jeered, 'Well, if you look like me, you ain't got a problem.' Victor smiled back. He would remember her arrogance. Make a note of it in his mental Rolodex for when Mandy came running in search of a favour. He merely held up his hands before him, as if he'd been stopped by Dick Turpin, and said,

'More champagne?'

Victor disappeared into the melee of freeloaders and returned with an armful of bottles. The remainder of the evening passed through its expected stages of increasing oblivion, all gauged by one's trips to the Gents. The first, a quick, dizzy visit. The second, a heavy gauntlet of stubbed toes and slurred apologies. The third, a swirling phantasmagoria of triple-vision and projectile puking down the express-tunnel of the khazi. Luckily, the third didn't occur. By visit number three, I had sobered up and just wanted to leave. But Mandy insisted on a ruse that demonstrated just how flippantly she treated Nick and Antonia. Somebody revealed that the exec whose party it was, far from being a visitor of prostitutes, was a happy bandit. All evening, it hadn't escaped our notice that he'd been doffing his cap at Nick. First a shy glimpse, then a languorous stare every fifteen minutes. Nick, by this time feeling like Dorian Gray, played up to it, to the great amusement of the girls. Then Mandy hit on the idea of seducing this man in order to land a deal with his new label. Nick would be his houseboy, like Bogarde in *The Servant*. He would bring this captain of industry lightly toasted snacks wearing a floral pinny. He would vacuum in his boxer shorts. He would work out before breaking the glazed meniscus of this guy's pool with an Olympic dive. After these suggestions, Nick's look was now more Alan Shearer than Dorian Gray. But by this time it was too late: the big man had begun his long cruise over. Nick was positively pale under his fringe by the time he was engaged by his combatant. He knew he'd have to make a go of it. That's just how things worked. Mandy would blank them both for ever if he didn't. Then came the cruel part. Mandy turned around, grabbed her glittery bag, and left the club.

I ran after her, into the February air, all the way up Shaftesbury Avenue. Eventually, I caught up with her at a bus stop. Panting, I said, 'What's wrong with you? You can't leave Nick in there with him! You didn't even say goodbye to Antonia.'

'I couldn't stand it all any longer. That queer. That prick who thought he knew it all.' She flung her deadly nightshade hair back from her shoulders. 'And you were giving Antonia the eye.'

'Come on, I only have eyes for—'

'Ah, shut up.'

'You flirt with Nick all the time.'

'Bollocks.'

I knew some kind of savage spasm was on its way.

'Anyway, what about trying to run your ex over?'

Her fist caught me on the left temple, causing her watch to fly off into the street. I crumpled into a nearby phone booth. That wasn't a girl's punch. That was a right-hand jab worthy of McGuigan. I stood facing the woman I had married two months before. But she wasn't looking at me, she was staring at her broken watch in the gutter. Her blue lips thinned and trembled. She looked as if she were concentrating on a tricky manual task, like the desperate act of forcing a big object back into a small bottle.

Now, many would conclude that I asked for it. That I deserved my first punch from mercenary Mandy. And to an extent I submit my *mea culpa*. After three bottles of champagne, I couldn't tear my eyes away from Antonia's bust. But no one could say that Harriet, our wedding photographer and trusted tenant, got what she deserved. One evening in late February, as I returned from the shop, I caught a glimpse of Harriet marching down the Holloway Road towards me. Among the evening crowd of scarf-wrapped, steam-breathing commuters I could see the poor girl clutching a handkerchief to her forehead and crying. Her topaz locks were fanned like a bird in flight, or a Rossetti dreamer. I was shocked to see her in this state. She seemed to be walking somewhere with great purpose. I caught her by the shoulder and asked, 'Harriet, what happened? Have you been attacked? There's blood on your face . . .' She seemed surprised and embarrassed to find me there, her eyes swimming with a kind of childish grief. She pulled away, though not roughly, accepting my concern but with an insistence that I could be of no help. The one sentence she spoke was uttered more with regretful anguish than anger. 'Ask your fucking wife,' she sobbed, then tumbled off into the human stream.

I climbed to the first landing of our Archway flat. Scattered on the stairs were Harriet's possessions. The awful sight of destroyed things. There were the hand-embroidered cushions that I knew she spent evenings making, a broken-spined book, an upturned ashtray, a camera or two. I picked up one of the Nikons to inspect the damage, and called out, 'Mandy?' There was no reply. Pushing open a door, I found her in the cramped communal kitchen, alone, smoking, with a cup of tea before her. Her white shirt seemed to be stained with brown dribbles. 'What the hell's been going on?'

She didn't like this interrogation. Didn't feel the need to answer to anybody. She said, 'I told her she had to go, and we had a fight.'

'I saw her on the street, she was bleeding.'

'That's her fault, the stuck-up bitch. I told her ages ago that I was raising the rent.'

'You can't just give people ultimatums. You can't just declare, "Get out now, I want to raise the rent."'

Mandy stood up with regal pomposity and ground the butt under her leather boot. She pushed past me onto the landing, shouting over her shoulder. 'She asked for it.'

'Asked for what?'

I followed her out and stood in front of the gaping door to Harriet's room. Inside I could see the flashing lime eyes of one of the cats cowering under a table. It struck me that I had never seen the interior of Harriet's room. The air seemed musty, long lived in. Since I had entered the house five minutes before, I had shared in the feral fear of the cat. Some invisible pall lay over the whole area, like the quiet that descends on a physical space after violent activity; the serenity of a battlefield after surrender. Mandy took no time in replying to me. She said, 'A kick in the head, that's what.'

I slumped down on the stairs, and rubbed my brow, maybe in some kind of subconscious sympathy with Harriet. My own left temple was still giving out unpredictable throbs from the punch Mandy had given me the week before.

'You know that's assault, don't you?' I asked, wearily. 'I wouldn't be surprised if she's back with the police.'

'She's too much of a wimp to do that. Anyway, she said her dad was coming tomorrow with his big posh Volvo to pick up her stuff.'

'You can't just go around kicking people in the head!'

Yes, the genie was well and truly out of the bottle. I often made an analogy between Mandy's escalating violence and the increasing recklessness of dictators or serial killers. Like Saddam and Aileen Wuornos, she acquired a taste for blood and found she couldn't stop.

I looked directly into her face. Amid the strident self-regard I caught a glimmer of guilt. From the start, Mandy had used her mother's death as a kind of *carte blanche* for acts of astonishing nastiness. I was only then beginning to see this clearly. Unfortunately, it was my nature to be placatory, appeasing. I didn't want further conflict. I just wanted, like the social worker with the delinquent, to understand, and use that understanding in some kind of cure. I also recognised that Harriet had served her purpose in Mandy's overall scheme, in her fantastic ambition. She had been chewed up and spat out. The previous summer, when I first started seeing Mandy, Harriet was about to be apprenticed to one of the leading London fashion smudges. Plus, her father was going to write about Fellatrix in the *Independent*. Neither the apprenticeship nor the piece had materialised. In Mandy's mind, she could afford to kick her dissenting tenant in the head. Harriet, as an instrument of advance-ment, had run her course. There would be no dire consequences. Even the police didn't worry her. I noticed Mandy's eyes were bulging slightly as they stared fixedly at my face. There was some-thing dreamlike about the situation – the crimson-eyed stranger of a wife screaming at me in an empty house. Just recently, when I watched her sleeping, I observed that the eyeballs themselves were unnaturally distended from the sockets, like Popeye or cartoon representations of an angry man. Everything about her seemed suddenly engorged, vitalised, on edge.

In a voice that couldn't disguise her guilt and self-hatred, she said: 'What's it to you anyway? I have to hold onto this flat, and she can't afford to stay here.'

I felt a queasy melange of emotions: disgust, regret, fear, sadness; even a kind of sick admiration that anyone could be so outrageous. That anyone could reach adulthood with so little idea of how to behave. Her actions always reminded me of the spittle-faced toddler in its high-chair throwing rusk at the wall when induced, against its infantile will, to eat. Bea's face came to me then: calm, forgiving, exquisite. I had exchanged my dove for a raven.

'What about all this?' I gestured at the scattered belongings, lying sadly where they had fallen. Mandy had probably thrown them at Harriet's retreating back as she made her escape into civilisation. The sight of broken possessions, the type of scene one witnesses after a burglary, always filled me with a gut-churning sense of dismay. A kind of meta-melancholy for the forlorn objects them-selves.

'It's her rubbish. She can deal with it. Anyway, she left the door open and two of the cats have disappeared.'

With these words, she pulled her red leather mac over her white shirt and disappeared into the icy street to look for them.

Three days later the police were indeed called to the flat, but this time it was Mandy doing the calling. The two remaining tenants, Steve and Matt, had been found one morning in the kitchen locked in mortal combat. It turned out that tension between them had been high for months, largely over Matt's propensity to linger in the bathroom Timoteing his Viking locks. When Steve decided to take his weekly shower – usually in his brief moments of sobriety – he had to take it there and then. Steve's repeated poundings and threats had been ignored for a full ten minutes. When the scrubbed and refreshed New-Ager emerged, Steve immediately placed him in the sort of headlock that turns your face blue. Mandy responded to this commotion by calling the cops. Even when the squad car arrived and removed Steve from the premises, Matt's face still resembled a grape about to explode under a wine-press. He vowed – in a voice surprisingly higher than normal – that he was leaving at the weekend. This suited Mandy fine. In her mind, Steve was never seeing his soiled room again either. Within two hours, Mandy had placed adverts for the three rooms in all the local papers and newsagents, the rent raised to a ridiculous level. This was to be countenanced, so I was told, by radical decorating.

When I heard about these bold moves, I realised one thing about Mandy: she was in motion all the time. Nothing lasted for long with her: friends, jobs, pets, ideas. Most of the time it seemed like change for change's sake. Change gone berserk. What was one way in the morning would always be different by the evening. The mood you left her in at midday would almost certainly be another by midnight. The decorating was completed during two intense weeks. This involved me being largely airborne, lying on planks balanced between two ladders as I reglossed the windows and stippled over the foul mushroom cloud of gunk on Steve's ceiling. A Puerto Rico of tobacco leaves must have gone into creating such a gargantuan stain. The two errant tomcats were never found, so the remaining moggie was divested of its Fellatrix badge and exchanged for three others at the Pet Rescue Centre. As grumpy and downright vicious as the three dismissed cats were, I was sad to see them go. Mandy claimed I was just being a sentimental fool who couldn't abide change, and there was a degree of truth in this. But the joy with which she welcomed the (admittedly slightly better tempered) new arrivals was unsettling. Did she feel no remorse for her three old musketeers? Her astringent smile would follow the new cats about the room as they gambolled in a spaghetti of guitar leads. She would spoil them with roast chicken and slivers of salmon. Christ, we were hardly eating more than boiled vegetables ourselves at the time. But it was pointless appealing to Mandy. She was too singular, too zealous. And change really turned her on. It filled her with a zest for more change. Made her think she was pushing the world around, instead of the world pushing her.

With the adverts for tenants came the usual identity parade of rapists and panty-wearing loners. A lot of these, believe it or not, were put off by *Mandy*. We finally settled on a female singer-songwriter, an IT consultant, and a businessman. The singer-songwriter turned out to be a junkie, the IT consultant a coke dealer and the 'businessman' one of the strangest individuals I have ever met, but all that came later, much later. The surface of people is all we have to deal with in the early stages. Human beings go to great lengths to conceal their real proclivities, processes, perversions.

One afternoon, around the time these jokers moved in with their false-bottomed suitcases and electronic scales, I found myself in central London with a couple of hours to kill. Martin had closed the shop at lunchtime in despair, saying it would cost more to heat and light the place than the pitiful trade we were sure to do. That week, Mandy had been forced to start part-time at a hairdresser's on Denmark Street, the elusive deal further away than ever. Funny how all girls seem to know how to cut hair. Even if they don't, they feign deep knowledge of scissors, basins and dyes. It must be a point of pride. Mandy was no exception, although she wasn't saving me much on haircuts as, increasingly, I didn't need them. I had been in the habit of surprising her after work, the two of us taking long wanders in the Aladdin's cave of shopfront windows, filled with spangled Gibsons, streamlined Stratocasters, glittering vintage Gretsches. Often we would go for a beer at the Twelve Bar club and then blag our way in to check out the latest band. That afternoon, with hours to go before Mandy finished, I thought

I'd take in a movie with my last guineas, a rare occurrence at the time. The film was Bergman's *Wild Strawberries*. It was a guilty pleasure of the highest order slumping down into the plush red chair; solitary, sans popcorn, and waiting for the first subtitles to appear on the screen. Much handwringing and religious doubt later, also feeling slightly disturbed, I exited into the freezing street and made my way to the hairdresser's only to find Mandy had just left. I belted up St Martin's Lane in pursuit. Then I ran around the shadowy back of the Centre Point building, a horrible London spot – I always imagined the ghosts of the poor from the demolished St Giles' Circus crying from the ground. In the February night, the black tower seemed to absorb the frayed light of the Tottenham Court Road: phallic, somnambulant, unanswering – a giant tombstone for the collective dead. Finally, I vaulted the railings and descended into the tube. At the ticket barriers I spotted her at once: only, from the scowl on her face, I rightly concluded she wasn't pleased to see me.

Deadpan, she said, 'I didn't think you were going to bother.'

My first instinct was always to appeal to a reasonableness I was convinced every human being possessed. Wrong move. I replied, upbeat, 'Don't be like that. Anyway, it can't be a surprise any more if you expect to see me.'

'Where have you been?'

'Oh, I saw a film. Nothing you'd like.'

This, evidently, was the worst thing I could possibly say.

'You've been lounging around in a cinema when I've been working my fingers to the bone! When this fucking band needs all the help it can get! When you haven't even finished decorating the rooms for the new tenants! When we haven't got a penny between us!'

Ah, the woe that is in marriage. I tried to answer, but the words, for once, didn't arrive. And anyway, there wasn't a suitable gap in which to say those words had they been available. The eye-bulging tirade didn't let up when we were past the ticket barriers. Nor did it abate as we waited for the earth-trembling train (what a long wait that seems now, in the memory). Nor when we were sitting in the jammed rush-hour carriage. There we were, three months married, screaming like council-house residents in a public place. As the choked train squealed into Camden, passengers delivering us their blackest looks, I made a risky decision. I would do something I had never done before. Because I could take it no longer. Mandy's voice at full throttle always sounded, to me at least, like a knife cutting vegetables very fast: chop, chop, chop, chop, chop. And it was this noise, and our personal life, that she was sharing with a hundred murderous commuters. As her slicing-machine reached banshee pitch I calmly got up, dusted the spittle from my collar, and stepped off the train.

'*Welcome to Great North Eastern railways. The restaurant car will be serving hot tea and coffee, fresh soup, gourmet sandwiches, and a wide range of crisps and snack products . . .*'

Not again! It dawns on me that I will have to listen to this excruciating announcement after every station. Eternal recurrence. Nietzsche, that walrus-tached sack of shit, would have understood.

'*. . . These include hot baguettes with fillings of roast beef, roast chicken, Christmas turkey and stuffing; toasted bacon and tomato sandwiches plus a wide range of home-made cakes, biscuits, pastries, hot drinks as well as a fully licensed bar. The buffet trolley should also be passing through standard accommodation shortly. Thank you!*'

The platform of Welwyn Garden City, with its decrepit Nabisco breakfast cereal factory opposite, is disappearing into the gloom. The works, a big, tumbling, brooding building, with its never-lit neon sign, stands next to a vast car park, big enough for a medium-sized airport. I know all these landmarks by heart. I am getting closer to the place where I misspent my childhood, my adolescence. Closer to home. The train will pass Hamford, where I grew up. I'm not sure if I'm looking forward to this or not. Why does this provide no comfort? More a kind of excitement or dread. A moment ago, sitting rocking slightly in my seat, I saw all those awful scenes from the early days of my marriage with a knifing clarity. Nick's terrible disclosure; the punch in the face after Stringfellows; Harriet's forlorn cushions on the landing; the bulging asinine eyes of my wife; the disparaging looks of the tube commuters as we headed back to what was supposed to be our happy home. The shame and the disturbance it all caused to my soul. That daily rancour now seems like a half-forgotten nightmare. How did I put up with it without stepping off the train – metaphorically speaking – every day? I must have been out of my mind. And I never did see Harriet again. Many times, from the top deck of a bus or at a lonely all-night garage, I thought I spotted her knotty orange hair flying in the London wind, but it was always someone else. A student or a young mum with a pushchair.

I can hear the clanking of the drinks trolley behind me as it makes its slow approach. People are straining to find the correct change; lining up the miniatures, with their plastic sun-hat cups, on little pull-down tables. There is the hiss of an uncapped bottle of Schweppes; a whiff of malt whisky. The fluorescent lights seem suddenly heavy on the eyes. Two seats in front of me, the Islington lesbian couple, loquacious since we set off, are having an intense discussion about a play they have recently seen. The stridently middle-class voice of the dominant partner has started to blot out all thought. In fact, it has blotted out the responses of her lover. This is a monologue she is subjecting us all to. I open my notebook and attempt to read back my last entry. This proves to be surprisingly hard work. There must be an orchard of plums in that voice. '. . . But of course the audience *en masse* weren't receptive. They didn't realise they were watching a representation of some kind of cultural epoch . . .' Cultural fucking epoch? How does she get away with that in normal conversation? Doesn't she realise how embarrassing she is? Look, she's even embarrassing her friend . . . Christ, I've been stuck on the same sentence for a full minute. And her voice. That accent. How did it get that way? I glance around to check if anyone else is sharing my outrage. Not a soul. Even Robin and Michelle both seem to be concentrating on their books without too much trouble. '. . . all the ideas were marvellous; so intellectually risky . . .' Jesus, she's reviewing it for the *Guardian* out loud, here and now. '. . . but it was the second act that struck me; it really turned all that post-post-modern revisionism on its head . . .' Maybe I should try to sleep, close my eyes. No, that will make me concentrate even more on her voice. I must persevere with this sentence. Nope, it's meaningless, she's blotting out the meaning. '. . . Yes, the second act was nuanced in a marvellously vigorous way, so fully achieved in comparison with the . . .' Fuck, if she mentions the second act again, I'm going to have to take someone's hot coffee and pour it all over her. Or at least ask her what play she's talking about. '. . . the total *specificity* of the role . . .' Okay, that does it.

'Anything to drink, sir?'

The benign eyes of the trolley girl stare into mine. Robin and Michelle look up, readying their wallets and placing their books flat on the table.

'No thanks. No . . .' My gaze has fallen on the black plastic bin-liner sagging from the back of the drinks wagon, into which all the spent miniatures and styrofoam cups will eventually be thrown. Something in this tableau makes me start to tremble. Perhaps it's the aesthetic distance between the shiny trolley, its cargo of inviting booze, and the quotidian household object stuck on the end. The promise and the fulfilment co-extensive, or something. (I think I may have swallowed the same dictionary as my Islington friend.) Or maybe it's because there is no more depressing sight in the world than a black bin-liner. Perhaps this is because they are the traditional receptacle for severed heads and torsos, sadly discovered on seagull-swarming landfill sites. Or because they are utilised by rough sleepers as makeshift duvets on punishing December nights . . . But this isn't enough, and I know it. I am well aware of what makes me shudder so. Three weeks ago, two bin-liners turned up in my hallway. I don't know who let them in, but there they were one evening as I returned from a solitary pint in the Prince Regent. And what they contained was, for me, worse than severed heads.

Inside the fullest sack was a sizeable selection of the books I had left behind at our marital home: mainly hardbacks, some with inscriptions from her ('to the sexiest Byron in the world, Happy Valentine's 199-'), nestling in what appeared to be a gunk of cat shit and litter. The second bag, though smaller, seemed to be heavier. It contained old vinyl, the onyx chess set we had bought together in Cephalonia less than a year before, Rudi's wedding gift of *The Illustrated Kama Sutra*, and many of my presents to her that she obviously didn't deem worth keeping. There was a wok, a flower vase, jewellery, the greatest hits of The Carpenters and (most painfully) the underwear she had worn on our honeymoon but had subsequently refused to even look at. Finally, my only remaining copy of *Hours of Endlessness*, the verse smudged by a substance I trembled to identify. This stuff must have been cluttering up the flat, the space she had long coveted as an abode for herself and her 'private life'; the latter a phrase she ludicrously used on a number of occasions. I would always holler back, 'You're married, for God's sake, this *is* your private life!' But Mandy was convinced she had another one, elsewhere.

I dragged the groaning sacks up to the hateful hutch of my room. The larger one split on the ascent, leaving an acrid trail of cat crap. Did she deliberately throw this shit in with my books? Or were the bags lying around for days while the cats used them as a latrine? Either way, I sensed that the zenith of my humiliation had been scaled. I crumpled onto my bed and began to feel choked from the very interior. I fell on the thorns of life. I bled! How could she? . . . How could she cold-heartedly return books with personal inscriptions, telling of our love, our long involvement? I instinctively reached for my cigarettes, then remembered I'd given up the week before after an incident where I had passed out drunk on my bed with a lighted fag, only to wake up the next morning with a tyre-sized scorch mark in the fire-retardant duvet and mattress. The shock of almost killing myself and everyone in the flat from such stupidity had scared me into quitting – and I was still undergoing the berserk tumours of cold turkey during every waking minute. The visit to the pub for a drink without a cigarette had been a hurdle I had just about managed. Instead of smoking, I set about placing all the callously returned objects around my room. After half an hour I gave up. Populating the tiny space was the debris of a married life – things cruelly transplanted to a location they were never intended to inhabit: videos in a hole in the wall; the chess set on the camping table, not the lacquered shelving we'd shopped for together and that I'd put up. I quickly returned everything to the grotesque ebony bags, then threw myself on the bed in the hope that sleep would come and behead the day.

The following morning, I surfaced with the curtains still open, the chestnut tree outside bare to its bones: a shrivelled autumn skeleton. At its feet was a waterfall of pale rust, the large paddle-shaped leaves in knee-deep piles. The wind shook its branches at rhythmic intervals – it looked like an old codger standing in a gale, every conceivable hue of decay around its battered shoes. Time had beaten it again.

There was a muffled knock at my door. One of the haggard croupiers, just returned from his shift, informed me there was a message on the communal answerphone. It was a woman's voice saying: 'The table is outside.' I knew at once that it was Mandy, and that the table she referred to was our large oval pine dining table I had spent weeks diligently sanding and varnishing. How considerate of her to return it. My heart felt giddy at this minuscule mercy. Maybe she still loved me. Maybe there was a slim chance that . . . I stepped out into the brisk November air to find no table. Then I realised she meant outside the flat *we* used to share. A flying visit to Seaham Road confirmed within the hour that it was no longer there. It had been nicked. Of course it had been nicked. If you left a coffee mug outside in that area it would be filled up in somebody else's kitchen in the time it took to boil a kettle. This, as you can imagine, felt like some kind of meta-zenith of humiliation. She had surpassed herself. Derision had made its masterpiece. You don't get up off the floor after a blow like that. You don't get up easily. And the fear is that you may *never* get up. There was nothing for it but to go and get drunk. And the venue for this pastime had been, for an entire month, Rudi's place.

That night it was Arctic under the stars. It was just as well I had packed in smoking, as Rudi's first gesture on arrival was usually to open all the doors and windows of his ground-floor flat and direct you outside. And this was a man who smoked the occasional cheroot himself. Yes, it was a freezing night, with long cumuli of steam issuing from the mouth of every damp commuter. The lengthy trudge to his bachelor lair always required a cigarette at the end of it. But this time I just walked straight in and threw myself and my scarf down on his leather sofa. Outside, the wind was raking leaves in the early darkness; also clanking something hollow in his back yard.

Rudi said, 'Come on in, spunker. Accept a pew and a wee tipple.' He squared his meaty shoulders to take a look at me. His rhinestone eyes seemed to say, yes you're the same self-pitying arsehole as last night and the night before. But his smile couldn't suppress relish at having company, or rather, a drinking buddy over on such a regular basis. He grinned like a Rubens satyr, then handed me a bottle of red to pour. 'What lies has she been telling you now? A lot ay shite, I expect.'

I took a plastic bag from my pocket and tossed it onto the icy stainless-steel coffee table. I said, 'She sent all my stuff back. In two big bin-liners.'

'Is that it?' said Rudi, and joined me on the sofa.

'Of course not. Open it.'

Out fell the basque and stockings from my honeymoon. Rudi's eyes brightened. 'Ah, the old returning underwear as ay gesture of contempt. Still, she could be wearing it for some other shite. It isnae that bad.'

'No, it's worse. She only left my table out for the Turks to nick off the street. The one we used to eat off every night.'

'Now that is pish, I have tae say. You don't fuck with a man's table. Here, have some more. In vino veritas.'

He made a lunge for the bottle and refilled both our glasses. I observed Rudi as his soft corpulent hands handled the silky lingerie. The glossy black of his eyebrows. The slightly pursed greedy mouth. The swirls of body hair escaping from a rift at the top of his red shirt. Rudi Buckle always wore red. Red and black. In his supple voice he suggested I was exaggerating my predicament: 'Like I say, Bry, the whole fiasco could be a lot worse. You've got a room, half a job. You'll make it through this, I guarantee you.'

I knew immediately that it had been a mistake to go over. In my condition, I should have been alone in a straightjacket or in a monastery. I knew my whole opera of disgust was boring to Rudi, and that he had nothing of any perspicacity to say on the subject. Yet still I went over. Night after bacchanalian night. And he always mentioned the room he had located for me as early as possible in the conversation. He obviously thought I should be grateful to him for evermore. Christ, I should have taken that room at the Y. His way of life frightened me too, after marriage. The selfish bachelor round of cooking for one, chasing women and caning it till God knows when . . . It all seemed as empty as the hull of a playboy's yacht. I could feel the furred tongue and fangs of the Singleton Existence closing around my aorta.

'She wouldn't even come to the door to explain herself,' I said.

'But you did talk to her?'

'Yeah, on her mobile. She said I'd once asked her to put all my stuff in the bin, just like she'd done with me. She implied she was only following my instructions.'

'Aye, in a battle of wits be sure to bring a weapon,' mused Rudi, sagely. 'Did she tell you what she'd been up to since she threw you out?'

'Oh, yeah,' I said, feeling a hot alcoholic tiredness behind my eyes as the first bottle of red found its mark. 'She's been holding parties for all her Spanish friends, renting the spare room out to Japanese students to pay my part of the rent. Doing all those things

I inhibited her from doing, apparently. And get this. She even wants me to pretend to the council that I'm still living there so she can pull off some kind of benefits scam. The final indignity!' My blood was up now. I looked at Rudi, that self-styled playboy and carouser of Kentish Town. His black, needy eyes, full of their strange appetites, had narrowed — as if listening to information anyone wise knew already. Yes, it was always me — the puny ingénue — who was the last to know the truth about the human condition.

'That's only to be expected,' whispered Rudi in his mellow, velvety, versatile undertone.

'From a psychopath like her, yes.'

'And are you gonna play ball? She already owes you two hundred and fifty bar from the last rent.'

'What else can I do?' I was on my feet now, making a Christ-like gesture with my arms. I knew Rudi found these emotional demonstrations intolerable. 'She's like an unbeatable force. She just steamrolls everyone and everything in her path. The double-dealing bitch!'

'Calm down, old fella,' said Rudi, and raised himself from the creaking leather. I could see evidence of the sunlamp on his flushed face and scorched neck. 'Since that last baby went down in a rather splendid fashion, I suggest you find another and get stuck intae the bevvy. Meanwhile, Rudolino here is gonna reheat a magnificent spag bol he cooked earlier. Are ye having a wee bit? It's choice.'

'I'm not hungry,' I said, and sat down.

'I take it that's an affirmative. You gotta eat. Strength is life. Howa y'ever gonna get stuck into some serious fanny looking like a pipe-cleaner?'

After dinner, Rudi made a big deal of clearing away the plates and saucers of Parmesan cheese. I could hear him throwing the debris into the dishwasher behind the polished expanse of his breakfast bar. I surveyed the pastel lighting of his bachelor den. The walls were invaded by framed Japanese posters of impeccable vulgarity. Comic-strip cartoon characters; futuristic blondes coiled in pythons; Akira with a machine gun — the sort of thing even Athena wouldn't carry. Then there was the cream rug of Tsarist luxury placed before an open fire, the grate of which always held a mound of amber embers. The location for his many seductions, no doubt. I shivered at the prospect of sexual contact with another woman. My night with Haidee had only left me feeling inept and out of practice; even more vulnerable to that dowry of smiles that is love. Despite the fact that the last two years of my marriage had been entirely without sex, Mandy had somehow inoculated me against intimacy and affection for ever.

Rudi sat down heavily and refilled both our glasses with dense red wine. He said, 'Now Bry, I was wondering whether you could teach me a wee bit about poetry. There's this—'

'—Bird you want to pull. What a surprise.'

'Aye, and she's a real classy number. Blonde, twice my height. Her last fella was a porn baron, but all she really wants is for a man to recite poems to her. In bed.'

'Give her Robbie Burns. That'll get her going.'

'Doesn't he play for Celtic?'

'He's your national poet, you maniac.'

'I just need pointing in the right direction. I'm shitein it for the next time she comes over. I told her I had a degree in politics and philosophy. She's a choice bit o' posh, I'm tellin' yuh.'

'What's her name?'

'Suki.'

'Well, that fucking says it all.'

'Well, you married a Mandy!' countered Rudi, suddenly defensive, his considerable shoulders flexing aggressively. The wine was beginning to clot my eyesight. I felt suddenly incoherent; angry beyond words. At that moment, I would have killed all of Rudi's family and pets just for a cigarette. The sure knowledge that I should be on my own returned again to mock me; scorning my dire laxity of purpose, my deficit of discipline. Why did I need this? Every night drinking myself into a stupor, sick with bitterness and regret?

I said, 'Tell her about your business and forget the poetry, Rudi. Drop the names of your latest big clients.'

'I cannae waffle about that all night. Anyway, I'm not getting the popstars and footballers any more, just these fuckin' high-rollers who look like they'd do you in if you clocked 'em funny, like. I mean, last week, one of my wee boys found a fuckin' machine gun under the back seat of this guy's Merc. Nae just an ordinary shooter, but a fuckin' Heckler and Koch nutter wiy ay silencer.'

'It probably belonged to the porn baron.'

'Aye, he's after me an' all, apparently.' Rudi looked at his feet for a moment, then turned to me, his dark eyes sparkling in the light of the rotund candle on the coffee table. 'Still, it's a million miles from radge old Hamford, eh? I remember the best we could do was go down the Duke of Wellington and drink pish-weak lager till we puked every night.'

I was in no mood for a reminiscence about the home town. My life seemed to be unravelling by the hour in London, and all Rudi could think about was pointless nostalgia and his next conquest.

'I can't believe she'd do me like this,' I said. 'Everything's down the khazi. I'm thirty.'

'Aye, and I'm thirty-one, spunker. They're all witches. They should be issued with broomsticks at birth.'

'Throwing me out of a flat I was paying for while she gallivants around Europe with Italian men. Returning all my things covered in shit. Throwing away furniture that I restored. Using my name to scam the council!'

'Well, that's foreign birds for yuh,' said Rudi, stoically.

'She was only half-Spanish.'

'Aye — half-Spanish, half-mad.'

I was spluttering by now, pure vitriol on my lips. 'I mean, most of the time she behaved like a man. You know, with that masculine swagger. When she hit me, I used to ask her whether she thought she was an honorary bloke, or something. It's not normal for women to have so many male hormones.'

'As ah says, you're gonnay come through this like a soldier. If you need any poppy, you just have tay ask.'

'Thanks, but I already owe you enough. It's not money I need.

It's . . . it's clarity. I need to work out in my head what this disaster was all about so it never happens again.'

Rudi sighed and scratched the abundant chest hair that always seemed to be straining, werewolf-style, to escape from his shirt. He said, 'You know, you always use such melodramatic language. A disaster. You were just the same in Hamford. It coulday been worse – you might've had a bairn, a mortgage.'

Again I saw a blood-flash of anger cross my vision. I was sick of Rudi's devil's advocate rap – and from a man who'd never committed himself emotionally and financially to another human being in his life. He probably thought he was telling me home truths that I badly needed to hear, rather than reciting page one from the Dictionary of Platitudes. What did he know? He wouldn't have lasted an hour married to that destructive, venomous little tyrant.

'She never wanted a child and I certainly wouldn't trust her with one. She throws her weight around like a man – you've seen her! And no one would lend the pair of us any money for a mortgage in a million years.'

This cut no ice with Rudi. The barely visible pinpoints of his eyes had a look of circumspection. He was a self-made man. A determined achiever. He pulled a cheroot from its slim packet and readied it for lighting. I felt a junkie lurch at the sight of this. In his warm voice he said, 'Mebbe that's part ay the problem. If you don't earn any money, they lose all respect for you. Endy story.'

'Why are you standing up for her now?' I shouted, incensed. 'Why did nobody warn me about her?'

'Cos nae bastard knew her except you and Nick! You makes your bed, you gottay lie in it.'

Rudi lit the cheroot and blew a smoke ring with his first puff; his glossy head leaning back at a critical angle. By this time of the night he always resembled some kind of gross Silenus – hairy, intoxicated, insatiable. I knew what was coming next. He opened his straining wallet and dropped a small wrap onto the sheeny coffee table.

'You don't understand,' I gasped. I had begun to gesticulate again with my clumsy hands; dangerously fired up. 'She was a nasty piece of work. A malicious shrew. A chronic moaner. A psychotic!'

Rudi shrugged. This squawking was altogether too unmanly for him; too much like the bleatings of a wronged wife. He merely said, 'Marry in haste, repent at leisure. Fancy a line?'

I stood up. 'No. I want revenge.'

'You gottay move on, Bry. You know, I saw Antonia and Nick the other day. I don't know why you didn't try it on with Ant if Mandy was refusing you action for two years. The rack on the wee lassie! You could stack a dinner service on there and still have room for a toaster.'

Rudi lowered his left nostril onto the funnel of an immaculate twenty and did his line.

'I don't care about Antonia. What I care about is this,' I said, and rolled up the sleeve to expose my right arm. Rudi stared at the mesh of deep diagonal scars for a moment. This was the only secret I had kept from him.

'Cocks and arses! Did she do that? Why didn't you tell me?'

'Because it's pretty shameful, don't you think?'

'I knew she was a loony, but not capable of that.' For the first time in the evening Rudi looked worried: genuinely engaged in what I had to say – as if the scars threatened him personally. 'Sit down and finish this charlie.'

I did as he asked. By that point in the proceedings I didn't care whether Rudi sympathised or not. The room was pitching like an argosy in a storm. The pastel lights seemed to stutter like oil-lamps as the juddering ship disappears into the tempestuous brine. In a quiet voice, he asked,

'Did you ever hit her back?'

'Never. Okay, just once.'

'Aye. I'd never hit a woman either, no matter how crackers she was.' I knew from deep experience that men who insisted they didn't hit women always did or had done. Rudi, I was convinced, was a dark horse such as this. There was too much shame in his agitated look for this not to be true. The empty clanking from outside seemed to have picked up in frequency and volume. I hoovered up the line that Rudi had lovingly prepared (with one of his high-ranking credit cards) then snatched up my scarf. He said suddenly, 'You're nay going? The night is but an infant.' Then he smiled to correct his concerned tone. I caught a beseeching look in his eyes. He would have done anything to share another bottle of wine. He was lonely.

I said: 'I need isolation, Rudi. Don't take it personally. Thanks for dinner. And the rest.'

'Ah well, when you gotta nash, you gotta nash.'

As I weaved towards the door I heard his voice. It was so quiet I wondered for a moment whether I was hearing things.

'Bry, can I keep the gear?'

I turned and said, 'How pissed are you? It's your charlie.'

But he was pointing at the pile of lacy lingerie, still in the sad supermarket bag in which Mandy had returned it.

'Sure. Who do you want it for? Suki?'

'Aye,' he nodded, 'for Suki. It looks about her size.'

But my resolve for revenge didn't last long. Immediately after I returned from Rudi's I fell ill. Some kind of debilitating gastro bug. All I could do for three days was watch the crabbed old miser of a tree out back get slapped around in the bitter wind; its shed skin of leaves yellow, rust, beaten copper, sepia, brown. I longed to see it towering in its May glory, an unimaginable sight as November slid grimly into December. For two of those days I was up all night in the unfamiliar communal toilet with astonishing stomach cramps – an agony akin to having one's abdomen excavated with a bread knife. I must've made thirty visits before each dawn. This was followed by cataracts of puking and the runs. I puked until I was retching stomach acid. Seventy-two hours of sweat-puddled amoebic gastroenteritis hell. I didn't pass a solid for a week. But like the ancients or the American Indians, I took it for granted that my ordeal was some kind of divine comeuppance or punishment. It had to be. I had sinned against powerful, ordaining forces. My version of forgetting to make the correct libations to Apollo was neglecting to remember that not all people were nice and kind underneath. Some were twisted fuck-ups who were positively hell-bent on your own downfall. For revenge; for recreation; for reasons known to themselves alone. Motiveless malignity. That was the only solution I could come up with for Mandy's behaviour.

By the end of my sickness I managed some dry toast and water. On that morning, a pale sun was refracting through the gauze of horse-chestnut branches, making the tree appear to be made from shards of broken glass. This effect was achieved only if one squinted at the correct moment. As I practised this, I recalled an era when actual broken glass had been a daily fixture in my life. Windows, mirrors, bottles ... all, over time, had been shattered. The first memorable incident was the summer after we were married. It was definitely summer because I remember Concepcion and Fidel playing in a square of sunlight in the big top-floor room before fleeing in terror as Mandy destroyed the twin icons of her mother's photographs. These sacred objects had been hurled against a wardrobe on a balmy afternoon just as I was retreating from a pointless argument. Mandy had been crying hysterically on the sofa when she suddenly snatched the large double-frame and threw it with all her might. It exploded against the pine doors in the same way a champagne bottle disintegrates against the hull of a tanker. Then she jumped up to finish the job. As she ground splinters of glass into the cascades of her mother's hair, the two slightly differentiated poses – one thoughtful, one more severe – disappeared like a dissident's mementos under a jackboot. Finally, she picked up the frame and pulled apart the hinge that held the diptych together. The two faces of Ramona dropped to the floor. They would watch us no longer.

———————

'Ladies and Gentlemen, we are now approaching Stevenage. Please make sure you take all your belongings with you. Any luggage left behind will be taken away and destroyed. Please hand in anything suspicious.'

With the memory of Mandy destroying the images of the only person she ever loved still fresh in my mind, I seriously consider handing *myself* in, to enjoy the privilege of being painlessly destroyed for free. But then sense prevails. Outside the train window stand the blighted Iron Curtain concrete underpasses of Stevenage. How anyone could conceive of something so ugly beggars belief. And this is a place I spent half my teenage years.

The glowing orange carbuncle of the Gordon Craig Theatre rears up in the half-light, even shabbier than I remember it. There is a cry of brakes, strange grindings and clankings. A scattershot of rain against the window. The train is almost at a standstill. Behind my forehead a strange amalgamation of pains has taken hold – headache, throbs from the suitcase strike, twinges from the strain of recollection. There is a metallic taste on my carpeted tongue. I must be sobering up . . . and this will never do. Turning my head suddenly to see if the drinks trolley has disappeared, I rick my neck. O fuck fuck fuck! For a full minute there is no more physically demanding action I can perform than staring out onto the grey vista: chilly inland gulls; empty buses circling a roundabout; eye-watering wind bending the umbrellas of the few forlorn punters who wait on the platform. The doors sigh open. Not many people stepping off either. I don't blame them. Christmas in Stevenage? I'd rather spend it in the Gulag . . . Then I recognise the swarthy slick-haired lover last seen at King's Cross breaking the heart of his girl, the one with the umbrella. He struts along the concourse, his shoulders slightly hunched, the veins in his big hands bulging. Well, he would live in Stevenage. Where else? Abruptly he stops. He appears to be jamming something into his suitcase, hampered by the quick rain. No, he's *extracting* something, with great difficulty. It's a bunch of flowers, slightly bent and dilapidated, but still presentable in their purple paper and bow. Someone appears at his elbow. A woman. And not the woman he said goodbye to in London. This one is taller, more animated, a glossy redhead. She produces a sprig of mistletoe, and he bends forward unsmilingly to kiss her. My heart gives a sudden jump at this secretly observed infidelity. How do people manage to keep others perpetually in separate compartments? To have private lives within a private life? Is no one satisfied with what they've got? Why this pathological appetite for change, for novelty? As if they were scoring points off God by trying to move faster than the speed of life? Why doesn't anything remain constant for more than a moment, when everything worthwhile in life seems to demand constancy as a prerequisite for its success? Love, for instance. Ah, gimme shelter from this chaos, this ever-turning wheel! I begin to feel the hot, familiar pain in my heart returning when I am distracted by a shrill noise. A mobile has gone off in someone's pocket. The sound doubles in rude volume as it is extracted into the open air. It belongs to Robin, and the ring is the tune of 'The Stripper'. The Wanker, more like.

'Hello, mate. Yeah, only at Stevenage. How's tricks? . . .'

Once again, I feel I must tune him out. For my own sanity. Why couldn't he have switched the bastard thing off? It's Christmas. The mobile – just one more example of the unwanted osmosis of information, of universal intrusion. If this is the Age of Information, there's too much of it. You couldn't say the same of the Enlightenment. You can never have too much light. Soon everyone will be having breakdowns from the stress of being *contactable* all the time, from being locatable; held answerable to another's catechism. Soon we will all be razzed to death in the street, or in our studies, or in the bath. Or on the train. And you can't just switch the damn thing off, oh no – that precipitates a whole host of other urgent enquiries: 'Where were you? I've been calling all day.' I know, I know, I JUST WANTED SOME PEACE.

Peace – I remember peace. If this is Stevenage the next stop must be Hamford. The location, for a few years of my life at least, of some kind of peace. Of stillness. The still point of the turning world. Before the mobile had been invented. Before the wider world had been embarked upon. When change constituted only predictable change – the slow revolution of the seasons; that pellucid illusion of permanence that is childhood.

4

Home

I remember home. And some days I remember it so vividly I am actually there, reliving each minute in consecutive detail. From time to time, one has to go deeper into memory to achieve this hallowed state, to visit places not usually accessed during the diurnal round. So where was peace to be located in my early life? Certainly, peace was present in my childhood bedroom – mother and father not yet up; early sun caressing the windowpanes with her gathered beams; the woo-wooing of wood pigeons unseen in the allotments out back. Heaven in all her glory shining. This combination, for me, equalled home, safety, predictability. Peace. Because children need predictability if they're not to grow, well, a little wild. But peace of a kind could also be found at my grand-mother's house in Barnet: a thirties semi on verdant Yew Tree Close, a short drive from Hamford. I can recall the intense antici-pation of lying on the rolling back seat as we approached the sooty car dealerships and synagogues of sprawling north London, the very intersection of city and shire. This was in the days when Des and Sinead were still nuclear, before the atom of our unit had been split by Delph. Once we had parked in the U-bend of the secluded cul-de-sac, I would race up the drive and part thick, tendrilling ivy to ring the deep-chiming bell. The door would tug open, allowing out the smell of furniture polish and burnt sugar. And there would be Granny Chloe, my father's mother, a tall, snowy-haired widow, a beatific smile playing in the creases of her mouth, though mainly around the eyes. Gran would smile from her eyes. They were a kindly brown, resonant with sympathy and calm; though also present were the residues of struggle, make-do, bereavement. She often seemed rather elegant to me, much too graceful for the plodding commuters who infested the close with their newly waxed Humbers and Granadas. She also knew how to handle children — she had great sweetness and strength of character; her large hands liver-spotted with sizeable dashes of rust, her eyes hooded and patient. And she always had a present hidden for me on these visits — a toy car, a soldier, a spaceship: anything — she knew I wouldn't care *what* it was as long as it was a present. I would race to the four or five known places of secretion in an ecstasy of suspense, often barrelling back in triumph before Des or Sinead were through the door.

Let me think of her house for a moment, its hidden recesses of cubby hole and wardrobe. The red sticky lino of the functional kitchen; the settled stasis of living room, with its gilt-spined leather volumes. The must and the dust; the tubular steel of the Art Deco armchairs; the aroma of flapjacks (often still hot on our arrival); the dark mahogany of the picture frames; the oriental trinkets behind glass cases; the valuable Buddhas under their glow of polish; her collection of snuff boxes. The house seemed preserved from another era — the 1930s, at least. There was always something deeply suburban about its odours of nut roast and vegetable garden (Gran had been a vegetarian since her twenties, way before medical science made it fashionable); its long-fermented tangs of camphor and gloom. There were objects in her house that puzzled me, that didn't seem in any way contemporary; as if they might have been constructed for an epoch that relied on bicycles and Model-Ts for transport. The big Roberts radio, or 'wireless' as Gran called it, for example – grilled and heavy, like a slab of wartime technology, with its three spare silver buttons for selecting wavebands and aerial as long as a fishing rod, which I spent hours extending until it snapped. Or the Victorian commode chair in her room, whose cushioned seat could be removed, revealing the mysterious and discreet hole to the basin below. Or the dark Edwardian wardrobe with its blast of mothballs on peering into the Narnian interior. Yet, I can never remember doing much at Gran's, except wandering gingerly around, endlessly investigating; with a child's inexhaustible curiosity. There are photos of Gran pushing me proudly in a wheelbarrow down the long, well-tended back garden that contained two park benches. Another of her kneeling next to me with a bubble-blower kit, her patient hand holding the plastic 'O' before the embouchure of my lips, sunlight catching the furrows of her forehead, her hair dramatically white. She had slow, calm movements and an interesting rasp in her voice. She always had the effect of making me feel safe, as if she had been waiting a lifetime to have this grandchild to hide presents for, or to prepare vegetarian salads for, with side-plates of thick-spread butter on gravid slices of brown wholemeal bread. The legacy of a life avoiding the flesh of living beasts was excellent teeth. Hers were strong-looking, white, orderly. And she didn't appear or behave like an overlooked woman – a widow who had raised three children single-handedly. She was always smartly but inconspicuously dressed; though there cannot have been much love for her in that life – love just for herself, like any woman needs, regardless of age. Towards the end I recall all forms of exertion tiring her. Once, when I asked her to heave down a World Atlas from a high shelf, she had to sit down for a breather, as if after a long, exhausting hike. 'I feel H and D,' she would say. Only years later, I discovered this was short for 'hot and dizzy'. Years later still, at her funeral service, one of the revealing readings stated that she loved 'music, beauty, walking, flowers and birds'. As a child of five, this information was unknown to me; hidden, arcane – part of the secret adult life I couldn't comprehend.

The polished Buddhas had an unusual history. My Grandfather, Brian – whom I never met, and who died when Des was himself a child – was a Civil Servant and Sunday painter. Well, rather more serious than that. He had a shed in the back garden, preserved under tarpaulins, with his painterly equipment still dustily extant. An artist's studio, no less, resembling the chaise-longue-littered attics of Beardsley or Augustus John. I loved to stare in fascination at the high easels and crenellated canvases; the ruptured tubes of umber; the dusty brushes in biscuit tins, and, best of all for a small boy, a real skull grinning from a lectern – a gruesome Yorrick of the suburbs. The Buddhas were part of this collection, along with intricately carved spice boxes, delicate Japanese prints of swift fishes, and a full set of Samurai swords. Brian had even exhibited a couple of times, and every available stretch of wall in Gran's house swarmed with his oils and framed sketches. Maybe this early exposure to the creative process, so flagrantly on show, so successfully executed, convinced me that art was a legitimate job for a grown man. I didn't know then that Grandpa slaved as a pen-pusher from nine to five in nearby Southgate until his last illness. One painting in particular fascinated me – the biggest in the house. At that age it seemed as vast as the side of a lorry, and depicted an Andalusian scene looking towards the sea: all hot yellow with burning vistas of indigo ocean. In the foreground was a flourishing cactus, an object that virtually blotted out the wind-beaten sierra. Not a Wild West cactus, but a broad-leaved thriving triffid. This plant struck me, at that impressionable age, with the force of myth. Like Van Gogh's cypresses, it was immovable from the imagination. What did it signify for him, so obdurately central, blazing and mad in the midday sun? I would have loved to have known. Another adult secret. I had dreams where I found myself walking through this landscape, stirred by the sudden moment of recognition as the six-foot cactus confronted me, like Barton Fink finding himself on the deserted beach with the horizon-pointing bathing beauty.

There were other more intimate pictures too. A number were of Gran herself. There was a profile of streamlined, elegant Chloe in a velvet fedora, her face a rich greenish hue, as if she had sat for the portrait in a semi-lighted hot-house. These pictures spoke of other times, of adult difficulties, joys, adversities, sexual secrets. The mysteries of a life that awaited me, full of the unknown things grown-ups do; the unknown places they go to work; the unknown conversations they have downstairs long after you've been put to bed. Another even smaller picture showed Gran in a lilac flapper hat, tight like a bathing cap; her face white as a lily – a young woman. I remember not being sure who it was. 'Is that you, Granny?' I asked, pointing at the beatific smile in the robust frame.

'Oh, yes, when I was a young girl,' Gran answered, with an air of slight regret. She didn't want to be reminded of her former glory, though she allowed the picture a place among the landscapes and sumptuous still lifes.

'It doesn't look like you.'

'That's because people change as they get older. Their faces change.'

'You fibber!' I said, genuinely bewildered. 'You always look like Gran.'

'No, I used to look like *her*. But I'm still Gran . . . come here!'

And she would scoop me in her arms and take me on the grand tour of all the pictures in the house. Though I had done this many times before, it never ceased to be an excursion of wonder. I used to think other children's houses were distinctly lacking when I saw only the Pirelli calendars and peeling noticeboards or Monet's tired poppies on the wall. She would take me up the staircase and stop to explain the sketches, many of them cartoons of political figures distorted by treasureable Groucho Marx noses and speech bubbles I didn't understand. In the spare room, where I would sleep if we were staying over, terrified by the dark creaking of teak furniture, she would point out a seascape painted in Germany, where she had taken Grandpa when they were courting; or a dense sylvan scene in the Black Forest; or an oil sketch of Des as a boy my age, engrossed with a toy bottle-green double-decker bus. I didn't know then that she and Grandpa were so poor that they both walked five miles into

Kensington every Saturday just to save the bus fare when visiting Brian's cherished galleries. Or that Gran would pride herself on finishing the housework by nine every morning so that there was time to do more interesting things with Des and his two sisters. Or that, after Grandpa died, she worked as a welfare assistant at a local primary school, making coffee and doing sum cards, and then for years as a dinner lady at another one. Or that she would arise early on tenebrous mornings to make bread and scrub the collars of school uniforms, also maintaining the long garden with its little pond and two park benches that Brian had created for the children he never got to see grow up. Or that, when Brian was gone, she couldn't bear to hear Kathleen Ferrier singing 'What is life to me without thee, what is life when thou art dead?' on her old Roberts wireless.

When it was time to leave, in evenings smelling of blossom from the cul-de-sac's many apple trees nestling among the yews, this bitter pill would be ameliorated by a further present, often some home-made flapjacks wrapped in kitchen roll; now cold but still the most exquisite flapjacks this side of that great bakery in the sky. On the long journey home through the dark and forbidding adult streets, I would fall asleep on the backseat (in an era when seatbelts were only 'clunk-click' compulsory) and dream of all the fascinating things I had seen: the wide-grinning skull; the pale orange fishes in the pond, like the ones in Grandpa's beloved Japanese prints; the hastily constructed concrete air-raid shelter still in the back yard; the tiny tin snuff boxes with their ripe and strange odours; the upright piano favoured instead of a television; the mysterious spreading cactus in the baking Andalusian scene, like Moses' bush about to catch fire . . . And once back in Hamford, still asleep, I would be lifted from the car (by tired and irascible Des? By Sinead? I never knew) and placed in bed, a gesture I loved more than anything else in the world. It spoke of a family as a generous, happy unit: and I suppose we were for a brief two-swallowed summer. There I was, stretchered into my own bed by doting, considerate parents. Home again safely, to dream of strange, sunbeaten shores.

★

So much for the dreams of a child whose life was about to change abruptly. For the grown-up there is only regret and damage control. Also, there is always an epicentre of dreams, dreams we have as adults, that, paradoxically, concern the important, never-forgotten places of childhood. Places formerly known as home. Once aware that we are visiting these locations during our nocturnal journeys, we quickly earmark them as sacred sites. Mayan temples of deferential worship and sacrifice, with all the fear of imminent excommunication. We greet them like old friends. They are locations that, when the soul arrives at them, deep in the early hours (maybe after an age of disturbed rambling through a deserted and crumbling seaside resort), we recognise as the inner sanctum, the master bedroom of significance. For me, this locus is the back door of number fourteen Dovecote Lane, the house in Hamford where I grew up. The White House, as we called it, since it was the only building in the lane to exhibit any colour other than brick.

Dovecote Lane was a little backwater of tranquillity in a medium-sized market town. Built on a gradient overlooking the town centre with an alleyway that took you down to the main road, the house itself was a three-bedroomed semi on an unmade lane facing allotments of land. It was at the bottom of this alleyway that I recall my mother getting whistles from lupine teenagers on our journeys to the shops. There were also tall silver birches at the side of the lane and conifers in our back garden. This glorified dirt-track was called Dovecote Lane due to the squat, now-deserted pigeon coops at the civilised end, the end that annexed onto Annesley Rise, a steep row of non descript family houses each with a fussy wrought-iron gate out front. To the west was a hospital-sized telephone exchange, an ugly impersonal monolith seemingly manned by robots or monkeys, and filled with the soft efficient whirring of computers – I never knew, as nobody I spoke to had ever been inside. Next to the exchange was Water Hill, a rough, parky expanse that bulged upwards towards a girls' school and a row of benches overlooked by a conical watertower. An Aonian mount for a young bard. The entire hill was man-made, a reservoir created to serve the surrounding area. From the hill could be seen the Lane and, on bright December days, I would sit on these benches and watch the towering sun-iced silver birches and their swooping gulls; the yellow haze of branches in front of number fourteen like an incandescent winter flame. From this vantage point, it was just possible to make out the uncivilised end of the Lane where a breaker's yard and an old school playground gave way to a large wooded wilderness.

In these dreams, these mythical homecomings, only the house is significant, though I know the rest of the town is out there somewhere, an ethereal context on the periphery. By the back door I mean the approach to it, down the tight concrete passageway that cleaved a thoroughfare between the grey, once-white bricks of number fourteen itself and the mysterious and tall privet hedges of Mrs Melbourne next door. In these dreams – which on average I have trembled through four or five times a year since I last saw Hamford – it is always night. The White House becomes the Black House. Good things of day have long since drooped and drowsed. A still night in an indeterminate season, neither winter-crisp nor summer-steamy, but an April midnight maybe; the softly permeating odour of privet as pungent as soil after fresh rain. There is often a tremulous yellow moon in the sky. The moon that is always rising. I am probably about eight or nine – ten at the most. And they all follow the same pattern. I am in a hurry. I am out of breath. I leave the wrought-iron gate clanging at the top of the passageway (where have I just been in these sagas? I never know), then I am bounding the short distance to the shrouded back door. The small garden is always sarcophagus-dark in its deeper recesses; two yards of patio illuminated by the strong light of the kitchen. The clutch of red-hot pokers, shorn of their furious crimsons and exotic yellows in the weird altered darkness, sway sagely on their moorings. The big stone flower tub is grave with neglect; the blustering evergreens like sinister sails . . . and the door, the door itself – eight squares of smeared glass in a glossy blue frame – is always locked.

And I never have the key.

What happens is that I peer through one of the panes, vaguely anxious at first as I notice the upstairs lights are on. This anxiety builds to a fever of agitation when I realise that pushing the door-bell creates no sound whatsoever. Somebody is in, but they are not *letting* me in. I can see the pale canary colour of the sunflower-print roller-blinds in the living-room window shift suddenly in response to an errant elbow – or maybe the shadow of an adult passing rapidly, plate or wine glass in hand. Yes, a gathering is in progress upstairs. This is strange as Des or Sinead never had anyone over, except at Christmas, and especially after Delph was on the scene, with Des wearing his horns on the other side of the English Channel. I can hear the swell and chatter of provoked laughter; the pump of seventies disco; busy bottles doing a round of refills. It sounds like they – whoever they might be – are having a swell time. But I am excluded, left to make the increasingly menacing acquaintance of the night garden, with its fecund odours, wind-rustlings and bottle-scattering tomcats.

At this point I will begin rapping with a coin against the glass, the chink-chink-chink sound unbearably magnified in the trans-fixed silence of the back yard. The thought of throwing stones at the first-floor window will be briefly entertained, then dismissed. There is the possibility of shouting also. Amid this, a fierce sense of paranoia, setting in for the night, like fog. The overpowering component in this paranoia is petrification, in the Greek sense of the word: to be made stone, like the heavy flower tubs, like the statues seen by Perseus. I become stuck in a trauma of inaction, of procrastination. If I peer in deep at the glass I can see the uneven, wine-purple tiles of the corridor stretching to the imposing bulk of the dangling coats at the far end. The same rack of jackets and scarves that – as an even smaller child – I would be terrified of passing on a night-errand to the dank downstairs toilet. Terrified because of the very real danger of sudden twisting arms darting out to grab my neck, or tangle epileptically in the air as I hop past on bare feet.

But no one ever appears. Just the inviting, quiet absence of the corridor and the disturbing vacated space of the kitchen, perhaps in a disarray of prepared food and empty bottles. A recurring dream in which nothing ever happens. Sometimes I am there for hours, heart racing – the party grinding on obliviously upstairs, me timidly tapping a two-pence piece against the pane in the tense solitude of the garden. *Chink chink chink*.

And that back door – locked, blue-glossed – is a cipher for all that occurred in that house: an eight-squared honeycomb of history. The portal through which life came and went at number fourteen Dovecote Lane; the front door being hardly used, except to admit post that needed to be signed for, or visitors on special occasions, or anything that required access by car. But that navy-framed back door is where I remember my mother, battered briefcase in hand, leaving for school every day. Or where she'd greet or adios dastardly Delph in my father's absence. Where friends would stream expectant of jelly and ice cream or the pink Eden of Angel Delight. It was also the location for the washing machine: a noisy corner (especially during the insanity of full-spin), where you would find a disorderly mound of boots and training shoes. I can picture it in high summer too: open to the garden, July wasps streaming in and out; the comforting sound of plates being stacked emanating from the kitchen, which shared the same cracked burgundy tiles as the corridor. Also on the ground floor was the cellar. While technically not a cellar in that it was situated next to a kitchen, the gradient the house was built into meant that its rear had three storeys, while the front appeared to have only two. So the cellar was lit by a grate that let in light and dust from the unmade road out front. A dark repository for timber, sallowing cardboard boxes, newspapers, work-bench, nails, tacks, screws, glues, private documents and all manner of secrets. In other words, a playpark for any boy aged between three and thirteen. This shadowy vault also added an air of unease to the bottom part of the house, what with the racks of coats and their phantom arms, the chill of the tiles and the rarely visited downstairs khazi, which seemed to contain every species of spider except those that absolutely *had* to have a tropical climate in which to survive.

Then there was the small matter of the ticking. Every room in the house had a ticking in it, even the ones that didn't have a clock. You thought you heard it. From the purple-tiled kitchen floors covered in dusty rush-matting to the woody, timber-creaking cellar, the house was abrim with dark, horologic resonances. Especially when you paused for a moment by the frosted panes of the mysterious blue back door – the door that led out into the wider world, away from home, into random and terrifying futures – with everyone upstairs on Christmas Day or New Year's Eve. And especially at the foot of the stairs, the heavy winter coats on pegs, thick with ghoulish hands ready to grab a little boy, like young Jane Eyre trembling before the red room. Suddenly there, out of the silence, you would hear the ticking of the kitchen clock, also behind an impenetrable frosted-glass door, talking away to itself with the only two syllables it knew: *tick, tock*. The silence on that lower level seemed alive, as if the house were a recumbent sleeper, its respiration slowing as it approached oblivion; the clock marking its cold exhalations. Time the heavy breather, always advancing, always winning.

Not that the place was haunted. I had discovered this with the aid of a ritual I always employed when forced to stay in a strange house or bed. I would find the quietest spot in the building, first making sure it was midnight and that no one else was awake, and then (with all the drama available to a ten-year-old) lay myself open utterly to any spirit whom I imagined was creating the strong presence. I would dare the apparition to make itself known. At number fourteen, this spot was at the end of the passageway – the blue back door. At the climax of the ritual I would ask out loud for anyone – or thing – to come forward. This was always a raw, bare moment, and luckily I only received a reply once, causing me to flee from my silent vigil at the garden-facing glass in white-haired panic. Well, not so much a reply as a demonstration of one of the laws of physics. The ghost had been my own breathing, condensing against the cold panes.

Ghosts. Unheard music. Supernatural clocks. But it didn't feel that threatening at the time. That's just a trick played by the memory. And I don't feel I am any closer to an explanation of what made it home. What is a home? A door that's always open – a place that offers unconditional safety just by being what it is, where it is. At number fourteen Dovecote Lane I cannot recall a time when I wasn't there – it was the house I was born into. It contained my first life memories. Something sacred and non-transferable – they will die with me, like everyone's. Home as a central point, like the spike of Donne's geometrical compass – no matter how far one travels or how long one resides somewhere in later life, the impulse is always to return. To crawl back to the comfort of known rooms, known voices.

The second floor at Dovecote Lane floor contained the runnered shelves that held my father's books. I can see them now, a precious emblem of learning; an uncharted rainforest for a child. The light from the sunflower-print blinds used to cast a saffron glow in the room – it often resembled a library under a Los Angeles smog. On the rare occasions when my father was around (in the tranquil days before the degradation and turbulence brought by Delph) I would ask him about the exotic titles: 'Eugene Won-jin. What's that Dad? Is that about a real person or a made-up one? You and Your Neurosis. Dad, what's ner-o-sis?' I remember his replies as scanty, evasive. He had that strange way of looking at me – a neutral evaluation from under hooded eyes. He was often preoccupied, not surprisingly considering the ructions that were going on behind my back at the time. He often smelt indistinctly of chemicals, of the lab. A short man, with powerful shoulders, bald-headed, handsome, opinionated, I nevertheless remember him as a gentle presence. Like Granny Chloe. His displays of temper would largely be confined to hand-wringing and expressive hisses or sighs, like a lorry letting off its airbrakes. His movements were quick and decisive, especially in the cellar where I watched him at his carpentry bench, planing a door or fixing a broken drawer with wood-glue and heavy G-clamps. I stood spellbound as a chisel made its effortless way through a plank of pine. A manly puff sent the shavings scattering. Same when digging in the patch of allotment opposite the house. The blade of the shovel would go in each time with a decisive *whoompf* as his rubber-booted foot struck it with great force. Yes, he could handle a spade, my father. This is all the more surprising when I think that he had no father himself to watch. No masculine role model. But then the world is full of orphans – orphans of the heart. I often ponder these facts: I am roughly the same age as him when he fathered me. Where are my tools? My workbench? My books and shovel?

Sinead, on the other hand, would always be there, omnipotent. If that omnipotence describes a good mother then that's what she was. To be everywhere at once; capable, all-seeing. In the top part of the house, the bathroom was her domain, with its cluttered shelves of potions and perfumes, the steam that took forever to clear. The airing cupboard contained folded towels of unimaginable warmth and luxury. This was in the days when she would always apply scent to her wrists and neck before leaving for the school – lavender, or occasionally sandalwood. Her morning ritual was often accompanied by vexed expressions as one minute her mauve headscarf kept slipping off, the next her magic wooden letters couldn't be located; then the toast was 'black as cinders'. A lapsed Catholic, she would use expressions such as 'Mary mother of Jesus!' during moments of high exasperation. The rough, bike-stealing boys in the lane who she had threatened to 'sort out with a big stick' had lately become my friends. But then there are always bigger, rougher boys waiting out there when we leave the soft harbour of childhood. We had formed a gang. This caused Sinead a great deal of pleasure as she was always exhorting me to go out and play. She didn't know we were a gang, however, until it was too late.

On a Saturday, I would call on the members one by one. Often there were only three of us. Not much of a gang, you might say. My first visit would be to the house of Trevor Thomas on Annesley Rise, who we all knew as the Little Kid. This appellation was due to his stunted, weaselly frame, his wiry knuckles and his choirboy voice. His earnest eyes were as wet and mobile as a dog's. Then, further up, towards the bad estates that bordered the town (always named after things they *didn't* resemble: the Sunnyside Estate; the Haywain Estate), we would knock for Nigel, a boy with learning difficulties, four years older than us, who was forced to play with younger kids due to the outright rejection of his peers. He was big-framed, with slow eyes black as the seeds of apples, overhung by a monobrow the length of a large slug. A bit of a pitiful gang, but at least it got me out of the White House, away from the boiling resentments and strained scenes. Initially our activities centred on building things – camps, treehouses, bivouacs, or, when it was raining, robots and contraptions that would never work, with circuit-boards and soldering iron. Then construction turned to destruction. By the end of our reign over the badlands of the neighbourhood, our escapades would involve either throwing, burning or exploding any object we could lay our hands on.

The wall to the overgrown sanctuary of the allotments always required a running jump and a leg-up. It was topped by a mons pubis of slippery moss. Although Nigel was tall enough to scale it by himself, he was too backward to act on this knowledge. Many a rimey morning the Little Kid and I would struggle, one clod-hopping foot in each hand, to push him over the top. He was as heavy as a sack of gravel. The wall was a good indication of how tall I had grown. Once the running jump became a brash joy, not a shoulder charge that resulted in flayed kneecaps and a twisted neck, I knew I was growing up.

One November day marked Game Over for us three bizarre musketeers. It was always cold in my memory of those months – the air a brace of metal against the forehead; earlobes crimson under parka hoods. But this short afternoon was especially bitter, the autumn mist and fog mustard brown and supernaturally abundant. We sloshed our way down the lane then hiked ourselves up the wall. Once among the birches and sycamores at the back of the allotments we began destroying one of our old tree-camps. Out of boredom, out of malice — we all fancied ourselves Jack from *Lord of the Flies*. The wooden observation tower was first to hit the leaf-mulch. Next, the swinging rope, which also doubled as an escape route in case the location was marauded by insurrectionists from one of the euphemistic estates. Finally, the machine-gun nest (complete with stash of toy guns and soggy ammunition) crashed into a mesh of blackberry bushes. The Little Kid appeared ecstatic at this carnage, though I was a little sad. I didn't want to destroy everything — if we did there would be nowhere to play and nothing to play with. Nigel, seeing that his stunted friend was enjoying himself, started to laugh along, producing a noise that resembled a mule under a load. A sort of strangulated sawing sound. It vanished quickly into the dense air. Like being suspended at thirty thousand feet, the sere November day disappeared into nothingness on all sides. The only other sound was the low cawing of the wood pigeons, with their extended second note: woo-*wooh*-woo.

Then it began to go wrong. We had devised a game whereby Nigel had to attack us, the last soldiers left defending the valuable strategic town that was the compost heap. This Nigel embarked on with abandon, all plodding limbs and rebellious black hair, the imaginary general of his own army; hurling sticks in a frenzied counter-assault. During this occurred the mishap that would reveal to my mother that I wasn't out collecting fossils or playing marbles. Nigel, like the ghost of Cain, seeing an empty emulsion can, picked it up and flung it full force at the Little Kid's head. A whoop of pleasure from the overgrown boy; a blood-curdling yell from the runt. Still echoing in my mind today is this scream of immeasurable decibels, emitted as he fell to his knees, holding the big red gouge in his skull together. I had never seen blood come so fast and copiously. Rushing to help the Little Kid, I discovered Nigel was still laughing, antic, unstoppable. He took matches from his pocket and began to torch the remains of the camp. The lighter fuel and ammunition we kept stashed in a waterproof box soon went up. At this point I remember Delph — newly installed at number fourteen, and eager to assert his authority — appearing on the allotments like a big-bearded Adam. My mother wasn't far behind. He ran through the fog, tall and sinewy, with one motivation: to put Nigel in the ground. As I cradled the Little Kid's bloody head in my lap, Big Nigel stood next to his pyre, a frown of confusion on his face. His laughter had transformed itself into strange, low mooing sounds. Burned into my memory is his pitiful look: crestfallen, confused; uncomprehending that the game must finish, his close-set eyes anguished under their low black brow. However, before Delph could reach him some survival instinct must have kicked in – he was off in a flash across the cabbage patches, still making the mooing noises, the athletic northerner in pursuit, shouting, 'Come here you little bastard, you fire bug! I'll kick your arse! Kick your arse!' Looking back, I still believe Delph indulged in this gallantry only to impress my mum, who by now was kneeling next to the Little Kid, trembling with butcher's hands.

In the end, poor Nigel was carted off to the Land of Nod known as council care. The Little Kid survived, though he had to spend four months with all his hair shaved off looking like an electrocuted gerbil as the twenty-five stitches did their reformatory work. For some reason he never seemed to grow any bigger, unlike the rest of us. And when we did grow bigger, the Lane grew smaller. The gangs and camps had become an official menace. Although our so-called posse had disbanded, I started running with the rough boys from the top estates. Soon you couldn't sprint, kicking up explosions of slate and mud, down to the breaker's yard at the bottom without encountering Mr Tombs and his two mangy sheepdogs. This self-appointed Cerberus was a rake-thin peggy old buzzard with a voice like a hacksaw who acted as guardian of the grounds after a series of burglaries. Mr Tombs was Dovecote Lane's oldest resident, and he would glower from behind the permanently chained gates to the breaker's yard with a look of harsh propriety. His voice would saw through a perfectly good afternoon with a sour threat: 'Scarper you little buggers, or I'll call the police.' We jeered at him until he rattled the wire meshing, eyes bulging: 'I'll give you some! If your mums and dads weren't just up the road, you'd have some from me, you buggers!' No one knew quite how far he would go. Behind his lizard-slit eyes and gummy scowl he was an unknown and terrifying quantity. I had nightmares in which he broke the skulls of little children to dust between his thumb and forefinger.

Once the kids got out of hand, it soon became clear that the lane was populated by wheezing, gossiping geriatrics – like some kind of terraced old-folks' home. Des and Sinead were the youngest couple on the block. This can have only contributed to my mother's boredom. The most magnanimous of these valetudinarians was Mrs Hewson, who lived in the last house in the bumpy lane, just before it dipped to the ivy-devoured wall of the breaker's yard. She had a breadloaf hair-do left over from the mid-sixties and boiled-sweet specs, behind which glimmered seemingly sane eyes. She didn't appear to mind the rolling gangs of boys pelting each other with half-bricks just outside her net-curtained home. But then she had Colin to worry about. Even at that young age I, along with everyone else, harboured suspicions about Mrs Hewson's son, so obviously unmarried yet in his early thirties. So obviously shy, yet simultaneously threatening. He was often seen at erratic hours with a plastic bag under one arm and a big snorkel parka done up in all weathers. The plastic bag undoubtedly contained pornography. Some of it ended up in our camps – left there purposefully? It wouldn't surprise me. He was always sneaking around, friendless, trembling. Still fresh are the odd, vertigo-like sensations on first seeing the crumpled glossy pages with their gleaming stilettos, anguished expressions and detailed seething clefts. It took years before I, and probably the other astonished little boys, realised these women were largely chimerical. For Colin Hewson, with his pursued expression glimpsed in a greasy halo of fur, this was probably the closest he ever got to a real woman. People claimed he had a voice like a Dalek, but I cannot remember him uttering a single word to anyone in ten years.

So it came as no surprise when, arriving back after a desultory camping holiday in Torquay, we were greeted by police officers and their streamlined shiny vans in the lane investigating the sexual murder of an old lady on the allotments. Colin Hewson was the prime suspect. It was a sultry August afternoon. There was a flurry of nervous excitement when a journalist knocked on our front door and asked if he could use our phone. At that moment, the van with the mysterious, tarpaulin-wrapped cadaver in the back rolled past. As our door opened we were met with a pack of pressmen hovering on the step to gain some height for the photograph. Everyone was afforded a brief, terrible glimpse. The corpse was encased in a raw ebony body-bag guarded by a policewoman. No part of the anatomy was visible, but this only invested the mobile sarcophagus with potent questions about the human organism and its final destination. So this was death, then. A tremendous stillness at the centre of things while the living take photos, wring their hands, cry hysterically. In death, it seems, the focus for a short while is on you only. How pleasurable, if only one were conscious to reap the benefits of that sudden celebrity! And then, somewhere unseen, the dutiful worms take their turn. The human body begins its eternity of neglect. One becomes obscure. Literally non-existent. Only after this process is completed does activity subside and one is granted some peace.

Many years later I discovered what had happened to this woman, my mother having hidden the local papers for weeks after the grisly event. She had been raped and strangled, with a broken broomstick pushed so far inside her that it was discovered only during the post-mortem. I remember feeling damaged and sick at this revelation; startled that human beings had such unreal, bestial violence inside them. It was like the occasion when I discovered what the word 'Holocaust' actually referred to. The word itself was phonetically scary. Was it really true? Or were the revisionists deeply afraid that this mechanised, industrial-scale slaughter could be part of a so-called civilised world? How could it have happened? And so recently in world-historical terms too. A paradigm shift we are only just beginning to comprehend. It all seemed very remote from my secure embryo-world of trees and camps. The world that was always quiet on Sundays, tempered by the lovely soporific pipings of wood pigeons. So remote that it might have happened on another planet.

After Colin's arrest, and predictable release, the crime went unsolved for eighteen months. Then new evidence convicted a young welder who lived on nearby Annesley Rise. A skinhead and member of the National Front, he had been under the impression that his victim had been Asian. In fact, she was Portuguese, of Romany blood – Gemma Fernandez, a woman who had lived and worked in the country since the Second World War. She had escaped the Nazis in 1945 and had lived in the same gloomy bungalow until 1976. Thirty years of quiet living after the fevered diaspora had deposited her in a dreary commuter town in Hertfordshire. That's a long time to believe you've finally evaded man's inhumanity to man, his butcherings, his holocaust. A long time to carry the illusion that you were one of the lucky ones . . . Her killer got life. He was, as I recall, one of the roustabouts who used to wolf-whistle my miniskirted mother as we dragged a shopping wheelie down to the market.

Neither the murder nor Mr Tombs stopped us from investigating the land beyond the breaker's yard. There we discovered the remains of an old school playground, the ramshackle schoolhouse gutted and overgrown. Populated by pheasants, foxes and blackbirds, broken glass crunched underfoot as we ran our heedless ways. It was overhung by tall silver birches and sycamores. Once I climbed one to retrieve an old man's flat cap, only to tumble from the branches, the hat teeming with a devil's cauldron of earwigs. I thought of Gemma Fernandez in the cold ground with only these for company. Here we would dig for fossils, play army, smash old TV sets, before it was time to return to the ticking house. Later, I would learn to cycle a stabilised bike on the gouged macadam, the tyres forever puncturing on scattered glass.

It was in the surrounding wooded wilderness, strewn with whacked-out radials and circles of bonfire ash, that Gemma had been strolling when she was attacked. Only cissies, however, let that worry them. By the time we were all approaching middle-school we knew every climbable oak and jungle shortcut in the area. Though sometimes, on darkening afternoons, venturing to the very edge of the wood, it seemed one would enter almost Narnia-like into another world. It was here we found the derelict remains of what once must have been a very grand house. There were submerged cellars with racks of blackened wine bottles, draped in a white mist of cobwebs. There was a drained swimming pool jammed with busted cookers and car bonnets, all dumped into a tarry inch of rainwater – water that seemed alive with belching, gangrenous frogs. Best of all was a piece of land which might once have been the tennis court. It was now a miniature meadow, over-grown and bordered on all sides by overhanging horse chestnut trees. For a brief time this became a very magical place for me, as no one in our loose agglomeration of tearaways seemed to know its existence, or were too busy hurling bottles and masonry into the drained pool to explore further. It is good to have an exclusive spot in the universe, somewhere that is yours and yours only – a virtual impossibility in adult life. It was a place I sought out, always alone, on summer days, to stand in the glossy waist-high grass and enjoy a resolute, uplifting solitude. The celestial light of July invested everything with the vivid stillness of a dream. The grown-up world seemed many years in the future then. A feeling of unparalleled peace, of timelessness, was achievable in that rectangle of hushing grasses. I can see now the blazing snow of elder flower; the quick-diving magpies hurrying to their partners in the dense chestnut canopies. It was as if the place were entirely and magically removed from the rest of the town, the world even. There I allowed the warm, giving silence of the field to fill me to the brim, like a slowly poured glass of wine; a towering summer paradise, the sun falling in retina-splitting arcs through the tree tops.

The memory of this experience has resulted in a peculiar idea: maybe there is no heaven – because we have had it already. In childhood. All notions of Eden may stem from this. A moment during a childhood day – not the photo-moment, misleadingly captured – but a real, living sun-gloried afternoon when time stood still. Usually in a sylvan setting. My hours in the long grass of the overgrown tennis court approached this notion of the paradisal. After all, the word 'paradise' derives from the Persian for 'garden'. It is a memory unique to each of us: plural, though defiantly singular in its particularities. A seafront somewhere; a taste; a safe hand. The Godlike hour afforded every man. If we were to locate this moment, this second caught in a windfall of light, on the grid of memory it would be at the centre, the very apex. The absolute centre of experienced time, by which we judge all other moments. That flash of high balance, with the sun so sympathetic to the leaves, the leaves so sympathetic to the sun. That hour of splendour in the grass. Our adult memories can never compete with this paragon, this near-Platonic recollection. What can we provide to compete with it? The wedding day? The best night of sex we ever had? The great meal with friends that gives one the sensation of life deepening sensually and emotionally? All are shadowed by time, corrupted by time. They all tear past too rapidly, are located on the outskirts of the brain's memory map. On the dim periphery. No, it is the childhood sun-epiphany that occupies the throne. It is eternal for as long as we are. So maybe there is no heaven. No eternity. Because we have had it already. In that moment.

Back at the ticking house, things were about to change for ever, though I did not know it then. One of the last occasions when my mother, father and their boy were together was the cold Christmas I was allowed to chop the firewood. I must have been six or seven years old. Frost had settled on the red-hot pokers of the back garden; Russian gusts troubled the high branches of the birches and evergreens. Puddles became mirrors, oozing up brackish water when broken with the heel. Inside the warm cocoon of number fourteen were a couple of sealed-up Victorian fireplaces that Des had uncovered with pickaxe and monkey wrench. He claimed that a house without an open fire was 'barbaric'. Once they were functional, he would sit close to the flames, a book open on his lap, Mendelssohn's violin concertos in the background. And my mother itching with tedium, no doubt. That Christmas, I was helping him to fetch the newly halved logs in a wicker basket.

'Are you really moving to France, Dad?'

He gave me his evaluating look and scratched his sweating pate. 'I'm afraid so, but you'll still see me. I'll be back every two weeks to keep everything shipshape.'

'Do you have to go? That means I'll be with Mum all the time.'

'I'm there for as long as Diatrix need me. And what's wrong with your mother's company all of a sudden?'

'She might bring Uncle Delph around again. I don't like him. He's a freak.'

My father ceased unloading the logs and looked suddenly apprehensive, though he quickly disguised this by seeming out of breath. He puffed, 'I think you'll find his bark is worse than his bite.' Then, thinking of Mum, he let out a bizarre chuckle. 'More's the pity . . . Come on, why don't you help me chop the last of the wood.'

In the easy way that children are distracted from their preoccupations, I gasped: 'Can I?!'

'Why not? You're getting to be a big boy now.'

In my excitement I started to dance around the room. I was aware that my father was sharing in my happiness – in a reserved way, of course: he always appeared uneasy during open displays of high spirits. Uncomfortable, as if he wanted them to end as soon as possible. He stood there with a look of broad approbation, a grin opening up his face. To hide his embarrassment at this pleasure he massaged his temples – both at once with thumb and forefinger spread, a characteristic movement. Then I did the worst possible thing: a silly spontaneous thing that still causes me inexplicable shame. I accidentally knocked his glasses off. They narrowly missed the flourishing fire and landed in the wood basket. At once this lit the blue touch paper of his temper, and he began scrabbling among the logs for his spectacles, hissing and cursing. In my panic and shame I ran outside into the failing light and waited for him. At the bottom of the garden the tall evergreens swayed like the conifers in Chagall's *Le Poète allongé*.

He soon appeared, glasses replaced, slightly less ogreish, but still hassled, impatient. He took up the hand-axe and demonstrated how the logs should be split. Severely, he stated, on no account should the axe be brought down while holding the log. Instead, the sharp edge should be tapped into the wood, allowing enough purchase to lift both at the same time. Then he did a practice hit for my benefit. Smack! The wood parted effortlessly on the block.

He didn't seem to have exerted any force at all – it was all in the angle, he told me. Then he passed the brutish blade to me. Of course, I immediately forgot his instructions. My trembling left hand grasped the dusty log. It was now or never. Upstairs, when he had assented to letting me chop the firewood, I had never felt closer to him. It was one of those father-and-son moments – my first and last, as I was to discover. But my act of rank clumsiness had left me feeling foolish, incompetent, degraded. An extreme reaction, you may ponder, but this is the Bildungsroman of a poet here, not an investment banker. I brought the axe down . . . and hit the thumb of my left hand with a square blow. Blood welled up, then a glimpse of bone; white and exposed like the dome of my father's head. Expecting fireworks, I was to be proved wrong. Des merely took the axe and quietly led me through the blue back door in search of a tourniquet; the tall trees now even more like Chagall's against a sky of furious purple.

Despite my bandaged hand dangling from a sling I managed to have the best Christmas Day I can remember. The nights preceding it were rich with an unforgettable excitement, the blue air deep and cold, ringing with carols. The opening of each gold-glitter window on the advent calendar caused an intolerable ache of anticipation. Then, on the magical morning itself, there seemed to be presents galore, some of them bought by Delph as an ingratiating gesture towards my mother, though I did not realise this at the time. I sat like young Stephen Dedalus, happy to see the real fire banked high and red in the grate, the Christmas pudding with its welding-torch party-hat borne in on a special plate. A sense of peace was the vital component here, the determining factor. Quietness and safety and excitement. The Christmases of childhood are always jewel-like, somnolent, special. Special in the qualities of the light: the gold and green created by the tall candles; the serene properties of purple enhanced by Christmas tree bulbs; the reflective silver bands on school-provided crêpe paper. Then there are the gilded, aureate flashes thrown by the Angel's Wheel, as small flames are lit one after another; the radiant seraphim slowly beginning their flight over the copper bowl; the celestial chimes making the most sacred and delicate sound. Church bells from beyond the stars heard. A hushed, exalted time, the year all guttered out into short afternoons of dismal December rain and walloping winds. Also, the quietness of the living room on Christmas Eve, chocolate coins ransacked to the last wrapper, and only the intense nest of the tree for light, a cargo of gifts at its feet. There is a unique preemptory quiet that belongs exclusively to that silent night – a deep, restful hush that seems to emanate from every house on the street, as if, after long agony, the whole world had finally downed its weapons for an evening.

Enter Delph Tongue. The jolly thriving wooer. Who the fuck let *him* in? Well, my mother of course. My mother who was always there. And against the best advice. After Des took up residence in Lille, the posturing northerner was everywhere, as cheap and brash as his Brut aftershave. He was a tall man, muscular, with corpse-like cheekbones white and drawn under a thin Viking skin. His cleft-chinned face towered over me like some statue of Stalin in Red Square. However, as much like Uncle Joe as he eventually became, this being the seventies, his role model was the Travolta of *Saturday Night Fever*, and in accordance he wore his trousers too tight and too flared: the awful bullybag on show at all times. In fact, this was at the core of my revulsion – in contrast to Des, he was an overly sexualised man: pheromonal, engorged, straining, erect. He carried an air of overmanning stupidity, of defiance and boundless ignorance. In those days, I used to bring my Gertrude breakfast in bed – and there they would both be, propped against the distressed pillows. There was a sense of urgency to this servile act – I had to be quick: with the two of them working in the same school, they left the house at different times. Stopped the tongues from wagging unnecessarily. There was also something inappropriate in the way Delph sat, naked down to his abdomen, among the luxurious covers as I handed him and mother the charred toast and milky tea. Mum would be deep in the duvet, a pinkish fresh look on her face that I hadn't seen before, her jet black hair fanned and ringletted against the fat pillowcases. I would be wondering when my father was coming back and what *he* would think about another man in *his* bed. But I never questioned the fact of an 'uncle' sleeping with my mother. This was just what adults did, I surmised, when they reached a certain age. As I deposited the tray and the post on the sheets, Delph would always have a witless witticism to hand, the trademark of the humourless man. Men with no sense of humour shouldn't attempt gags, that way they at least retain the kudos of the strong silent type. But this didn't deter Delph.

'You're a cheeky one,' he'd say, 'barging in on two people with no clothes on.'

Where's the wit in that? He would be smiling, as if he'd just delivered a devastating one-liner at the Carnegie Hall; waiting for the raucous applause.

'Leave him alone, Delph,' my mother would groan. 'It makes a change to be waited on hand and foot.'

'Aye. He's like a little butler. Little Lord Fauntleroy!' he chided, laughing indulgently.

Once mother had left for the school, and while my 'uncle' climbed into his paint-spattered overalls, I was regaled with gruesome stories about the hell-holes he had worked in: mental homes, meat-factories, sewers. Apocryphal or not, they were the kind of tales he probably thought would amuse a young lad. But instead they had a deeply disturbing effect. Before rising to the rank of school caretaker, Delph had worked as a mortuary assistant and grave-digger. One morning, as he zipped up his blue-cotton boiler suit, he said, 'When you die, make sure you don't leave your gold fillings in.'

'But I don't have any gold fillings. Mine are black,' I replied, slightly bewildered as to why people wore gold where nobody could see it.

'Oh aye, just make sure you don't.'

'But why?'

'Cos those were the first things me and Tommy had out. Then the wedding rings. One got stuck on this old bloke's finger. Like a bloody limpet, it were. We tried soap, hot water, everything. In the end we just chopped the bugger off.'

I gulped, 'Was there . . . was there blood?'

'Dead people don't bleed, lad.'

'Are they cold?'

'Cold as ice. Well, they been int' freezer. Best gag I played on Tommy was when we were switching shifts. I dressed one of the stiffs up in my clothes and sat him in a chair for when he came in. You shoulda seen the look on our Tommy's face!'

'Did you tell Mum this story?'

'I wouldn't blab about that to your mother, if I was you.' He looked at me, and I saw all the animal cunning of his Aryan features. A kind of threat mingled with a base need for acceptance. 'You should respect your mother. That's your problem. You're too cheeky by half. In my day you would've got the back of someone's hand for telling on folk.'

Yes, these threats and mirthless practical jokes were his stock in trade. A sort of substitute for wit. I remember him concealing a real spider in a bathtowel for my mother to find, almost scaring her into a state of catatonia. Not a joke spider, you understand, but one of the eight-legged fiends from the downstairs can. There was an element of cruelty in these pranks, and of control, too, of dominance. As the years of his tenure drifted past he would try to assert his usurper's authority in different ways, but at the time there were these chilling ruses. He also made it very clear to me that I would never beat him in a fight. Never. Not even when I was eighteen, twenty-five, thirty-five. He would strut around in a yellow posing pouch (which bore the laconic legend: 'Danger — Long Vehicle') and flex his pecs.

'You'll never win a fight with me. Even when you're bigger. I'd *bray* thee.'

Ah, the archaic thees and thous — so shocking at first, so alien and impertinent to the ear, ludicrous in any context lacking an altar and a lectern. But every sentence seemed to contain one of these pronouns culled from the King James Bible. 'Thou's just a little sprat — skin and bone.'

Finally, on these strange mornings, he would challenge me to an arm wrestle. I crumpled, of course, but I felt I couldn't lose face by backing down. And he always asked me to touch the straining, vein-throbbing heft of his biceps as he pretended to struggle: 'Go on, feel that. Hard as bastard granite! Like Rocky in his flicks.' Then my knuckles hit the canvas. I like to think my dad could have won such a contest, and looked forward to the day when *I* would, regardless of the threatening nonsense he poisoned me with.

Of course, this was the honeymoon period for Delph and Sinead, the golden summer of their 'shenanigans'. They celebrated this with a nauseating, declarative ardour that was unsettling to behold. Delph would turn up at number fourteen with gift-wrapped bouquets of sickly carnations; trinket boxes containing necklaces and cheap-looking diamond rings; his 'n' hers dressing gowns, and all manner of gaudy crap. But there was no disguising the smell of something rotten in the county of Hertfordshire. My mother suddenly and mysteriously took up keep-fit, putting in half an hour of aerobic stretches before work. Her wardrobe changed, too. Banished were the simple black suits that matched her eyebrows, in were seventies rollnecks, wigwam bell-bottoms, clingy tops and ringletted hair like Farrah Fawcett-Majors. Yes, the seventies had everything to do with the tastelessness of their epic *amour fou*. The dyspeptic dribble of free-love and bra-burning that had started in late '69 had now morphed into a garish tide of anything-goes. The mid-seventies: nipples everywhere and inadvisable Stuart-era bouffants on every man. Powercuts, political scandal, peccadilloes. The disturbing physicality of disco. Instead of Mendelssohn, the house now bopped to those slick four-to-the-floor productions, all played off quaint 45 rpm singles. RAK, Columbia, Tristar. The high watermark of white flares. YessirIcanboogie. Saveallyourkissesforme. Youmakemefeellikedancingdancingdancing. Also never off the turntable, the eternal Christmassy harmonies of Abba. Sinead and Delph would mince around to this soundtrack for hours on their forbidden weekends before sitting glued to the television, seemingly joined at the hand and lip.

Naturally, their eternal summer started to fade. I remember the terror I felt on first overhearing a violent argument between them. My mother shrieking from the kitchen downstairs; the explosions of broken crockery; the leonine male voice roaring above it all. How could two people so detailedly devoted to each other find themselves in such combat? How could reechy kisses so swiftly turn to blows? It was a sickening paradox for me. Worst of all were the discordant scenes over food. Those unquiet meals made for many ill digestions. I remember Delph calling my mother 'an ungrateful bitch' at the dinner table, after she'd expressed mild dismay at a disastrous lasagne that he'd slaved over. The rest of the meal was sat out in excruciating silence as Sinead sobbed quietly, the food suddenly forlorn and inedible on everyone's plate.

Delph would be in the habit of doing the weekly shopping, a great bootful of bags that filled the freezer to bursting point. This extravagance was in direct contrast to the occasional trips to the market for vegetables and fish that used to satisfy the palates of Des and his wife. To add to this abrupt reversal, Delph often spent time at the rickety kitchen table clacking out mini-printer sell-by dates which he affixed to every item before they were stored. A psychiatrist could probably make much of this prissy compulsion coupled with his strident masculinity. In fact, he exhibited all the unwitting campery that goes with overpoweringly masculine men. I always related this to the awful seventies virility of the Bee Gees — beards, gold, cream trousers. Their measurement of libido in a *walk*. So this was what it meant to be a man? Two decades previously it was a short-back-and-sides and doing your National Service that made you a man. Now it was a falsetto and a Colgate grin. I can recall my father, years later, when Sinead and Delph were unhappily married, calling his usurper a 'woofter' to a friend. Was there a touch of lavender in their later marriage? I was too young to tell, although I always found something anomalous about Delph's flatmate, 'Mike', who we occasionally saw before my new uncle had his size elevens under the table. Now, that would have been a double insult. My mother sharing a pavilion with a guy who hadn't even sorted out which side he was batting for.

All in all, Delph Tongue was a very strange smalltown Casanova. He was one of those men who had no friends outside of his rela-tionship. Not a single one. I don't remember a phone call or a letter. He would disappear for months at a time, God knows where. Up north? Amsterdam? A loony bin? In the end one can only speculate. All I know is that, for me, my childhood family was interfered with by an invading tool with a ludicrous name. The wrecker. The home-destroyer. The nest-destroyer. The Pluto. The Caliban. The Grendel. The distillation of every stupid and base virtue. A poison to give to your child — who never forgets.

Add to this the strong meat of a single fact: in over ten years of imposture he never once took this little boy out to kick a ball around. Amazing. Obviously, football didn't interest a man such as my father, but with Delph there was always the possibility of an afternoon of glorious headers and turf-stained knees. The truth was — and this became clearer as the years progressed — the gimp just wanted me gone. I was an obstacle between him and my mother. Nothing would have pleased him more than to see me break my neck playing in the woods beyond the lane. And this was a man who, I later learnt, passionately wanted a child with my mother. Why, when he had zero talent for them? All very mystifying. In fact, I only remember two pleasing acts performed by Delph Tongue before things became really nasty. The first was buying a pet for the house. One crushing summer day of sweat and maxi-pops I found myself idly kicking up stones in the lane. Then the beep of a car horn: it was Delph tearing down the road in my mother's car. Parking rapidly, he flipped up the boot. He had that smile on his face, the one that looked like a grimace, or an awful cunnilingual leer. Then he was advancing towards me with a package behind his back. Not a moocow coming down the road, but Uncle Delph with a cardboard box, pocked with breathing-holes containing our first cat. Even the fact that it was later christened 'pussy' – something that Sinead and Delph used to laugh mysteriously over – could not arrest my joy.

The other act of contrition was a trip to the park in Stevenage Old Town, at my mother's behest most likely (Stevenage being a place I thought was so named because it contained so many Steves). We stayed for three hours, Delph pushing me on the swings in the seventies sunlight, snapping photographs which I still have. Byron Easy in his Six Million Dollar Man T-shirt, smiling in the sun that is young once only. I almost got to like him – after all, Des would never consider spending three hours in the park with his boy. The only object missing was a football . . . You may remember me saying I hated Delph. Well, there's a problem with that: as a child whose real father had mysteriously disappeared to another country to work, I experienced a strong urge to love this *de facto* father. But he was ultimately unlovable. Just as shit is ultimately inedible. All attempts at affection were rebuffed – and my natural instincts were revulsion at his hot, showy, self-conscious, campy, aggressive behaviour and gestures. His egregious mix of sadism and sentimentality. His innate coarseness and bestial lack of sophistication. Bear in mind, he was first inculcated into my bloodstream at the age of six. I had to put up with this menacing, proud, ignorant man until I was almost eighteen. That's an awful long time to dine on shit.

Oh yes: 'ignorant' – Delph's favourite word; a word beloved of profoundly stupid people everywhere. Deeply insecure about his lack of education or knowledge of virtually any subject except school caretaking (and on seeing Des's massed living-room library, who wouldn't be?), Delph used to append this word to everything he didn't understand or was threatened by. Rude behaviour was 'ignorant'. No, it wasn't, it was rude. Me not finishing my cabbage was 'ignorant'. No, it wasn't, it was common sense. Me contradicting my mother or sneering at Delph (anything more vocal was answered by his hand cracking me across the forehead) was, apparently, 'ignorant'. No, it wasn't, you freak of nature, it was the natural reaction of a very scared little boy.

As promised, Des made his weary, chemical-smelling return every fortnight and we ate together unhappily as a family. But the house didn't belong to him any more. During the week it vibrated to disco, to blood-curdling rows and other unnameable, uninhibited noises. My father had waived his authority to the oracle from Yorkshire. He had abdicated. Our jaunts to Granny at Yew Tree Close became rare. Instead, we began visiting *Delph's* dim and blighted family up in Wakefied. The contrast was stunning. The long drive would find us on the outskirts of a rain-blasted wooltown: slag-heaps, impoverished pits, boarded-up working men's clubs, flat caps, chippies. His parents' house was a tiny miners' terrace on a row that resembled Coronation Street. Instead of glowing Buddhas, oil paintings and stimulation, there were hours to kill by the damp fire, with Delph's dying tubercular father in a continually made-up bed. He was still black from a lifetime down the pit. I couldn't believe that the seams of soot in his mangled hands would never wash out. His phlegmy voice and accent were almost impossible to follow and his fits of dry coughing and retching frightened me. Overall, my dominant feeling during our stints up north was that of being a spare part; offloaded, as I often was, onto whatever cousin or inbred for a day of mischief on the wind-torn estates. I hated them and they hated me, little Lord Byron Fauntleroy, *a child from another relationship*. Central to these memories is the Saturday morning football. I remember enduring sub-Alaskan temperatures, my flimsy plastic coat covered in icy drizzle, my feet frozen solid. Then there was the torture of waiting for the ref's final whistle, the charging boys, the strong conviction that I shouldn't be there. In addition to this, Yorkshire seemed to free Delph to explore the full stupidity of his personality – he didn't have to pretend to be cultured up there, with his own. The first time he was truly menacing towards me occurred after a wedding reception I was coerced into attending. We arrived at the half-finished barn of the social club to be met by the full desolation the north had to offer: gale-blown car park; sad confetti among chip forks; cold-looking ushers with draught-excluder moustaches. Then inside: seventies perms; Babycham; cheese nibbles (anything 'foreign' or with garlic left untouched). My mother in an awkward sequinned dress. Delph in black tie like an undertaker. And something disharmonious in the pickled-onion air: a sour argument between Delph and Mum had prevailed since our arrival, like the thin drizzle. Vicious whispering. Black looks. Delph's raised hand and my mother's flinch. In fucking company too, the madman. The stomach-upsetting fear all this aroused in me . . . Then it was time to be deposited back at his parents' house as it was past my bedtime. Delph elected to drive me there, insulting my mother as he careered out onto the blowy street. I recall the palm-sweating anxiety of being alone with him, the pleasure he took in the violent slamming of the car door; the glorying in his own capacities, his *range*. Then . . . then it all goes blank and cloudy; occluded. A terrible event occurred, but I cannot remember what it was. It will have to wait. Yes, it will have to wait until the cloud cover lifts.

Once back in civilisation, a mooted trip with my father to France seemed like sweet manna from heaven. We finally made it over there one Easter, Des driving the two of us onto the ferry, eating toothpick-thin french fries with arterial ketchup. We stopped off in Paris first, and stayed in a hotel opposite Marie Curie's house. Of course, Des knew all about her – with him you had the guided tour, the history of radium, her martyr's death. And he wasn't just reading it off the plaque outside her house. After my radioactive exposure to Delph, I had forgotten that adults *knew* things: they possessed know-how, working knowledges, facts and figures; code-breakers for the world at large. Then there was the Parisian soundtrack. My Proustian response to music probably began here with the tape that was never out of the new-fangled Philips cassette recorder. It was, I'm ashamed to admit, *Tubular Bells*. I only have to hear the pure, crystalline arpeggios of its opening bars, and I am back in Paris; hounds barking under a blue midnight sky, streetlamps gleaming off unfamiliar Citroëns, the smell of sweet refined choc-olate that the French used for their Easter eggs. Strange that the hot, hopeful emotions that well up on hearing those notes are significant only to me – it feels they should have a bigger signifi-cance in the world: a transferable, communicable meaning.

In the end, me and Dad struck a deal – if I didn't mention Delph, he would let me go to the pâtisserie every morning and order *'une baguette, s'il vous plait.'* Also, take me to see *Close Encounters of the Third Kind* dubbed into French. This arrangement worked very well until we arrived at industrial Lille, where I let slip that Delph had been using his workbench and tools. At the time my father had been chopping vegetables for his one and only dish: spaghetti bolognese. This final indignity made my father's shoulders shake. It was hard to tell whether this was down to the onions or the information, but I'm sure I saw globes of tears behind his glasses. Him being my dad and everything, I'd like to think it was the onions.

At the end of Delph and Sinead's honeymoon period, something inadmissible occurred. A nocturnal fracas that only now puts me in mind of Mandy and the Archway flat, when the new tenants started to move in (and out) one after another. How I recreated an earlier hell in a different location, I don't know, but the overpaid behavioural analysts always state that this is inevitable . . . It was an incident that reinforced my notion that a house is not a home if it vibrates to the dark forces of violence, maliciousness, hatred. Rather a narrow ledge for eternity, like the pad of Prometheus, than that shit.

Delph and Mum had taken the train to London to see the gruesome musical *du jour*, Andrew Lloyd Webber's overblown *Evita*. They had played the album for months. I was as sick of 'Don't Cry for me Argentina' as I was of disco. Deep beneath my disgust was the conviction that they were connoting the lyrics with their turbulent love: 'All through my wild days, my mad existence, I kept my promise – don't keep your distance.' Anyway, they must have taken these melodramatic passions back to Hamford, because I was awoken very late not by my mother, but by the mother of all rows. Not just shouting, but the loud crashing of objects as they were hurled around the living room. I tiptoed onto the top landing, heart beating like crazy. Immediately, Mum appeared in an arc of light; her mauve head-scarf askew, panda-eyed from her liquid mascara. 'It's all right. Just go back to bed. Do you hear me now? Go back to sleep. It's all right.' But it wasn't all right. She returned to the jarring sound of bitter curses; the raised male voice like the auditory equivalent of a phallus. Dominant, accusatory, heedless. Of course, I didn't go back to bed. I was too terrified. Like the clichéd child listening to his parents row, cowering behind the banisters, I waited in intolerable suspense for it to finish. Except these were not my parents. Just my mum and some lunatic. This added to the sense of danger. Anything might happen. It sounded like she was going ten rounds with Tyson down there. More gut-churning bangs and splinterings. The abominable sound of a table going over. Then sweeping lights outside, the policeman's insistent knock. Delph, looking especially tall and equine, bolting down the corridor to intercept them. The blue arm pulling him out before he could start his mendacious explanation. My mother weeping, broken, shaking; a bruise over her left eye, her long straight nose quivering in anger and fear.

She took a look at me and vanished shamefully into the living room. I followed, and was met with an unbelievable sight. Every object in the room was upside down or destroyed. The coffee table on its back like a floored wrestler; pictures torn from the walls; broken flower vases on the drenched carpet; Des's shelves of books staved in; a lampshade in the fireplace. And worst of all, a giant rip in the saffron blinds, like a huge eye letting in the night. My mother left for a moment to talk with the police, then returned. She came close into my personal orbit and knelt down before me. 'Now, this didn't happen, okay? This is our little secret. You won't tell anyone, will you?' She was trembling, an unusual look of fear in her rain-coloured eyes. I didn't answer. She continued, 'If you say yes, I'll let you stay up and watch TV.' She had never allowed me this privilege before, but I felt, for the first time ever, in control of an adult. To be honest, I could have named my price. I tremulously asked, 'Is he coming back?' She smoothed her hair and said quickly: 'No, not tonight. He won't be back tonight.' So I sat in front of the mono-chrome screen for two hours. I watched *Match of the Day* and then some play about slum kids on a day-trip to the seaside, while my mother set about resurrecting the room. It was the emptiest pleasure I ever experienced.

Delph disappeared for six months after this outrage. My only glimpse of him was when my mother drove me to Stevenage swimming baths for our weekly dip. The return journey was always undergone in pitch darkness, the stars rich and abundant over the open fields of Hertfordshire, the car stinking of chlorine and damp towels. Often we passed the coaches leaving for northern destinations with forbidding names: Sunderland, Wetherby, Barrow-in-Furness, Wakefield. One ink-black evening I glanced out of the window as the illuminated flank of a coach swung past, and saw the ghostly face of Delph at the back. Unmistakably him, all pretence of shallow charm cancelled from his long Aryan face. A rare glimpse down the toilet of his other life away from my mother. There he was: solitary, brutish, unrepentant. I started shouting, 'Mum, there's Delph, there's Delph! You've just missed him on that coach.' She didn't look at me.

'Oh, I didn't see,' she said with forced insouciance. But I knew by the agitation of her fingers on the steering wheel and the way her teeth caught her lower lip that she had.

———

Entropy is a useful word. The autodidact is always on the lookout for useful words. I won't patronise you by stating that it means the tendency of all systems to chaos. A 'measure of the degradation and disorganisation of the universe' (COD). From the Greek *trope,* meaning transformation. The centre cannot hold. It is an apt word for describing the union of Sinead Easy and Delph Tongue. Because marriage, or a relationship, is a system like any other. And it always felt as if the situation was close to spiralling out of control. That this was the direction it was fated to take. Over the years, the White House became just that, a house, not a home. A housing. A shell with a shaky centre. If anything defines home then it is stability. Things should not be in a constant state of flux and transformation; instead things should endure. A state of entropy could also describe the home I tried to build with Mandy. Living with an endless succession of tenants might help to pay the rent, but it dilutes any sense of permanence or peace. Nevertheless, you try to make places permanent because you can never make people permanent.

The big flat in Archway started to feel like a hotel, or rather, a B&B, a *pension*; the worst kind of flop-house. As I might have mentioned, the three pretenders who took our newly decorated rooms were soon unmasked. The female singer-songwriter was discovered fixing up heroin in our shower. She spent weeks dressed only in a scabrous flesh-coloured dressing gown, crying audibly in her room before Mandy was forced to eject her into the night. The IT consultant was also involved in Class As, only he was a coke courier, his mobile incessantly ringing, leaving at all hours to deliver his wraps to the youth of north London in pubs, tube stations and their private abodes. He also had to go.

The so-called businessman was by far the oddest human being I
had met up to that point in my life. A squashed-looking man of
forty, Ukrainian or Macedonian, he once brought back two
hundred eggs which he attempted to store in the communal
fridge. We returned home one day to find defrosting pizzas in
all the cupboards, and a sulphurous smell that didn't leave the
kitchen for weeks. Every morning he would leave the flat in his
dry-cleaned suit for an unknown destination, carrying an expensive briefcase. Once, we surreptitiously opened this case to find
it contained nothing but sand. As far as we knew he never used
the bathroom once. Instead he would douse himself in scent.
Then there was the moaning in the night. In the small hours he
could be heard babbling in his native tongue, then gargling and
whinnying. In the end we didn't have to throw him out. He
performed this task of his own volition. We heard him attempting
to shoot the moon at four a.m., but were too late to catch his
swarthy hands on the door-latch. All we found was his television
set abandoned in the hall. In his room was the briefcase, still full
of sand.

So all three rooms were standing empty. Inevitably, the rent had
to be lowered to below its previous rate. Then came the real scum
of the earth. The rootless, itinerant flotsam and jetsam who answer
small ads with all the unconvincing bullshit they can muster. *I'm
just down from Liverpool and need a place for a couple of weeks.* Sure, no
problem. *I don't have a deposit, how about an eighth and a fake Rolex?*
Fine, move in when you want. *People say I've got a dodgy face, but
I'm honest, trust me!* I'm sure you have, and are: come and share all
the intimate spaces of our life. Because that's what sharing a flat
amounts to. You cannot live with people you wouldn't choose to
stand next to on the tube. But that's what Mandy and I ended up
doing, just to make ends meet.

With these desperadoes came real disruption, discord, chaos.
Human excrement left in the shower, and no one owning up to it.
A lad from Manchester who split owing three months, leaving only
a pair of jeans and a heartbreaking note to the effect that it was all

he had of worth to give us. The teenager from a loaded family up in Highgate who neglected to tell us he'd been thrown out of his parents' mansion, rather than leaving it of his own accord. After a while, his folks had our full sympathy. Every night his room, which was situated next to ours, would shake to the subterranean bass of techno, hardbag, ragga. A posse of pot-smoking trust-fund skankers would be over every night, swearing, whooping and farting until we unplugged the master fuse for the whole house. One by one, all our kitchen utensils started to disappear: cups, plates, corkscrews, the lot. Eventually they were discovered in his room like guilty errant children. Pans of week-old baked beans were uncovered under jazz mags, growing anemones of mould. Finally, one day when I was at the shop, he tried to behead Mandy with a baseball bat. Entropy had reached its full operational capacity, its disintegrative zenith. She was forced to break down his locked door after repeated appeals to turn his music off were ignored. The floppy-haired fool, stoned out of his mind, grabbed his bat and pursued Mandy around the house, destroying everything he could see, eventually overturning the coffee table in our room. I raced home from the shop, the familiar sight of a police car in the street outside. But it was the vision of the coffee table that arrested me, that welded me to the spot. Mandy, shrieking that she could have been killed, shook in the doorway, while I stood there distractedly, staring at the four legs upright in the air, like a dead animal. I couldn't speak. I was back in Hamford, the night after *Evita*, the little boy behind the big banisters, walking in on that scene of unforgettable destruction; my mother's rain-coloured eyes full of rain.

The restaurant car opens its smoked doors with a reassuring whisper, allowing me free passage to the bar. The buffet car. I have come in search of a drink. And not just any drink, oh no. Only a vat of wine or a distillery of whisky will do after recalling so much trauma, so much terrible beauty. Granny and her gallery. Delph and his straining dong. Des and his onion tears. The dead table, on its back with rigor mortis legs ... The only problem I can foresee, as I wend my way through the baubled crowd with their double-bacon-and-brie combination sandwiches, is that Great North Eastern Railways don't do proper drinks, they do improper drinks. They do excuses for drinks. Those Lilliputian miniatures with their silly clear-cup hats; the squat bottles of weak imitation Jerry beer; the minuscule shots and their rabbit droppings of ice ... I park myself in the queue by the window and drink in the tearing fields instead. How shocking and tawdry the present day seems after all that recollection, that orgy of reminiscence. In the distance, past the boating lake with its outcrops of children, its simple sails, the bundling countryside seems lighter, more surreal the further towards the aft of the train you go. Almost as if it were daylight once more; the diurnal revolution somehow in reverse. The rain appears to have abated. Outlines of ruined abbeys – pale Elsinores – are visible on the horizon. A late shaft of divine sunlight, emitted from a troubled grey cloud, is strafing distant enclosures. The shadows of cringing trees seem suddenly otherworldly – as if the whole of Hertfordshire were lit from below by some seraphic arc-light ... I rub my eyes. There are no sails, no children, no Danish castles. Of course there aren't. It is only a trick of the failing light.

The only other problem I foresaw with scoring a drink, as I left my memory-booth in carriage B, was the smoking problem. I think I mentioned my slight accident with the unextinguished dog-end and the thankfully fire-retardant duvet. It's been over a month now and I'm not sure of my resolve, my iron-in-the-soul. A month since I nearly immolated myself and my three patient flatmates. The thing the anti-smoking lobby tries not to emphasise is that cigarettes are one of life's kingly pleasures. The fact that it is a pleasure never free from the shadow of death – the sovereign's sovereign – seems all the more apposite. The notion they will never admit to is that nine out of ten cigarettes taste ambrosial and relieve a mental hospital's worth of anxiety. They also give you something to do with yours hands, something to look forward to, and a stance of unanswerable cool. Christ, they're good. In fact, the more this puritanical synod – the anti-snout zealots, the professional *smirkers* – tries to persuade you with phrases such as: *dirty little habit, makes you impotent, kills you in the end*, the more one longs to take up smoking as a vocation, to complete one's PhD in advanced inhalation. They neglect to mention that a cigarette and a glass of whisky occupies a space in the higher echelons of sensual pleasure. Also the fact that, clinically, it's easier to kick heroin.

Of course, none of this helps me, or the weakening tungsten of my resolve, as I sway in the Christmas queue. My body is screaming for nicotine, like a starved child. Then I notice something on the horizon. Or rather, it notices me. A familiar church spire, like a poniard in the sky's murky underbelly. An icon from the past, so familiar, so condensed, it feels like it has been burnt onto the retinas for thirty years. But there it is: St Cecilia's church, Hamford! A sick desire to return to my seat before the express shoots through the station grips my intestine. A disabling yearning for the companionship of my notebook. All thoughts of a drink and a soothing pipe of tobacco are jettisoned. I begin to barge my way out of the queue and towards the smoked-glass doors. 'Excuse me please . . . Gangway! . . . Mind your backs!'

Through the bleared windows of carriage G, I can see that the train is making its approach to Hamford station. I search the fuddled Filofax of my mind to recall my carriage designation: B? Yes, I am definitely in B. B for Beatrice, my lost love. That means four more swaying gauntlets to run. Eight sets of smoked-glass doors. One thing's for certain and that is we won't be stopping. Because the express never stops for Hamford. It is a blur on life's memory map. No, it won't stop. I know it won't stop because I have made this journey many times before, as passive passenger, as dumb interlocutor with the vast mouth of the past, its secrets held only in the bowed trees and glimpsed lanes now flashing by the windows of carriage G. Outside, a kind of vivid half-light, a crepuscular photo-negative, is illuminating the convex sweeps of Hertfordshire fields. I can see rooks, like heavy grapeshot, making fast patterns in the sky. A beached tractor on the perimeter of the ploughlines is beam-black and peopleless, as vacant as the scarecrow crucified against the dripping horizon. Then I see the silent mouth of the disused railway tunnel, and feel my own heart in my throat.

Carriage F.

The tunnel, lying between heavy banks of nettles and wild grasses, begins a grave excitement in me. The kind of excitement only felt when place and memory make their intersection. The deep, ungraspable disturbance – so amorphous, so slippery! – of the past happening in the present. The moment is tagged with a ticket: prepare to meet your past. One is powerless to disobey this notice. And it is never just a single recollection, but a compound containing many memories, all vying for examination, for primacy. As I trip over the dragnet knees and feet of carriage F, I see my sixteen-year-old self running towards the disused tunnel. A brittle, skeletal October day of mutable silver skies. The day I left school. The day I returned to find all the locks on my father's house changed. Et tu, Des. I remember running without purpose to the edge of town, where the railway sends its looms of cables deep into the countryside, towards other towns, other futures. The afternoon had that crisply realised clarity of new and keenly felt suffering. The brown already-rotted leaves were shredded and dust-like underfoot. The leaves that were falling amounted to a snow shower of vivid crimson and angry yellow. The air was ice ingested into the lungs. My nightmare of being locked out had finally become a weighty reality, though the White House was long gone. At sixteen, I had been living in Des's bungalow on the outskirts of Hamford. It was there I had decided not to bother turning up for school one day. He had responded by shutting me out with the aid of a master locksmith. Another door had been barred, deadlocked. And I was to live where, exactly? With my mother and Delph in their immaculately tasteless hutch on the blighted Barratt estate, with its nightly rows and vibrations of harm and violence? In Rudi's hammock? On the streets? I ran on, with the autumn sun brave and yellow on the trunks of stripped trees. The leaf-carpeted macadam gave way to a farmer's track of obdurate, uneven earth. The furrows of the old railway tracks were intermittently visible. And there it was: the sightless O of the tunnel, with its sewery vapours, scattered syringes and rich atmosphere of danger. A void. The kind of darkness you don't encounter that often. A secretive and forbidding absence of light. I collapsed under the mossy putrescence of the tunnel wall; heavy with failure, even at that age. Out of breath, out of hope. Tears might have come, I don't recall. Like Dickens and his sojourn in the blacking factory, this was the very worst thing that could possibly happen to me. I knew I would bear the scars a lifetime, with all the attendant self-pity and shame. I remained there for an hour, maybe more – at least until the trees had lost their tinge of sulphurous October yellow, and the light had dimmed. Yes, in the big O of the disused railway tunnel I sat down and wept.

Carriage E.

And now the tunnel is gone, disappeared into the dark backward abysm. As I vault the obstacles of stray suitcases I can see that the train has gained higher ground. We are shooting over a blackened bridge that reveals a mini-roundabout in the recess below. Hobhouse Road! How many years has it been since I saw Hobhouse Road? Like an old friend greeting me with open arms. The intersection of many drunken memories, many childhood journeys in Sinead's Mini to the shops, to the school; inevitably to the hospital. The long straight gorge up a hill to the town centre is quickly effaced by the blur of a housing estate. The Barratt estate! Where my mother moved to set up home with the errant Delph; otherwise known as the Poets' Estate, as every vacant cul-de-sac was named after a substantial versifier from days gone by. Keats Way. Byron Close. Mase Field. Ah, I always liked that last one.

Carriage D.

'Oh, get out of the fu—' I have to be in my seat when we whoosh through the station. Nothing else will calm my rattling nerves. The noise of the train fills my ears as another set of smoked doors makes way for me. I feel the rumble and tilt, the *Sturm und Drang*, the chatter of rails; like Saleem returning triumphant to Bombay, hearing the abracadabra made by the sleepers. I must get this down, this deluge of the past, all masticated by the churning wheels of the carriages. I must fix this horrid equinox in ink. A brief collision with a pensioner exiting the loos and I'm into . . .

Carriage C.

A bridge is fast looming up out of the sepulchral mist. But not one we will travel over. This one we will pass under. It is a flimsy footbridge suspended above the swaying cables. The same one I shivered over on all those three-mile treks to school from the Poets' Estate. It is unnervingly unchanged from twenty years ago: the blue panelling with its streaks of birdshit; the iron railings cold with rain that I used to skid my finger through, schoolbag over hunched shoulders. We can't be far from the station itself now. In fact, the station has to be the next thing. The next stop we never stop at. The final doors seethe open and I gain my writing desk.

The station! Hamford station, with its approach of chalk cliffs wreathed in rain. The pines and their dangerous tenure in the gradient. The sudden ramp of the platform, taking us up, up, up. The screech of the Intercity horn warning passengers that this train, this bullet through time, will not be stopping. Then the hanging baskets with their spectrum of petals, maintained even in the dead of winter. Purple, pink and yellow. Chrysanthemums and lilies. Those quaint hanging baskets swaying from the Victorian wrought iron; the ornate metalwork with its numberless coats of black paint. How they remind me of the day I boarded, all those years ago, the banal escape shuttle heading in the opposite direction – heading for the squall of London, its ice-ages of poverty, its semi-psychotic Spanish women. Then the sudden awning of the ticket office, with its drenched Christmas Eve stragglers; the berserk compression of air stopping their ears.

I used to love this town! And hate it, too. I couldn't wait – as the cliché goes – to leave. For what kind of return is this? Certainly not some kind of Zionist's utopia? It's not a homeland, an Israel or the African interior. This is no-place, some-place; the location of my own personal 'forgotten boredom', my childhood. Except that it isn't forgotten. It lives – and vividly. Hamford is somehow equated with Spenser's Cookham in my mind: the prosaic market town whose countryside – those haunts of ancient peace – could be reached if you continued walking in a straight line for three miles in any direction, a landscape which played host to strange, inexplicable events. Maybe not resurrections in churchyards, but an ineradicable myth system of its own. Spirits seen from the side of Water Hill; leylines under outlying wellheads; mysterious screams heard on July midnights. The old woman, Gemma Fernandez, dead in woodland at the end of our lane, felled by Pluto's dart after escaping the Nazis. The surrounding fields alive with midsummer dryads and maenads. A secret spring of water near my old man's bungalow where depressives came from miles around to drown themselves. The spinneys of trees on high hills that attracted summer Satanists, leaving behind their mysterious rings of ash. And all this enclosing a collection of residential streets, shops, car parks and timbered Tudor buildings. Ah, maybe that was it. Hamford was old, very old, an ancient settlement on the Icknield Way, with its river and Norman church. Groaning up from the ground were the ghosts of Alfred's warriors and their code of wyrd; inoculated into the soil was the blood of strange sacrifices, offerings to Norse gods; or the passage of English kings and queens who hunted in the fertile woodland. And all the time the feral countryside impinging on the frail mead-hall, or what is now a shopping arcade. Chaos pressing its nose against the lit window. A silence that filled the town, especially after dark, after the bells of St Cecilia's church had ceased on an August evening. Yes, when it was dark: that was when the rank blood of pagan slaughters welled up from the chalky soil! With no place of safety except the mind-constructed ones of religion, family, love.

A shrouded sign gives two alternatives: Town Centre and Station. But I don't need the Town Centre because I am the centre, the emotional centre, the locus of memory. Achieved at last. And just as I left it ten years ago. The palimpsest of the past, strangely altered, with its new trudgers through the December mist, new shopfronts and chain bakeries. This dump was what I used to call home, this random collection of dormitory estates, schools, shopping arcades, bleak footbridges.

The station now guzzled down the throat of Advancing Time,

I can see the dagger of St Cecilia's again over the market palisades. I have a sudden sinking sensation caused by the knowledge I am halfway there; halfway towards my destination, like the moment in the cinema when one realises the long-anticipated film must end, just like everything else. *A quick flash of the station approach and its puddles of blinking neon, the lights like exotic fish in an aquarium. The same road where I took my first bedsit with its folding camping table and gunged mini-oven. Its bath on the top landing shared with a mysterious Caribbean gentleman who always left a barber's shop of afro curls and a London Particular after his three-hour soaks. The two-drum laundrette where I washed black jeans till they frayed to a white nothingness. Then the curve of the road that led to my landlady's bungalow at the top, where I made my monthly pilgrimages. Mrs Pincer. That crooked black widow! I remember her manicured front lawn and childless kitchen. The need to make a good impression, to be polite, well-thought-of, non-threatening or rent-dodging, always high in my mind. I hated myself for this dog-like deference, but it came over me automatically.* Going, going, going . . Soon the dark stage curtain will call time on these memories. St Cecilia's disappears, replaced by a junkyard of rail spares and exhausted rolling stock. Get it down! Quick, before it goes. *Mrs Pincer's. Not so far from the Poets' Estate. Why does my mind always stray back to that rabbit run? As if directed by some Global Positioning Device of the psyche. Because so little happened there? Or because so much was reckoned there, in spite of this? It is all behind me now, in the big December darkness, somewhere down the line. I have no choice but to locate it in the interior . . .*

Adieu, adieu, my native shore! Going. *Going.* Gone.

After Dovecote Lane, we lived for five years at number nine Southey Close. On moving in, shades of the prison house immediately darkened its walls. What ghosts must haunt it now? It was situated on a satellite estate, its dismal vistas ludicrously at odds with the ambrosial waft of high culture conjured by the street names. Yeats Drive. Tennyson Avenue. Vaughan View. Imagine if you will, agile reader, a provincial Los Angeles of featureless Barratt hutches, all constructed to house the shoddier end of the commuter market.

Concrete walkways overlooked by the sentinels of sad saplings in mesh cages. Busted Ford Cortinas on tarmac and quartz driveways. No shops for a mile and a half. Each house with the same comfortless layout: kitchen and living room downstairs, two box bedrooms upstairs. Okay, so not the privations of a Rio slum, but a world away from the White House and its cramped Victorian cosiness, its orange grove of books and secretive corners. There was nowhere to play, either. Gone was the Lane and its towering silver birches, allotments and concealed gardens. Gone the rich compost odour of November bonfires, replaced with the constant stink of someone burning plastic and the endlessly depressing tinkle of an ice-cream van. And, behind the flimsy windows with their winding-sheet nets, the rooms were always cold. With no double-glazing or central heating (a system of storage heaters had been installed at all three hundred and fifty addresses), the sleep-deprived poet would find himself braving a nippy bathroom every morning only to douse himself in a chill that lingered till evening. One moment we were at the White House, with Delph hugely, inappropriately, presidentially resident, the next we were at Southey Close watching moustachioed mechanics waxing bonnets every Sunday. The move was just another decision that was never explained: bewildering to a child, completely unacceptable. Why did they have to inflict this orgy of ugliness on me? And for how long would it last? Was it permanent? I felt confused, disrupted, undermined. After all, Des was still living at Dovecote Lane. I would be ferried over there every fortnight when he returned from Lille, then ferried back to the estate every Sunday night in time for school. But somehow this made it all worse. Why couldn't I live at one address or the other? To see the childhood house in juxtaposition with that gaudy dump was unbearable. The adult reasons for moving were never shared with me. It was just the next thing. Another stop on the great general movement away from the Centre.

The new place showed pitiful evidence of an attempt at cultural betterment. This was the satanic work of Delph, pathologically insecure that my mother would miss her weekly dose of Mozart and Radio 4. Though, in Des's absence, this was always doomed to failure. One day I braved the Arctic bathroom to find myself pissing in front of a mini Michelangelo's *David*. Worse still, next to it was a ten-quid repro of Rodin's *Lovers*, a vile token of Delph's affection for my mother, no doubt. I shuddered at the muscular hand of Paolo on her thigh, the awful submission in the curve of Francesca's back. Not only this, he had invested in a set of leather-bound classics (Mrs Trollope, Gaskell, Fanny Burney, G. B. Shaw's plays), cassettes of classical music and a Matisse throw. But Delph had got it all wrong, as people with no innate cultural bearings always will. The books (ordered from a coupon on the back of a Sunday tabloid) were mainly stodgy nineteenth-century melodrama at its worst – all destined to remain unread during his tenure; the classical tapes were monstrous low-fi compilations of marching-band staples; and the Matisse throw was – to anyone with a pair of eyes – gruesomely at odds with mother's delicate William Morris cushion covers, then back in fashion. How I remember my father guffawing at this very definition of vulgarity when I described it to him. He was sitting in front of his log fire at Dovecote Lane, listening to the Winter adagio from *The Four Seasons*. In full petit-bourgeois effect. Often at these times his hooded eyes and lunar pate would look profoundly solemn, until I began to relate the arrival of each new grossly tasteless *objet d'art*. 'Last week, they got a poster of two people kissing. It was sickening.'

Des looked up absent-mindedly from his toilet of despond and asked, 'Who was it by?'

'I don't know, but it was kind of like wallpaper – like a pattern made of gold. And he was holding her head at a funny angle, like he was trying to break her neck. It didn't look comfortable at all.'

'Klimt?'

'Yeah, that's the bloke. But it wasn't signed by him, it was signed by someone called Athena.'

At this Des took off his glasses and exploded into hoarse laughter. His tearful shaking had a strange effect on me – it made my heart leap to see him smile, but it also bequeathed a lifetime of cultural confusion. As much as I despised Delph's cack-handed attempts to embrace Art, to breathe higher air, to imbibe a beaker of something other than Dr Pepper, I hated my old man's easy, self-satisfied, lower-middle-class elitism. It is a legacy I still feel today when reading a tabloid: hatred and guilty pleasure combined. Hatred at their salacious reporting of the latest nonce trial at the Old Bailey, replete with gym-knicker snapshots intended only for a jury, but joy over a liberating editorial attacking the funding of a nobs' opera house 'when people are dying from want of a hospital bed'. Still, these cultural faux pas of Delph's raised a chuckle from Dad, and that's all an eleven-year-old wants when he thinks his father doesn't give a shit whether he lives or dies on a distant housing estate. Eventually, my fortnightly visits would bring forth a tissue of lies and exaggerations. I started making things up just to see him in a mood that wasn't irritable or clinically depressed. In fact, marital separation and moving house didn't seem to have made either Des or Sinead any happier. Often, I would finish the three-mile walk from school to find Mum sitting alone in the darkening kitchen, staring off into space. When I asked her what she was up to she would reply, 'Thinking'. If I put the light on, she would rise to turn it off, then continue sitting until the yellow beaks of the streetlamps threw sad paths of sulphur over her face and the cheap linoleum.

All this struck me as quite odd, because two events at the White House the previous year had led me to believe that her liaison with Delph and the subsequent move would make her deliriously happy. The first occasion I will never forget. I was sitting on the cushions in front of the black-and-white set, watching *Jackanory* when she crouched down before me, obscuring the view as she uttered the immortal words, 'There's something I have to tell you . . .' I remember the shock of seeing her eyes full of strangled compassion, or something approaching the difficulty of explaining an adult and complex fact to a simple and childish mind. Besides which, she had been crying: the tropical-lime seventies eye-shadow was smudged into the dark pits of her eye sockets; her peacock headscarf loose

HOME

over its cargo of ebony hair. She went on: 'Your father and I don't
love each other any more.' I felt a burst of adrenalin at this statement of the absolute obvious. O my prophetic soul! She had been
seeing Delph for five years, for Christ's sake! The man had been a
permanent fixture of the house for the last two. But to hear her
articulate it, in an unusually gentle voice (a voice which excluded
the harsh tones of 'Get down here at once and finish your greens!'
or 'Right! Bedtime, young man!') was indescribably stirring. I knew
I would remember this for the rest of my days. The official
announcement. I hesitated before finally saying,

'That's pretty obvious, Mum.'

She straightened slightly at this, allowing me to catch a glimpse
of the TV screen. She was spoiling *Jackanory*, after all.

'Well, it means we'll be moving to another house.'

'With Uncle Delph?'

'Yes, with Uncle Delph.'

Something like panic or anguish or shame appeared in her face
now, emotions I hadn't seen before and didn't want to see again
in a hurry.

'What about Dad?'

'Your father is going to stay here. You can see him whenever
you like.'

She paused slightly after this statement, as we both knew it was
inaccurate. I would not be seeing him 'whenever I liked' because
he was never around. Filling the room now were her imploring,
tear-ruined, green-rimmed eyes. The million objections I had to
this plan, this caper of hers, seemed to lodge in my larynx. They
remained there without the extra aid of effort needed to make
thought into audible speech. Instead, I just said,

'Okay.'

And went back to watching the patient storyteller on the screen.
To me, not loving someone was not a good enough reason for
upping sticks and enduring the stultifying boredom of a Starter
Home estate for the rest of your life. Hating someone, perhaps.
Hating someone, and loving someone else – however erroneously

· 249 ·

– yes. But not just the absence of something. Love then, for me, became merely an abstract noun. After all, what was love? I didn't feel it. I just felt kind of in the way. So I simply said, 'Okay.' It wasn't as if my opinion on the matter would have made any difference. The decision had been taken. They just wanted to run it past me before the removal van crunched and wobbled down the unmade lane, and the tea-drinking men in their tea-brown overalls entered the familiar white house to dismantle my childhood.

Like I said, always too easy.

The second bombshell arrived when I had just turned eleven, in the back of Sinead's Mini, ferrying a bootful of rubber plants to the new address. A bright morning in early September, the birch trees on Dovecote Lane resembling a New England fall. Apropos of nothing, my mother said to me from the driving seat, 'Now, how would you feel if you had a little brother or sister?'

Ooh, I don't know, how about . . . *Horrified? Scandalised? Sick to the very pit of my stomach?* I knew at once with childish intuition (and the weary tone of her voice) that this wasn't her idea. It was Delph's. This Caliban, this pig with no talent for his lover's existing child, wanted one of his own, and sought to coerce my mother – the unfortunate owner of a womb – into bearing it. I would have felt better if she had admitted, on that pellucid morning of falling leaves, to be carrying the very progeny of Satan himself. Because any nipper of Delph's would surely have the number of the beast tattooed somewhere on its cranium. If the child were a boy, it would have to be named Damian; if a girl, Rosemary, after its mother. How could she contemplate carrying the devil's own spawn for nine months? Let's look at the facts. Delph was almost certainly a confused latent homosexual. His family were white trash gargoyles who spoke in funny accents with an archaic vocabulary of 'thees' and 'thous'. The man himself was a glorified handyman with no prospects this side of the circus. What's more, this being the late seventies, all the evidence pointed firmly to the fact that Delph Tongue was the Yorkshire Ripper.

Now, fragile reader, you are probably sighing that this reaction marked what Portnoy termed the culmination of my Oedipal drama, but the suspicion that Delph was in fact the most wanted man in England had firm roots in reality. For the simple reason that, after the wrenching move to number nine Southey Close, he was never around. He deposited his horrid droppings of cheap repro sculpture in our bathroom, then fucked off into the night. For months at a time. 'Up north', apparently. I was never sure where, or when, if ever, he would return. And Sinead didn't know either, unless she was keeping facts from me, which was always a possibility in those turbulent days. And 'up north' was where the eyes of the country's many police forces were focused. Inevitably, it was the tape recording of the suspect's voice that confirmed my worst fears. At that tender age, I somehow confused the glottal Geordie tones of this hoaxer with the soft wide gormless vowels of Wakefied. A northern accent was a northern accent, after all. Too scared to phone the police, I would tremble with anxiety as I made my way home after school, expecting to find Delph in the kitchen, ineradicable bloodstains on his hands, the now familiar look of feigned innocence on his murderous chops. It also occurred to me that Delph might have murdered Gemma Fernandez, and that I might be sitting on important evidence . . . So my mother was to bear the child of the most wanted pervert and killer in the country. Oh, how I wished I had stayed in that womb! But this wasn't the worst aspect of those dark days. The worst thing was a place I started to think of as my third house, the Stevenage council slum owned by an obese friend of my mother's called Barbara, or Babs as she was hideously abbreviated.

Babs was probably the largest homo sapiens I had ever laid eyes on. Her colossal folds of flesh seemed to be somehow regenerating: the existing mass producing more pulpy cellulite by the hour. Every time I was left overnight in the cramped, sick-smelling bedroom with her two infants I expected to find her exploded over the kitchen walls come morning. The reason for this residency was that Delph had begun working nights as a security guard, and needed total quiet to get his serial killer's shuteye. Or that was the story, anyhow. After a single night there I knew I never wanted to return. But return I would, unexpectedly and often, whenever Delph's work required him. I hated the wretched cardboard house this strange woman laboured in – husband in the nick or at sea, I never did find out. I loathed being abandoned in the baby-smelling bedroom, juggling the two emotions of badly wanting to return to Southey Close and *never* wanting to return there, with its rows and bolt-holed Rippers. I gagged on the curdled Weetabix I was expected to eat every morning, sunk in warm milk (that I imagined had come straight from Babs' Krakatoan breasts) and topped with barnacles of cheap white sugar. Plus, I missed my mum.

In the end, circumstances prevailed. My sojourn at Babs's co-incided with two unfortunate events: I began wetting the bed, and my mother announced she was pregnant. I don't know which was the most harrowing, but within less than a year I had used up a department store of linen (Babs fitting a plastic incontinence sheet to my camp bed) and I had a little sister, who they named Sarah. Instead of the spawn of Satan, she turned out to be a solitary star, and – I tremble to admit it – the inaugural love of my life.

The first day at an all-boys comprehensive school is an experience that all bedwetters should undergo. It certainly put an end to one form of nocturnal emission, though happily coincided with the commencement of another. One hundred and twenty pallid First Years all gathered on a concrete playground in their starchy blue uniforms, like the trembling internees of a concentration camp. Nobody knowing where to go. Farts and burps and kicks in the balls. The awful thought you might have to play rugby. Not what a young poet needs, I can tell you . . . There is an inescapable air of the messdeck or the barrack hall about all-male institutions. This in itself wasn't surprising. What was a constant source of wonder during my five years at this establishment was how many individuals (boys and teachers) *liked it*, sought it out, revelled in it. Yes, those bluff Taffy games masters and crooked-backed sadists thought there was nothing strange about spending the lion's share of every day in the company of so much testosterone and male hormonal panic. They were in clover! Didn't any of these perverts long for the confection of perfume, the brush of female hair in a corridor, a high voice? Something in a skirt? No, it seemed the entire staff relished this socially implausible situation. And the boys too, after a couple of years, began to fear and hate anything feminine. The conditioning had worked. Of course, there were a couple of women on the staff, but they were harassed out or grossed-out within a couple of years. Two terms of being asked for a blow-job every morning or coming in to find the board chalked with a hundred spurting erections was enough to deter even the most broad-minded French mistress or buxom P. E. beauty. And, of course, there was the obligatory paedophile for a head. Mr Cave – or the Reverend Cave as he was known, since he regularly preached pious bullshit in a stentorian voice every Sunday at St Cecilia's church – was an egregiously confident boy-fiddler. This danger-to-society had a pinched nose that flared his nostrils to the width of an anteater's. His stiff upper lip was constantly moist with a film of sweat. In retrospect, I wonder how he lasted so long in the job. Why didn't anyone blow the whistle on him? Didn't the parents, our supposed protectors, suspect anything? Perhaps it was his brisk and plausible manner, his advocacy of cold-shower discipline, his *dog collar*, that kept him in the job for decades. Maybe *everyone* knew about it, but the etiquette of the time forced parents to wave their hands and look the other way. It came with the territory, I suppose. The funniest thing was that Mr Cave seemed to think nobody knew he was sticking his hand down kids' pyjamas on school excursions. What is it about the nonce that makes him imagine nobody knows what he's up to? With the Reverend Cave it was screamingly obvious to anyone half-awake that he had a feverish and frothing interest in young boys' bottoms.

It was at this sewer of chalk-dust and thrashings that I first encountered Rudi. A burly boy with brilliantined hair, and a dark look in the points of his pupils. He approached me in the playground on a sun-sliced morning in January. I immediately felt the need to impress him, so I said,

'Hi. My stepdad's the Yorkshire Ripper.'

The big boy shot back: 'Well, mine owns British Aerospace.'

Nonplussed by this, though slightly perturbed by his garrulous Glasgow accent, I allowed a silence to develop, as many would in the years to come. But Rudi always seemed more than able to fill these lacunae. The icy rink of the playground was blue in the early light, the cries of boys mingling with the sound of inland gulls. Stretching before us both was the prospect of double maths and a cross-country run of unimaginable brutality. Rudi said,

'Fancy a wee bunk-off this afternoon?'

'Wee – that's rude.'

'No it's not, spunker, it's just the way I talk.'

He appeared to be slightly affronted at my suggestion. Rudi was about the same height as me, but wider and stronger; with more meat all round.

'So is that word,' I said, seeing how far I could push him. I had witnessed other kids rag the swarthy boy in this way. He seemed to accept a degree of this as legitimate, his family having just moved from Scotland.

'What?'

'You, know . . . spunk.'

'D' yuh want a burst mooth?'

But there wasn't time to answer. In a flash we were rolling around on the diamond-hard tarmac, crowds of boys surrounding us shouting, 'Bundle! Bundle! Bundle!' Once we had been separated, my mouth indeed burst and bleeding, and had been forced to shake hands in the sinister presence of Mr Cave, we became buddies. Rudi and Byron – inseparable friends for the next five years.

We went through a lot, me and the hirsute Scotsman, when we were young and full of grace. Truancy, drugs, rock 'n' roll, girls, failed exams. My first gig, first draw on a Camberwell carrot, first fumblings with the unopenable bras of pneumatic fourth-formers were all experienced with Rudi somewhere in the background, his tremendous nose throwing a shadow well worth casting in bronze. When he began wearing the knot of his school tie in a fat, insolent triangle that obscured his shirt, I followed suit. When he ditched his Adidas schoolbag for a skinny leather satchel stencilled with the logos of rock bands, I slavishly copied him. Only when he started shaving the comical bumfluff from his upper lip a year ahead of everyone else was I unable to imitate his initiative. And what did he gain from me? Cultural instruction, I suppose. A Virgil to guide him through the inferno of the third form; an advisor on the right books to read and the cool films to see. Because, when all was said and done, Rudi was not terrifically bright. He had spirit, spark, a certain entrepreneurial savvy, maybe even a devious cunning, but he was no Newton. So Rudi got to look more intellectual than he actually was when hanging around me (always a major point-scorer with girls he asserted – 'Just look at Arthur Miller') and I had a burly Scottish bodyguard to fend off the bullies that plagued this skinny boy who was already showing signs of losing his hair.

A couple of years after this, towards the end of the long, baking O level summer, Sinead and Delph decided to move house. My kid sister Sarah was five years old, about to start school, and the house on the Poets' Estate was getting too small. Small for what? you may ask. For a sensitive, already receding boy who loathed his volatile stepfather? For the daily rows that startled the neighbours behind the cardboard walls? For the all-engulfing aura of sadness that surrounded the project of my mother's affair? Yes, for all these reasons. And for one other that I wasn't informed about: Sinead and Delph were planning to get married. They wanted to move up in the world: to a bigger house, to bourgeois respectability, like people born into fuck-all always do. Only, this was doomed to failure. You can take the man out of Wakefield, but not the Wakefield, et cetera. Once we did shift our tea chests (some still not unpacked from the last move) half a mile up the road, Delph performed his usual trick of permanently disabling us from meeting the neighbours' eyes with any degree of confidence. He achieved this by immediately causing a public scene. This time it was over my first real girlfriend, roly-poly Rhianna, who I had brought back for an hour of furtive fumbling and spliff-smoking in my bedroom.

Once Rhianna had cycled off unsteadily into the summer night, Delph approached my door and knocked rapidly. He was still terrifying, even at the age I was – his features atavistic and gouged with indignation, his voice suddenly loud. 'What's going on?' he shouted. When I had frantically dispersed the smoke and opened up, he confronted me: 'Did you ask if you could bring someone back here?'

'No, why should I?' I said, fronting it out.

'You bring back some tart to fool around under my roof, while we go out to work all the hours God sends?' Christ, could he fit any more platitudes into a single sentence? 'You should ask our permission.'

'She's not some tart, her name's Rhianna. Now if you don't mind—' I went to shut the door, but he jammed his boot between it and the frame, his lips curling into that familiar sexual grimace. I knew he wouldn't be able to let that pass. No, there was no way he could let that go unpunished. He had to have access, reach, power. A power that, in my mind, had no legitimacy.

'Are all the girls in Hamford on bloody heat, or what? You were playing cheeky with her, weren't you.'

'What does that mean?' I asked, cringing at the Yorkshire phrase. 'Playing cheeky?' At this point Delph's whole anima, his verbal expressions, his rangy physique, his dullard's soul were nauseating to me, almost to the point of implosion.

'You know what it means. Any more lip and I'll knock you to the end of the bloody garden.'

I pushed past him; my gorge could stand no more. But he was after me, with a heavy tread, following me out onto the front porch where . . . where the couple from next door, entering their house with a ton of shopping, witnessed the full fury of his vengeance. His continuing vendetta against the personal affront of my existence. The end result: a shiner the colour and texture of Jupiter's angry puce spot.

A black eye is not an attractive facial feature to wear to a wedding. Especially not at the self-conscious age of sixteen, when the eyes of the world seem to be evaluating you with the steady scrutiny of a CCTV camera. A fortnight later I was crammed into a dusty pew witnessing the tiring sight of my mother at the altar saying vows to a man I would gladly see sent to the electric chair. On my face was the now-sallowing result of walking into a door, or so I told everyone. Little Sarah stood close in attendance, a beaming bridesmaid. It was all over. All hope of a reprieve was cast asunder. Marriage being a final thing, or so I believed then. A white wedding too, with all the trimmings: the spruced-up guests, the tottering cake, the opulent reception held under a marquee in our new back garden. Sickening. As the mournful voice of the vicar intoned their full names I imagined I saw the shade of Des, a few pews down. The displaced father with his horns polished for the ceremony. Later, I would ponder the degradation of seeing your own mother marry a man you hate, two weeks after he has beaten you up in front of your neighbours. Ah, hate . . . such an alien emotion to me then. I didn't know I hated Delph until I was twenty-five. Because I tried to love him so much. But love couldn't admit such a monster, such a Claudius.

The congregation filed out into the June glare, a tasteless vintage car bearing bunting humming in the gutter. Confetti was blowing on the deleterious wind. Ahead of my mother, Delph was the first to step into the vehicle, characteristically forgetting his manners. Back then, I had been doing a great deal of thinking about people with human qualities (warmth, empathy, insight) as opposed to those with predominantly animal or reptilian traits (lust, brutality, sadism). Delph was one of the latter: on the surface a human being, with charm and human friendliness, but motivated underneath by bestial appetites, by cunning, by savage energies. He had to have immediate gratification in every domain. He had wanted my mother and he had got her, regardless of what he had to destroy to attain his goal. He had wanted a child and he had been presented with one. So it was only natural that he should forget decorum and get into the burnished car ahead of Sinead. A selfish slip. I thought only I had noticed this faux pas, but I registered a minuscule twitch of disgust on the chauffeur's face as he held the wide door open for the galloping groom. Then I felt a tugging at my shirt sleeve. A small hand curled around the cuff of my hired suit. It was Sarah.

'Aren't you going with them?' I asked her.

'I want to stay with you,' she smiled.

'But you have to get in the car. They're your mum and dad. They're also the rules. Aren't you happy?'

Of course she was happy. She had got to skip around all day in a bridesmaid's dress; shy as an antelope, a bouquet of lavender in her tiny hand. She was overjoyed for them both. Delph was, after all, her biological father. I shivered for her, for what she might have to endure, for how she would feel penitent for every abuse perpetrated against her over the coming years. Because, as we all know, children blame themselves.

'Okay, then,' she said after a slight girlish pause, and ran towards the newly respectable couple.

Sarah climbed into the big car. She was so small she had to use her hands to hoist herself up. Once inside, the weighty black door heaved shut. Then they rattled off into the sunset.

Fast-forward four months. The fifth week of the sixth form. October. Already the new house cowered to the sound of harsh words. I remember feeling queasy when I heard Delph storming out one night shouting, 'Why did I bloody marry you?' Horrible to hear that sort of thing so soon after the happy day. Ho hum. And not because of the noble pathos evoked by a similar expression of the Moor's, but because of Delph's utter ignorance of how much this marriage – this folly – had cost everyone. The GDP of toler-ance and faith that it had exacted from the family he had walked into and destroyed. But by then I didn't give much of a fuck. Because the day after this outburst I had, in my father's absence, begun spending nights at his bungalow. There Rhianna and I would smoke half an eighth of resin and play knackered vinyl till the small hours. The idea had been floated one night that I wouldn't return to school. What was the point? Sinead and Delph didn't care whether I furthered my education. They were relieved to have got shot of me. There was the strong sense that nobody was at the rudder. Except myself. Byron Easy and his small pile of unpublished and unpublishable poems. So, the next morning, I didn't go in. And that weekend Des changed all the locks on his house in order to deny me admittance to this last sanctuary. The following Saturday, that skeletal October day of silver skies and Sisley trees, found me running across the lumpy fields to the disused railway tunnel where I sat down and I . . .

But you know all that. I remember the evening when it was all decided. Me and Rhianna in the rimey garden, nerves blazing after a cloudy bong, kissing those delicious kisses of sixteen. The emancipating feeling of knowing I would never return to the schoolhouse with its cast of gargoyles and perverts. By the time we pulled the patio doors to go in, snow was falling, gently at first, but seemingly dispensed by the hard bright moon above. Snow in October; the crescent of a Damocles cutlass dangling from the velvet cushion of the sky.

———

I am lying under a bush in Camden Square, an inch of snow in my ears. It is cold. Very, very cold. The latest Rhianna in my life is not a sweet, slightly corpulent sixteen-year-old, but a mad bitch named Mandy. Let me explain . . . A year after getting married, I too was also having a screaming row with my wife every night. I too was enduring the words, 'I wish I'd never married you,' spat in my face at the slightest provocation. The latest of these fights had seen me trudging the slush-banked streets of Holloway until midnight. A frozen January in London. I had taken in a movie. I had bought cans of strong lager. I had sat in the late-night café and eaten a fried-egg sandwich. But I still couldn't contemplate going home. Because it didn't feel like home. Just four walls and a lot of grief. Ah, the old familiar. Instead I had found myself in Camden Square by a sort of homing instinct – back at my old crash pad. I

even looked in at the hushed curtains, but was unable to see the
new occupants microwaving their midnight cups of cocoa. Lucky
them. Instead, I made myself a bed on the hard ground, the big
bare trees clashing overhead in the bitter wind. O! What a miserable night I passed! The cold stars shining above in their mockery.
And in the morning, a fresh fall of snow: deep and crisp and even
in the stunning sunlight. A spiritual stillness in the air. And frostbite
threatening my toes. I brushed off my clothes, looking for the St
Bernard, and made my weary way to A&E.

Just another average scene from a marriage . . . The previous
month, Mandy and I had driven to Slough to have Christmas
dinner with her father, the first since getting married. Progress
reports were expected. Forced smiles were the order of the day.
Nobody had any appetite for these deceptions, and anyway, Mandy
had said her only motive for going was to borrow some money
and visit her mother's grave. Ian Haste had recently purchased a
big black Labrador, to keep him company. The gaunt widower
had never remarried, and spent his time slavishly redecorating the
old family home. Of course, we still had Fidel, newly separated
from his beloved Concepcion, so we took him along. Despite his
traumatic severance, he was in a gregarious mood. By the end of
the long afternoon, the two dogs were on more than friendly
terms.

'That is a *male* Labrador, isn't it, Dad?' Mandy suddenly enquired.

'Of course. I don't want litters of puppies around the house.'

No, that would mess up the immaculate cream carpets that swept
regally from room to room, like an Arab potentate's love nest. The
two dogs were merrily frolicking under the big, resinous Christmas
tree, licking noses.

'Mum never had dogs. She was a cat person. It won't feel like
home now.'

'When did it ever feel like home, Mandy?' said her father wearily.
There were new smudges under his dark eyes, black baggage. 'After

she died you couldn't wait to get out. To start the world.' I was about to tell Mandy how lucky she was, having this palace to go back to if the going got tough, when Ian Haste turned to me, lighting a long Dunhill. 'What about you, Byron. Are you getting any peace?'

'What's that supposed to mean?' said Mandy, indignantly.

Mr Haste knew his daughter well. That much I had ascertained about my father-in-law over the past year. His evaluating eyes settled on me. He still considered me to be a waster and a loser, despite my stabilising influence on Mandy. On the mantelpiece, an early photo of his daughter watched us: she was sitting on a tin of Quality Street holding a rabbit. It was all there, the bossiness, the hauteur, the spoiled black bulbous eyes, the way she headlocked the forlorn bunny like a wanton boy.

'Well, there's been the odd disagreement,' I sighed, catching Mandy's admonitory glare, 'but nothing that would make the papers.' A lie, of course. Many of Mandy's outrageous acts over the last year wouldn't be out of place in *Who's Afraid of Virginia Woolf?* This was a woman who would scream the house down when she couldn't find a hairgrip. Who would hurl alarm clocks across the bedroom when she didn't want to get up in the morning. Why did I stay with such a woman for more than five minutes, you may well ask? Well, it was hard to locate an answer to that at the time. Something to do with the permanence of marriage, the emotional investment one makes, the sorry fact that I still loved her. Because maybe Mandy was my last shot at love, my last chance of continuity, of forgiveness. After every eruption I would always place an inordinate value on the little cards we left for each other; cards of contrition, usually bearing favourite animals.

The circumspect father turned to his daughter. 'It's not easy setting up home together. Not when the roof over your head depends on the health of your relationship. That's why I bought your mother's half of the house out.'

'When she was having her flings, you mean?' said Mandy, eager-eared for information. Ian Haste paused, stretched his long drainpipe legs to let out the tension, and took off his orange party hat. Addressing us both, he said,

'That's right. If you can't trust your wife with your friends, why should you trust her with your joint assets? Get out while you can. Now, I'm not saying you two are having any problems, but you have to watch what you get tied up in. Wait till you know how each other behaves. Under pressure, that is. Use a little nous.' He pronounced the final word as if he were referring to Jack Ketch.

'Well, at least she had her fun before she died,' said Mandy, scornfully.

I reflected on Mr Haste's cunning, some of which had obviously rubbed off on his daughter. Buying out your own wife while she's still married to you. Not bad.

'Plus a house is not a home,' I volunteered. 'Especially if all the love's disappeared. It's just four walls and a leaky ceiling.'

They both looked at me as if I had no right to comment upon the amount of love present in their household. Then a bark, from behind us. We all turned. Fidel, a dog a quarter of the size of Mr Haste's black Labrador, was attempting to mount his new playmate on a marital bed of Christmas wrapping paper. The big dog turned to us with a mixture of panic and sorrow in his eyes. He gave another bark, this one louder, although he knew his pleading to be fruitless. As we were well aware, once Fidel had set his heart on someone, he had to complete the conquest, from bouquet to post-coital cigar.

All three of us began laughing, thankfully shifting the emphasis from the clotted reprisals of the dinner table. Mandy asked her dad,

'Has he got a name yet?'

'I've tried a few, but none of them fit his sad eyes.'

Fidel's flying haunches, thrusting uselessly against the Labrador's back legs, gained in speed. Oh, yes, he must have thought, I'm taking someone from behind whose name I don't even know. And maybe I'll never bother to ask!

'How about Macca?' suggested Mandy. *Macca* was Catalan for queer.

'Now, what would your mother think?' said Mr Haste.

'Or JFK, perhaps?' I said. But their blank looks told me no one got the joke.

On Boxing Day Mandy drove us to the graveyard outside Slough where Ramona had her final resting place. It was a blowy, brumal afternoon, the gales making our eyes smart and stream. I was glad to park up in the little enclosure before the chalky path that led to the graves. We had continued a sour argument about money for the whole journey. By the time Mandy ripped the handbrake from the floor of the car, neither of us were speaking.

We passed the gatekeeper's stone house and the big bending yews on the outskirts of the cemetery. Ahead of us were mechanical diggers, then a few bedraggled women laying flowers at a new stone, the marble all black and glossy in the distance. But mainly there was the path. How long was that path to her mother's plot! It was the first time I had made the journey. Mandy hadn't visited in over three years. She walked slightly ahead, leading the way, her arms embracing the tired yellow-and-white chrysanthemums. All paths lead this way, I thought grimly. This is where the long and winding road terminates. This is our ultimate home, where we finally get some peace and quiet.

At last, we neared Ramona's unprepossessing stone. Once before it, I could see her full name – Ramona Haste-Arias, and her dates, horribly close together in time. Below it a simple inscription: 'To the Best Mother in the World.' Mandy bent to lay the flowers, the wind taking on the edges of the wrapping paper.

'Hold that,' she said, passing me one of the bouquets as she wrestled the other from its constricting elastic bands.

'I will,' I said, in a reverent whisper; all past rancour vanished in the humbling, wind-torn no-man's-land of the cemetery.

As she stooped to fan the blooms, I saw a sudden humanity in her, not witnessed before, or at least not in its entirety. She was a little girl again, needing her mummy. She took the other bunch from me and said softly to the stone, 'You're better off where you are. They never understood you up here.'

Up here. I thought about her statement for a moment. Yes, up here, one is still vulnerable to the daily slings and arrows. At least down there, posterity's cruel judgement cannot harm you; that is something we have to administer, have to deal with. We all fear the cruelty of posterity. Its awful flippancy. Its retrospective shallowness about lives that had to be struggled through. Its reductive vocabulary that can only admit a man as having been one thing: a hero, a conqueror, a cuckold . . . I pondered what sort of woman Ramona really was. By all accounts, demanding, bossy, eccentric, beautiful. Much like her daughter, then. I thought of the two photos, the magical diptych, that Mandy had ground underfoot earlier in the year. Ramona in her flowing promiscuous prime, her warm skin alive to a lover's touch. Then the cruel desecration: once by the tomb; again by Mandy's foot. Does anybody's memory deserve that? Or do we deserve all that and more from the people we hurt, we disappoint or leave behind? Finally, I thought about the reality of down there. Whatever consciousness we had, if it survived, was perhaps facing the blue-void blankness of eternity. As hard as this life is, surely that must be harder?

Before me, Mandy was having a quiet moment, her back resolutely hunched. It was cold. I suffered all the pangs of up here. Soon it would be time to return to the car, to the deceptive warmth of Mandy's childhood home.

I turned and looked about me. Death, finality, everywhere. The unsquareable notion that all these skeletons had once been breathers, had once visited others' graves with flowers and pondered the same unimaginables. Well, they were out there somewhere, with all the mysteries solved — untameable as the breeze. And if they weren't — if there was nothing to come — their remains, their obdurate relics rested underground: unappreciative of the florist's shops that bloomed above them in the dark, shunting wind.

5

Asmodeus

'*L*adies and Gentleman, this train will shortly be arriving in
Peterborough.'

We are past midway now. The Rubicon has been crossed.
Too late to turn back. What has been embarked upon must be
endured. If only I could feel the heavy weight of a revolver in my
pocket! How placated must the suicidal farmer be, seeing the blun-
derbuss or shotgun above the mantelpiece every morning as he goes
out to corral his dwindling herds. The comfort of knowing he can
always turn back, and with a single quick and easy stroke, too. Back
to the soul's default state: free-floating, without its cumbersome
cargo of flesh. No drawn-out drownings or excruciating overdoses
of rat poison for Farmer Giles. With a gun, the potential is perpetually there, like a friend one can always turn to. The promise of
merging with the wind. The gateway to a blue eternity. Ah, if only
the Everlasting had not fixed his canon, et cetera.

I turn to my old friend the window. The far fields always melt
my heart. *There you will find the grey rump of Lincolnshire in undecided
weather, the thundering carriages numbing your ears; the fleeting flecks of
poplars under talons of cloud; the bruised gradients, stippled and hacked; the*

ordered patchwork created by the enclosures; the quick whoosh as you pass under a road bridge in the hermetically sealed tube; the long perspectives afforded by the sweep of the firmament . . . I am writing again, unable to cap the flow or the pen. Unable to come to terms with the strange, emotional animal that I am. The curse of self-reflection! How different must be the consciousnesses of those who lack the habit of self-reflection. How alien is the poet to the normal man, with his easily met appetites for money, car, holiday and family; the management consultant, say, with his prosaic and easily satisfied aspirations; the cancelled visor of his suit and tie. And this is the man Mandy, deep down, dearly wanted me to be. How useless to the common good, to women especially, are my particular qualities of self-examination. And for sound biological reasons, too. The species little needs a man hell-bent on contemplating his own errors and infirmities, when he should be protecting his mate and providing for his young. Strange how one's thinking reverts to these Darwinian modes. It makes me wonder what Mandy, or any woman, ever saw in me. Traditionally, the males compete for the female until the female takes her pick from the competing males – that's how the majority of mammals go about it, and we are no different. And compete I did. Half of London seemed to be in pursuit of Mandy for a time. And pick she did, for obscure reasons of her own. No, I don't have those qualities that a woman looks for: security, tenure, stability, muscly forearms, a cock that would honour a horse, et cetera. I am a strange, emotional, passionate, turbulent, stunted figure, just becoming loathsome to myself after all these years of self-deception.

The low fields in their coats of sere and rust; the telegraph poles, smaller cousins to the pylons, latticing the land; trees blown in an elemental wind; an airstrip; goalposts; toiling cars; broken birches and sad willows weeping tendrils into chilly streams; canals and causeways; the over-arching dome of the sky, grey as a sea lion.

Peterborough! Where I once came to collect a new passport. With its stationary Pullmans on curving tracks, its big-rippled river. Then a grid of buffers; a blue bridge; the dour frontage of the Great Northern Hotel; sooted chimneys and cylindrical silver tanks girded with ladders; a stalled recovery unit yellow as a sunflower; floodlighting; rusted rails; tenacious heather trackside; dandelions and couch grass; unhappy houses with their weeping windows . . .

Unhappiness. If I had to isolate one defining feature of my marriage it would be its unhappiness. Why had the pursuit of happiness brought me unhappiness? Why had the pursuit of women, the universally accepted mission to find a mate, resulted in so much sorrow? Were the qualities I looked for in women the wrong ones? Most men, if the truth be known, just want a housekeeper who is also a good lay. But then I felt myself far from being a normal man. Maybe I even conceived of myself a favoured being, in Wordsworth's phrase. So what were these qualities? Maybe it was all a project of fantastic narcissism. In reality, I wanted myself but with tits. A soulmate of such under-standing that they were indistinguishable from *me*, though in female form. But I only managed to find parity in turbulence and hysteria, not in understanding. I mistook a mutual corruption of the psyche as proof that we were made for each other. We both intuited something similar: a hurt, a damage, a rebellion, a scar. The only exception to this pattern being Bea, and I hoped sincerely that she was now married to someone kind, sane and honest, and had two beautiful children with plum-coloured eyes.

I look across to Robin and Michelle, wanting very much to ask them why they chose each other; why they singled each other out over-and-above all the other human options on planet earth. They don't appear to be unhappy. But I find myself unable to disturb their reading with such urgent, ludicrous questions. When the heart is full, as someone once said, you should keep your mouth shut.

———

The final place Mandy and I moved to, where our great unhappi-ness found its proper tenure, was on the Seaham Road, near Finsbury Park. This came after an interim flat rented from my old friend and landlord, Keenan Peach. Well, we arrived there after a whole string of addresses, each upheaval motivated by Mandy's inability to be patient with a property. A whole saga of madness. Once we had decorated the latest pad from skirting board to ceiling and got to know which corner shops opened past midnight she was already perusing the papers for another place. Like I say, change gone mad. A whirlpool of depth and danger. Change for the sake of it. You could not invest in a volatile commodity such as Mandy. Maybe one day I will be able to rationalise this peripatetic episode, but at the time it felt like I was being led by the nose like an ass. Before the endgame played out on the rungs of the Haringey Ladder, I dialled Keenan's number as a last resort. After all, he always said I could call him, even in the 'direst of emergencies'. It just so happened that he was subletting a ground-floor place in east London complete with back garden for next to nothing.

Once we arrived, in early April, with all the meshed saplings on the Leytonstone High Road showing pastel eruptions of blossom, we realised why the rent was so low. The place was infested with cockroaches. Not only that, but the stink from the hairdresser's next door (Cut-Off Point) produced by the perming process was unendurable as the weather became hotter. Mandy took this to heart, blaming me for phoning my old Wottonesque landlord.

'This is just your style, Byron,' she scolded. 'If I leave anything up to you it ends in disaster. You can't be trusted with practical things. God knows how you managed to live on your own for eight years without a woman to wipe your bottom.'

We were awaiting the first visit from Rentokil. The phone call to the pest control agency had been delegated, as Mandy had been too busy recently with Fellatrix. They were at the crucial stage where everyone in the music industry had heard of them, or seen them, but no investment had materialised; presenting the real danger of the pot simmering off the boil, never to heat up again.

'That's not true. I managed to iron my clothes for almost a decade without you.'

'You can't even iron a shirt properly. I had to teach you that.'

'Well, they were too busy forcing us to play rugby at Hamford Boys' School. You never learnt any skill you might need in later life.'

The depredations caused by a year and a half of this sort of sparring (and much worse) had taken their toll on both of us. She had to make a quarrel, whether she could find one or not, every day. I found I was tense from morning till night in her company, always on my guard for the next conflagration or skirmish. My hair had started to exhibit white patches at the scanty temples, like the parched grass of summer.

'Well, don't let Rentokil palm us off with some pissy mousetraps. I know what a pushover you are.'

'Hey – it's not such a disaster. When I described our friends over the phone, they told me they were only German cockroaches. They're half the size of the big bastards.'

'I don't care what nationality they are. It's an infestage.'

'You mean infestation.'

'Don't correct me all the time!' she bawled. 'How can we unpack anything into cupboards when they're swarming over the walls? I can't even eat in here without wanting to puke.'

It was true that the situation was urgent. The moment we had closed the door on the removal men, a small earwig-sized insect had scuttled across the work surface towards the kettle. On opening the big larder cupboards we were met with what looked like black paint. However, the disturbance of air caused the paint to start moving, like a layer of living tar. The entire wall was alive with them.

'Leave the talking to me.'

'Yeah, like I left you to talk to Quentin.'

'It's Keenan.'

'Whatever.'

The man from Rentokil came and went, spraying all the floors with an evil-looking canister of poison, leaving hundreds of sticky traps. He would be back to perform this operation every month.

But the cockroaches were not the worst of it. The most melan-choly aspect of this new habitat was the ramshackle ugliness of east London, expanding into Essex like a malignant urban bacillus. There was something uncared for and jerry-built about every square inch. After a while I couldn't bear to look at it: the long narrow rows of Victorian workmen's tenements punctuated by neon kebab houses, always empty except for estate-dregs playing the gaming machines. The peeling old men's boozers on every corner, with blacked-out windows, their long-antiquated adver-tisements for Choice Ales from the Hand Pump, or Fine Dining Upstairs. The phone boxes graffitied with swastikas. Something claustrophobic or lightless in the air. Whole districts without a post office or record shop or restaurant; the hordes of poor with their horrible buggies and clothes and nasty eyes. A Balkan feel to the area, with everything broken or useless or in short supply. Then the mournful sounds of the afternoon: distant ice-cream vans with their naive tinklings, or the squall of children playing at lunchtime from the nearby school. Or the sight of importunate commuters at tube-mouths shoving their way into the unfresh air; awful to observe in winter, always hurrying home with their animas of disconsolation or expedience. Stepney, Mile End, Stratford, Bow. A wasteland whose barren vistas worked on me in a terribly undermining way.

Spring didn't seem to happen in east London. The meshed, nascent trees shed their blossom quickly, which rolled around like miniature pink tumbleweeds. The skies glowered angrily all May, occasionally crying a dank drizzle that seemed to hover in the air like mist. There was something blocked or obstructed about the whole enterprise of regeneration. Also, for the first time I found myself stranded miles away from Rock On. Since my only mode of transport was my battered bicycle, I would bike it over to Royal College Street whenever I had work; pedalling like a madman past the Lea Valley reservoirs, the wind slapping me and the distant water around with an easy hand. After dark, the return journey often took two hours. The dilapidation of the area, the sense of peripheral panic and boredom, was so different to the bright cosmopolitan hubbub of Camden. I felt as if I were living in some scoured dormitory town rather than a great metropolis. We were far out. But, at the same time, it all felt apposite. The movement, me and Mandy's movement, was forever outwards, like some tremendous entropic unravelling.

The flat never saw the back of its cockroaches. After a brief abeyance, the oppressive blooming heat of late May saw their numbers escalate. They would show up everywhere: in the sugar bowl, the turn-up of a pair of jeans, Mandy's handbag – a rank impediment to every day. It didn't help that faithful Fidel was scared of them. He would circle their spasmodic movement for a curious moment before whimpering off to his stinky bed under the dining table. A fine and dashing Casanova he turned out to be. God knows how he would have reacted to the sinewy cat-burglar, crowbar in hand, crack-habit to feed. A budgerigar would have provided a better deterrent.

For most of our time out east I remember Mandy as either ill or swinging the lead under the cloud of one of her imagined ailments. I knew this to be a ruse to avoid the nasty and unedifying fact of work. Come eight in the morning, if it wasn't a migraine, it was chronic back pain, or irritable bowel syndrome, or fever, or period cramps. The only shop I knew well on the high street was the chemist's, as I was forever loitering under its fluorescent lights, dutifully scoring pills and remedies or repeat prescriptions. By the time it was established she wasn't going in to whatever fly-by-night job she had at the time (so far that year she had evaded regular work as an estate agent, bargirl, canvasser and pharmaceutical guinea pig), she would beg me to call the indifferent employer and announce her incapacity as sincerely as I could manage. 'This is a surefire way to get the sack, you know that?' I would grumble while dialling the number. 'Oh, but please, Byron, I'm sick, I can't go in, I just can't! Do it just this once.' But it was never just the once. Then she would adopt her little-girl's voice that had surely been effective with her father and numerous dupes in the past. Of course, I would always lose her the job. As every employer knows, only someone with lesions to the larynx and their neck in a brace would be incapable of calling themselves in sick. Then it would all be my fault. I often took the full broadside of her fulminating rage for not putting the correct note of plausibility into my voice during the call. 'Couldn't the fact that you've spent more days sick than you've actually worked have something to do with the situation?' But that appeal always fell on deaf, half-Spanish, ears.

If I happened to be around on these days of malady she would always be up and about by midday, feeling much improved. Often, by five, when it was time for her to drive to rehearsal, her poorly condition would have been all but forgotten. Throughout the day I would have been playing the good doctor Byron, making her hot *caldo* with *fideos* or massaging the strange route her spine took up her back. How I hated wasting my time in this way. How I despised her epic malingering – it drained one of the will to live. Yet her self-enforced condition of passivity often gave me some peace. She couldn't be her usual volatile self with a thermometer under her armpit. However, towards the end of our tenure in Cockroach Mansions, she spent a week in bed defiantly refusing to show her face at her new job, that of travel agent at the London offices of Iberia. Monday saw her placid with a fabricated concoction of migraine and aggravated muscle spasms. By Thursday she had become petulantly hopeless, crying, 'I wish I was dead' whenever I tried to persuade her to at least phone in herself. The receptionist had got to know my voice so well. She would say, '*Buenos dias*, Byron!' after I cleared my throat. On the Friday I limped home exhausted from the shop after my bike had suffered a puncture on the Tottenham Hale gyratory system. Rainwater sprinkled from my cape as I forced the front door ajar. Once I had stamped my boots and stashed the maimed tubular steel frame in the hall I knew something was up. The lights were all off. There was a tense hush to the kitchen. I creaked open the bedroom door. Mandy was still on our low double futon where I had left her that morning.

Tentatively, I approached her with a cup of tea. She turned over as quick as a cat, enormous eyeballs bulging, her long black hair dishevelled.

'I'm dying,' Mandy told me with panic in her voice.

'Don't be absurd. What's the matter with you?'

'These pains in my head,' she grasped her temples melodramatically, tears streaming down her face. 'They won't go away.'

'It's just a migraine. Have you taken those preventatives?'

'Just a migraine!?' she howled, sitting up in bed, her voice raised by ten decibels. 'What the hell do you know? It's probably a brain tumour. Call the hospital!'

We had been through all this many times before. Numerous brain scans had proved beyond doubt that she wasn't suffering from a malignant cranial tumour. Irritation at this drama started to grow inside me. I was exhausted, soaked to the skin, hungry. I said,

'I'm not calling the hospital again. Drink this and see how you feel in a couple of hours.'

She snatched the cup from me with the sort of noise wrestlers make when their hide hits the canvas in a double nelson. Then she catapulted it across the dimly lit bedroom and started banging her head against the wall.

'Don't'—*Bang!*—'you'—*Bang!*—'understand? I'm *dying*.'

'Please don't do that, you'll hurt yourself.' I went to intervene, but she tore my hand from her shoulder. I could see blood on her crown; her thin but powerful arms trembling.

I surveyed the sad fountain of tea now indelibly decorating the recently painted walls. Great. Fantastic. Why don't you just smear them with excrement too? Then I heard a faint noise like a child's whimper from the back garden.

'What on earth's that?' I demanded.

'Don't ask me.'

'You must know. You've been here all day.'

But Mandy had turned and buried her head in the pillows. She was weeping and shaking uncontrollably.

I ventured into the rain-racked garden to investigate, flashlight in hand. The muscular wind blew the door to the outside can like a weather vane. A strange feature of the Victorian properties in the East End was that they all had unusable brick shithouses crumbling next to their gutter pipes. It reminded me of Wakefield. Of poverty and darkness and privation. The noise, like a child trapped and in distress, increased in volume as I walked to the end of the dark strip of grass; overgrown now in the early summer, overhung by birches cowering from the storm. Finally, I parted brambles at the back by the compost heap. And there was Fidel, dejected and wet; shivering with great wrenching spasms.

'Hey, come on boy. This is no night to be outside.'

I was shocked. Such a domesticated hound as Fidel would have done anything to avoid braving the elements on a night like this. Normally he would be stretched out in front of the gas fire, twitching in lascivious dreams. Something had to be up. His pitiful eyes met mine along the beam of the flashlight. 'Come on, up you get.' I turned and motioned for him to follow. Instead, he let out a pitiful yelp. I would have to pick him up. Transferring the torch to my other hand I scooped him from the bushes and put him on the grass. He promptly keeled over. One of his back paws was broken.

I would later discover from Mandy, after much interrogation, that she had thrown poor Fidel against the door in a fit of rage when he had demanded his daily bowl of Chum.

A week after this unforgivable incident Mandy was back at work. She didn't want it mentioned. It was regrettable, in the past. Her mood was up, effusive, future-facing. There had been some kind of breakthrough with the band. Privately, I didn't hold out much hope. More than once during that strangled spring I cadged a lift to work from Mandy, as she had managed against strong odds to keep the job at Iberia. In the vexed toil of the rush hour she would tailgate cars as we took corners at fifty miles an hour, her slickly polished shoes working the pedals. Often, we would be gridlocked for tense interludes on the bleak Forest Road, during which the conversation turned to the urgent need to find somewhere else to live. Always the next thing with her. Her long straight nose twitched as she brainstormed desperate plans: benefit scams, identity theft, escort work. The stripey red and white of her uniform resembled a barber's pole made from fabric. She announced, with unanswerable assertion, 'You might like living in a squat with bugs and an outside toilet, but I'm not putting up with it. My dad's a stingy bastard, but he'd be appalled to see me there. I deserve better. And that stink from next door. It's worse than an abattoir.'

'Okay, okay,' I groaned, observing her patience unravel like a loose seam, 'I'll call Keenan on Monday. See what else he's got.'

'Forget about Keenan. He's the reason we're in this mess. Antonia reckons there's a place just round the corner from her, on the first floor. You're much less likely to get vermin on the first floor. I can't stand this hole with nothing to do, and all the people looking like they live on a council estate.'

'I thought you liked east London. Cheap and cheerful, you said,' I muttered, watching a thin patina of disgust disfigure her features.

'It will be okay when they finish fucking building it. Anyway, that was then, before the reality kicked in – no one comes to visit you here. They all said they would but how often have we had people over?'

I thought about the flat above the yeasty bakery, with its numerous parties, the phone always ringing. Just up the road, the shuttered, turreted houses of Highgate and Crouch End, with their milk-cheeked children growing up in an atmosphere of safety, Chopin, macrobiotic pulses and the *Independent on Sunday*. Yes, there was a sense of grand isolation out here, fenced off from civilisation by the Hackney marshes and the great dolorous reservoirs.

'I was getting sick of all those people traipsing in and out.'

'You get sick of everything, that's your problem. I like meeting new people, new friends. Plus it's miles away when we have to rehearse. We've got these big gigs coming up. It's make or break time. And I never go out any more. You have to show your face on the scene or they forget who you are.'

If they haven't already, I thought to myself. But I didn't share this fear. Instead, I said, 'But what about the money? That's why we moved here, because we couldn't afford to live over there.'

'I don't care, I'll work all the hours I can get.'

I frowned at this statement, but directed my expression out of the window at the furious stationary drivers. It wasn't worth the argument.

'Okay, I'll see if Martin can give me some overtime.'

'That's just pocket money,' she sneered. 'I want things. I want holidays, a new car, new clothes. A new life.'

'There's only one problem. What about the money we owe Keenan?'

'Well,' she snorted ostentatiously, 'he can forget about *that!*'

Ah yes, the small problem of the money we owed Keenan. Close on two grand in back rent. Which we didn't have. In fact, we were nowhere near the rent. If the rent was a famous summit and we were climbers, we wouldn't even be in the foothills sorting out the guide and the map, we'd still be at home saving up for the plane ticket. On Mandy's orders we had initially withheld payment until the infestation had cleared up. But that was three months ago. In the intervening time she had frittered the money that should've gone to Keenan, who was probably fuming about this fact at that very moment in his Bond Street boutique. This left us with no choice but to shoot the moon, owing thousands, and hope he never caught up with us. An operation that would eventually lead to us assuming different identities for large portions of the week and looking over our shoulders all the time. The date for this subterfuge had been set for the end of June, just before Keeney was due to arrive to inspect the creepy-crawlies and collect his wad.

You may have noticed, sagacious reader, that time has been zipping and speeding past at a furious rate without due reflection on a number of troubling incidents. I had been married for over a year. My wife had just thrown a living animal against a bedroom door with the intent to injure it. Why didn't I press that the RSPCA take poor Fidel away, or at least that Mandy seek a psychiatrist? Why did I stay with her and what did we do with our time together? All difficult, intelligent questions. The first being the easiest to answer. Over the months, I had become softened, brainwashed, acclimatised to her behaviour. Not that I thought it was normal or legitimate, rather that I didn't see such madness as strange any more. It took a while for me realise that Mandy was morally and mentally deranged: these things aren't immediately apparent in people, they're revealed slowly, like mercury poisoning. My major aspiration was just to get through the week intact. And also, I suppose, to retain what I thought was her love; to impress her with my diligence; to hold up my side of the marriage bargain; to prove to myself that I could pay my way and not let these incidents derail the institution of holy matrimony. Again, I found myself in the position of coun-sellor or social worker, gently persuading the delinquent away from its destructive behaviour with the positive example of love. Love given unconditionally. Love, the best tonic. She always managed to appeal to this capacity in me. On the rare occasions that Mandy actually went to work she came home tearful and distraught. Nevertheless, she always received the full quota of care and concern from me. My role had become that of helper, not husband. Mandy – that irksome, brawling scold – was sick, in every sense of the word. I now think she suffered from a recognised condition: 'Histrionic Personality Disorder'. Look it up, it's in all the textbooks. She was an invalid. And everyone suffered and sickened in her slipstream. Poor Fidel. Our vet, Mr Morris, didn't believe for a moment that he had broken his foot chasing a randy female sheepdog in Walthamstow's Water Park. The perceptive eyes in his square head held a grave admonishment as he inspected the whimpering Fidellino. Of course, I covered for her with a load of persuasive bullshit, just as I did when she threw the vodka glass at my face. By this time she knew I would . . . So part of me remained with Mandy in order to improve her, to make sure she never took out her Juno's rage on other living creatures. A very womanly impulse. Somehow her imbalance of hormones (or even chromosomes) had feminised me, made me passive. But I had a strong desire to help her. In this I wasn't passive. It had become an altruistic enterprise.

As to the other questions, I really don't know what we did with our time. It just seemed to slip from us, like the leading horse in the Grand National, nosing ahead effortlessly. Our days and evenings were filled with work; endless squabbles over money; the machinations of her time-hungry band. All supposedly fruitful and purposeful activity, but looking back I just see a void. Everything seemed to get us nowhere. My time could have been more rewardingly spent lying on the couch reading, an activity that was tantamount to masturbation in Mandy's eyes. I had to be seen to be *doing* something at all times. The scowl of the world when it catches you dreaming! It was enough to give you cancer, ulcers and turn your hair white. At the time I equated her with the philistine tyrants at school – those brute-force bastards who just can't wait to give you a playground pasting, or smack a football into your head, or pour Lucozade down the back of your shirt, or fart in your face in the rugby scrum.

By the time we reached the East End, an invisible barrier had been erected between us. Something obfuscatory had got a hold. Ultimately, I knew all this pointless activity was just a front, a racket to cover our lack of intimacy. Without realising it, we had stopped having sex. The frequency of our violent rows seemed to advise against this activity. After scarring each other physically and verbally, the last arena you want to get involved in is one where strong and spontaneous emotions are hard to hide. I would watch her dress in the morning, sliding her terrific legs into tights and boots, as if I were watching a movie. Her body became a statue in a museum, an unimpeachable Praxiteles, and equally untouchable. Also, it was anomalous to me that someone with such a great figure could be so non-sexual, could have so few carnal needs. Erotic love was off the menu, seemingly indefinitely. So, for a quiet life, I would assent to virtually everything she said. The cost of conflict was too much for my own interior economy. If I had won victories in the past, every one was pyrrhic or indecisive, and liable to revision by her selective memory if they ever came up in conversation.

Predictably, on the sizzling morning of our escape from east London, with the removal van waiting on the street, the phone rang. The voice on the other end of the line said, 'Ah, Byron – you're in. Now, the rent.'

It was Keenan – timed to perfection.

'Yes, we've been having a bit of—'

Mandy, with a heavy box under each arm, knifed me with a look, as if to warn against any infirmity of purpose.

'Yes, I know you've had problems with little creatures, but I can't wait any longer. I have to bank the money by Monday.'

Money? What money? He meant the rent, of course. The explorers on that particular expedition had perished from frostbite months ago. I played for time: 'Have I ever let you down before?'

He gave out a sort of strangled titter at the other end, as if somebody had their hands around his throat while simultaneously tickling him. Unfortunately, his next sentence confirmed that they didn't. 'Frequently, Byron. Now, to save you the trouble of coming all the way to Bond Street you'll be happy to hear that I'm just down the road. So I thought I'd pop over.'

It was too late to deter him. As this information went around, panic broke out in the ranks. The unfortunate removal men were asked to shift an hour's worth of packing cases in ten minutes, with me and Mandy frantically helping; our sweat sprinkling the dust-dry pavements of June. As the hulking van took us away from the East End for the last time, Fidel rubbernecking passing dogs as he sat on my lap, I thought I saw Keenan rounding the corner at the end of the road. But it was only a mirage of summer, one of many that year. A paranoid calenture. My landlord turned out to be a lumbering Nigerian in a rainbow-hued traditional shawl. I had mistaken this blazing cape-of-many-colours for one of Keenan's waistcoats.

'You don't want to look inside the oven,' Mandy said once we were across the threshold of number seventy-two Seaham Road. As this kind of imperative always invites disobedience, I immediately opened the door to the cooker. On the middle shelf of the lard-begrimed oven was a dish that contained half a meat pie, possibly chicken, but most likely steak and kidney. A pathologist could probably have told us with a degree of accuracy the cause of death and how long it had lain in situ, but we estimated three months. Too long anyway, for its rank stench caused us to hurl the windows wide and dispose of it with all the precautions reserved for clinical waste. But this wasn't our most disheartening discovery, oh no. On top of one of the high kitchen cabinets were two aerosol canisters: one of air freshener, the other the strongest insect repellent you can buy over the counter. Sure enough, the wretched flat had cockroaches. Not a Teutonic infestation, but a population of the startlingly large and shiny brutes that look and move like tropical beetles. This time, Mandy took charge and phoned Antonia at *Acquisition*.

'They're as big as mice. I can't believe you didn't warn me about this.'

Ah, the irony of it all was finally making me smile. I wasn't sure that I didn't quite like cockroaches by this stage. They were, after all, just another of God's creatures. I could hear Antonia's golden public-schoolgirl voice at the end of the line – croaky, enunciated, blind to ridicule. As I watched the window to see if Keenan had followed us, I idly pondered whether I would get bored of breasts as big as Antonia's if I had married her instead of Mandy. I turned and surveyed the empty echoing rooms of the new place – just four walls and a ceiling again, not a home. And there was my wife, that master of living well on nothing a year, standing in the middle of it, her long glossy mane absorbing the sun, directing operations once more with her silver baton.

'Darling,' the muffled voice rasped, 'don't panic. I'll send my father round this weekend to advise.'

Antonia's father ran a big farm out in Suffolk. He would know the practical measures that should be taken in such a situation. Infestations were his bread and butter. I suddenly felt a deficit of male know-how. Surely, as a husband, I should be the one exterminating vermin and putting up shelves. Not for the first time, I felt complicit in my own emasculation. Christ, outdone by the father of your wife's best friend! With Mandy as circus master, as per usual. If I had possessed hair to cut off, this Delilah would have exercised the shears. Being a constant passenger in Mandy's car (literally and metaphorically) didn't help either, nor did the fact that she seemed to organise everything with her extravagant energies. Why didn't I learn to drive and take the helm in these masculine matters? These were pressing questions at the time. I suppose the answer was that I was too involved in my own inner life, and its metaphysical demands. The need to respond to life by the perverse and non-remunerative act of writing poetry. Post-pamphlet, I had been hit by a writer's block that was threatening to be terminal. But these were not legitimate ways, in Mandy's eyes, to spend one's time. If I did write in those days, it would necessitate creeping from our futon in the small hours and settling myself by the small, cat-shaped table lamp, where I could allow my thoughts to soar and fly. I would never reveal in the morning what I had been up to all night. This was another iron curtain to any intimacy that might have feebly arisen between us. I had my own world of inner concerns, of wrestling with strong mental opponents like the existence of a deity or the possibility of an afterlife, whereas Mandy's world was all outward engagement. And boy, did she engage. In our first month at Seaham Road, she sold the Peugeot and bought a vintage Triumph Stag from the dealership round the corner. The fact that the oily-vested mechanics delighted in her flirtatious and slinkily dressed presence had nothing to do with the massive discount she received, or so she insisted. Other mad profligate escapades saw her acquire a laptop, a new mobile and the complete recordings of Paco de Lucía in a lavish boxset. All in the space of a weekend. Who tabbed all this? Ramona's bequest, mainly. I knew she felt a rich sense of entitlement about these purchases. It was her money, after all, she argued. The wisdom that it's never your own money in a marriage was dismissed with a curl of her Catalan lips. We immediately fell behind with the rent. A pink Fender Stratocaster was purchased in anticipation of the big showcase gig at The Dome pencilled in for the end

of September, for which Fellatrix were vigorously rehearsing, seemingly day and night. I, meanwhile, plodded on with my midnight
metaphysical ministries and barren days in Martin's shop.

The gig didn't go well, to say the least. Fellatrix were headlining,
though you wouldn't have guessed by the numbers in attendance.
I stood at the back of the half-empty venue watching executive
after executive head for the exit. The guitars were out of tune.
Mandy looked nervous but defiant behind the big pink Stratocaster.
A lone plastic glass smacked into the drum kit as the last chord
rang out. Tears appeared in Mandy's darkening eyes as she hurled
the Strat into her amp and stormed off the stage. If a week is a
long time in politics, a year is an ice age in the music business.
Nobody was interested: the band were, if not checkmated then
zugzwanged, washed up, finished. Nervously, I headed backstage. I
found Mandy in conference with the sly and unshaven figure of
Victor Moore, one of the few people on the guestlist who had
demeaned themselves by showing up.

'Told you she was a fickle mistress,' I heard Victor drawl, on
nearing Mandy. 'You should change your name. Write a new set
of songs. And sack that drummer – my daughter keeps better time
on the saucepans in our kitchen.'

'I don't care about your daughter,' said Mandy, brushing her
tears away fiercely with her sleeve.

'That's just a random example,' added Victor with a self-satisfied
air, his cunning eyes doing a once-over of the dressing room for
any signs of coke.

'I thought you liked the songs!' Mandy said imploringly.

I took this criticism of Victor's to heart, as I had sweated blood
in writing all the lyrics.

'Yeah, well,' he muttered, and stared at his big, practical
Caterpillar orienteering boots.

'Anyway,' countered Mandy, high malice in her voice, 'what
do you know about music? You're just a plugger. And why should
we change the name just to satisfy those idiots who walked out? I
thought you liked the name.'

'But it's past its sell-by date! If you're not careful you're gonna have that loser dust all over your shoulders,' smirked Victor. 'It's deadly dandruff.'

Mandy could take it no more. She stood up and pushed Victor out of the way.

'Fuck you, weasel,' she hissed.

I felt immediate admiration for this outrageous act of defiance. Go, girl! But it was obviously suicidal. Victor held his hands up in surrender, a grin on his face. He didn't care that much anyway. He had another three bands to check out that night, all with guitarists less volatile than Mandy. He wouldn't have to exercise his power of making Fellatrix music-business pariahs – they had performed that task themselves, by hanging around for too long, by being generally surplus to requirements, by telling a well-known industry professional to fuck himself. They were off the radar, dead in the water, shut down for good, banished for ever from the vanity fair of the London scene. Mandy would take a while to digest this information, weeks and months in fact. But the damage had been done. I tentatively went to put an arm round her shaking shoulders.

'Is the guitar okay?'

She said: 'And fuck you, too.'

Dios mío. If that wasn't prickly enough, things became substantially hotter back at Seaham Road. The van journey resembled a funeral cortège. Each member of the band solemnly dropped off with their gear, hopeless expressions on faces. Few words had been exchanged; maybe the odd conciliatory pat on the back had passed among musicians unsure of when, if ever, they would see each other again. Once through our front door, the high stack of her flightcased amp blocking the passage, Mandy produced the guestlist; a long printed roll-call of all those absentee VIPs. She took out her lighter and held it under the paper.

In the gloom of the hall I asked, 'What do you think you're doing?'

'What does it look like? I'm burning rubbish.'

The flames spread through the paper, soaring upwards as if the thing had been doused with petrol. Then she disappeared up the stairs to our flat, still holding the flambeau. I followed, only to find her calmly walking through the rooms, applying the flame to curtains, clothes and wall posters, which took immediately. My heart, always unsteady around Mandy, started to rattle like a fire bell. This done, she flung the torch into the recycling box which was full of tinder-dry newspapers. It flared up at once.

'You're crazy,' I said. 'You're going to kill us all!' But Mandy wasn't listening. She went to sit sulkily on her big limousine-length sofa, awaiting immolation, like an impassive sati widow.

I raced out to the hall for a non-existent fire extinguisher. Panicking, I barged back and was forced to improvise with a wet tea-towel instead. By the time I had smothered the curtains, the recycling box was a towering inferno. By the time the recycling box had been doused in the bath, the posters were scorching the ceilings, leaving sooty circles the size of car tyres. By the time the last flames had been mastered the whole flat reeked like a gutted factory after an arson attack. I crumpled to the floor in front of Mandy, exhausted, waiting for her to speak harsh words. But, to my surprise, I found her face unexpectedly gentle. She stared at me beatifically; stared a hole right through me. In the low light, tears dripped steadily from her chin, like jewels from an icicle.

There were other ways of living, but I couldn't envisage them at the time. On every occasion I tried to picture this better life, it shifted shape or ran beyond my peripheral vision, where it hunkered down and waited. In the absence of this modifying spirit I made the best of things, on a day to day basis. You can't just get up and walk away from a hellish marriage. It isn't that easy, as anyone who has been in the same tiring predicament will testify. Instead, you make amends. The mind, if it is reflective at all, constantly circles the pros and cons: the reason the union happened in the first place; the daunting consequences of breaking the Gordian knot. The ramifications. A great deal of time is spent in not wanting to seem a failure in other people's eyes. Also, not wanting to *look* into their eyes. A marriage is different from the common or garden relationship. It is supposed to be holy in the eyes of the Invisible Man. It has legal implications. Parents get involved. Children, if there are any, have to be taken into account. Friends wish you well and are always enquiring about the health of your marriage, as if it were a living third party, dependent on the correct nutrients and vitamins. You feel obliged to produce a progress report every couple of months. Then there are the intimations, forwarded by others, that your partner is less than faithful. There's nothing worse than the jealousy between two people who have started to despise each other. Not the noble loving 'not wisely, but too well' of the Moor, but a corrosive covetousness that one clings to, as it supposedly produces evidence that – despite burning flats and flying fists – you still love each other. This non-nutritious and possessive jealousy is hard to walk away from.

The day after Mandy's band went up in smoke, she retired to bed with a high temperature. Not as high as that produced by the flaming curtains of the previous night – the thermometer indicated nothing above normal – but high in the sense of highly strung. Ready to snap. By six, I was locked into an argument over the subject of Antonia, whose lovely twins had graced The Dome in a melon-coloured tank top, which seemed to produce a measurable tensile stress (on the material and on the men). Apparently, my tongue had been on the floor all night. An hour of attacking my behaviour had degenerated into general swipes at women and personal-level abuse aimed at Antonia herself.

Mandy raised herself from the futon (her semi-permanent home) to deliver her peroration: '. . . Then there's all those *putas* in their tight tops giving people's boyfriends – or worse, husbands – the eye! Whores! They're all whores!'

She slumped back down again, shaking from the strain of so much concentrated pejorative thought.

'Well, you've really put your cards on the table now,' I countered. 'It's not my fault Antonia was wearing that top.'

'That silly slut! She should have her stupid page-three tits removed. Surgically removed.'

'I thought she was your best friend.'

'Not if she's wiggling about in front of everything in a pair of trousers all night she's not.'

'Christ, if she could hear you now.'

'She's too busy flirting.'

'And you've never flirted in your life, right?'

'Plus she's got cellulite. Can you believe it? At twenty-four!'

'Oh, who cares!?'

I thought it curious that, taking into account the fact that Mandy and I were no longer sleeping with each other, she seemed to want to exercise all her wifely privileges of sexual possessiveness. I knew she was innately competitive with anything female (Jesus, she even used to become jealous over poor Concepcion when I cradled her in my arms), but this was an incoherent attitude of hers. Obviously, this was in the days when I still expected some kind of logic to her insane views, some consistency or integrity. After the vodka-glass incident, her rank jealousy had manifested itself in gentler ways. A joke developed between us where, if we found an unknown but wholly innocent phone number the back of a cigarette packet, we would comically interrogate each other in silly voices. 'Whose number is that?' 'Ve haff vays of making you . . . ,' et cetera. This had the effect of diffusing the troublesome unexploded bomb of jealousy. Only, just recently, her old termagant edge was back. If I mentioned any other woman, whether a customer in the shop or someone seen on an escalator, she would become Cleopatra, demanding to know her competitor's age, height, the sound of her voice or whether there was 'majesty in her gait'. At a Fellatrix gig in the spring she had thrown a lit cigarette at a girl I just happened to be asking for a light in the audience. A subtle shift of emphasis from throwing objects at *me*, but worrying nonetheless.

And, true to form, there was a double-standard at the heart of this. While I wasn't allowed to so much as glance at another woman, she could have all the handjob-fatigued suitors she wanted. There used to be a queue of them after every gig, insisting she autograph their spotty buttocks. However, just recently her fury had been newly directed towards her own gender, her fellow sisters. I put this down to the delayed influence of the old señora, Montserrat. Largely brought up by her dotty grandmother, who never hesitated to pronounce a woman a *puta* for the slightest transgression, Mandy seemed to be turning into the bitter old dame at a rate of knots. But she had never accused Antonia of being a whore before now. Maybe she only thought it. This was a new development. She was slowly alienating herself from her own sex. In fact, if I examined the situation, Antonia was her only female friend. There was no getting away from the fact that Mandy was that most terrifying of female quantities, a man's woman. She gloried in the intense and seedy attention of the men, a natural sunlamp to her ego and vanity, but spurned the knotty Sisterhood.

I could no longer tolerate this high bitchery. I made to leave the room in order to search for the mobile, that we shared.

'. . . Not only that, but she was fluttering her eyelashes and talking in that fake Marilyn Monroe baby voice. I can't stand that husky shit. You know that's a put-on voice, don't you? Just for the benefit of men? If you ever visited her parents' farm you wouldn't hear her using that silly accent. She sounds like a bumpkin up there.'

'Can't you give it a rest? Anyway, where's the mobile? I need to call Rudi before he's kneecapped. He's been mixed up in all sorts recently.'

But Mandy wasn't listening.

'And Nick's just as shallow. He's such a poseur. All he's bothered about is being seen with the correct pair of shoes.'

'Okay. Whatever you say. She's a slag and he's a poseur. Where's the phone?'

Mandy paused, and said, 'I don't know. I think it was on the bed.'

Our eyes met for a beat. Mandy rummaged around under the covers and sure enough produced the phone. She had been lying on it. The weight of her cellulite-free, non-flirtatious thighs had pressed the call button. She confirmed the worst. The number dialled had been Antonia's, who, we later found out to our unlimited shame, had been crouched next to the phone with Nick for the past hour, listening to our real opinion of them both.

———————

'It's like the Bromley PTA dinner and dance in here,' said Martin Drift, sucking on a red Marlboro in the underground gloom. 'What's wrong with these young people? They all look like surfers or hippies. Not to mention those grave-robbers in the white make-up. In my day you had gobbing punks.'

We were standing in the patchouli and dry-ice melancholy of the Electric Ballroom watching a beyond-forty alcoholic finish her final song on stage. Even the band seemed to have become suddenly embarrassed by the strangely uninhibited hand movements and cater-wauling with which this woman chose to climax her performance. The name of this band of risibly unsmiling Goths was Rose Masquerade. Unquestionably, this was a rose long overdue pruning. Without looking at Martin, whose skin I knew would be glowing in indignation under his salty beard, I shouted, 'You were – sorry, are – a hippy, Martin. It was bands like yours they wanted to destroy.'

He shouted something back but it was drowned out. I couldn't attack Martin on a point of cool for the simple reason that we had both capitulated. We had embarked on a night of barrel-scraping. On the unreliable advice of Pat Coffer we were, indeed, contem-plating Eurovision. The great man himself was near the lip of the stage, attempting to hold a conversation with Mandy, whose features appeared and disappeared in a fog of dry ice. This was just as well, because nobody else wanted to talk to her. Anybody remotely connected with the music industry had either blanked her, smirked or frozen her out on first encounter. A few had ironically made the fellatio gesture behind her back, with a curled hand held to the mouth, tongue visibly in cheek. This, of course, was in tribute to her late unlamented band, named after an act that Mandy had never performed on me, and one which, she insisted, she never would even if the temperatures in hell dipped below zero. To be honest, I was glad she had taken Pat off our hands. I could sense Martin also dreaded delivering the final verdict that his Eurovision hopeful – Miss Moonstone, currently curled in the foetal position on stage as the last waves of feedback shredded ears – wasn't up to scratch. In fact, so far from qualified was she for the job of singer, popstar, sane human being, that almost anyone with functioning limbs randomly picked from a crowd could have made a better go of it. In terms of talent, she made Martin and I look like Bacharach and David. Why such a comparison? Because ever since acccepting Pat's offer of the Eurovison songwriting gig we had been frantically thinking of ways to renege on our promise. The latest, cooked up while standing dumbstruck in front of the monitors, was to claim that we were both secretly illiterate. Write her songs? We would sooner sign our own certification for the madhouse. *Nul points*!

Pat Broke off from Mandy and began to search for us through the Waterloo of dry ice.

'Quick,' Martin said, 'he's coming our way. Let's scarper to the bar. We might be able to lose him there.'

'What about Mandy?'

'She'll do the same if she has any sense.'

Not sure by this stage of my marriage that she possessed any, I downed my diluted lager and left the plastic pint glass sticking to the venue's floor. Martin tugged the sleeve of my jacket and started to force the milling punters aside, like Moses through a Black Sea of leather jackets. Once at the bar he stood with his curled fiver, demanding service with his peculiarly astringent grey eyes. He had determination, Martin, that I would grant him. Sometimes I thought he was the only sane person I knew. He was a compact, sinewy, elegantly evolved man who placed a high value on loyalty, diligence, grit – the old values. Quick to form opinions, he nevertheless proved to be quite shrewd about human behaviour. I couldn't think of a single assessment he had made that hadn't, over the years, proved correct. Mandy did indeed turn out to be Mad Spanish Mandy, with all the slavering suitors in the world. Pat did indeed turn out to be one of the most persistent lunatics in the asylum, not just a harmless old pisshead.

The very contemplation of writing a song for Pat's Eurovision turkey had only arisen because of the sharp downturn in Rock On's fortunes of late. By November, the apparently never-ending downward trajectory of the shop seemed to have reached a nadir; at which point it turned a corner and just continued in freefall during the run-up to Christmas. Little Johnny, it appeared, didn't want that spangled Gretsch Country Gentleman with pearl inlays any more, he wanted a sampler and a digital mixing desk. December had seen tumbleweeds blowing across the dusty floors of the Royal College Street shop. I had been downsized to one afternoon a week. Desperation was in the air. Every time I arrived just after lunch-time, Martin would be stepping out into the bitter wind for a Londis chicken slice, like Oates leaving the godforsaken tent. But he was determined to see his family through this 'lull in the performance', as he liked to call it. With debts like his, he had to be. Plus, his wife had finally persuaded him to move the family from the crack and pitbull estate where they had resided since the eighties to a purpose-built council block in Belsize Park, thus unfortunately doubling the rent. Despite his limpet-like resistance to movement or change, he had reacted to this upheaval with a Senecan shrug. 'You have to expect everything in this game,' he would say, as another Thursday afternoon's sale of three guitar picks was banked. I was surprised by his resilience. Somewhere Martin had hidden reserves. So, when Pat had marauded in on the last Friday before Christmas, invigorating us afresh with his Eurovision dreams, we had told him he could count us in. I may as well admit that I too was hoping beyond hope that Rose Masquerade's singer was not the flapping festive dinner she turned out to be. I too was vainly dreaming of big paydays; Green Room nerves, Terry Wogan's melting brogue, hairspray, glitter, and a ticket out of Sing-Sing. I hadn't really believed that Mandy's band would disappear down the great rock 'n' roll khazi in the sky. It had been such a central plank of her – our – existence. I hadn't known a time when she wasn't living the dream day and night. I trembled to think how she would fill her days now.

Martin handed me a urine-coloured pint of warmish lager and asked, 'Are you still using that wedding present?'

Up until that moment I had totally forgotten his gift of a phallic-shaped lava lamp, delivered personally on the evening before my wedding day. The undulating green and pink patterns in their joke-erection plastic tube had to be hidden when Montserrat and Leo visited the following spring. Not long after that, Mandy had belted it to the floor in one of her apopleptic rages. I felt a sudden chill of shame at this. It had been such a surprise to see Martin at our door (the first occasion he had visited), cold and hungry, on the way home from the shop, his car coughing exhaust at the kerb, green novelty-cock under his arm.

'Yeah,' I said shakily, 'I think it's still in a packing case some-where.'

'Only, I didn't see it when I came over to see your new place. Now, if you didn't like it, if you thought it was gaudy rubbish and belonged in a knocking shop—'

'No, no,' I said, knowing how easily his feelings were hurt. He really was a sensitive soul under that dense beard and grizzled skin.

'—I just thought it would tickle your fancy. I burst out laughing when I saw it down the Lock Market.' Martin glanced over my shoulder. 'Aye, aye. Here comes trouble. Pretend we spent most of the set here.'

I turned to see Pat Coffer limping towards us, a rock 'n' roll Long John Silver, dragging his unwilling right leg with a tattooed hand. His puce complexion and concrete-grey eyes shimmered under the distant strobes. He was an Irish mountebank or Covent Garden costermonger from the old tradition.

'Gentlemen, I knew I'd find ya here, propping up the counter. She's the dog's, isn't she?'

Martin suddenly had his business visor on. He said, 'Who, Mandy?'

'Nah, Moonstone. She's got what it takes, eh? A real performer.'

'I'm afraid we sat most of it out, Pat.'

'Ah, but I saw you both spellbound for the grand finale, eh, eh?' He slapped Martin on the shoulder and winked at me. 'I don't half fancy your missus, Bry. It does an old wanker good to be seen out with a pretty bird on his arm. Reminds me of the days down Studio 54 when—'

'Pat,' Martin said with icy finality, 'she's shit. I've never seen worse in thirty years of exposure to shit. She wouldn't even make it on a cruise ship. And I think Byron might want his wife back at the end of the evening.'

Martin gave Pat a harsh look at this last statement. He knew the old carouser's ways too well. For a small man, Martin could be enormously forceful and charismatic. But Pat refused to look crestfallen.

'Give her a chance! I spent six months of giros on her singing lessons.'

Despite the fact that Moonstone was one of the worst singers in the world and of world-class ugliness, my soft sentimental nature, my innate easiness, made me feel sorry for Pat. He had been through the mill and had been spat out the other side with his gammy leg and his tormented enthusiasms. At that moment, I felt a strange affinity with him. As if we were brothers in adversity. Plus, I had been regaling Mandy with visions of a better life for a week, all flowing from the golden chalice of Eurovision victory. In the end I caved in, just like I did when Pat touched me for a twenty earlier, his unignorable confrontational eyes sparkling.

'Okay, Pat, I'll write a few lyrics.'

Martin rounded on me. 'I won't let you, Byron. I won't let you waste your time. Pat's made a career out of wasting people's time.'

Surprised, I said, 'Ah, what harm will it do, Mart? The man's in need.'

Martin addressed Pat, his usually gentle and equanimous eyes steely. 'Sorry, mate, but I won't let him. He's under contract to me.'

This last statement was ludicrous, and we all knew it. We stood there in the smoky blue-lit cavern of the ballroom, like a Mexican standoff.

'But, why not?' croaked Pat, his voice suddenly full of pebbles.

''Cos he's an old friend,' said Martin.

To my surprise, my heart expanded at Martin's words. Maybe I had been under great emotional strain of late, but tears smarted in my eyes, disabling me from further speech. This was a far cry from the knockabout badinage of the shop. I didn't think he would defend me like this. I felt the sudden upheaval burn briefly inside me, like the ghost of an old wound.

Finally, Pat said, 'And what am I, then?'

'You're just old,' said Martin, and motioned for me to follow him in search of Mandy.

The day after my Eurovision dream crashed and burned, me and Martin went for a curry, and laughed off Pat's desperate importuning. A year previously, I had sat in the same bijou balti house with Mandy, my mother, my half-sister, Sarah, and her boyfriend. I still tremble, sober reader, at the memory of this night, one of the most bloody battles ever recorded in domestic history. However, up until this watershed, Mandy's deep eccentricity sometimes warmed me. This didn't quite cancel out her periods of spectacular suffering, but it went some way towards it. I loved the evenings when she danced around the flat to salsa and mambo in front of the big mirror as a prelude to a night out, eye-shadow glittering on the exotic anemone-like bulges of her eyelids. Or when she cooked paella with cockles, still full of sand, from the market. Or when she bought me books for no particular reason, with effusive inscriptions on the fly-leaf. Yes, there were some good times. Brief moths that danced erratically before the light. Like the afternoon we watched *Casablanca* together under a duvet as the rain bucketed down outside.

Or when we drove all the way to a Surrey village dog-show one July and Fidel picked up a rosette for third place. All the pastimes of a married couple: gilded rings on fingers declaring our exclusivity. Then there were the nights when we played cards around the big varnished dining table that I had spent the summer sanding and waxing. I still loved it when she spoke her fluent mellifluous Catalan or machine-gun fast Castilian. Or when she cooked with olives carefully picked out and weighed from the Cypriot grocer on Green Lanes. She was fiercely pragmatic in the wider world of getting and spending. Her fastidiousness sometimes had its upsides: only the best would do – for her wardrobe, her bathroom products; for her kitchen. I secretly admired this attitude – me, who would always settle for second best to avoid a fuss. Once upon a time this attitude had extended to her band and her three long-gone tomcats. To me, even.

Recalling that evening in the intimate mango-light of the Indian restaurant – my mother, sister and her boyfriend before me like an interview panel, Mandy sullen and playing with her food on my left – is like falling off into a troubled afternoon sleep. I feel as if I am walking through a house, each room deeper and darker and more dangerous to enter than the one before. The sight of us there is painful to the touch, to the very eyeball. I can see the waiter bringing over the poppadoms and laden tray of chutneys; smell the cigarette smoke curling into the incense air; feel the coolness of the lager on my tongue, cooler than the misty December night outside on the Holloway Road. I can see Sarah and her slightly dull, wary-eyed boyfriend making a start on the yoghurts and dills, holding hands on the linen table cloth, while Mandy looks contemptuously on. I can see my mother, Sinead, heroically preserved Sinead, slightly shrunken by the years, her sable hair dryer and more troublesome than I remember, the dewlaps of middle age just beginning to form under her chin. I can recall the feeling of troubled incipience; that we were all getting to know each other at last, with Sarah just about to finish her A levels, with mother living so far up north. The evening had commenced promisingly, with a drink at our flat in Seaham Road, Mandy putting on a brave face after a day of migraines, pills and explosions of temper. But some transformation had occurred in the cab over. My wife had reverted to type, or to the feline venom that seemed to be her default state. And she knew the evening meant a lot to me, that it had been long-organised, that I hardly saw Sarah and had never met her boyfriend before. Her new mood of barely concealed intolerance, boredom and spite didn't make for an easy journey. I could see by the expressions of my companions that they were wondering what had gone down, what had changed her tide in a matter of moments; whether it was something they had said or done. But these were all fruitless questions with Mandy. It was rarely anything anyone had said or done. She would turn for deep childish reasons known only to herself. She hadn't yet learnt how to behave. That evening, I would feel the full gravity of this diagnosis.

As the main courses arrived, in sizzling iron urns borne on chocks of pine, I asked Sarah, 'So tell me what they do for English A level nowadays.'

She smiled at me, her eyes as fjord-grey as my mother's. She had also inherited some of some her vital, vibrant energies. Three years ago, before Bea, before Mandy, I had the heart-troubling notion that I was falling in love with her; my own half-sister, such a pure pebble in the clear stream of her youth, so vivid and in the moment. And so forbidden. I remember watching her sleeping on the sofa of my mum's living room during a rare visit to Yorkshire. The down on her apple cheeks was like cotton-wool fibre, white and wispy, her chest rising and falling like the ocean. She had said one evening when Sinead was in the kitchen making mulligatawny soup that she loved me and wanted to marry me when she grew up. That was the moment I put a stop to it. I told her she was only fourteen and it was against the law. As the oval saucers of pilau rice were set down, her boyfriend David eyed me suspiciously. He was a pharmaceutical assistant, upright, pragmatic. The collar of his Marks and Spencer shirt, rising crisply from the navy pullover, advertised his sexless conservatism, his unbearable reliability. Maybe she had told him something of this outlawed love, though I doubted it. He had that close-set, circumspect look that passes as intelligence and attractiveness in men but is merely the vigilance of a dog.

'We're doing *Moll Flanders* at the moment,' said Sarah, 'It's brilliant. She gets to go to America and sleep with all these men, and she's still having babies in her forties.'

'And that's a good thing, is it?' frowned David.

'It's brilliant. She's so free – so emancipated! For the time, that is.'

Mandy looked coldly at my half-sister. I could tell she was examining the corpulence that always threatened Sarah's upper arms, the bright sea-fresh gleam to her skin. I could tell she didn't know what 'emancipated' meant.

'Did you ever read that?' I asked my mother.

Sinead paused before this familiar question. Her long, straight nose twitched animatedly. Untouched by the depredations undergone by the rest of the body, it was the nose of a twenty-one-year-old girl. 'Anything I read your father had looked at before me – he always explained the plot so I wouldn't be lost with his snooty friends. To be honest it saved a lot of time.'

I thought I'd ask Sinead another familiar question. The question I always asked on the rare occasions we met. 'Do you, er, ever see anything of Delph?'

My mother bristled at this. She looked frail, worn-out, ill. I wanted to ask her if she was poorly, but the company advised against it.

Instead, Sarah jumped to my rescue. Changing the subject, her sparkly voice said, 'Let me tell you about what happened to Demjanjuk the dentist! I've been dying to tell you all day.'

'Does it involve a slow and painful death?'

But my mother didn't want the subject changed. To me she said emphatically, slowly, 'I haven't laid eyes on him for years.' Then she turned to Sarah. 'You'll see your father at Christmas, won't you?' Sarah nodded in assent. For a beat there was a tense quiet around the table. 'Now,' my mother suddenly smiled gamely, 'is everybody's food here?'

Delph and Des. Fathers and the past. Subjects that were always off-limits during these meetings. I knew Sarah had her own book of grief concerning Delph, but it was a closed book. If she shared it with anyone she rarely opened its pages to me. Maybe this was because she sensed that, if I ever laid eyes on Delph again, I would baseball bat his head into something resembling Sainsbury's economy mince. These two men had become the unmentionables – they had been written out of history, like the butchers of Treblinka. I thought it best then to avoid the issue, or at least involve Mandy in the conversation, as long experience told me that her silence indicated she was going down fast, like a plane whose propeller had stopped.

'Well, I only wanted an update,' I muttered. 'Nobody tells me anything any more.' The previous night, my mother had paid a visit to Stevenage to see her friend – and my old nemesis – Babs. I longed to ask whether Babs was as fat as I remembered, but this seemed off-limits too. I turned to Mandy. 'Surely your father's not still on his own?' She didn't make eye contact, instead she merely continued trailing a fork in her untouched chicken jalfrezi. The peppery pickles and chillies were beginning to raise the temperature. She shrugged her shoulders. 'Only he didn't seem that happy with just a Labrador for company last Christmas. You know, there are plenty of dating agencies for the over-fifties.'

Mandy said, 'Dunno.'

Perhaps unwisely, I pushed the matter. 'But it's been nine years since your mum died. It's not natural. For a man.'

A pause. Then she mumbled, 'You know he's still on his own. You couldn't replace *my* mother. Anyway, he deserves everything he gets.'

Sarah and David exchanged glances. They were probably wondering how the confident, friendly woman of an hour ago, so intent on showing them photographs of Tarragona and her family, had changed into a brooding and morose wielder of monosyllables. Sarah offered to bail her out: 'No one deserves everything they get, don't you agree, David?'

I could tell Mandy was thinking, *What do you know? You're only eighteen*. But for the moment this went unvoiced. It was stored, like molten magma underground. The moment had arrived for David to demonstrate whether he had a sense of humour. After all, many people deserved all they got, and more. Hitler, Stalin, Pol Pot, Delph.

'I think that all depends,' said David, failing at his task of diffusing the situation with a well-turned bon mot or slicing aperçu.

'Depends on what?' said my mother, not really interested. I could tell she gave no quarter to Mandy's childish silent mood. Characteristically, she would only involve herself in conversation with those who were willing to talk. If Mandy bore grudges – against her father, against Sarah, against the world in general – then she wasn't about to nurse it out of her against her own will. My mother's arthritic knuckles closed around her napkin. She looked pale under the pastel lights of the restaurant; her ageless piccolo nose and dark eyes had gained in dignity over the years. She had the same aura of settled understanding, of calm engagement, as Goya's portrait of Isabel de Porcel. Rearranging her white scarf around her frail collarbones she awaited David's answer. He was on the spot now, against his volition, flailing in the strong waters of his own lack of spontaneity.

Finally, David said, 'Well, it depends on how great their sin is.' He turned to Mandy, who was rolling a crumb of rice around under her elegant forefinger. 'Now I don't know a thing about your father, but parents always get the blame for everything, don't they?'

'They fuck you up, your mum and dad,' I interjected happily.

'Thanks!' said my mother in a stern bark.

Sarah's champagne eyes glittered at this. She always delighted in me saying or doing the wrong thing, a talent lacking in her diplomatic boyfriend. Her throat showed whitely in the drab light. Framed by the velvet caresses of her black gown, it was sexual, scandalously exposed. Everyone had dressed up for the occasion. Even I had ironed and sewed buttons onto my only white shirt.

'No, that was a misprint,' smiled Sarah. 'It was, they *tuck* you up, your mum and dad.'

Everyone, apart from Mandy, laughed at this. At last the icebreaker was on its way from the North Sea to the choppy waters of the Pole. My wife fixed Sarah with her basilisk stare, while I gazed lovingly at her. In my peripheral vision, I could sense that something volcanic was stirring, but I couldn't think of a way to stop the eruption. We had tried to involve her in the conversation, but she had been resolutely opposed to any such banter. She looked gravely serious, as if we were all fools on a day out from the madhouse. All eyes were on Sarah now, and Mandy loathed this, loathed not being the bright centre of attention. More pertinently, *my* eyes were on Sarah. She couldn't stand my engagement with anyone female other than her for more than a few seconds. At last, she pushed the table from her, winding Sarah in the folds of her voluptuous stomach.

'You're just a stupid fat whore,' spat Mandy, very close to Sarah's shocked and terrified face. Then she turned to me. 'And I'm going home.'

Mandy grabbed her glitter bag and strode terrifyingly fast towards the door, barging smiling waiters asunder and eliciting glances from the surrounding diners as she did so. Then she was gone, her profile expressionless in the biting December air. A silence that actually felt medically dangerous descended over the table. Sarah looked first at my mother, then at me, then at David. But Sinead had fixed her attention on her cooling chicken korma, while David appeared to be pondering a tricky chemical equation. For a moment, nobody felt much like saying anything. Mandy's words were too busy resonating in everyone's ears. '*Stupid*' (clearly Sarah was anything but unintelligent), '*fat*' (she still bore traces of puppy fat around her chin, but all the same . . .), '*whore*' (that was the clincher, the worst thing she could have said, and in front of my mother, too). The food was cold, inedible. My old spasm of disgust at unquiet scenes at the dinner table flashed through my guts. Except this time I was responsible. I had gathered everyone here for a pre-Christmas balti with high expectations of cordiality and tolerance. Instead, my beloved sister had been frozen to stone by this woman I had married, this incomparable tragedian.

'I'm sorry,' I muttered, 'she hasn't been feeling well.'

David looked up, the dog-like stance of defiance again present in his eyes. He said, 'That's not really good enough, is it?'

'What else can I say? I'm sorry, sorry, sorry. Sorry that you had to be witness to that.'

My mother let out a long sigh, the sort that accepts a situation isn't salvageable and that the fallout out will be long and complicated.

'Sorry that you married her?' said David, gleams of anger in the corners of his eyes. He was getting into his jacket. 'I know I would be.'

'Oh, come on,' said Sarah in a voice softer than she had used all evening. 'She's been ill. We all lose it from time to time. Where do you think you're going?'

David was on his feet. He shoved the chair under the table. 'To have a word. She's out of order.'

'It won't do you any good.'

'Nobody talks to my girlfriend like that.'

'Hey,' I said, 'she's my sister, too.'

Before I could stop him he was at the door of the restaurant. I looked briefly at my mother and Sarah, both on the verge of tears, then ran after him. By the time I had negotiated the deluge of cars streaming south in the frigid air, I could see David, a distant figure along the road, haranguing a tall woman by the tube station. I caught them up, only to hear the last sentence of David's furious torrent.

'Me and you −' he shouted pointing at Mandy's defiant nose, '− me and *you* aren't talking. Understand?'

He turned, surprised to see me behind him, then took a step sideways and began to stride back to the warm glow of the restaurant. I stared at Mandy, and said,

'You fool.'

She didn't answer. Her eyes were completely unreadable: full of contradictory messages: contempt, surprise, arrogance. Then she disappeared into the dank entrance of the underground.

★

Question: when, during a relationship, does one know inwardly that it is doomed? When does that final straw crack the whinnying camel's back? There is always a moment, a quiet interior voice that whispers home truths to your soul. It is the voice of self-preservation. The voice of ultimate sanity. It was this voice that became my secret interlocutor as I returned to the Indian restaurant that chilly night. It said: *Get out now. This is going to keep happening again and again. You have married a nightmare, a walking incubus. A follower of Xantippe. An obstinate, meddling Circe. A domineering, controlling, feckless, wrong-headed fool. An abuser of others' generosity. A person who absolutely has to spoil everything, whatever it is, everywhere. A deeply insecure, horrible human being. An erratic, emotional, theatrical, sadistic, self-destructive personality. She should have a sign around her neck that says: Unsafe Building – Do Not Enter. To witness her rage, my friend, is like having a brief glimpse of hell – every day. Oh, and,* the voice added in joyful whisper: *what a stupid person you are for marrying someone so stupid.*

When I reached our table my mother was already paying the bill. It was too late for further apologies. I embraced my sister, my hands grateful for the softness of her velvet dress; her wounded confidence making her somehow less physically robust. I didn't know when I would be seeing her again. I suddenly visualised her as a bridesmaid at Sinead and Delph's wedding, wheeling around in the blizzard of confetti, reluctant to get into the big car. It broke my heart to see her now, humiliated, putting a brave face on a scene it would take all of us a while to forget. I briefly shook David's hand, but our glances fell among the swirling paisley patterns of the carpet.

By the time I reached Seaham Road, I had already downed three bottles of strong lager on the bus. I began thinking about how unhappy I was, at bottom. A deep, iron-riveted, insurmountable unhappiness. Then I recalled the unforgivable, inadmissible thing Mandy had uttered. My blood was up, racing through my veins like fast-acting poison. Mandy was in the bedroom, face down on her polyhued Latina bedspread. I can't remember what I said to the nearest syllable, but two years of anger had suddenly been unleashed. I was an avenging gladiator striding into the dusty arena of the coliseum.

'How fucking could you?' I yelled at her. 'In front of my mother, too. Do you have to destroy absolutely everything, or are you going to leave something standing?'

She shrugged her shoulders. I aimed a dart straight for her heart. 'Oh, you have nothing to say now, is that it? We can usually rely on you to give your loudmouthed opinion on everything. For your information, she's not stupid, she has a place at Cambridge waiting for her. Secondly, she's not fat – and so what if she was? You're a fascist, that's what you are! A body fascist. What are you going to do when you're sixty and nobody's whistling at you on the street any more? And lastly, she's no whore, which is more than I can say for you, with all that tarty crap you wear.'

It was true that Mandy dreaded the day when she would no longer feel the enrichment provided by the male gaze – when it would disappear overnight (when men would look right through her to the ripe teenage blonde behind), causing her to shrivel like a date in its absence. Hearing my own blood thumping in my temples, I took another swig of beer. I felt suddenly like the worm that turned. But Mandy maintained her ominous silence. Usually she would have responded to a tirade such as this by screaming the house down. Yes, the empty vessel certainly makes the louder sound, I thought, as I watched her pathetic shoulders heave up and down. And I had exchanged deep water for this shallow pool? I shuddered at the reality . . . There were two plain facts in the electric air at that moment. One: she didn't give a toss, and two: she wasn't scared of me. Or not enough to do me the decency of acknowledging my presence. Why would she be scared of me, standing five-nine in my Converse trainers, balding, reasonable, easy? And she the big hitter, the terroriser of tenants and small animals, the fearless verbal sadist. I had never hated another human being more in my life.

Instead of saying another word on the matter I threw my newly opened bottle of Hofmeister at the bedroom window. It went clean through, with a deafening spew of glass, landing in the street below (in the morning I would find it on a patch of grass, intact). But it had the desired effect. She looked up from the bed, craning her incurious head over one shoulder, her eyes dark with scorn.

Obviously, her violence had taken its toll. Usually passive and compliant, it had infected me. I had performed a similar act of mindless destruction about a year into our marriage. It had become clear that there were certain things, sexual things, that Mandy refused to even contemplate. We're not talking about anal ticklers and hot-plates here – just wholesome oral sex. Like a 1950s prude, she said these acts were 'dirty'. 'Don't tell me you've never read *Cosmopolitan*!' I had exclaimed on learning this. Thus, after a drunken evening of sexual frustration, Mandy had become outraged when I had tried to go down on her after our formularised, missionary-position, post-pub lovemaking. Thinking she would have liked it, thinking that I'd never slept with such a puritanical woman, thinking that I was too pissed to care, I threw a bottle of red wine against the wall. She was stunned, not imagining I had such rage in me. 'Most women would be delighted!' I shouted. But it was a pale imitation of her behaviour, and we both knew it. I was so aggrieved that I slept half the night on the floor naked, as if someone had died.

But this time was different. I would make her pay for what she had said to my sister. As I approached Mandy's figure on the bed, I thought just once, just this once, I saw a flicker of fear in her face – as gratifying a sight as I had seen all year. Then the red mist descended before my eyes.

———

London town. The very late 1980s. I don't think I finished telling you how I found myself in a situation envenomed with irrevocable wrong. Back then, I felt myself to be moving at a considerable pace. Despite the fact that I was living a life of Communist Bloc scarcity (clothes washed so many times they were almost transparent, et cetera), there was quick-moving fire in my soul. The carbon-monoxide-leaking red buses and grand canyon thoroughfares of the city were a galvanising wonder. They carried me along on their steel streams. I felt stirred by the hammer and shimmer, the impersonal variety, the heterogeneous maze. Oxford Street! That boulevard of broken bards, that (in De Quincey's words) stony-hearted stepmother. I had just moved to my first bedsit in Harlesden, with its nightly police chases and streets that resembled, on a Sunday morning, a landfill site. That spring, I had left my job in a steel-casting factory in Hamford for the brittle uncertainties of the big city. I felt small, scared, sociopathic, fast-travelling. I wasn't yet twenty. The factory had calloused my hands and filled my lungs with metal dust. My blue overalls stank with manly odours after ten-hour shifts of fettling and pouring molten aluminium into pig-casts and dies. I eventually found these mysterious ingots were destined for the Ministry of Defence. Shamefully, it turned out, I had been involved in making objects intended to destroy other human beings. I left behind a world of tea, tabloids, cloying canteen dinners, farts and round-nosed files. A provincial subculture of sub-normalised men, many of whom still lived with their mothers until well into their thirties on the outlying estates.

So London was a big deal. I knew no one, but at first that didn't bother me. I felt like the incognito hero of *The Day of the Jackal*, or all those Raskolnikovs and superfluous men that had lurked unhealthily in rickety rooms before me. I read Colin Wilson's *The Outsider* and got myself a job on a building site. I stood on those open-air tube platforms of west London: Queens Park, Willesden Junction, Kensal Green; feeling volubly poetic, my dusty boots spotted with spring rain, the sky overhead blue as a movie star's eyes. Though I was still toiling with men who looked as if they wanked three or four times a day, and who introduced me to the bookies and roll-up cigarettes, nothing could beat working outdoors. The site was on top of one of the big Park Lane hotels, with sheened limousines pulling up every thirty seconds to be attended by a squadron of obsequious doormen. Apart from shifting huge chunks of masonry into a service lift, one of our tasks was to carry scaffolding over vertiginous gangplanks at the very top of the building. At that altitude, all it took was the wind to catch on the bending ends of the poles and your balance was fatally lost. We had to time our forays between gusts, like crack soldiers waiting for a break in enemy fire. Unsurprisingly, a delicate petal like Byron Easy lasted all of a fortnight under such conditions. Hard as it was to say goodbye to my work chums, Gibbo, Tosser and Irish Danny, the danger money didn't compensate. I told them that my death by falling from the twenty-seventh floor would be a serious loss to world literature and took my last pay packet. Its bulk of notes and coins in the green-windowed mini-envelope felt good in my hands.

If I did get sentimental over the old home town it was only to ring Rudi, already powering ahead with his valeting business, and possessed of that innocent-sounding deviousness essential for climbing the greasy pole of commerce. Mother and Sarah had moved up north. There was no reason to physically return. The town slowly became mythologised in my memory, halted, as it were, in my teenage years; caught in the bird lime of time. My next job had the attraction of being both dangerous and boring simultaneously. After reading Henry Miller's exploits at a dispatch office in New York, I found myself working as a bicycle courier on the fast and mean streets of the City. Houndsditch, Cornhill, Poultry, Old Jewry. The very names are impossibly evocative to me now. That freeing, scary, headlong whistle down Fleet Street, satchel on back, radio crackling your call-sign, nostrils full of black gunge. Ah, I could regale you for hours, patient reader, with the dangers I passed. But I shall spare you that particular summer of loneliness and Lucozade. I fast felt that I was wasting my time, skating over pavements on two wheels for promised bucks that never materialised. It wasn't exactly demanding, mentally, after all. To be honest, they hadn't asked for many qualifications, just a bike and two functioning arms and legs. My greatest Hamford fear had been realised – that of making a living as a glorified postman.

This led to my one and only brush with higher education, the vain attempt to infiltrate academia already alluded to. For a long time I had kicked around the idea of bettering myself. Despite the negative evidence of my O levels, I had managed to wangle an interview in the English department at one of the major London colleges. A degree. A new life. This rite of passage was set for the spring.

The first thing that struck me about the cosy, book-infested office was the heat. Whew, they keep ivory towers hot, I thought. How do they manage all that stringent mental effort, all that translation of Old Icelandic under such conditions? I took off my leather jacket and secured it on the back of the uncomfortable green-cushioned chair and awaited the arrival of Professor Valerie Organ and her co-interviewer, Dr Schnitz. I was tired and anxious, and not a little nervous. My hour-long sojourn in the common room hadn't been promising, I must say. The proliferation of impeccable middle-class accents, the students coming and going with takeout coffees and volumes of Kierkegaard in duffle-coat pockets hadn't served to bolster my confidence. For some reason I expected bearded youths playing acoustic guitars on the campus steps, an atmosphere of welcoming liberalism. But they all stared at me in a most condescending way! As if I had 'intellectual leper' felt-penned on the sweating dome of my head. What's the matter, never seen a balding mature student before? Eventually, the last kids filtered from the common room, Hampshire vowels rolling in the rarefied air. One hearty quarterback shouted to his girlfriend, 'I'll see you in theory.' This puzzled me for a while, not to say impressed me mightily. I spent five minutes marvelling at the cerebral force of students who were satisfied with *virtual* meetings, until it dawned on me that 'theory' was a lesson, or lecture, or seminar – I didn't know the lingo yet. The only other intrusion, as I stole as many books as I could stuff into my courier's satchel, was the appearance of two equine female undergraduates in the de rigueur uniform of black overcoat, square shoes and pinching, daunting spectacles. They idly checked their pigeonholes while I watched furtively from the far corner. Their names, I gathered, were (you couldn't make this up), Emily and Pippa. As they made to leave, Emily, the most insufferably confident of the two, began to issue orders into her mobile phone.

'Can I have the usual table . . . Yah, it's just for the six of us . . . and Daddy's favourite wine? . . . Oh, splendid, Juan. We'll see you Tuesday.'

Emily had a theatrical voice, so low and cello-deep it resembled none other than that of the possessed teenager in *The Exorcist*. Then Pippa piped up. 'Won't that conflict with reading week?'

'You mean skiing week? Not bloody likely!'

Giggling like cockatoos, they left me to ugly thoughts. Jesus . . . I was barely twenty-three, but I felt twice their age. Though paradoxically, I also felt younger, like their stable boy or butler. These two, I pondered, have done everything that's it's taken me years *not* to accomplish. They probably possessed banners of credit cards in their bulging wallets, their own cars back home in the Shires, sexual partners in double figures. They could ski! Christ, *you don't book restaurant tables by mobile phone when you are a supposedly penniless student of nineteen years of age!* I reflected on my gruesome past. These were two girls who probably returned at every opportunity to the bosom of the affluent thatched villages from whence they originated, with parents who adored each other, never raised their voices (let alone hands) in anger, and resolved arguments by talking things through calmly. I felt suddenly sick and sour in the quiet of the common room. I was singularly unfit for the job of student, for competing with these hot-housed whizz-kids, these garglers with silver spoons. Convinced I should leave, I stood up and swung the satchel over my shoulder. Who was I kidding, thinking I could walk in here and—

'Mr Easy?' a voice broke in from the doorway. It was the admissions secretary. 'If you'd like to follow me.'

Too late. In minutes I was sitting in the stultifying office, waiting for the entrance of Professor Valerie Organ and her sidekick, or brain-colleague, Dr Schnitz. I glanced at the heaving monuments to erudition that were the bookshelves. At least, I reflected, the academic world being what it was, if the worst came to the worst, Professor Organ could always open a second-hand bookshop.

The door yawned open and two women walked in, one small with brutally short greying hair, the other much younger, awkwardly tall and conspicuous. The older woman held out her hand with an impersonal smile, and said, 'You must be Brian.'

No, vigilant reader, she hadn't made a mistake. I've been lying to you again. In fact, I've been lying to you for a considerable amount of time; since you began reading, unfortunately. My real name *is* Brian. You didn't really believe that I was honoured with the name Byron by my mother did you? The story goes like this: when Sinead was eventually informed that the author of 'I wandered lonely as a cloud' was in fact William Wordsworth and not Lord Byron, she gave up the idea of naming me after the great Regency swordsman. My father thought it would be compensation enough to be called after his father, Brian Easy. So Brian I became, on my birth certificate, until mother told me the whole saga of the mix-up. Naturally, I was outraged. How could she exchange the noble 'Byron' for the less than rakish 'Brian' without first consulting me? So, I simply changed it back. But, for the purposes of my National Insurance number, the Inland Revenue, the medical profession and institutions such as universities I am Brian. It just makes things so much easier, for them at least. Still, I think first ideas are usually the best, don't you? First ideas identify the essence before the mind gets too bogged down with existence, or second thoughts. A friend of mine at Hamford Boys' School was called Terry. His surname was Towel. It took his dim parents a number of years to realise they had saddled the poor boy with the name T. Towel. But by that time he was a Terry, through and through. He had grown into his name with consummate assurance. Every time he closed in on the box with his superlative halfway-line sprint, the cries of 'Terry, Terry, over here!' or 'On the head, Terry!' would've sounded completely wrong had his name been Philip.

Anyway . . . I'm sorry, okay?

I stood. 'Yes, that's me. Brian Easy.'

'I'm Professor Organ,' said the older woman in an exaggeratedly quiet voice, so quiet that I had to bend forward slightly not to miss anything. 'And this is my colleague, Dr Schnitz. We just want to ask you a few questions about what you've been up to, what you've been reading, *et cet-erah*. Oh, do sit down.'

I sat and watched the two academics gently take a pair of seats dangerously close to mine. Women whose occupation is the life of the mind move slower than other mortals, I reflected. They were certainly an odd pair. Professor Organ had a compacted, serious presence; a round ruddy face, with spokes of irony etched from the corners of her eyes. She wore no make-up, her lips as thin and pleasureless as a man's. She made a big deal of not making eye contact with me, as if the answers to her imminent questions were not to be located in the corneas, but in the cerebral caverns of the ether − measureless to man, of course. Dr Schnitz, on the other hand, stared at me from the off, with a fascinated evaluating scrutiny. This I found rather unnerving. She had a long banana-shaped nose, beady black eyes and so much foundation and powder that she seemed at times (over the next treacherous hour) to resemble a bon-bon under a blonde wig. Both were terribly dressed (supermarket training shoes with drainpipe jeans). Both were spectacularly unattractive. But attractiveness is not the name of the game in academia, oh no. In fact, being a bit of a poster-boy-or-girl can seriously work against you in this racket. Look at Plath, or Fitzgerald or Hemingway. All suspect from the start. No, the more divergently Sartrean your eyeballs in this business the more seriously you are taken, the more the mind seems to hold supremacy. Ugliness, for some reason, equals legitimacy. Look at Shakespeare, with his chinless smirk, or Dickens with his musket-barrel nostrils. No, to be a bit of a looker is a sin of the first order.

The equatorial heat basted my face with sweat. They commenced the interview. The only time I remember being this embarrassed in front of two women was with my mother and the midwife at my own birth.

'So, what did you read to get in the mood for today?' whispered Professor Organ.

'Sorry, I didn't catch that.'

She repeated the question.

'Oh, a bit of, you know, app–apposite criticism,' I stammered.

Silence.

'I see.'

'Well, I thought it best to start, to start – with the major schools of thought.'

She looked victorious for a moment, like a chess opponent to whom one has just offered a mug's opening move.

'Of whom, may I ask?' she said, leaning closer in her chair. I could tell Dr Schnitz, observing me as if I were a rare specimen, was dying to speak. 'Apposite criticism of whom?'

'Erm. The Bard. I mean Bradley. On *Othello*.' I felt like a hedgehog as the juggernaut bears down, klaxon screaming. Professor Organ scratched her slightly stubbly chin.

Another lengthy pause. I thought these brainbos (brainbox bimbos) worked quicker than this. She glanced at her colleague, as if to sanction her contribution. Jesus, this was like good cop, bad cop.

Dr Schnitz's magpie eyes flashed. She spoke for the first time in a staccato treble: 'How did you think he dealt with the question of Shakespeare's double time-scheme?'

'I thought he, er, dealt with it very comprehensively.'

Professor Organ smiled at my non-answer. She would have to use a different instrument. A sharper scalpel. To save my embarrassment (or maybe to increase it – by this point I wasn't sure), she said, 'Yes, what do you think are the advantages of starting a narrative *in medias res.*'

In medias res? Christ, my brain cells felt pulverised by the gladiatorial effort. That's Latin, right? Or is it a place? Is it in St John's Wood? No, that's a *des res*. Giving up, I allowed my gaze to fall on my shoes. For a full minute. So powerful was Dr Schnitz's stare in its effort to burrow under my brow that I thought she might have some sexual interest in me. As roasted as I looked, this didn't surprise me that much. Universities are very sexual places; all that dry-as-dust learning must give everyone the horn. They are indeed perverse institutions. What else is there to get worked up about? All those Bard madmen and blue-stocking imbibers of Keats, too timid to drink their warm beakers of the south directly from life. They need a shot of real sex more urgently than the rest of us. And Dr Schnitz didn't appear overly fussy. The thought of this made me feel much, much worse.

Professor Organ put an end to my misery by changing the subject. 'Tell me, Brian, what poetry do you like?'

My mind went blank. I felt like the losing contestant on *Mastermind*, flailing in his ebon chair. But this, surely, was my subject? How could I be unable to name a single well-known poet? All I could think of were the smutty verses of Lord Rochester that I had been perusing in the common room.

'Well, I'm a big fan of Rochester,' I managed to squeak, relieved that I had located an example from, you know – the past.

The professor shot me a patronising and disapproving look down the lines of her nose.

'And when did you first come across Rochester?' she purred, but not nicely.

At this I almost laughed out loud. 'Erm, perhaps that's the wrong choice of verb!'

Her unkissed mouth gave a kind of mirthless grimace to the thick silence of the room. She rephrased her question. 'Okay, when did you first *encounter* Rochester's verse?'

'Just now, in the common room. Sorry, I'm not doing very well, am I?' I said, and shifted in my seat.

'Oh, I wouldn't say that,' grinned the tall doctor. Oh God, she definitely fancies me.

Professor Organ took the reins once more, with a sigh of vexation. 'Okay, Brian, what fiction has stimulated you lately? Doesn't have to be the nineteenth-century novel – old, contemporary, anything you've liked.'

At last: a question I could answer! I wiped a slick of sweat from my brow and said, truthfully, 'Blimey – everything from Norman Mailer to Henry Miller to Bret Easton Ellis.'

Organ and Schnitz exchanged worried glances. By this I assumed that Mailer, Miller and Ellis weren't their favourite authors. That they were somehow – what's the phrase? – uncanonical.

'And what, I'd be interested to know,' said the professor almost inaudibly, 'recommended you to these . . .' she paused for maximum pejorative impact, '. . . writers?'

'Oh, you know. Their energy mainly; their manly take on modern life. And, it has to be said,' I announced with a glint in my eye, 'the nooky.'

Schnitz leaned forward. 'Sorry, the what? Synecdoche?'

'No, the sex. I mean, it's how we all really think and feel isn't it? Sex on the brain, most of us. Not like all that repressed Jane Austen stuff. How can you trust a forty-year-old virgin to write with authority on human relationships? I mean, when it comes to sex, Jane Austen's just,' I searched for the correct adjective, 'crap.'

Relieved that I had made a start (though somewhat worried that my thesis had been all selling and no substance), I was perturbed to see a deep frown materialise on Professor Organ's robust face, like the first furrow cut into a wedding cake. Her colleague appeared to be suppressing a laugh.

'And how,' said the older woman with skyscraper-high disdain, 'would you describe their treatment of women?'

Some sort of contrarian voice – a goading yob-voice – had taken up residence in me over the past few minutes. 'Well, it's horses for courses, isn't it. I'm sure men got a hard time from, what's her name, the one that looked like a wrestler – mates with Picasso?'

'Gertrude Stein?' asked Dr Schnitz, raising an eyebrow and so elongating her nose to the length of a largeish courgette. This fiendish double act, these weird sisters, were beginning to seriously upset my equilibrium. The job of bike messenger suddenly seemed very appealing.

'And how would you describe the work of Gertrude Stein?' said Professor Organ with impatience. '*Crap?*'

This hit me straight in the guts. The penny had dropped. Somehow, I knew in that moment, with the repetition of my somewhat generalised adjective, that I had failed the interview. For the rest, it was a season in hell. During the remaining forty-five minutes the word 'crap' would be fired at me again and again with the relentless accuracy of a Bosnian sniper. I counted thirty of them. At least. My lack of knowledge on every topic known to man was subjected to a strenuous investigation. The heat just never let up. I felt – to repeat one of Dr Schnitz's classical allusions that I had to look up later – like Ixion on his wheel of fire.

In the end, they both politely walked me to the door. With great insincerity, Professor Organ shook my hand and delivered her standard final line, as her colleague smiled libidinously in my direction.

'Thank you, Brian. Feel free to look in on the library before you leave.'

I closed the door and breathed fresh, uncontaminated, non-gender-specific air. Set alight by two feminist academics! Grilled to a cinder by gynocentric goons! My dream of a degree, of water-fights in the dorm, of a timber-floored London flat rich in reference works, of a better life . . . like cold ashes in the mouth. On unsteady legs, I staggered down to the library. But I didn't have the stomach to enter. Instead I bumped into Emily and Pippa, exiting the canteen.

'And don't forget to bring me your Hobbes and Locke . . . Ciao!' said Emily, her voice thunderously deep as before.

Something turned direction in me then. Like a flank of timber breaking free from the log-jam. Something bitter and sour and encrusted took offence at their casual sense of entitlement to all this. The gravy train of privilege that they clung to until they were kicked off screaming. No – they didn't need to cling to it and were never kicked off. The world welcomed them with warm, adoring arms. Like high-ranking credit cards, there was nowhere (and nothing) on this earth these girls were refused. Inevitably, I thought of their parents. Yes, you are to blame, I decided, for your Little Pippas and Poppets and Emilys learning nothing worth knowing in twenty years. I've had enough! Understand? You fucks with your two February weeks in Chamonix, your kids with Latin to A level, your million-pound houses ringing with accomplishment, cello-practice and the traditional songs of your Norwegian nannies! Your cats named Sophocles and Aristotle. Your four-wheel drives and teary compassion for those little 'golliwogs' starving south of the equator; your Sophies, Tabithas and Natashas with their own ponies and shelves full of Austen and Brontë by the age of ten; you muesli-eating, *Guardian*-reading covert yuppies (for that's what you are in spite of your earnest altruism and leftist bravado) – you have no idea, as you leave your Rembrandt exhibition for an evening of 'magical' Verdi at the Royal Opera House, that somewhere (in Camden, Toxteth, Middlesbrough, East Kilbride) A SINGLE MOTHER IS TAKING IT UP THE ARSE FROM HER PIMP JUST SO SHE CAN AFFORD ENOUGH CRACK TO KEEP HERSELF ALIVE IN ORDER TO KEEP HER *BABY* ALIVE FOR ANOTHER WEEK!

Forgive me. I think I need a little lie-down.

'Your move,' says Robin, and takes his hand from his bishop.

Michelle smiles at his foolish blunder, her grin reproduced in the black windows of the train. She pretends to um and ah over her next move – this little piggy went to market, this little piggy went . . .

'Uh oh,' I say, over the muted thunder of the sleepers. I watch her bony hand reach for her queen, as spontaneously as she can make it.

That's the problem with women, they're always pretending to

make decisions when they've already made their minds up. Hours ago. Weeks ago. Why do they do this? Why do they play this transparent game, this tired ritual? Ah, the mendacious mores of the gentler sex. One of the oldest subjects known to man. Quite obviously Homer's Penelope didn't exist. Before the stereotype-hacks identified the sluttish toga-babe, the Elizabethan temptress, the Augustan bodice-burster, *she* was the first male fantasy figure. Certainly chimerical. No woman was ever so constant in real life. Wait twenty chaste years for some geezer while he gallivants round the Med with nymphs and sexy sorcerers? I think not, somehow. In real life she would've been twice divorced with another teenage son. And teaching those suitors a few positions, too. The only thing Penelope really did was to perform an operation every night that she wasn't entirely honest about the following morning. That much smacks of real life, of real insight into the feminine psyche. That's how I know Michelle is only pretending to her husband that she hadn't decided on her next move ten minutes ago,

'Check,' Michelle announces, trying not to sound too triumphant.

A cloud passes over Robin's brow. Outwitted and unmanned, sir! I have been watching their game for half an hour. Or rather, I have been watching Michelle let Robin think he had a hope in hell for half an hour. They've been quite chatty with me, all told. Amazing how friendly people can be if you make the effort. They even told me more about their plans for their first child, down to possible names for both genders. A baby – something they can both cherish and celebrate, that will inaugurate their long future together. How a marriage should be, really. And all this I didn't anticipate when we left King's Cross two hours ago. Takes all sorts to make up a world, I suppose.

To save Robin his embarrassment I clear my throat and ask a question.

'Big wedding was it? Last July?'

Michelle looks up from the board with a dreamy grin.

'Two hundred guests, a country church, and a horse and carriage to the Chinese restaurant in the village afterwards.'

Robin straightens proudly in his confined train-seat at the memory.

'I tell you – my speech, mate. What a classic. I can still remember it line for line. Shame I couldn't then!' At this he bursts out laughing, his jellied black hair shaking on his crown. Of course, I had to make the mistake of asking them how they met. In ten minutes they'd privileged me with their entire life stories. I just had to know why they chose each other; had to know the secret of happiness and why it had proved so elusive for me. I also wondered, but didn't ask, about their sex life. I was curious to know if they were still doing it with the same frequency and at the same rate of knots as when they first met. Were they still doing it at all? After all, once Mandy and I had co-habited for a year, the only sexual activity in our house was the dismal sight of Fidel attempting to fellate himself night after night. I glanced at the suitcases under Robin's eyes and decided he looked tired. Very tired. Yes, they were still at it, all right. Like laboratory rabbits, if I guessed correctly. I bet Michelle, with her enthusiastic, energetic hands, never allowed him a moment's rest. And probably after he'd endured a gruelling day advising on capital gains tax, too. I really felt for him. What is it about women always wanting sex when you're at your most exhausted? You take them away for the wicked weekend in the Cotswolds with the two dozen red roses and the Bollinger on ice and they're not interested. Then, after the month from hell at work, when you are at mental and physical breaking point, they will – completely against expectation – choose to treat you to the basque and sheer hold-ups concealed under colourless jogging attire . . . They don't want a quick one with the lights out, oh no: they want to draw a real first-night performance from you. A proper neck-ricker, with a month of foreplay and the sort of gymnastics that would kill a parallel-bars Olympic gold medallist.

'Yeah, my speech wasn't up to scratch either,' I say. 'Still, you only have to do it once. Hopefully.'

'Well I couldn't go through the hangover again,' observes Michelle brightly. She was absent-mindedly twisting her wedding band on her finger as she spoke. Yes, I used to do that, I admit to myself with a simultaneous plummeting of my spirits. The ring. My Argos-bought wedding ring. That golden emblem of exclusivity. I remember how it felt on the finger itself, heavy and solid; how people looked at you and treated you differently; how inwardly altered you felt. As if one of life's great hurdles had been finally vaulted. And now there is a pale welt where it used to be, like the ring a vase of flowers leaves when you remove it from a table to throw the dead blooms away.

Robin's face has darkened again on contemplating the board. You're up Crap Creek without your mobile, Robin – just admit it. I feel I should ask his wife about the unmentionable that everyone keeps mentioning: the Millennium. Everyone seems willing to talk about the forty-eight-hour rave they're planning to attend, but no one wants to go into the unspoken fear that this could be it. This could be the end of the world as we know it. Fuck your Cuban Missile Crisis or the eclipses of 1605 or Cassandra wailing about the fall of Troy. This is the day of judgement. The long-awaited global catastrophe. Let's hope we've all settled the tab with the Big Man upstairs and packed our souls. The thought that has *definitely* crossed everybody's mind is this one: what if, when they release the balloons on the twelfth stroke, the heavens are suddenly rent apart and a Pythonesque hand reaches earthward for all the ant-like sinners, like in some nightmare by Fuseli? The earth groaning under its own weight of humanity, malignant and benign alike. Molten streams of people, like a second flood. Except it won't be Pythonesque. It will be unthinkable. We are standing, after all, on the brink of the unknown. Great and terrifying forces may be released. *Twothousandzerozeropartyover*, and all that. But nobody, apart from cranks, Seventh-Day Adventists and children under ten, is actually talking about it. They're just thinking it. Extraordinary.

'So, what have you got planned for the big night?' I ask, forgetting that, if they interrogate me, I have no satisfactory answer.

'New Year's? Oh, we're having a quiet one with Robin's mum.'

I nod, and allow myself a glance at the train window. I can see my own broad forehead, projected with the image of three looming pylons, the dark countryside beyond. So everything's going to be just the same as we left it come January the first? Christ, I'd like you to be right, Michelle.

'I might have a quiet night in myself,' I tell her. 'Anyhow, I'm just off to the smoking car.'

I excuse myself and rise on jelly legs. Oh yes, another thing that slipped my mind – I have capitulated to smoking. Some time after we rumbled out of Peterborough I snapped. I couldn't handle the bleakness, the sensory deprivation. With no proper booze on offer and this song sung blue on constant replay in my head there seemed little alternative. The ambrosial fire of a Rizla full of cadged Old Holborn marked my fall from grace. Abstinence was just too much like purgatory. I guess I don't have that iron in the soul, that strength of character that holds out to the death under enemy torture. What a depressing fact to learn about oneself.

The smoked-glass door opens obsequiously before me, like a mechanical courtier. I find an empty seat among my fellow chortling chokers, those other deferrers of reality. Flattening my notebook out on the Formica, I try to recall the last evening Rudi Buckle visited the shared flat. It was only three weeks ago, but it feels like the previous century. The sunset over the gardens behind the house had been much like the jagged, apocalyptic cataract of colour that is streaking the skies outside my train window. I remember writing, *it won't last long – it never does. The pale pink of a late November afternoon as it slides into dusk. The shivering, transitory sky and its canopy of tiny clouds, its billows of birds. The leaf-graveyards of the gardens out back with their mulch of wet yellow, peaty bronze. Woodsmoke smells; plumes of white above the huddled terraces. Everywhere a sense of oncoming and increasing emptiness; the terrible firmament full of metal and last light . . . The big chestnut stripped down to fibres, its hardy skeleton – its leaves filling the whole garden like a deflated parachute. It stands in a kind of agony: a hand-wringing mother shaking in a winter gale, all night grieving for her dead children; like a Niobe of the urban forest.*

Five minutes later, and a startling new palette in the heavens. A glowing salmon sun behind the fixed spires of poplars; a stripe of gold dotting the high clouds. Forlorn bushes and early lights coming on in windows . . . steady change: minute by minute; the light sucked down from the sky to a fluorescent horizon. Elsewhere, that strange greyness unique to late November. Whatever is present in the sky will not last long. No, it won't last long – it never does.

Rampant Rudi sat in my kitchen in a slippery red shirt, lighting a cheroot from a candle stuck in an old whisky bottle. He had been growing his hair long, and looked like a chubby version of Salvator Rosa's *Self-Portrait*. With his suede-soft voice, he said, 'In my experience, Bry, when a woman is sure of her man, that's when she starts behaving badly.'

'They take advantage, you mean? Once you've fully committed?'

'Precisely.'

I sat opposite him over the big, wax-spattered kitchen table. The two croupiers had left for their evening shift and the viola player was working a wedding in Tunbridge Wells. I had made a rare foray into the kitchen, sadly cooking a meal-for-one of plain pasta and Tesco pesto mixed with olives, when Rudi had called round unexpectedly. His movements were becoming harder and harder to trace just recently. He had made an unusual number of enemies in a short period of time, and thought it best to be constantly on the go, like a shark patrolling the endless oceans. I had just wiped away my tears (precipitated by the olives you understand – they were, and still are, like onions to my soul) when the doorbell rang. Five minutes later and I was bending his poor Scottish ear off once more.

'That was the problem. She took me for granted. Expected me to be always there. I don't suppose my jealousy helped.'

'Aye, the green-eyed marauder,' said Rudi, and drained another beer from the bottle factory at the centre of the table. 'The more you suspect, the more you push 'em away. It disnae matter how hard you try tae put a lid on it. It seeps out in the end.'

'And they can sense this, can they?'

'Aye. Witch telepathy. Developed over hundreds of years.'

'But how else could I react? You saw how she behaved, towards the end, I mean.'

It was true that the last months of my marriage had seen Mandy disappear on holiday without me three times. The first occasion was a jaunt to Italy with Antonia, leaving me and Nick behind to drink maudlin pints of Guinness in the Prince Regent, wondering what the hell they were getting up to. The other two trips were solo adventures in the Levant, during which she removed her wedding ring (and everything else, I imagine), probably becoming the busy adultress I always accused her of being. However, I will never know. She denied any impropriety on her return, even though men called Emilliano were constantly phoning the flat and asking in thick accents if Mandy was '*en casa*'. No, I had no way of ever finding out what abominations she had committed. She would deny everything until her face was the colour of a sailor's uniform. The fault lay with me, I was confidently told – in my over-active imagination. How could I expect an attractive 'single' woman in the libidinous cities of northern Italy to be up to anything untoward behind her husband's back? What a pathological fool I must be to suspect that! What a dribbling, misguided Leontes!

'She was certainly putting it about a bit. Geographically, I mean,' said Rudi, stroking his deep-pile chest hair.

'But you think I overreacted?' I asked, meeting his black eyes.

'Not exactly. But it disnae mean she wasn't up to something.'

'She took pleasure in my not knowing. Of that I'm certain. She was probably being diddled by every Juan, Pepe and Carlos on the block. It was another way of exerting her power. Christ knows, it was her idea to get married in the first place. She loved seeing me twisting on the end of the line.'

'*Schadenfreude*,' Rudi said quickly. I was impressed by his sudden insight, his verbal resourcefulness. Rudi had watched so much porn in his time that, over the years, he'd become almost fluent in German. Although, it has to be said, his vocabulary was fairly limited. And I hardly think he'd acquired this word from *Analnacht* or *Spermtroopers*.

'Spot on. She enjoyed my suffering – or rather, she allowed herself to enjoy it because she never believed in any rules of behaviour. I mean, why did she want to get married if she couldn't make the necessary sacrifices, or play by the rules? Hold on – not the rules – the fucking *vows*.'

I allowed the last word to resonate while feeling the concrete waders begin to exert their pressure on my chest. The truth was, I felt complicit in her abuse. I had lowered myself in making a union with her. Mandy had abused my good nature, my trust. I could comfort myself by imagining she knew she was worthless in comparison to me – a lesser human animal – and had sought to castigate me for choosing to be with her. Just like when a dog chases you if you're stupid enough to show it fear. But it was cold comfort: I was to blame. I received a mug's comeuppance. In this sense, I deserved all I got. I thought of all the fools undergoing the same treatment across London in that present moment; the goddess Hymen lynched and hanging from a tree in the garden. If only we could open the roof of every house and witness the pain of those marital bedrooms!

'I was an attentive husband. Considerate. Patient. All the things you should be.'

'That's part of the problem. You were a wee doormat. I mean, maybe there were some things you couldn't give her.'

'Like what?'

'Diamond rings. Rough sex.'

'She didn't want *any* kind of sex, let alone rough!'

Rudi was rubbing his temples. The melancholy crimson of the sky through the kitchen windows was the same colour as his shirt. He sighed, 'There's nae point obsessing over it. You have t' move on. Believe it or not, I've got hassle of ma oon.'

I looked accusingly at his handsome, ladykiller's brow, wondering what problems he could have that compared to my cyclone of disgust and regret.

'Like what? The taxman?'

Rudi shifted evasively in his seat, then said: 'Remember Suki? Well, that sleazy sugar daddy of hers is after me.'

'What's the worst that can happen? A broken nose? A scratch on your Hyundai?'

'The bastard's put a contract out on me. Two grand to maim me with a blunt instrument. Three if it's a sexual injury.'

'Like a crowbar to the tackle, that kind of thing?'

'Exactly.'

I cracked another beer and passed it to my old friend. 'That's pretty . . . full-on.'

'Aye, to be honest, that's half the reason I called round. I couldn't kip on your floor tonight, could I? Only I'm . . .' He couldn't get the word out. His sense of masculinity, his legitimacy, was compromised by it.

'Scared?' I ventured.

'. . . Shitein' it. To go home, that is.'

'Hey, nothing's too much for an old buddy.'

We cheersed glasses with a hopeful chink.

'Thanks,' he said in a mealy-mouthed whisper, looking profoundly ashamed at my acceptance of his proposal.

I am back in my seat watching Robin topple his king. Predictable. The capitulation of men to the will of women. So widespread these days that it barely merits comment. They always have their way in the end.

'That was quick,' says Michelle to me, a smile widening her pale face.

'I couldn't bear it for long,' I reply, aware of the humming ashtray stink emanating from my clothes after five minutes in the smoking car.

She gestures to her husband, 'Robin's seen sense and called it a day. You always want to play best of three if you lose, don't you Robin?'

He doesn't reply. Instead he snatches up his book and settles back in his seat. I decide to ask a question that has been much on my mind.

'So, er, who takes care of all the practical things between you two? Only, we could never agree on anything when I was married.'

'He does all the DIY, the heavy lifting and takes the rubbish out,' Michelle explains. 'But if any calling needs to be done, that falls to me. You can never understand a word he says on the phone. He mutters.'

'Not so,' mutters Robin, from behind the pages of his lad–lit paperback, which bears the unpromising title, *Salad? Chilli Sauce? Everything?*

'Only, I'm interested in how other couples operate. You know, where I went wrong and all that.'

'I'm sure it wasn't all your fault,' says Michelle, with her deeply concerned therapy-face.

'It's always the man's fault,' sighs Robin, with good–humoured resignation.

I digest the dynamic between Robin and Michelle as I sit before them, the soporific beat of the rails beneath us. A gently confrontational remark like the one Michelle just uttered would have caused an incendiary scene between Mandy and myself. I suppose that's how normal people do it – they *let things go*. It's the only way. Otherwise the knives come out if the rubbish doesn't go out, as they did many times for me. I observe them there, Michelle unpegging the travel chesspieces, Robin gurning over his knockers and kebabs yarn, and decide they have isolated an essential ingredient in the happiness recipe. To let things go. As young as they are, as simple and easily pleased, they are twenty times more sophisticated than me and Mandy ever were. Jesus, it was a wonder we could even feed ourselves. And Robin, for all his lairy deportment, his tepid soul, is twenty times the man that I am. He earns steady money, he puts up shelves, he slings the bins out without complaint. One day he will probably make a perfect father for Wayne or Robinetta. What good is existential angst and whining to any woman? Observing this happy couple, I think of myself, thirty years old, newly separated with divorce on the horizon, and know just how badly I blew it. I fucked up because I expected happiness to result from such meagre ingredients, such a paltry larder.

Happiness? I had always thought people who expected happiness from life were deluded crackpots. Who told them that was on the menu? They look at the world with all its genocides and cruelties, its gassings and random murder and expect felicity? A pathological aspiration, surely. No, better to be content with just being *lucky* . . . and what do I expect from a visit to my mother's, with all this weighty heart-baggage, this incapacitation of mine? Not happiness, surely? The whole project is dragging me into the earth, I think, as the train flies like an arrow into the night. How can I force my face into a smile after three months of grief-swallowed days? With my mother on her own too. I think of the last time we shared December the twenty-fifth. A pair of losers together around the cooling turkey; the clotted cranberry sauce. To spend Christmas at home with a family that has stayed together is to be part of, to be proximate to, *success*; or a success story of a kind. But to do the same in a broken family is always to take part in failure; and with weary reminders of that failure at every turn. The empty place at the head of the banquet, where the absent father should sit. The unpulled cracker. The missing relatives and their propitiatory cards hanging from the eaves, all of them having far happier Christmases elsewhere. It is a kind of anti-celebration that brings out the Scrooge in everyone. The sense of life becoming, year after year, ever more shallow – rather than deepening, or expanding like the concentric circles of an evergreen tree.

I allow my notebook to fall open at random, and see the entry for the fifteenth of November. My heart races at what it discloses. I had forgotten her card. Mandy's card. Not a Christmas card, oh no, but a slim missive pushed under the door of my shared flat; waiting innocently for me one evening. It depicted a trellised Mediterranean house overlooking the sea, an amateurish watercolour with sentimentalised hanging baskets of crimson bougainvillea swaying over mysterious windows. *The heat of midday transforming the distant waves into a platinum shimmer. Vines looping the veranda and*

backs of benches. A settled calm in the dusty street winding up the moun-
tainside. A frivolously daubed black cat, its tail in the air like a question
mark, just exiting the front door. A slatted bench scattered with simple
things: a loaf, onions, a pitcher of olive oil, white wine, pescado *fresh from*
the bay. A tangible sense of life moving slowly, incrementally, at its natural
default pace; not the sick hurry of London and its soul-shaking ructions
. . .

'Excuse me,' interrupts a voice. It is Michelle. I look up from
the page to be met by her inquisitive smile. 'Sorry, I couldn't help
noticing that you've been scribbling in that book since we set off.
Are you a writer?'

It takes a while to get my bearings, to orientate this question in
my mind, what with my heart beating so fast at the memory of
Mandy's card. Well, am I? A writer, that is? If passports still declared
vocations, is that what it would state? Excited, despairing, feeling
dangerously righteous, I realise I cannot read another of my own
words.

'Writer? That's pitching it a bit high. Here,' I say, then rip the
page from my notebook and pass it over to Michelle. 'Take a look.
It's rubbish, really.'

She flattens it on the table and reads with eager eyes.

. . . *But mainly the egregious red of the bougainvillea, their homely*
baskets; well-kept, tended daily no doubt. And not a soul around, not even
a goatherd on the distant hillside rolling with pines. Wasps in the deleterious
air; cicadas probably, if one were to go there. If one were to feel the warmth
of that sun. Lastly a single white butterfly, a tiny smudge from the end of
the brush, dancing weightlessly over the lintel.

Why did she send me this card? With its impossible message? The
message which consisted of two sentences:

'Our little home. We'll find it one day.'

Michelle looks up from the crumpled page, and says: 'That's
beautiful . . . the cow!'

6

Less Haste, More Speed

Only when you stop moving do you realise just how fast you have been travelling. Like calm water in a sheltered ravine after the insanity of rapids. The bleak stillness of a platform after the berserk thunder of the train. The first day at home after a month on the run. Early in the spring of the second year of my marriage, after Mandy had irrevocably marked her card with my mother and my half-sister (not to mention with Antonia and Nick, both still seething after Mandy's unwitting telephone transmission of genuine spite), I stood outside the Hampstead flat-share that used to be occupied by Bea all those marquee moons ago. I say 'used', as I wasn't sure she didn't still sleep on that hard double bed in her raftered room; another hand peeling her Marks and Sparks knickers down her inexplicably erotic thighs. That lambent morning, I had a sudden feeling of stillness: as if, after long and violent movement, I had been brought short. Stopped dead.

Misty Victorian footpaths. Elegant frontages. Children late for school, climbing from sparkling people-carriers. Toddlers in three-wheeled buggies. Wicker trees. The sun aperture colourless and infinite . . . Ah, the children we never had! The coherent and productive life we never made. Nostalgia and sentimentality curdling to make their bilious brew. On the one hand, I was confident that I sought to explicate the present by an examination of the past. On the other, I felt like a stalker standing there, with no particular errand, attempting to peek through the slatted pine blinds. No, the Expressionist prints didn't appear to be on the walls. Little sign of the three out-of-work gallants, either. Most likely they all found posts in the City, in the theatre, on the grubby streets of London's medialand – I couldn't be sure I didn't see one of them reading the news the other night, but that might have been his father. I considered rapping on the door, but thought better of it. The idea of buttonholing passers-by and informing them that, once upon a time, here lived all love, all beauty was briefly entertained. It occurred to me then that I was still in mental contact with Bea, that I conducted imaginary conversations with her, or with her ghost. The people we have mind-conversations with – lovers or friends from the past, the dead, even – are very important. To our current coterie they seem like marginal, never-mentioned people; but to the inner life they are central. Long after Mandy had usurped Bea, she made a point of bringing her up in conversation, mainly for the purpose of ridicule. She said, 'That name, Bea, it sounds like a dog's name,' or 'I don't know how you could've put up with somebody so dull: she never went to parties, looked like she bought her clothes from a charity shop.' I would tolerate these snide, rampantly jealous attacks in silence. The subject of Bea was never ventured by me. Instead, I was the loving curator of her museum, visiting the gallery of our memories with increasing frequency, holding those imaginary conversations. It wasn't as if Mandy's thin drizzle of poisonous calumnies didn't have an effect, though. I began to question whether I truly used to like everything about Bea: her reticence, her rather too-wide shoulders, the way she made me feel, in Austen's phrase, the inferiority of my connections. Then I saw sense. Bea had that rarest of attributes in a woman: ultimate indifference to what people thought of her. Usually, women lose their self-consciousness only when dealing with children: their habitual monitoring of their own behaviour and appearance disappears as another, stronger prerogative takes over. Sure, she used to swish her chestnut hair neurotically, lovably, from her eyes all the time, but her attitude to the whole package was: 'Take it or leave it, baby.' And, like a fool, I left it.

The London morning was full of a stirring clarity: deli smells, the breath of filter coffee, frost on the rear windows of banked cars, the noisy shutters of a florist's going up, the narcotic odour of petrol. I felt like a kid with his nose pressed up against the glass of my past, loitering there outside Bea's old bedroom, with no particular place to go. I didn't even know what had drawn me there that morning; there was no special anniversary to commemorate. I had just cycled blindly across the peeling vistas of the Haringey Ladder, up the strenuous Shepherd's Hill and past the bracing heath, the February wind making my eyes pour. But, it appeared that Bea was no longer resident in her timber floored flat where we spent so many candlelit nights around the kitchen table, a fug of sweet smoke from her Silk Cut Ultra Lows in the air. And even if she had been there, what would I have said? Sorry for dumping you, for having no faith in myself or you or love? Sorry for relinquishing our nascent passion for marriage to a barratrous harpy? It was all too late, I concluded, and I should sit out my purgatory like a man. I crossed to the railings on the other side of the street, unshackled my bike, and cycled off down the big hill.

I should stress this wasn't an isolated incident.

If the truth be told, after this initial visit I could be found there, once a month, for a whole year. My eventless morning vigils at Bea's reminded me of a similar pilgrimage undertaken in the early nineties. Only this was a poetic pilgrimage, not just furtively hanging around an old girlfriend's flat. On the morning of February the eleventh 1993, I walked briskly from my Camden crash-pad to Fitzroy Road near Primrose Hill. The weather conditions had been strangely similar to my first return to Bea's: the same washed-out chilly watercolour sky, the same slicing freshness to the air, the same grey London dawn with the thousand hands raising a thousand shades in a thousand furnished rooms. The purpose of my visit had been to commemorate the suicide of Sylvia Plath thirty years to the day – the barefoot, perfected woman with her head on the oven's floor, discovered by her children's nurse on a routine visit. My heart raced as I rounded the corner, whistling posties oblivious to the significance of the date on their postmarks. I had expected coachloads of Japanese tourists, the dismal peanut-crunching crowd, or at least a few fey dawdlers in overcoats like myself. Instead – nothing. The street as bare and empty as a Chapel of Rest. I stood very still in front of the solid-looking house, with its plaque celebrating Yeats' brief sojourn, and felt a thrilling solidarity with my fellow bards. But still no flutter of activity. For some reason I expected the front door to open. Maybe that would occur later, I thought, when the guided tours with megaphoned poetry recitals from open-topped buses showed up. But I doubted it. The dead require no extra effort from the living, just lip-service to their 'tragedy'. I took a last look, fixing the scene photographically in my mind, then walked on, pretending to have other pressing business. It had all been dramatically eventless, like the repose a family must feel after a relative's fitful existence has come to an end. The speeding life suddenly stopped dead, brought short with a terrible finality. As I passed the great, blackened, unused drum of the Roundhouse I pondered all those artists who had taken their own life; who had left their beautiful pearls behind but found the life that bore them intolerable: Van Gogh, Woolf, Plath, Hart Crane, Hemingway, Berryman. When thinking about that odd morning mission I also reflect on those who checked out further down the line: Kurt Cobain, Richey Manic, Sarah Kane. Now just T-shirts on Camden High Street; the living, sentient human beings all gone into the dark.

Mandy changed without the band to organise her life. She became (if that were feasible) brasher, more bitter. With the implosion of her great dream, she had no idea what she wanted to do with her time. Predictably, she lost the job at Iberia: not by failing to turn up, but by kicking the front door in after the area manager had disciplined her over uniform anomalies. Her skirt had been found to have a sluttish split from knee to hipbone; not what the airline wanted to promote in its junior staff. The police were called and Mandy was sacked on the spot. A verbal and physical tirade, one that few of the placid customers booking flights to Rio de Janeiro would ever forget, was unleashed by my wife as they hustled her from the office. When she arrived home that evening she tore the red-and-white barber's-pole shirt from her back, exposing her strangely elongated shoulder blades and crooked spine pinned under a black bra. On occasions, there was something of a ten-year-old's tantrum about her rages. I would have laughed, if it wasn't for her capacity for extreme and frightening violence, and the fact that we now had no source of income. Martin had been forced to lay me off indefinitely at the start of the year. He had said, with an odd gravity in his Bromley whine, 'I wish I could tell you to sit by the phone and await my call, Byron, but I can't be certain it'll ever come.' I had nodded quickly at this, observing how his brow pinched anxiously when delivering any kind of bad news. He added, 'Anyway, you should be living in the real world, sorting your family out. I'm sure Mandy doesn't appreciate the fact that you can never buy her anything or take her anywhere.' He had a point. And he was genuinely sad to see me go. As I watched Mandy seethe and genuflect while ripping off the uniform that she had wasted 'hard-earned' cash on, I thought to myself: not content with alienating your tenants, our two best friends, my own mother and half-sister, you have to plunge us into penury by another rash masterpiece. *Four hundred years ago they would have burnt you as a witch.* Instead, I asked, 'Are they going to press charges?'

'What do I care? They can't discriminate against what I wear. We're not at school any more.'

'What if you get a criminal record?'

'I won't get a fucking record from that, you idiot!' she yelled. 'Are you thick or something?'

It was a trope I had long noted in Mandy (and one which I

related to Delph's use of the word 'ignorant') that she used to call into question my IQ by labelling me 'thick'. Not just occasionally, but all the time. And she really meant it too. For her, I wasn't the full peseta. I had come to the conclusion that it was the trademark of the super-insecure, dim-witted of the world to slander the intelligence of others by using either 'thick' or 'ignorant' as insults. It was a more reliable test than any Mensa could provide.

'Well, they won't be very sympathetic at your next job when they find out how you left this one,' I volunteered, fearing her volcanic anger. I was getting dangerously used to her ways by now – the ostentatious scorn, the wallowing in the pejorative.

'I'm not getting another job. Here –' she spat angrily, 'help me with these.'

Mandy was attempting to zip her legs into her favourite pair of leather boots, lying flummoxed on the kitchen lino while Fidel wagged his tail in her face wanting to play. 'And get rid of that stupid mutt.'

'Fidel!' I said sharply, pleased to have any authority in my own house. He ceased flailing his tail and looked penitently in my direction. 'Outside.' At this command he trotted towards the dog-flap I had installed in the back door, his ears flattened to his head. After two years he had finally begun to respond to his name. I approached Mandy and tugged the obstinate zipper. 'So what the hell do we do now? You know Mart can't afford me at the moment.'

'That was only ever *pocket money*,' she sneered. 'I tell everyone I know that you're a kept man.'

I felt the sharp incision of this comment. It was true Mandy had been paying for almost everything recently to help my cash-flow crisis. Her many mysterious accounts held funds I could only guess at. This certainly increased my sense of helpless emasculation. Since the start of the year we had been choked with money problems: ulcer-giving, cancer-forming dough-headaches that would challenge Houdini to find an escape. I felt cornered, checkmated to the nth degree. Most days I couldn't afford the carfare into town or a pint of milk. The balance in my account stood at £1.75. As a punishment I was relegated my own separate shelf in the fridge until I started earning again. This often held the elliptic form of a single egg. What with the sex embargo, the situation worryingly resembled my bachelor hell of a couple of years previously. I felt embarrassed and humiliated if I ever had to beg money from Mandy, like a trembling wife approaching her husband for the housekeeping. Although she rolled her globular eyes when I did, I knew she secretly revelled in wearing the trousers. However, it wasn't a situation I did enough to question or remedy. Possibly this was a legacy of the all-pervasive rampant feminism of the 1970s. Any boy growing up in this decade was subjected to the most indoctrinating epistemology concerning the emancipation of women. They were at least equal, if not superior beings, the mantra went. They deserved to be treated with greater respect, remuneration, sympathy and reverence than they had been for the previous two millennia. They demanded – no, deserved – houses, jewellery, cars, holidays, childcare, skincare, promotion and regular orgasms. And this was everywhere: on the news, in sitcoms, on savagely defaced patriarchal advertising hoardings. Coming to consciousness in this environment allowed me to think that it was never otherwise – who were these hypo-thetical creatures, these sympathetic Eves, who soothed babies to sleep in 1950s sweaters, or cooked a man a hot meal when he returned from the pit? All I could see were brassiere-burning furies, and the insolent, intelligent face of Germaine Greer exhorting her sisters to drink their own menstrual blood. This was coupled with a corrosive negativity towards the male gender. According to the new nostrums of radical, militant feminism, we were all worms, scum, potential rapists. And these ideas went in, travelled deep to the centre of the psyche, waiting to be proved correct on the battlefields of the sex war. So it didn't seem odd, when the going became financially choppy, to allow Mandy to take the reins for a while. After all, the buried indoctrination said that is what all women secretly desired. Not parity, but *supremacy*. However, it's strange when confronted with financial catastrophe how quickly men and women revert to primitive type. What was I, the supposed breadwinner, doing sitting on my arse all day writing poetry? she would scream. Are you a man or a mouse? Oh, I'm sorry, I thought you wanted some equality, some liberation from those tired gender stereotypes. *Excuse* me.

'I won't be a kept man for ever, though,' I offered limply.

'No,' she said, rising to her full height, 'and I'll tell you why . . .' I noticed how much she loved talking to me from this position. Her favourite spot to start an argument was when I was lying on the bed reading. Apart from this activity being tantamount to having a handjob in public for her, she revelled in the height advantage, scorning me along the twin barrels of her flared Catalan nostrils. '. . . Because we're getting together all the crappy clothes in both our wardrobes and going down Camden market to flog 'em to the Japs.'

I sighed at this latest escapade. Not only did it sound like hard graft to me (and I tried to hoard my precious gold-dust writing time in the knowledge that all other activities were chaff on the breeze), but it was doomed to failure with her as mastermind. I said,

'Okay, who's got you a pitch there?'

'Your pal Rudi, if you must know.'

'Rudi? I thought he was king of pricks in your eyes.'

'Yeah, well, he's got his head screwed on when it comes to money.'

I had been surprised the previous week, on coming home from Martin's depressing redundancy meeting, to find Rudi sitting in my kitchen playing ball with Fidel while Mandy did the washing up. Rudi was always adept at finding something manly to do when in the company of women. If they complained about the car, his head was under their bonnets within moments; if the garden was overgrown, he would drop by with his turbo-charged diesel Flymo to perform the favour of cutting their lawn. This he would do stripped to the waist if at all possible, beefy shoulders swarming with fuliginous hair. In fact, he had done just such a service for Antonia a number of times the previous summer when Nick complained haughtily that he wasn't born to be her groundsman. That evening last week, I was met by the sight of Rudi tickling Fidel's tummy with one hand while wrestling a ball from his snarling jaws with the other. Both males were growling. He had popped over to pick up the battery charger he had lent Mandy (ignorant as I was of cars, I imagined they had to be hotwired like in the movies). But there had been no mention of any market project.

'Don't tell me,' I said, 'he's owed a favour by one of the goons who run the stalls and is bequeathing it to us. He'll never let us forget his gratitude if we accept, you realise. I know Rudi, that's how he operates.'

'So what? At least he can pay for a roof over his own head like a man.'

'You always bring it down to a slur on masculinity.'

'Whatever. Anyway, I want to go on holiday. I'm going to save up for it. I want to go to Cuba, get away from this pissy island with its pissy weather, and all you dull *English* people.'

I knew it was pointless arguing; a waste of time to oppose her Niagara of bile. When she made up her mind to do something she was invincible, haranguing as many people as possible into the bargain. She was an inveterate recruiter. As with the band, everyone in her orbit would be called upon to help out, to join her cause. If they malingered or implied they had better things to do with their time or their own lives to lead, Mandy would subtly ostracise or punish them. Or not so subtly, in my case. If I didn't conform to her schemes, she would make my life a daily hell. Thus I always capitulated, from writing all her lyrics, to rent scams, to moving house every other month, and now the market and her cockamamie idea of going to Cuba.

I had other objections to her plans. One was that she gave up on everything, abandoned every endeavour. Despite the protestations from everyone (usually people like myself who had worked long and hard to support her) not to forgo her band, she just chucked it all away at the first obstacle. Taking Victor Moore's cynicism to heart, she thought his Confucian utterances demanded she give up for good. Secretly, I was disappointed by this surrender: if she gave up at the first hurdle on her lifelong ambition, how would she treat her marriage? It revealed a hitherto unseen weakness to her character, a hairline fracture in her iron will. It is only when you spend time with such a person that you realise how much we invest in 'sticking it out' or 'seeing things through' in life. How much of our general fibre is built upon the age-old values of endurance, the protestant work ethic. Also, how corroding the reverse of these values can be: to be around someone who *gives up* all the time breeds feelings of futility and emptiness. If they, the instigators of these schemes, cannot be bothered with them, where does that leave us, the loyal supporters?

Then there was her devout hatred of anything English, despite the fact that she was half-English herself. The market caper was merely a means to the end of escaping the British Isles. Somehow, Ramona's genetic legacy seemed to be the only one operative in her body. For her, this sceptred isle was full of rude, gloomy, spendthrifts who had no idea how to *fiesta*, and who could only use their summer holidays to spread ugliness on the beautiful coastlines of southern Spain – 'her' coastlines. Normally, I let this rank xenophobia go; I knew her father and myself were implicated in this slander: we were the pasty remnants of empire, of everything sunless and morally lax (the Catholic Church coming in for much praise when it suited her, even though she didn't understand a word she was crowing about). To her, we bulldog Brits stood for washout summers, lying tabloids, career politicians, caravan holidays, unvirile men, and inedible meat teas with suet pudding. We were the unsexy impediment to every avenue of fun that she pursued. We couldn't dance, cook, make love, make films or treat a señorita the way she should be treated. Our very hairstyles thwarted her enjoyment of walking down the street. This pathology grew over the years. It began as merely noting that English men were 'unfriendly' and 'cold' in comparison to their grinning Levantine counterparts. She neglected to observe that these Lotharios, after their Castilian courtships, often insisted their women become chaste, baby-producing kitchen–drudges, forbidden to so much as say *qué tal* to another man. Her mania culminated in rubbishing everything English or North European on a daily basis, reserving a special opprobrium for any woman with ginger hair – or 'ginger minges' as she unfunnily called them. I finally sympathised with her madman ex-boyfriend who had repeatedly begged her to 'fucking move over there' if she hated Blighty so much.

So it didn't surprise me that she wanted to do this market job in order to escape the isle of dogs for good. To Cuba, where she foolishly imagined there would be a fiesta every night in the street, with the joyous populace (proudly wearing their multi-coloured Che T-shirts) all smoking cigars and rattling their ration of rice in honour of Castro.

Hoping to swiftly put an end to her unrealistic ambitions, I said, 'Mandy, you do know that Cuba is still a communist country.'

To which she answered (I shit you not): 'What does that mean?'

A fortnight later, we were trundling up Buck Street in a second-hand Bedford Rascal, the back bulging with flares, coats, boots and heavy clothing-rails. The kick-off for the markets was usually six a.m., five-thirty for the die-hards or the old crooks who had flogged their leather belts and Harringtons there for twenty years. Even in late May it was freezing at that hour, the recalcitrant pigeons picking their way through a detritus of noodle cartons and frosty fag ends, the sheepskinned regulars blowing steam into their takeout cappuccinos. It took us a while to get set up. By midday, I was still struggling to pin home-made handbags to the canvas roof of our stall or re-erect the clothing-rail that collapsed at the very touch of a tourist. For the first week we made the grand total of thirty-five quid. This I saw as vindication of the idiocy of the whole enterprise. I would sit there for hypothermic hours, stamping my feet in time to the discordant hardbag then in vogue, while attempting to plough on with J. M. Bradawl's *The Nexus of Unstable Definitions*, a book which I was currently reading at the rate of a sentence per day. Against all expectations, Mandy, far from wanting to throw in the hand-embroidered Mexican towel, insisted we persevere and try a second week. After all, the pitch was free, and the weather threatened to get warmer. Sure enough, week two saw a crazy reversal of fortune, with an influx of the hallowed Japanese buying Levi flares at our absurdly optimistic prices. The yen they had to burn was incredible. By Friday we had cleared three hundred quid. Mandy celebrated by bringing Fidel down to the stall, as he had been confined to the garden for a whimpering fortnight.

Fidel became a fixture of our business from then on, his lovable big brown eyes and powerfully masculine charm helping us to shift many a gold and pink *Charlie's Angels* T-shirt. He was tethered to the clothes-rail, a constantly replenished bowl of water under his busy tongue. I was newly impressed with his strength as, when any female dog appeared within a half-mile radius, the clothes-rail would start to move as if by a poltergeist, Fidel tugging it in her direction with a carnal determination. It also surprised me how many people you run into when you become a barrow boy. I suppose it's akin to standing still for any length of time in London – you're bound to encounter someone you know. Six degrees of stagnation, I think they call it. For one, I didn't think all these faces from the past would be interested in seventies suede overcoats with fun-fur collars, but there they all were: square old schoolfriends, girlfriends, ex-friends, customers from Rock On, distant relatives, even old teachers back from hippy odysseys in Goa. One day Martin drifted past, and did a double take, surprised to see us there, shov-elling hats into bags, and banknotes into our pendulous bumbags. I didn't want him to think I was doing too well, just in case he refused to give me the old job back when things 'came right'. Inevitably, Rudi was a regular visitor, often looking over his shoulder for fellow shafters that he didn't want to bump into. Occasionally, he and Mandy would disappear to sort out some business with the major-domo who ran the place, leaving me with Fidel for company. This annoyed me, as Rudi was my old chum, though Mandy would always ridicule his clothes and accent on her return. Then, also inevitably, Antonia and Nick showed up, the latter exchanging polite greetings, while Antonia hurried past with her home-counties nose in the air. This produced a stream of scorn from my wife. She seemed somehow proud of her orgy of bridge burning. Mandy didn't know that I had been secretly meeting with Nick for the past few weeks, usually in the lightless snug of the Prince Regent for a pint of Guinness. Nick had managed a stall himself, after all, and it was he who was instrumental in the success of our operation. For example, he had advised me to visit all the charity shops in Kentish Town on a Monday morning, as that was where you usually found pairs of cool trousers going for nothing, which you could mark up to make a six hundred per cent profit. He also alerted me to a wholesale place near the Brent Cross flyover that had warehouses full of leather jackets bound for Amsterdam, and whose owners were willing to cut favourable deals. After months of fiscal emasculation at Mandy's hands, I enjoyed playing the shrewd operator, stuffing fivers under my Fagin's coat.

It was in the Regent that I rendezvoused with Nick one evening at the beginning of summer.

'I suppose she thinks it's all a result of her impeccable business acumen,' said Nick, his fringe undulating as he blew froth from the top of his pint.

'Of course she does. I'm just a passenger as far as she's concerned.'

I surveyed the clientele of the Prince Regent with my usual nose-diving spirits. Frazzled navvies, ketchup-faced fantasists and retired prostitutes were the order of the day. The pasty passengers of life. All seemed too inert to even visit the bar. Instead, the mutton-chopped landlord would bring a pint of their usual to their tables at half-hourly intervals, keeping score on a chalkboard. There was even one middle-aged character who would leave the pub to take urgent calls on his mobile every ten minutes. Nick and I were convinced he was merely talking to himself. As he smiled and gesticulated on the street beyond our window, we were unable to imagine he had any friends whatsoever, let alone one who possessed a mobile.

'You know Antonia's prepared to forgive and forget,' said Nick suddenly.

I was surprised by this. 'What about the other day at the stall? She walked on by like Queen Victoria.'

Nick hesitated to reply. He was still too sensitive about what he had overheard that day himself, and recognised my complicity in it. My answer didn't show enough contrition. 'Well an apology has to come from Mandy, does it not?'

'Christ, you know how difficult that is to obtain. She still hasn't forgiven her mother for dying in a car crash.'

'That was hardly her mother's fault,' stated Nick axiomatically, with his clear-eyed look that sometimes surfaced from beneath his veneer of languid cool.

'Exactly. Neither is it Antonia's fault that she's got big . . .'

'Say it,' said Nick, amused, 'I don't mind.'

'Big tits. It's just petty jealousy and bitchery. I mean, they used to be best friends. All I heard when we met was how wonderful Antonia was.'

'Yes, strange how the weather can change direction,' mused Nick. Despite the tension between us, I knew we were both enjoying the freeing novelty of being in a pub without the wives or girlfriends. It was good to feel the warmth of heterosexual brotherhood; of unimpeded lechery, of mutual grievances aired — the high emotions of manhood, all the higher for being repressed most of the time.

I said, 'You know, I'm really sorry.'

'Why is it —' started Nick, with a tone of measured philosophical inquiry, 'that everyone but Mandy apologises for her actions? What makes her so special?'

He had me there. For a long time I thought this was the trade-off one endured when one married a beauty. Different rules seemed to apply. And this latitude was constructed not by the women themselves, but largely by men. These giraffe-pinned Amazons could throw as many public tantrums as they wished, could insult waiters and bellboys, even their husband's own mother and still get away with it as long as they looked a million dollars from morning till night. Ah, the pride and the pain of being shackled to the most desirable object the world has to offer: a desirable woman. And the unspoken truth, understood by both dutiful husband and preening wife alike, is that, if you cannot put up with this, there is a queue ten deep who will. As Henry Miller drolly commented, he'd never seen a pretty girl starve. Lionised from an early age, these beauties usually have an unrealistic expectation of how they will be treated in later life. They expect adoring looks, opened doors, capes thrown over puddles, a husband with a painstakingly maintained musculature and bank balance who will present them with a gift for every day of the week; a gift for getting up in the morning. And lo and behold, when they grow up, they find this is indeed the treatment the world offers them. Now, just imagine what all that does to the ego! How different are the expectations of the plain wife, embarrassingly grateful not to have been left on the shelf, willing to accept the crumbs from the beauty's banquet. Yes, beauties operate by different rules. They make you glow with pride just to be seen on their arm for an evening, but know how quickly they can turn that pride to agonised jealousy with a deferment of their gaze to another suitor. The strongest man is but a mouse in their claws. As one battle-hardened Venetian exclaimed, O curse of marriage that we call these delicate creatures ours!

'I can't answer that, Nick,' I said after long deliberation. 'Sometimes she scares me. I've never encountered someone with so much anger and spite before. A woman impudent and mannish grown. It's taken a while to know how to handle it.'

'And can you handle it?' enquired Nick, raising an eyebrow. He seemed distracted, like there was something terribly important, pertinent to mine and Mandy's relationship, that he wanted to get off his chest.

'Do you want an honest answer?'

'Of course,' said Nick, glancing up to the wall-mounted TV in the corner of the pub. Manchester United were heading out of the tunnel. His eyes lit up. Usually Nick wasn't impressed by anything, and I disliked this in him. People who don't have any enthusiasms, who are universally unimpressed, are usually without talent themselves.

Only football ruffled his quiff, filled him with an admiration for human endeavour. I waved a hand in front of his face to get his attention. His unusually sensitive eyes found mine.

'No,' I answered. 'No, I can't handle it. Not this time.'

———————

A chirpy, clucky Yorkshire accent interrupts Nick's response in the Prince Regent.

'Hello, I'm Clare Thompson, your teamleader for the day . . . for the passengers that have just joined us at Grantham, I should inform you that smoking facilities for standard-class passengers are provided in coach H, which is situated to the rear of the train. Smoking is not permitted in any other area of the GNER service . . .'

Nick's face, his popstar's lips as they speak his debilitating reply, begin to fade before my eyes. What he said, the importunate plea for me to get divorced while there was still time, will have to wait. I must again engage with the tedious present. Big-boned, ruddy northern lads are hauling hockey bags down the aisle. The train begins to pick up speed. My, my, we are moving fast. I didn't even realise we had stopped. We have shed a few passengers though. The denim octogenarian hobbled off, with an unusual vigour for the size of his suitcases. A girl with an intelligent continental mouth did indeed disembark. Robin and Michelle are dozing in front of me, their heads heart-stirringly making contact at the temples. Outside, I can see Dales-stone in tightly packed walls running alongside the galloping train. The winter light is fading. The winter light appears to live in my heart. The sky is a grey shroud. I can see a churchyard with sodden copper leaves heaped up under the stricken trees. A gold legend on the church spire's clock reads 'Redeem the Time'.

I suddenly apprehend, with a peculiar intensity, that I am on the scrapheap of future romantic involvement – florid-cheeked, broke and exhausted, a hot date with my mother the only thing on the horizon. I feel bitter and weak, with all hope of a coherent future diminishing into the darkness, like the disappearing lights of Grantham seen from the wind-stripped countryside. The body prepares itself for separation from a loved one, like a death. The body does what it has to do, takes care of itself – seems to know the drill. Certainly, the body's job is to keep up with the soul, and to stop looking so old all the time.

The major problem, I ruminate, sitting here wanting another fag, is that I never notice anything but my own inner workings, my sad mechanism. I walk through the world rapt with a kind of over-attention, but it is all self-focused. I miss things, even when I think I am taking them in. In London, for instance, I walk out into the streets, onto pressure-cooker tube trains, along pavements alive with heterogeneous flicker, but it all seems dreamt in retrospect. When I arrive home and close the door to my tiny room in the shared flat, I think, did I do all that? Was I really there? Me, among all that clamouring, vital, arbitrary, ever-exfoliating life? My real attention was elsewhere. It was on myself – inward-facing, an endless communion with the soul and its daily fluctuations, its general health and position. Whole weeks fly by when it seems I was involved in the world and its transactions only to find that I was really elsewhere. The essential part of myself was surveying *itself*. It was never engaged in the larger public life. This was not its primary occupation. I had been soul-watching. Just recently, when standing before the mirror in the lime-shaded bathroom, I have seen the eyes of Rembrandt's later portraits in my own: foolish, bankrupt, sick of it all; the pleading vulnerability of a child, housed under the fatigued lids of a fifty-year-old man. Facing this mirror – usually on those off-guard moments after a shower when one catches one's reflection, surprised that the physiognomy belongs to the mind that is surveying it – I think, is this face *mine*? Where do these eyes lead to? Do they lead to me? Are they the mirror of the soul, or are they a phenomenon we shouldn't be concerned with, cursed as we are with consciousness? Why are we fascinated by this Cartesian split, this always-spellbinding duality? This dialogue between soul and body? Because both parties seem mutually inhibiting. Stopped there, arrested before the glass, puckered and hacked about in the steel light of morning or the warm perishing glow of dusk, I can hear Echo's voice receding into the forest. Except there are no tears to distort my vision. The moment is always too candid, too raw, too full of unanswered questions (about the past, about destinations we may never reach). But the moment always seems to announce: *this* is the destination, or at least one of them. Here you are again, in front of the mirror, trying to connect the centre that speaks and flies and sings with the astounding, familiar contraption of flesh and cartilage; the skull that will look just like a million others when we eventually thin out. Usually, I cannot help noticing how the body hasn't managed to keep pace with the soul it houses; how the years have altered the visage, the bestial visor. How the veins in my cheeks have splintered and split, finally lying there dead under the surface of the skin; two clown-like port wine stains, a Santa Claus patina on skin no longer supple and clear. Or how the hair has abdicated its tenure on my scalp, leaving a surface on which it is impossible to imagine that anything living had ever been present. The body decays, but the soul seems to remain ageless, birthday-less. There are no anniversaries for the soul. So why this valetudinarian ache? Possibly, it is the tension, the disparity, between the static inner and the kinetic outer, as the body undergoes its predictable somatic cycle, that makes us feel old. Often during these mirror moments, I remember the skull in my grandfather's studio: leering, ineradicable, dead. And I am convinced that the owner of that skull (whose skin it once covered to make his face) also stood before a mirror and asked the same questions, and also returned to his room, towel around his shoulders, water in his ears, without any satisfactory answers.

I decide a cigarette is a very good idea indeed, and make to get up, bracing myself for my addict's trek to the smoking car. Then I notice a poem in my notebook, staring up at me from the facing page where it fell open. Blimey. I had forgotten even writing it. But not the feelings that forced me to pick up the quill. Scribbled one night in the last week of my marriage, the final few days in the marital home, it was suggested by seeing a lonely item of fruit in the wicker basket in our kitchen during one of my nocturnal vigils. It was entitled (with Hardyesque simplicity, I thought), 'The Orange':

> The single orange in the basket,
>   Now overripe in full decay,
> Is like a teardrop in a casket:
>   Swollen, yet not dissolved away.
>
> Of life and fruit we know two things:
>   The first, that both run out of time;
> And second − this one really stings:
>   For certain words there is no rhyme.

Metaphysical, *n'est ce pas*? Or maybe more firmly in the Cockney School of rhyming. Well, those closing lines never caused me any satisfaction. The fact that certain words have no rhyme is a condition only of life, or language, not of fruit. If the ballad form had permitted me to write 'for certain *citrus rutaceae* there is no rhyme' as well, then that would have made all the difference. Ho hum. And I think you can guess what the orange, you know, symbolised.

A cigarette has to be in order.

I ease myself up on feet that have gone to sleep. Steady ... my legs feel like phantom limbs. Though it is almost completely dark outside, I can just make out the long reach of a canal with its surprising swans disappearing into the dusk. The crisp filaments of the trees seem impossibly delicate, austere. In the bleak midwinter, indeed. How I long for spring, for Proserpine's return to earth after the squalor of Pluto's captivity.

———

Meanwhile, back on Mandy's farm ... Things were going from bad to unendurable. After a summer cleaning up on the market she changed her mind about the Cuba jaunt. Instead, she spent the money on clothes and going out. None of it made her happy. Nothing ever did. She also became hysterically aggressive. It didn't take much to set Mandy off. There was a long list of pet hates that could precipitate these incendiary, ungovernable assaults. They sound like the comical preamble to a joke about a superannuated pedant, but the results of these phenomena were anything but comical. They included, among many other prosaic things, the sound of anyone chomping gum in the vicinity; her sugary tea being insufficiently stirred; cigarette ash on a carpet; foreign accents (Yorkshire, Scots, Yank, Aussie); my buying magazines or newspapers; my getting drunk; anyone chewing their food audibly (especially children); anyone who reeked of the pub; the shower curtain not being pulled across properly; the pans completed before the plates when washing up; anyone overweight, or with a fat behind, and girls and other women of all ages and ethnicities.

In fact, Mandy's obsession with weight and food increased and diversified as she got older. Not technically anorexic, she had a curious regime. I began to realise that she maintained her coltish figure by wasting exactly half of every meal. This, I believe, was a habitual dieting practice inherited from Ramona. Time after time, I would watch her approaching the halfway mark of a dinner, then see her contemplate putting the fork down. 'You have it,' she would say, with a tint of disgust, as if the food had been cursed, then scrape the remaining half onto my plate. 'But you're still hungry,' I would protest, 'I know you are.' She would ignore this accusation and slope off for a cigarette, restlessly peckish, but unable to ignore her own stringencies.

As winter approached, her seismic eruptions took a turn for the worse. We were always running in those days. Running to stand still. One morning, on the uphill cycle to work, a voice had called out, 'Hey – Byron! Byron Easy! So this is where you've been hiding!' It was Keenan Peach in a blazing waistcoat, taking his poodle for a walk. I crunched the bike up the stiff gradient in first gear as Keenan and his dog ran absurdly behind me, just out of reach, like a Keystone Cops movie. 'Come back! You owe me, my friend! You owe me big time!' But he never caught up. And he never got his money back. Just as well, as we were once again without a pot to piss in. Mandy began interviewing a stream of foreign-language students to share our intimate space. This line-up of verbally challenged Brazilian and Japanese lodgers proved to be among the last straws for our marriage. They would come in at all hours, sullenly drunk, only to overhear the most excruciating scenes. Mandy at this time was close to out of control. In the space of a month, she attacked me in Safeway's car park (because, as she later explained, the way I said the imperative *tranquila!* 'made her violent'), then elbowed me in the head while taking Fidel around the park. She also threw a steaming plate of spaghetti puttanesca at the wall, hurled a set of keys at the back of my neck and punched the steering wheel of her car for no discernible reason. Further to this, she decimated her old turntable and cut up her CD collection with a pair of scissors because she walked in one day with a headache and I happened to have music on. She smashed a cup to pieces against a mirror after an argument over how many people could fit in the back of her Bedford Rascal van. Annoyed at my drunkenness after a night out at Rudi's, she hurled the cat litter tray down the stairs, adiosed a stool through the landing window, then broke a bottle of olive oil and threatened to glass me. Outraged that I had kept my old letters from Bea, she dumped them in the bins outside, then threw a dish at the mantelpiece destroying Martin's green and grotesque lava lamp. Stressed out one afternoon, she flung envelopes in my face then exploded her favourite yellow mug with the hammer I had been using to put up shelves. Awaking one morning with migraine, jaw-ache and back-ache, she began punching herself in the face with her own fists and a jug. Walking in after work, she upturned the chilli con carne I had spent the afternoon preparing because she had a bad back. Waking up at six a.m., she battered the clock radio about the bedroom because she had nothing to wear. Driving to her father's, she almost killed us both when she took both hands off the wheel to grab my hair, hitting the kerb as she did so. Finally, she demolished the kettle, all the cups, the kitchen table and one of her mother's favourite vases because she couldn't find her lighter. *Twice.*

And none of it made her happy. At the height of this madness, I would look at the framed black-and-white photo of Mandy and me on Brighton pier; clothes low-slung, hand in hot lover's hand, future-facing and optimistic. It was almost too much to bear. Too antithetical to the 'lots of fun, lots of sex' promise she had made. Okay, a lover's promise is not a political manifesto, but by this point I thought they shared the quality of containing no truth whatso-ever. When I found myself in one of the locations where we had spent our brief happy time, that summer of solid shadows in Finsbury Park for instance, I was overcome by a stately heaviness. Walking past the windows of our old place above the bakery in Archway, I remembered the sybaritic afternoon I leant out of the wide sash frame and relished a sense of high balance in all of nature: the sun so sympathetic to the leaves, the leaves so sympathetic to the sun. Now, with the poor terrified lodgers witnessing such ructions, I felt it was all over bar (literally) the shouting. I experi-enced an intense urge to abandon the sinking ship once and for all.

Unfortunately, it is when you most want to jump off the train in life that you often discover it is moving too fast.

———

'*There are lesbians in the building!*' Montse's voice had wailed, in the hysterical tones of a village señora exposing a heretic during the Inquisition. The setting was the landing of Leo's airy flat in Tarragona, and old Montserrat was indeed correct, there were lesbians in the building: one of them was her daughter.

This terrible discovery had been made a month before Mandy's aunt and grandmother paid their threatened visit to us after the second Christmas of our marriage. The ancient matriarch, no longer puzzled as to why her surviving daughter hadn't been near a man for a quarter of a century, had concluded that Leo was no longer a sexual being (hard as it was for her to ever conceive of either Ramona or Leocadia as sexual beings in the first place). This assumption was reversed one afternoon when Montse awoke from her siesta to find her daughter sitting on the kitchen table in front of a young woman she had previously known only as Carmen, a young colleague from the mental hospital where Leo spent her days bed-bathing schizophrenics. This wouldn't have made an especially unusual tableau, except for the fact that Carmen was kneeling on the tiled floor with her head buried underneath Leo's skirt, the older woman moaning in beatific transport. It took a while for Mandy and I to learn the full shocking details from the splenetic old woman, but the resulting heart attack she almost suffered sent her out onto the landings and balconies of the apartment block to proclaim the outrage. 'There are lesbians in the building! Get out as soon as you can!' the octogenarian shrieked, her heavy bosom heaving, as if she were warning of a blazing inferno.

As this tale was related to us in the cramped galley of our kitchen in Seaham Road, we tried to suppress our laughter and intensify our looks of surprise. Because this was not as shocking a piece of news to us as it had been to Mandy's grandmother. We were preparing to take the selectively deaf old bat to Grease at the London Dominion, a production which, I had read, was famously loud for the theatre, more like a rock gig than a West End show. Both Mandy and I were rubbing our hands at the prospect of Montserrat turning up her hearing aid. Leo, meanwhile, had been relegated to their Bayswater hotel for the night. Mandy's grandmother had assented to travel with Leo (she felt unable to get on a plane without 'assistance') but refused point blank to be seen in public with such a degenerate. She imagined that Leo would walk down Oxford Street salivating Sapphically at every young woman they encountered. We, meanwhile, were secretly relieved that the greying auntie wasn't around as the real purpose of her visit to England was to palm Montse off on us, preferably in our flat, or in a house nearby which she was, incredibly, willing to buy, in order to be shot of the old dear for ever. This is how much Leo wanted to make a home for herself and Carmen in Tarragona, feeling, as she strongly did, that she had done her time in the dungeon of filial duty and that it was now Mandy's turn. My intemperate wife reacted with horror at this suggestion, and to be honest, I shared her reluctance. The idea of a life with both Mandy and Montse was a Dantean vision of purgatory. Usually I'm softened by the presence of women – a strange influence that I cannot account for – but not by that of Mandy or Montserrat. Their company was like being trapped in the Big Cat house at London Zoo.

'I tell you –' foamed Montse in our kitchen, 'I have nothing against them in principle. *Dios mío*! In the war, Barcelona was full of them. But my daughter! *En mi casa!*'

'Gran, it's Leo's house, not yours. And we should be getting on. You'll make us late with your hysteria.' Mandy had been holding her grandmother's coat for the past twenty minutes as the *vieja* stalked the kitchen like an elderly elephant. We had known for some time that Leo was a lesbian and thought it wonderful that she had finally plucked up the courage to start a relationship under the pejorative eye of Montse. Mandy had revealed to me one evening on our honeymoon that the real reason why Leo's marriage had mysteriously failed in the sixties was that it had never been consummated. Confused by her own sexuality, the imperatives produced by a wedding night had shocked Leo into an acceptance of her own nature. This made relations very uneasy between her and the virile toreador she had married. Subsequent to this disaster, any affairs had to be conducted in secret. With Franco coming down hard on miniskirts let alone open Sapphism on the streets of Tarragona, Leo's sojourn in the closet had indeed been long.

'You will never understand what shame this has brought upon me, *chica,* upon my good name. All our good names!' she appealed to Mandy. 'If my Pepe were alive, he would have had none of it, I tell you! He would have sent her to her room to wash out her unholy mouth with *jabón*. Every day is hell. I cannot face my neighbours. Marisa ignores me on the stairs. Henriquetta stares at me on the street. *La morvida*. Ay, ay, ay!'

'That's because you went and told them all,' said Mandy. 'How do you think Leo feels?'

'Perhaps if you moved somewhere else . . .' I suggested to Montse. At this, Mandy shot me a look. 'In Spain, that is.'

'Ah, *mi vieja corazón*,' she moaned melodramatically, clutching her breast where she imagined her heart to be. 'I don't have long to live. You will all *fiesta* on my grave, I know it!'

'Don't be foolish,' snapped Mandy, with real impatience. 'Now get your coat on.' It was like dealing with a reluctant child.

Montse appealed to me, her stooped form only slightly shorter than mine, and hissed, 'You don't think it's right, do you? Do you? She is only defending Leo because she has always hated me.'

'Perhaps now's not the time to go into it,' I muttered.

Briskly, Mandy said, 'I don't hate you, Gran, now get your coat on.'

There was the parp of the cab from outside.

'I think we'd better hurry up, Señora,' I said, relieved not to have to answer her question.

But the question of whether it was right or wrong lingered over the roomy seats of the black cab, a mode of transport we hadn't seen for a number of years, such were the dire straits we were in. Unfortunately, Leo had got wind of our penury, and had spent a month on the phone to Mandy attempting to bribe us into taking Montse off her hands. When this had failed she reverted to the old standard of filial duty and its importance in the building of character, something which she doubted Mandy possessed. 'My dear,' I had overheard Leo saying on the crackly line from Tarragona, 'I have had forty years of the old woman, the least you can do is show willing. It is your duty to your grandmother. You knew this was something you may have to take on one day.' Mandy had replied to this with unusual tolerance: 'But only when you're dead, Leo!' There had been a pause; just static on the line, during which I thought her auntie had indeed kicked the bucket from such a display of ingratitude. 'Well, I don't intend on doing that for a while yet!' So the situation had reached an impasse, a deadlock. Privately, I knew Mandy's iron will would never countenance such a move, even if Leo offered us a million quid. She had always resented Leo's patronising ways. And Leo, in turn, had always hated Mandy for her insouciant airs and graces, her feline body, her freedom.

As the cab sped through the jewel-lit streets of Euston, past the illuminated phallus of the Post Office Tower, Montse said,

'You young things – your problem is that you have never had to live through a war.' All pretence of deafness had now vanished. She was as alert and persuasive as a defence lawyer. 'When I think of how we held out against the fascists. Starvation. Rats running over the bodies of our brave men. No water for days on end. That is hardship. And my own daughter repays me like this!'

'You have to live and let live, Gran,' said Mandy, wearily.

'Ramona would have had an opinion on the matter, I can tell you!'

'My mother had an opinion on everything, but I'm sure she wouldn't have minded. What's the big deal? You have to let Leo get on with her life, lesbian or straight. God knows she's done enough for you.'

Montse put her hands over her ears theatrically. 'Don't ever use that word! What do you know of the injuries she has done me?' I expected to see the evidence of tears around her surprisingly young-looking eyes, but her rages were always conducted without waterworks. The olive oil she applied every night gave her skin the texture of kid leather. Just like her granddaughter, she was a formidable engine of determination. I suddenly wished myself anywhere but there, in that cab, heading for a night of sub-standard acting and outworn tunes. 'She wasted all my savings on her trips. I never knew where she was for months on end.'

'It wasn't months, Gran. She went to Barcelona every spring for a weekend.'

'And what perversion was she up to there? Eh? She was never the good one, the pretty one. God will repay her for spitting on the Bible, *imbécile!*'

'Gay people even get married these days,' announced Mandy

with a smile. 'Imagine that,' she said, turning to me and grinning. 'Leo and Carmen wearing wedding dresses and exchanging rings.'

Montse let out a moan as if she had just been stabbed in the side. She was shaking her head pitifully. 'I will never accept it. *Nunca.*' Leo had shown us a picture of Carmen in the lobby of the Bayswater hotel. She was very pretty, with the wide lascivious mouth of southern Spaniards and eyebrows that met in the middle, just like her greying paramour.

'Come on, Gran,' said Mandy, taking her arm in preparation for leaving the cab. We were now outside the towering frontage of the Dominion. 'We don't want the cabbie to cancel his holiday in Benidorm.'

The performance was indeed very loud. Prior to the show, Montse had repeatedly insisted her hearing aid wouldn't be powerful enough to pick up 'the lovely voices'. It caused us great pleasure to see her continue in this assertion – with the intention of garnering our pity, of course – for the whole evening. Repeatedly turning the volume control up to max, *Grease* must have sounded like a speed-metal gig inside her head. When we exited onto the lairy pavements of the Tottenham Court Road, old Montse really was deaf as a post.

The following day she was due to return to Spain. Mandy drove us all to Heathrow in stony silence – Montse still furious at her only-surviving daughter's deviance, Leo fuming that her grand plan had come to nothing. Ian Haste had agreed to meet us in the departure lounge to see them off, as he had always got on tolerably with Leo. I knew this was not because Leo reminded Mr Haste of Ramona – no, she couldn't have been more different from his wife: Leo was timid, restrained, decorous. It was rather that they were old allies against common enemies: first his truculent mother-in-law, latterly his impossible daughter.

We sat over cooling cappuccinos, Ian Haste's endless legs absurdly unaccommodated by the low table. The subject of conversation turned to Montse's proposed ejection to England.

'Are you sure this is your final word on it, Mandy?' said Mr

Haste, his tired face looking more like a skull on every encounter. There were smudges of strain, almost as black as boot polish, beneath his eyes.

'Don't tell me you're on her side, now?' Mandy groaned.

'He's on the side of reason and fairness,' said Leo, with a properness to her English diction.

'You two always gang up, I remember—'

'*Corta el bacalao*,' Montse said to herself.

'Translate please,' I asked Mandy.

'It means, "Whoever cuts the fish decides", and comments like that get us nowhere, Gran. You can't expect me and Byron to put you up. We can't afford it.'

'But I will pay for everything!' Leo said brightly.

'It's not the money we can't afford, Leo. It's, it's – the nervous breakdown. Look at her! She would drive a priest to suicide.'

'That's no way to speak about your elders,' she said, but gently, persuasively. Despite her doctrinaire manner, her school-matronly hips and hands, she was a big believer in diplomacy. I could see how important her new life and freedoms were to her. There was something super-sensitive and soft about the old auntie; on the last lap now, before sixty. She was transparent, her soul visible in the quick wrinkling of her brow or tiny twitches of her hirsute upper lip. I felt sorry that she had to deal with the old Señora. She deserved better.

'*Ah, de perdidos al río*,' burst out Montse, with a vigour that belied her four-score years.

'*Qué?*' I said, to Mandy.

'From lost to the river,' my wife translated, unhelpfully.

'Whoever wants me can have me,' moaned Montse. At this point she called over the waiter. 'Hey! *Guapo!* Do you like experienced women? *Sí?* Then live with me. I am no trouble!'

'Mother,' said Leo angrily. 'Keep your voice down. You'll embarrass him.'

'Embarrass him!' Montse cried. 'What about the shame you have caused me? I cannot even stand to sit next to you on the plane with thinking of the filth you have performed with an innocent girl.'

'She's not innocent, Mother,' said Leo. 'Carmen is thirty-five and has a *niño* to take care of.'

'*Ai, ai, ai, dos y dos son cinco!*'

'Just quieten down,' persisted Leo.

'*Me cago en la mar salada . . . me cago en la puta,*' snarled the old woman.

'*Escoria!*' snapped back Leo.

Now I was completely lost. I said again, 'Translate please.'

'That's unrepeatable, I'm afraid,' said Mandy. She turned to the trembling old woman. 'Now, we'll come and visit you as much as we can. I know Leo has bought you some nice things from Harrods for your special diet. It will be spring soon and you like that, don't you? Flowers and newness and light. And Leo, you know this is not for ever, don't you? It's just the wrong time. She can't walk into our lives like this and expect us to cope.'

I looked at Mandy as she said this and felt the stirrings of my old admiration. She could be remarkably even-handed when it suited her. I know I would have caved in years ago faced with the perdition of the devious old dear and the quietly steely auntie. No, I was too easy for that double act. I thought, with a twist of anguish, about Grandma Chloe, and how sane and sweet she had been. I pictured then her liver-spotted hands and prune-like face, blowing bubbles from the bubble-blower kit in the back garden of Dovecote Lane. Her human essence rich in sympathy. The distance between her elegance and the maddened old señora stretched before me like a chasm.

As the flight was called, Mandy's father said: 'You say it's not the money, Mandy, and you can't afford the time? Is that correct?'

'That's right,' she lied. I remembered the story of all the dodgy ruses Ian Haste had had to employ to make his loot, and the even dodgier ones used to hang on to it. Coming from nothing, from a stinking tenement in Bow, he knew how difficult it was to get on when you knew no one and had nothing. And even more so when you bore these handicaps in big letters on your face. His dark eyes held sad knowledge about the tides that run in the affairs of men.

'You shouldn't look a gift horse in the mouth. She's offering to buy you a bloody house,' said Mandy's father, his voice suddenly making use of the blunt importuning vowels of the East End. He no longer relied on incremental movements of his greying brows to register annoyance.

'We can get by without you lot, thanks all the same,' said Mandy.

'But Leo's made you a very good offer. You could all live together in this place; stop pouring money down the toilet on rent. Those landlords of yours must be laughing all the way to the Caribbean.' As he said this, his eyes met mine. Over the years he had changed from being a suspicious and protective father to an enthusiastic detractor of Mandy and her crazy ways. Not quite a confidant or ally, but more certainly on my side than that of his capricious daughter.

'Yeah, somewhere a landlord laughs so hard he pisses his pants!' I volunteered, quoting Lou Reed. There was a sudden silence around the low table. This wasn't a good idea. All eyes fell on me, containing varying quotients of outrage. 'Sorry,' I said. 'It's a song . . .'

Mandy gave me the evil eye and got to her feet. She looked at her father, Leo and Montse in turn, then stated with finality: 'Sorry. No can do. Now, let's get you back to Spain.'

———————

Thirty, that famous and dispiriting summit, that Mont Blanc of the psyche, was staring me in the face. In the last few months of our marriage, before that dreaded line in the sand, we took our final holiday together. A package trip to Cephalonia. For once I had managed to save some money by working a band-saw at a furniture restorer's on the Camden Lock market (a job which played havoc with my twisted recalcitrant spine), so I was able to pay my way. Incredibly, Mandy would later travel to Italy three times before the summer was out, where she would have to rely on the kindness of strangers. But I quickly found my new dough meant nothing to her. It was 'pocket money' again. I had thought this might have reestablished some parity between my wife and myself, but I was sorely mistaken. It was the holiday from hell.

It started promisingly, however. There was a great feeling of life decelerating, of a tense string slackening, when we disembarked in the warm air of Argostoli's airport. As Venus stepped onto the tarmac (Mandy was looking especially good in those last months: fragrant, sexual, magnetic) followed by her trusty bag-carrying Vulcan, the sun greeted us like a loving father. Helios, present in an unbroken sky for a week, his grand paternal gestures sweeping the glittering oceans, soon to infuse our limbs with a daily warmth. We sparked up by the luggage conveyer belt, sweat bubbling on the concave hotplate of my head. 'This is paradise,' said Mandy 'Yeah,' I concurred. 'I feel I could even do some writing.' But she didn't like that last observation.

The ramshackle coach to our apartment, high in the hills near Mount Aenos, creaked past monasteries ruined in the great earthquake of the fifties. Newly painted pastel churches now filled the old sites, with ornate iron gates casting detailed shadows on the sun-basking stucco. Cicadas sang in the early evening and great insects came in at the open windows of the coach, landing with a friendly softness on your knee before flying off. Everywhere was a scent of pine cones on the sea breeze. Our luggage followed behind on a flat-bed truck, like the entourage of an English lord. There was something about the quality of the light on the island that struck me immediately – a splintering clarity. I realised I hadn't actually seen light so powerful and pellucid before. What I had witnessed during an English summer was merely a poor artist's impression: soggy, cloudy, reluctant to hang around for more than a day at a time. We stashed our baggage in the marble-vaulted apartment, said hello to the maître d' and his leering teenage son, and went for dinner on the high terrace. It was sunset, a blood-soaked sheen of dying light that infiltrated everything. With the smell of the sea and the potent herbs of the kitchen it felt like a perfect hour of existence.

After coffee (which Mandy refused to drink because she claimed it tasted like sweet mud), she suggested we take a look at the night beach. This represented a re-emergence of her old rebelliousness, as the beach was two miles down a steep dark road. With great trepidation, wanting Hector's courage, we descended the heady gradient in the star-hung darkness. As Mandy went ahead, we tiptoed down the wrong track for an age, past goats tethered silently in the blackness; then, retracing our steps, we began the hour-long hike towards the ever-louder sound of the sea. We encountered rabid-sounding dogs howling viciously, concealed in the bushes; also blind-eyed peasants seemingly watching us from terraces. Sleeping in ditches were cars that looked abandoned, but were merely evidence of Greek parking. At last we started to kick up sand from the approach-road, the big ebony horizon flat before us, breakers softly sighing up the pebbles. We slumped in two low deckchairs and a tense silence developed. I had registered fear of the dogs on the road down, and I knew she was deeply contemptuous towards me because of this. Sitting there, in front of the great Ionian Sea, felt like the adventure two newly-lovers undertake before returning to their hotel for a night of arduous passion, or, even better, sex on the fine sand itself. But I knew such thoughts couldn't be further from Mandy's mind. Remembering the black night of our honeymoon in Tarragona, I said, 'Shall we go now?'

She paused for a moment before asking, 'Are you happy?'

This question astounded me. Never in nearly three years had she made such an enquiry. I felt quickly depressed; low as I'd ever been, the negative energy crawling back into me from nowhere. We were in the final stages, and we both knew it. However, it had to be gone through, endured.

'Yes and no,' I eventually replied.

But she said nothing further on the matter. I knew by this that she wasn't happy either. Instead she said: 'Let's go.'

Back in the hotel room, exhausted, we retired wordlessly to bed. This was the cue for us to have our first argument, I thought. The brief harmony of the airport and the nocturnal beach were gone. A pitch night was showing through the taverna-style windows, an ancient night like the ones Odysseus must have known as he lay in wait outside the gates to his old kingdom – black, many-starred, sealed.

'You know we haven't had sex for a year and a half,' I said from my single bed in the cell-like silence. My appeal sounded inert, impotent – almost as if it expected derision, rebuttal, laughter. Single beds had been Mandy's idea. Just lately she was openly scornful of anything carnal or bodily. Once upon a time she called her sexual feelings 'being amorous', and I used to love the quaint innocence of the phrase. Now, in the moonlit room, my voice suddenly loud and echoey from the marble, I lay winded on my blanket brandishing my useless, unwanted hard-on. It also occurred to me then that every hotel room in every hotel in the world had been the location for an act of fellatio. Well, this one wasn't going to see any tonight, I thought.

'I don't like it any more,' she said.

'Why is that? You used to.'

Her voice came back from the other bed, small and clear: 'I don't know, it just grosses me out somehow.' She rustled her sheets as if she were turning over to go to sleep.

I waited for a while before asking, 'Is there someone else?' I hated feeling like this: rejected from every failed initiation and curdled with jealousy. My tongue felt suddenly too big for my mouth, bathing, as it was, in a moat of saliva.

With a firm simplicity she said, 'No. Now put it away and go to sleep. I want to get down to the beach as early as possible.'

Ah, the beach: her great mission. The getting of a suntan. For months before going away Mandy would always take a bottle of Ambre Solaire frying oil and a towel to the sunbed shop that annexed the local hairdresser's. Here she would swap ribald tales with the three hard-faced peroxide blondes who cut hair and pumiced nails all day. Tanning was an obsession with Mandy. If she began to get pale, she would grab the non-existent extra inches around her tummy and exhibit them to me with real disgust. 'Look at this. I look like a pasty *English* person.' In fact, before her visits to the fast-tanning shop and its weird sisters she had even bought a sunbed on the never-never from one of her many catalogues. This was installed, like some monolith from a Second World War operating theatre, above our futon, so she could irradiate herself every day. I tried it a few times myself, and enjoyed the peaceful, amniotic slumber it gave you. The plunge back into cold reality when it clicked off at the end of its cycle was like a death.

So Mandy had to make the beach early. We stepped out onto the bougainvillea-hung terrace and contemplated the big purple mountains across the bay. The restorative light was a marvel. Descending the same cicada-singing roads as the previous night, the sound of Orthodox bells in the hot thick air, we marked our spot for a day of epic sun-worshipping. This, I gathered, was all Mandy wanted to do for a whole week. I flattened out my Rilke on the molten sun-recliner and gave in. Whatever she wanted, went.

The evenings were similarly predictable. We would hike out into nearby Argostoli, past tiny, elaborate Byzantine churches, and sit on low walls in the amber squares eating Greek breads and drinking bottled beers. Often, Mandy wore her ankle-length denim coat, which raised a lot of heat from the Cephalonian boys on their guttural mopeds. Her charms struck their sight with unmistakable force. But then, she always did get the looks, with her stacked heels and swagger, her sweep of sable hair glossy under the pinkening evening sky. Back at the hotel, with the chicory smell of kebabs and meat pizzas from the barbecue, the maître d's teenage son wolf-whistled her as we entered in under the ivory arch.

Of course the clear skies couldn't last. On the Wednesday, she smashed a jar of olives in the street. Thursday saw a horrible ruction that I tremble to revisit. A vicious, tempestuous fit, caused by nothing at all, in the sizzling heat of the hotel room. She tore up my Rilke. She spat in my face. She screamed. She threatened to get the first flight back by herself. The savagery of her outburst shook me considerably. At its height, she was like a cornered hell-cat. It felt like the zenith of our misery. Concluding that all the tears cried in the history of mankind could probably refill the oceans twice over, I decided to go down the long road to the beach on my own. In the heat, a pike in my heart, I cried so much I thought I would faint. Where do tears emanate from? How can the psychological produce such a physical result? If one is depressed one's skin doesn't turn black, so wherefore tears? For women they are a relief, for men, torture. Ever since we landed (apart from the first night) there had been the constant background hum of unrest, discord, depression, of the unsatisfactoriness of everything. Of the final stages. Even in paradise she couldn't be happy, this woman coloured ill. I felt a panic come over me as I stood on a high crag overlooking the luminous waters, as if my soul were expanding to fill and burst my body. I had to close my eyes, like I was going out of my mind.

The rest of the afternoon I paced out with solitary hours of swimming across a cove little frequented by tourists. The glass of the water felt good over my head as I dived to the golden grid of sunlight at the bottom. It resembled a baptism. I surfaced and looked at the hills with their intricate patterns of bushes and rocks, like tiny tight afro-curls. The sea was warm and supportive, the colour of agate or jade in the near shallows, deep navy further out. By five I had had enough and allowed myself to drift on the soporific currents. Mandy's poison was leaving my system: I felt free, relaxed even, strangely indifferent to my fate. I could have drifted there, seagulls scattering overhead, until I reached the Pillars of Hercules. I closed my eyes – trying to squeeze out the salt along with the clotted pain – and kept them shut; the sun a white presence behind the lids. Quite gradually I became aware of a rocking motion to the water, the distant drone of a boat some way off. I flipped over and noticed at once how far out I'd drifted. The high crag where I had stood was a dot on the great curving sweep of the hillside. I began to swim for shore but the rocking motion increased, making it impossible. Ominously, the noise of gulls, from a nearby buoy, seemed very loud – I felt they were sizing me up as carrion.

The faraway hum of an engine had belonged to a large pleasure cruiser that was producing a formidable rip-tide in the bay. I felt a twist of fear. Trying to swim was so impeded it seemed I was doomed to stay treading water until it got dark – the rhythmic undulation of the pull was tugging me further out, dragging me down. I considered crying for help, but nobody would have heard me. The big cruiser now gone, its after-effects were causing havoc in the bay. I could see foaming breakers hitting the beach in florid explosions. My head went under, and I opened my eyes foolishly to see the limitless blue beneath my struggling feet. I surfaced, heart pounding, and began an agonising front crawl that seemed to take me nowhere for two minutes. Quite calmly, another part of me was thinking: so, adios, then, Byron Easy. This is right on time, to drown aged twenty-nine like Shelley, on an ill-advised outing, my heart stung from foolish ructions – it all served me right. And anyway, what did I have to return to? Maybe old Percy Bysshe entertained such thoughts as the *Don Juan* went down, the volume of Keats still in his pocket, his heart strung out on another man's wife.

But eternity cannot have been ready to welcome me into its white radiance. Slowly, very slowly, I began to get somewhere. The beach became nearer, its unsuspecting figures running joyfully or kicking sand out of sandals on the tide wall. I wasn't going to die after all. The colour of the water changed from a heavy navy to a welcoming turquoise. I thought then of the occasion I almost drowned during a desultory fortnight on the Norfolk Broads with Mum and Delph. I had stepped off the slimy stern of the barge, ratchet in hand, expecting to open the lock, only to find myself up to the top of my head in thick, green, dark, mossy canal water. I had experienced a second or so of high panic, a flash of the ever-lasting. The end: not later, but now. Then a strong hand fished me out.

Closer still, and I managed to put a toe on the bottom. The relief felt like a homecoming. Then a foot. A web of dancing reflections surrounded it. In a moment I was dragging my trembling body up the steep gradient of the beach, face stinging and sun-struck, heart pounding but grateful.

When I limped back to the hotel in the evening I found Mandy by the pool, slurping a pina colada and teaching Spanish to the priapic teenage boy. I sloped off to the shower. I never told her what happened that afternoon. Somehow, I didn't want to give her the satisfaction.

On the penultimate day I managed to persuade her to do something more active than lying like a piece of steel under the welding-torch glare of the sun. With my remaining drachmas, I had booked us a trip to the underground caves at Melissani. She reluctantly agreed to go, fixing her shades to her head, where they remained until well after nightfall. On the coastal road in the rotten reeking bus, I stared at Ithaca in the misty near distance, a glowing blue of promise and mystery. For the past few days I had had the strong intuition that Homer was born on Cephalonia. If he had been, the sight of that sister island across the bay must have seemed like some Elysian home, some final destination where a man would be glad to hang up the lyre. Of course, they say he was blind, but I found it hard to believe he never saw the world, in every sense of the word.

After the inland drive, we finally reached the caves and spent a cooling hour underground slipping on stones and staring at the giant pendulous stalactites the Germans had used for target practice during the war. The ghosts of executed soldiers, the sites of forgotten pogroms, made me very melancholic. After this grim refreshment we walked to the underground lake where I had what can only be described as a peculiar, perplexing experience.

As we queued for a free boat under the dome of dank rock, open at the top like a volcano, I thought I saw someone familiar disembarking from one of the rowing boats that ferried tourists around the caves. The Greek oarsmen were singing traditional songs, full of forced vitality from the strain of repetition. I focused and refocused my eyes in the rippling light and became convinced that, fifteen feet ahead of me, chaperoned by an Adonis-like boyfriend, was Bea, her chestnut hair glossy, hallucinatory. She was wearing a colourful top of a rich, subdued red. I was staggered at the seren- dipity of this: of all the places in the world to come face to face with Beatrice, standing in line for a pleasure boat with the woman I chose instead of her. I had travelled to the lofty peak of Hampstead and stood vigil outside her old window for a year and had returned disappointed. But here, in the death throes of a catastrophic marriage, I was to come face to face again with all love, all beauty. The girl was laughing and squeezing her boyfriend's hand, heading up the narrow stone path to where we were standing. Closer. Then closer still. Yes, it was definitely Bea: the same steady intelligent eyes with their air of fragile intensity, of depth. I froze up, my heart in my mouth, having no conversation or explanation ready. I asked Mandy to swap places in the queue so I was on the inside. Bewildered, she complied. Mandy had never seen Bea in the flesh before, so there was little chance of her causing a scene. Bea was now a couple of paces away. I wished she would speak, so I could hear her voice and have final confirmation . . . then . . . then the woman passed and I saw it wasn't her. Too tall, more Mediterranean in close-up, her hips swaying in that libration characteristic of Levantines. I felt breathless, relieved, off-balance. Grasping Mandy's hand, I saw my wife was looking at me confrontationally. It had been a long time since we held hands.

Ignoring her look of confusion as we pushed forward for the first available boat, I stammered, 'I think I need my eyes testing.'

On the final day, our baggage stored in the hotel's kitchen, awaiting the flat-bed truck that would ferry it to the airport, we took the bus to Metaxata for a last swim. Away from the tourist trail, overlooked by the calm craggy mountainous outposts high above the bay (the ones that had almost witnessed my drowning a couple of days before), we spent the morning running into the surf. An hour before it was time to kick the sand from our towels and head for the airport, I heard

Mandy shout excitedly from the shallows. 'Byron, come quick!' Her voice was shrill, like a cry, with a child's excitement. 'There are fish!' I ran across the foot-torturing pebbles and waded out. The sea was the temperature of a tepid bath. Sure enough, when I reached Mandy, there were currents of silver darting fearlessly between her legs. She stood there, thin and brown, her black bathing costume tight to her spine, her hair up, as the shoals came in eddies out of nowhere. The water was so clear, you could see their eyes. Some bigger creatures, a foot long with flexible green spines and delicate markings stayed with us longer. So friendly, familiar and curious were they, it was like being joined by one's children. Mandy trailed a hand through the crystal Aegean and tried to touch one, but it proved elusive. It darted away under the glassy ripples. She smiled at me; a smile from long ago in the past, a smile I hadn't seen since she asked me to marry her on Brighton pier. It made me very sad to see this smile after the scarring scenes of the week. I glanced over my shoulder at the two vacant stripes of our towels on the beach, then smiled back. I didn't have to say anything. We both remembered the time.

Darkness. The train is sighing relentlessly to a stop. The sun has finally dipped below the horizon. What a long time that took. We seem to be very far north. I can see Doncaster station half a mile away on a bend in the tracks. The amber sparkles of the town resemble Christmas-tree bulbs that no one bothered to spend much money on; uniform in colour, carelessly distributed. They glitter like those fish, silver and rapid; forming ever-dilating circles and shoals. I can still see them, feel their intimate touch against my bare legs, Mandy smiling that long-ago smile.

Outside my window, even with such a lack of light (and I have to press my face very close to the glass in order to make anything out), I can see all the melancholy preparations for the festive season. I open my notebook and record: *A cloud of rooks over the carrion of a starter-home estate; a six-foot inflatable snowman in a drive, huge-bellied and sad despite the smile under his phallic carrot; a Christmas tree in every window; flashing decorations like landing lights (holly, ivy, Santa, Rudolph, sleighs) probably visible from space . . . further on, wreaths of tawdry tinsel on doors; stars of David; meagre homes with their satanic satellite dishes.*

Then the approaching station: trackside always belching up the worst and most depressing objects, as if God had emptied an ashtray from on high. Corroded drums; forgotten bales of fencing; plastic bags caught in sharp branches; upturned chemical containers; wheel-spares; buffers embedded in the ubiquitous sea of volcanic pebbles; isolated signals; coils of steel cable; scorched warning signs, bumble-bee yellow; dripping flagstones and capstans upended in a wilderness of couch grass; a rank of floodlights disbursing an icy blue-and-white glow; a lunar illumination for a peopleless wasteland.

I settle back in my seat and try to meditate on why my marriage had to end. It seems important to get this straight before I alight from the train. There might be awkward questions, after all. There are only another couple of stops before Leeds and time is most certainly cracking on.

Once back in England after Cephalonia, I remember something snapped in Mandy. There were no more smiles like the one she gave me in the sunlit bay below Metaxata. Back were the mood swings of a toddler. Her inner recklessness, her genius for fits, her true ugliness, found its full expression. Miss Haste had become Mrs Hurtle. Did this mean it was finally over? How much more of this spirit-destroying nonsense could I put up with? Did I have the energy to cut and run? No, I stood still and endured it all – everything she had to throw at me. And a lot got thrown, I can tell you, during her blind tantrums, the scorching disruptions that appeared out of a clear blue sky.

In early summer, when my bank account was finally shut down after years of overdraft abuse, I persuaded Mandy to make the journey to the Holloway Road and open a joint one. We were refused, prompting Mandy to hurl the account documents at the cashier. Once outside, she propelled the jam tarts she had been carrying at a woman innocently queueing for the cashpoint. O, that

Knave of Hearts! Within the space of a month, she kicked in the glass kitchen door at Seaham Road, pummelled the video recorder to pieces, threw a Walkman through the kitchen window, smashed up all our wedding photos, then, out of pure impatience at having to queue so long, hurled a tin of dog food at a cashier in Tesco. Not content with this, she attacked me twice in one evening with her Struwwelpeter nails and flung my bike down the hall because I came in late. The following day she threatened to stab me to death with a knife and then bit me in the neck. Unwilling to go to work one morning, she decimated the clock radio I had replaced after its predecessor's destruction, then broke a plate over her own head during a hysterical screaming fit brought on by a migraine (yes, I also told her that it wouldn't make it any better). Unforgivably, she ruined my thirtieth birthday by coming home from the restaurant and slamming the front door ten times, later lashing out at me with a fork. Finally, she smashed the telephone to pieces. *Three times.*

Thank God for the invention of the mobile, is all I can say. Mandy: an adult with the emotional equipment of a child. Turbulent as a Ruisdael landscape, she was what anger-management therapists term the classic 'exploder'. She couldn't sit in the discomfort of her own feelings for more than a moment without lashing out.

The *coup de grâce* came during a bust-up over her first planned holiday to Italy with the newly reconciled Antonia. I couldn't believe she had the funds for another trip after Greece, but one of anything was never enough for Mandy. That evening, our customary row had been going round in tedious circles for an hour: me imploring her to travel when she could afford it, her telling me to stay out of her 'private life', when she suddenly rose from the sofa with Amazonian purpose and punched me hard in the mouth. I felt a sharp pain, like a razor cut, then saw a gout of blood dollop onto the carpet. My errant incisor, the one that had prevented me pronouncing many Spanish words over the previous years, had gone clean through my lower lip.

As I sat in a green cubicle at Accident and Emergency getting stitched up, I reflected on how Mandy had performed the same action on me. Private life? It seemed like an oxymoron at the time, but Mandy the moron could not see this. A married couple, I lectured her, were a publicly and legally recognised social unit. To do anything in 'private' (especially something sexual, and it was this that I was afraid of when Mandy was in Italy) equalled adultery. After her attack, I resolved to allow her to pursue this illegitimate 'private life' and not give a damn. But I was suffering, all the same. Something obdurate on the interior wanted to have a loyal wife, even a crazy one – or no wife at all.

I still have the scar from that punch. It hurts sometimes to drink anything too hot or too cold. More poignantly, I still have the tan, in both senses of the word, from that week in Cephalonia. It smarts more as time progresses – nowadays I can't get through twenty-four hours without crying. It also strikes me (as the train sighs regretfully to another stop), with the guilt and shame of the puritan who has succumbed to the dissolute life, that I wasn't drinking back then. What a fall from grace I have undergone since! A vision of a particular morning a couple of weeks back confronts me, seizing up the ventricles. This, surely, was rock bottom.

I had been up all night at Rudi's, downing gallons of red wine and vacuuming up the copious charlie that was always magically replenished on his coffee table. A villainous chaos of dice and drinking. We had talked, we had broken bread, we had gone through the whole tedious saga of my marriage one more time. By nine in the morning I was back at the Heartbreak Hotel, still flying at thirty-five thousand feet, with that keen, invincible, garrulous sensation one has after a night on the Posh. I remember somnam-bulantly divesting myself of my clothes and sliding into the paltry bedding, first making sure I left the curtains open, as I had to be at Rock On for ten-thirty. An hour's sleep should suffice, I thought, as I caught sight of the big chestnut tree out back strafed in December light. Its trembling branches were bare as wires; its leaves now a dead mulch of browns and greys at its feet. The metallic sky allowed brief visitant flushes of sunlight through, momentarily turning the tree silver. I must have sat for a while watching this sublime sight, naked, my knees up under my chin against the cold. A million ideas and connections prevented me from sleep, my nose dripping coke-filled tears onto my borrowed bedspread. Downstairs I heard the two croupiers letting themselves in from a hard night at the casino. There was the sound of the kettle going on, jangling keys, stentorian coughing. Then something forgotten occurred — a lost interregnum. Time change. Something must have happened in this interim, because when I next looked at my watch it was eleven in the morning and I was locked in the TV room at the front of the house, my trousers around my ankles. In front of me was a wrap of charlie that Rudi had evidently slipped into my jacket pocket for luck. The fact that it contained only a few crumbs of white powder told me that I had been at it for a while. The fact that my limbs fizzed and ached with a directionless erotic energy also vouched for the fact that I hadn't just been drinking coffee in preparation for a hard day's work.

Worse than this, on the silent screen before me, three satyr-buttocked Germans were humping the same woman in the usual orifices. She appeared to be in considerable pain, but, with the sound turned down, it was hard to tell. Her face was contorted into a rigor mortis grimace, her teeth slightly blurred by the bad quality of the video. Yes, this video was the other item Rudi shoved into my pocket as I tripped from his front porch into the weird light of dawn. With what implacable force were these Jerries going for it! It was hard to countenance that this ridiculous involuntary movement of the hips had brought us all into being. The endlessly involving sight of other people screwing, all tenderness absent, just the animal seeking pleasure and satisfaction from its fellow animal. It held me spellbound. How simultaneously familiar and alien were her beseeching hand gestures and intimate contortions. Did all women look like this while making the beast with two (or in this case, four) backs? And the male of the species? Did we all use such uncontrollable violence, such main force? Obviously, in more ways than one, these humping Huns were not as other men. Not every bloke is possessed of a schlong that would win first rosette in a village Prize Marrow Competition. But I guess we must all resemble them in some intrinsic way. I tried to recall, with averted eyes, the last time . . . It must have been the night with Haidee, her whispering French nothings into my ear, me inexplicably guilty that Mandy would find out, even though she had dumped me the previous week. Those old, uxorious habits die hard. No, we had not resembled these Teutonic porno fiends with their greedy needs, their furious faces. That night – our one and only night after the shipwreck of my separation – Haidee had sweetly cut the lights and lowered her strawberry-spotted underwear before climbing into bed. There was a degree of awkwardness, which I found surprising, having just turned thirty. There was also something strange and thrilling about a new intimacy, the unlearnt language of her flesh, the shaky esperanto of the somatic dance. There was certainly no gymnastic ramming, no brutal wheelbarrowing around my tiny room. Maybe she would have liked or expected this, I didn't ask. No, it wasn't one of those nights when you can reflect, after the twenty-sixth position, that you're no longer in it for the sex – more as a researcher for the *Guinness Book of Records*.

Afterwards, she brushed a swipe of hair over my balding crown and murmured, '*À demain,*' a fine valedictory phrase from a lover. The moment resembled a French film whose lithe heroine spends most of the time unclothed behind pale, jaundiced blinds. I almost expected to see a subtitle to appear on my misted window. Then, when it was finally morning, I awoke with a start to find her watching me, her head on one side, an intent childish look on her face, like a toddler mesmerised by a flame. An unseasonal glow of sunshine illuminated the peeling walls. Her clustered curls fanned the pillows like golden coins. She smiled at me, baring perfect orthodonture, small and heartbreakingly white. And I, in turn, smiled at her, thinking: there lies the thing I love, with all her errors and her charms; her Gallic vivaciousness, her endearing bronchial cough the result of too many Marlboro Reds. Ah, she could have saved me but she chose not to! With this vision before my eyes I slipped into unconsciousness. When I jolted awake again at midday, she had gone.

I switched off the sweating Germans and pulled my trousers up my tingling legs. I had supp'd full with squalor. Feeling like a cliché – the dumped husband who turns to the bottle or drugs – I buckled my belt and noticed the white seam of the scar on my left thumb where, years ago, helping my father to chop wood, I had almost amputated my hand. Arrested there, I could see it all vividly before me: the whipping winter wind; my dad furious that his glasses had been knocked off (why so angry? Because he had been momentarily rendered myopic?); the swaying of the red-hot pokers in the back yard. I remembered the moment I forgot his careful instructions; my panic, my eager desire to please him; that strange need for approbation that all sons feel in the presence of their fathers. The next instant: a shocking gash, with its revealed knob of bone, the quick bloom of blood.

Feeling stirred and hot around the neck, I slumped down again on the tissue-strewn cushions. The glass of water that held the wrap – which I had been soaking to extract the last dregs of coke – looked suddenly nauseating, undrinkable. My jaw ached from two hours of grinding my teeth. Outside, an ice-cream van miles away played 'The Camptown Races', curdling with the austere sound of the viola from next door. Then nothing. The viola was gone, but I still heard its maudlin vibrations. Unheard music . . . It had been ten years since I spoke to my father, ten bewildering winters. I wondered what he would make of this scene, this debauch, if he could witness it: his only son watching porn, coked off his face at eleven in the morning, recently separated from the wife he never met. A vortex of dissipation. I pictured the look of censure from his hooded eyes, the finger and thumb of his right hand massaging his temples in vexation. I imagined he would conclude that this was 'always where I was destined to end up': a bad end in a freezing north London rooming house. Hard as it was, I attempted to see it from his point of view. I also tried desperately to visualise him, after his years down under, with anorexic Emmanuelle at his side, tending the barbie on the beach for his new family. Maybe his skin would be a rich leathery brown; the remainder of his hair grey, alpine white even. Possibly he was even shorter, with that curious shrinking that accompanies age, despite the expansion of paunch and jowl. Quite probably he hadn't shifted in his inflexible views. Despite this I realised that, for what seemed like the first time in ten years, I missed him. Other people had fathers, why didn't I? We both knew where to find each other, so why hadn't we?

There is something about cocaine that makes one contemplate communicating with people one really knows better than to communicate with. Something about the gregarious intensity of one's own perceived wonderfulness forces phone calls or letters that should remain strictly unventured. At that moment I felt an uncontrollable desire to get in touch with my old man. I seized my notebook and began scribbling, in an illegible hand, words that I once heard at the start of a record: *Dear Dad, things didn't turn out quite like I wanted them to . . .* But I was too wired to continue. An impenetrable scrawl would only make him despise me more, if despise me he did, though I wasn't so sure of that. The feelings weren't so grand and classical between us as to accommodate hate. Instead, there was banal evidence of indifference . . . No, a phone call would be better, while I still felt up to it, while I still felt confident enough to confront him. I remembered my mother had given me his Australian number years ago. Unlocking the door to the television room and barging back into my lair, I began ransacking my old diaries and address books. The chestnut tree in the back garden looked strangely surreal. It was full of magpies, full of light. Alone in the cuboid space, the loquacious sparrows expressive in the gutters, the deep smell of the damp garden intensifying the beiges and muted ochres of the walls, I finally located the number on a yellowing strip of Rizla and descended downstairs to the communal phone, first listening on the landing for a moment to check the coast was clear. Sitting at the rickety phone table, the number quivering in my hand, I began to dial, a giddy recklessness inside me. It felt like the kamikaze moment before coming face to face with a blind date, the heart full of a Dutch courage that it knows it cannot sustain. Far away, on the other side of the world, a world where the water disappears in a different direction down the plughole, I heard a ringing.

Then the door to the kitchen was shoved open. Standing there was the elder of the two croupiers, looking haggard, unshaven. He said,

'Shit, Byron, aren't you at work? Martin's been ringing the phone off the hook all morning wondering where on earth you'd got to.'

A voice on the other end of the line – the other end of the world – was now saying in a heavily French-accented trill, 'Allo? Allo?' Emmanuelle. My father's wife. His second wife. It was the first time I had heard her voice.

I put the receiver down. I had completely forgotten about work. Sliding the piece of Rizla into my pocket, I thought: Goodbye, Old Man – it was never meant to be.

'Did he sound angry?' I said quickly, hoping nobody had blundered into the television room and discovered the troglodytic scene. I swallowed hard to prevent the gnashing of my teeth.

The croupier laughed with a horrible knowingness: 'No, but I'd be surprised if you still had a job.' Leaving the room, he added, 'By the way – did you know you've got a nosebleed?'

Not surprisingly, Martin had been less than elated that morning, waiting, as he was, to hop out and visit his missus in hospital after a gallstone operation. I remember the walk to the shop, through strange insidious-looking trees and jarring perspectives. Even the rubbish piled up on the Camden Road made me paranoid. Being wired to the eyeballs indoors is a different experience to dealing with the great swarming, super-real population of London. I was aware that I was grinding my jaw and giving quick shakes of my head, like a chaffinch taking nuts from a bird table. I was vaguely conscious of an all-encompassing inability to do anything competently. Crossing the road was fraught with danger and something approaching inexplicable despair. My lungs felt as if they were cased in lead, so heavy was my descent, my come-down anguish. By the time I made it to Royal College Street and the lacerated frontage of Rock On, I felt as if I were losing my soul. However, once I had been there for five minutes, and had put up with Martin's ostentatious frostiness (he found it impossible to lose his temper), I quickly sensed his attitude change. He looked me square in the face and went off to fix me the strongest cup of coffee ever made. This he followed by producing a litre bottle of water from the fridge and insisting I drink it if I ever wanted to work at Rock On again. As he monitored me in this task, despite his brisk annoyance, I was aware of a generosity behind his gestures. His hand went back to scratch his grizzled ponytail as he watched me there in the empty shop, drinking like a man who'd staggered halfway across the Sahara. He had seen enough casualties in his time to know that I was fucked; done-for; off-my-tits; a stretcher-case. If he hadn't had to go and rattle his wife's stones in the pewter dish, I'm sure he would have stayed to talk it all over – man to so-called man.

———

A flash of movement on the platform brings me back to the present. The train has been stationary for five minutes. Robin and Michelle are still asleep, both snoring in gentle crescendos. Tracksuit Man is absorbed in the back page of his tabloid. But out there, in the darkness of Doncaster's main station, the lunar landscape is no longer without human activity. Something is kicking off – literally. A drunken scuffle has erupted between beered-up lads in their brightly coloured pub shirts, the type designed to be worn outside the trousers, the collars pinned back with prissy white buttons. All eyes on my side of the carriage peer out of the window for a better view. A headlock, of the professional variety learnt in martial-arts classes, has a British-Rail employee on the ground. There are shouts and oaths, an awful crunching noise, then . . . What is it about violence that is uniquely watchable? I ponder this as the Station Master weighs in to break it up. The tension pins one to the spot. It strikes me that I've had little experience of this sort of violence before: bestial, group-led, mindless. No, that's wrong. Scratch that. What exposure I've had to it was brief, but the violence involved was of the particularly nasty kind, the type that stays on un-erasable videotape in the mind's vaults for ever. The type one *feels* when one witnesses it being meted out. Sure, I've seen lingering drunks rolled across flagstones by Darth Vader bouncers, or interminable street bundles where two massed armies of estate psychos have detonated, with mountain bike seats and the predictable Becks bottles halved on junction railings. I have even had a Stanley knife waved in my face by a twelve-year-old as I made my way up the Kentish Town Road after an evening watching football with Nick. But all the protagonists got up again afterwards. That was the important thing. Literally and figuratively. They, we, all of us including the exhausted observers, dusted themselves down and lived to brawl, or watch, another day. All of us surfaced the next morning feeling like fruit that had been containered from the Cape to Southampton in a hurricane. I had even seen Rudi Buckle, on the razzle one night up West, half throttled by a doorman, who blacked him out so effectively that his lifeless arms couldn't remember to break his fall when he was eventually shot-putted onto the concrete. But he still creaked himself onto his knees, blood water-pistolling from his once great nose, cackling like a maniac.

This was not the case, however, with a nasty incident I was unfortunate enough to bystand a month ago. It was a few weeks after my final split from Mandy. Battered and bruised as I was, I had agreed to accompany Rudi on some mission of skulduggery in W5. A London night with all the winners and losers on the street, along with those that slip in between – the inconspicuous ones like me who appeared to have neither won nor lost, but were just suspended in perpetual stasis. A freezer-interior night in West Ealing. (Night – why do these things kick off at night? It's as if daylight, simple common-sense lunch-hour daylight, has a curbing, limiting effect on men's always startling capacity for violence.) A vault-like, breezeless midnight with me waiting in Rudi's car as he bullied a couple of take-outs from the 'Time Gentlemen'-yelling barman. Then a bustle of activity: three six-foot-plus lads exit the tenebrous portal of the pub's saloon door followed by a fourth, slightly shorter, Algerian-caste man. I thought, quite naturally, that he was their friend. I was wrong. Within seconds, quick fists were flailing inaccurately. The Algerian took a punch and crumpled to the frost-forming concrete, his hands outstretched in supplication, contrition, surrender. But that wasn't sufficient for the tallest attacker in his puke-orange puffa jacket. Oh no, not nearly enough. From the muffled interior of the car I overheard a terrible sentence, a verbal detail that would be as hard to erase from the memory as what happened next. What the tall man said was:

'Do you want to fucking die?'

Then his boot flashed out – the right foot, with enough range and acceleration to suggest he'd somehow taken a run-up. He kicked the Algerian as hard as you would kick a football from the halfway line, connecting with the fiercely vulnerable bullseye of his right temple. A death blow, really – had to be. Reckless, cautionless force. I would like to say that the man's head went back instantly, like a catapult sling, and met the flagstones with the crisp retort of a rifle shot, like in the movies. But, amazingly, it didn't. Something far worse happened: it juddered slightly (and the surprise for me was that, from contact with a blow of that velocity, the pounds-per-square-inch impact, that his head was still on his shoulders). It quivered with a game resistance until his disembodied voice emitted a groan, an almost feminine sigh of disappointment. And only then did his skull ricochet back, taking his shoulders and white-flag-waving arms with him.

The three big men walked off. Casually, defiantly. A queasy aftermath silence in the air. And then I noticed that the street was absolutely empty – I was the only witness to what was surely cold-blooded murder. Slipping from the car, I tripped on the kerb in my alacrity to reach the starfished figure dramatically alone on the wide pavement. It suddenly seemed even colder under the black midnight sky. London after dark is full of street-kickings, squalling domestics, wino-pastings, tired altercations, but this was something quite different. This was something else. It was only when I was a foot away from his quiescent bulk, close enough to see the stitching on his flying jacket, that any kind of timidity or caution entered my approach. 'You all right, mate?' I found myself asking once, twice, maybe three times. With a lurch of my colon, I noted that his face, which I had taken to be quite still, was actually in rapid, detailed motion. It was trembling as if a low-level electric current was being passed through it via a socket in the back of his neck. I could hear, also, that his tongue was making a phlegmy, staccato, gargling noise against his upper palate. But it was the eyes, his eyes, that really got to me. As I stared down into his face, like a surgeon over a patient in some hellish field hospital, I became aware that he couldn't see me. Even though he was making full eye contact, the lids alert and taut under his North African brows, his gaze plangent, demanding, he couldn't see me. For him, I didn't exist. He was somewhere else entirely. Not on this scarred, time-suspended November street, but on some vivid plain – infancy, childhood, love-life, all zipping past like antelope on a screen behind his eyes. I prodded him. No reaction. Dully, the realisation began to immerse me, like a sweat of ice across my back: he couldn't feel anything either. Seconds later, he was convulsing – fitting; epileptically energised. And there we both were, on the Godless, solitary, ransacked street – him dying, me watching. Slowly, a fleck of blood appeared on his protruded lips, like a Levi's tag or the red ladybird that globes up after a needle is withdrawn. That's all I needed to see. I was into the pub like a shot fired from a cannon, smacking spectacularly into the exiting Rudi and scattering his hard-bargained-for take-outs over the step.

'What thay fu—'

I hollered for an ambulance, assistance, a doctor. The barman pointed to a fat Irish woman in the ambered snug who was apparently a nurse. Then we were back on the street, the fast-deteriorating man on his side, now shrouded with the weak placebo of somebody's jacket. The next twenty minutes were a fuzz of lime-jerkinned paramedics and radio-crackling cops; all demanding statements, unrecallable details. Intermittently, I glanced at the Algerian surrounded by the many feet of onlookers, helpers, officers, and thought how apart he was, locked in the drama of his own mortal crisis. I thought of the cadaver of Gemma Fernandez in the childhood lane, surrounded by people, but immaculately isolated. He was slipping in and out of consciousness, two crimson scars now apparent under the crew of bristly hair: one where the toe cap had made awful contact, the other a present from the unforgiving paving stones. The fat Irish nurse kept asking him: 'What's your name, love? Do you know your name? Come on, tell me your name and we'll laugh about this over a drink next week. Please tell us your name?' Over and over like a mantra. But no name, no sound of any sort, was forthcoming.

A stretcher appeared, and he was shoehorned on to it; the throng parting to allow the catastrophe, the *goner,* through.

Next thing I remember I was in Rudi's car, silently watching the flashing night-time stripes of Shepherd's Bush – the razed, rubbish-tip streets whipping past like a movie beyond the windscreen. Towards Marylebone, I asked him, 'Did you get your business done?'

'That was the business, big man,' said Rudi in his silky voice.

'What do you mean?' I turned to him, shaken. 'You had someone done in?'

'Aw, naw,' he chuckled. 'That bloke, the Moroccan. That should've been *me.*'

The fracas on the platform is over, only a few jeers and shouts can be heard under the steely lights. Very soon we will be heaving off into the blackness . . . That kick, that boot in the head, the crucial death-dealing blow, had been intended for Rudi. Whatever he had got mixed up in was murky indeed; a black well of coshings, garrottings and pay-offs in dodgy Ealing boozers. Recalling that incident put the platform jousting in a different light. There were levels of violence, and I had witnessed, or been on the receiving end, of many of them; had felt that unique typhoon of adrenalin. Only, Rudi currently seemed to be an intrepid explorer into a new and frightening arena. An uncharted midnight.

A whistle blows. Silently, the train begins to move off, towing us all into the dark.

7

Night

November. The Macbeth of months. When night's black agents descend at three-thirty in the afternoon; when feeble, propitiatory, citrine streetlights flicker into life on misty streets. A month before I married, there was a particular November night Mandy and I spent in the tiny recording studio at Rock On putting the finishing touches to Fellatrix's new demos. Strange that this should come back to me now, but something unexpectedly nasty occurred that I have blanked out or erased over time. Curious. I had thought that the vodka-glass incident was the only outrage that gave me reason for concern in those ebullient pre-nuptial days. But this was worse, somehow. More unprovoked, more depressing. I can see it all clearly before me: Mandy's languorous legs hooked under her PVC miniskirt as she sat listening on the studio sofa; the Starship Enterprise constellation of the red lights, the sweet smell of scented candles and incense burning in the corner; and me struggling with the electronic gadgets, eager to please.

It was one of those nights when even the firework terrorists and banger-bandits find it too miserable to venture out. Scything cold.

Green-coloured rain descending in a kind of freezing gauze. Shuddering winos. The streets of Camden black as bin-liners. Add to this the disorientating effect of London darkness lasting twice as long as London day. A day in November which never really brightens from dawn onwards. It may even have been Bonfire Night itself, the troops of party-goers sodden and melancholy on the cold pavements, some waving sparklers against the big wind. But I can't be sure – those days seem to blend and disappear together into an oblivion. There was a closeness between us that evening, the unique closeness of two who have decided to relinquish all others, to take the fatal leap.

'Funny,' I said, in the snug glow of the studio as the tape whirred back to the start of the final track. 'It usually sounds like the Blitz outside at this time of year.' Mandy smiled at me from the couch, her big brown Catalan eyes even larger and moister in the candle-light. She lit a cigarette and allowed a hoop of smoke to ascend over her head.

'Much too cold to be out on a night like this,' she murmured, her voice suddenly quiet in the new silence. 'How long will it take to mix this? We've been here since Martin locked up.'

'Oh, we'll be here all night,' I said, with the confident authority of past experience. 'You can't rush art.' Many times in the past I had curled up to sleep on the sofa on which she was amorously reclining, wrapping the unzipped sleeping bag around me like a winding sheet.

Mandy seemed surprised at this. Her expression darkened. 'We can't kip here! There's no bedding. It's getting cold.'

It was true that the temperature of the night was trying the skylight with its icy fingers. Condensation had formed, which dripped dangerously close to the electrical equipment. I yanked the burn-pocked sleeping bag from beneath the mixing desk and tossed it over to her. 'Here, you have this. I don't suppose I'm going to get much sleep.'

'Whatever you say, lover,' said Mandy, but I could tell she resented roughing it. Nobody had prepared her for the fact that life in a rock 'n' roll band may not be as straightforward as going

into the office five days a week and collecting your salary at the
end of the month. The hours were anti-social, to say the least.
There was no security, no pension-plan, no paid holiday, no degree
or certificate you could produce to say that you had finally
qualified, now-give-me-a-job, please. No, the CD-rack browsers
had no idea that the music they played in their car, that they
danced to, or used for the purposes of seduction or hoovering,
came to them via the most mangled and circuitous route imagin-
able. It was a miracle anything got to them at all. Mandy was
affronted by any endeavour that didn't provide an immediate
return: like a child she demanded instant gratification. There would
be many things, I told her, that wouldn't pay off for years; many
gambles, many things taken on trust, much taking of two steps
back in order to make the vital one forwards. Much sleeping
under the mixing desk and touring the Highlands in a broken
van. Maybe even much sleeping with the producer. After these
lectures she would always smile knowingly, as if I were the dogmatic
voice of enforced drudgery, as if she knew better. Her hidden
weapon, she always insisted, was that she could be a bitch. I sighed
at this bravado, thinking how many bitches had been kennelled
over the years in the pursuit of fame and fortune. Better to be a
lap-dog for the strutting patriarchal powers-that-be than have
your teeth removed one by one. Submission to the beast was
what brought success, for a woman, at least. Madonna included.
But her smiles turned to worrying sneers when I voiced this. At
first, I secretly hoped her belligerent attitude towards the grim
realities of the music industry would somehow fast-track her to
the top. She was too impatient to do the obligatory five years of
starvation on the dole before The Man condescended to putting
his hand into his voluminous back pocket. But now I could see
she was merely unrealistic, a work-shirker, a something-for-nothing
merchant. I didn't mind mixing her recordings, cold and tired as
I was after a long day in the shop. She had recruited me into her
schemes, as usual, without me realising it. And it felt good, just
the two of us there in the creamy candlelight, me happy as the

old maid who has just been married off to the county squire. I was, after all, doing it for love.

'Why don't you put your head down for a bit,' I suggested tenderly. 'Tomorrow's another day.'

But I could see her eyes were already closed; the high-domed lids, glitter-covered, tense and occasionally trembling. Breath from her slightly arrogant, dinted nostrils evaporated in the dank air. I crossed the room and gently wrapped the sleeping bag around her bony brown shoulders and tucked her long legs up under a couple of cushions. She was sleeping soundly. Something about her snoring there defencelessly made me suddenly paternal – worse, made me want to have children with her. I fondly imagined her there with our future offspring, a touching pietà under a tarry fog of fag-smoke.

It was indeed a long cold night. My feet went dead in my shoes, which felt water-logged somehow. By five, with the darkness still sealing up north London outside, I finished the final mix and sought the small kitchen to empty the ashtrays and fill the kettle. My face looked surprisingly white in the tall mirror. The curlicues of age were trying the corners of my eyes, drying my scalp which once grew luxuriant hair in the days of Dovecote Lane. I found it hard to believe that I was on the verge of marriage. The events of my own childhood should have inoculated me against it somehow, but there I was, aged twenty-seven, with my wife-to-be sleeping like an infant in the next room. How did I get here? Whatever route had led me to this November dawn, I felt almost euphoric as I washed two foul tea cups under the cold tap. I smiled to myself as I dried them, and caught my own foolish face in the big bright mirror. No, I shouldn't smile so much, I thought. I look gormless and big-cheeked when I smile, like a hamster at feeding time. The kettle reached its steamy climax and clicked off. I stirred three spoons of sugar lovingly into Mandy's tea and took it through.

Bending over her recumbent form, which had assumed a tight embryo ball during the night, I gently shook her shoulders and said, 'Tea up. Your mixes are done.'

Her big eyes flipped open with a look of unsteady confusion.

She didn't seem happy to be there. She didn't seem happy to see me. In fact, she looked furious. A change had come over her while sleeping. Her bedraggled cascade of hair was stuck under her left shoulder, and she rooted it free angrily, like a horse tossing its mane. She paused for a moment, scratched her head, then took a swipe at the offered cup with the back of her hand. Hot tea arced across the room, painting the already spattered walls and falling into the precious circuits of the mixing desk. The cup clattered to rest, unseen. I was stunned.

'Why the fuck did you make me sleep here?' she seethed and got up violently.

'We had to finish your mixes! Jesus, look at what you've done. You've probably ruined Martin's equipment.'

'I don't give a damn. I'm going home.' And she lurched past me, arms wrapped tightly around her – shivering exaggeratedly as if she had just been retrieved from the deep-freeze like a leg of lamb. This was probably our first or second disagreement or falling out. So I decided to tread very carefully. To give her the benefit of the doubt. Ah, how naive I was to think it was merely a temporary aberration, the time of the month maybe. Then I began to feel hot-headed myself. I was angry that I might lose my job. The desk was probably destroyed – not from the liquid, I knew, but from the sugar (which only Mandy took), which would gum up the components, making it impossible to repair.

'Well, you'd better explain the mess to him,' I asserted as her back disappeared through the door. 'You know – I need this work.'

All I heard from the kitchen was an echoey complaint; soul-deadening in its bleakness. It was the first of many occasions when she used the same sinful phrase to end an argument. Five words which I would grow to hate and fear. She said:

'I wish I was dead.'

Tarragona. New Year's Eve. The last night of our honeymoon. Another long day's journey into night. Why do ructions, gross scenes, fights, always occur under the cover of darkness? Not many people have arguments at sunset or dawn – maybe we are poetic animals after all, receptive to beauty even when we're hating each other. I might as well let you in on the full story, unburden my marriage secrets. What have I got to lose? You've seen us both at our worst, full of sour hatred, wishing each other not divorced but dead. The first inclination I had that Mandy hated me, really despised me, came a week after we married. Far too soon! you might exclaim. But maids are May when they are maids – the sky changes when they are wives.

I think I told you, generous and patient reader, that there was some kind of altercation on the beach during my honeymoon. Now that it's dark I feel I can revisit the scene and tell you what really happened. It's hard to continue while keeping such a heavy burden to myself – we are arrested and trepanned by the past while attempting to function and deal with the present. That midnight, terrible words were exchanged, contemptuous words that should not pass between man and wife after twenty years, let alone seven days. Words that cause intense suffering at their recollection.

Let me share them without restraint.

We had decided to take a walk on the sand. The horn-tooting Barças had fled into the night on their tinny mopeds, hollering *Feliz año nuevo!* and guzzling wine from goatskin gourds. We were both drunk: me with a tottering unsureness of foot, Mandy under the gathering black cloud that always accompanied her inebriation. Far out to sea, the dark breakers shot white foam up the beach under a scroll of fog. A constant, rhythmic threshing sound accompanied these waves, the low foghorn honking somewhere near the harbour. Mandy walked apart for a moment, then started swaying towards the shoreline. By this I knew something was up.

'Hey – can't you slow down?' I called. 'Why are you always walking off?'

I caught her up, and tried to peer into her face. The lash of her forehead scar seemed to glow in the moonlight.

'I've got my headache back.'

'What, the migraine?' I asked.

'What do you think?'

The alcohol had made me less than patient with her. Somewhere within, I felt anger at her stubborn determination to be true to her moods, to be obstinately herself. I also felt scorn for myself: the base anger a tourist feels when he buys something shoddy at a bazaar. My patient approach hadn't ameliorated her caustic moods over the nine brief months I had known her, and I still wanted reparation for the glass in the face, the tea thrown over the studio.

'I don't know, I'm just asking,' I said with rising heat. I was concerned. 'Shouldn't we go back now? You can't go for a swim at this time of night.'

'Do what you like,' she snapped, and tossed her hair back with the quick dynamic movements she used when she was approaching boiling point.

'Why don't you tell me what's the matter?'

Without looking at me, she said: 'You were thinking about Bea earlier, I could tell by your silly expression as we did the grapes.'

Astounded at this telepathy, I said, 'Don't be ridiculous. Come on, let's go back now. It's cold, it's dark.'

But she continued walking. 'Don't bother lying to me, Byron. It was written all over your fat face. You haven't stopped pining since I told you to dump her. What's the point of marrying me if you're constantly mooning over some silly cow, with her stupid university degrees? With that dog's name, too. God, that would've sounded good in the church with her mother looking on – Beatrice and Byron, I do thee wed.'

I was stung by this, as I always was by any mention of Bea. And I knew the jealous reference to Bea's mother arose because she was thinking of Ramona, dead now for many a New Year's Eve. It struck me that this may have been the very beach where Mandy's mother played as a child, tearing along, brown as a walnut under the coruscating heat of a Spanish August. The beach where Mandy may have played herself, Ramona proudly observing behind caramel shades. I changed my tone, ashamed that I had been so insensitive not to predict this delicate area. Why the hell had I said yes to a walk on this tainted sand in the first place?

'Come on, I love you, Mandy. Don't be so venomous, we've only been married a week.'

'And what fun that's been. You haven't even bothered to learn two words of Spanish. What are you like, giving my Gran dirty looks every time her back's turned – all that awkwardness with Leo? They won't bite your head off, you know. They're only human beings.'

'Come off it, Mandy! People's relatives are hard work.'

'I'm a sociable person. It's not my fault you're a hermit who hasn't seen the light of day for seven years.'

'Wait a minute, you clammed up when you met my mum at the wedding.'

'Only cause she hated me.'

'She did not hate – for Christ's sake – I hadn't even seen her myself for a couple of years. She was nervous. She was shy. Weddings aren't her favourite thing, you know. She's twice divorced, or did you forget that?'

It felt odd defending my mother there, on the vast expanse of nocturnal sand, the foghorn sounding far out to sea. Mandy had taken a course parallel to the waves now, and they were loud and furious in our ears, a gush of salty spray spattering our faces.

'It was *obvious* she hated me, Byron. I can read people, you know. I've always prided myself on that. Antonia tells me I'm good at that. Your mother took one look at me and wrote me off as a Spanish floozy. I could tell she was wondering why I was getting married in a miniskirt and why I didn't have my own mother there.'

'For fuck's sake! She knew your mother was dead.'

Mandy span round, her brown eyes now crimson in the difficult light. 'Don't talk about my fucking mother like that!'

'I'm sorry,' I said, scared of her shaking shoulders and feline countenance, as if she were ready to pounce. As yet, I was unaware of her capacities, her boundaries. She hadn't actually hit me thus far, but I realised she dearly wanted to. I decided the best form of defence was attack, always a terrible error with Mandy. I continued, 'I can't stand around on a beach in the middle of the night being screamed at by you. It's not my idea of fun, you know! I've tried my best with your crazy grandmother and Leo lecturing us day and night about children and earning money and God knows what else. I put up with them at each other's throats last year when I first met them, what more do you want? And another thing – so what if I was thinking about Bea? Is that an offence now? We went out with each other for almost a year. She was a good person. A well-meaning, gentle person. What did she ever do to you? You got what you wanted, didn't you? You got me. It doesn't show you in a very good light when you're always laying into her with both barrels blazing. You know, why do you hate people so much? I can't stand to hear it – it poisons the air. And I can't help mentioning mothers now and again, you know. People have mothers, they're everywhere if you look hard enough! And it's not those people's fault if your mother's dead.'

The night had taken on a surreal quality, with the aerodrome noise of the waves, the strange fog and the desert-like vistas of sand. We were dangerously far out. I was afraid of tides, of being cut off, of strange wanderers in the darkness, of Mandy punching me in the face. I noticed that both her fists had remained clenched during my rant. I also noticed that her face was dripping with tears. But not sorrowful tears: instead a cataract of loathing and thwarted supremacy.

'You're full of shit,' hissed Mandy.

I went to touch her, badly wanting contact, but she pulled away viciously. 'Don't say things like that, it breaks my heart.'

Every memory of Barcelona, of the recent glorious days, slowly soiled by her sentence as it lingered in the brutally fresh air; as if a fundamental barrier of respect had been crossed. It was as if she desired the destruction of everything beautiful she ever encountered. I couldn't believe so many cracks had appeared so quickly. She had her game, combative, ready-for-anything face on now.

Neither of us was very drunk any more. Yet, the world felt turned upside down. When I glanced towards the water, the sky seemed to be the sea and vice versa, so disorientating was the fog and the blackness of the waves.

'You're just a short-arsed little prick!' she spat, like a haggard regurgitating a kill. 'What do you know about people dying? About real life. You go around in your own head all day, with your useless books. Sometimes I can't bear to look at you. Like tonight, eating those grapes like a pig, one after another. You're welcome to that fat-arsed Beatrix or whatever her name was.'

'Please don't be like this!' I said pitifully, and went to touch her again. But she threw my hand off with superhuman violence. I felt as if I'd touched an electric current.

'I wish I'd never married you,' she sneered, and strode off into the black, obscure night.

Full of booze and tired beyond reason, I watched her walking away; her shoulders hunched, pushing her diminishing head forward at an angle. I sat down in the sand and grabbed great handfuls of moist gravel and shells. It felt good to make contact with the cold wet ground. Letting the handfuls go like sand through an hour-glass, I smelt the stirring female odours left by the tide. The foghorn sounded, low and mysterious, like an unearthly valediction. The waves were so close now they began to seethe over my trainers, drawing back with a shush like a giant intake of breath. My heart was full of stones. Of intolerable disappointment and anger. The tide was coming in. I tried hard not to fall asleep, though part of me wanted to float out on the great black current, through the Pillars of Hercules and out into the open Atlantic. It seemed like days before I stood up on prickly limbs and made my way to the tide wall, where I walked for an hour before the yellow light of Mandy's cab appeared.

If you had to come up with a defining characteristic of human beings, then it would be mental suffering – not physical suffering.

All creatures great and small undergo physical pain, and I hope my portion of it on this earth is small, but . . . there, I've just illuminated my point: that 'hope' is a kind of suffering too, a phenomenon not experienced by the dog about to be drowned, or the monkey waiting in the vivisectionist's lab. In terms of pain, anticipation forms the larger part of the burden. Claudio couldn't be absolute for death – he had too many visions of nothingness to contend with. It is a mercy, I suppose, that a dog or a monkey doesn't have to prepare its soul for the Everlasting, doesn't have to imagine the agony of those it leaves behind. Until the murder or torture commences, it is blissfully ignorant. If you have to identify the worst thing that's ever happened to you, it probably involved mental suffering. A bereavement. A separation. Physical torture is rare. Not many of us have undergone six hours of having our fingernails pulled out while drops of water batter our foreheads from a pipe in the ceiling – unless you count the Eurovision Song Contest, which Martin and I foolishly declined to enter, as Rose Masquerade eventually made the heats. Of all the love-disasters, a separation that occurs while you're still ostensibly together is probably in the top five of the mental suffering hit parade. The water is all around but not a drop of it is drinkable. When she's in, you make sure you are out. And vice versa. It's hard to be pragmatic about the realisation that your marriage is a catastrophe, but that's what I was forced to contemplate after returning from our honeymoon. What to do? All the top manuals advise you to 'work on it'. But what course of action is there, when working on it makes it worse?

Mandy didn't hit me during that Stygian night on the beach – that came later, after the noisy debacle following the soiree at Stringfellows with Ant, Nick and Victor Moore. That was the night the genie really sprang free of its bottle. Maybe I should tell you what really happened.

Of course, after the first punch, it's all over. You can never return after that firebreak is irreversibly crossed. Things are never really the same again. Strange, because hitting is everywhere – in Western saloon-bar brawls, in books, on TV. They make it look so effortless, balletic, free from comeuppance. But they don't deal with the aftermath, with what the heart feels after the body is struck by another human being. After that first blow it was open season as far as Mandy was concerned. And she used that awful phrase on me a number of times. Not that echo of Mariana's, 'I wish I was dead.' That was merely her daily mantra. No, after her first swing, 'I wish I had never married you!' rang out along Shaftesbury Avenue in the February night. Those seven words seemed to go straight to some essential core, reminding me, as they did, of my stepfather and his peevish, rancorous tirades at my mother. They are, of course, the exact words Delph had used on Sinead, heavy with all the ingratitude and meanness of spirit, all the lowness and spoilt nastiness that it is possible for a human being to summon.

That night, waiting at the bus stop after Strings, me out of puff, Mandy furious that I had spent the night mesmerised by Antonia's heaving bosoms, the cat of violence was allowed to come spitting and scratching out of its bag. She punched me so hard I went back against the phone box, eliciting a terrified look from a Japanese girl inside calling Tokyo. Mandy's expensive watch catapulted into the filthy gutter, where it lay in a trench of rain, the water the colour of despair. She stared at it for a long while, her eyes bulging psychotically, as if the watch was to blame. Then she turned to me.

'Look what you've done.'

I wiped a smear of blood from just above my ear. It looked black on the back of my hand, like soy sauce.

'Like that was my fault, yeah?' I said, feeling nauseous, fractured somehow from the adrenalin shooting around my system. I motioned to pick up the watch, but she went for me again, kicking and scratching and pushing until at last I fell into the gutter. At this, I had to laugh. I lay there as a number twenty-nine rounded the corner and began to bear down on me, laughing into her face at her ludicrous scene, her imitation of a prize-fighter.

'I wish I'd never married you!' she screamed. And it seemed like the whole street turned around to see just who this man could be,

unwanted in matrimony, lying, as he was, in the road with a bus
heading straight for his head.

You may well ask, stern critic, what I was looking for in such
experiences. After all, they tell us that we secretly hang around
what is bad for us, drawn like moths to terrible flames, when every
self-preserving instinct informs us to get out fast. Like the battered
wife who keeps returning for her monthly black eye because she
finds the insecurity of freedom terrifying. They also hint that such
women wouldn't be able to survive without the thrill of having
their self-esteem lowered by a total bastard on a regular basis, but
that never finds its way explicitly into the textbooks. That would
be outright misogyny. But there is something tiresome about the
banal central strut of psychotherapy – the doctrine that, if you state
something one way, you secretly desire it the other. If you claim
to abhor violence you covertly desire it, feeling, as one really does,
in need of such punishment or abuse. That to protest too much
equals a cast-iron case of guilty as charged. All I can say to that is
– absolute balls. Protesting too much more often means that something terrible has been perpetrated against you. Where does one
put the full stop in this protesting? At what point does legitimate
protest turn into superfluous protest?

So there I was on the London street after dark, decked by my
wife. And it didn't end there, either, as you can probably guess.
I'm ready to tell you about Mandy's *pièce de résistance*, her
defining atrocity. You may well recall the night I visited her after
work by surprise. The Hairdressers' Ball. She had just left, so I
ran the gauntlet of the Centre Point junkies until catching up
with the world's angriest woman. What was I after? Why did I
persevere? Well, part of my inability to act derived from a deep
sense of pity that anyone could be so lost, so completely incontinent when it came to their aggressive impulses. Amend that. I
mean that any *woman* could be so incontinent. Violent women are
always fascinating, an anomaly. And I suppose part of me wanted
to play the anthropologist, the therapist, while I helped her on

the long road to knowing how to *behave*. Why do we quake in the irresistible glare of the violent woman, the virago, the tornado of female spite? Because they're not supposed to behave like that, of course. Programmed as they are to bring us into the world, to nurture us, to give suck and buy us toys, to keep us from harm, there is something contradictory, counter-intuitive about women swinging like street fighters and swearing like sailors. To find a tiger's heart wrapped in a woman's hide is a self-replenishing form of astonishment.

And it was with the anthropologist's steady gaze that I observed her on that tube train, sharing our personal strife with a hundred disgruntled passengers. Or at least I tried to keep my head analytical. I think I mentioned that I did something I had never attempted before with Mandy: ignored her. Stepping insouciantly from the carriage at Camden Town just as her voice attained the velocity of an automated bacon-slicer, I resolved for once not to give a damn. According to her, taking in a movie while she was doing that rare thing (a day of work) was some kind of war crime. So take me to the United Nations, I thought. Drag me to the Hague in an armoured car. What are you, my mother? Do you have to dictate my every-fucking-breath? Do I have to consult you when I go to the khazi, just to check the flush doesn't coincide with one of your migraines? Do I really have to apologise for enjoying myself? Haven't I spent the last year of my life trying to get your wretched band off the ground? (Oh, and before we leave the subject – as you might have guessed, Fellatrix were shit. They virtually defined the substance. Despite my valiant attempt to improve them with my lyrics, they were one of the three most talentless bands to have arisen in the northern hemisphere over the past decade, barring the French ones. What else could they have been?) Do I really have to listen to your hysterical voice – like a knife chopping vegetables very fast – laden with threats and personal-level abuse when I have just spent two hours in the divine company of Bergman's solemnly lisping Swedes?

It was with these righteous and pertinent thoughts that I alighted from the tube carriage, recklessly believing that it would put an end to the argument. I had worked up the courage to ignore her, to blank her, to snub her, to freeze her out. And this did take a degree of courage with Mandy. She could be terrifying. I could see the fear in the uneasy eyes of our fellow tube passengers. There was something very ancient in her rages, her spitting onslaughts – a deep pan-gender fear that apprehended the ghosts of Clytemnestra, Medusa, Procne. But I defied all this for a moment. Turn me to stone if you dare then, I thought, as the tube doors clanked shut behind me.

Bad move.

Like in all the worst horror films, the pursuer had pursued me into what I imagined to be my place of safety, the platform. In retrospect, I must have been foolish to think Mandy would take that snub on the chin in front of all those people. No, she would have to save face, have to exact retribution, have to bake my children in a pie. I immediately felt two claw-like hands grasp my hair from behind: two haggard falcons alighting on my head simultaneously.

'You fucking bastard!' her voice raged behind me.

Then the toecap of a boot made contact with my arse. At that point I should have turned and put a stop to it – a stop to her. Instead, I kept on walking. I remember thinking, why do these aberrations always happen at night? Is it true that women are really moon-controlled; that terrible unmanageable energies are unleashed? Still fresh in my mind was the eager sprint I had made behind the Centre Point building in order to catch her up. Past the great dead needle of the tower itself, sentinel over the charred ground of St Giles: the voices of the poor wailing from the palimpsest of paving stones. Strong night forces were at work in the blackened alleys and concrete arches, littered, as they were, with syringes and the humps of dossers in sleeping bags, like rocks at low tide. Once trapped there, you truly knew the bright day was done. The shadow of the great building seemed to suck everything under it into a void. A deathly stillness pervaded among the junkies and clippers. Despite the distant sound of sirens, theatre-goers, boisterous lads on a night up West, I could hear my own heart beat strongly in my temples as I half-ran, half-marched towards the mouth of the tube. And now I was walking calmly up the escalator, with my wife of two months viciously kicking and rabbit-punching me from behind, trying to make me turn, to acknowledge her awful anger.

But I didn't turn.

I kept on walking. I almost felt calm as I took these blows. Not that they didn't hurt, they did. They were directed with fearsome accuracy, each kick and right-hook like a featherweight's well-placed jab. Even when I caught the astonished eyes of the rush-hour hordes pouring down the opposite escalator in their raincoats and well-cut suits I kept my countenance. It was only when I neared the crest of the escalator that a wave of panic swept over me. What if she didn't stop? I didn't mean then, in the immediate future, but ever? What if this was her true nature, her true colours? What if everything that had come before was an elaborate ruse, an undercover operation to ensnare a man so she could enact her pathological fantasies of revenge. Because this punishment in no way fitted the crime. This, for watching a film? Even though I hadn't met her eye since we stepped off the train, I knew she was enjoying herself; that this represented a primal release, with all guns blazing, the very thing she had longed to do to all males from childhood onwards. Maybe because I sensed the great catharsis she was obtaining from this I continued to participate in it for so many unendurable minutes. She knew I wouldn't retaliate, after all. In retrospect, it must have been wonderful for her – it combined the three things she had always craved in a single prolonged act: public recognition, revenge upon men, and proof of her physical strength, all at once. Because she always had a big Amazonian thing about physical strength. She became affronted if things were lifted for her or doors held open. Even her father said she drove like a man, and this was intended as no kind of compliment. She also had a score to settle. Specifically with men. And there I was taking the rap on behalf of every male who had hurt her, left her, mistreated her. As the ticket barriers came into sight, I made a number of mental notes: to seek professional help on her behalf the moment she calmed down; to call her old man and tell him she also punched like a man; and to buy a gumshield in case anything like this occurred again.

I slipped my ticket into its slot, with Mandy still using my rear as an archery butt, noting the wary looks of the station personnel. *Domestic.* I read their thoughts. *Best leave them to it.*

'That's fine, guys,' I said in passing. 'I can handle it.'

But the fury at my back didn't let up.

'Had enough yet?' she shrieked, 'You lazy bastard!' And hurled another punch my way.

An irrational thought struck me as I exited the station, and that was: I'm not dressed for this. Ever since Mandy had started on me, I was aware that I had chosen to sport some of the clothes she had picked out before the wedding in order to transform me from a sartorial joke into someone she could tolerate being seen with in public. I had on blue cord flares, a dagger-collared shirt and an even bigger, half-size suede jacket with fur lining and a chunky zip. Adorning this was a neck tie, borrowed from Nick, tied in a kind of Noël Coward knot, fashionable (believe it or not) in the mid-nineties. It struck me as I ascended the escalator that I must look like some kind of dandy, inscrutably taking my punishment for a bad gambling debt.

Effeminately dressed, too full of forgiveness, not up for this kind of combat, I stepped into the rich navy night of Camden. The smell of onions and peppers and char-grilled meat smacked me in the face. These odours emanated from the risky-pizza stalls opposite the World's End, where mid-week revellers and winos were tumbling past. Gelid, fluorescent light gave the post-work crowd a cadaverous look as they bought their evening papers, grinned into mobiles, or clasped tight the hands of their loved ones. Black cabs swung through the lights of the big intersection, followed by buses lit up like aquariums, the ghostly fish of commuters staring with bored curiosity at an overdressed man getting beaten up by a woman. At that moment, a white van with three bum-crack cowboys sitting up front halted at the pedestrian crossing. The wag nearest to my side of the road pulled the window down, tore the bacon sandwich from his grinning mouth and yelled,

'Oi! I'll teach you how to punch, mate!'

Ah, how that sentence has resonated down the years. I will never forget it, his kind offer of tuition. Almost paternal in its comforting supportiveness. Many aspects of it have struck me as inherently wise, almost philosophically acute, in the ensuing months and years. *I will teach you how to punch, mate.* Apart from its trenchant humour, its mordant drollery, its utterly apposite comment on the situation, I found it referred to a hidden standard of male behaviour that I had somehow neglected to assimilate over the years. It seemed to imply, not only is a man's pride intimately connected with his ability to dish out violence, to *handle himself,* but to handle himself with women. You know, when the old lady gets a bit uppity, a bit out of line. A bit above herself. When she starts (God forbid) swinging punches at you. Because that's just not on, is it? That's out of order. That would mean you were some kind of punch-bag. Or woofter. Somehow less than a man – a boy that was still getting his hair pulled by the girls in the playground. That would imply that she has requested entry to (and been admitted by *you*) into an elite club: that of assumed physical parity, of a kind that exists only between men. Because all men have to assume they have parity – every prompt to fight is a challenge to this assumption: 'Outside, then'; 'Come and have a go if you think you're hard enough'; and, best of all, 'Do you want some?' In other words, *prove it.* All refer to an essential eliciting of proof, of putting one's fist where one's mouth is. Prove it, or stay a poof, is what is generally assumed by this nostrum. Of course, no bird, the leering chippie would assert, could ever win a fight with a bloke. She would be foolish to even try. Inferior strength and all that, let alone deficient brain wattage. And if she did, she knows what she can expect. No, there is no admittance to that exclusive male club of violence, because who knows where it would end? They'd be off fighting wars next, or flying planes, when they should be at home furthering the human race with a baby's bottle in one hand and a new nappy in the other.

In fact, that Neanderthal in the white van looked like the sort of bloke who winced whenever he heard the phrase, 'the men and *women* of the armed forces'. Or saw books with titles such as, *Sacred Autonomy: Radical Feminist Readings of the Policing of Female Behaviour.*

Nevertheless, he undoubtedly had a point. As the van sped off towards Kentish Town in a rodeo of beeps and jeers, I considered how utterly right and wrong his statement was simultaneously. Wrong, because the liberal consensus is that you should never hit women, and wrong again because I didn't need to learn how to punch – I needed to learn how to avoid getting involved with this type of maniac ever again. But the statement was right in the respect that, by letting it happen, I had lost my self-respect. There I was – being pasted by a woman in the middle of a London street. Where the fuck *was* my self-respect? And did I ever have any? These were important questions for me at the time. Yes, along with the sincere urge never to encounter any of the people from the platform, the escalator, the station, or the van ever again in my life, I really had to look into the issue of self-respect.

But the question, or problem, of Byron Easy's self-respect had begun early on, in Wakefield, during a night I am working up the courage to share with you. In fact, there are many heart-troubling incidents that I am working up to. I feel as if I have only told you half the story so far, dear reader, that I have stopped short at the vital moment, a kind of coitus interruptus of the psyche. I feel duty-bound to dish the dirt, to push on with my journey into darkness. To share with you the nasty, perverted truth about these so-called human beings.

Believe me, I wish this didn't all sound like condemnation. I have looked repeatedly for redeeming features, mitigating circum-stances – Mandy's bereavement, Delph's impoverished upbringing. My, they all had it so bad. And didn't I get to know about it! There is another tenet of psychotherapy (a course of aid that I have never undertaken, I should again stress), that urges the patient to forget about the past. To forgive the abuser, because if you don't,

QED, they have won. You are still, in effect, being abused. Only then can one proceed to that great abstract notion, that laughable chimera, self-love. A cute idea, nevertheless. And attractive too, in one's optimistic moments. It's comforting to believe that you can relinquish the past by a sort of mental trompe l'oeil; eradicate the pollution from your mind by the simple act of forgetting it all. But wholly wrong, and dangerous too. The past, as we all know, is part of the present. Where else can we experience the past except in the present? Memory is a function of the present, of current consciousness. The unwarranted memory is the worst – the unpleasant and arresting reminder of former abuse that makes the heart pound, appears without invitation as you are walking down the street, doing the laundry, watching television. We are open to these assailants no matter what mental regime of amnesia we exert. If it was all so easy, Macbeth would have been able to turn his back on the air-drawn dagger and gone for a taco.

How weary all that 'get a life', 'stop living in the past' rhetoric makes me! That one-cure-fits-all nonsense. Dangerous nonsense, too. 'Stop perpetuating the pain by remembering it,' the mantras read. I recall Rudi, that king of mindless bon mots, once insisting that I got some kind of vicarious thrill out of recounting episodes of violence.

'Admit it, Bry,' he had said while uncorking another costly bottle of red. 'You get a kick when you go over this stuff with me. I can see the excitement in your wee eyes.'

Yeah, right. Would he say the same to a rape victim; that they derived a kick from recounting their ordeal? He stated this with arrogant confidence one epicurean night at his place. As if I was there for my own amusement! As if I was some guinea pig for his shallow psychological systems! And Rudi, of all people, pontificating in his carmine shirt like some kind of world authority on pain. Rudi and his purportedly 'happy' childhood. (I am always suspicious of people who announce that they had a perfectly 'happy' childhood, thanks very much. I mean, how did Rudi turn out like he did if he had such a blissful upbringing?) All this irked me, as what we do with pain is very important. Sure, say the textbooks, pain only lasts a second – it is up to us to decide whether we want to sustain it by moping and blaming our parents or past lovers for the rest of our lives. But that doesn't take into account what the writer does with his pain – the man whose response to life is to write it, investigate it, dissect it, like a curse. He doesn't want to forget, he wants to enter areas most are too scared to even approach. Fundamentally the writer, the 'man of imagination' as Coleridge put it, is interested in the nature of violation. He wants to examine it for his own rehabilitation, granted, but he is also journeying, torch in hand, into the darkness for all our sakes. Creation being an act that is at once both supremely selfish and altruistic. The writer demands an answer, not just happiness (that great misleading goal of all psychotherapy – who the hell said happiness was ever on the menu?). He wants to explore the human transaction that has taken place. He doesn't want to listen to platitudes such as Rudi's. That would be a double violation. And, that night, I became angry with him; forcing him to grin sagely. 'That proves you ken what I'm saying!' he hollered. Again, absolute balls! Of course, legitimate affrontedness looks the same as the anger produced by recognising a bad truth about yourself. But how can the observer tell? They cannot! And the more one protests, the bigger the hole beneath one's feet appears. As easily influenced as I was (and as pissed), I remember checking myself for the verity of Rudi's allegation that I enjoyed being a victim and, almost at once, found it lacking.

'I'm trying to believe in higher human conduct . . .' I struggled, knowing that Rudi had already made up his mind. 'Not the world you believe in.' Which was, I knew, a world of deception and perversity. A world reduced to a mesh of submissive and dominant relationships, an index of cruelty.

'You're just living in the past, Bry. You gottay move on.'

'Maybe, but I stand by the legitimacy of feeling my own pain till I die. Good for you if you've mastered your own anguish – though I thought you didn't have any. But I don't believe it for a moment. Good for you if you're not perpetuating your own pain by morbid memories. It's just not the best method for me.'

Ah, Roman times! And I don't mean the carousing at Rudi's, but the epoch when we were nearer bestiality, in a historical sense. Human excoriation at the coliseum. Sacrifices to Apollo. I can see the atavistic residue of this in Rudi's conception of the world. A theatre of cruelty and emotional blood-lust. Throw me to the lions, why don't you! Tell me I spend most of my time dwelling on violence and revenge. Much more time than my timid face would suggest. If he had been the victim of such violence, then he might not be so quick to make careless pronouncements about me 'getting a thrill from receiving it'. Because this is the saddest thing about those really in denial: their refusal to believe they were ever victims. The Californian rhetoric utilised by the self-help guru (greying, pony-tailed, with moist beaming eyes) attempts to convince these spineless fools that nothing was ever done to them. But, of course, it was. They were all victims of another's appetite, sexual or other-wise. At least I could admit I was a victim. And the world would be a healthier place if everyone else could too. As for the thrill bit: of course, cathartic violence is thrilling, but only for its progenitor. I could tell Mandy was deriving much pleasure from pistol whip-ping me up that escalator, just as I enjoyed hurling that bottle through the window the night she refused my kind offer of cunni-lingus. But being on the receiving end a thrill? I don't think so, somehow.

Against the brutalities of ancient Rome, of current psycho-analytical thinking, I offer the innocence of my first five years. Things were better then, when I was boy eternal. Everything was right. Everything was forgivable. And how the human animal demonstrates altruism or forgiveness was of great importance to me just after the split. Even though we are the only species to exact revenge, we also have the capacity to swing the other way: some people seem to have a forgiveness that is meta-Christian. Unfortunately, it is the Nietzschean view that has inculcated us against so-called weak and foolish reactions to violation, the 'slave-morality' that tells us to turn the other cheek. And maybe he had something. All the evidence indicates that the meek will not inherit the earth, oh no. The meek shall get the shit kicked out of them and then get told by their best friend (and probably their greying, pony-tailed, moist-eyed therapist) that they enjoyed it.

That night of tears and madness in Camden didn't conclude with White Van Man's wonderful aperçu about teaching me to punch. There was a dire postscript. As I walked up the Kentish Town Road, turning the other cheek, I felt the intensity of her blows and verbal onslaught increase. Gone was the teeming life of the station, replaced by the charcoal portal of the Devonshire Arms, a Goth pub that always seemed livelier than the spartan old men's boozers dotted along that strip of road. The cumin and garlic stinks of the noodle bars had been replaced by the odours of wet sand, dust and sewage from the building works near the lock. The stars were dazzling in the sky, throwing down their spears on the fighting fools below. Once on the hump-backed bridge, where the canal slithers sullenly below the road, with its moored barges and glittering vistas of reflected light, I became aware that Mandy had stopped following me. I turned and was met with the sight of my wife stretched out in the centre of the road, her sheeny blue mac beneath her, like Joan of Arc waiting for the first torch to set light to the kindling. Luckily, there had been a lull in the traffic, but a stream of cars had broken away from the distant lights, heading straight for her.

'For Christ's sake! 'I shouted. 'Is that what you really want?'

She didn't reply. It was too late to quibble. I ran over and dragged her, kicking and struggling like a toddler, to the safety of the kerb before the first car swept over the hump of the bridge. So she had finally gained my attention by offering to kill herself. For a long time afterwards I wondered what would've happened if I had just let that car roll over her. That would have taught her a lesson, I thought. But, of course, like most lessons given to the stupid, the pedagogue is the main beneficiary.

The fall-out from that appalling night resulted in a week of non-communication. I felt, bruised, ill, anguished, confused . . . You are the first person I've shared this with, and I'm still not sure I can trust you with the knowledge. This of course is part of the special trouble I referred to earlier, that you might have difficulty understanding. Not the usual writer's trouble, money-trouble, soul-trouble; but crazy scenes such as these. I mean, have you ever experienced anything similar? And if you have, what did you do with such moments? Under what heading did you classify them? What taxonomy can encompass such unleashed spite, mania, martyrdom? Even Hazlitt, in his *Liber Amoris*, would struggle to write up this sort of stuff and keep his sense of humour.

So, did I ever learn to punch? Well, later that year, as Mandy lay on the bed after the abysmal scene in the curry house, I had my first lesson. Terrible to admit it, but it felt quite natural, hitting a woman. It all came easily, as it does to many men, programmed as they are for violence. I think I mentioned that evening witnessed one of the most bloody battles ever recorded in domestic history. Well, there was blood and for once it wasn't mine. After my bottle of lager had sent shards of glass over her Latina bedspread she looked up at me with bored scorn. Then she turned contemptuously away. Her words to Sarah from earlier resonated in my head. 'You – are – a – stupid – fat – whore.' No, there was no way she was getting away with that, I thought, as the red mist descended before my eyes. No way she could flagrantly insult people dear to me. It was at that moment that I realised I really did have people dear to me – strange how the saying of vile, forbidden things should clarify one's own thoughts. I really did love my sister; unspotted and undeserving of such calumny. And my mother too, sitting there patiently in black, as if, like Chekhov's Masha, in mourning for life itself. I really didn't want Sinead exposed to such perverse hatred, not at her time of life, after all she had gone through, after all she had done for me. This finally pushed me over the edge.

Approaching Mandy on the bed, I thought I saw a gratifying flinch of fear in her face. This, after all, was just what she had counted on me never doing. As she rolled over, she laughed at me. Then I smacked her in the face.

———

My heart is pounding at the recollection of all this. I didn't like the man I had become that night, full of curry and beer, knocking the missus about. No, I didn't expect such things in my life . . . The train is rollicking through the dark enclaves of the North – Dales gates and low cottages. It really is impossible to see any detail outside the smeary window, just the racing cables rising and falling. Beyond that, nothing. Darkness visible. Forcing one to peer inward. The darker it gets beyond my window as the train hurtles towards Wakefield, the more, paradoxically, I find I can see.

Michelle is still sitting before me, writing text messages (most probably effusive Christmas greetings to her friends and family), while Robin has vacated his seat to 'spruce up', as he termed it. We are getting closer to the end, closer to the final destination. The feeling of warm incipience at King's Cross has been replaced by contemplation of final things. We are all saying goodbye somehow. I take out my battered notebook and balance it on my knees so Michelle cannot sneak a peek at what I'm writing. That was a bad move to show her the passage about Mandy's card earlier on. Pearls before swine, and all that. *That card – the corny but touching bougainvillea curling from well-kept window boxes, the simple Mediterranean light evoked by a wash of powder-blue from the watercolourist's palette. And that heart-rending message, in my wife's all-too-familiar hand (I hadn't seen it for a couple of months, but I recognised it instantly: from birthday cards, inscriptions on flyleafs, cheques written for goods we couldn't afford).* 'Our little home. We'll find it one day'. *And which day was that to be?*

Why did she give me such false hope? Such final cruelty. My heart thunders when I think of that last card. 'Our little home' — admitting to the dream of safety, of permanence, of becoming each other's family (in the absence of parents) that we had both secretly entertained before getting married. How could she so be so arrantly contradictory? How could she leave me, deceive me, then write such nonsense? She must hate me very much, I concluded, to send this masterpiece of contradiction. What perversity! 'We'll find it one day . . .'

It is getting late now, late in my curve or journey: it is now a question of racing time to its inevitable conclusion. An idiot-check on the Self. What do I have left? Thirty years at the most. The best is past. I am closer to the end than to the beginning. Why not put an end to it now, the sad and sorry dance, the flicker of shadows on a screen that passes for this life. I could get off at the next station and put my head on the line. No, too much anticipation, too much mental suffering. And way too much blood. What about pills? My mother is sure to still have her apothecary's kitchen cupboard full of potions. Why wouldn't she? Yeah, pills would do the trick; to flow out gently on the current — through the Pillars of Hercules, shaking hands with Thanatos as darkness descends before my eyes. Hold on, I really don't want my mother to find me dead in her house! Now that would be an insult. No, somewhere private where I won't be disturbed. And a gun. If only I could find one! A gun is always the best option. Swift and clean. The quick gesture with the tensed finger and the longed-for oblivion. Hopefully.

There arrives a time in one's life when you forget what you came here for. Especially once you've hit thirty. Like the visit to the corner shop where you wander around annoyed, racking your brains, wondering what the hell it was you needed. What did I expect to find, on the plateau of my thirties? Peace, harmony, children, a break in the battle? Success, respect, vindication, a happy marriage? Career and family? No, none of these are present in my life, aged one-score and ten. The famous summit proved to be an optical illusion. Instead, all I encountered was more of the same: intense death-anxiety, regret, failed love, thwarted aspirations, stagnation, saliva.

Of course, a shrink would conclude that I had separation anxiety, or abandonment issues — that I should learn to say goodbye more easily: to people, to my twenties, to this vale of tears we all eventually have to relinquish. And he would be correct in saying so. Extend that anxiety to places and the seasons and he would be even more acute. I could never leave a house, or a summer month, without intense, childish sadness. Leaving my mother's place the last time I saw her caused great upheaval, agony even. I remember taking a moment to myself on her balcony that overlooked the usually dour Leeds–Liverpool canal. At once the sun came out, piercing, pastoral. A stolen pleasure there on that ledge: the buffeting gusts and sun-supernovas on the ripples, like beaten panels of adamant; the armadas of mallards arriving for a feed; the dreadful flame in the poplars; everything shockingly bright, afterlife-bright; everything tainted, somehow, with death.

'That bog doesn't get any cleaner,' announces Robin, breaking my reverie. 'Looks like a football team has puked down it.'

'I think I might have contributed to that,' I confess weakly from my facing seat.

Ignoring this, he turns to his still-texting wife and asks, 'What's the next station, Mich?'

'I think it's Wakefield, darling.'

At these words my heart seizes. I had forgotten that the dreaded wooltown was the next stop. I feel a hot humming in my ears, my chest expanding with unmanageable emotion. I really don't need to see Wakefield.

'Excuse me,' I stammer, getting to my feet. I will have to sit this one out in the smoking car. All the negative capability in the world won't get me through the sight of the raw name on the platform sign. Wakefield – the very noun in its first syllable is somehow treacherous, dangerous, foreboding. Our visits there in the 1970s always felt like some kind of wake. The rain, the satanic mills, the graveyard streets. A funeral for my mother and real father – the death of childhood.

Bursting through the five adjoining carriages I feel as if hornets have taken residence in my stomach. First I have to find someone from whom I can cadge a cigarette. Helps if you're female, I always reflect . . . I am in the sparsely populated, overlit smoking carriage,

a rank cloud in the air, like the aftermath of an explosion. I survey
the booths and choose my victim. A man with high Aryan
cheekbones is sitting with his back to me in row F. He is bearded in
that self-consciously rugged way men adopt when they want to co-
opt some extra quotient of masculinity: he's too young for it – like
Kris Kristofferson in *Alice Doesn't Live Here Anymore*. I clear my
throat and the man turns. Suddenly I am face to face with Delph
Tongue.

———

Wakefield, the mid-seventies. Where my self-respect made its
last stand. For some obscure reason, I always associate the place
with child molesters. Why, I have no idea, because nothing of
that order ever happened to me there. Some of the men just
resembled nonces, that's all. Not the feeble-framed flasher with
his rheumy eyes and comic chuckle, but a harder, altogether
more professional beast. The man (usually a family man, maybe
even a pillar of the community, like the football manager or
school governor) dedicated to a career of self-justified paedophilia.
His face meaty and ingenuous; his look stern, opaque, plausible.
There he'd be at the five-a-side game of a weekend, leering the
boys on, leading the whistles and applause. In his more casual
moments, he would take the guise of the donkey-jacketed
bogeyman, with his tremendous impunity, walking his mutt by
the monumentally depressing slag-heaps or closed-down collieries.
Hanging around the swings, 'playing cheeky' with his dog, as
Delph would put it. Of course, he would discreetly disappear at
any sign of an adult. Undetectable to any but a trained eye. But
once you notice, he is *everywhere*.

So why should I notice, and why should I care? No pillar of
the community ever tried to put his pillar into me. Because it didn't
happen up there, it happened at home, where these things have a
habit of happening. I might have to deal with some unfaceable
things here . . . There comes a time when we all have to face

unfaceable things. I may as well tell you a few more secrets I've been putting off for some time, reader. After all, we don't know how much longer we'll both be around. We must speak now while we still have the chance, still have the time.

The hour is midnight (when else?) and I am ten years old. I have just been very naughty (an unremembered and unremarkable misdemeanor), requiring a back-hand blow from my friendly 'uncle' Delph as I cowered at his unusually loud voice. After this he ordered me to get in the bath and prepare for bed. Where is my mother? I don't remember. No, that's right — Delph is 'babysitting' — ironic as he is a baby himself, savagely overgrown. It is a Sunday night, or the Sabbath, as Delph insisted on calling it. My mother is out, and I have sensed her dangerous absence all evening. With her not present, anything could happen. The curious thing is that the evening had been harmonious up to the predictable eruption. An inedible tea of baked beans and burnt bangers. An episode of *Charlie's Angels*. The construction of a Meccano robot claw. But a ruction was always a sure-fire occurrence when alone with Delph. He would have to play the tyrant before the day was out — for a man like him it was irresistible. For half an hour I had struggled quietly with my bolts and washers as he smoked and guffawed at *Man About the House*. I had stayed silent while he made mysterious calls on my mother's phone. Then I put a foot wrong. I wish I could recall the offence! As his intimidating frame towered over me, male to male, all the more soiling for the concord of the evening thus far, I felt guilt for upsetting the applecart. But was it my fault? Something I said, most likely, inflamed his righteous opprobrium. And I had to let his fury run its course. He had to ruin everything — that was an absolute rule with him.

Number fourteen Dovecote Lane had felt big and empty that night, all the lights burning uselessly, like a showroom. (Why do I remember this detail? Because Mum always insisted on the lights being extinguished in an unoccupied room, that's why.) Corner lamps glowed, softening the vulgar black-and-orange-spored design of the bouncing sofas. Sudden noises were magnified. A torque of strain could be registered around the whole house. After his explosion, shaken, humiliated, scared, alone, I ventured down the stairs (which seemed bright as Crystal Palace) to say goodnight as instructed to Delph, who was sitting brooding, massively spreadeagled on the sofa.

'The little heathen's ready for bed then?' he grinned mirthlessly from his perch in front of the telly. I hated being called a heathen. Even though I had no idea what it meant, I knew it was derogatory.

'Yes,' I said in a small voice.

'Why don't thou come and sit thyself down next to me. The God-spot's just about to come on. That'll improve yuh. One day your mouth will get you hung,' he said, though in a quieter voice than before. His legs were dramatically splayed, a great distance between his bony kneecaps.

I didn't want to comply, but there seemed no choice, no mother to run to, no excuse at hand. More worrying was his changed, conciliatory tone. The old hot-and-cold routine. He had utilised this before after a cataract of violent rage – it was disorientating in the extreme. My dressing gown felt big and cumbersome over my pyjamas. I could smell the apple shampoo that I had used on my hair, which I had been permitted – with seventies *laissez-faire* – to grow long. There was something threatening about the forced amity of Delph's half-smile. A kind of Fagin's leer. I stood for a moment before walking forward and depositing myself at the far end of the sofa; the adrenalin of humiliation making me unusually aware of everything. My hands felt hot and too big, like the flesh pinnacles of delirious dreams. I could smell the reek of Rothmans from Delph, sitting a foot away, examining me with an evaluating smirk. I could hear the drip of rain from the lane outside, the odd car rumbling past. I wished very much that one of them was my mum's.

'Why don't thou cuddle up next to me,' he said, his voice egregious in the silence.

'I don't want to,' I answered in the sulky tone available to all children, the one that constitutes their only defence. Children learn the value of their consent, their volition, at an early age. Delph's invitation was really quite stunning. At no point in his sojourn had he ever made any physical contact with me, other than blows. He wasn't what you call touchy-feely. He was a cold, vain, dynamically unpredictable man. The notion of sitting next to the tyrant of minutes before was a nauseating thought. And perplexing, too. At that age I couldn't reconcile anger and contrition, violence and warmth; the capricious swing from one extreme to another. I also knew there were adult appetites in play, phenomena I didn't understand.

'You might catch cold after your bath.'

His eyes were burning a hole in the side of my skull. I remained resolutely fixated on the Archbishop of Canterbury who was expostulating with a furrowed brow on the black-and-white screen, wringing his hands. Then, with a big easy movement to the left of me, Delph's rearing arm reached over and scooped me over onto his horrible lap.

My heart pounded as I murmured, 'It's not that cold. You don't have to.'

'Aye, but I want to,' he said, with a sentimental burr.

The scene before me is extremely vivid. The things you think you miss at the time are the things you remember for ever. I can picture the saffron blinds, whose job it was to keep out the night, lifting and falling in the breeze. Our cat curled almost once around itself in an embryo-like huddle on the paisley beanbags. The smell of the ashtray, acrid, with its raw dogends-and-beer stink of pubs, unavoidable a foot away from my nose. The squirls of peacocks on the shade of the standard lamp. The steel couplings on the underside of the square Habitat coffee table, the table that would spend half its life on its back. And the big, inadmissible hands of Delph, hugging me to him, stroking me with an overmanning tenderness which, he probably imagined, conveyed all his shallow contrition.

I suppose he must have copped a feel. Every part of my body was touched in time. His strong, hot sentimental grasp wouldn't let me go for what seemed like an hour. I remember him cooing soft, penitent sentences into my ear as he did this; shame for his loss of temper earlier. I don't remember exactly what was said. I was too confused by this unprecedented scene, the fact that he was holding me in a manner which healthy adults would term 'inappropriate'. But he was sorry. That much I understood. So very sorry for scaring the wits out of me. He wanted to make it up to me somehow. He wanted to show me, to give me as much affection as his foolish, hasty hands could afford. I don't suppose it went further than that, but his hands that had greedily appropriated everything in my life (my mother; my self-respect) must have irresistibly found their way to my unprotected parts, and taken whatever twisted pleasure they could as he fondled them. His satyr-like rapture continued until he was startled by the sound of a key turning in the lock. With surreal alacrity, he pushed me to the other end of the sofa and set my dressing gown straight.

Seconds later, my mother was in the room, face to face with her lover and small son, innocently watching the archbishop arguing the finer points of Anglican theosophy with an interviewer who resembled Gary Glitter.

I didn't tell a soul. Especially not my mum. I didn't want to cause pain by revealing that her trust had been betrayed; that Delph was a dissimulator of the highest rank. I didn't bother to inform her about a similar betrayal that occurred on a schooltrip to Wales either. This time, more predictably, it involved that old short-eyes, Mr Cave, the headmaster.

The formidable, salt-laden, sin-laden air of Anglesey, exposed as it was to the broadsides of the grim Irish Sea, was just what Hamford Boys' School deemed invigorating for their first years. The April after my eleventh birthday two minibuses of farty, boisterous lads made their way to Wales for a week at a ramshackle bed and breakfast. A week of awful teas and orienteering in depressing windcheaters. Of course, any excursion that admits only males comes to resemble military manoeuvres. This pleased the martinet Reverend Cave very much. His chastising voice could be heard in the early morning outside our doors, rousing us for a bracing dip in the medicinal waves. Army discipline, conflated with the rhetoric of Christian soldiery, was what us 'orrible little oiks required, apparently. You can be certain that we were all out of our blankets like a shot. We all complied. Any delay would have him charging into the room and plunging his hand (reduced to a freezing temperature under the cold tap beforehand) down your pyjama trousers. And nobody desired that. Nobody wanted to see his sweating upper lip (thin as a curl of ham), hear his despotic voice, or behold his gloating, sly, confident eyes behind coke-bottle specs appear in the room when they were in a state of *dishabille*.

One night, towards the end of that comfortless week, I developed a stomach-ache after the beastly evening meal of fish pie and spotted dick with custard. There was nothing else for it but to seek help from teacher. A visit to Mr Cave after dark was strongly inadvisable, but at ten o'clock, my guts aching and lurching, I was forced to knock on his door and request aid. As I rapped my knuckles on the wood (faintly, so he should not hear me), I was shocked to find him already waiting there, like a praying mantis, his air of faux formality slightly ruffled from whatever furtive activity I had disturbed him at. Book marking? Orisons? Masturbation? Or some awful combination of all three?

'Sir, I've got a tummy upset.' My voice was loud in the drab hallway, the yellow lights abruptly flickering off as their timer expired.

'Well, well, well! Mr Easy has a tummy ache, has he?' gloated the headmaster. 'Let's see if I can be of assistance to a wounded soldier.' His sealed eyes, slitted as a lizard's, full of fraudulent friendliness and malice, assessed me. They were alive with excitement.

'That's all right, sir. My mum gives me bicarbonate of soda, if you've got any of that. Or a Rennies.'

'How do I know what to give you if I haven't examined you?!' roared Mr Cave, forgetting for a moment that he was a reverend and not a doctor. 'Come in and take a pew.'

The door closed behind me and I took in the room, with its

sickly light. It was bigger than our dorm, with two cases neatly stacked against a wall and a desk which bore a Bible and a spare pair of thick-lensed reading glasses. For a moment he circled me, then went to what I assumed was a medicine chest in the strongly lit portal of the bathroom. I felt I had to say something to fill the silence.

'It's okay, sir,' I trembled, my voice cracking beyond control. 'I'm feeling a bit better all of a sudden.'

'Now, now,' he chuckled, like a demented Faustus in his study. 'You're just a bit anxious, I can see that.' He was in front of me now, reptilian and hungry, bearing a glass fizzing with Alka Seltzer. 'What I'm about to give you won't hurt. Quite the opposite. It will set you right . . . my, my, you are a wounded soldier.' He gave me the glass, invading my personal space, a perfunctory smile on his pursed lips. 'Never doubt the wisdom of your Dr Cave. The lion must lie down with the lamb. Drink it up now. To the last drop.'

It didn't take long. He had to resort to scriptural quotation on every occasion. That was part of his salesman's patter. And he was trying to sell me something. An experience I had to buy whether I wanted it or not.

'Thank you, sir,' I said, my knees knocking together, wishing very much that he wouldn't stand so unbearably close.

'Is it all down?' he asked, taking the glass from me and examining the dregs under the pale yellow light in the ceiling. 'I saw one of our coloured brethren earlier – Singh. He had an upset tummy too. Informed me that it was against his religion to eat such a repast as the good Lord gave us tonight.'

Ah yes, the race issue. Mr Cave would often start assemblies with the phrase, 'Children whose parents are from hot countries . . .' Singh's parents, as we all knew, were born in Luton.

'I think the word he used was "rubbish", sir.'

'What?'

'Not repast – rubbish.'

'Well, that's as may be. Now, I just need to examine your

abdomen, to check there's nothing seriously wrong. Take off your pyjama top.'

Terrified, I did as I was told. Mr Cave's unusually cold right hand pressed my stomach and I flinched. It felt like a fish fresh from its packing of ice.

'Are you as obliging as your name suggests, Mr Easy?'

'Your hands are cold, sir.'

He pressed again, even harder. 'Now, that didn't hurt did it? Believe me, boy, I've seen it all. There's nothing new under the sun. Ecclesiastes.'

'If it's all right, I'd like to go now,' I stammered, and swallowed hard.

'All in good time,' he grinned, his broad face colossally near to mine, like a lover's about to bestow a kiss. I observed that his respectably greying temples were narcissistically trimmed and neat. His brisk and cordial glance had narrowed to almost nothing, like gun-slits on a pill-box. I felt uniquely powerless, as his white, slab-like hands journeyed lower. Hands that held hymn book and Bible every Sunday while he advised his congregation how to live.

'Now, let's just check if your waterworks are in order and we'll be finished.'

His free hand gripped my shoulder to steady us both for the possible recoil. Then he fondled me for what seemed like fifteen, twenty seconds. I thought, in those dismal moments, of Mr Cave's wife – often at the school, mute and shy, a silly gormless prude. I wondered whether she knew he got up to this. Picturing her tiny body and mouse-like hands (an almost representative picture of suppliant femininity), I pondered whether Mr Cave thought of little boys as he did it to her. Even if she knew his true proclivities, I concluded, she would have no say over whether it was right or wrong. She would conspire with him, forgive him, in the Christian manner. She would try to understand him; let him have his way. At any trial in a court of law she would cite St Paul and the sacrosanct doctrine of a husband's supremacy in every matter. She obeyed, and enjoyed her subordination. Yes, Mr Cave had chosen well in his wife.

The abominable, arrested moment over, Mr Cave withdrew his hand and became dismissive in his manner. His top lip was glossy with sweat. He was doing the perfunctory dance of the lover who has taken his fill. 'Everything seems shipshape, young man. Now, get to your bed. If you need me, you know where I am.'

He gave me a last look, one that seemed mired with depravity; with the joy he took in his own dissimulation. I bolted towards the door, hastily pulling on my pyjama top.

'Easy!' he shouted as my hand found the brown plastic knob.

'Yes, sir?' I said, startled.

'What do you say?'

'Thank you.'

'Thank you what?'

'Thank you, sir.'

Then I was out into the abyss of the corridor, scrambling in the dark for the timer-light switches that were nowhere to be found.

He'd been at it for years, I later discovered. Decades of experience and practice had gone into that moment. There was a definite feeling that Mr Cave delighted in doing something well, with swiftness and skill – almost as much as he delighted in the sexual objective itself. A vain, narcissistic conceit, the flatulent stench of powerful abilities successfully demonstrated, had filled the sickly room that night. For years I marvelled at the ingenuity and persistence of men such as Delph and my headmaster. The brazen fraudulence of their actions. But then, how skilled do you have to be to stick your hands down the pyjama trousers of a terrified child? Not very, I concluded. And maybe I got off lightly. Maybe other boys had tales of sodomitical terror that would haunt them for the rest of their lives, whereas I only had the cold, fishlike hand of Mr Cave cupping my balls to contend with.

The fact I found hardest to reconcile at that age was that both Delph and Mr Cave were either married or soon would be. How could men who dug chicks find such practices arousing? When my mother tied the knot for the second time, on that nuptial day in

June, the vision of Delph on the sofa came back to me as I watched his big hands push the wedding band up my mother's fleshy finger. The vicar stood impassively, unaware of who he was dealing with. But did this vicar also secretly fondle little boys, or worse? Was the world just a stinking cesspool of lies, evasions and perverse sexual desire? Or was it the Eden I walked into after the ceremony, with Sarah skipping through the late blossoms outside the church?

A parallel question could be, how skilled do you have to be to hit an eight-year-old boy? How much talent does that take? To hit another grown man demands a high degree of courage and skill. Tactical, physical, medical even. There is a great deal of prior assessment to make in that moment before the blow is dealt. One has to consider: will this result in great pain, injury and even my own death? Or will I get away with it – will I be vindicated through a combination of strategy, physical strength and dexterity? Not so with an eight-year-old. To all intents and purposes an eight-year-old is a punch-bag, the softest of all targets. The one thing any man contemplating hitting an eight-year-old boy can be sure of is that it doesn't take much skill. Also that he won't receive a pasting in return.

These latter considerations must have been dimly, atavistically, present in Delph's mind as he slammed the car door that night in Wakefield after the wedding reception and thrust forward in first gear. Everything I mentioned before about that night was only part of the story. Things got a lot worse. I could tell at once that he was in the mood for a scrap. If he thought an eight-year-old boy wouldn't put up a fight he was wholly correct. Because after we left the razed community centre and its pube-bearded ushers (facial hair which denoted manliness up north, but would've raised an eyebrow in even the hardest Old Compton Street gay bars down south), a terrible event occurred. I remember the rain-dripping intensity of the black Wakefield streets as the car did sixty over hump-backed bridges; Delph's hunched, cleft-chinned visage bent over the wheel. The veins improbably big on the backs of his hands. Through the rear window of the vehicle I could see the blue cloud-cover had parted, magically revealing the moon, cold and voiceless and ancient. A disco song – Elton John and Kiki Dee's 'Don't Go Breaking My Heart' – had been the last disc spun by the DJ, and was now on a loop in my head. Moments before the record had come on, Delph had been trumped in some argument with my mother. He had insulted her. Threatened to hit her. Now he was a seething pressure-cooker of pent-up fury. Muttered curses rose over the rapid, grinding gear changes, the tyres squealing around the bends of residential streets. Heart pounding, hoping we would reach the blighted hutch of his parents' house soon – a surprising desire, as I despised being there – I held onto the back of the passenger seat. But I could tell we were nowhere near. We seemed to be on the outskirts of the town: big raw-smelling stretches of water were suddenly visible under stone bridges, lit by the strange lunar glow. Nearby, the crowning lamps of unfamiliar estates whipped past, with their steam-blowing men walking unhappy dogs by dank walls. Dead flowerbeds on municipal greens appeared as plots in a graveyard; the chained gates of failing collieries black, meshed and mysterious in the moonlight.

Eventually the car slowed and we turned into a cul-de-sac. With a wrench of the wheel, Delph pulled up in a narrow driveway and turned off the engine. He swung round to face me.

'Now you just stop here and say nowt,' he snarled, showing his big square teeth. Then he added for good measure: 'You little bastard.'

Booting open the car door, he headed up the drive towards the pale orange gleam of a porch. I trembled, not knowing where we were or what would happen next. A figure of a woman, big and voluptuous, obscure in the murky light, appeared in the doorway. Delph quickly disappeared inside.

Waiting there, the car at an angle on the steep drive, the moon big and sinister through the misty back window of the Vauxhall Viva, turned out to be one of the central moments of my childhood. But negatively central. Not the sun-epiphany you carry forever like a brimming bowl of milk, but its opposite. The yin to its yang. A cancer that coils malignantly inside, feeding on the healthy body for years to come. There was an oppressive silence in the car, with me straining to hear noises from inside the house, wondering who on earth this woman was, where the hell we were, what my mother was doing on her own, and, ultimately, what Delph would do to me. My heart was high in my mouth for what felt like hours: sodden, desultory hours, my soul as wet and heavy as a sheet on a washing line. *Don't go breaking my heart. I couldn't if I tried.* To revisit that scene is like standing in the anteroom of Hades, with Pluto waiting in the central labyrinth, biding his time until my arrival.

Then a rankling, ratcheting sound as the front door opened fiercely, expelling Delph into the night. I heard voices, suddenly loud, that must have been speaking all along. The mysterious woman was straightening her top in the orange light, an angry defiance in her stance. Delph tumbled back into the car, flicked on the engine and roared in reverse down the drive in what seemed like one continuous movement. With me more terrified than ever, we tore along until we reached the first set of lights. I sensed that Delph was angrier, if that was possible, than before. His contorted, papery-skinned face turned to me as we stood on red.

'This is all your fault, you little bastard,' he sneered, the grimace distorting his features, allowing his full ugliness to appear in his face. 'You're in everybody's way. Can't you bloody see that at least?'

Then a back-hand blow sent me flying onto the stinging plastic seats. My head span with white points of light. There was psycho-pathic force in his punch. Some inwardly monitoring voice told me this was all consistent with the behaviour of a bully – they wait to get you alone and let you have it. That way, any testimony after the event can be made to seem like your exaggeration. But there was no time to ponder this as the car catapulted forward, throwing me into the footwell as we took off.

No, it doesn't take much to hit an eight-year-old boy. Not much courage or skill. Not much in the way of adding up the pros and cons of his retaliation. Because he won't retaliate. Because he is weaker and smaller. Delph, bullied at school before he in turn became a bully, knew the ins and outs of picking on somebody weaker and smaller. You could be a bully too, he discovered, if you chose your mark with care. As my head swam with stars, I recalled his boastful tales of drowning puppies in the canal as a boy, or dressing up male corpses in women's clothes at his mortuary job. Gratuitous cruelty to things weaker and smaller – if not actually dead – was his speciality. I watched his enraged hands grip the wheel as we tore back towards the centre of town, the car now flying through red lights. His speed was reckless. I worried more for pedestrians than for our safety. Every time his cigarette burnt down he scrambled for his pack of Rothmans on the passenger seat and lit another with the butt of the last. The blow to my face now started to smart. A flash of powerful pain, modulating to a leaden ache by the time his parents' terraced street was in sight. The song again – '*Woo hoo . . . nobody knows it . . . but when I was down, I was your clown.*' A bubble of self-pity welled in my throat, but I stayed it. Something told me that crying would do me no good. Tears would act like drops of petroleum on the embers of his scorn, so I held them in – water behind a dam.

At long last the car's speed dipped, and we pulled up in front of the dimly lit miner's house. I contemplated with dread the scrubbed concrete stoop, the gaggle of empties, like gossiping women, left out for the milkman. A comfortless inner sanctum where alien-accented, resentful strangers awaited me. Delph killed the engine and ordered me from the car. Something super-intensified about the reflections in the street struck me. The cobbled road was silver and platinum. I turned to see the moon again, a big eye at the end of the street.

'And I don't want to hear a peep out of you,' he snarled.

'When's my mum coming back?' I asked, panicky. The first words I had uttered all evening. I could feel my pulse thundering in my eardrums.

'Never you bloody mind,' he snapped, and pushed me towards

the front door, which opened as if on command. 'Now get up those stairs, you little wretch!'

There was an edge of insanity to Delph's unmediated aggression, with all force utilised at once, and no thoughts of the consequences. I felt I must communicate with someone – anyone – sane, and tell them I was in the care of a lunatic. I badly hoped that there were people still awake in the house. As I took hold of the banister I glanced in at the snug front room and saw old Mr Tongue in his bed beside the fire. The white sheets appeared grimy, tousled, like the aftermath of a torrid afternoon. I could see his beak-like profile, and the pale, death-ready skin of his neck. He resembled a grotesque bird. A cup of tea in a mug commemorating an Ilkley horse show stood on the washstand. He hawked and spat into a handkerchief, examined it, and seemed satisfied. The flames of the fire in the tiny alcove appeared to emit no heat, instead they jumped and rippled among the coals like restless tongues. No, the old man couldn't help me. I could cry out, but it would be useless. I was among strangers.

'I said get up them bloody stairs!'

Delph's voice, deep and ferocious behind me, was followed by a kick in the pants and a push to the shoulder. I went forward onto my nose. Banally, I noted that the carpet on the first two steps of the staircase had been worn away, also that it didn't extend to the edges but was held in place by antiquated stair-rods. I hoped very much that this wouldn't be the last thing I ever saw. Something hot like mucus began to run down my chin.

'I won't tell thee twice!'

Running now, I gave one last glance towards the old man, but he didn't stir. I suddenly remembered he was almost totally deaf from tinnitus caused by a mine-shaft explosion. He was doing some horrible movement with his mouth and gums, as if he were trying to rearrange his false teeth. Then another kick, harder, making me stumble.

The dam behind my eyes was beginning to give way. Tears joined the hot substance now flowing into my mouth. Behind me, a force-field of pure malice; a kind of madness in the increasing recklessness of the kicks. *Right from the start, I gave you my heart.*

I made the top step but was floored by another great boot to the buttocks.

'Now get to thy bed, you little bastard!'

The door to the room I shared with Mum and Delph was pushed open by the flat of my future stepfather's palm. Again, I noticed the huge veins on his hands, big and bulbed like tubers about to burst. He shoved me through and I collapsed on the makeshift bedding. Grabbing me by the shoulder, he turned me around.

'Wipe thy nose,' he ordered, and pulled a handkerchief from his pocket. 'And your eyes while you're at it, crybaby.'

I took the offering and did as he said. As he went to leave the room, I noticed something triumphant in his eyes: as if he had successfully completed a long overdue mission. I suddenly saw how happy this kicking had made him. A perverse joy fluctuated in the pupils of his intense eyes. He had delighted in this wanton destruction, this furious vengeance. 'Get to bed right now. I'll be back in five minutes to check on you.'

Then he was gone.

In a kind of trance I went about the room, shedding my clothes, the bloody handkerchief stuck to my nose. I felt black and blue; dirty, humiliated, destroyed. My chest was rent by huge spasms. Sobs alternated with exhausted panting as adrenalin raced around my system like a motorcycle on the wall of death. The very novelty of the experience was startling – its unreadable newness. Then came trepidation over the immediate future. Would he come back to finish me off? Would I make it through till tomorrow? As I shivered into my pyjamas, their cold material adding to the damp wretchedness of my humiliation, I was at least thankful to be alive.

Then the doorbell froze me in my tracks.

My mother! I stopped to listen by the bedding, desperately attempting to decipher the leaden northern vowels. No – it was a man's voice. A late caller. Delph's perfidious baritone was welcoming somebody in. The front door scraped shut. Then the rustling of divested coats. Footsteps. More unrecognisable banter. The sound of the whistle-kettle being filled and its clunk as it made contact with the hob. My heart sank at these sounds, like a stone in a loch. *Honey when you knock on my door, I gave you my key.* Catching my face in the dressing-table mirror I saw eyes that were big and red with bawling. All I could taste in my mouth was the salty tang of tears and blood intermingled.

At once I heard footsteps on the frayed stairs. Unmistakably the heavy tread of Delph. He gained the landing, breathing heavily. One step, two; then his knuckles on the door.

I opened it.

He seemed embarrassed, crimson-eared. 'There's a visitor for you, you mithering git,' he announced flatly, his cleft-chin towering above me. 'That Postlethwaite fella, who wanted to pick thy brains, remember?' I recalled the man – a gormless, open-faced enthusiast who once worked with Delph's father down the Rochdale pit. On his last visit he had cornered me by the fire and asked about my hobbies. For want of an answer I blurted out that I liked fishing, thinking that was the sort of boyish pursuit I should enjoy. Although I had once been given a couple of angling magazines, I hadn't been near a fishing rod or river in my life. And now this man was here, wanting to talk to me, demanding an audience. Me – in the state I was in, at this time of night.

I didn't know what to say.

'What's the matter? Cat got thy tongue?' There was a dull monotony in Delph's clichés; the dullness of a man with no interests outside himself. But also an anxiousness: with this unexpected visit there was a distinct danger of exposure. There was much at stake, and we both knew it, though Delph affected nonchalance. Grudgingly, he said, 'Well, he's come to look in on our pa, and he wants to talk to thee. So you better wipe your face and come downstairs.' Then the satyrish look of earlier appeared in his eyes. 'And not a bloody word about anything, okay, or you know what you can expect.'

So I followed Delph downstairs to endure my humiliation. As

I reached the bottom step I peered into the room with dread. Sitting on the opposite side of the fire to the impassive old man was Mike Postlethwaite, erect in a green waxed jacket, his face younger and more convivial than I remembered it. Despite the late hour, he seemed eager to talk. He was slurping tea and expanding loudly on the topic of pit closures, the decrepit miner in the corner nodding occasionally in assent. If there was anything I felt less inclined to do at that moment, it was talk about a subject I knew nothing about to someone I didn't know; with my eyes all puffy, my heart crushed. A rule in life was presenting itself to my young mind: you always have to endure what you least want at the worst possible moment. It was an infallible rule. But there was no escape. Delph ushered me into the tiny front room and the two men looked up.

'Here he is,' said Delph with his Janus chuckle, presenting me to them as if I were a Turkish boy at a seraglio. 'You just caught him. About to turn in.'

The old man in the corner made no reaction. The sooty ingrained lines on his hands were like seams in the coalface itself: indestructible, compressed. A faint smell of mouldy potatoes and cabbage rose from the unaired pen of his bed. Postlethwaite stood up diffidently and offered his hand. A strange gesture towards a boy of eight. I took it lamely, though I couldn't meet his eye. I was self-conscious about the crust of blood around my nostrils, the obvious evidence of tears.

'Hello, little man,' he beamed.

'Hello, Mr Postlethwaite,' I answered weakly, my face averted. His unselfconscious bonhomie was just what I didn't need.

Delph produced a tiny chair for me and set it next to the fire. My bruised backside stang as I sat. I was close enough to see points of sweat glittering on the man's forehead. As I turned my face towards the coals I felt the censorious gaze of Delph monitoring me. It was too late: the pantomime had to be gone through.

'I know it's almost midnight and that,' started Postlethwaite in hale and hearty tones, 'but I thought I'd drop by and check on your granddad. Then I remembered the little lad that were round who wanted to talk tackle.'

I intended to say, he's not my granddad, but felt Delph's degrading glare burn the side of my face. The three men were arraigned around me like some hellish tribunal: Minos, Aeacus and Rhadamanthus, with Yorkshire accents. I tried vainly to think of something, anything, to say, but it was as if I were looking at a blank sheet of paper. Instead I found myself unable to do anything other than shrug my shoulders. Undeterred, the bubbling stranger continued. 'Any road, what rod are you using now?'

'A green one,' I offered, stupidly.

'Aye,' he said impatiently, 'but what make?' He was attempting to crane his head around and make eye contact, but I shifted my face in shame. He had that over-keenness for engagement of those with no talent for children. I had no answer for him. Seconds dripped by like hours. Where was my mother?

'I – I can't remember.'

'That's not much use to Mr Postlethwaite, is it?' said Delph sinisterly from the shadows. I could hear the stir of flames among the embers. For a moment I thought the old miner had fallen asleep or even died, but movement in his rheumy eyes confirmed otherwise. My face felt hot, suddenly screened with sweat. A wet sensation under my armpits made my pyjamas feel constricting.

The eager man went on: 'First one I had was a wonderful splitcane rod made by Hardy's. Before your time I should think.'

The implausibility of this stalled conversation after the exponential violence of a few minutes ago lay heavy on me, like a leaden hand. The whole charade seemed ludicrous and sad at the same time. I felt soiled, interrogated; useless in my inability to answer his questions. To fill the silence I stammered: 'I'm only eight.' Tears, globular and warm, welled up in my eye sockets. I wanted to run from the room. *And nobody told us, 'cos nobody showed us . . .*

'Aye, you're just a nipper. But at your age I had all the gear. Flies. Lures, gaffes and nets, and a Hardy's reel made in 1890. A real treasure it were. An antique – just like me and your uncle Delph.'

At this he roared with laughter. His hand reached out and touched my arm. I flinched. Delph sat silent, observing me, waiting for the slightest whiff of defiance. He also knew the charade had to be endured. It was a torture for him too, though in a different sense. Postlethwaite leaned forward in his seat at his own soggy wit. He repeated the inert joke. 'Like me and your uncle! Ha ha!'

The unbearable catechism seemed never-ending. I wanted my mum. I wanted to live on Mount Everest for the rest of my life. I stared at the fire, but instead of amber coals I saw the Vauxhall Viva tearing through the bleak Niflheim of the Wakefield streets, the mysterious woman (his bit on the side?), the flashes of moonlit collieries, the big-veined hand lashing out, the rain of blows to my back as I struggled up the stairs. The song in my head.

'Oh yes, I had all the tackle at your age. My father's creels, his otter.' The man paused conceitedly. 'I can tell by thy expression that you don't know what an otter is. Well, we were put on this planet to learn. By otter I don't mean the little furry animal that lives on the riverbank that they made the film about – Tarquin, I think it were. No, an otter is a contraption you slide down the line to knock your spinner off if it gets stuck.'

He let this pointless fact linger in the room, like a gigantic fart. I wanted to vomit; his mystifying talk was curdling with the shame in my heart. Every note sounded was false, like some awful seventies TV play. He must have seen straight off that I'd been crying but chose to ignore it. Like ignoring the fact that you've surprised somebody naked. There was a terrible tension in the room unavoidable to everyone. The mute, tearful boy. The insidious silence of Delph. The desiccated miner. But somehow, this prating fool was blind to it all. Like a man who whistles while his own house burns down, he was inflicting this nonsense on everyone. For a moment Postlethwaite paused for my reaction to this fine nugget of knowledge. I looked into the fire and said, 'Oh, I didn't know. That's – that's fascinating.'

'Well, I'm sure – you're like me – it's not the bits and bobs that take you to the river. It's being close to nature that counts.' He sat back with a self-satisfied sigh. 'The gentle waters, the solitude. No darkies playing their jungle music at top volume. Then your first catch of t' day! I remember my first trout when I were out for carp. Heaven!'

I gazed into the flames in an attempt to tune him out. But this must have convinced him that I didn't believe his statement. I felt all the shame of Rousseau, made to walk before a spit of meat as he went supperless to bed in front of his elders.

He persisted, 'Honest! I can tell thou thinks I'm fibbing, but it were a beauty . . .' I decided as long as I concentrated on the fire he wouldn't be able to see my appalled crimson face. I was aware he was stretching his arms to demonstrate the size of the trout. But I couldn't turn. 'It were this long, ain't that a fact granddad?' But 'granddad' didn't respond. He too was conjuring pictures in the coals. 'That were my split-cane rod's doing, that were. Amazing, cos that day I had an English lure, but the Yankee ones made by Heddon are the best . . .'

I could feel the water against the dam again. Insistent, unstoppable. I sniffled to keep the tears in. The man's voice was a tyrannical dirge. Elton was singing, *Don't go breaking my heart*. Then Kiki's confident, trilled reply (how her voice makes one believe her): *I won't go breaking your heart!*

'Hard as it is to admit that the Yanks do anything better than us, but—' Postlethwaite paused and examined me candidly. At last the penny had dropped. 'Is everything all right?'

Too late. A sizeable tear ran down my face and trembled from the bottom of my chin, a bright icicle. I sniffed monstrously to keep in a deluge of snot. At that moment I felt there was a danger of my head imploding.

End, please *end*, I thought helplessly.

Delph's voice cut in, suddenly loud, as he stood up in the posture of the jailer eager to return the prisoner to his cell. He could sense the game was up. 'That's enough now,' he barked coldly. 'Get thee to bed.'

'Sorry Mr Postlethwaite,' I said quickly, my tears now pathetically obvious. And I was genuinely sorry for him. Sorry he'd been so generous with his time for a little heathen whose mouth, like young Oliver's, would one day get him hung. 'Thank you for a lovely evening. Maybe one day we can go fishing together.'

Like Hyperion to a satyr, Des and Delph. Ah, if only it were that simple. If only Delph were that glamorous, Des that noble. The fact was, my mother didn't find a man such as my father useful after a while. It always boils down to utility value in the end. And what did women want, after all? Moses Herzog reckoned they all ate green salad and drank human blood. Ultimately, once the sexual obsession has worn off, they want security. So what went wrong if Des was more able to provide this? There lies the rub. Delph probably perceived his handicap atavistically. This was perhaps his Achilles heel. Unfortunately I was too young to pierce it with my arrows. The vain fool certainly tried to improve himself over the years, with pointless evening classes and failed forays into the air of higher culture. He must have been terrified of losing my mother when she discovered his only future was painting white lines on playing fields. So why *did* she choose a barbarous ram over Apollo? Perhaps it all boils down to excitement. My father could offer her financial security, a house on leafy Dovecote Lane, steadiness, exposure to classical music, chess. But he couldn't offer her excitement. That was too much of a tall order. And Delph certainly came with a spurious promise of it, the sort guaranteed to lower a woman's self-esteem in the end. He, after all, could offer gross physicality, height, disco dancing, unpredictability and a good slap if you crossed him. Maybe that's the crux, the perverted truth, about human love. Delph was physically bigger than my father – his hands, his shoulders and probably his cock. Ultimately, it seems what women want – what they will sacrifice a family for – is heft. Bigness. They must need this male bigness in order to feel protected, or, logically, on the other side of the coin, threatened.

In the animal kingdom, the female chooses her mate based on body-size and aggressiveness. The Alpha male. The leader of the pack. Someone to throw them around the bedroom, to protect their young. Physical power is unanswerable. Brute force, main force, will always triumph in the end. As the years plunged that agreeable evening of chat about fishing tackle further into the abyss of time, I thought about the relative sizes of my two surrogate fathers. If Des had discovered the truth of that brutal beating, would he have challenged Delph? (Because I wanted him to.) Was he big enough? Spiritually, I mean. If he had done, it would have served very little purpose. Every fact indicated that the bigger man, this posturing ignoramus who usurped a rightful father, would have given Des the pasting of his life. Those big-veined hands (calloused from grafting at the school, from working out with dumbbells kept behind our sofa) would have made mincemeat of Des's frail and balding scalp. He would, in Wall Street parlance, have out-dicked him.

So when it came time for my father to throw me out of his house, I knew he wasn't up to the job. Physically, I mean. Though I had just turned sixteen, I was a good two inches taller than him. The flashpoint was my decision to leave school. What was the purpose, I thought, with the arrogance of youth, of continuing the academic grind when there was no one at the tiller to steer the ship? The October Saturday evening I announced this – the air still sickly soft with summer, the big trees slow to shed their load of leaves – I found myself surprised at the vehemence of his reaction. Sequestered in Lille for weeks at a time, oblivious to my life, or the tyranny of Delph, he suddenly seemed very concerned for my future. Though this manifested itself in a kind of cowed, distracted, spitting rage. Not for him the grand physical gesture; instead he crackled impotently in my bedroom as the maples lost their red leaves outside. At the time my hair was unfashionably very long, and this seemed to form the crux of his argument, the focus of his recoil.

'You bloody shaggy-haired fool!' he railed, shaking his fists like a pint-sized Popeye. 'You're a *fool,* that's what you are! Thinking you can disappear to London and live off the state. Taxpayers like your mother and myself.'

'Since when did you care so much?' I countered, shaken by the strength of his scorn, his Richter-scale reading. 'For the last ten years you've been getting on with your lives as if I didn't exist, as if I was a burden.'

'Get your hair cut!'

That morning I had been looking at photos of my younger self, gathered on the tatty yellow bedspread. There before me was the abortive camping trip to Cornwall with my mother and Delph. A snap of their car recalled the vicious argument they had chosen to have on the way, lasting two hundred miles. Another evoked the flummoxed tent, the two weeks of torrential rain, the dire fish and chips eaten from soggy newspaper every night. Each tableau held some kind of heavy pain. That morning I saw clearly how *in the way* I was, on those expedient holidays, to all concerned. I could perceive the strain in adult faces; everyone wanting to be somewhere else, with someone else. The final picture of my father, vexed parallels scoring his brow as he posed awkwardly on the steps of Dovecote Lane, me smiling over his shoulder, told only one story: kids are a life-sentence, and adults are really only killing time before the little buggers leave home. So why he reacted like he did when I announced I was jacking in school was mystifying. My father shook with rage as he informed me of the error of my ways: 'You'll come to nothing! You're a loser! There are only winners and losers in this life, and you're starting to fall into the latter category.'

I stood dumbstruck at this, the red and saffron maple leaves toiling in the strong wind outside. 'I'm only doing what you've all wanted for a long time.'

'And what's that?' he bellowed, finger and thumb massaging his temples like pincers.

'To get out from under your feet.'

'Don't play the burning martyr with me!'

As the day darkened outside, as my father held forth savagely against youth, time, folly and Mick Jagger's hair, I pondered the subject of winners and losers. I tried, in my jejune way, to see it from his point of view. The discarded cuckold, with all that heavy humiliation to bear, must have keenly felt what it was to fail. It was amazing that the plane that took him to France every fortnight didn't ditch in the Channel under the weight of this heavy knowledge. Here was a man whose marriage had failed, who, from financial imperatives or his own desire, had no relationship with his only son, and who had been usurped by a man who thought Paris was the capital of Italy. What a loser! It must have felt like a medieval pressing to carry that axle-load around. This hissy fit he was having, as the unequalled beauty of autumn leaves gloried in their decay, was merely a momentary lifting of that tonnage. All his thwarted scorn for my mother, for Delph – for everything he found impossible to express or shoulder – was now working its way out in his righteous spasmodic rage. His self-hatred was awe-inspiring in its power to intimidate. Because Des had been true to his name – he had been way too easy with everybody. Unable to keep his wife in his own bed (or another man out of it) he had allowed the world to walk over him, like an Old Testament trampling. As if he had stood before the hordes exiting Egypt and invited them to use him as a carpet. And now he had had enough. I was certainly impressed by this unexpected assertiveness. I knew its value, its weight-shedding importance. But I had to let it run its course. Though he was shooting the messenger, I found myself overcome with emotion that I had provided such an outlet. It was necessary, to let him have his say one last time. It was also necessary to conceal my feelings of love, or to convert them into aggression, just as I knew he was doing as he staggered around the room castigating me without shame. We were male, after all. In the wake of Delph's drubbing – his emasculation – of us both, it was good to finally learn this. I wondered how he would remember this moment, years down the line. Saying what you most want to say relieves you of a weight, but it also has the habit of coming back to crush you in later life. Moreover, the outcome he desired – my capitulation and return to school – was not going to happen. He had lost that battle already. Fatherly authority had for many years been passed, through the loving hands of my mother, to Delph. Des was no longer the parental oracle. In fact, neither was Delph. From then on, I was to be my own oracle, for better, for worse.

I heard him out, then pushed past him, ravenous for fresh air. I intended to stand in the golden kingdom of fallen autumn until the wind turned my hair white. I would run like an abandoned dog to the wide 'O' of the railway arch where I would sit down and cry.

'Stuff it,' my voice said in a strange treble. It sounded pipey and unbroken after my father's fulminations.

The following morning, all the locks were changed on his house.

Let me tell you about the last times I saw my fathers. Yes, fathers, plural. I got rid of one and the other got rid of me. The wrong father, as it turned out, did the leaving. But what is youth for if not for fucking everything up in grand style?

A year after that autumn evening, my father called at my mother's place. I had just turned seventeen. There was no particular errand that Des had to run – maybe he desired more of the punishment the cuckold secretly relishes, the saga of self-pity that it becomes legitimate to publicise once you become a rejected man. He would have seen the depressing hump of the caravan that Delph – still grimly married to my mother – had purchased so they could 'get away at the weekends'. He would have observed the 'his and hers' tea mugs, the bookless shelves, the prissy banality of the home Delph had stolen from him. The ambrosial waft of high culture a world away. He would also have been aware of the rotten atmosphere, like an undetectable smell of bins, pervading everything. The odour of things rank and gross in nature had obviously risen to the surface. For months prior to this occasion, an escalating tension like the whistling of an unattended kettle on the hob had filled the house. Until a week ago I had been signing on, shuttling between my mum's and my old man's whenever he was absent in France (he had let me back in, conditional on searching for employment). Unwanted at both houses, I endured this situation as I was too cowardly to grab the rope and swing away. Despite my grand plans of a year ago, I still wasn't in London. Instead, I was broiling in a stew of drugs and booze, vacillating as my middle-class friends flew their loving coops to university halls of residence, or (the working-class) started jobs that saw them owning powerful cars in a horrifically short time. I knew I was malingering, clinging to a domestic situation that I vaguely hoped would improve. But it didn't improve. In fact, the shrieking kettle had become unbearable. A week before, I had blagged a job hulking crates at a garden centre, only to discover that Sinead wanted the vast majority of my insulting 'pay'. I was informed that I was 'in Delph's way', and I felt his cold choked animus on the back of my neck every time we crossed paths. A mass murder, or a coup at the very least, felt imminent.

The night of Des's visit, I had been uncharacteristically delirious with joy. This was because my job had provided a solution to the whole problem. With work, I discovered, the world suddenly allowed you in, with time-honoured stupidity, to its exclusive club. The winners' club. Regardless of whether you're a junkie or a serial killer, the overweening powers-that-be react to the fact of one being in paid employment by opening their legs and begging for it. As many times a night as you want; no orifice a problem. To my amazement, a visit that morning to an estate agent had produced a breakthrough. They (the world, to whom membership is always subject-to-status) had allowed me to rent a small bedsit in Station Road for twenty-five pounds a week. Carumba. A month previously they had scooped me from their offices like a turd when I had admitted that I was on the dole. So my happiness, which knew no theoretical bounds, was intruded upon by Des. The knocker and moaner. The arch deflater of every plan or aspiration, threatening notions which illustrated to him just how safe he had played his life. Gore Vidal's maxim about dying every time a friend succeeds was personified by my father that night. He seemed personally offended when told that I had got myself together and found a job and a flat.

'What? You're going to live on your own in a stinking bedsit?' he guffawed. 'That's the outcome I always predicated for you.'

As he stood on the landing, I saw all the gloating charmlessness he could exhibit when he wanted to. Not as unattractive as Delph's psychotic rages, but disappointing all the same. Hopefully, Des was feeling my withdrawal sharper than a serpent's tooth in his buttocks. As he laughed I found it hard to share his sense of humour. Inscrutably, I watched him twitch at the foot of the stairs. My mother felt she should say something.

'Well, that can't be so bad for you.' Her voice was conciliatory as she addressed my father. 'You'll have the place to yourself at weekends. No more funny people calling round day and night.'

By funny people she meant the dealers and weirdos who seemed to gravitate towards anyone with a bit of blow. I looked back and forth between my mother and father – the weary, subordinated woman, her dramatically black hair now seamed with grey; the chuckling old man, bald as a ballpoint. I couldn't comprehend that they were my parents, that they had ever had anything to do with each other, let alone me. So this used to be a family, then, I thought – once upon a time when I was too young to remember. Did they envisage that this day would come? They were referring to me as if I were some sort of chattel to be disposed of. I broke my silence.

'No thanks to you,' I said to my old man, 'I've sorted something out.' My earlier euphoria had dissolved into anxiety and antipathy. Anxiety that he was right (and it's hard to ignore the testimony of a father, no matter how distant they have made themselves), and antipathy towards his attitude, which seemed to view my future with a satiric smirk, or at least as a target for assassination. I felt alone, without help; scorned and burdensome, like the grand-parent staggering through the first strange seas of Alzheimer's. My sudden comprehension of my father's emotional frailty was not present this time. I said, 'You've got what you both wanted – me out of the way.'

My mother wailed pitifully, 'None of us can help the things life has done to us, Brian!'

'Don't call me Brian!' I snapped back.

My father was still laughing.

'And – and, this job,' he sneered. 'Shifting crates for a bloody horticulturalist – is that the best you can come up with?'

'It's better than nothing, Des,' said my mother, her pale eyes showing the first signs of tears.

I remained silent at this. My heart-sore vulnerability had hardened to something nastier. Here was this man, my own father, laughing in my face at my humble station in life; flagrant, full of self-pity and scorn, insane with self-righteousness, with no other solution than to turn my struggles into some sort of charade that he found amusing. *I* was an outcome that he found offensive to even look at. He was pissing his pants. Presume not that I am the thing I was!

'You're a loser,' he laughed.

'Maybe so,' I said, fixated on his hooded eyes, trying to read subsidiary emotions beside that of anger. I felt all my violence, Delph's violence, well up inside me like a shamefully powerful infusion.

'It's not that bad a job,' said my mother.

I went to barge past him, but he restrained me. The only other components in his shrouded eyes were surprise and fear.

'Just you try it,' he threatened, impotently.

In a firm voice, I said: 'Hurry up and die,' and pushed his head out of the way with the flat of my palm.

Seconds later I was in the street, the night fresh as the inside of a fridge, the stars puncturing the firmament in a blaze of diamonds.

And that was the last time I saw one of my fathers.

The last time I saw my other father, the big-veined oracle, wasn't as dramatic, but just as shameful. An autumn evening. I had just stepped out of my Station Road bedsit to check on my laundry as it made its mournful turns in the blackened doorless cabin across the street, when a big car shot past, stopped, then reversed up to where I was standing.

The passenger-side window wound down, and there was Delph Tongue. I hadn't seen him for a year. Occasionally I would visit my mum, and see the caravan, that symbol of dull marital togetherness, parked stolidly in the drive – but my stepfather had been mercifully absent from the vicinity every time.

'Thou's out late,' said Delph through a big-lipped sneer. He had aged too, like the rest of us, the skin tighter below the eyes, sprigs of grey at the temples. He still had those high convex cheekbones and eyes like two dark currants stuck in the head of a gingerbread man. And still that dynamic charmlessness, the machine-like energy of the eloper or *cavalier servente*.

It was an awkward moment. We had always hated the very sight of each other.

'Just checking on my laundry,' I muttered, as if this was knowledge he was already aware of and I was updating him.

'Aye, it's not much fun with no machine of your own,' he ventured tritely.

The man in the car, this Belial from past, this kerb-crawler, was suddenly a stranger to me. Here was a presence who had dominated my life for almost two decades, and yet there we were, like shits that pass in the night. His was just another car heading home, or away from home. I looked around at the puddled neons of the road, the evening traffic ferociously pushing through, the commuters walking wearily back to their soap operas of debt and failed marriage. Certain women, dressed in shell-suits, who I knew to be prostitutes, pulled up their leg-warmers impatiently as they loitered on the corner.

'No, I suppose you're right,' I said, bowing, as ever, to his supremacy.

'Your mother says thou hasn't called for a month. I think she deserves more, don't you?'

I didn't answer this. I could tell he was aggrieved at the loss of his authority. For years that kind of comment would set off a churning sea of bile. I merely shrugged. He had lost his mark.

'Where you off to?' I asked, not interested. I knew that his marriage to my mother was practically over. It existed in all but name, within the antiseptic walls of their house. I hoped secretly that he was leaving town for good and that his boot was stuffed full of his meagre possessions, the unread gilt-tooled books, the statue of Rodin's lovers.

'To 't dump,' he said in his bludgeoning Yorkshire tones, his equivocal smirk still registering with me as a sneer.

There was nowhere else for the conversation to go but its grave.

'Okay, then,' I said, as I saw him put the car into first gear, ready for the off. I observed his hands and tried to comprehend that they were the hands that had once hit me, sexually interfered with me. But this knowledge did me no good. It enlightened me no further, gave no answers to the mysteries of consciousness, morality or our eventual destination. Without thinking, I said: 'Take care.'

As soon as the words left my lips I knew he had me. He would pounce without mercy. The strong desire to love this *de facto* father was never far from the surface. And Delph knew it. I had said something generous and he would have to rebut it, trample on it, piss on it.

'Sod off,' he snarled, his lips curling into a leer, a look of all-encompassing derision on his horrible face. That look, that disyllable retort of maximum animadversion, was an apt peroration to the whole sorry affair.

Then he wound up the window and drove off into the night.

The layer of fumes in the smoking carriage judders slightly as the train pulls away. Like a gust of cannon smoke after the firing of ordnance. Amazing that a body of chemical emission can behave as one, in concert or unison. I take a last drag and watch the carriage expel itself from Wakefield station. Glad to be gone. Wouldn't you, delicate reader, be glad to be gone from this region of endless cold and everlasting night? From the soiling admissions of the last twenty pages?

Of course it wasn't Delph in the train seat earlier. Just someone who looked like him. His doppelgänger. I had hallucinated Delph, just as I had hallucinated Bea in the Missolonghi caves. The man I asked for a cigarette was an ice-hockey player from Wombwell. He informed me, for ten eye-searing minutes, of all the fun a young man can get up to when on tour with a sporting team. His high Germanic cheekbones jutting out, almost into the aisle it seemed, like the very image of my stepfather. But it wasn't him. Ten minutes? It felt like more, somehow.

On unsturdy legs, longing for a drink, I wend my way back to carriage B. Despite the strong probability that I would have swung for him, had the hockey player indeed turned out to be Delph, the one burning question on my lips had been a curious one. Who was that mystery woman in Wakefied that night after the wedding reception? I never did find out. Somehow this fact had multiplied in importance over the years – it felt like the lost piece of a jigsaw. Was Delph being unfaithful to my mum at the same time as she was being unfaithful to my father? This was important to know. For a long time, the only comfort, the one redeeming feature of the whole saga had been the notion that at least, out of all the destruction, true love had triumphed over the suburban oblivion of a dead marriage. But was the adulterer, in turn, cheated on? Was this shady woman some fancy piece that Delph had locked away in the rainy wastes of Yorkshire? As I stumble through the hissing vents of the train, the outskirts of Wakefield rocket past, just as they did that night twenty years before. I can recall the chained collieries, sunken in darkness, some flattened by bulldozers, the old wool mills, the clinging estates, the moon like an eye at the end of the street. That song . . . But, in the distance, all I can see is a coral reef of amber streetlamps under a fog of drizzle. The year starting its long recuperation from its darkest night: the dreadful equinox of the twenty-second of December.

I reach my seat and nod to Robin, who seems startled that I'm still alive.

'Only been for a fag,' I say, buoyantly. But his response is a dismissive snarl. I feel suddenly full of chronic nausea and weariness. His sneer of non-acknowledgement recalls Delph's last look ·from his car window. I had intended to open my notebook and write up my North Yorkshire odyssey. But now I feel almost unable to pick up the pen. Is this what ages us, what hardens us? The aggregate of all those times we said something generous or naively informative to people who secretly despise us for our daily beauty? Those disparaging Malvolios, Angelos, Iagos.

Perspiration, not inspiration, I think, and open the black covers at random. The entry for the second of October confronts me. The day I left the marital home: *I'm so angry I can barely hold the fucking pen. I've been fooled, I've been had. She pretended she was someone she wasn't. So this is it. Starting again at thirty with nothing, absolutely nothing to my name. Feel small and useless. Today my wife told me she hated me and hated having sex with me. That all her orgasms had been faked. 'Even on our honeymoon?' I asked. 'Especially on our honeymoon.' she said, triumphantly. The bitch! A whole summer living beyond her means in a flat that I've grafted to pay the rent on, running around like* La Belle Dame Sans Merci *in Italy with God knows what winking, cheaply lascivious Romeo . . .*

Enough already! I cannot continue. Let me tell you instead, while we are on the subject of last meetings, about the last time I saw my wife. The mesmerising presence who had turned up at Rock On three and a half years previously displaying the white frill of her knickers over the waistband of her trousers, who had given off all those uneasy vibrations from under her canvas of butter-coloured skin, who had finally turned into my worst nightmare. A woman impossible to deal with: stern, obdurate, flinty, rough, remorseless. Whereas I had foolishly expected all the qualities of the good wife to emerge as I administered the cure to her troubled soul – a wife who was dutiful, attentive, faithful, supportive, *gentle*. In the final analysis, my marriage had been a Grand Guignol; a Spanish tragedy.

The last flat-destroying marathon took place one night three months ago. A terrible nightfall. After an hour of deadlocked verbal combat, she had reiterated the sentence ('I wish I'd never,' et cetera) that had come to seem like a mantra. Only this time she added a chilling caveat. After repeatedly punching me in the head, turning over the bookcases – which went down like collapsing tower blocks – Mandy screamed: 'I want you out of my flat! Do I have to call the police to get you out?'

I was on the sofa. She was towering over me, like some awful Clytemnestra. 'Your flat? Suddenly it's all yours, is it?'

'Right, I'm calling the police.'

'Do what you want! You've already ruined my life.'

I could see this baiting would get me nowhere. Almost stoically, she disappeared into the narrow kitchen and returned brandishing two knives, like a martial arts fighter.

'Put them down,' I said as calmly as I could.

'Now – are you going to get out?'

Though pretending not to care about the sudden escalation of threat, I retorted, 'And where will I go? You know I've got nowhere.'

'I don't care!' she screamed, with an unhinged intensity almost turning her cross-eyed. 'Go to that prick Rudi's, you're virtually a couple as it is!'

'That's pretty fucking low!'

Then she lunged forward with deadly accuracy. My hands went up before my face to protect my eyes from the flashing blade, but she caught my middle finger, slicing off a chunk like the tip of a carrot. I yelled out, horrified to see my own blood on the sofas we had chosen together at Ikea. I remember thinking: this is as bad as it gets, a life, a marriage.

'See what happens if you don't get out?' she taunted.

'You've lost your fucking mind!'

'Get up, you wretched idiot!'

The knives flashed out again, slicing patterns on my right forearm, creating the wounds that I would have to hide from Rudi and my future flatmates. Aware that there was a real danger I could die, seeing the tawdry headline in the Sunday red-tops (Mad Spanish Bride Knife Frenzy – Chihuahua Witnesses Husband's Murder), I grabbed both her wrists at once and yanked her forward, the descending blades narrowly missing my chest. A strange sense of timelessness descended during this pivotal struggle. There was no going back from this – everything was being decided at once. Noting quietly her scar from when she put her hand through the window during our first months of love, I saw again how strangely proportioned she was – both physically and mentally. At that moment, with Mandy twisted across the sofa as I grappled for the blades, for my own life, her bottom half didn't seem like it belonged with her top half. The two sections of her body seemed as anomalous as her punishments that never fitted the crime. In those suspended seconds, I thought about how much she resembled Ramona in the two long-gone photographs; how Mandy had evolved to her destined maximal condition: the unstoppable Spanish fury – her mother. To put a stop to her, I administered a fierce Chinese burn to both her wrists. Shrieking, she dropped the knives but managed to grasp my T-shirt, ripping it diagonally, as if pulling up something by the roots.

I had disarmed her. The moment of shimmering equilibrium had passed.

Mandy collapsed on the floor and started screaming hysterically. Panting, I examined my wounds. Staunching the blood with what remained of my T-shirt, I decided that I would live. Then I felt a sudden absence around my neck. Something was missing. Not my head, but my chain, bearing the cross that Mandy had bought me in Barcelona. My only piece of jewellery, it had never left my chest since that day. Now I saw the crucifix lying on the floor next to its severed silver chain, drops of my own blood surrounding it like spilt Eucharist wine on an altar. The wreckage of the bookcases, of the cats' mischief-centre, of our marriage, suddenly melancholy in attendance.

A knock at the door silenced Mandy's awful imam-like wailing. I heard the crackle of a radio. There was no need for her to phone the cops. The neighbours had saved her the trouble. Outside, a cold blue light oscillated in the darkness.

8

One More Stop

Some deaths are too horrible to go through with sober. One, I imagine, is blowing your head off. Despite the ubiquitous vision that has assailed me for the past three months, the weighty barrel entering the delicate, infant flesh of the mouth (like a morbid act of fellatio), the reality would require a great deal of courage. Or whisky. Or both. If discretion forms the greater part of valour, then inebriation forms the greater part of suicide. Only world-class ascetics and the insane have managed to top themselves sober. This I conclude as I peer through the thick windows of the bucking carriage, the train racing towards its final stop.

All the available methods, come to think of it, don't actually warrant close inspection. Even contemplating them impartially fills me with a kind of animal dread. Let's look at the options. Cutting your wrists in the bath? All the candles, incense, soothing music and sellotape in the world won't prepare you for the egregious sight of your own lifeblood filling the water like spilt ink. As suicidal as you might have been, the instinct, surely, would be to jump out and attempt to drink back that lost blood, that ebbing essence. Then there's the leap from the motorway bridge. The fact of your

altitude, the wind and traffic sounds heightening your own aware-
ness of the conscious moment, argues against the motorway option.
No way do you want to be that alert as you check out. And think
of the mess, the road pizza you would create. Worse, you could
end up in the front seat of a family saloon and take out some
perfectly innocent couple heading for a day-trip to Bangor. No, the
plunge from the motorway bridge is beyond contemplation. The
old belt around the timber joist? Forget it. There's the strong
possibility of dangling there and slowly turning black for half an
hour. Pills? Too risky. Get the dosage wrong and you wake up in
a hospital bed a paraplegic or brain-dead. Exhaust pipe through the
window? Better, but gives you too much time to contemplate the
road back. Self-immolation? Horrific in the extreme. And what if
someone managed to turn a fire extinguisher on you? You would
have to spend your last hours like a peeled grape as the body
dehydrated down to nothing. Drowning? Now, there you would
discover that you were your own worst enemy. The organism, in
its very DNA, carries the instinctive will to live. The genes would
order you to grab the lifebelt as you went under for the third time.
No, I know all about almost drowning, voluntarily or not. Also,
as with immolation, there is always the possibility that some passing
hero would jump in and drag you kicking and screaming back to
the problems you wanted to leave behind. The only options, in
the end, seem to me what you might term Roman: the sudden
strike to the heart with the broadsword, the cutlass across the throat
– the bullet to the brain. The sudden eternity. Obviously, out of
the last three, the gun wins hands down as the most savagely effective. Brutus probably took upwards of an hour to die. One tiny
movement, one command from the mind, one electrical spark across
the synapses and you're through. The *felo de se* that's as quick as
changing channels on the television. It virtually defines that nonsen-
sical phrase: the easy way out.

The only problem is: I don't have the courage for any of them.
Not even the easy option. Nor do I have any booze. More pertinently, I don't have a gun. But the frequency of the vision, the

cold barrel in the hot mouth, must mean it's something I deeply want, deeply desire. And this is typical of the kind of thinking I do about death (constant, non-conclusive). It precludes the other, normal kind of thinking people do about it — the kind that leads to decisions over cremation versus burial, or how to meet a friend's passing without hysteria.

Outside, the fields are tumbling by under darkness. In the summer, when I last made this lone journey to visit my mother, the hurtling landscape looked marvellous: the hedgerows dense, the green foliage oily and fresh, the air alive, the expanses of water scintillating. Hayricks dotting the sloping fields under the warm, yeasty breeze. The fields seen from the train not flashing by, but seeming to *revolve* in a kind of circle: the near distance moving faster than the far horizon, with its almost static pylons — an intensely graceful move-ment. It had almost lifted my heart. Now there is just a void through the bleared window. Anxiously, I wonder whether eternity holds a similar absence, a corresponding blackness, and turn away. The reflected, artificial light of the carriage is tiring in the extreme. My eyeballs feel melted, corroded to the core. A rank, tarry taste from the cigarette is in my mouth. The beginning of a hangover is trying my cranium with its exploratory instruments, its dental picks and incisions. My legs prickle sleepily, and I do indeed have the first warnings of hospitalising indigestion. The journey is almost over. A few passengers are stirring, checking watches, stretching, yawning. Soon it will be time for them to haul their leather cases from the racks or the over-clogged pens between carriages, then descend onto the floodlit platform, the big runway of Leeds station, and jump into the arms of loved ones.

Soon, also, it will be time to tell you about last things, about where everybody ended up. I don't feel I've given a proper account of these significant others. Oh, I'm sure they will be all sleeping soundly in their beds tonight, waiting for the felicitous footsteps of Santa as he makes his rounds. Take Martin, for instance. He's spending the holiday with his family, as he always does. Oh, and he gave me my old job back. Did I tell you that? Out of pity, mainly. He told me he knew what a failed marriage felt like; that he had special insight into the debilitating feelings of despair and self-hatred. Nice to think you're not alone. He also surprised me with some facts pertaining to his past life. Last week in the shop, with the tinsel sadly draped over guitars that nobody wanted to buy their sons for Christmas, he told me an interesting fact about his ex-missus. Apropos of nothing, he said, in his smoker's growl: 'Sharon used to hit me too, if it's any consolation.'

I stood there embarrassed, two flight cases in my hands, as if I were going on holiday. The past few months had drained me of the ability to feel empathy with anybody else's nightmare but my own. Not knowing what to say, how to inject the right note of concern into my voice, I adopted the neutral tone of the interviewer. 'I thought you said it was the drinking that put an end to that one.'

Martin shifted slightly behind the counter. The corrugated skin on his face burned a delicate crimson. His posture was that of a man about to reveal all to police inspectors.

'That was a factor, make no mistake. But it was her – her temper – that really finished it off. We had this record shop on the Camden High Street. In a year she had pissed off all our customers. Every one.'

'I see,' I said, putting the flight cases down. It was unusual for Martin to talk about personal stuff, but the shop was empty. The sound of Slade's 'Merry Christmas' from a passing car was suddenly very loud, then distant. 'And how did she do that?' I asked, fearful of revelations too similar to my own sorry history.

'She once punched out a bloke trying to flog all his Bowie vinyl. Offered him five quid for the lot – said the eighties' albums weren't worth the electricity used to record them. Then decked him when he called her a philistain.'

'Stine.'

'Whatever. She wouldn't listen to the appeal of reason.'

'Sounds familiar.'

Martin continued, taking the elastic band from his greying

ponytail and raking the hair back with his free hand. It was costing him much to confide in me like this. 'For three months after we got married, everything was great. Total bliss. We opened the shop, she seemed happy enough. Of course, I was drinking a bit then, but that was a hangover from the Drifter days.'

The moment was too solemn to indulge our usual banter about his forgotten group, but he paused anyway to allow me the opportunity.

'Go on,' I said, feeling somewhat relieved that I wasn't the only man in the world who had married a maniac.

'Then she started going for me for the slightest reason. Over dinner, in the shop, in the car – Christ, that was scary. And I mean full-on punches, too, not slaps. She almost caused a motorway pile-up when she jabbed me in the knackers on the M4.' I didn't ask why she had behaved in this way, as I knew there didn't need to be a 'why'. 'I lost count of the amount of times I moved out only to move back in a week later. I should've stayed away, but that's the problem – you're not thinking with your head.'

Martin stopped, frustrated at his inability to articulate any of this properly. The question that filled the silent shop was: In what other organ does thinking take place? However, I felt like helping him.

I said, 'I know. You're thinking from the heart.'

Pleased with this distinction, but uneasy that he might have said too much, he tried to grapple with the subject in general terms, his grey eyes gleaming. 'Thing is, only now do I see it for what is was – abuse. It's hard for a bloke to admit that his trouble and strife is knocking him about. Other people – other men in particular, just laugh. Women think you're a wimp. The police don't want to know. But it is abuse. No two ways about it. And abusers tend to go for people who love deeply, because they know their victims will put up with it for longer. They know they will keep coming back. They know their loving nature will prevent them from fighting back.'

We both expected a customer to walk in and break the spell. But none did.

'Sounds like Mandy,' I said. Martin looked a little guilty at this, as we both knew that he was complicit in encouraging us to get together. She had been Martin's acquaintance long before our marriage.

'Well, people keep a lot hidden. I kept wishing Sharon would turn back into the woman I first knew. But she was always like that, underneath, I mean. Deep down. The fact is, an abuser will figure out how much you can take then play you like a fish on a line. They will push you to the limit of your endurance, then, when they sense you're about to snap, they back off and tell you they love you, or manipulate you with guilt, or both. They give you crumbs of hope, and hope is always fatal for people who love deeply.'

'Why is that?'

He couldn't answer. I hoped very much he wasn't about to cry. Eventually he said, 'Because, if you're not totally cynical, hope is just another way of saying you still believe in people.'

Martin cleared his throat and looked down. I searched for something to say. In that instant I wanted to escape from the imprisonment of my past, the vortex of dismal human beings, of abusers like Delph and Mandy. I floundered around for a subject that would bring us back to the present.

'Anyway, how's your wife's stones?'

Martin brightened, snapping the elastic band tight on his ponytail. He had been holding it, like Yorick's skull, through his difficult oration. 'Fine, thanks! She has to go back in Feb to see if everything's settled down . . . I'm flattered you remembered, with all you've got going on.'

'Well, I'm not that busy,' I said, forlornly. 'Just loneliness and masturbation.'

We both chuckled at this.

'Anyhow, are you going to put those guitars away in the stock cupboard? I don't think anyone's going to buy them at this late stage.'

'I haven't got the key.'

'I'll get it for you.'

I watched Martin's retreating back as he ventured into the office to search for the key. The place was such a pigsty I knew he would be a while. It hit me with the force of revelation that Martin had been my father for some time. He seemed to have always been there − patriarch, provider and rock: all those chimerical things. It struck me then that Martin had taught me things, in the manner a father is supposed to instruct his son. The things they don't teach you at school. Not the practical things, like how to run a shop or work all the recording equipment, but priceless things a father never taught me − discipline, circumspection, optimism, uxoriousness, how to handle money and difficult characters, how to trust your instincts, correct cynicism, childlike enthusiasm. And not just that, but how much he had imparted about how to behave, about masculine conduct. Superlogical, calm, shrewd, precise Martin. And fearless, too: to this day I take his who-gives-a-fuck example of walking through the London streets after dark as some kind of gold standard. He never cared − leaving the tiny studio at midnight in his brown bomber-jacket to traverse some of the most dangerous estates in England. He could handle himself: alone. Walk softly and carry a big stick. What father ever taught me that? As a man, no one ever teaches you The Rules, but he came closest.

Standing there, waiting for him to return, I wondered what sort of men Des and Delph really were. Why hadn't they been so wise and supportive? Martin Drift, a surrogate father, who had survived electrocution and alcoholism in the name of rock 'n' roll. Now, that's what I called a dad! And maybe he felt a hint of the same filial feeling. He only had daughters, and there was some of the wistfulness of the father who longed for a son about him. I thought then of Des and his second wife Emmanuelle thousands of miles away in Sydney − stick-thin Emmanuelle who had borne him two children I had never met, and who didn't know a word of English. I tried to calculate his age − almost sixty now, an old man. I felt a sudden pang of regret, always present, but unavoidable in that empty shop, the December winds hailstorming dead leaves against the window. Outside the day was freezing and winter sere – full-blown decay everywhere; Thor trying the roofs of houses; the leaves squashed by car tyres into the tarmac making a honeycomb mosaic until the rain destroyed their patterns. Des's ten-year absence from my life had seen an ecumenical change. The landscape, the emotional landscape, had altered beyond recognition. If one were to keep score, then we had both been losers in some things and winners in others. As Martin hurried back to the counter with the key in his hand, I thought maybe I should pick up that phone before it was too late. As much as I loved Martin, as much as he had been a good surrogate parent, I decided I should leave my third father and see what my real one was up to.

'Eureka!' said Martin triumphantly, smacking the key onto the counter, his astute eyes meeting mine.

I smiled at him. He had heart, Martin, that much you had to give him. The secret, of course, is to have a lot of heart. Because if you don't have heart, all you have is a point of view. All you have are opinions.

A week after I shoved my three filthy cardboard boxes into the shared flat, Mandy helpfully dropped some post off for me. She didn't want me to come round and collect it, and, with the cica-trices of my wounds still sore under my sleeves, I had no intention of doing so.

Amongst the junk mail was a birthday card from Leo in Spain. I had always thought her remembering the date was a nice touch. But the Spanish are like that. Despite the fact that she must have been considerably resentful of both me and Mandy for not going along with the house idea for mad Montserrat, she had included a long note. She told me, in a flowing longhand of formal English, that she had found a solution to the whole problem. Instead of buying a house in London, she had put all her savings into a security-monitored apartment for her mother near the sea. Far from being an old people's home, the place was palatial, allowing Montse maximum independence, with a mentor who visited twice a day to fix her special meals and check she hadn't murdered the neighbours. Thus, Leo and Carmen could live quietly together in the big, airy, tide-smelling apartment. She had managed to claw back her life while still doing her duty.

The note signed off wishing me well, and hoping that one day I would publish some more of my poems, which she had never read but was dying to see. Another Spanish trait – they took their poetry and poets very seriously. Unlike in England, where their status, despite the Bard and lip-service to the Laureate, is akin to that of paedophiles or estate agents in terms of social currency. I put the card on my mantelpiece, where it still sits, next to the spew of loose change and that other card, the one from Mandy with the Mediterranean scene and the sentimental, heartbreaking message. I remember thinking for a long time about Leo, the day already dark outside at three, the croupiers just stirring in the kitchen below. She also had a lot of heart. I tried to picture her cooking for her lover in the Tarragona flat, standing squat on the stone tiles, the air scented, her greying hedge of hair wrapped in a scarf. Still with her air of properness and self-restraint; finally out of the closet after forty years. Very much on my mind at the time were the people I might or might not see again. People become partisan when a marriage breaks up. What other choice do they have? With Leo, I thought the chances of ever having any contact with her again were next to zero. What excuse did I have? Initially I had thought of her as a gentle, timid presence – weak even. But she was a woman whose interior was arcane, occult; a secret – like precious documents in a bank vault. She made me think again of my people-blindness, another subject that kept me awake at night, clutching the mouldy borrowed duvet. She was a grown-up, with deeds done: her passions evolved and modified by a life lived – and how many of those did I know? People really are very mysterious in the end: their consciousnesses coinciding with ours in the little windows of opportunity that we are afforded. Sitting there, with Leo's card staring at me from the bare mantelpiece, I hoped she was happy. I also concluded that human beings were like artichokes – they exfoliated inwardly: you never got the true picture, even when you were in close proximity for years.

Around the same time, I had an unwanted and chilly phone call from Ian Haste. He wanted to know, principally, when Mandy and I were going to get a divorce. Were we aware, for example, of the financial implications of staying each other's next of kin? His voice, always holding at bay those cockney vowels, was a surprise when it came on the line. After the small talk and formalities were out of the way he informed me, 'If anything happens to either of you, the remaining partner gets the lot. You do realise that?'

I told him I didn't, but added, 'There's nothing to divide up anyway. There is no "lot".'

'Maybe not for you. I don't want my daughter to be forced into giving everything she has to you.' He sounded circumspect, ostentatiously frosty.

Knowing I probably wouldn't see him again, I said, 'What does she have? It's not like she's successful or anything. Most of that stuff in the flat belonged to both of us and I don't care if she keeps it.'

'That's as may be, but from my own experience, you have to get things straight.'

He was talking with the easy assurance of a man who had seen all this coming. Maybe I was the only one who hadn't. This made me want to take the train to Slough and desecrate his fastidiously maintained lawns, to smash the tacky Renoir over his head.

'I'm not in a position to think any of this through, Mr Haste. I'm still trying to get my head around it.'

I knew he would loathe me even more for this statement. His ethos was practicality, common sense, endurance. For him, an artist was a genetic aberration, like a homosexual.

'I can start the divorce proceedings myself if you want, at the local county court.' I had already had a communication from his solicitors, Openwork, Gallipot and Allwit, stating the benefits of dissolving the marriage forthwith.

'No, don't do that,' I said, panicked. My consent or otherwise to a divorce was the only feeble straw of power I had left against the steamroller that was Mandy. If she wanted to marry one of her Italian lover boys she would just have to wait. For eternity, if possible.

'I see you're going to make things difficult for everyone,' he said coldly.

'Difficult!' I exclaimed, heart-sore and shocked. It only took a slight flesh wound to set me off. 'Isn't your daughter the most difficult person in the world? You know, I'm not convinced she didn't plan this. Didn't plan to end up with that flat and everything in it. It's all run too smoothly for it to be otherwise.' There was a silence at the end of the line. In the past, I had successfully appealed to his sense of his daughter's waywardness, but not now. He had come down firmly on her side, on the side of kin. A sour egocentric man who never gave his daughter anything but a prominent white scar on her forehead. I said, 'Why don't you all shaft me a little bit more? Go on, I can take it!'

Ian Haste said, 'You're a little geezer, aren't you?'

Flabbergasted, I asked, 'What's that got to do with it?' He had sounded just like an East End gangster.

'I'd love to knock your block off.'

'You don't know where I live.'

'I can find out,' he said menacingly.

'We'll see,' I replied, and put the phone down.

For a number of days after Mr Haste's heartwarming call I tried to imagine him there in his big tasteless house with only his black dog for company. Had I been blind about him too? There he was, planning revenge, this Longshanks of the suburbs, chain-smoking Dunhills with his bat-like hands. His reticent manner in the past always hid an overweening stubbornness, a slyness, an antagonism. And this wasn't just paranoia, although much of my thinking at the time bordered on the insane. I gave strict instructions to the croupiers and the classical musician to vet all my calls. If a male, pseudo-elocuted voice came on the line, I had emigrated to Australia to be reunited with my father. One night soon after the split, I was handed the phone in the kitchen.

'Byron, it's Sarah,' a small voice said.

'Sarah!' I had only talked to her once to her since the awful night in the Indian restaurant. She sounded effusive and bright.

'I thought I'd call and see how you were. It took ages to get your number.'

'I'm okay, I suppose,' I said, not wanting to burden her. 'How did you get it, by the way? Not from Mandy, surely.'

'That hysterical bitch? You're joking aren't you,' she said, and I felt happy, like I always felt when people took my side. It's amazing how many so-called friends play devil's advocate after a break-up, as if your emotions are some sort of game they feel they can judge without examining the evidence. 'No, I got it off Rudi.'

'Yeah, he gives my number to everyone. How's college?'

I had heard through the grapevine that she hadn't made Cambridge, and instead was studying medicine at King's in London. Our proximity hadn't encouraged me to track her down. I felt somehow responsible for what Mandy had said that night — after all, I had inflicted my wife on everyone. I had opened their eyes to behaviour, to human capabilities, I wouldn't wish on my worst enemy.

Sarah said, 'It's going really well — only another six years to go. Listen, I have some news for you. Do you remember that girl you went out with ages ago?' She paused to giggle for a moment, 'Sorry, of course you must remember. Beatrice, long brown hair, plummy voice. Well, she's doing a PhD at King's. Can you believe it?'

'Really?' I felt, suddenly vulnerable at this information. Open on all flanks to considerable emotions. My one thought: it doesn't get any easier as you get older, does it? 'Did you talk to her?'

I tried to imagine Bea now, with her chestnut hair and deep-set eyes that had a melancholy look when you caught them at a certain angle, her unreadable feelings.

Sarah said, 'We had a chat, yeah.'

'You didn't give her my number, did you?' I asked with some urgency.

'Now I'd never do that without consulting you first. But that is what I am asking you.'

'Sarah,' I said, 'I don't feel up to talking with anyone right now. She's probably forgotten me. She's probably married to someone sane with a couple of sane children running around. The last thing she needs is to be bugged by the man who dumped her three years ago.'

'Well – okay. I always imagine old friends want to catch up. The past is just blood under the bridge.'

'I – I don't feel at all well at the moment. Maybe we – we could meet up soon.'

'Name the time and place. I've missed you.'

In the end Sarah named the time and place as I'm always hopeless at such arrangements. Unintentional harm is often done by my random choices of location. I always pick the train station where they broke up with the love of their lives on days when they've just had a long course of colonic irrigation.

But we didn't meet. I kept cancelling. Because I was in no fit state, no fit state at all, to interact with healthy humanity. During that call she told me Delph had disappeared again, up in the wastes of Yorkshire. What little contact she had with her father had dwindled to nothing over the years. Her relationship with him was complex and painful and we hadn't discussed it as much as my greedy, emotional heart would have liked over the years. What was it with me that I had to get to the bottom of everything, that I had a hot and urgent need for elucidation? Why couldn't I just let it all go?

But I knew why. Because I missed these people, even the ones who had done me wrong. Especially those ones. I had an urgent need to get even, to exact revenge, to inculcate my strongly held beliefs. It was the dear and the good whom I couldn't face – those to whom I had done wrong myself. The thought of a meeting with Bea had terrified me. Ever since her apparition had floated from the quayside of the subterranean lake in Cephalonia I had been childishly scared of bumping into her on the street, on the bus, at Rock On even. Why? Because I would have nothing to say except sorry a thousand times over. Maybe I was becoming more acute in this, the game of people. Perhaps I was long overdue a harsh lesson in this subject after Mandy. After Sarah's call I thought about the people I would really miss if I topped myself. Apart from Sarah herself, pitifully few presented themselves to me. Martin, certainly, and possibly Nick. Oh, and Fidel. Christ, would I miss my trusty Fidellino! While Mandy and I had gone into meltdown, Nick and Antonia had kept an aloof distance. During the summer, the happy news that Antonia was pregnant came to us via a text-message. All I could think about at the time was how relieved I was that Mandy had exchanged her milk for gall and was incapable and unwilling to have kids. The situation was hideous and terminal enough as it was. The news didn't exactly surprise me. If any woman was born to rear children it was that fertile, nurturing, earth-mother, Antonia. It had been abundantly obvious that her job at *Acquisition* was only a way of marking time until her real role in life was undertaken. Nick, aloof and dandyish, guarded about his freedoms, had put off the vexed subject of children for as long as possible. But Antonia, with her fur-lined voice and acres of land where her many dogs, chicken and sheep ran free, was not to be confined to the city for long. She had always talked about moving to the country and becoming a baby-machine, something that Mandy sneered at behind her back.

I had been happy for Nick at the time, but we had lost touch. He knew I was free-floating, that I had been ejected onto the periphery of life by Mandy. I had the loser-dust on my shoulders, thicker than the dandruff on a third-former's collar. That's why I was surprised when, in early December, he invited me to the Regent for a drink. Of course, I declined. I turned away from his magnanimous gesture. I was deep in the dungeon of despond, loathsome to man or beast. A Quasimodo, unfit for human eyes. But he wasn't to be deterred. He had something to tell me, so he claimed, that couldn't be turned away from.

The door to the Prince Regent crunched shut behind me and I saw Nick at once, a pint of Guinness before him, the paper flattened on its front, showing pictures of grimacing footballers. Courteously, he stood and went for his wallet.

'Lord Byron! Long time no see.' We shook hands. 'What are you having?'

'A triple Bell's. No ice please,' I said, feeling lousy, in need of plastic surgery and a full blood transfusion. Nick disappeared to the bar and I surveyed the old familiar joint. Chapel of rest lighting. Mangy carpet. Unattended fruit machine. Unshiftable smoke. Ragged drinkers, looking as if they had been discontinued from the human race. Nothing had changed.

'Here you are,' said Nick, carefully unzipping the change purse on his wallet and filling it with coins. 'Cheers.'

We chinked glasses: his big and brown topped with a meringue of froth, mine small and vinegar-coloured, the glass slightly warm. I took a sip and followed its fire all the way to my stomach.

'Here's to marriage,' I muttered, 'that sad, sour, sober beverage.' Three Irish drinkers watched us from the sanctuary of the pool table, probably thinking: *poofs.*

'Christ,' said Nick, eyeing me intensely, his quiff falling in front of his eyes.

'What?'

'Can I say something?' he asked, a concerned look filling his face, as if he had just noticed a facet of me that he'd never seen before.

'Sure.'

'You look – you look terrible.'

I knew this was coming. But it was bracing to have someone else confirm it: a third party that wasn't my bedsit mirror. I was aware a fortnight of stubble had given the impression that I was trying for an Islamic beard; that Nick may have indeed supposed I had converted and bought a prayer mat. There was the matter of my unslept eyes, shockingly crimson on their inner rims, especially at the bottom where they seemed to be permanently full of fluid. I had also lost a great deal of weight. Unable to contemplate the empty ritual of cooking for one in the months since my break-up, I had subsisted on four-for-a-quid noodles and cheap red wine. Tyre-black smudges had begun to appear under my eyes, with newly revealed dents in my balding scalp also highlighted in the same way. Then there was the matter of my clothes. Nick, a man ever-vigilant for clothing errors or offences, would have been the first to notice that I hadn't changed out of a toothpaste-spattered jogging top for a fortnight, and that my supermarket trainers in no way matched the frayed black cords. Also that I was wearing no socks, my bare ankles resembling the sad pictures of the dead in war zones, prostrate after being shot by snipers on the way to shops.

'Thanks,' I said, and toasted Nick's glass again.

'No, seriously. You look like you've been in a concentration camp.'

'I feel it, believe me. You're not looking so bad yourself.' Nick smiled awkwardly and sat back, knowing that he had touched a nerve. He had changed too. His limbs seemed stronger, less fey and *fin de siècle* than before, his clothes rigorously ironed. I could detect that pre-emptive adultness that comes over people about to become parents. 'Have you been in training?'

'I've been putting up a few shelves, if that's what you mean.' Nick actually blushed at this. Any activity seen as uncool, especially that apogee of domestic servitude, DIY, could not be freely admitted to. But there was a defiance in his response. Out of all the people I knew (and this category was diminishing by the hour), Nick was the least worried if people liked him or not. Despite his destiny as a paterfamilias he still had his *sprezzatura*. He wanted to be admired, that went without saying, but whether you took him to your heart or not he cared not one ounce.

I took another sip of the whisky. It acted on my whole system, making me wince. I was slightly apprehensive about Nick's reason for bringing me here.

'You haven't dragged me out just to tell me that, have you? I've been lying low for a while. I really don't feel up to human company.'

'Yes. I can see that,' said Nick slowly. He looked at his paper for a moment, lost for words. The footballers grimaced back at him, caught in mid-air gladiatorial combat, gurning coliseum warriors. I decided to help him out.

'Are you and Antonia going to – to tie the knot?' I asked gingerly, 'I wouldn't be surprised if you didn't. After my terrible example.'

'Byron, don't blame yourself.' I became aware of a schism of pain in Nick's voice, also an unprecedented degree of compassion.

'Well, are you?'

'I haven't asked her yet. But it's on the cards. It seems like the obvious step, to make an honest woman of her.' He was prevaricating and we both knew it. Nick leant forward at this abruptly, as if to confide something in my ear. Whenever he did this I was always reminded of his surname. Cranford. Like crane-forward. It struck me that I had never shared this useless information with him, but his grave face deterred me from doing so now. He whispered, 'The truth is, I'm terrified.'

I laughed at this, the first time I'd laughed in weeks or so it seemed. The very muscles felt out of use, atrophied, making my face ache. I surprised myself by saying, 'There's nothing to be scared of. It will all come naturally, if you're still in love. Of course, you have to believe in every word. The vows, I mean. You are in love aren't you?'

'I adore her.'

'That's not the same as being in love.'

'Well, that's the best she's getting.'

'How is she anyway?'

Nick looked wary, before saying, 'She started talking to Mandy again.'

'I thought they already were – talking, that is.' A sharp pain was again present in my heart. It seemed I heard about my wife's life third-hand now. Maybe I should get used to it – used to the general conspiracy. I had been disappeared from everyone's life, like an Argentine dissident. 'I mean – they went on holiday together to Italy. Women can't do that without talking.'

'I know, but Antonia was still keeping Mandy at arm's length. They were best friends once.'

'How can I forget?'

'I thought you may like to know a cheering bit of trivia.' Nick leant forward again. 'Do you remember that dog you and Mandy had? The first one? The smooth-coated chihuahua?'

'Concepcion?' Trust dog-mad Antonia to keep track of Mandy's mutts. 'Yeah. We sold her to a loony granny up in Hampstead who lived in, like, a turreted castle.'

'Well, the other week Antonia announces she wants a pedigree dog. Not content with the fact that her father's farm is swarming with them, she insists she has to have one that very day. Hormonal, of course. One minutes it's M&Ms by the bucketload, then Angel Delight, now pedigree dogs. So she carts her bulk over to Hampstead and finds this mad old woman wanting to sell three smooth-coated chihuahuas.'

'Don't tell me, the mother was called Concepcion.'

'Dead right. And she apparently had these puppies just after you sold the little terror to her.'

'But we were told she couldn't give birth. That it would kill her . . .'

'Well, she was a freak of nature. So that means the father must be—'

'Fidel!' I said, and felt a hot pain well up in me. Dangerously unstable, sensitive as a thermometer, over the past few days the slightest things had forced tears into my eyes. A chipped cup. A certain song. The look of the towering chestnut tree out back fencing with the wind.

Nick sat back smiling, as if a valve had opened and pressure had been let out from his neck. I would miss Fidel terribly, that I knew. Pride, nevertheless, for his paternity, after we had done so much to obstruct it, swelled inside me. Then a sadness that Fidel would never get to see his children. In the end, he would be just another absent father. I fought back the strong impulse to weep and said, 'So is that it then? The purpose of this meeting? I thought you had something important to tell me.'

'Not exactly.' A strange squint in Nick's eyes told me the game was up now.

'What, then?'

He took a deep breath and said, 'When did you last see your friend Rudi?'

The subject of Rudi very rarely came up with Nick. They had disliked each other intensely from the word go. Nick thought the Scots wheeler-dealer a barbarian and Rudi, in turn, had Nick down as snooty poseur. I said, 'The other night. No, last night. Why?'

'Did you know that Rudi fucked Antonia?'

Stunned, I said, 'Jesus. No. When?'

'A couple of years ago. He came round to fix her car and I found them hard at it on the back seat.'

I started to tremble nauseously at this revelation. My jogging top felt wet with sweat, as if I had just completed a half-marathon. I knew Rudi was always leching after Nick's girlfriend, but he did that with every woman. To see him in action was a marvel: he had to be the most sexually successful male on the street at any given time. Argus-eyed Rudi – out shopping with his latest squeeze, but still checking out every piece of tail on the pavement: white, black, oriental, pubescent, menopausal. Rudi with his philanderer's toolkit: toothbrush, condoms, deodorant, *A–Z*, importuning sexual stare. And he always said Antonia was the ultimate: stacked, petite, and young, too. But there was a paradox here. Because, though seemingly an equal-opportunities skirt-chaser, when it came to close liaisons, any woman past twenty-five was a write-off in his universe. According to him, once they started to wither on the vine they turned into neurotic old biddies – or became less malleable, depending on how you viewed it.

For a moment I thought this might all have been a big fib on Antonia's part to keep Nick interested, then I remembered he had had the ocular proof. I stammered, 'What did – how did you react?'

'I offered him out, of course. You must remember that black eye he had. It gave me great pleasure to see it lasted for almost three months.'

'He told me that was from a ruck outside a boozer.'

Nick said sniffily, 'Well, he would say that, wouldn't he.' He preened himself on the creaking wooden chair. I suddenly admired him for doing what any man automatically should under the circumstances. Men had evolved strangely. Clubs at sunset had probably metamorphosed into pistols at dawn, and so on into mere words wielded by generations of passive eunuchs. Or was that just me?

'I'm stunned.' Then a horrible thought crossed my mind. 'The baby. Antonia's – your – child? You don't think it's . . . ?'

'Not a chance. She swore blind. And just to be sure, I've booked the DNA test.'

'Rudi Buckle! The slimy jock bastard!'

Nick cleared his throat and said, 'Fancy another?' I looked down at my glass. Without realising, I had finished my whisky. Then he added, ominously: 'You're going to need it.'

Moments later another triple Bell's and a Guinness were on the table. Nick's sensitive eyes caught the low pub lighting as he said, 'That's not the worst of it.'

'Well, that's pretty bad.'

'Remember when we came here that time after the market?'

'Yeah. The good old bad old days.'

'And the football came on. Man U versus Bayern Munich in the final?'

'Whatever.'

'Well I was about to tell you something, but unfortunately that contest was too good to miss.'

This was typical of Nick. No sense of proportion whatsoever. I scratched my stubbly chin and took a sip of fire water. On an empty stomach it was already making my head spin.

'Well, the season's over. Feel free to fire away.'

Nick looked grave, as grave as I had ever seen him as he said: 'Rudi fucked Mandy too.' I went to open my mouth but no sound came out. Instead I swallowed back a mouthful of vomit combined with the finest Scotch whisky. Shaking his head in that mock-weary way of his, Nick continued, 'And not just the once – he still is.'

———————

I was never cut out to be a philanderer. I knew this for a fact when I was fifteen. Conclusive proof came when Rhianna, my first sweetheart, took me to the youth-club disco one Friday night. There, under the eternal mirror balls, her best friend Monica slipped her phone number into my pocket, with the urgent message 'Call me – your Lordship' written under it in a girlish hand. When I examined it later, with my heart racing at an accelerating rate of knots, I noted that the biro 'i' of Monica bore a love heart instead of a dot. This almost caused me to ejaculate on the spot. The truth was, Monica had been giving me the eye for months. She never missed an opportunity to gently touch my arm or giggle flirtatiously in my presence at parties. Nubile, slim-waisted and fond of suede miniskirts, I can see Monica now playing havoc with marriages as she slips her mobile number into the pockets of her girlfriends' husbands at sophisticated dinner parties; a lipsticked kiss under her name, the same love heart over the 'i'. A singular man-stealer and goer. I spent the following weekend in a riot of testosterone-driven panic. Monica filled my dreams like the archetypal erotic enchantress: Salome, Carmen and Clara Bow rolled into one. Then, finally, on the Sunday night, I flushed the number down the toilet. Why? Because I loved Rhianna. I thought we were going to get married and live in the country with dogs and books while she raised my heir. She would get fat (or fatter), but I would be faithful. This is the first mistake that a would-be philanderer can make. To be troubled by your conscience virtually counts you out from the off. The seasoned womaniser or girl-gourmet knows that whoever he is going out with or married to will either never find out, or if she does, will suddenly agree on the spot to an open relationship just to keep him. This is the first rule of the roué: never let anything so unfashionable as morality bother you. For a split-second. Wait too long and someone else might be in there, yanking off that suede skirt with his teeth.

The second rule is: never pass up an opportunity. Life is short, shorter than any of us realise, and no one wants to be sitting there at eighty, like Betjeman in the wheelchair, tartan travel rug over his legs, moaning that he didn't have enough sex. The professional philanderer or crumpeteer knows the world is full of women and will set about them systematically, if not alphabetically, then at least geographically by country of origin. When I was contemplating marriage with Mandy, I thought with real regret about all the sex I would never have, that I was disqualifying myself from by prom-ising fidelity. The raunchy afternoon encounter with the unmarried mother of two (the dressing-gowned greeting, the unbelievably professional fellatio); the pneumatic sugar with her voluminous folds and dusky aroma; the trapeze-artist Chinese with her versatile waist and flower-like hands (who will walk on your back and crack your bones); the ice-maiden Swede with legs as long as the Baltic channel; the three-in-a-bed romp with two pierced punkettes met down the Electric Ballroom on a cider binge; the businesswoman in her night-black stockings bent over the hotel mini-bar; the Jacuzzi encounter with a notorious dollybird or Page Three regular; the identical twins who both resemble Farrah Fawcett Majors in her goddess period; the willing cheerleader; the five-grand-a-night hooker; the girl next door; the nymphomaniac dominatrix; the list of platonic girlfriends as long as your arm; the schoolgirl; the slut; the Vestal Virgin.

None of the above, atrocious reader, I reflected, would I ever get near. The philanderer, on the other hand, wouldn't see marriage as an obstacle – he would see it as *cover*. And that highlights another handicap, another reason why I would never make it as a practised tail-chasing skirt-merchant: I am the world's worst liar. My overly candid eyes, too impercipient for a man of thirty, have a habit of dilating and announcing, *look at me, I'm lying to you very badly*. My inept mendacities would land me in the divorce court within hours of any forbidden encounter.

Lastly, and most importantly, I wouldn't be able to stand the strain on the soul. As much as the hyperactive running around town, the jellied legs, the struggle to remember so many female names is exhausting, the stress on the soul is greater. The inner emptiness, the animal cunning, the sheer fraudulence required to be a top-notch screwer of women (an Alfie or a Mark Antony – pick your model) would send me to the loony bin. Byron Easy: poet and failed womaniser. Mad, sad and not very dangerous to know.

None of these scruples, however, troubled my dear friend Rudi one whit. Honest, honest Rudi. According to Nick, it turned out he had been balling my missus behind my back, virtually from day one . . . It fills me with relief to get this off my chest, to lay my palms flat on the Formica before you, reader. It may go some way to explain my behaviour, or the strange mental areas I was leading you into. The special trouble I referred to earlier. Maybe this will elucidate my pathological anger. If there's any divine justice Rudi will end up in the Ninth Circle, with all the other prolific betrayers, with Brutus and Judas. But the world as it is tonight tells me there is no justice. I'm not making excuses for myself, don't get me wrong. I'm just relating the facts as they are, in reality. It wasn't such a mystery after all. Because it all adds up. Only a blind man would not have noticed it. But then, many things just recently have confirmed me to be partially sighted at the very least. The frequency with which the Scottish carouser of Kentish Town was getting away with it was spellbinding. I should be issued with a guide dog! That ubiquitous Sir Smile! His stocky presence in my kitchen when I came home unexpectedly, the secret late-night calls by Mandy, her frequent disappearances from the market stall with Rudi to 'talk business', and, more recently, more flagrantly (and my heart boils to recall it), the way he insisted he keep the honeymoon underwear that Mandy returned. You guessed it. It wasn't for Suki, the poetry-mad gangster's moll. It was for my lawfully wedded wife.

When Nick told me all this in the Regent I blacked out. Five minutes later, covered in whisky and spittle, a mad dog on a chain, I was forcibly restrained by the three Irish pub hardmen who lurked by the pool table. 'I'll cut them to pieces!' I howled, as Nick helped by getting me in a headlock. 'The fucking both of them!'

But I didn't, in the end, want to be seen as one who loved unwisely.

The train is thundering, hurtling, plummeting to its destination . . . an arrow in the night. The blue gardens of Leeds are splashed with moonlight. In the distance is the vast, humming, orange glow of the urban conurbation. Cold, impersonal as a circuit board. It won't be long now . . . Not long till I meet my mother; not long till we all hear the dreadful twelve gongs of Big Ben that signal the end of a millennium. No, the end is close to being achieved.

It all seems pretty obvious now. Like my father before me, I had been royally cuckolded. There was a sweet symmetry to it all; an ordered sense of proportion and rightful return that I found almost soothing. Like father, like son – and I formerly thought we had so little in common. Sobering to finally find out where you stand in the majestic roll call of men, of history. All great men have been heroes, conquerors and cuckolds in their time, or so spake the great poet. I was the drunken patsy, the motley-wearing fool jeered at by the court when he believes he's making them laugh. Nick had known for almost two years. I wonder how many other things he had withheld from me. Thanks, friend. I won't bother talking to you again. What to do with Rudi, though? That was the question I struggled with for three long weeks. During which time I saw him almost every night. That was a test, as you may imagine. Maybe I'm stronger than I give myself credit for. I didn't act immediately, of course, that would have been hasty. But instead of writing an ottava rima on the weekend's events – my usual instinct – I began to make fiendish plans in earnest. I wanted to cook up something special for both of them, those two actors, those Oscar-winners. Something Biblical, something Shakespearean. I also needed to broil in my own goulash of self-reproach for a while.

It wasn't until last night that I cracked it. Last night, the twenty third of December – the day after my wedding anniversary of course, with delicious apposition – I paid a visit on my old friend Rudi Buckle.

He had been expecting me. The hefty-shouldered Scot ushered me in, then automatically went to undo the latch of his patio doors at the far end of his bachelor lair. This was a Pavlovian reaction to the cigarette I always sparked on arrival. His movements were slow, solid, plausible as ever. The picture of innocence, I thought!

'That's all right,' I shouted to him, aware that my voice was as chilly as the night air. 'I gave up, remember.'

Rudi stopped in mid-movement and pulled the door back. He surveyed me curiously, suspiciously. Our long acquaintance informed us both instantly when something was up with the other. We could sit in silence for half an hour at a time and not feel the imperative to speak, or say a single sentence and convey something was amiss. I didn't want the latter. I wanted to play him along for a little while. To wade up to my neck in the sewer of shit one more time. I smiled, and he smiled back.

'What can I get you, big man?' He was wearing his customary red shirt, with an undergrowth of eager chest hair escaping uncontrollably from the collar. His large, white, fleshy hands looked warm and pillow-soft, the nails bitten. The bangs of his hair, now grown long to his shoulders, flopped like oily fronds onto his shirt. His black eyes glowed under his strong brows, garrulous and arrogant, the whites yellowish, off-colour.

'A beer. No, make that champagne.' I knew his fridge always held champagne, and I knew he wouldn't refuse.

'You all right, spunker?' he asked in his tactful Scottish voice, and took a step towards me as if to assess me better. I felt the maleness of the moment. Two stags in a clearing. 'What's there to celebrate?'

Throwing my coat down on the scuffed brown leather sofa, I said, 'You'll find out, by and by.'

'I'm fascinated. Champagne it is then.' Seemingly placated, he disappeared to the ceiling-high fridge behind the breakfast bar. I looked around the room and tried to not to think, as I had done for the past three weeks, of all the places he and Mandy might have made love, or fucked, as you would more accurately term it. The unusual or non-obvious surfaces: the tumble-drier, the step-ladder. The positions they used. The things he said. The noises she made. The luxurious rug before the fire bore no evidence, no used condoms, no telltale ruffles. Why would it? Neither did the big armchair, the kitchen table or the dark aperture to the bedroom scream their secrets at me. The framed prints of world-class taste-lessness on the wall kept their counsel: silent, vigilant, neutral. A fire burnt in the grate as usual: aureate, like whisky held up to the light.

He returned with the heavy bottle of bubbly and sat down on the sofa opposite, still a little wary. His guilty eyes (and oh how guilty they now seemed to me, as guilty as a little boy's who had transgressed against paternal authority!) evaluated my posture, which was tense, crabbed, ready for anything.

'Relax, pal. It's Christmas in a couple of days. The time for goodwill to all men.'

The cork popped, and vapour rose from the dark gun barrel of the bottle. An arid ejaculation.

Flatly, I said, 'How's your hassle progressing? Heard from the porn baron lately?'

Relived that I hadn't opened with a personal question, Rudi leant forward and filled my flute to the brim with champagne. He went into his routine of strongly vexed evasion, his brows pressing down heavily like two black slugs, 'Och, you dinnae wanna know.'

I chinked his glass with mine. 'Cheers.'

'So what's the occasion?'

'You'll find out.'

His distrustful look returned. He could tell something volcanic was bubbling under in me, magma-like, waiting for an opportunity to vent. He said, 'Your good health, sir,' and returned my gesture with his glass. Like an old friend.

'I mean the contract they had out on you. Two grand for a maiming with a blunt instrument. Three for a sexual injury.'

Rudi winced. I bet he felt that one. 'Aye, that's still in the air. I seem to be keeping the bastards at arm's length though.' I almost said, 'That's a shame', but let his slimy lips continue the story. He revealed that, the previous night, his foray into the London under-world had culminated in him driving a getaway car to north Wales after an abortive warehouse raid. Once over the border on the return journey, expecting to find five hundred cases of Silk Cut and a kilo of coke, all they discovered were bags of manure and pig feed. He continued, 'Take the other week for instance. The Welsh fiasco. Because I was the new man on the job, they thought I staged the whole thing as a wee set-up. That I had all the loot in mah hoose. I told them they could come back here and poke about to their heart's content.'

'And did they?'

'Aye,' said Rudi and sank bank onto the groaning sofas. He rolled his shoulders like an oxen under a yoke. He was at ease now. Sure that I hadn't found him out. We were playing cat and mouse. I decided to show my claws.

'Did they find anything?'

Rudi flushed red, intensifying the barbecued effect produced by his sunlamp. 'Not a crumb. But I had half a kilo of resin in my pocket from the back of the car. The stupid Taffy fuckers who did us over must have left it with the fertilisers by accident.'

'I bet that required a lot of acting,' I said, and drained the cham-pagne. Courteously, Rudi reached forward to replenish my glass.

'I was shitein' myself,' he roared. Outside I could hear the same curious clanking that was always present at Rudi's, like a cowbell relentlessly struck.

'But you always were good at acting. I remember your Kowalski in the school play. Tough, uncompromising, irresistible to women.'

Rudi puffed up at this. He loved flattery. 'Aye, that was choice. Hey, you're knocking that back.'

'Well I'm celebrating, am I not?'

'Aw come on man, tell me the occasion,' he importuned.

'I'm celebrating a breakthrough. I've turned a corner.' I drained my drink and set it on the table. With the effervescence provided by two glasses of bubbly, I fixed the dark points of his eyes with mine. 'No longer will I pine after Mandy. I've seen through her. She's as transparent as – as this glass of fizz. That's all she was, really. Froth in a glass. She was no fury, no termagant.'

'That's ma boy!'

'Do you still do much acting, Rudi?'

He shifted uncomfortably in his seat, cradling his glass in his groin. 'No. Why would I? What do you mean?'

'How long has it been going on?'

Silence. Except for the hollow clank clank clank from the darkness outside. I watched Rudi seemingly diminish in his seat as his eyes recognised my implication. No need for lengthy explanations between old friends. He knew. I knew. We both knew. His shoulders, hands, chest, head seemed to shrink visibly. The whole room felt suddenly small as a diving bell.

But still no answer. For a moment I thought he was going to bolt from the room. From the inquisition. The expected reprimand.

In his soft dexterous voice he said, 'About two years. I'm sorry, Bry.'

An electric pause.

'You were my best man.'

'What can I say? She made all the running. Honest.'

'You were my best friend.'

'I know, I know,' he looked at his feet, the fireplace. Anywhere but my eyes.

'Do you know what I'm celebrating tonight, Rudi?'

I took the phallic bottle from the centre of the table and poured us both another glass. The fizzy head overflew the rims and surged down the stems, blackening the wood of the table. Under normal circumstances Rudi would have pulled me up about this, but he had no choice but to sit and endure my supremacy.

Sullenly, like a little boy, he answered, 'Naw, man. Why don't you tell me.'

'I'm celebrating the end of our friendship. It's been, what, twenty years now? We've been through a lot. School. Girlfriends. London. But now I've finally seen what a bag of shit you are.'

Rudi went to stand. I thought he was going to hit me, but then I saw the glaze of tears in his eyes. Sentiment and deception. That tired old pantomime horse. My nerves were tingling with the arousal of vindication. A hollow excitement sensitised my skin, as if I were plugged into the mains. A hollow high, with all the blowback of an empty victory round the corner, the inevitable turnaround. I held out a hand, and he sat.

'I'm sorry. What more can I say?' Rudi pleaded pathetically. His charismatic voice was now flat as beer left out overnight.

'You don't seriously expect us to be friends after this?'

'I didnae think you would find out, especially now with you two being split up and all.'

'It must have been hard to keep it a secret. For both of you.'

'Aye,' he muttered, shamefully, his gaze fixed on the floor. He looked like a broken man, cumbersome; a bag of spuds in a glitzy crimson shirt.

'The market, for instance. The nights you drove her home after gigs.' Rudi merely flinched at these concrete examples. He resembled a man undergoing the torture of a thousand cuts. I felt like kicking his head off his shoulders like a football, but I restrained myself. 'Then there was that time earlier this year, after I burnt Mandy's breakfast and she—'

'Who told you all this?'

'What does that matter?' The helpless look in his eyes was giving me great pleasure. 'Okay. It was Nick,' I said with some satisfaction, knowing Rudi hated him.

He sneered, but refrained from a tirade of righteous disgust. That was my arena. I continued. 'You were lucky I didn't catch you at it that day. I almost followed Mandy after she stormed out.' The morning – the morning of my appointment at the Eastman Dental Hospital, where Mandy threw my copy of *Culture and Society* in the bin along with the burning bangers – she had exited with her high hauteur, her immense attitude, the ceiling light plunging to the carpet as she slammed the door. And in reality she was off to fuck Rudi. My, oh my. I was about to tail her, to make amends, even if it meant getting a cab to follow her Volkswagen, but reason had prevailed. Of course, she hadn't gone to the supermarket, as she had told me later. 'Nick said he saw the two of you hand in hand in Waterlow Park that day.' That last detail had hurt me considerably. It had been years since Mandy had held my hand, let alone consented to sex, or marital duty (as I never saw it). God knows what depravities they had enacted, maybe in the very location where I was sitting guzzling champagne. I felt a constriction in my intestines just imagining it. The champagne was reacting with the acid in my stomach. But these two – Rudi and Mandy. You had to hand it to them. What a pair of consummate thespians. And what a credulous fool I was. It must have been easy. Easy as taking candy from a – easy as pulling the trigger at a pogrom. I gave them every opportunity to display their acting skills, and boy did they take me up on it. An uxorious, patient, loving fool. Now enduring a badly needed lesson. What pedagogy, between them, did they exhibit! It was almost laudable.

'I didn't want to, Bry, but . . .'

'But it was too good to turn down, wasn't it? In a way I don't blame you – no, I do blame you, a lot. With a body like Mandy's, I mean—'

'She made all the running, Bry, God's honest truth! After the first time I didn't want to carry on!' Rudi's eyes were now wild with appeal, sweat bubbling on his meaty forehead.

'But you did carry on, didn't you,' I said coldly, pinning him to his seat. He couldn't answer for a moment. The room had now transmogrified into something larger, strangely altered, differently lit; the pastel bulbs of Rudi's seducer's lighting burning a lemony yellow. The hollow gong outside a death knell.

'Aye,' he said ruefully, like a schoolboy before the headmaster.

'How could you live with yourself?'

'I dinnae know.'

'How could you sleep at night?'

He shrugged foolishly, 'You've got me there.'

'How could you have me round night after night for the last three months, listening to me disintegrate? Bold as fucking brass?'

'I had to, didn't I?'

'Did you? What was it, some kind of penance to listen to my shit? Your single act of contrition?'

'Maybe.'

'But you don't know, do you? Because you haven't got a clue about anything. You tell me I'm your friend and then fuck my wife. You sit downwind of my disgust and then say it's an act of penance when I put the idea into your head. You twist the truth with me, then think you can apologise and make everything okay. You probably twisted the truth with her for all I know. Certainly with yourself. If you think you've bullshitted me, its nothing to the porkies you've told yourself. There's nothing to you, Rudi. You're a blank. A nothing. A waste of space!'

Rudi took this verbal kicking in silence, like a condemned man. Then he caught my eyes from a lateral angle, like he was framing a picture. I knew what was coming. His explanation. His mitigating circumstances.

'But I tried to put a stop to it, from the start! It was all a big mistake, with a mate like you, Byron. I think she did it because she, how can I say it . . .'

'Say it.' I was interested, even in his garbage.

'. . . Because she hated you. She said she'd grown to hate you. It was awful to hear, with you being mah best friend and that. I used to try and shut her up, but, after that first time, she was ringing me up day and night.' I shifted in my chair at the confirmation of this. Something that Nick couldn't verify, only the guilty parties. Mandy's punishment quickly went from suffocation, or a merciful strangulation, to burning at the stake. I felt dangerous sitting there, my heart pounding, my stupid feelings on fire. Rudi continued, 'It was like a tidal wave of phone calls. Mainly at work.' Again, I took a sharp intake of breath. So she phoned Rudi at work, just like she used to harass me until I finally gave in. In a smooth voice, Rudi went on: 'I never thought she liked it that much, but she said I was her only excitement in life, that her marriage – you and her, like – was all but over, that she only used you to pay the rent. I told her to stop using you and get a divorce, but she wouldn't listen. I hated lying to you, Bry, honest, you've got to believe me, God's honest truth, I know I like to put it about a bit, but I never wanted to do this to a mate. It was always a point of honour with me never to—'

'Stop!' I shouted as loud as I could manage. I couldn't bear any more of his cheap excuses. I stood up and faced him down.

Rudi looked stunned at the reverberation of my voice; scared, uncertain. Tentatively, he asked: 'What are you going to do to me?' I saw at that moment the full loneliness of his life. How much he needed me. How much he required a stooge, a scapegoat, someone to deceive, someone to destroy. Without such another he truly was impotent. Also, how much he needed someone to drink with; to play at full-blown masculinity in the company of another man. Although a chick-connoisseur and dedicated tail-chaser he didn't actually like female company. Hated it, in fact. Bored him to death. Nauseated him with their banal pronouncements, risible vanities. No, Rudi only wanted one thing from women, that Holy Grail between their legs. And once that had been achieved the conquest was over and he sought out male company. The only problem was that the Holy Grail often belonged to his friends or business associates. He would continue incorrigibly in this fashion until he died – which wouldn't be far off if I had anything to do with it.

'Do?' I enquired. 'I'm not going to *do* anything. Except maybe get another bottle of champagne.'

He seemed confused, relieved. 'Help yourself, big man.' His eyes followed me to the fridge. The tension had been broken momentarily. The room seemed to assume its normal proportions once again. I returned to the table with another bottle of bubbly.

'Shall I do the honours?' he asked subordinately; the question a distant reminder of the old days, like light from a collapsed star.

'You're welcome to each other, for all I care.'

'Don't say that, Bry. I feel terrible. I've never felt worse.'

Secretly I thought, Oh, you will do, and stifled an inner compulsion to giggle, to start dancing.

I smiled. 'I'm serious. Do you think I wanted her back anyway? Christ, after what she did to me?'

Rudi seemed tangibly to relax. His paddle-shaped hands grasped the bottle and swiped off the golden sheath in an easy movement. This, however, was all part of my plan. To placate him. For I had to work fast, skilfully.

'She is a psycho, ah'll give you that!' he grinned, as if we were two friends finding mutual fault with a woman we had both willingly shared. But we hadn't willingly shared her.

'She used to slag you off too.'

'Did she?' said Rudi, suddenly affronted, very keen for information.

'Oh yeah, all the time. Said you were a pisshead, and that somebody should cut your balls off.'

'I can take that,' he said quietly, revealing that he couldn't.

'Also that your clothes were shit, you were ignorant and had bad breath.'

He smiled at this, seeing Mandy's bile as acknowledgment of his two greatest qualities: his ability to drink and his ability to score. 'She had a tongue in her head! I'm a bit surprised you only hit the stupid hen once.'

'I thought you didn't believe in that.'

'Aye,' he said uncertainly, another can of worms creaking open.

Rudi popped the cork, still unsure that I wasn't going to bludgeon him to death.

'She also said you were a stupid Scottish poseur with a fat face and arse.'

Rudi muttered solemnly, 'I don't know what to say.'

'Then don't say it. It'll spoil my celebration.' I held his gaze. 'Still, despite all that, she still fucked you. Women and their sexual choices, eh?'

Holding both glasses as he poured, I continued staring intently at Rudi, mainly to distract his attention. Go on, you beauty, pour your last glass! This was also part of the plan. As the top-notch Bollinger fizzed rapidly I dropped two colourless pills from the palm of my left hand into Rudi's flute. Go on, you priapic waste of oxygen, come to Byron! And *santé*! They were, after all, his pills. That night he had crashed at mine, running scared from whatever goon he had aggrieved, a small transparent packet had dropped from Rudi's trousers as he shed his clothes to kip on my couch. Fascinated to get anything on him at that stage, while I planned my grand revenge, I dexterously pocketed it and took it to the croupiers in the morning. Both were experts in drugs of every kind – at the casino it was part of the job description. They were unanimous. The pale, wheatgerm-like pills were Rohypnol. So this was another of his methods! Shocked, I concluded that I had been ungenerous towards Rudi in thinking him merely a master philanderer. He was a rapist too.

'Cheers!' I said.

Rudi looked surprised. 'It doesn't feel right to say that now.'

'No? I'd like you to, though.'

Between his discoloured teeth, Rudi said, 'Cheers' and drank deep.

Yes!

Betrayal. Depravity. Filth. Dissolve away! I drained my glass in one and took a look around the room. Feeling calmer, I thought: it won't be long now, my friend. We all go into the dark, eventually, you sooner than most. The liquid amber flames in the grate fluttered every time a gust came down his chimney. The breakfast bar was scrupulously wiped, the appliances gleaming on shelves, the wine rack stocked and hefty. I noticed that his bins were a series of plastic supermarket bags tied with bows queueing by the door. Disappointed that he didn't have bin-liners for his own body parts, I suddenly remembered Mandy's underwear that he seemed so keen to have that night, my wedding present to her in Barcelona, encased in their dismal plastic.

I looked at Rudi. His eyelids were already drooping. 'One more question.'

Groggily, I thought, he said, 'What's that, Bry?'

'All that gear of Mandy's. The stockings and suspenders you said you wanted for what's her name—'

'Suki.'

'For Suki. Did you ever use them with . . .'

'You don't want to know that,' he said, shaking his head wearily.

'That means you did, didn't you.'

'I cannae say.'

'But you have to.'

'Why do you want more pain?' Rudi suddenly looked at me reproachfully, like a small boy. Then his chin flopped onto his chest.

My God, that was fast! And I must act fast, I thought, climbing swiftly to my feet and running over to the bulked form of my ex-best-friend. I felt his pulse. Still alive. But he was out cold, like a marionette whose strings had been cut. Rapidly, I went through his pockets for his keys. The warmth of his thigh through the trouser material was strangely intimate, too redolent of the human animal and its needs. Because I didn't want to see Rudi as human now, not with what I had to carry out.

Finding his coil of keys, I ran to the pine-floored master bedroom and knelt at the safe. A feature of the flat, which had been a clothing manufacturer's office, the place contained three of them. Rudi liked to boast about these unmovable pre-war safes. Big and green with brass handles like a submarine's periscope, the largest was situated in his bedroom. The first key didn't work. Neither did the second. Finally, the weighty door swung wide with a sure oiled motion. Open sesame, bastardo! Inside was a sizeable amount of currency and a Jiffy bag. I wasn't after the money, he could spend that in hell. Instead I took the Jiffy bag, which was unusually heavy, closed the safe door and locked it.

Back in the living room the pastel lights seemed to conceal Rudi's slumped figure. Without his personality, his life-force, he was invisible. The flat seemed doubly empty with only me intent on performing an act of rank craziness. I tweaked his fleshy shoulders through his shirt. Not a peep. Then I emptied the Jiffy bag onto the coffee table. In front of me was a Browning automatic pistol, black and chipped, and a handful of five-pound notes. Originally a decommed weapon, or so he said, Rudi had bought it from one of the market goons. This skanker had had it doctored so it fired one shot at a time, the automatic function sadly defunct. Never having handled more than a starting pistol, the very thing frightened me, lying there with its potential for revealing a sudden eternity. I picked it up and checked the magazine like they do in the movies. It appeared full, the butter-coloured brass bullet casings topped with slugs of dull lead. Rudi had proudly showed me this fearsome weapon a month ago. We had spent the night arguing about it, like a married couple. He insisted the people he was mixed up with wouldn't hesitate to wipe him out if they found he had shafted them. It was his only form of protection, he told me. I lectured him that he had never fired a gun before and they would probably use it to blow his head off. Not so, he stated. These nutters carried machine guns so they didn't need his pissy pistol. And anyway, he had been in the army cadets at school.

Rounding on Rudi, I knelt beside him.

'Sorry, big man,' I said into his deaf ear. 'But you didn't expect to fuck her and for me to like it, did you?' Heart pounding like crazy, I poured another flute of champagne, downed it in one, and suppressed the urge to burp. I took the gun and placed it softly, lovingly at his temple. For some reason I started to laugh. It sounded indecent in the quiet of the room. The jubilant peal echoed as if in a canyon. The empty clanging from outside had finally ceased. This gun, I thought, originally bought for Rudi's protection or the bank job that he insisted he may at any moment be asked to perform, was now going to end his life. It was so wonderfully funny. And those pills, used to silence dollybirds so he could get his end away, were even funnier. I said, 'You're funny, Rudi. The best you can do is steal other people's women or rape them when they're out cold. Christ –' then I felt a thread of anger unspool deep in my stomach. An escalating wire of rage. He had lied to me for years, bare to my face. Mandy – well, she had lied too. But lying was her modus vivendi – her first instinct in any given situation. She couldn't do otherwise. No, with Rudi it was personal.

I pressed the gun harder to his temple and said, 'Adios, old chum.'

We're here! The train is slowing down! Imperceptibly, inexorably. The grinding, remorseless iron wheels decreasing in speed. The velocity dimmed. In counter-thrust, in sorrowful abdication of movement. I crane my stiff neck at the window, pressing my nose against the cold glass. The rivulet of water is back in the corner of the pane, a quivering vein. The bend of Leeds station is perhaps a quarter of a mile away, the floodlit silos for the many trains awaiting us. Rain, fast and nasty, is coming down in sweeping torrents. The station lights illuminate every detail: glitter-showers of jewels, more impressive and torrential in the icy glare. As hard and unappeasable as my heart.

Suddenly all around is movement. Robin jolts awake, nudged by an elbow in the ribs from Michelle. Ah, married life, I remember it well. Looming figures are everywhere: stretching, yawning, brushing mince-pie crumbs from beards; burping, coughing. They haul rucksacks from above my head. An infant, terribly upset to be woken, bawling like he did at his birth, his mother shushing him on her knee, looks at me through his tears.

And over so fast, like everything in life. Time is not a long-distance runner, he's a sprinter; in training for all eternity, he's faster than all of us. He's crossed the finish line before we can even leave the blocks. Over before we knew it even began. Time throws you out of the way of experience too fast – no sooner are you involved in it than you are travelling away from it. My day-long psychomachia has left me with remarkably little to remember. What stands out most are the memories. And that's no good. Because you cannot spend your whole life remembering; worshipping the goddess Mnemosyne. But, unfortunately, life is not linear – we're arrested by the past while dealing with the present. Though we pass through each metaphorical station (never to visit them again) we somehow take them with us, accumulating mental baggage as the journey goes on. The beaming shrinks would assert that this is an attitudinal thing: we *choose* to carry this baggage – the station is past; we should feel luminously free at any given moment of our lives if we choose to perceive it as such.

'Looking forward to turkey and all the trimmings?' says Michelle with an ingratiating smile. 'Your mum will be pleased to see you.'

I smile back. A smile doesn't cost anything after all, as Grandma Chloe was fond of telling me. 'I've got to find her first. It's been a while since I paid a visit.'

The bony woman stands up, constricted by the table, and thrusts her paperback inside her rather formal handbag. The dominoes and travel chess have long been stashed. 'I hope it all works out for you in the end. It's good to get things off your chest now and again.' She smiles once more and looks for Robin who seems preoccupied with his phone, one hand readied on his case which he has just dragged down from the luggage racks.

The train is at quarter speed now, the machinery crackling, undercarriage grumbling as if in the wrong gear. Sheets of rain can be heard lashing the tracks.

'Well, thanks,' I mutter, still in my seat. 'Have a good Christmas. Both of you.'

At this Robin looks at me and thrusts out his hand, his oiled hair mobile as the legs on a spider.

'Cheers, mate. Mind how you go.'

I shake his hand.

'Yes, life has but one entrance and a thousand exits.'

Awkwardly, by way of consolation, and perhaps feeling the need to match my maxim, he adds, 'Remember, what doesn't kill you makes you stronger.'

'Nietzsche,' I mumble.

'Who?'

'Never mind, safe journey.'

The aisle is now full of passengers. Aunties and uncles, long-married grandparents, stroppy teenagers wearing clothing I don't understand. My, my, if anything makes you feel thirty, then it's not knowing why certain trousers look like they're on back to front, let alone the name of the popstar who made the aberration fashionable in the first place. Everybody seems awfully anxious to get off the train, to not be in motion any longer. How wrong is that saying, 'It's better to travel than arrive.' It's *always* better to arrive! Human beings are waiting to arrive their whole lives. When really travelling, getting there is everything. And most people spend their existence merely commuting – just another form of stasis after all – while under the illusion that they are going somewhere. These weary travellers certainly look happy and relieved; though mixed with this is the anxiety that accompanies Christmas, with maybe a twist of urgency provided by the Millennium and the thought that it may be their last. The boisterous crush has taken the form of a daisy-chain down the whole length of the carriage. Then the sudden static of the tannoy. I brace myself for the anodyne message.

'*Ladies and Gentlemen, we are now approaching Leeds. Please make sure all your luggage is with you before departing the train. On behalf of GNER we wish you a very merry Christmas and hope you've had a very pleasant journey, also that you travel with us again in the near future. Thank you.*'

It didn't disappoint. Suddenly heartsick, I pull my single shoulder-bag from under my seat and push out into the queue. Ten passengers ahead of me, beyond the bobbing heads of Michelle and Robin (his hand touchingly linking hers) I see the rearing bulk of Tracksuit Man tugging his case from the luggage pens. Silent since Stevenage (I had hoped he had disembarked somewhere – anywhere – along the way), he now appears horrifically active and awake. His two children minister around him in obedient silence. With a sough of brakes, the train reaches virtual-zero speed, inching up to its buffers, the rain outside monsoon-like in its intensity. A growl from the engine, making the floor shudder. Then a gentle shunt. It is over! The long ordeal is finally at an end. Umbrellas are flourished as all the doors open at once. The queue starts to move.

But there's an obstacle. This is not good. Tracksuit Man cannot find his luggage. I shake the prickles from my toes as the snake of people takes me closer to him. Hopefully he's had a skinful and doesn't remember his old adversary. Or maybe he does and will take out his frustration at his lost or stolen belongings on me. A flush of fear makes me suddenly sensitised, wide-awake. We seem to be on a collision course. Hold it, his daughter has found his bag. A smile breaks his face, like a rip on a rugby ball. He's off. I am out of danger.

Once on the platform, I realise this is not quite the case: ahead of me, a hunched obdurate form is taking up half the thoroughfare. I see Tracksuit Man has abruptly stopped. At five foot six he still looks formidable. My goodness, what is he doing? He appears to be petting a small dog held in the arms of a tweed-jacketed lady. The dog, I notice is a chihuahua. He seems more familiar than ever. Then it hits me, with the force of a bullet, where I have seen Tracksuit Man before. He's – he's Steve, from the flat in Archway. The builder. The nutter. Memory, I have the key! Older, with flecks of grey in his savagely razed number-one crop, but none other than the same man. It is too late to avoid him now. His children notice me staring and tug his arm. He turns. His look, diligent reader, is not initially welcoming. Slowly, a weird transformation morphs his trademark moronic snarl into a smile.

'Hey!' he calls in his deep voice, clicking his fingers as if to aid his memory. 'It's Rock On, it's whatsyourname.'

'Byron,' I say, moving forward.

'Ron, me old mate, from the shared flat!'

'Steve – thought you looked familiar.'

'Yeah, I thought I'd seen you inside, or something . . . Pentonville nick.'

Simultaneously, the shame of our earlier enmity enters our faces.

'Well, er, what have you been up to?' I offer awkwardly.

'You know, bit of this bit of that. No hard feelings eh, about earlier.'

'God, no,' I say, and smile at his petulant daughter who received the back of his hand in what seems like another lifetime. Before me is the deeper past: the trip to Brighton, with Steve emptying the plastic bag of cans one after another on the back seat. The tremendous waves against the pier. The offer of marriage from the beautiful girl with the flying ebony hair. Further back still, the first evening in Mandy's room with Steve's paintbrush thrust out like a weapon towards me, the stink of paint in the June night air, the twin photos of Ramona on the mantelpiece.

'How's it going with mad Mandy?'

'Oh, we – we separated. Not long ago actually.'

'Ah, well. Times change,' he says, fixing me with his surprising ultra-blue eyes. And there was nothing more to say. We never did have anything to say to each other.

'Nice to see you again, Ron. Take it steady.'

'You too, Steve,' I say, already heading for the ticket barriers.

Then a roar at my back. Deadly, full of accusation and anger.

'Oi!'

Jumping spontaneously at this shout, I turn and see Steve's beaming face.

'Only joking, Ron!'

We wave and walk on.

And I didn't even know he had kids. Well, well, well – all around you, unseen, people's lives have been evolving, hurtling to their conclusions, then you encounter them again. And it's never who you really want to see, is it? The ghosts of old lovers or enemies always turn out to be just that: ghosts. Bea in Greece and Delph on the train: apparitions – chimerical projections both. What else could they have been? And now I bump into a man I spent most of my life avoiding when I was shacked up with his landlady. Who gave me a sock on the forehead with his case which is still smarting dully. Who once subjected me to his Fucking Amazing Heavy Metal CD on a summer night when I was falling in love. Time, coincidence, serendipity: all meaningless.

My passage into the square main area of Leeds station (obstructed by a two-sided glass box with an official operating each barrier to allow the crowds through) was brisk and unfettered. Alone in my dangerous state of excitement and despair I witnessed many scenes of repatriation – tall, virile young men swamping tiny girlfriends in huge arms; rucksacked grandparents receiving kisses from in-laws and dawdling children. All that family! All that meaningful exchange! Under the soupy lights, feeling the breath of winter on my neck after the soporific interior of the train, I struggle to extract the map from my meagre bag. The automatic doors hiss open before me as I catch a final glimpse of Robin and Michelle disappearing into the off-licence cubicle for some last-minute yuletide tipple . . . And now the rain-torn expanse of the shopping plaza. Midnight. That makes it Christmas Day. With street plan in hand I step from the station awning and brave the full violence of the weather.

Oh, you didn't really think I shot Rudi through the head did you? It was tempting, I must admit. He looked so contrite there, his head bowed, out for the count. The thought of Mandy letting herself in with the key she surely has and discovering his headless corpse was also a strong incentive to go through with it. But the strong disincentives of sewing mailbags and completing my PhD on a government-issue manual typewriter didn't appeal. The plan was always to wait, to lie in wait for her to come, to meet her lover boy, only to find *me* there. Waiting with a Browning automatic in my hand. Determined, confident, sick. I might have made her kneel, I wasn't decided. Or take the gun into her mouth in an act of mock fellatio before I pulled the trigger. But you didn't expect me to be capable of such perversity, did you? To have that capacity? A poet and a seer; a boy who wet the bed until age eleven, and started again aged thirty. No, in the end I spared them both, though they didn't deserve it, the clowns. I decided to leave Mandy to live her life – her private life. As for Rudi, he's probably only coming to consciousness now. My croupier friends said the effects of Rohypnol can last up to eighteen hours. Round about now he will see the champagne bottles arraigned like skittles on his coffee table. He will go to his safe and discover that his gun is missing. He will take up the religious life, like the penitent Henry II after his slaughter of Becket . . . There was always the thought of turning the gun on myself, as they say in news reports of mass shootings. Was I capable of that? Am I capable of that?

I must never get my hands on a gun.

Anyway, Mother's house. Turning from the shopping plaza into the deserted, grilled and boarded-up Commercial Street, I feel the weight of the pistol through my shoulder-bag. I am afraid I lied to you, again, stern critic or reader. My last lie. I promise this time. I told you I didn't have a gun. But I do. Kurt sang that he didn't have a gun, but he most certainly did. He had plenty of guns. Shotguns, pistols, bazookas, you name it. But I have just the one. Big and unwieldy and yet to be used. Sheltering in a doorway, the rain showering in rivulets from my scalp down the back of my neck, I transfer Rudi's pistol from its Jiffy bag to my coat pocket. I walk out into the downpour. It produces a pleasing heaviness as it sways.

Twenty paces up the street, I decide the rain is too intense and return to my shelter. In the nook of the doorway, I flatten the street plan on a wheelie bin and use my cigarette lighter to make sense of it. Skinner Street, Skinner Street. Somewhere east of the town hall, museum and art gallery. Ah, there it is – across a motorway bridge. I always remember the motorway bridge. I traversed it in the summer when I last visited. On the way, the sun had been strong in the big canopies of the chestnut trees, the air hot and spore-filled, with the old tram lines in the city centre gleaming like scimitars in the light. Children had swarmed fish-like to the convoy of three ice-cream vans parked up next to an expanse of green. Characteristically, with their headlong shrieks and cries, they made me think of death – or rather, how children are the torch-bearers of life in the face of adult decay. Once you get to a certain age, I mused, all one has to look forward to are deaths: one's parents', then one's friends', eventually one's own. I remember stopping there in the grandstanding sunlight, and writing these useless thoughts in my notebook, more sure than ever of the pointlessness of my so-called insights; convinced that they were quite possibly the symptoms of some mental illness.

Even with the gun in pocket, my bag still feels too heavy. I take out my black notebook and decide that it feels a lot lighter without it. Then something turns in me – a tumour of self-derision, of ridicule. How I ever thought those morbid musings would be of worth to myself or anyone I don't know. In a shaking fury, I go to the entry for that summer day and tear it cleanly out, the fast rain making the ink bulge and run in a matter of seconds. Hold on – why not the whole sorry lot? Why not drown your stillborn sons? Opening the domed lid of the wheelie bin, I hold the note-book trembling in my hand . . . then let it fall. A cloud of gruesome-smelling refuse detritus erupts in my face. That I didn't need.

Once I move off, the sheets of rain like stage curtains shifting and churning rapidly, I see the signs for my mother's district. Great puddles holding blurred neon reflections block my way. A small course of rapids seems to be flowing in the gutters, the drains greedily drinking the foaming water. Not a soul around. Where did the exodus from the train disappear to? Into snug cabs and family saloons most likely. I note the sadness of the Christmas lights festooned over the barren streets. And the silent shops, which prob-ably began their onslaught of festive advertising two weeks before Halloween. Jesus, in the future it will be Christmas *all year round*. Walking purposefully now, I hope it's not too late for mother when I arrive. In the past she would leave out a light snack downstairs, maybe a beer or two. She's good that way. Thoughtful. But then she was a teacher. You have to be thoughtful when you're devoting your sanity and your life to taking care of other people's futures, to that noble profession – like the fire service or nursing, a dirty job most people pray someone else will risk their lives doing.

Hold it, I've read the map incorrectly. This may take a while to fix . . .

It is much later. Some time has passed. It feels like I've been walking for hours. I *have* been walking for hours. You take one wrong turning and then never find your way back. The funniest dead end I wandered into in the last God knows how long was the industrial estate cul-de-sac which held, amazingly, a shackled pit pony shivering on the blackened earth. I gingerly approached it with a tube of sugar taken from the train, half expecting a shaft of incandescent light over a manger and the Three Wise Men to appear. Its tongue felt hot and rough on my freezing hands. Then it licked my face in one big sloppy swipe. It was probably the most affectionate gesture I have received from another mammal in the past six months . . . My watch tells me four in the morning. Jesus, what have I been up to? At least the rain seems to have let up. Strange comings and goings in my head, thoughts I cannot account for have been assailing me for a while. I think I shared a few with you. Did I? I honestly cannot remember. At some point during the night I passed the town hall, the museum and the blackened Royal Infirmary, the latter doing a brisk trade by the looks of it, with its Christmas Eve ambulances pulling up every five minutes or so. I must have spent a while there because I remember counting twenty-five, their revolving lights flashing under the troubled skies. Something curious has happened to time. I cannot remember when my train got in. Something odd must have happened because every-thing feels present. Everything is happening at once, simultaneously, inside my head. There is no past tense. Everything is now. Eternally now . . . So when did my train get in? It seems a long while ago now. I hope Mum is still waiting up.

★

Just stopped for a bacon sandwich and a cuppa at one of those all-night hutches that look like garden sheds on wheels. I literally stumbled across it. And a moment ago I was lost. I left Merrion Street and turned into the great long curve of North Street, which, if I remember correctly, will take me over the motorway. I am on the right track now. It took me a while, but I made it. These all-night transport caffs are always lots of fun. The characters you meet at four on Christmas morning, I tell you! After the tattoo competition and the ragged fight over who gets the last onions on their hot dog, I leave the company of my fellow humans and stand apart in contemplation. There's not much else to do but sip my boiling tea, swathed in the smells of grilling. Time is indeed behaving oddly. I feel out of time – above it slightly, like Boethius posited God must be for the universe and predestination to work. If this is the case, then it means I have become God in the time it took to walk from Leeds station to this blighted van parked on a sliproad somewhere. And this is the kind of thought I can do without.

I hear the drone of cars. I must be very close. This must be it, the motorway.

Once across the bridge (with its temptations to hurl myself over) I feel brightly optimistic that I'm almost there. Keep passing those open windows, I tell myself – how could I cheat my mother out of a last meeting? Also, I can't tell you how surprised I was to pass a Byron Street a while back. I wonder why mother never told me about it. Well, I was always Brian to her. I take my map out again and see I am just around the corner. The sky above is that broiling blue of nowhere-time, Eliot's uncertain hour before dawn. My watch says six a.m. I wonder how it's taken me so long? Voilà! Here we are – Skinner Street. All the houses look the same, so I have to be careful. I don't want to knock on the wrong door. At this time of night, that would be like waking the dead. The grass on the approach to her place is dark and squelchy underfoot. Yes, I remember how the grass runs out and gives way to a long path. Damn, they all look so similar in the dark. I try my cigarette lighter but it's gone, kaput, dead. Ah, ha! I knew it was around here somewhere. I look up at the sky and notice the moon above a spire, big and ocular behind sprinting clouds. I stand before my mother's front door. Usefully, I don't have to go by house number. The big marble doors on her street all have the names of their occupants chiselled in definite lettering. Hers reads: In Loving Memory, Sinead Mary Maguire, 1939–1999.

The funeral was held at the end of July. I remember the train racing in splintering light past stretches of water so blue they seemed to belong in the Mediterranean. Distant rows of poplars flamed in the strong light, the sky full of surreal architectural clouds. Time seemingly motionless. Every mile or so, a corn field blazed richly up a slope as the carriages streamed under dappled canopies of trees. A sensation of farms, towns, villages, cities passing in quick succession kept my mind from the ultimate destination, the church on Skinner Street, where the small pine coffin awaited surrounded by men in charcoal suits.

The cancer had started as an unobtrusive lump in her throat. About the size of a green bean; but hard, very hard, like a bullet; unyielding to the touch. She had been ill that night in the Indian restaurant, but hadn't told anyone. Characteristically, with the wisdom drawn deep from a life of suffering, of divorce and separation, of rash action and prolonged consequence, she chose to keep this part of her private life private. A morning like any other had revealed it, in front of the grey mirror in the tinctured light of early dawn, before the routine day in the classroom, only months away from retirement. Arranging her hair into its bun so the scarf could be tightened around it, her fingers had tugged at the necklace that had become snagged in the silk material. And there it was. So revelatory, so surprising, so hard, like an amulet under the skin. How had she never noticed it before? Now her fingers had found it, she couldn't stop worrying the dark bead under the pale Irish skin. What was it made of? What colour was it? How long had it been there? Was it black? Was it death? Finally, irrefutably death? Panicked, she had dropped the scarf and phoned her GP, thinking all the time: this is it, this is how it ends, not a heart attack, not a speeding car, but here with the discovery of a rock-like, unappeasable impostor in her own body.

They operated a fortnight later, and showed her the tumour in the kidney dish. It was indeed black, redolent of death; as menacing as the voided sleep of eternity. For a couple of months she was in the clear. But the doctor's warnings had proved correct. The cancer had spread, like a multiplying tar throughout her body, down to her lungs and diaphragm. A corrupting inimical progression, invisible on the exterior. And her with no one to go home to, an empty dinner table and double bed in her Yorkshire semi, washed up there after the rapids of life – no one but her errant son, now married to a difficult half-Spanish woman, and her younger daughter, fathered by a man she no longer saw, whose very face, the face that had at times seemed to her as handsome as a Viking's, was now banished from every photograph album, every conversation, even her own memory. And those vital energies, which seemed to vibrate her long aquiline nose as she spoke, now quelled by a cowardly disease, one that says it's gone, never to darken your door again, when all the while it is still there inside wreaking havoc, turning you bald via chemotherapy, giving you pain that you hadn't experienced since childbirth, killing you by degrees.

As the train neared Leeds that summer day, I thought of her alone in her house, on the dark mornings as her strength failed, as the cards from work colleagues collected on her simple dresser, like cormorants on an outcrop of rock, until they were all moved to her hospital bedside, along with her favourite books.

Sarah was the first person I saw on arrival, suffering terribly from hayfever if I remember correctly. It was hard to tell the real tears from the deceptive ones, as it had been in Lille with my father as he chopped the onions. I gave her a tissue and she said, 'Thanks

Byron, you're always so well prepared.' Once outside, after the numbing eulogies, the priest dark-eyed and deep-voiced, we watched the surprisingly small yellowish box as it was lowered into the grave. The earth was thrown in, great handfuls containing small stones, and smelling richly of the ground. The light came streaming through the yews, causing an old friend of my mother's to express a worry that she may get sunburnt.

At least, I thought my mother had endured an empty bed . . . In the modest chapel, with its monochromatic mourners, there had been a number of people I didn't recognise. The pews were crammed – mostly men and women in their sixties and seventies, with the ravaged, hacked-about faces of anyone who's seen three-score-and-ten; plain-as-spades Yorkshire faces, black suits tight under armpits, dewlaps resting on crisp collars, all the accoutrements of mortal difficulty in their eyes, skin, cancelled expressions. After a reading, by my half-sister, of Tennyson, she rejoined me at the front, the buoyant cadences of Vivaldi's 'Summer' filling the church. She nudged me in the side and pointed to a tall, head-bowed man with abundantly healthy head of dark hair that seemed at odds with his deeply creased face. This, apparently, was Benjamin Brown, with whom my mother had shared her last years. A decent, hardworking man neither Sarah nor Sinead had informed me of. I was flabbergasted. Not only at how little I knew of my own mother, how little I had enquired, how unobservant I had been in her house, the hospital and, finally, in the hospice that held her cradled form in her last days, but also astonished that I was the last to know anything. And also startled at my own feeling of happiness in knowing, in the end, she may have been happy.

The box gone into its beastly hole in the earth, I lingered with Sarah in the relentless glare. A towering goldmine of a day: the azured vault stretching to the near horizon, the light touching the leaves with its gentle fire; the full-bloom hedgerows unbearably blue with lavender, the indolent summer breeze speaking of wild fertility. And no rain anywhere to remind me of her rain-coloured eyes.

As Sarah gripped my arm ever tighter, her defiant eyes staring sightlessly into the ground, the axing finality of it all almost knocking me off-balance, I thought of Mandy by her mother's grave that chilly day. The barren afternoon I stood as she laid a wreath and spoke to her mum as if she were alive under the soil, a matter of feet away. With me enduring all the pangs of 'up here'. Well, now a kind of parity had been reached between us, I could understand her better. Mandy, whom I knew to be wrong for me even as we kissed forbiddenly for the first time like Paolo and Francesca, the sunlight pouring through the open sashes. Mandy who would eventually shop me to the cops for supposedly knocking her about when they were called that night of our last awful fight. Mandy, exigent in the extreme, a victim when wrong, a martyr when right. Mandy, that splendid actress and manager, full of zinging efficiency and purpose, who would use those qualities in the professionalism of her betrayal, though I didn't know it then. Mandy – that festering lily! That Cressida! And yet . . . until you encounter the same pain as someone, you have no idea who they really are. Because that pain, that bereavement, becomes part of them, like the ossification of bones, or the indelible spilling of ink onto paper. The subject and the abstract emotion are merged for good. If I ever came close to forgiving her it was then, by that gaping hole, into which rushes all our projections and hypothetical conjecture about what, if anything, comes next. The hole next to which it is proper to feel the torment of things never said, of thanks never given, of time never shared. The black rectangular gouge in the ground by which we contemplate the bottomless mystery of what it is to be alive, to be in motion, to be assailable by the world we're born unwillingly into.

Sarah tugged my sleeve and whispered through her sobs, 'David's here.' I turned and nodded hello to her meaty-faced boyfriend – still slightly dog-like and in his element in a situation that didn't require humour. He was accompanied by a woman I hadn't seen for years. My mother's friend Barbara, or Babs, with whom I used to stay at her child-infested council house in Stevenage. Sure enough, she was still the largest woman I had ever seen, with her folds like black cushions absorbing the light of the unforgiving sun; she too was weeping uncontrollably. Seeing her there made me think of Delph in his seventies prime, and feel for once a measure of *his* pain: walking into a marriage with a child he knew no other way to discipline other than to hit, as he in turn, so my mother had told me, had been hit by his father. And later, desperate for a family with a woman nearing her forties, eager for something meaningful in his life; excluded, marginalised, playing second-fiddle to somebody else's soap opera, the product of another relationship. It could have all worked out so well for everybody, if he hadn't been held powerless in the grip of uncontrollable appetites. If he had had an ounce of mitigating intelligence to inform him of *what he was doing* with the emotions of other people, not just my mother's. If, when he had forced Sinead into having a child by him, he hadn't taken for granted her unimpeachable sacrifice.

Behind me, I was aware that Sarah, David and Babs were talking softly. But I didn't register a word — all I heard was Sarah's soft, confident voice like a bird singing in the solitude of a deep wood. Instead, I stood with the sun idiotically and unsympathetically warming my face, staring into the dark hole, and saying in my head all the unsayable, unrefinable things that come from love.

———————

It all looks very different now, the graveyard, in the darkness, with its long indistinct path, the heavy clouds rolling above, the first glimmers of dawn in the sky — although the latter could be an optical illusion. It occurs to me, as I trace my finger along the wet grooves of my mother's name on the stone, that the blue-black void of the sky is similar to the sight my mother's soul is experiencing. In other words, nothingness. If that's the case, I really have nothing to fear. Maybe I should give you, tired reader, the satisfaction you deserve and blow my head off right away. Maybe. But first some last words.

If I glance around I can just make out the shadowy presences of tombs: Victorian family plots with their carved angels missing heads or wings; long slabs with information desecrated by moss and the vandal's aerosol; newer stones like my mother's, the black marble catching glints from the moon which journeys fast above, behind intermittent clouds. Nearer still is a Jewish grave, with its touching pebbles arranged in arcane patterns; rain-wet, devoid of the wilting flowers deemed appropriate by the gentile. I surprise myself by how at home I feel here, with time itself seemingly arrested, my heart broken, yet brokenly living on. There is a clarity to everything around me, the stones, the blades of grass silver in the moonlight, the beached diggers, the crisp shadow of the church on the blue ground – although, it has to be said, a lot of the graves look poorly maintained. Shame on those relatives. I hadn't thought death could look so ugly. But predominantly there is the feeling that I have finally arrived at Now, that finally I am living in the present tense, with all impetus to future action cancelled, all lust for revenge dissipated. Ah, revenge. The moment for actual revenge has passed. I let Rudi and Mandy live – the latter mainly because now, and at that summer funeral with the July sun outrageously at odds with my gravid heart, I have a measure of how she felt. I too wondered, as I wonder now, whether Sinead is watching me, like Mandy imagined her mother was. Now I know what it feels like to wish for a mother's touch of deep redemptive tenderness and know, finally, that none will ever come again. No, out of all the feelings or naive notions about human behaviour that brought me here, revenge is the worst, the lowest. Because, although reputed to be a dish best served cold, it resonates for me with the casual violence of the world – like the spear in Christ's side – easily meted out, but taking centuries to correct. So, any kind of real retribution will always be off the menu. However, if you abuse people emotionally or physically in this life you can expect to be revenged within the pages of fiction. It's the least you can expect. In fact, you (whoever you are) should be fucking honoured – think of Dickens's villains, immortalised with an affectionate hatred. That's a small price to pay – nothing to the foaming calumny of a wife, the blows from a man who pretended to be your dad, the sexual abuse of a headmaster.

Sexual abuse. Why is it when I think of something shameful from my past – some aberration or incident – immediately there flashes up this image of a gun blowing my head to pieces, my own finger on the trigger? It is an infallible synaptic process. And why does it always come down to sexual abuse in the end? Why does it make Hitlers and suicides and junkies? The world of adult appetites crashing in when you didn't know they even existed. Delph. The Reverend Cave. The satanic agents of my downfall. They couldn't keep their hands to themselves. Maybe they had had it done to them. In that case, one can really ascribe it to ignorance – the blithe lack of insight that what hurt them might in turn hurt others too. And such a cliché, to be hurt by it, to be fucked up by it. On my gravestone, if there's enough room, they should inscribe – Here Lies A Cliché.

But I forget. There won't be a gravestone. Only a midnight burial at the crossroads.

Sitting down now, in the long wet grass, I take Rudi's pistol from my pocket and lay it on my thigh. In the gutter I can see the stems of cut flowers, decaying orange peel and sweet wrappers from the day's visits. There's a strong wind in the high yews, making that old sound. And all around me – a homunculus surrounded by giants – the dead, wringing their hands on their plinths of stone. Irrationally, I find I'm scared of necromancers or Satanists or deranged lovers disturbing me in the act. And what act is that? The act of self-destruction. Here I am, possibly surrounded by the ghosts or souls of my significant dead (mother without her trademark headscarf, Grandma Chloe without her beatific eyes, Ramona lacking her seemingly ineradicable flesh) thinking about topping myself. I must, after all, be my own worst enemy. What more terrible enemy can a person have than a self that is hell-bent on destroying itself? Born to be my own destroyer! I should have died in a duel with Rudi, like Pushkin. That would have automatically conferred immortality. Is that what I'm looking for? *Non omnis moriar*? Or is it merely oblivion – an end to the tiring vicissitudes of life, with its relentless wheel that dashes hopes as soon as they are raised. One thing's for certain, I have been spectacularly unsuccessful in exercising any negative capability. Pre-Freud Keats, unbeknown to him, stumbled on one of the main tenets of psychotherapy, one of the central things it tries to inculcate – the ability to sit up to your neck in your own mental shit, assailed by unendurable stinks, yet still function. The fact that the barrel of Rudi's gun is making the short journey from my thigh to the back of my mouth confirms this.

Lying down with my mother's stone at my crown, like a marble headboard, I see again the sky in its array of bruised greys and incipient blues. Still that uncertain hour. How I long for the rosy-fingered dawn, et cetera. Again a three-tier colour hierarchy in the sky – a dusk in reverse – difficult to distinguish the two occasionally. Something tells me I should learn to endure my going hence instead of continuing with this stupid, cowardly caper. Isn't that what everyone else has to do? I should learn to take death less personally. After all, what is fairer than death in its benevolent democracy? Death, as the poet said, will be a quiet ride in some green lane. Or did I say that? At least I don't think I'm God any more – now that would be worrying. However, there is an amazing stillness in the air now the wind has died down. A preemptive calm. A delicious freshness that is life itself . . . It makes me wonder whether I regret anything. If you regret your youth, then why live? What else – now let me see. My impercipience? My people-blindness? Well, I've paid the price for that. I suppose if I regret anything it's not picking up that phone and speaking to my father. It's bad luck not to resolve things before death – I fear an unsettling meeting in the underworld, like Odysseus' with Achilles. Nonetheless, as a symbolic act for a father, you can't get worse (or better) than locking the doors on your own son. And as a verbal act from son to father you can't top 'Hurry up and die.' I think, on balance, my act, my words were worse. As Coriolanus said, 'Often, when blows have made me stay, I fled from words.' These vicious acts must hang around somehow, like radioactive debris, long after their perpetrators are pieces of dubious bone in a rusty casque. Yes, it's a shame I won't get to see my real father, after my rejection by the wicked father, then the relinquishment of the good father who came third, Martin Drift. I certainly won't regret leaving these curious times behind. Things are always much worse in apprehension – the Millennium will more than likely bring, well, nothing – a prosaic continuation of what went before. Nineteen ninety-nine will seem, in retrospect, a more genteel time, full of deceptive panic, but in reality the calm before the hurricane of the twenty-first century. Yes, I am doing the right thing in getting out while I can. In leaving this warm, sensible motion for good. In the words, once again, of my namesake, I must forsake the earth's troubled waters for a purer spring.

The barrel of the gun has been in my mouth for so long it feels warm. Uncomfortably, it sits in a moat of equally warm saliva. The stillness around me really is scintillating. I have chosen my ground well. My final resting place, my home, where I may get some rest from the onslaught of change, temporality, life. The trees swell soundlessly in the gentle breeze, the light above them still undecided. Then a startling sound, a bird – not the soft coo of a wood pigeon, but a harsh cuckoo! Its blunt notes ring out again, like a reproach. I can see the bird itself on a low, rain-black branch of the nearest tree. Well, hello, friend. The noise I'm about to make will be much louder. My finger tenses around the trigger as I resist the urge to close my eyes – I want to see it all, down to the last dregs, the stones, the church, the sky, the world. Oh, well, I think – no time like the present . . .

It's no good. I can't do it.

But I was prepared for this. I knew it would be a struggle, right to the very end. After all, I could have done this in Rudi's flat and saved myself the effort. But, crucially, I wanted to remember every-thing first. To fix those moths of memory under glass once and for all. It's difficult to act when thinking shows you every angle, when you plough the pros and cons until the ground of action is fallow – and all along there is the suspicion that everything you do *is an act*, a hollow, non-conclusive pantomime. Well, this is intended to be the final conclusive act. An escape from this whirlpool of lies, the nothingness of life, the battle with Time and its bigger army. This world which passes like flowers fair.

Cuck–koo!

That's okay, my friend, you go right ahead. It's over. The woods no more us answer, or echo to our ring. Clenching my eyes tight, I commend my soul to the Everlasting. Then, very gently, very slowly, I squeeze the trigger.

It's . . . it's . . . not much different to being alive. The view, that is. Except, if possible, stiller – nothing is moving; the static stones of my last resting place immovably still. The cuckoo frozen on its branch. So *this* is what the soul sees after death – not blackness, but the *same thing*. Of course! This is where the soul begins its journey: in the same place it divested itself of the cumbersome body. And the soldier was right! I heard no bang whatsoever – the speed of sound being a notorious slowcoach. It was all remarkably painless, too. I can recommend shooting yourself in the head to anybody. As quick and effortless (and meaningless) as pushing a button.

Hold on, the cuckoo just moved. Flitting noiselessly to the branch below . . . now it is in flight. And the light, the light has changed too. Barely perceptible, but a definite lightening has taken place. I can see inscriptions on stones that I couldn't before. I gingerly try to unlock my fist from the pistol. My God! I am still in my body! We are still coupled in that intolerable bind Marvell couldn't abide.

I try shifting what I think is my right leg. It moves! Flux – Heraclitean and vital – tells me I'm definitely not in the underworld yet. Now I am on my feet, dizzy in the gathering light of dawn. The ancient movement of wind in the trees is not only affecting branches and twigs but also lightly caressing my face – and now it is deep in my nostrils; taken down into the lungs in greedy gasps.

I stop to examine the gun in my hand. Fiddling with the stock, the magazine drops into the wet grass. I retrieve it and examine the cartridges. A gurgling, trembling laughter fills my whole living body.

'Rudi, you bugger!' I say out loud, my voice startling to me. 'You were shooting blanks all along!' Just as Rudi was a facsimile of a human being, the gun appears to be a replica; the bullets dummies. Then something even more astonishing, even more welcome. A beam of light, strong and yellow, the first of the new day, surprises me from behind the church spire. I drop the gun and close my eyes in rapture. The sun, even at this chilly hour, feels warm and restorative behind my lids, like hot amber. I luxuriate in this sensation for as long as I dare. *Yet though I cannot be beloved, let me love!* Opening my eyes again, I decide to walk – one foot lame from my long recumbency in the grass – towards the true, non-deceiving light.

Acknowledgements

Thanks to Anna Webber, Zoe Ross and Jessica Craig at United Agents; Tom Avery, Jason Arthur, Emma Finnigan, and all at Heinemann; Becky Swift, without whom, etc. (www.literaryconsultancy.co.uk); Deborah Rogers, Hannah Westland; James Cook, Ian Tuton, Riet Chambers, Daisy Falconer & family; Robert Newman, Dan Jenkins, Ben North, Waheed Khan, Jeannette Robinson, Kelly Wilkie, PJ Harling, Pete Chapman, Paul & Jonny, Steve Necchi, Dave Pearce, Andy Naughton, Wayne Burrows, Sean Gascoine, Jaspreet Pandohar, Caffy St. Luce, Mike Scott, Rose Gledhill, Yvonne Enright, Geoffrey Cook, Laurie Ip Fung Chun, Jamie Fewery, Anna-Sophia Watts, Glenn O'Neill, Richard Skinner, Aki Schilz.

Also the following inspirational teachers and academics: Jeff Wood, Neil Rogal, Mike Shearer, Helen Hackett, John Sutherland, Kasia Boddy, Mark Ford, John Mullan, Greg Dart, Paul Davis and Neil Rennie.